Fear settled over Kacha.
Whatever Medeoan did, there was magic to it.

"Beloved?" he inquired, as he moved softly forward.

Medeoan sat deep in concentration. At last she looked up to smile. "Forgive me, beloved. I am at a working. This will be a girdle to help us be sure the lords master are loyal. Am I not clever?"

Clever enough to be truly dangerous, if only you knew it. "But will not such an open display of your power make your lords master nervous?" Prince Kacha said.

"Yes. No one will be able to hide from us," she said, "but somehow you will ensure they are not too upset."

"I will set my mind to it," he assured her. "I live to serve you."

Watch her, cautioned the voice that never left his mind. *You must watch her closely. That girdle might be used against you.*

I've thought of that, answered Kacha silently. *It could also be my own tool when I bind her thoughts forever. Then she will no longer be any danger.*

"*A Sorcerer's Treason* is a sumptuous tale of subtle magic, malevolent sorcery and twisted loyalties where nothing is as it first appears—I can guarantee you won't regret venturing into Sarah Zettel's world.

—Sara Douglass, author of
The Wayfarer Redemption

P9-DXT-013

Books by Sarah Zettel

Fool's War
Reclamation
Playing God
Kingdom of Cages
The Quiet Invasion

Isavalta
A Sorcerer's Treason*
The Usurper's Crown*

FORTHCOMING:

The Firebird's Vengeance*

* A Tor Book

The Usurper's Crown

A Novel of Isavalta

Sarah Zettel

TOR®
fantasy

A TOM DOHERTY ASSOCIATES BOOK
NEW YORK

THE USURPER'S CROWN: A NOVEL OF ISAVALTA

Edited by James Frenkel

A Tor Book
Published by Tom Doherty Associates, LLC
175 Fifth Avenue
New York, NY 10010

www.tor.com

Tor® is a registered trademark of Tom Doherty Associates, LLC.

ISBN: 0-812-56518-5

First edition: April 2003
First mass market edition: February 2004

Printed in the United States of America

0 9 8 7 6 5 4 3 2 1

*This book is dedicated to my friend
and fellow practitioner of the
writing arts, Karen Everson*

Acknowledgments

The author would like to once again thank the Untitled Writers Group for their honesty and support. Many thanks also to my editor, James Frenkel, and my agent, Shawna McCarthy, without whom this book and this series would not have seen the light of day.

In the lofty chamber, at the river mouth . . . a fair maiden stands, stands and decks herself, commends herself to valorous folk, glories in deeds of war.
                    —*from a Russian spell of protection in battle*

Prologue

Medeoan will not yield.

Those words echoed inside Avanasy's head as he stood in the vestment room of the god house, one eye pressed against the rough, wooden door so that he might watch the wedding. Shame weighed on him. He had not found in himself the strength to leave while any chance remained for Medeoan to change her mind. Therefore, he must hide like a thief waiting for a household to settle into sleep. Avanasy was under sentence of banishment, and if he were found today within the borders of Isavalta he would be killed. So, where did he choose to harbor himself? In the heart of the Imperial Palace of Vyshtavos. Emperor Edemsko, Avanasy's patron, would have snorted at that, had he known, and pronounced it "arrogance typical of a sorcerer." Then, however much the emperor might regret it, he would carry out the sentence his daughter Medeoan had laid down.

Medeoan will not yield.

A rush of air swirled the scents of incense and burning candles through the cracks in the door. By pressing his right cheek against the door's pitted surface, Avanasy could just barely see the tall, gilded doors open to let High Princess Medeoan pace gracefully but deliberately into the god house. As she glided past his vantage point, he saw how the assured glow of a maiden's love had taken on a sharp edge in her face. This was her decision. Against council and advice, this love was all hers, and he could see clearly that she felt pride as well as joy in it. Her parents on the dais and the statues of the gods on their pedestal watched her approach with the same stately equanimity. Avanasy's jaw tightened as the courtiers' murmurs reached him. The poets and the gossips would doubtlessly set out a banquet of approved words to describe this sight. All those assembled in the god house would later be said to have noted how the color in the high princess's cheeks rivaled the roses in her wedding crown and girdle for brightness. They would say her sapphire blue eyes shimmered with joy the way the golden symbols of luck, happiness, and fertility embroidered on her blue gown shimmered with the light of braided candles set in every corner and cornice of the gilded room. Ballads and romantic themes would be composed on the heir of Isavalta and her great love.

Those themes would not last. Avanasy knew that fact as he knew that the sun would rise the next morning, and the knowledge burned his heart. The pain only grew sharper because he could do nothing. Finally, his restless, discontented student was happy. Finally, she was at peace with her place in the world.

That peace, however, rested on a carpet of lies. He had tried to tell her this hard news, but Medeoan had just stood before him, her jaw hanging loose in stunned disbelief.

"Why are you saying this, Avanasy?"

They had been in her private chamber, the only place he could possibly utter his accusations. They stood on opposite sides of the central fire pit so that he seemed to see her standing in a patch of flames. Beyond the princess, her ladies-in-waiting sat in their alcove, her wedding veil stretched out between them so they could work on its embroidery. All of them bent studiously over their work, pretending very hard not to hear anything that was being said.

"Because it is the truth." His voice had been soft, then. Anger would not serve. Medeoan had always looked to him for sympathy. He had to show her he felt that sympathy still. "Kacha means to use you to gain Isavalta for himself."

"He does not need to use me," countered Medeoan doggedly. "Once he becomes my consort, Isavalta passes to his heirs, our children. His bloodline will have Isavalta."

As it has been denied its native land of Hastinapura. Avanasy met her eyes, willing her to hear what he truly said. "Medeoan, you are a sorceress. You may not conceive easily, and you will most certainly outlive Kacha." He did not say, why do you think your parents had to negotiate the marriage treaty so carefully? He did not say, why do you think those who sit on the Pearl Throne offered you the son of their emperor's brother rather than their heir? Medeoan already knew these things, however much she might wish not to. That knowledge hung in the air between them like the scent of the wood and charcoal burning in the fire.

He expected anger her from her. Indeed, he hoped for it. Anger would mean that she had heard him, and that his words had reached beyond the walls she had erected in her heart and her mind. Instead, she drew herself up, her whole bearing showing an unfamiliar resolve. "You think I do not know that my existence is shaped by politics? I know that as I know my name. The needs of the empire shape every single facet of my life but one: Kacha loves me."

Kacha. Now, he waited for his bride beside Bakhar, the keeper of the god house. Kacha's narrow, rugged face was appropriately solemn as he watched Medeoan's approach. Like Medeoan, Kacha wore the imperial blue, but his elegant kaftan was covered by a white coat embroidered with silver. He would not officially obtain imperial rank until Medeoan accepted him before the gods. Then, that white coat would be removed, and his crown of white roses would be replaced with a crown of gold and sapphires, and he would have all that he wanted.

"Politics shapes your existence, yes." Avanasy rounded the fire pit and stood directly in front of Medeoan. "It also shapes Kacha's. His father should have been on the Pearl Throne, but he is not. It galls him. His son—"

"Is his route to empire," Medeoan cut Avanasy off sharply. "Why does that matter? I am marrying him. His father will have the empire he desires." She turned from him then, gripping the back of a gilded chair. "It is done. There is no need for this treachery you would dream up."

"No need, perhaps," said Avanasy to her back, "but I fear that owning the future of Isavalta is not enough for them."

Medeoan whirled around then, at last truly angry. Avanasy suppressed a grim smile at that anger. At last, at last, she was beginning to hear him. "How can you say such things?" Medeoan demanded. "What proof have you?"

"You require proof?" Avanasy said gently, taking another step forward. "Answer me this question. Where is Kacha now?"

Medeoan frowned, her brows drawing together. "He is meeting with the Master of the Treasury and the under treasurers."

Avanasy nodded. He had known the answer before he spoke. "Were you not supposed to be in consultation with them?"

Medeoan hesitated, but she covered the pause with a dismissive wave. "I must see to the wedding clothes. There are sigils that must be properly prepared."

"I could do that with the aid of your mistress of the weaving sheds, as could any of the court sorcerers." Avanasy spread his hands, encompassing the room and leaving her nowhere to turn. "Why are you not in consultation with the men who will most likely be your ministers when you assume the throne?"

"Because I wish to be here." Medeoan pronounced each word carefully and clearly, but her voice trembled all the same.

Forgive me, thought Avanasy silently, as he pressed on. "Kacha said he would take care of these matters for you, did he not?"

Medeoan had a ready answer. Avanasy had known she would. "I wish the Council of Lords to become used to him and his position of responsibility."

"So it was your idea?" He raised his eyebrows. "He did not suggest to you that he sit through this dull meeting while you are more agreeably occupied?"

Medeoan stood silent.

"And how many other meetings in these past months has Kacha shouldered the burden for?"

Her fist knotted against the back of the chair. She was so young yet. She believed she had finally found the escape she had always sought, and it grieved him to force her to see the truth. But how could he be loyal and do otherwise? "He is the first person who wished to make my life easier rather than more difficult."

"He is the first person who wished to cut you off from the functions of the government that will be yours, or should be yours."

That was his fatal miscalculation. Medeoan turned away.

There were those who had heard of Avanasy's objections and cautions regarding the marriage and looked askance at him. They wondered if he had fallen in love with his imperial student. He kept his silence at these whispers. They were not entirely wrong. He did love Medeoan. He loved her as a daughter or a sister. So he told himself, most days. He was too honest with himself not to admit that there were times, when they sat together in confidence, and she told him of her fears, that other loves were stirred in him. He loved the brilliance of her mind and of her magic, and he was by no means blind to her beauty. To see her so utterly overcome by treachery and flattery left him devastated.

As was required upon entering the god house, the High Princess Medeoan paused to kiss the robes of Vyshko and Vyshemir, the house gods of the imperial family. Vyshko lifted his pike high, and Vyshemir spread her hands, offering her cup and knife to the assembly. Coins and velvets lay heaped at their feet, the gifts of the ones who stood before them. Those who were close enough, and those who knew Medeoan well, knew she did not observe the gods dressed in their finest indigo silk for this ceremony. Instead, she stole covert glances at her groom, who had already processed in and honored the gods with treasures from his southern homeland. Now, he waited for Medeoan. Doubtless, she saw how fine his chiseled features were. In her memory she heard the sweet words of love and sympathy that he poured endlessly into her ears.

Perhaps they are right after all, the ones who call me a jealous fool. Avanasy bowed his forehead against the vestry door. *Perhaps she was right to exile me.*

"He's told you you'll be free, hasn't he?" he had said to Medeoan, his voice growing harder with each word, even though he knew it was a mistake. He knew he should stop, he must stop, or he would drive her away, but he could not stop. There had been then only himself and her, and the fire burning beside them, echoing the anger and fear burning in his veins. Nothing else registered in his mind. "He has told you that you can have the one thing you have longed for, as long as you trust him."

"He is helping me," said Medeoan. "Is that not what a

husband and consort should do?" She walked up to him slowly, deliberately, far too close for courtesy. "Is that not what a teacher should do?"

"Is a consort supposed to bribe the treasury ministers?" shot back Avanasy.

Two bright spots of color appeared on Medeoan's cheeks "What?"

I'm sorry. I'm sorry. "Your ministers have been the recipients of several small but expensive gifts from the hand of your consort-to-be."

Medeoan ducked her head, pretending to turn her attention to the ladies working so diligently on her veil. "He is generous to all who serve well."

"To all who serve *him* well," Avanasy corrected her.

"I have heard nothing of this," Medeoan said without looking back at him.

"No," said Avanasy. "Because you have ceased to attend meetings, and because Kacha has not told you."

She whirled around then, and Avanasy saw fear behind the anger blazing in her eyes. She believed him, at least in part. She remembered that he had never lied to her, and so she must know that now he spoke the truth.

Had not Kacha walked in at that moment, everything might have been different.

Avanasy heard the sound of something scrabbling against wood, and realized it was his own nails scraping against the door as his hand curled into a fist.

Kacha stood beside the keeper of the god house, waiting patiently while his bride poured out a small heap of gold and sapphires at the feet of the gods. He was handsome, for the most part. Although his face was narrow, the rest of him was broad and well sculpted. As suited a prince of the Pearl Throne, he had been well schooled in the arts of his homeland. He could read, and he could write several languages, which was more than most nobles of Isavalta could say. He could judge horse flesh, cloth, and gems. He could dance, sing and play music, and write a letter that could singe a maiden's soul. He could speak politely but firmly in front of his elders, and he could weave a web of words to get what he desired. He had only two flaws. His right hand was twisted and withered like an old man's. The flesh around his right eye was a network of white scars, and the eye itself was sunken and somehow aged. A chariot accident, he had said. He had been thrown, his hand becoming entangled in the reins and then crushed when the car overturned and his face had been pressed hard into the dirt. These outward signs that he had suffered in his life seemed only to draw Medeoan closer to him.

That scarred and aged eye glittered at Avanasy. As his suspicions had begun to deepen about Kacha, he had tried to find out the truth of the story of the chariot accident, but he had no bond of blood or vow with Kacha. That lack had caused his scryings to fail. No other sorcerer at court could be persuaded to so doubt the word of the young man who would soon be their emperor.

"Forgive me, Medeoan," Kacha had said then, his gaze darting between Avanasy and his intended. "I did not realized you were occupied."

"No, come here, Kacha." Medeoan held out her hand. Kacha, his gaze fixed firmly on Avanasy, crossed the room in a swift stride to take her fresh, unlined hand in his withered one. "What is being said here concerns you."

Kacha's eyebrows rose minutely. "Then I am anxious to hear it."

They did not look at each other. Their gazes both fixed on Avanasy, Kacha with the mildest of curiosity, Medeoan with cold anger. "Avanasy, who has never lied to me, says that you have been giving bribes to the treasury ministers."

Kacha bowed with his palms pressed against his eyes, as was the fashion of his homeland. "Avanasy does not lie."

What little blood she had left drained from Medeoan's face. "Then it is true?" she breathed.

Kacha bowed again. "It is true." He spoke casually, and as he lifted his head, Avanasy saw how the prince's eyes shone.

Before either Medeoan or Avanasy could speak, Kacha asked, "Did Avanasy tell you why I did such thing?"

Avanasy felt his heart go cold. "Tell me why," said Medeoan.

"Because your father's Lord Master of the Treasury has

been stealing." Kacha held up his hand, forestalling protest. "I have been reviewing the ledgers. I have some proof, but not enough. I needed spies."

"And why did you not see fit to inform the emperor of this?" asked Avanasy evenly. He must not accuse, not now. He must not lose hold of his anger.

"The emperor is a sagacious man; he will require more than my word as a prince when I say that one of the high families of Isavalta harbors a thief," countered Kacha. "Which is why I needed proof."

"And why did you not see fit to tell me?" asked Medeoan quietly.

Kacha dropped his eyes. "I was afraid."

"Of what?" Medeoan stepped closer to him. "Of me?"

"No." Kacha shook his head, and lifted his eyes, and stared straight at Avanasy.

It was a gesture Medeoan could not miss. "Of Avanasy?"

Kacha reached into the breast of his kaftan and brought out a tiny silver mirror. The surface had been carefully etched with a complex series of crosses and knots. A single human eye had been drawn in the center. "My servant told me Avanasy had asked for this to be placed in my chamber. He was told it was an amulet of protection. There are books in the library that say otherwise."

Kacha handed the mirror to Medeoan, and Avanasy knew the young prince, the would-be emperor of Isavalta, had made his mistake.

"Highness, I swear on life, blood and soul that is no work of mine." Avanasy stretched out his wrist. "Take my blood, work your will, and see for yourself which of us lies."

He hoped she would take his word, but knew she could not. Medeoan carried a knife with the small bundle of keys that hung from her girdle. She raised it now, and cut his palm, the swift, shallow slice he had taught her to make. Avanasy held himself completely steady. One, two, three drops of blood fell from his wound onto the mirror. Medeoan breathed deeply, calling up the magic that was part of her soul, part of her world. She traced her finger through the tiny puddle of blood drawing a new pattern, as complete and precise as any he himself could make. The air tingled cool and sharp against Avanasy's skin. It was a sensation Kacha could not feel. Medeoan shaped a spell of understanding. Had the watching mirror in truth been his, the blood would be absorbed into its surface. As it was, it would fall away like water, and Medeoan would know the truth. It was Kacha who lied to her, not he.

But the mirror drank in the blood until every trace of red was lost.

Avanasy's soul plummeted. Medeoan raised her face to his, and her skin had gone paper white. He saw the flash of triumph in Kacha's eyes, his scars standing out very white against his dark skin, and Avanasy knew like a sickness in him that he was lost, and that the fault for the loss was his own. He had grossly, stupidly, fatally underestimated how well Kacha's father had prepared his son for the role he was to play.

"Get out." Medeoan's voice shook with her fury. "I ban you, I banish you. If I find you within my country again, you will be killed!"

"Medeoan . . ."

"Do not speak my name! Be grateful I do not have you killed here and now for the traitor you are! Get out!"

As the memory of her cry made its echoes in his mind, Avanasy made himself watch Medeoan, trembling with excitement, complete the journey to her waiting husband. Part of him mused that this voyeurism must be his own punishment for his arrogance. This was how he sought to deepen his own guilt and at the same time justify his fatal boldness.

And it is just as useless. He watched the court, resplendent in its golds, silks, and velvets, reverence, bowing deeply from the waist with their hands crossed upon their breasts.

Medeoan will not yield.

Those words had been spoken by Edemsko, the emperor of Isavalta. Medeoan's father, relieved that his only living child had finally ceased to sigh against the burdens her birth had placed on her. Avanasy had felt a traitor going to the emperor in private to ask that Medeoan's order of exile be rescinded. But how could he not? Now that he had seen the depth to which Kacha had laid his plans, how could he abandon her? So, he had finally managed to work his way past

Iakush, the lord sorcerer, and gained audience with Medeoan's father to lay all his suspicions before the emperor.

But Emperor Edemsko was not one of those who believed the heir to the throne should be kept from power. Medeoan had never been supposed to be the heir. Her older brothers had been stout princes, but one had been thrown from his horse into a freezing canal, and the other had succumbed to fever, leaving only Medeoan to take up the burden. No effort of the court sorcerers could produce another living child from the empress's womb. So, from her youth, the emperor forced Medeoan to attend council sessions. He had insisted she have practice in direct governance, knowing that she would rule when he was gone. Now that she had seen fit to give an order of her own, he would not overrule her, even when that order was to exile the teacher the emperor had chosen for her.

Avanasy watched Keeper Bakhar gesture with one strong hand so that the court could rise and watch as he placed Kacha's mismatched hands into Medeoan's fair ones.

No, he said in the silence of his own mind. *No, Medeoan. Stop.* His eyes turned involuntarily to the emperor and empress. They sat on their thrones on the dais behind the keeper, laden with pride, sphere, scepter and crown. They glittered more brightly than even the gods. Today, the royal regalia seemed no burden as they watched their daughter tilt her happy face toward her husband. No doubt, they were blessing fortune that political necessity could be married to happiness. Isavalta, fledgling Isavalta, Isavalta called eternal but really just a babe in its new borders, would be safe now. This union, this happy union, would assure it. There were plenty of other sorcerers at court. Kacha would be well watched, by them, and by the emperor's own informants. Were it true that Medeoan was in danger, it would be seen well before any plan could be completed. Such a discovery might even be useful during future negotiations with the Pearl Throne of Hastinapura.

"Now I do call on those all here assembled to bear witness." Medeoan's voice rang strong and clear through the god house. "High Princess Medeoan Edemskoidoch Nacheradavosh being well pleased with the form and the offerings of Kacha *tya* Achin Ejunlinjapad do take his hands under the watchful eyes of Vyshko and Vyshemir, now and forever, as husband and consort, as Beloved Prince before the Pearl Throne of Hastinapura and High Prince of Eternal Isavalta."

"Let Vyshko and Vyshemir hear," intoned Keeper Bakhar. "Let all pray to Vyshko and Vyshemir for their aid and blessing."

Avanasy closed his eyes. He did not want to see the contentment glowing on Medeoan's face. He did not want to see the satisfaction of her parents.

Stop this. Stop her, he prayed, but whether he prayed to her mortal parents or immortal ones, he did not himself know.

But no word broke the holy silence. There was only the rustle of cloth, the occasional sigh, and one badly suppressed cough. If the gods watched, they watched in silence.

"It is done, Avanasy," said a quiet voice in Avanasy's ear.

Avanasy stiffened. Slowly, refusing to betray any fear, he straightened and turned around. Behind him stood Captain Peshek Pachalkasyn Ursulvin, fresh and stern in his best uniform coat. Peshek's breastplate had been so brightly polished that Avanasy could see his own comical look of surprise in its surface. He gripped his poleax in one hand, and carried a bundle of cloth in the other.

No words came to Avanasy, so he just spread his hands. In response, Peshek shook his head.

"Our good keeper thought you might need help getting out of here today." He pressed the bundle into Avanasy's hands. "Put this on."

The bundle proved to be a guard's coat and helmet. Through the door, Avanasy heard Keeper Bakhar speaking again, extolling all the duties of a virtuous consort toward their sovereign. To be strong, to be constant, to bend mind and skill to the service of the sovereign, who in turn would shape them to work for the good of Eternal Isavalta.

Yet, the solemn, celebratory words said to Avanasy only that all was done. No one mortal or divine had seen fit to intervene.

"You will be much more use to all of us alive," said Peshek earnestly. "You have friends enough, Avanasy. There are plenty among the high families who do not trust this treaty with Hastinapura. You can be well hidden."

Avanasy shook his head. "No. This is my fault. I accept my punishment." He slung the coat on over his plain kaftan and pantaloons. Its hems brushed the top of his boots, hiding his everyday clothes. The helmet shadowed his face, and Peshek passed him the pike to complete the hasty disguise.

"At least I will know you are alive somewhere, then," muttered Peshek. "Before, you simply made a mistake. Now, you're playing the fool."

As ever, there was too much truth in Peshek's words. "Then let me play my role as I see fit."

Peshek let out a derisive snort, but said nothing else. He held silent even as Avanasy turned back to his spy hole in the door and made himself look on Medeoan, his student, his responsibility, his sovereign, and his judge, one last time. A cluster of rose petals had fallen from her crown and lay like a puddle of blood beside the hem of her wedding gown. An omen? Avanasy did not know whether to wish it was so, or that it was not so. He only knew that he could stay no longer. Peshek, as he had been so many times before, was right in this. He should already have been gone, but he could not bear to leave while any hope remained. But now the choir raised its voice in song, and Medeoan stood on tiptoe to kiss Kacha full and warmly on the mouth. Now there would be prayers and more exhortations. Hours of ceremony were yet to come, and none of it meant anything. Medeoan had spoken her acceptance, and that was what mattered before the law and the gods.

Avanasy turned and nodded to Peshek. Peshek rolled his eyes heavenward to say *finally*, but no word passed his lips. He simply lead Avanasy through the vestry, silently opening the side door to the library and striding through. Peshek carried the authority of the House Guard in his straight back and measured gait. No door could be closed to him, especially today when it was so important that the palace be absolutely secure. Avanasy made himself copy Peshek's demeanor.

The library with its long walls of books and windows was deserted. Indeed, the whole palace was still. In the courtyard, the patrols of the house guard stood at attention. Even the servants had paused in their preparation of the feast so that their minds could be occupied in prayer and thanksgiving for the wedding they were not allowed to witness because there was no room left in the god house. None would stir until the bells rang. None but himself and Peshek, who would die as surely as Avanasy would if they were caught now. The realization that Peshek's safety hung in the balance put speed into Avanasy's steps. If he should die, that was one thing, but Peshek was loyal to Medeoan and Isavalta, and she was going to need such loyalty.

Outside, the spring sun was warm, but the breezes were chill. For all it was beginning to deck itself out in green and blossomed finery, the world still remembered winter. The canal that flowed past the marble steps of the palace had thawed, however, and it had been a full two weeks since word had come to him that the ice on the great river had cleared. That was all that mattered. He could leave now, leave eternal Isavalta, leave the world and sail for the shores that waited beyond the Land of Death and Spirit. There he would never have to hear the name of Medeoan spoken. There, only memory would speak of how she had turned on him, or how he had failed her, and memory would fade.

Chapter One

The bed frame creaked, and Ingrid Loftfield instantly opened her eyes. Moonlight streamed in through the mended curtains, laying a silver skin across the room's sparse furnishings. It was more than enough to show Ingrid the silhouette of her sister Grace climbing out of their sagging bed. Unblinking, Grace rounded the bed's foot. Ingrid held her breath. Grace's hand strayed out to pick up her knitted shawl from where it hung on the post, but her eyes did not turn to see what her hand did. All her attention remained fixed on the bedroom door as she padded across the bare boards and out into the hall.

Ingrid kicked back the quilt and jumped to her feet. She pulled off her nightgown to reveal her dark skirt and work shirt. Her jaw firmly set, she bent down to stuff her feet into her worn boots.

Tonight she would find out what ailed her sister.

"She just wants a good shaking," their brother Leo had announced.

"You're too free with the girl." Papa had glowered at Mama. "You should not let her go galloping across to Bayfield whenever she pleases. It's some man, you see if it isn't."

"You must watch her, Ingrid," Mama had whispered in the back kitchen as she banked the fire for the night. "The Devil's finally got to her."

Devil or man, I will have my answer. Stepping as lightly as she could, Ingrid followed Grace into the hallway. Her sister was already down the stairs. Grace did not look back once as she slipped soundlessly out the front door.

Ingrid herself was halfway down the stairs. A floorboard creaked behind her. Ingrid twisted to see back over her shoulder. Her mother stood at the top of the stairs, a candle in her hand, and her face pale with some emotion Ingrid found she could not name.

"What is it, Mother?" she heard Papa's gravelly voice call.

"Nothing," Mama called back. "Nothing at all."

Ingrid swallowed hard, and hurried out after her sister into the chill of the late-spring night. The brisk wind smelled of pine resin and the ever-present cold of Lake Superior. Grace all but flew down the footpath toward the rutted track that served as Eastbay's main road. Gathering up her hems, Ingrid followed, her teeth gritted until they ached.

Tonight we put a stop to this.

The settlement of Eastbay popped up here and there out of Sand Island's wilderness like a cluster of spring mushrooms. It called itself a town, but it was little more than a scattering of dwellings connected by meandering dirt paths. Despite the fat, full moon that lit the night, the houses seemed blind and distant. Even the forge squatted darkly back in the woods. The trees loomed large and all the night noises—the rustling, hooting, rushing sounds—filled in all the empty spaces, leaving Ingrid with the unaccustomed sensation of being a trespasser. *This is not your place,* the whole world seemed to say to her. *Go back to your bed until the daylight comes. Leave her to us.*

But Grace hurried on before her, a pale ghost in her flannel nightdress, and Ingrid could not even think of turning back. Mama was trusting her to find out what was happening, and to do it quickly. If Papa found out Grace had gone out of sight of the house, unaccompanied, at night, Grace's life would be made unbearable, whatever the reason turned out to be.

Grace's illness had begun in May, just as the island's short, late, spring was beginning to warm toward summer. Grace had been across on the mainland in Bayfield, earning a little extra by doing for Mrs. Hofstetter who had just been delivered of twins. Papa had objected to her going, but Grace had just faced him with her sunny smile and said—"Well, Papa, you can lock me in the shed if you choose, but unless you do, I'm going."

Grace could do that. Grace could smile, and laugh, and glide her way through any storm of shouts or tears. Sometimes it was maddening, but most of the time Ingrid clung to her sister like a sailor clinging to a lifeline. She willingly shouldered Grace's share of the work around house and field so that Grace might go to Bayfield. So that Grace might keep that easy smile.

Then, a squall had come up, suddenly, as they would in the spring, and Everett Lederle had burst into the back kitchen to tell Ingrid he had seen a great, gray wave swamp the small tug carrying Grace back home.

Ingrid had run then too, her skirts hiked about her knees so she could keep pace with her father and brother, sprinting through the driving rain down to the bay to help launch the boats and bend her back to row against the waves toward where the tug had last been sighted.

Lake Superior was the provider for everyone on the island, but it was also their collective enemy. No one would be left to its mercy while there was any chance she might be saved.

They pulled Frank and Todd Johanssen out of the frigid, grasping waters, but although they strained their eyes and shouted until their voices were hoarse, there was no sign of Grace.

Ingrid was blind with tears and rain when her father ordered them back to shore. Shaking, she'd climbed over the gunwale onto the sand, brushing aside all the hands that reached out to help. She would have to be steady when they told the little ones. Fiercely, she'd knuckled the water from her eyes, just in time to see a white shape burst from the gray lake. Leo saw it as well and threw himself into the water, grasping Grace by her shoulders before she could disappear beneath the surface again. Amid the cheers of their neighbors, Leo had dragged Grace shivering to the shore. Coats and oilskins had been thrown over her, and her family had led her home to a bright fire and a warm, dry bed.

She'd been sick for a time after that, to no one's surprise. Mama had tended her with mustard baths for her feet and strong tea for her stomach. After three weeks, though, Papa began to ask what could possibly still ail the girl, and Mama urged Grace to come to the breakfast table. Leo and Papa frowned, sure she must be better by now, and equally sure she was lazing. But Ingrid looked at Grace's pale cheeks, and saw how listlessly she picked at her porridge, and Ingrid knew in the depth of her heart something was still wrong.

The color in Grace's cheeks did not return, nor did the saucy light that used to dance in her eyes. Instead, her skin remained as white as if she had just been pulled from the lake. If left to herself, she would stand at the front window gazing across the tiny, weed-choked yard. Mama or Ingrid could nag or cajole her into lending a hand with the work, but they found they had to keep a sharp eye on her, or her mind would drift and the copper tub for the laundry would be overturned, or on baking day the fire would be built so unevenly the loaves came out charred lumps.

"What is the matter with you, Grace?" Ingrid finally demanded in exasperation.

"I don't know," said Grace, tears brimming in her dimmed eyes. "I don't know."

Ingrid hugged her sister hard then, and let the matter drop.

After another two weeks of this, over even Papa's grim objections, Mama summoned the doctor from Bayfield. He could find no crack in Grace's skull, nor any irregularity in her eyes, heart, or breath. Nor did he find what Ingrid suspected was the greatest fear—that Grace was with child. He simply counseled patience and packed up his black bag.

But that same night, Grace began walking in her sleep. They found her first in the front room, kneeling on the horsehair settee and staring out the window. On the next night, she was standing in the front yard, staring hungrily at the closed gate. On the next, she was halfway down the track toward the bay, for all that Mama had locked and barred the doors for the night. When they questioned Grace afterward, she could give no answer, no hint of a reason for her behavior. In fact, she stopped talking at all. During the day, she would not get out of bed unless lifted bodily. She would not eat. Only Ingrid sleeping in a chair before the front door kept her inside at night.

It was desperation that had made Ingrid decide to follow Grace instead of barring her way tonight. Papa was talking about sending Grace away, and Mama's tears told Ingrid that she would wail about such action, but she would not stop it.

Mama's tears only came when she was not going to take any other step.

Now, the darkness itself seemed to part for Grace's effortless, hurrying feet. All the purpose that had drained from her during the daylight had returned and even when she took a sharp right turn off the road, her gait was sure and unhesitating. Ingrid was left to stump behind her, blessing the full moon and cursing the brambles and tree branches snatching at her hems and elbows.

Where are you going? Ingrid thought, torn between frustration at her sister's silent purpose, and fear that her noise would wake Grace from her trance at any moment. If Grace woke, she might simply return to her stupor, leaving Ingrid still without answers. *Much farther and you'll be in the lake.*

Indeed, the shore was in sight. Lake Superior spread out black and silver below the gentle rise which Grace had climbed. Ingrid ducked behind a wild blueberry bush, catching her breath and narrowing her eyes suspiciously. *Grace, if this truly is because you are meeting some fisherman, it's not Leo you'll be getting your shaking from.*

The water was calm tonight, Ingrid noted. The moonlight highlighted only the barest ripples in the night-darkened water. She could just hear the sound of water lapping at the stones under the whisper of the wind through the trees. Grace paused for a moment on the top of the short bluff. In the light of the moon and a million stars, Ingrid saw her sister scan the shore, searching for Ingrid knew not what.

Then, Grace began to run, down the slope, right down to the narrow strip of sand at the water's edge. Ingrid peered between the branches of the spindly shrub that sheltered her and watched Grace kneel beside what appeared to be a large stone.

"I came." Grace's voice drifted up to Ingrid on the chill, steady wind blowing off the lake. "I promised I would."

"Cold," answered a shivery man's voice. "So cold."

Ingrid shot up to her full height, uncertain which of the two on the shore she was going to murder first. But even her sudden motion and all the noise of it did not cause Grace to turn her attention from the man beside her. While Ingrid stormed down the hill, every fiber in her tight with fury,

Grace just took off her shawl and draped it across the man's shoulders.

"Is that better?" asked Grace.

The man was little more than a collation of indistinct planes and angles in the moonlight, but Ingrid saw him reach out one hand to pull the shawl more tightly around himself. "I never dreamed it would be so cold."

"Let me help you," urged Grace.

Which was all Ingrid could take.

"Grace Hulda Loftfield, what do you think you're doing!" she shouted as she strode onto the sand.

The sound of her full name seemed finally to reach Grace. She tore her attention from the man. Ingrid planted herself before her sister, hands on hips. Grace stood slowly, her own hands dangling at her sides.

"Ingrid . . ." she breathed weakly, as if the strength that had brought her here had all flowed away.

"The whole family has been an uproar for weeks!" cried Ingrid, flinging her arms wide. "I thought you were ill, and all the while you were just waiting to sneak out to meet some man! Papa will thrash you within an inch of your life!" Ingrid rounded on the man. "As for you, sir . . ." and her voice froze in her throat.

The man had also stood up. He was sopping wet. Water dripped from the bedraggled ends of his curling hair. It ran in rivulets from down his naked shoulders and his sodden canvas trousers to puddle around his bare feet. Grace's shawl clung to his shoulders, soaking up quarts of water. His chest was so sunken that Ingrid could see his ribs.

But it was not this that robbed her of her voice, nor was it even his hollow eyes or his gray skin. It was the silver sand behind him. Ingrid could see Grace's moonlit shadow spreading clearly across that sand.

Beside her, the man cast no shadow at all.

"What are you?" Ingrid croaked. "Grace, come here." She stretched out her hand. "Come away."

"Ingrid . . ." said Grace, but she did not move. She just swayed in place.

"No," said the man, whatever he was. He knotted the end

of Grace's shawl in his gray fingers. "Don't leave me, Grace. I beg you."

"Come here, Grace," ordered Ingrid, fear and dawning comprehension giving her voice strength. "Now!"

Grace slumped her shoulders. "I can't."

The drowned man—against all reason, Ingrid knew that was what he was—clutched Grace's shawl even tighter. "You promised you would help me. You promised you would not leave me here."

"I won't." Grace lifted her foot to take a step toward the drowned man, but Ingrid dodged between them.

"Leave her alone!" she cried. Now that she stood before the ghost, she felt the cold. It rolled off him in waves and bit straight into Ingrid's bones. It was cold beyond winter, beyond ice, beyond the waters of Lake Superior. It froze her blood in her veins and threatened to reach through to her soul. Ingrid staggered backward, trying to push Grace more fully behind her. Then, because she could think of nothing else that might help, she began—"Our Father who art in Heaven, hallowed be thy name . . ."

At the sound of the prayer, the drowned man's face twisted into a horrible scowl and a light came into the hollows of his eyes that filled Ingrid's heart with fresh fear.

"No!" shouted the ghost, and his voice was like the winds of a winter storm. "There is no God where I am! He left me there in the dark but I will not stay! I will not stay!"

Ingrid snatched at Grace's hand and turned to run, but her sister might have been a block of marble for all Ingrid could shift her. The ghost now gripped Grace's shawl in both fists. "She promised," he said grimly.

"I did." Grace's voice was as pale as her cheeks. "I promised. Under the water."

"She's mine." The ghost slid closer.

"No." Ingrid stepped back between them, trying to stiffen her spine against the all-consuming cold. "Jesus, Joseph, and Mother Mary, help me. You shall not have her."

"She's mine by her own promise. We made a bargain. No name can keep her from me."

The ghost reached out and Ingrid pressed back against her unmoving, unmovable sister. Her heart beat wildly in terror at the idea that the apparition and all the cold he carried might reach straight through her and engulf Grace as if Ingrid were not even there.

A flash of movement caught Ingrid's eye. A fresh shadow dashed headlong down the beach. Moonlight glinted on metal as the new shape leapt forward. Ingrid opened her mouth to scream as the knife blade came down. With all her strength she threw herself backward, knocking Grace to the sand. The ghost's cold rushed over them, and for a time, Ingrid knew nothing more.

Ingrid woke to the scent and sound of a fire. She lay on her side, her back against the bracken-covered slope that led to the shore. A smoky blaze smelling of pine and moldering driftwood burned on the sand and a man's form sat beside it. Stiff with cold and damp, Ingrid pushed herself upright immediately. As she did, she saw Grace, also lying on her side, her fair head pillowed by her own arm.

Ignoring the man, Ingrid crawled to her sister, laying an anxious hand on Grace's throat. Fresh relief washed through her as she felt the warmth of Grace's skin, the beat of her heart, and the slow draw of her breath. Only then did Ingrid lift her eyes to meet the gaze of the man beside them.

The moon had set and the morning sky filled with clouds, so she had only the fire to see him by. The resinous, red-gold light showed her a lined face with a hawk nose and deep-set eyes. She could not make out their color. The hair swept back under his fisherman's cap was a dark gold, and his hands, although tanned, showed themselves to be surprisingly long-fingered and delicate as he reached for a fresh piece of driftwood. He broke the branch easily in two before tossing it onto the small fire and raising a fresh shower of sparks.

Ingrid was suddenly extremely conscious that she was rumpled, and half-covered in sand. In the next heartbeat, she cursed herself for such ridiculous vanity, especially at such a moment.

"Thank you for your help and company, sir." Ingrid attempted to gather her composure and her manners. "My sister has not been well, and . . ." She dropped her gaze to the fire, intending to find some sort of lie to explain how two young women came to be out on the shore after dark. As she did, she saw the scraps of knitting among the ashes of the fire and realized that they belonged to Grace's shawl.

The man followed her gaze with his own. He gave a tight smile that was at once amused and grim. Before Ingrid could recover herself, he asked, "How long has this haunt plagued your sister?"

Ingrid opened her mouth and closed it again. She had absolutely no desire to speak of this to a total stranger. In truth, she had no desire even to remember it. She felt her mind scrabbling for explanations that were other than what had happened. She knew she could give in to them quite easily. There had been tricks of shadow and moonlight. Grace was simply more ill than anyone had realized. She needed the doctor again. She needed a rest. That was all.

The only problem with any of those thoughts was that Ingrid knew they were all lies. "About two months," she made herself say. "Why did you burn her shawl?"

"The ghost touched it," said the man as if it were the simplest reason in the world. "If it was not destroyed, it could be used as a talisman against her."

Ingrid felt her throat tighten. "Grace touched the . . . ghost." *Say it. Call it what it is. It is ridiculous. It is impossible. It is also the truth.*

The man nodded, all trace of the smile gone from his face. "I thought she might have."

Ingrid brushed Grace's hair back from her cheek. Grace did not stir at all, even as Ingrid stroked her shoulder and arm. "Will she be all right now?"

"No," said the man matter-of-factly. "I am afraid after this she will be much worse."

The answer sent a stab of anger through Ingrid, but she suppressed it. "What must be done, then?"

The man turned his eyes from her, back toward the flames. "I don't know," he said. "I wish very much that I did."

"I see."

They sat in silence for a moment. The man appeared to be ready to stare calmly into the fire until Kingdom Come, but Ingrid felt no such composure. Part of her was frightened and angry about this stranger and his pronouncements. Part of her was already shivering from imaginings of what Papa and Leo would do if Grace were caught out. Then there would be the scenes with Mama, and then if Grace got much sicker . . . Mama might not send for the doctor again, not after last time.

Yet another part of her was still reeling with disbelief at all that had happened, and desperately seeking a way to deny it, but here she was, in the slowly dying night, and here was Grace all unconscious beside her. She knew a hundred ghost stories, of course. She had entertained all her siblings as they were growing up with stories of drowned men, sunken ships, strange lights, and seers who predicted disaster. She'd heard the men speak of mystic dreams, and of the Indians with their hosts of goblins, the Windego, the Bear Walker and Nanabush. These were part of her world, like Lake Superior surrounding her island home, but not this, this, thing that laid claim to her sister.

"Who are you?" she made herself ask the man. She had to root herself in the here and now. She could not let the coming daylight lull her into disbelief.

"My name is Avan."

The name struck a chord with Ingrid. She had heard it from her father and Leo. He was a new man, come up for the fishing season. He was good with the boats. That brief statement from Papa was like a soliloquy of praise coming from another man. Leo had thought he was a Finn, although he had been vague about his origins. Papa had gone out with him two or three times now.

The realization should have been reassuring, but it was not.

"What brought you out so late?" asked Ingrid.

"Luck," he said, poking at the ashes with a long stick, tucking the remains of Grace's shawl deeper into the coals. "I could not sleep for too much thinking. I walked along the shore, and I saw you and your sister, and the ghost." He paused, watching the sparks and smoke rise from the damp wood. "That was brave, what you did. It should have worked, but I fear your sister has given this dead man too much."

"But you were able to drive him, it, off. I saw a knife."

"You did." Avan reached inside his coat, and pulled out a short-bladed knife that glinted dully in the firelight. Ingrid stared, for she had never seen such a thing. The dark blade was not all of a piece. Instead, it was three separate strips of metal, braided together and twisted into a wicked-looking point.

"The blade is cold iron," he said. "Such is supposed to have power over spirits and haunts. I was glad—" He broke off the sentence, and began it again. "I was glad to find out such sayings were true."

"And is the haunt gone then?"

"Only for tonight. The iron tore your sister's shawl, which was holding him here despite your calling her and the holy names you invoked. But he himself is not injured, nor could he be by such means." Avan looked at the blade with an expression of regret, and then tucked it back into his jacket.

"And how did you come to know so much?"

"I was well taught as a boy."

Which was no answer, and Ingrid saw in his face that he was clearly aware of the fact.

Before she could ask another question, Grace stirred under her hand. She gasped once, sharply, as if in pain, and her eyelids flew open.

"Where . . ." Grace pushed herself upright. Ingrid expected her next words to be "am I?" Instead, Grace stared wildly toward the lake. "Where is he?"

Ingrid knelt down in front of her sister, putting her body between Grace and the water as she had put herself between Grace and the ghost. "Who is he?" she demanded, grasping her sister's shoulders. "What has he done to you?"

Grace's eyes searched Ingrid's face without recognition for a long, painful moment. "He is cold," she said. She spoke slowly, dragging each word from somewhere deep inside her. "He saved me. I would have drowned, but he freed me from the water. I promised I would not leave him alone under there."

"Ask her if he told her his name."

Ingrid started, almost letting go of Grace. For a moment she had forgotten Avan. She frowned at him.

He had laid his stick across his knees. "She will not be able to hear me. She is too far gone to hear any but those of her own blood."

Ingrid nodded once, as if she understood what was happening. She tried to catch Grace's gaze again, but Grace was stared over her shoulder, searching for the ghost. Ingrid grasped her sister's chin as if she were still a child, and pulled it back down so that Grace would be forced to look at her.

"Grace, what is his name?"

Again, that heartbreaking pause while Grace came at least a small ways back to herself. "I don't know. I just know I promised. He's alone. It's so cold."

Grace began to tremble, and Ingrid's determination to find immediate answers melted away. She wrapped her arms around Grace's shoulder. "This is no good. I have to get her home. Our family will be . . . frantic."

"Yes." Avan stood, still keeping hold of the stick. "Can you manage her?"

"Since she was in diapers," replied Ingrid. She stood, keeping a firm grip on Grace's shoulders. Grace struggled briefly, which Ingrid found she expected from the way Grace's gaze would not leave the shore. But Grace seemed to lack the will to fight for long, and sagged against Ingrid's chest. "Although, I swear, I wish this were as simple," Ingrid breathed.

Ingrid found herself grateful that Avan pretended he did not hear that.

Avan let Ingrid lead the way, holding tight to Grace and pulling her forward one staggering step at a time. The farther they moved from shore, the weaker Grace seemed to become until Ingrid found herself supporting her sister's entire weight. She looked toward Avan, intending to ask for help, but then she saw the way he walked, stiff and alert, his arms ready at his side, clutching the stick the way he had clutched the knife. He walked like a soldier, she thought, as if he was expecting an ambush. Perhaps he was. The thought of that sent a fresh thrill of fear through her, and Ingrid kept her mouth closed.

She had no choice but to stick to the road, although dawn

was turning the sky silvery gray and soon the men and boys would come trooping down the rutted track to the bay and the boats. They already thought Grace struck down by madness. They would stare, and they would talk.

Well, the Devil take them if they do. Ingrid found she felt far more worried about what she would tell their family. It was already too late to disguise the disappearance. If she told what had really happened, Mama would insist on a priest. Under the circumstances, there could be worse ideas. Papa, thought . . . What would Papa think? He had been raised a strict Lutheran, and it came out of him at odd times. There would be words with Leo, no matter what happened. And what on earth would they tell the little ones?

"You must persuade your family not to try to send her away," said Avan, as if reading Ingrid's thoughts.

"Why not? She's not safe . . ."

"I fear no boat with her aboard would make it across the lake."

Ingrid felt her cheeks go pale. The words "is that possible?" hovered on the tip of her tongue. Of course it was possible. If all the other things that had happened tonight were possible, so was this.

"But you don't know," she said, cradling Grace's lolling head closer against her shoulder.

"I know she's being called. I know that in a moment of fearing for her life she bound herself to a dead man. I know that he will not let go that bond easily, and that he is restless under the water."

"Then what are we to do? We cannot surrender her to this . . . thing."

"No." Avan hung his head and was silent for a long moment. Ingrid could not see his face well in the morning shadows, but she felt he was reaching some decision. "Give me a day. I will find an answer."

Ingrid looked down at her fainting sister. It wrenched at her heart to see Grace so worn down, and in such a way. Mama had spoken softly of her fear that Grace's boisterous nature might lead her astray, but this . . .

At the same time she distrusted the stranger. There should

be a priest, there should be a doctor . . . but then again it was Avan who banished the ghost.

"Ingrid? Ingrid!"

Papa's harsh voice called from the morning shadows, followed quickly by the sound of heavy boots pounding the dirt road.

"I will do what I can," she breathed quickly.

Papa, Leo, pale Mama, and what seemed like all the men of Eastbay poured up the road.

"*Ach, Gott!*" Papa cried, seeing Grace collapsed against Ingrid's shoulder. He swept his second daughter up in his strong arms as if she weighed nothing at all. Mama laid her hands on Grace's brow.

"No fever, but her breath's so shallow . . ."

"What happened, Ingrid?" demanded Leo. "What did you see?"

Ingrid glanced at Avan, and she shouldn't have. Leo saw, and Leo, of course, jumped to the wrong conclusion. "What've you to do with this?" he demanded, stalking up to Avan.

Avan looked down at Leo, and for one of the few times in her life, Ingrid saw her brother looking spindly. "Your elder sister found your younger on the shore near the bay. She enlisted my help to bring her safe home."

"If we find Grace's been meddled with . . ."

"Leo!" thundered Papa. "Enough. Excuse him, Avan."

Leo did not appear to wish to be excused, but he did keep his mouth shut.

"There's nothing to excuse." Avan held his hand out, and waited. Leo, glowering still, shook it, and the tension in the air eased a little.

"What are you fools standing about in the damp for?" demanded Mama with unusual brusqueness. "Is she not sick enough for you? Get inside, get inside, and you as well, Miss Ingrid." Mama also had a hard glare for Avan, but it was plain to Ingrid it was not Grace she thought he might wish to meddle with.

Under the eyes of their neighbors, the Loftfields turned for home. Offers of assistance came, and were rebuffed by Mama and Papa.

"Thank you for your help, Mr. Avan," said Ingrid, careful not to look back at him as she followed her parents and brothers. She realized absurdly that she did not know for certain if Avan was his Christian name, or his family name. One more small mystery of this long, strange night.

As they neared the yard, Grace moaned and stirred in her father's arms. When they were all inside the front room, Papa set her on her feet and Grace stood, swaying in place.

"Take her upstairs, Mother," said Papa softly.

"I'll do it." Ingrid moved forward.

"No, you will not." Papa's cold words stopped her in her tracks.

Mama, her eyes already brimming with tears, took Grace's elbow. Grace offered no resistance as she was led away, but Ingrid thought she saw her sister's eyes flicker back, looking for her, pleading for help.

Ingrid swallowed and faced her father and brother. They were both square men, fair-skinned and auburn-haired, as she was. Hard men, shaped by labor and by the expectation of hard work and hard weather for the rest of their lives. The stubble on Papa's chin had gone gray, and his hands were thick with years of calluses.

Ingrid stiffened her spine, ready for whatever might come. It was then she saw the eyes of her two littlest sisters and their young brother peeping through the door to the back kitchen.

"Well there's a fine thing," she said. "All of you listening at doors when there's work to be done. The kindling is not gathering itself, nor are the hens going to give up their eggs without asking."

"Out into the yard, all of you," added Papa without taking his eyes off Ingrid.

The door swung shut as the children retreated.

"Now then, miss," began Papa. "What do you have to say for yourself?"

"I thought to see where Grace was trying to go," replied Ingrid steadily, folding her hands in front herself like a child saying a lesson.

"You thought!" snorted Leo. "You thought to humiliate us in front of all our neighbors. There won't be a man on the boats not asking me when you and Grace can come out again."

"Such a trial for you," snapped Ingrid. "I am so sorry that your sister's illness has brought you to such grief."

Leo took a step forward. "If she were ill, I would grieve. But she is either shamming, or she is mad, and you had to make sure the whole of Eastbay knew it."

Ingrid did not even blink. "The whole of Eastbay does know it! What do we think we're hiding in here? They'd help us if we let them, but no, we have to stay shut up in our house and deny our neighbors' concern."

"That's enough." Papa dragged the words out through gritted teeth. "You will tell me which of you the man Avan has to answer for."

Ingrid said nothing. She had known the question would come, but now that hung in the air, anger sealed her mouth.

Is that all you think of us? Of her? Is that what you think of any woman who smiles?

"Answer your father." Mama stood at the foot of the stairs. She wore her black hair pulled into a severe bun, and at the moment her bright blue eyes were dim with disappointment and resignation. She had been an Irish beauty once, Ingrid was sure of it. What had happened? In her heart, she believed she knew, but she had never been able to speak the words aloud.

"Answer him!" Mama clenched her fists. "Or has the Devil taken your tongue as well?"

Ingrid forced her chin up. She had only two choices now, she could either lie, or she could tell the ludicrous truth.

"It was a ghost," Ingrid said. "Grace is haunted."

Leo threw up his hands. "God in heaven!" he cried to the ceiling. "Are all the women in this family mad?"

"You asked what happened, and I've told you," answered Ingrid, calmly and firmly. "You can call me mad, or possessed, or any other name your stubborn mind can conjure up, Leonard Loftfield. It changes nothing, so, you may as well save your breath."

Hot, hard anger showed plain on Mama's face. She was going to start yelling in Irish and Papa would bellow back in German and Ingrid would have to shout at them both, or retreat with the little ones out back, when what she wanted was to go up to check on Grace.

But Mama did not yell. She just collapsed on the reed-bottomed rocker beside the fire, and hid her face in her apron. "Mother Mary, help your daughter," she whispered. "Jesus, Mary and Joseph, help your child."

"That's enough of that, Bridget Loftfield." Papa walked up to Ingrid, and all at once, Ingrid was a little girl again and she had to work hard not to shrink in on herself. "I've thought many things about my children, but I never thought you would be the liar."

"You also can call me what you want. I've told you the truth."

They stared at each other, neither one blinking, and Ingrid refusing to flinch. Behind them, she was aware of Mama in the rocker, her hands covering her face. Mama believed, and that was something. Surely that was something.

At last, Papa turned away. "Get into the kitchen. There's work to be done. Leo, it's time we were gone."

Ingrid turned and marched into the back kitchen. Once there, she gripped the edge of the table so hard she felt that it must break off in her fingers. She listened to the tramp of the men's boots as they marched out the front door. There was no other sound from inside the house, except the faint squeak of the rocker where Mama sat and wept her useless tears.

For a long moment, Ingrid let her anger burn. Then, at last, she willed it out of her, willed it through her hands down into the wood of the table, anything to get away from her. It did her no good. It was as useless as Mama's tears. She had to think. She had to decide what to do.

A knock on the lintel made her jump. Her hand pressed against her chest, she looked up to see Everett Lederle standing in the threshold.

"Hello, Everett."

"Hello, Ingrid," he said, pulling off the battered, blue cap he'd worn since he'd come back from the war. "I'd heard Grace had a rough night. I wanted to see if there was anything I could do."

Hard labor and time had worked their way with Everett,

like they had the men of her family, but with him it was
different. Him, they had polished, like a stone on the shore,
making him strong, patient, willing to let all the world flow
around him and ever able to wait. He was certainly willing
to wait for her. Everett loved her. She saw it in every look
and heard it in every word. The shame of it was, she found
herself unable to return that love.

"No, I'm afraid there's nothing to be done at present," she
told him. "But I thank you for stopping in."

"I'm glad to, Ingrid, you know that."

And she looked at him, earnest, steady, strong and
thoughtful, and for her lack of love of him she felt suddenly,
deeply sorry. "I do know, Everett, and as I said, I thank you
for it."

He waited a long moment for her to say something else,
but she had no more words for him, at least, she had none
he truly wanted to hear. But perhaps, after all, there was
something he could do.

"Everett, there may be something." *I should not do this. I
should not use him so. It will give him false hope.* Ingrid
could not love. To love would mean to leave Grace to be
worn down by the burden of caring for their hard family.
She'd thought of it, of course, she'd thought of it a hundred
times. Everett would at least take her to another house, but
to promise him love when she felt none, that would be so
much worse than what she did now. "I need you to speak
with the fisherman Avan tomorrow. I need to know if he has
any message or news for me. He knows what ails Grace, and
I would know if there was . . . news."

She saw the curiosity in Everett's face, and she saw disappointment. He did not want to be running errands to another man for her. But he said nothing of that. "If that will
help, that's what I'll do."

For a moment, Ingrid thought to squeeze his hand in gratitude. But no, she knew how he would take that, and he
would take wrongly. "It will. Thank you, Everett."

Everett nodded, put his cap back on his dark head and
stepped away across the yard. He was too late to catch the
boats going out. He had lost himself today's work to come
here to her.

Why do I not love him? Ingrid closed her eyes, and there in her private darkness, she saw Avan in the firelight, and she saw his long, graceful hands. Swiftly, she opened her eyes again, and went upstairs to Grace.

Grace lay still as a corpse under the faded quilts, her unbound hair spread out on the pillow showing the snarls the night wind had teased in it. Her eyes were open, but Ingrid had no idea what she saw.

Ingrid sat on the edge of the bed and picked up the comb that lay on the chest. Slowly, gently, she began to run it through her sister's hair, singing softly.

> *"Hushaby, don't you cry.*
> *Go to sleepy, little baby.*
> *When you wake, you shall have*
> *All the pretty little horses."*

"Ingrid?" Grace's voice was little more than a whisper.

"Yes, Grace. I'm here."

"I didn't mean to . . . I was under the water. It was so heavy, I was so tired. I was afraid I would drown. My lungs were freezing. He held me. He told me he would keep me safe. I cried to go home. He said I could, but that I must promise to come back. He was so lonely. I promised." She paused, and her chest heaved in a silent sob. "I don't want to go, Ingrid."

"You will not go." Ingrid gently teased out one more snarl. "I promise."

"He calls me. He calls me by my promise and he is never quiet. I didn't know before, but I do now, and he calls . . ."

Ingrid gripped her sister's shoulder. "Do not listen to him, Grace. He had no right to bind you so. You must not listen."

"So cold." Ingrid bit her lip to hear how much her sister sounded like the ghost.

Ingrid wrapped her arms around Grace and held her close, rocking gently back and forth. "He will not have you, sister. I swear by God in Heaven he will not have you."

———

Avanasy watched Ingrid Loftfield fall into step with her family, her back straight, and her hands gathering up her hems to keep them out of the way of her long, swinging stride. Her auburn hair had come loose during her night's adventures, and fell in dark curls down the back of her neck.

"Well, well, the one that got away, eh?" A hand slapped him hard on the shoulder. He turned his eyes from Ingrid to see Roman Thorfeld, a bony, blue-eyed man grinning at him, showing all his tobacco-stained teeth. Avanasy cursed himself for staring too long.

"I was just thinkin' about her poor sister," he said mildly, falling into the lower speech the fishermen favored. "Gone right out of her head I figger."

"*Ja, ja.*" Thorfeld, like a number of the men grown up on the shores of Lake Superior seemed to speak a blend of three or four different languages. He was not a vicious man, just of a coarse upbringing, and now he shook his head heavily. " 'S a shame too. They're good people, the Loftfields. 'S a sorry shame."

"And we're doin' nuthin' 'tall for 'em by standin' here," announced Elias Ilkka, a squat, dark Finnishman, tough as tarred rope and the nominal leader of the itinerant fisherman who clung to the shore of Sand Island. "Let's get to it, boys."

The men voiced their agreement in their various tongues, and trooped to the docks in a mass. Avanasy stayed with them. It was not what he wanted, but he feared that if he begged off, it would direct more talk at the Loftfields and plenty of that already swirled around him. Every incident, every encounter or interaction, especially involving the unfortunate Grace, was remembered, kicked over, examined, and improved upon. It went on all through the day, even out on the gray waters with the sharp wind pouring over them and all the work of rope, sail, net and the great loads of silver-blue fish to attend to. Omens for the misbegotten voyage were remembered, and Grace's wild ways. Her mother was a Catholic, it was said repeatedly, with many a sagacious nod, and her sister at twenty-three showed no signs of marrying, even with Everett Lederle hanging about her door like a hungry dog.

With all this gossip, all of it relishing its own stories, all of it essentially wrong, Avanasy found it hard to lose himself in the work, as he usually did. By the time they came in at late afternoon, it was all he could do to make himself help with sluicing the decks and hanging the nets up to dry. As soon as he was able he retreated to the shack on the shore where he lived amidst a cluster of other fishermen, each in their own summer shack. Come winter they would all head across to the mainland and turn to timbering for the season.

Come winter, what will you do? Avanasy dropped into his rough chair and stared at the banked coals in his tin stove.

After a time, he got up, poked the fire to life, put the remainder of the morning coffee on to heat, and lit his pipe with a splinter. He'd acquired the habit of both the brew and the bowl shortly after coming here, observing them to be the norm for the men around him, and he had to admit he found them both pleasant enough, if harsh. Like the backbreaking work on the boats, there was a rough enjoyment to be had in them, along with the singing, the gossip, the drink, and the wild beauty of the islands. He'd thought himself content. Not comfortable, to be sure, and there were days when the easy familiarity of his fellow fishers could still slap up hard against his pride. But content. Content enough.

Until last night.

He'd lied when he told Ingrid he'd been awake for too much thinking. He'd woken because he'd felt a change in the air. Something unchancy, Roman Thorfeld would have called it, and that was as good a word as any. He'd felt such things before in this world on the far shore of the Land of Death and Spirit, but those sensations had been fleeting, momentary brushes with whatever spirit powers this world held. He'd felt nothing so strong and so steady since he'd left Isavalta. All his blood sang in his veins at the touch of power, real power, and he'd gone to meet it like a lover.

There he'd found Ingrid Loftfield facing down a dead man, and about to die for it.

He hadn't even thought. He'd drawn his knife, and charged. Thankfully, the ghost had with him something of the living world it was using as an anchor, or else Avanasy would have done little more with his blade than annoy it.

Not that the burning of that shawl has driven it off for

more than one night. Avanasy sucked on the stem of his pipe, noticing only absently that its fire had gone out.

He had not worked any magic since three days after he landed here. He'd woven himself a simple spell of understanding that he might speak with the people who now surrounded him. Or it should have been simple, requiring that he take pains and be precise in his workings, yes, but otherwise it should have been of no great moment. But the effort of it had laid him low for almost a whole day. Among the many strangenesses of this world was this truth—that the magic was buried deep in the fabric of soul and soil and it would be coaxed out only with great reluctance. So, Avanasy had abandoned the work of magic for the work of fishing. It had seemed no great sacrifice. He had believed that exile and Medeoan's turning away had left him with little desire to continue as a sorcerer.

But then had come that touch of the other world last night, the brush of power, and he'd woken hungry for it. No, ravenous. It could have been anything, any monster, any trickster, anything at all, and if Ingrid and Grace had not been there to bring his other instincts into play, he might have done anything at all to keep it by him, to feel that touch of power that his blood so missed.

"I spent my life telling Medeoan she could not change what she was," he murmured to the fire. "It seems I did not listen to my own good teachings."

And I have given my word to help. He chewed on the stem of the pipe. He did not move to relight it. What did his word mean here? The word of a fisherman? The word of Avan? Nothing. He was no one in this place, with neither reputation nor honor to guard, and better off so. Power, and the revelation of power, could endanger him, forcing him further away into this world.

And the next time a power finds you? How much worse will it be next time?

Avanasy sighed. He removed his pipe from his mouth, knocked it out against the edge of the tin can he kept for the purpose, and stood. In the corner of his shack waited a heavy wooden chest which he kept locked with an iron lock, and which he now opened with an iron key he wore on a thong around his neck.

Inside lay his old clothes and boots, wrapped in oiled brown paper he'd purchased after his arrival, along with some gold stored up against emergency, and three silken scarves, woven with his own hands, each of them tied with three different knots.

Avanasy chose the blue scarf, and tucked it into the pocket of his coat. After locking the chest again, he turned to consider the contents of his cabin. He really should have wine for this, but there was none. He set some fresh coffee on to brew, wrapped up a packet of tobacco and his spare pipe, and set out some bread and smoked fish on the least battered of his tin plates. Rough fare, but the best hospitality he had, and that was what would count.

As the coffee finished, he went outside and laid a fire on the sand, lighting it with kindling of pine needles and splintered driftwood. The night was silent, except for the noises of wind and water. The other huts were dark and the men within them snoring loudly in their sleep. Avanasy laid his offerings out on the far side of the blaze and drew the scarf from his pocket. He spat on the knot and breathed across it, and tossed the scarf into the fire.

For a moment the fire burned bright blue, and a shower of sapphire sparks rose from the flames, then it shone red, and then white, but gradually, the pure white light faded, and the fire glowed golden again, as if it were nothing more than a blaze of driftwood. Avan sat down on a stone, and waited.

The moon had worked its way another inch up the dome of the sky when the rabbit came hopping down the beach. Its round black eyes reflected Avanasy's firelight as it advanced, hopping tentatively forward a few inches at a time, pausing to sniff the air. At last, it sat up on its haunches, combing its ears and twitching its whiskers.

Avanasy stood, and reverenced in his best courtly manner to the creature.

"I would be honored, sir, on this chill night, if you would join me at my fire, and share my poor fare."

The rabbit cocked its head to one side, considering. Then it hopped up to the plate bearing the smoked fish and bread.

It used its teeth to drag one scrap of bread off the plate, and began to eat. It ate all that bread, and the next piece, and the next, and then all the fish.

Then, it ate the plate.

Avanasy held himself very still. The rabbit advanced on the tobacco, snuffling it eagerly, drew a leaf out and ate that, and the paper it was wrapped in, and the pipe. Still, Avanasy did not blink, although he could not hold back some regret that he was about to lose his coffeepot. The rabbit stuffed its face into the coffee mug and drank it dry, swallowing the cup whole when it was finished. It knocked over the pot with one blow of its paw and crawled halfway inside, guzzling up the hot brew.

Then, to Avanasy's mild surprise, it withdrew its head, and sat up again on its haunches. And it was no longer a rabbit. Instead, it was a fat little man with copper skin and black hair bound in thongs hanging down past his shoulders. His ears were as long as his hair, and the lobes dangled down to his chest. His face was merry, and he smelled of sweat, tobacco, and coffee.

He belched loudly, the force of it shaking his long earlobes and making his round belly bounce. "You're a long way from home, I think, magician," he said.

Avanasy bowed his head in acknowledgment. "I am, sir."

"And why have you come so far to set out such a feast for Nanabush, eh?" He leaned forward. "Must want something, eh?"

Again, Avanasy bowed. "I have heard it said it is ever the way with us."

"Ha! Too true. Now, let me see if I can guess what ails you." Nanabush tugged at one pendulous earlobe. "There's a ghost, and there's a girl, and she's a fool and he's a bigger one, and you're the biggest fool of three."

Avanasy said nothing.

Nanabush spat in the fire. "Knots and bindings, nets and weavings, that's your business, and you want Nanabush to tell how to get yourself untangled."

"Is there a way within my power to remove the haunting from the Loftfield family?"

"Nets and knots with you," said Nanabush, picking up the

coffeepot and squinting inside with one round eye to inspect the bottom for more liquid. "Always nets and knots. Poor tangled magician."

Avanasy reminded himself of the absolute need for patience. "I believe I have had dealings with a relation of yours. She is queen of the *lokai*, the fox spirits, in my homeland."

"The Vixen. Yes." Nanabush held the spout of the coffeepot over his wide open mouth and let the last drop of liquid fall in. "She speaks of you." He smacked his lips loudly and belched again.

"Of your courtesy, tender her my best respect."

Nanabush stuffed his fist into the coffeepot, running one fat finger down along the bottom. "She says if you stay here you will live longer."

"I thank you for that news."

"Poor tangled magician." Nanabush sucked on his finger thoughtfully. "You fish. I've seen you."

Avanasy bowed. "It allows me to earn my keep."

"And it is not that different from shore to shore?"

"No, but one must know the waters."

Nanabush raised his finger to make his point. "And the fish themselves."

He was getting close to an answer. Avanasy could feel it, but he must not appear too eager. "I have heard, sir, that you know the waters and the fish better than any."

"Ha! It's true, it's true." Nanabush tapped his finger on the edge of the coffeepot. "These waters are deep, and they're dark. Many a soul is lost down there looking for the fish."

"So I have heard," said Avanasy gravely.

"But it's not just the soul that one must find." Nanabush shook his head, his earlobes flapping and flopping against his chest. "No. It's the bones. The bones of the fish that must be found and warmed. Bones bind as tight as any net."

"There is great wisdom in what you say."

"Ha! You will profit from listening to Nanabush." He shook his ears, tossing his lobes over his shoulders. "But others listen too. And others know things. The fish know that the dark of the moon is the time for fishermen, and they know that is the time for catching little fish, as well as big fish."

"Things do not so much differ from shore to shore."

"Not as much as some might think." Nanabush contemplated the coffeepot one more time, then dropped it onto the sand and kicked it across to Avanasy. "Nets and knots. Stay clear of the bindings and you'll live longer." His eyes twinkled. "Unless, of course, it is the bindings and their undoing that save your life."

Then there was only the rabbit, hieing itself fast across the sand and disappearing into the brush. Then, there was only Avanasy and his fire, and his empty coffeepot.

Avanasy picked up the pot. Well now he knew. Perhaps he knew too much. That was the risk of calling upon the spirits. He knew he could save Grace Loftfield. He had to raise the bones of the ghost at the dark of the moon, the very night the ghost would call Grace to him for the final, fatal time.

But, he also knew that should he ever return to Isavalta he would die. Unless, of course, he would live.

Nets and knots. Poor tangled magician.

Chapter Two

Medeoan stood at her mother's bedside and willed her to keep breathing.

The empress's private chamber was dark except for the light from the two braziers burning their pungent mixtures of charcoal and cleansing herbs which the physicians had prescribed as an attempt to clear the mucus from the empress's lungs.

Without daylight, the rich apartment seemed as robbed of its vitality as the woman lying still and sallow under the layers of goose down and royal blue velvet. The skin sagged around her throat and jowls, hanging in folds like the heavy curtains around her bed.

At least her eyes were still open, thought Medeoan as she reached out to try to smooth her mother's burning brow. At least some small sound still escaped her throat. Father lay in his own fever as if already dead. None of Medeoan's tears or pleading could rouse in him any sign of life.

The waiting ladies had all retreated to give Medeoan and Kacha a moment in relative privacy with her mother, and now those ladies stood in the shadows like ghosts waiting to come out and lay claim to the dying empress. Medeoan remembered as a little girl being brought by her nurse before those five ladies, and not being sure which one she was supposed to reverence to and call Mother. She had burst into tears at her confusion. The closest, tallest lady, this lady who lay so slack in her bed, had come forward and taken her hand.

"There, there," she'd said, smoothing Medeoan's fingers. "Don't cry. A great prince never cries where others can see, and you, my daughter, will be a great prince."

But not yet. Not yet. Medeoan's throat tightened, even as she forced herself to gently cradle her mother's hand. *I will save you. I promise.*

Normally, Medeoan's sorceries were kept out of sight. She was well trained, yes, and well read and she knew her own strength. But her actions were to be those of the mortal world whenever possible. No one, Father had said in a particularly blunt moment, wanted a ruler who appeared to strive for more than mortal greatness. But all that was laid aside for this. The court sorcerers had proven themselves useless in this matter. If there was to be magical aid for her languishing parents, the task fell to Medeoan. Already she had worn her fingers to the nub from two days of preparations while the others milled about trying to trap the life that spilled from the imperial vessels.

You cannot die yet. I'm not ready. I will not permit it.

As Medeoan straightened up, Kacha pressed close behind her, reminding her of his warm presence, and trying to ease her shivering.

Medeoan kissed her mother's hand. The skin was far too

hot against her dry lips. "You must bear with this for a little while longer, Mother." She tried to keep her voice steady. Mother's eyes were wide and shining with their fever. The empress let her head fall sideways so that she could look at her daughter, but the only sound she could make was a rasping cough. The physics said that the fever had swollen her tongue so that speech was impossible.

Medeoan sighed as Kacha pulled her close, not caring about the eyes of the ladies who surely watched them from their places in the shadows. He lifted her hand from her mother's, and she saw how his thoughts, as ever, were all for her.

"You have cut yourself," he said, looking at the delicate red lines that spread across her fingertips.

Medeoan only shook her head. "The threads for the weaving. They wear on the skin after a while."

But Kacha would not let the subject be dismissed. "You should rest before you go, beloved. You are exhausted." He touched her forehead, perhaps searching for some trace of the fever that wracked her parents. As ever, the knowledge of his love sent a small thrill of delight through her heart.

Despite that, Medeoan shook her head. "They are too ill. An hour could make all the difference."

"Then do it here," Kacha urged. "Surely their home is a stronger place for them than the woodlands."

"And if I draw out the sickness here, it stays here. I have to take it away from this house." She smiled weakly and pressed her husband's hand. "On these matters, I must ask you to trust me. I know how the magic must be worked."

Kacha frowned down at their hands.

"What is it?" asked Medeoan.

He ran his thumb across her knuckles. "You know what magic Avanasy thought best to teach you. I wish you had some other advisor for this part of your life."

Medeoan sighed. Kacha could not forgive. She would have been well pleased never to hear her old teacher's name again, but Kacha could not bring himself to cease worrying about the wrongs Avanasy had committed, no matter how many assurances Medeoan gave him. "It was not only Avanasy who taught me," she assured him. "Beloved, I ask you again, trust me in this. I will save them."

"Of course, my heart." He smiled. "In this I am but a few months old, whereas you have a lifetime of knowledge. I will be quiet."

No, dearest, that will never do. "You must always speak your fears to me, and your hopes. How else am I to know my whole mind and my whole heart?" She laid her hand on his chest. "We are two halves of one being, after all."

He lifted her wounded fingertips and gently kissed them. "Every time I look into your eyes, I am reminded of how much that means." He released her. "Go. The lords can wait. I will sit vigil over your mother."

"Thank you, beloved. I will be back before nightfall."

She kissed him then, allowing herself a moment to savor again the passion his touch sparked in her, and then she turned away. To look back would be to see Mother, her skin yellow and sagging against her bones. She could not carry that image with her into the woods. Her workings could not be tinged with despair. She must be all hope, all determination now.

Straightening her spine, Medeoan marched out of the sickroom to join her escort.

Kacha watched his wife sweep out of the room. Truly, she was beautiful, and when she allowed herself to be, she was a power in her own right. What a consort she would have made. He shook his head. Well, the Mothers did not always place one where one would thrive.

He felt the empress's gaze upon him. Kacha turned to face her. Her eyes were little more than dark holes in her yellow skull, they had sunken so far back. Her hands, so tenderly cradled a moment before by her daughter, plucked nervously at the coverlet, one of them struggling to lift itself up, to make some sign or gesture.

"Now then, Mother," said Kacha, stepping close to the bedside. "Do not bestir yourself." He leaned across her, hearing her breath rattle in her shriveled throat.

"The empress is overheated," he announced to her shadowed waiting ladies, as he straightened up. "She asks for a bath. Let her physicians be advised to draw one." He pointed to the first of the aging attendants. "And you had best make sure her broth and milk are cooled before they are brought in," he said to the second. "And a change of clothing might be advised," he added to the last two.

The women, one at a time, reverenced before his orders. They had been scolded into obedience of his words by Medeoan's swift and accurate tongue, shortly after her mother had fallen prostrate to the fever. They removed themselves from the bed enclosure to go pass the orders to their underlings, which gave him only a few bare moments of true privacy with his mother-in-law.

"Forgive me, my mother imperial," he whispered. "But this is necessary."

From his kaftan, he drew a kerchief, and then a velvet bag. Using the kerchief to shield his one wizened hand, he pulled an amber bead about the size of his thumbnail from the pouch. The bead had been cunningly carved into delicate human hands, their fingers intertwined. If one looked closely, one could see how tightly those fingers gripped each other, as if they were the hands of corpses clenched in the rigor of death.

Kacha once again leaned over his mother-in-law. She shrank from him, burrowing as far as she could into her pillows and goose down coverings. Her fingers stiffened all at once, as if they sought to scream for the woman who could no longer make any noise beyond a rasping cough.

"Now then, Mother," said Kacha softly. "It is but the work of a moment."

Swiftly, he caught her behind the head. Her mouth opened to cry out, and he popped the bead inside it, pressing her dry tongue down so that the bead must roll back into her throat, then sealing her mouth shut with his other hand.

"Swallow, swallow, Mother," he ordered her, massaging her throat with his free hand. "Swallow, and it will all be over."

Swallow, damn you. I have not much time.

She pressed feebly against his grip, trying to rise. Her hands flapped on the ends of their wrists, but at last, he felt her throat convulse as she swallowed the bead, and the spell it had been fashioned to hold. He released her, and she fell back down on the pillow, her eyes wide, frightened, and accusing. At the sound of footsteps which signaled the return of the empress's ladies, Kacha stepped away. Her first waiting lady rounded the edge of the screen, even as her empress's eyes rolled up, and their lids drooped closed.

"No!" The woman screamed, grasping her mistress's hand and pressing it against her breast. "Ofka, summon the doctors! She is in a stupor!"

Within moments, a flock of doctors and ladies surrounded the bed. Kacha stepped backward, letting them near her. Two of the court sorcerers hurried in to join the throng, and only then did Kacha allow himself a moment's concern.

Yamuna, this had best be swift, or these fools will be able to hold her life until Medeoan does her work.

Kacha might find in his bride naive in many ways, but he held her magical skill in great respect. It was that skill that made her dangerous. If her suspicions were ever roused such that she would choose to use it against him, the plans laid for her and for Isavalta would be at grave risk.

Be swift, Yamuna. Be sure.

With all eyes and minds directed toward the revival of the empress, Kacha walked out of her apartments, unobserved, and strode quietly down the hall to look in on the emperor.

Medeoan, High Princess of Eternal Isavalta, stood beside the mossy pool, several hours by canal from the palace of Vyshtavos, clad only in her shift, trying not to shiver.

You'll be warm enough soon, she told herself, as she watched Prathad, foremost among her waiting ladies, set the consecratory bowl down beside the pool. Beside it lay the cloth Mother had used to wipe Medeoan clean the day she was born, and next to that burned the stub of the candle Father had lit when she first drew breath.

Medeoan turned. Vladka, second among her ladies, held out the pillow upon which lay the girdle Medeoan had spent the last two days and nights weaving. The girdle's plait had been made up of silken threads twined with her hair, as well as her parents', and the blood and breath of all three of them tied together in the seven tassels that hung from its belt. She spat on the ends before she tied it around her waist.

Her parents were dying. The physics and the sorcerers turned their faces and said that Grandfather Death spoke to them, that he stood by the heads of their beds. Medeoan cursed them all. Her parents were not ready for death. She was not ready to surrender them. Not yet.

Prathad held out the silver knife with the golden hilt. It had been made over five hundred years ago by the first court sorcerer of Isavalta, when Isavalta was still merely one province among the northern countries. It was used only by the members of the royal family who were also born to magic.

Medeoan's was the first hand in four generations to hold it.

"Why are we born so?" she'd once asked Avanasy.

"None knows," he'd answered, shaking his head. "Perhaps because we are needed."

Medeoan shut her mind against memories of Avanasy. Avanasy was a traitor. He was banished. He was nothing. If no other sorcerer could help, he could not have done anything had he been here. It was foolish to long after him. This was her work. She was the one who was needed.

Medeoan waved her hand. Prathad and Vladka stepped back. Medeoan stooped until the knife's tip was a bare finger's width above the ground. Schooling her mind, as Avanasy had taught her (no, no, don't think of him now), she reached down inside herself and reached outside to the world around. She touched the magic, pulling it in, drawing it out, and she walked in a circle around the bowl. The air grew heavy and hot around her. The weaving had begun. She continued the tracery around the candle, the bowl and the cloth, linking them all together with her pattern.

Medeoan knelt before the bowl, the cloth and the candle, holding palm and knife over them. "I have gone into the deep country. I have stood beside the mossy pool. I have drawn the clean water. I have claimed the consecration cloth, the consecration candle and the consecration bowl. I have claimed the blood of my beloved parents and the blood of my own self." She pressed the knife blade against her palm.

"I have drawn the transparent line, and in the open country I make a great cry. Over cloth, over water, over candle, over blood, I charm my beloved parents." Hot. Hot. The air was on fire. Sweat beaded on her brow and trickled down her spine. So hot, hot with fever, burning, as her parents burned in their bed. *Good. Good. Let me summon the fever. Bring it to me.*

"I banish from you the fearful devil. I drive away the stormy whirlwind. I take you away from the one-eyed wood-goblin, from the alien house-goblin, from the evil water-sprite, from the outlaw witch and her sister, from twitchy-eyed mermaids, from the thrice-cursed Baba Yaga, from the dragon, the Vixen, and all their works. I wave away Yvanka's children and the screeching raven. I protect you from the flood, the fire, the frost, the quaking ground, from the twelve fevers that clutch and burn, from the black magician, from the warlock, from the savage shaman, from the blind cunning-man."

Pain now, running through her sinews. Her hands trembled, and the knife shook. She clamped her hand tighter and clenched her teeth.

Do not cry out. Do not break the weaving of words. This is their pain, you can hold it, they cannot.

Weak with pain and nearly blind with heat and effort, Medeoan took the knife in both hands and drove it straight into the ground.

"As the earth surrounds the blade of the knife, so shall my protection surround Edemsko and Kseniia." She panted against the heat and groped for the bowl. Her hands grasped the edges and she struggled to lift it. "As the pool swallows up the water," she tipped the bowl over the pool's edge, her hands quivering to hold onto it. "So will Edemsko and Kseniia's illness be swallowed." Her fingers slid apart and the bowl thudded to the ground. "As . . . as . . . as . . ."

Hold, hold. You can compass countries if you let yourself. Feel the words as you feel the threads on the loom, and the flames of the fire. The pain is nothing. It will be gone in a moment.

Avanasy's voice filled her. Avanasy exiled, traitor, and yet it was his words that rung around her head, that guided her groping hand to the candle, that allowed her to spit on her fingers, and pinch out the flame.

"As the flame is extinguished by my hand and spittle, so is Edemsko and Kseniia's illness extinguished."

Medeoan forced herself to her feet. Her ears sang with the effort it took to raise her arms. "This is my word, blessed by Vyshko and Vyshemir, this is my wish, and this is my seal upon it. Be done! Be done! Be DONE!" She screamed the last word with all the force her heart held, and with that scream, the heat, the pain and all the summoned magic rushed through her body from her heart to the soles of her feet, and was gone.

Medeoan collapsed onto the ground. She heard Vladka gasp and start forward, then stop. Perhaps Prathad held her back. She was too numb to look up, too numb to do anything except lie on the cold ground and breathe.

Done, done, done, her last word echoed in her mind. *I am done, they are done, it is done, all done.*

But done, Granddaughter, too late.

Medeoan jerked her head up. There, across the pool stood a figure in black robes, its face indistinct, as if shrouded by shadow. It reached one fine, unmarked hand into the pool, and impossibly drew forth a wave of water.

"No," gasped Medeoan, pushing herself to her knees. "No, Grandfather, I beg you, it cannot be so."

Grandfather Death stowed the wave in his deep sleeve and turned away.

"No!" Medeoan lunged after him, breaking her own, useless circle, running into the pool without even noticing.

"Highness!" shrieked Prathad. Hands grabbed her, hauling her backward out of the water.

The knife lay on the ground, and the candle burned beside it. Nothing. All for nothing.

"What is it, Highness? What has happened?"

"Ah!" cried Medeoan. "Ah, they are dying. I failed. I failed and they are dying!" She buried her head in her hands. She felt Prathad hold her close, weeping her own hot tears. Distantly, she heard the murmuring of the guards who surrounded her working. Gone. The emperor, the empress, were dying. The high princess had failed.

"Highness," said Vladka in a tremulous voice. "Highness, if it is as you say, you must return home, and quickly. You have . . ."

"I have nothing!" Medeoan snapped. She clenched her fists. "What do I have?"

"A husband who waits to hear from you," said Prathad. "Let us take you to him."

Kacha. She knotted her fingers in her hair, as if seeking to pull it out by the roots. How could she have forgotten even for a moment? She ached to feel his arms around her. Too late. Too late. But it could not be too late. Everything had worked, she had felt it. One or the other of them must still live. They were not both gone. She had not completely failed.

"Quickly." She pulled away from her ladies.

They all but threw on her skirt, her sleeves, her bodice, knotting each lace as swiftly as possible, and tossing over all her outer coat, her veil and coronet. Prathad called out for little, pale Anka the page girl, who ran for the guard to form up the escort. Medeoan did not wait for the canopy to be raised over her. She strode down toward the river's edge where her barge waited. The guard followed in haste, reforming around her with the girl pages who all seemed as white as their kaftans. Let her ladies follow as they could. The captain would have left men behind to escort them. She had to get back to Vyshtavos. She had to know who lived and who died. She had to find Kacha. She had to know how she had failed.

But Vyshtavos and its parklands lay beyond the city of Makashev, and although the captain sent the small barge ahead with a man to cry that the high princess (just princess still, she had not completely failed) was on her way, it did little good. Barges and coracles and rowing boats made a stew of the watercourse. The drawbridges were clogged with carts, and carriages, and old people on foot, and horses, donkeys, mules, dogs, all in the way, all streaming out of the streets between the wooden buildings with their peaked roofs and gilded spires and fat onion domes so that they could watch her pass. The river's breeze brought down the smell of the summer city, all mud and garbage, smoke and cooking food, and Medeoan felt that with every passing moment her heart must burst for beating so hard as she clutched the rail of her bench and willed the oarsmen to pull faster, and faster yet.

The lock to the imperial canal was at least open, and the keepers reverenced as her men pulled them past. The buildings cramming themselves up to the shore gave way to willows, pines, and sloping, groomed banks planted with lilies and bluebells, rare orange poppies and bleeding hearts. The air was fresh again, filled with the scents of the green and the growing. Birdsong replaced the endless gabble of people.

Which meant they were close, but not close enough.

Then the barge rounded the canal's great bend, and the trees parted to show the red-and-white granite of Vyshtavos, the palace built by her grandmother to show that Isavalta was a united and peaceful land, and that its rulers had no need to hide themselves behind castle walls. The imperial dock was imported teak wood inlaid with ivory. More uniformed bargemen waited there to receive the ropes the oarsmen tossed them.

But Medeoan saw them only for an instant. Her gaze skimmed past them to the broad, white granite steps, where the Council of Lords stood, with Kacha before them.

Her mind went numb. She could not feel her body anymore. It was a paralysis even more profound than that which had taken hold after her failed spell. Her utterly failed spell. Prathad and Vladka had to grasp her arms and propel her forward before her feet would move. They had to walk along the dock and climb the steps, carrying her between them.

Kacha was the first to kneel. He would be. It was so very like him. The first to bow his head and murmur, "Imperial Majesty."

The first to catch her as she tumbled to the ground in a faint.

The next hours passed in a blur of moving color and the rustle of cloth. Crowds of people whose faces she could not make herself see kept on marching solemnly up to her to kneel and bow their heads and call her by her mother's title.

At last, her ladies took her back to her private rooms. She stood as still as a wooden doll while they removed her daytime finery and dressed her in her nightclothes. They laid her in her bed and covered her over with velvet and eiderdown, and she still did not move. She lay staring up at the canopy, trying not to think of what had happened.

Mother and Father had to tried so hard to prepare her for this time. She, in her turn, had tried so hard to hide from it. Her efforts were of no use, however. The moment had found her, and all her evasions had accomplished were to make sure that it had found her stubbornly unready.

"My heart?"

For once, Medeoan found herself with no answer for Kacha. She heard his soft step as he passed the screens. She felt the feather beds sink as he sat beside her. She rolled over, huddling like an infant before him. His warm and welcome hand laid itself on her head and stroked her hair.

"I thought there would be more time," she whispered.

"I know," he said simply. "I believe everyone does."

"I don't know what to do. They spent years teaching me, testing me, lecturing me, and now I don't know what to do."

"That will come. What is important right now is that you realize you are not alone." He grasped her shoulders and raised her up until she knelt on the bed before him. "I am here with you. Together we will be the autocrat for Isavalta. You will be the flesh and blood, and the oh-so-passionate heart. I will be the bone on the inside, supporting and binding."

"Yes." In the darkness, her mouth sought his to kiss him hard and desperately. The press of his body against her held all the promise of life and the future. Together, as they were, they would know what to do. Together, hand to hand, skin to skin, and she would never be alone or confused again.

Some time later, Medeoan woke again to darkness. She lay for a time, listening to Kacha's breathing and feeling the warmth where his hand almost touched her shoulder. Beyond the curtains and screens that isolated them, she heard the soft rustles and sighs of her ladies asleep in their truckle beds. It was deep into the night, she felt that in her bones, and knew it by the sounds of sleeping around her.

Gently, Medeoan drew back the covers and slipped from the bed. Her black-and-gold mourning robe stood on its form waiting for her in the faint light of the brazier smoldering at the bedside. Before she could reach it, one of her ladies, in the dim light she was not sure which one, was there holding it out for her. She slipped into its warmth and let herself be buttoned in. Wrapping her sleeve around her hand, she gestured for a brazier's dish, which the anonymous lady brought so that she might have some light to see by. By its muted flames she could see it was Vladka who stood before her, ready to accompany her wherever she needed to go, and it was Vladka who she waved back to her post as she made her way between her sleeping ladies to the chamber door. The soldiers of the house guard and the young pages stationed there snapped to instant attention as she padded down the broad hall with its inlaid wood, its murals and mosaics.

The god house lay down the south stairs and at the end of the Gilded Corridor. Tonight, its wide doors stood open, releasing a flood of incense and candlelight. The double-wicked, braided candles that she had last seen at her wedding would be burning all night tonight. Those were the candles of Vyshko and Vyshemir, and their light called the gods to watch over the dead as well as the living. The court sorcerers and the keeper and his assistants moved about the room, shadows in all that gold and light, going through the forms of the ritual, keeping the vigils that were necessary to ensure that no ghost or goblin took advantage of the presence of death to make mischief.

Medeoan handed the brazier dish to one of the page girls and with a sharp gesture ordered her escort to stay outside.

The god house shined like a cave of jewels and fairy gold in a midwife's tale. The gods stood on their pedestal dressed in mourning black, and Medeoan imagined she could see tears shimmering in their glassy eyes. She looked up at them because she had no wish to look down to see the biers that flanked the gods' pedestal, piled high with flowers and green branches. Translucent white shrouds had been draped over her parents, so she could not see the yellow tint to their skin anymore. Those shrouds had been woven with care by the court sorcerers and contained spells as well as flaxen thread. Spells of peace, spells of protection, spells to keep the spirit from attempting to return to the flesh it had abandoned so that all things would remain in their proper orbits.

They would have fresh graves. The graves that had been dug in case of imperial deaths in winter were filled in when spring came. Medeoan had, more than once, walked through the cemetery with its stone monuments to see the gaping hole laid open for her, just in case she died while the ground was frozen hard. Every year it got a little bigger. There was a shroud for her too, somewhere.

So much laborious preparation for this ending. So much of life spent getting ready for death. This was what she had fought against since she had been old enough to fight, that her whole life was to lead up to this moment, to this end.

Well, now the end had passed, and here she still stood.

"Majesty." Iakush Vtoroisyn Gabravin, Lord Sorcerer to her father and Lord Sorcerer to Isavalta until she said otherwise, stepped softly up beside her. "It is not time for you to be here yet."

Until she said otherwise. "I have decided to be here," she answered him. "Therefore it is time."

"You wish to speak to them," said Lord Iakush with a sigh. "You have something you want to say, or something you want to hear."

Medeoan bit her lip, unable to answer. She had not thought her plan so evident.

"I stood beside my father's bier, just as you do, Majesty," Lord Iakush said. "I still remember the feel of his shroud under my fingertips. But my teacher was there with me."

Medeoan swallowed. "My teacher is a traitor."

Iakush paused only a moment at that. "Then I must ask you to hear me. It is a dangerous thing to call upon the newly dead. They remember too well the touch of this world, and if called back to this place they have loved, they may not wish to leave."

"But the living are always stronger than the dead." The words sounded hollow in her ears. She did not feel strong. She felt weak as water.

"Stronger, but sometimes not so desperate, nor so frightened, nor, at the worst, so angry," Iakush told her gently. "Your parents did not die easily. To call them back from the Land of Death and Spirit so soon will be to call them back to their hearts' best loves and worst fears. They may not be able to let go again."

"If I bring them back, I can send them away again." Medeoan did not look at the lord sorcerer. Her gaze remained fastened on the white-shrouded figures that were all that remained of her parents in the living world.

"It will be a struggle, Imperial Majesty. Would you wish on them more struggle now that they have gone to rest?"

"It is Vyshko and Vyshemir who are your living parents now." Keeper Bakhar rounded the pedestal of the gods, coming to stand at her other side. "They protect you, and expect your duty in return."

Medeoan turned her gaze up to the gods in their black gowns, especially to Vyshemir with her cup and her dagger, the tools she had used to save Isavalta when Isavalta was only one city and Vyshemir was only a mortal woman. It was Vyshemir's sacrifice of her life that saved Isavalta from invasion from the barbarians of Tuukos, and blessed it so that it could grow into the empire that had been placed into Medeoan's hands.

Not so long ago she would have cried, "But I do not want this duty!" She had, so many times, thrown herself prostrate at the foot of this pedestal, begging the gods for some way out. She was too small, she was too scared, she did not know enough, she did not want this duty. They had not listened. Instead, they had taken her parents and left her here.

"I know what you feel," said the keeper gently. "But if the gods trust you to rule their house, in their name, how can you fail to trust yourself?"

You are the heir of Vyshemir, her mother had told her long ago. *This is not a gift that can be returned. In the end you are the one who will decide how to make use of it.*

She had scorned those words then, and if she had not stormed out of the room on that occasion, she had on many others.

"I just wanted to tell them that I understand now," she said, wondering at her own words, but knowing the truth of them.

"When death comes so close, we find we understand many things," said Keeper Bakhar. "Come, Imperial Majesty, let us not trouble your parents, but pray for their rest and comfort."

So, for the first time, the new empress of Isavalta allowed herself to be advised, and let the keeper of her god house lead her to the audience alcove so that she might speak to her parents properly, through the gods. So that she might say she would do her best.

So that she might say that she truly did understand.

Kacha lay in his wife's bed for a time after Medeoan left, listening to how, after a few dozen heartbeats, the rustlings of ladies disturbed by their mistress's passage faded once more into the sounds of gentle breathing and sleep.

The withered fingers of his right hand tapped restlessly on the covers. He could not be absent when Medeoan returned, nor could he risk one of those ladies waking up and finding him engaged in improper activities. His fingers tapped more urgently, reminding him that he had other concerns.

You will simply have to be quick. Kacha slipped from his wife's bed. The darkness confounded his left eye but made little difference to his right. He waved the attending lady away and moved surely across the dank stone chamber to the unprepossessing door that led to his own suite.

The room on the other side was also shrouded in darkness, and his own flock of attendants snored in their rude beds, except for the two on night duty who sprang to their feet as he entered. He waved them back and did not spare them any other thought. Many of these were men he had brought with him. Those who had been assigned to him by the Isavaltan court, and could not be bribed, had long since been replaced by those who could. All of them knew better than to take any undue notice of what their master did after dark. Soon he would have to take similar measures with Medeoan's ladies.

The single advantage to the eternal cold and everlasting stone of this place was that there was always a fire burning somewhere. Kacha carried the smoldering brazier from his bedside behind a carved screen to the inlaid work desk where he wrote his letters. He set the brazier carefully in the waiting stand. He uncovered it with his right hand and blew gently on the coals to raise a cluster of delicate flames.

As the flames strengthened, Kacha felt a hunger seep into his mind. It flowed from his right eye and his right hand. Fire was gate and guardian. Fire was power and peace. These were truths he had not understood before his transformation, but now they were as much a part of him as his new eye and hand.

Prepared ink and paper waited for him on the desk. With his right hand, Kacha picked up the pen. He spat on the silver tip before dipping it into the thick black ink. Closing his left eye, he forced himself to relax and let his hand work. It was never easy, but it was necessary. Kacha knew himself to be a tool as well as a prince, and this was hard knowledge.

His hand worked busily at its task, sketching out particular sequences of letters, not to form words, but to form patterns, waves, tight, interlocking circles, and stars. His right eye saw the work, and it reached out to see beyond ink, spittle, and paper to places Kacha's mind would never touch.

When eye saw that hand had finished, hand laid down the pen and picked up the paper. Sweat prickled Kacha's forehead and the strain of his spirit reaching outside his flesh made his temple throb. He turned to the brazier and laid the paper down atop the coals. With his right hand, he smoothed the flames over the page.

Pain flared down through his skin to the bone. Kacha clamped his jaw closed to keep from screaming.

It does not burn. It does not burn. He tried to fill his mind with that thought. He had done this before and he knew his skin would emerge whole. If he had been a sorcerer in whole rather just in part, there would not even be any pain. But he could not stop his hand. He could not even pull it from the fire, so he must endure. Tool as well as prince. Conqueror and surrendered. But it hurt, by the names of the Seven Mothers, it hurt.

But while the fire blazed and filled him with pain, to his eye it appeared to have lost the power to consume. His skin, although it was surrounded by flame, remained untouched. So too did the paper on the coals. Only the ink began to smoke. It bubbled as if boiling in a pot. Kacha's fingers stirred the flame. The ink sizzled and the smoke took on a bitter smell. At last, all the ink turned to black steam and drifted away.

Kacha's hand twitched the parchment out of the flames. The pain ceased at once and the chill air was like a blessing against his skin. Relief buckled Kacha's knees and he dropped to the floor. Tears of remembered pain and present relief mixed with the sweat running down his face.

Kacha impatiently dashed the tears away with his left hand. His right hand smoothed the paper out against the floor. He peered at it closely and his right eye saw a series of faint, gray tracings, pale words that seemed to have been written with nothing but smoke.

I do not like that Medeoan has left your side now, read the words. *Keep close watch on her. It may be she has realized she can no longer play at being free from her birth. Concentrate your efforts on the Lord Sorcerer and the Mistress of the House. If we may secure those two, nothing may be done or said within the palace walls without our knowing of it.*

Soon it will be time to move to the Summer Palace. Before then, you must find your way down into the Isavaltan treasury. There you will be able to find the means to secure your wife should she begin to pull away from your side. Send word to me as soon as you gain access, and I will guide you further.

Kacha nodded in thoughtful silence at what he read. As usual, his father's sorcerer, *Agnidh* Yamuna, spoke with keen understanding. Kacha allowed himself a moment to pity Medeoan. His child bride would lose her empire without ever having truly gained it. It would be sad to watch her when she realized what happened.

Her death, when it came, would surely be a relief to her.

Chapter Three

"I'm taking the soup down to Mrs. Whitkoff," called Ingrid to her mother, bundling up the two crockery jars in the burlap satchel. "Is there anything we need from the store?"

Mama remained bent over the washtub and shook her head. For a change, Ingrid was glad of her mother's indifference. Since Mama stopped watching her, her task had become much easier, although her life had become that much lonelier.

For two weeks, Grace had languished in her bed. Ingrid had spooned broth, milk, and beer down her, and she swallowed, but it brought her no strength. At least she had stopped her nocturnal roaming. Avan's advice had done that much already.

Everett had made good his promise the day after Ingrid had seen the ghost. He'd come to the kitchen door at dusk and stood there with his worn, blue cap in his hands. "He said," Everett did not bother to use Avan's name, "that you should tie a piece of iron around her neck, and put another under her bed. This will keep her in the house. He has begun work on a stronger cure."

Iron. Of course. When Ingrid was small, when Mama still felt inclined to tell fairy stories, she had said that cold iron was proof against magic. Hadn't Avan said as much last night? "Thank you, Everett."

She expected him to bow his head bashfully then, as was his usual habit. Instead, he fixed her with a look of unusual determination. "Ingrid, what is happening?"

Ingrid took a deep breath. He had earned the truth, but this time it was she who could not look directly at him. She watched her fingers pick at the edge of the kitchen table. "Grace is haunted. Avan has knowledge of these things. We hope to lay the ghost, and free her."

"You believe this?" Incredulity filled Everett's voice. She could find no fault with that.

Ingrid nodded. "I saw it."

Silence stretched out long and tight between them until Ingrid saw Everett's shadow move across the table. She looked up. He had taken two steps inside the door, coming in just far enough to touch the tabletop, as if by touching the same surface she did he would be able to create some vibration of communion between them. "Is . . . is there any way I can help?" He did not doubt her. He would not. Everett dealt honestly and expected honesty in return.

For the thousandth time Ingrid wondered why she looked at Everett without love. He would marry her in an instant. Papa and Mama would raise no objection. He would build a new house for her and they would live in it together. He would never raise his voice to her. He would never think of raising his hand to her or their children. It would be so easy. All she had to do was say yes to him.

Perhaps, after all, that was the reason. It would be too easy a release. She would never know if she went with Everett out of love, or out of a final need to escape her parents' house. Without that certainty, she would have to live with the fear of her heart's life washing out of her, as it had washed out of her mother. "I will let you know, I promise."

Her words caused a gentle grin to form on Everett's face. "I'll hold you to that, Ingrid." He started to turn away.

"Everett . . ." Ingrid raised her hand as if to snatch at him.

"Yes?" He looked back over his shoulder, his eyebrows arched.

"I can't . . . I don't . . ." Ingrid's voice shook, and her hand fell to her side.

But Everett spared her the necessity of finishing her sentence. "I know." He shrugged easily. "It doesn't matter."

But it does, she wanted to say. *You should love someone who is able to love you in return. You should be happy.* That, however, was not something Everett would want to hear, and she would not disgrace this moment he had given her by saying it. Instead, she said the only words left to her. "You are a good man, Everett Lederle."

He smiled. "I am at that. I'll look in on you later, Ingrid."

"Thank you, Everett."

He waved his cap as a farewell before setting it back on his head.

So she had done what Avan said. She fetched a broken and rusted hinge from the shed and tied one half around Grace's neck on a piece of twine, and slid the other under her side of the bed. That night Grace had struggled, and she had cried out, but she had not risen.

"I hear him, Ingrid," she whispered.

"I know." Ingrid had tried to smooth out Grace's brow. "But not for much longer."

The Whitkoffs lived on the edge of Eastbay nearest the cove that gave the settlement its name. Mrs. Whitkoff was down with the croup, leaving her eldest daughter Lucia to manage on her own. Mrs. Gustavson was coming in to help, though, and so far the Loftfields' gifts of bread and broth were not being turned away, although no one seemed to have time to stand and chat anymore. Perhaps no one wanted to take the chance that Grace's madness was contagious, or perhaps it was just Papa and Leo's scowling at every man on the island was finally beginning to wear on their neighbors' patience.

Lucia Whitkoff, who had dark circles under her bright blue eyes, met Ingrid at the door with a broom in one hand and her infant brother balanced on her hip. Ingrid left one of the two jars on the kitchen table, and hurried away before Lucia had time to get really uncomfortable. She had no time to linger anyway. She had her own errand to complete, and she could not take long, or Mama would want to know where she'd been, and Ingrid was fast running out of lies.

The sun sparkled on the bay, turning the water silver and blue. Despite the warmth of the summer sun, Ingrid wrapped her shawl around her head, so that from the boats out on the lake, she'd be an anonymous woman with an anonymous bundle tucked under her arm. If Papa saw, if Leo saw ... it didn't bear thinking about. But now was the time she had to come, because now was the time when the fishers' shacks were deserted, and there was no one to see her scurrying between them. No one but Avan.

We must bring the ghost's bones up from the lake. I am making a net for the purpose.

He'd delivered that message by Everett. Ingrid kept it tucked under her pillow as if it were a love letter. It was written on a scrap of brown paper with grease pencil in a bold, flowing hand, like none she had ever seen.

At the dark of the moon, we will go fishing. Come find me when you can.

But as she approached his rickety shack this morning, she did not see a plume of smoke rising from the tin chimney. Worry struck her. She rounded the hut to the door, and knocked for form's sake.

"Avan?" she whispered, when there was no answer, pushing the door open.

Avan slumped in the hut's one chair, the great net he had been weaving spread out across his legs like a quilt. Ingrid gasped, almost losing her grip on the jar of soup she carried. Avan's hand twitched, scrabbling at a single knot, and even in the hut's gloom, she could see the blood staining his skin.

Quickly, Ingrid set the crock down by the door and ran forward. She pulled the net out from under Avan's hands, letting it fall in a heap onto the ground. As soon as the strings slipped from his fingers, his hands stilled and fell limp at his sides. The weight of them threatened to drag him out of the chair, but Ingrid caught him under the armpits.

"Come, you must help me," she grunted as she heaved him to his feet.

Avan didn't even groan, but he must have had a little strength in his legs, because he staggered beside Ingrid as she hefted him over to the rickety wooden cot that was his bed and dropped him onto it. She snatched the frying pan off the stove and ran out to the lake, scooping up some water to set on the stove. Upon opening the stove's door, she found three coals still glowing amid the ashes and was able to coax them to life with some of the tinder from the woodbox.

Avan groaned. Ingrid strode to the bedside, taking off her apron. She saw no cleaner cloth. His skin was fever hot against hers as she wiped away the blood from his tattered finger ends.

"What in God's name happened to you?" she murmured.

He'd said the task would be hard. He'd stopped going out on the boats to save his strength, he'd said. She'd become used to seeing Avan growing more pale, but this, this was gruesome.

Steam began to rise from the water on the stove. She washed his hands again in the hot water, cleaning away the scabs so they could bleed freely for a while. She propped them up on her apron. She'd have to find something to use as bandaging. She surveyed the hut and saw rope, and sacking, and two chests, one bound in rope, the other bound in iron.

"Forgive the intrusion, if you will." Ingrid opened the rope-bound chest and found a spare shirt and trousers, some linens and socks and four huge, worn, but serviceable handkerchiefs.

"Thank goodness. I've enough explaining to do. I come home without my apron or with my petticoats torn, I'd never be let out of the house again."

She pulled the chair up beside the cot and wrapped one handkerchief over his fingers, making a crude mitten. As she did, she saw again how graceful his hands were, and she could not help but notice that his calluses were fresh, as on the hands of a boy who had just started out regularly in the boats, not like the ancient knobs that coated her father and brothers' hands. He had scars too, three long, white slashes on his palm, and a whole series of old nicks on his wrists.

What are you? she wondered, winding the second kerchief around the first and tying it tight to make a secure, if improvised, dressing. *What are you doing here at all?*

She picked up his left hand and felt the tips of her ears heating up. His hand was heavy and warm against hers, and from her secret self came the sudden wish to press the back of it against her cheek, to feel how that smooth skin would feel touching her face, how it would be to press her lips against it.

By the time she tied the second dressing off, she knew she was blushing furiously. She pressed her palms against her cheeks, willing herself to calm.

Then she saw Avan's eyes open and watching her, and all the blood in her heart rushed burning to her face.

"Keep still, sir," she said, rising swiftly to her feet and turning away. "You need a cool cloth for that head . . ."

"No," he croaked. "Don't leave me."

"I'll be back in a heartbeat." She moved away, but she hesitated.

"No," he said again. "Please. Stay here."

Ingrid's heart thumped hard against her ribs. "All right." She pulled the chair back so she sat by his head. "But you shouldn't talk . . ."

"Yes," he said. "I must. I must . . . come back. Too far gone." He had to drag in several long breaths. "Too long away. I must touch earth again."

Ingrid frowned in incomprehension. "What can I do?"

He rolled his eyes toward her and said quite seriously, "Sing for me."

Ingrid wanted to protest, but only for a moment. The time for questions would come later. She must have Avan strong and well to save Grace. So she licked her lips, and began.

> *"Oh yes, my lads, we'll roll a-lee,*
> *Come down, you blood red roses, come down.*
> *We'll soon be far away from sea.*
> *Oh, you pinks and posies.*
> *Come down, you blood red roses, come down."*

She did not look at him as the verses wound along, the slow, old song of a man coming home from sea, sung to keep time while hauling on the ropes. She wanted to keep her mind on Grace's need, on how she might explain her lengthy absence to Mama, and how she would get out of the house tonight, but her hands still tingled from touching Avan's hand, and she could not pull herself away from the sensation.

> *"Come down, you blood red roses, come down . . ."*

"Thank you," he said when her song was finished, and his voice sounded stronger. "That cool cloth would be welcome now."

Ingrid all but ran from the hut to fetch a fresh pan full of water.

Avan lay silent and patient as Ingrid sponged his face down with a rag she found by the stove. He had no cup, so she held the hut's one tin bowl to his lips so that he could swallow some of the water.

"Thank you," he said again. "Now, Ingrid, I must ask you to listen closely to me."

Ingrid said nothing, she just leaned forward to better hear his rasping voice.

"The net is finished, but the working of it has shattered me. I thought myself strong enough, but I was not." His voice was flat as he said it, but Ingrid had heard the disappointment, and the reproach for himself. "If you want to save your sister, you must do as I tell you."

"I will."

"After dark you must take the net to the water's edge. You must have a fire going, a good one, with plenty of coals to make it hot. You must cast the net into the waters. The net will retrieve the dead man's bones onto the shore. You must cast them, net and all, into the fire."

Ingrid nodded.

"He will try to prevent you. You will have to be strong. He will work through your fear, and your cold."

"I understand." She spoke the words quickly, meaning only to use them to silence him. She was startled to realize that there was some truth behind them. This insanity had begun to make sense, the way a story of fairies or ghosts made its own sort of sense. As such stories had a deep familiarity to her, so this had all started to feel familiar. She felt at once reassured and disturbed by this realization.

Cloth brushed Ingrid's wrist as Avan reached for her. "Your sister will be called tonight," he said hoarsely. "There is not enough iron in any world to keep her safe."

"I understand," she said again as she folded his arm fussily back across his chest. He did not need to be agitating himself right now. She was surely agitated enough for them both.

He did not protest, nor did he stir again. "I will be there if I can."

Ingrid just shook her head. "You have done so much already. You have all my thanks."

"I hope it is enough." He turned his face away.

"Avan . . ." Ingrid rubbed her hands together. He turned toward her again. "Avan, where are you from?"

Avan's mouth twitched as if he did not know whether to smile or frown. "Isavalta," he said.

"Isavalta," Ingrid repeated the strange syllables. "I've never heard of it. It must be far away."

"It is."

"What did you do there?" Ingrid was not sure why he she had decided to quiz him, especially since a moment ago she had been convinced he should not agitate himself. Perhaps it was to convince herself of his reality. Perhaps part of her expected him to vanish away when all this was over, just another part of this ghost story in which she found herself. She already knew enough to know that if that happened she would be greatly saddened.

Whatever Avan might think of her questions, he answered mildly. "I was hired by a great family to teach their eldest daughter."

An image of Avan in a long-tailed black coat standing beside a little girl in ribbons and frills and a worktable piled with books flitted through Ingrid's mind. It felt unaccountably wrong, and yet, she did not believe he lied. "Why aren't you still there?"

The blanket rustled as Avan shrugged. "The daughter got married, and I was no longer needed."

"So you came here to work on the boats?"

"As you see."

"It seems strange that you could not find another teaching position."

"Yes, I imagine it must." Ingrid knew he would answer any other question she asked, but she also knew that he hoped she would ask no more.

"I will find some place to stash the net." Ingrid got to her feet. "It would not be good if I were seen here after dark."

Understanding and gratitude both glimmered in Avan's tired eyes. "None of this has been good for you."

"No. But I do not need to make it any worse." She bent

over the net where it lay and found one of its corners. She began to roll the great mass of knots up into the tidiest bundle she could manage. It was surprisingly heavy, despite the fact that the strings from which it had been made were far too delicate to contain any fish she knew of. The strings radiated out from their knots making patterns like sunbursts, like snowflakes. She had never seen such a net. She felt somehow she could become lost in those patterns if she stared at them for too long.

"You must bear your sister great love."

Ingrid bowed her head over the bundle in her arms. "She is the one happy thing our family has ever made." Then, heavily regretting those words, Ingrid strode toward the door. "I shall do as you say tonight."

She did not give him time to reply. She had stayed far too long already.

Ingrid stashed the net deep in a tangle of tall grass and fern. She marked the spot with three gray stones. She hurried over the bluff heading for home, snatching up branches of dry wood and pausing to pluck up wild thyme as she went so that her arms would not be empty, and her absence would appear less remarkable.

But she had barely reached sight of the family yard when Thad, her youngest brother, came running up the track.

"Papa's home."

Ingrid's back stiffened and her step faltered, but she recovered. "Well, it's early for him, isn't it?" she said as brightly as she could manage. "Help me with this." Thad held out his thin, nine-year-old arms dutifully and Ingrid loaded them with wood. He trotted around the house toward the back door. Relatively unencumbered, she opened the front door and strode into the house.

"So, is it you?" Papa's voice rumbled out of the back kitchen, and the man himself followed a bare instant later, with Mama and Leo in tow. "And where have you been, miss?"

"As I am sure Mama told you," said Ingrid calmly. "I have been taking soup down to Mrs. Whitkoff." She passed him as if nothing was wrong, laying the thyme down on the bare dining table.

"And is that all?" demanded Leo. "Or did you have other goods to deliver?"

For a moment, Ingrid did nothing but breathe in the sharp clean scent of the wild herbs. Then, she stiffened her shoulders and turned to face her accuser. "What wrong do you suspect me of?"

"Our sail tore out." Papa started forward with his shoulders hunched up almost to his ears. "We had to come in early. As we tacked around, we saw a woman going in and out of the fishers' huts. It was remarked by more than one how much she looked like you."

Ingrid swallowed, her throat gone suddenly dry. *You knew this would come. You cannot pretend to be surprised.*

"The man Avan says he has a way to help Grace," she said flatly. "I sought only a remedy for my sister."

"And what did he seek, eh?" sneered Leo.

That was the final straw. "Curb that evil tongue of yours, Leo, even if you cannot curb your thoughts."

"Ingrid . . ." began Mama.

"No," snapped Ingrid. "I tried to tell you what was wrong with Grace, and you only worried about whether the neighbors would believe we had both kept our virginity safe."

"Ingrid!" thundered Papa.

"Well, I will tell you what the neighbors think of that." She barreled on, too hot and angry to stop. "The neighbors don't care! Half of them are bastards of one stripe or the other! But for God knows what reason you have decided that Grace is wicked, and that I am implicated in her supposed wickedness, because I care what becomes of her, and you don't."

"You will not speak so in this house!" Papa raised his heavy hand.

Ingrid did not even flinch. "Go ahead," she said. "Strike me down, but I tell you this. That blow had better lay me in my grave next to Grace, because if it does not, I will leave this house and I will blacken our name from Sand Island to Bayfield and right down to Chicago."

Mama had gone paper white. She moved forward, a slow, sleepwalker's motion that reminded Ingrid of watching Grace slip forward in the darkness.

"If I ever hear it you speak so again in this house, mine will be the hands that throw you out into the dirt."

"How can you?" Ingrid flung her hands open wide. "She's your daughter."

"Do you think for one instant I have forgotten?" spat Mama. "I am responsible for her. I am responsible for whatever deviltry has taken hold of her! God forgive me, this is my fault!" Mama buried her face in her hands. "My fault!"

Ingrid wanted to feel sorry, she wanted to feel pity, but all she felt was tired. "Listen to me. I am going out. I will return by morning. If all goes well, Grace's affliction will be lifted. After that you can do as you like with me. All I ask is that you consider that I might have been telling nothing but the truth."

She meant to leave the house then, but even as she turned she realized she could not leave Grace here. Who knew what Papa and Leo would do when she was called out to the shore. So, instead, Ingrid stormed up the stairs to her bedroom.

Grace lay under the covers, as still as any corpse.

"Come, little sister," said Ingrid gently. "Let's get you dressed, shall we?"

Through the floorboards, Ingrid could hear the voices of her family raised in argument and blame. She tried in vain to shut them out as she moved about the room, gathering Grace's clean linen, her thickest skirt, and layers of shawls. Grace's skin was horribly cold to the touch and Ingrid had to dress her as if she were a rag doll. Grace's eyelids did not even flutter under Ingrid's attentions, and nothing passed her lips but the sigh of her breath.

"Perhaps I should become a nurse," muttered Ingrid as she sat Grace up. "I seem to be making a profession of hauling the sick about with me."

At the same time, she knew she would never be able to carry Grace all the way down to the beach. Biting her lip, Ingrid pulled the string holding the scrap of iron off from around Grace's neck and tossed it onto the bed.

As the iron thudded against the quilt, Grace's head jerked upright and her eyes flew open wide. Her gaze lighted for a moment on Ingrid, but then slipped past her to the door. Her hand tightened briefly on Ingrid's arm as she used Ingrid to pull herself to her feet. She took three faltering steps, and collapsed, measuring her own length on the floorboards.

Ingrid dropped at once to her knees beside Grace. Grace lifted her bedraggled head and saw Ingrid, truly saw her for the first time in this whole hellish month.

"Help me, Ingrid," rasped Grace. "Help me go to him."

"Yes," said Ingrid, although the word choked her. "We are going to him now."

Ingrid raised Grace up, shocked at the strength of her sister's grip. One step at a time, they together made their way down the stairs to the front room. Their family stopped their arguing and stared in a silent astonishment as Ingrid supported Grace to the door.

No one spoke. What was there left to say? No one would stop them. There would be time enough in the morning, if morning came, to worry about whether they would once again be admitted into their home.

The road to the lake's shore had never seemed so long. Grace stumbled over every rut. Children and old women came to their doorways to stare at their strange, limping progress. A child's voice laughed. Another's called a name. A clod of mud arced through the air and thudded softly at Ingrid's feet. It was of small consolation that this was followed fast by the sound of a sharp rebuke and a ringing slap.

Ingrid did not allow her attention to waver. She kept her mind focused sharply on the road, and on Grace. Grace's eyes shined with an eager light. Her sunken mouth trembled. Ingrid knew that her lips would be shaping the name of her ghostly lover, if only she knew it.

What will I do if she decides to run into the lake? Ingrid wondered with sudden desperation. *How can I possibly stop her?*

But there was nothing for it but to continue on their way, one weary step at a time. Against her will, Ingrid found her thoughts trailing behind them, all the way back to their door. She could not have said which made her heart heavier: the fear that their family might follow, or the fear that they might not.

At long last, Ingrid and Grace stumbled onto the beach below the bluff. When they reached the sand, Ingrid let go of Grace, although her entire soul screamed at her not to do so. She had to see what Grace would do. Once free, Grace tottered forward a few steps and sank down to the sand, her knees pulled up against her chest and wrapped her arms around them.

"He will come for me," she said. "After dark. He says so. He sings so to me."

"Well, we'll just have to wait," said Ingrid with a brittle briskness. "Will he object to a fire until then?"

If Grace heard, she had no answer. She just continued to stare hungrily out across the water, listening to a voice Ingrid could not hear.

At least she wasn't going anywhere, which would require that Ingrid sit with her. Activity allowed Ingrid to keep her mind occupied with things other than the coming night. She dug a pit in the sand with her hands and pieces of driftwood. She gathered driftwood and tinder, ranging as far afield as she dared to bring back fuel. She did not want to risk running out of wood. Her foraging also kept her from having to watch the sails from the returning boats, knowing that any one of them who looked toward the shore could see her and Grace, and would wonder about it. Oh, they were now surely the nine days' wonder of the island. Even if Mama and Papa took them back in when this was over, what then?

Ingrid Loftfield, I'm ashamed of you. How can even be thinking of that now?

But she was. Evidently, something of her parents' teaching had sunk into her heart. She made herself sit back on her heels and look at Grace—bright, sunny Grace—trapped by a dead man, lost in a ghost story. That was what mattered. That was all that mattered.

Ingrid squatted down beside the fire pit and lit her tinder.

Slowly, the sun lowered itself behind the island and the trees stretched their gray shadows across the beach. The sky and the water darkened to black and the stars, undimmed by any trace of moonlight, lit their own fires one by one. Ingrid's driftwood and pine burned down to white coals. She could feel the heat beating hard against her. At first, it was a comfort in the rapidly chilling air, but as she continued to lay fuel on the low, hot flames, the heat grew too much for her and she had to stand back several paces. *Surely, that is enough,* she thought, looking at the glowing nest of coals and feeling their heat against her face and the backs of her hands. *Surely that will burn whatever I may have to throw on it.*

"Ingrid."

Ingrid whirled around to see Avan standing behind her. He leaned heavily on a pole of roughly trimmed hemlock, her makeshift bandages still swaddling his hands. Even with nothing but fire and starlight she could see he was far too pale.

"You are not well. You should not have come."

"I fear I could not help myself," he said ruefully. "Bring the net. It is time."

Ingrid retrieved the net from its hasty hiding place. As she brought the bundle to the edge of the water, she watched Avan walk in a widdershins circle around Grace. He seemed to be struggling under some great burden. She could hear his rasping breath even over the sound of the wind in the trees.

"Now, Ingrid. Now!"

With all her strength, Ingrid cast the net into the water. It spun into the air, fanning open to display its whirl of patterned snowflakes. It dropped onto the black water where it floated for a moment among the flecks of moonlight, and then sank from sight.

At that same moment, the ghost rose.

He shined like the stars and the white coals of Ingrid's fire. He should have been magnificent, but loneliness rolled from his presence in choking waves. He huddled frightened in the midst of his own light and it was all Ingrid could do to stand where she was and watch him, balanced on the lake's tiny, night black waves. Abandoned, abandoned by God to the cold of the lake, and all he wanted was some small warmth. That was all. Surely, that was not too much.

Grace climbed to her feet. "I am here. I am yours, as I promised."

"No." Avan spoke the word in a whisper, but nonetheless it carried across the water, and Ingrid knew the ghost heard it as clearly as she did. "She is not yours."

"You cannot keep her from me," replied the ghost, lifting

his dripping head. The holes where his eyes should have been were as black as the waves, and without any trace of moonlight in them.

"I have drawn my circle about Grace Hulda Loftfield," said Avan heavily, and Ingrid had presence of mind enough left to think this a strange reply. "I have walked five times around her and each circle is a wall of stone and locked with an iron key. The key is hidden in the egg of a duck, in the bottom of the spring, beneath the white stone, at the roots of the tree, on the Isle of Shukerepia, in the river of Zagovory, at the end of the world, on the shores of the Land of Death and Spirit." Avan's voice faltered, but he straightened and began again. "I have drawn my circle . . ."

"Grace!" cried the ghost. "He cannot hold you. Come to me, my own! Come here now."

Grace screamed as if she was being torn in two. Avan's voice droned on and on in his strange recitation. Ingrid felt as if all the air had become a riptide drawing her forward, and it was all she could do to stand against it. She didn't dare move to put her arms around Grace, because if she did, she might break the circle. But Grace screamed and screamed and would not stop, and the ghost called and Avan called and there was not enough air in the whole world to breathe because of the weight of their calling.

Then, the lake began to churn white with foam, and, impossibly, the net she had cast out rose again, something bulky tangled in its rope. Ingrid added her own cry to the cacophony and launched herself forward, grabbing the net and hauling it to shore. Bones, gray with rot, heavy with water and despair, clacked dully against each other.

All the world fell suddenly silent, and it seemed that all light vanished. Ingrid gasped and clutched at the net. The bones clacked again, and she saw the flicker of her fire on the beach. How had it gotten so far away?

"Where do you go with my bones, woman?" asked a voice from the darkness.

"Away from here." Ingrid grit her teeth and struggled toward the fire. The bones were so waterlogged she felt like she must be pulling half the lake behind her.

"You have no right."

"I have every right. She's my sister."

"Don't answer him," said another voice, a tired voice, a weak voice, but compelling nonetheless. "This way, keep walking. Don't let the bones touch you."

"Give back my bones."

"Don't answer. Walk toward me."

"Give back my bones!"

"This way. You are almost here."

The bones were so heavy, the drag so powerful. Ingrid was strong, but she was tired, and the burden hung awkwardly. She heaved the net up behind her. One wet, soft bone brushed Ingrid's skirt.

"*Give me my bones!*"

The cry reached through her like a hand and clenched itself around Ingrid's heart. Cold, instant and burning, tore through her flesh and veins and the pain seized her so hard she could not even scream.

"Mine!" shrieked the ghost. "You steal all that is mine, mine, mine!"

"Ingrid! Ingrid Anna Loftfield! Come here!"

Name. Her name, it tugged, toward the voice, toward the fire. The fire she could see, the fire she had built. But she couldn't make it carrying the bones. They were too cold. She had to let them go. The cold squeezed her heart and the voice cried in her ears "mine, mine, mine, mine!"

No, thought Ingrid desperately, as she took another step forward, and another. *Mine. My bones, my heart, my sister, my fire. Mine.*

"Thief!" cried the ghost.

"Thief!" croaked Ingrid in reply. Too cold. She shook. She couldn't hold the net any longer. It was heavy as the whole world and cold as death. She couldn't feel her fingers or her feet anymore. But was the fire closer? Was it close enough to warm her? If she could reach the fire, if only . . .

"Grace is here, Ingrid. She needs you."

Yes. Grace. Grace needed her, needed the bones, needed the fire. The name sent a sliver of strength to Ingrid's collapsing heart. She could do this. She must. She dragged herself and her burden forward.

She couldn't breathe. Hands tightened around her throat,

crushing her windpipe. Ingrid tried to scream and her hands dropped the net to rise to her neck and try to claw at her attacker, but she touched nothing but cold and air. She saw now, she saw the glowing, distorted face of the ghost, she saw the fire, just inches away, and she saw Grace straining against her prison, and she saw Avan drive his knife into the ghost's ribs.

The chokehold faltered, and Ingrid collapsed beside the net. The cold fell again, crushing, killing, and with the last of her strength, she shoved net and bones into the fire.

The flames exploded outward as if she had thrown a bomb. In that single instant, Avan raised his arms high in exaltation, Grace threw herself backward from the water and the ghost dissolved in the circle of his own light. In the next heartbeat, the roar and the heat bowled Ingrid over until she lay flat on her back in the sand, blinking stupidly up at the stars.

Stars. She could see the stars. Hands, heart and throat tingled painfully with the memory of the clutching cold, but they were hers again. Ingrid got her hands under her and pushed herself upright.

"Ingrid! Oh my God, Ingrid!"

"Grace?"

It took her a moment to focus, and in that moment, Grace launched herself into Ingrid's arms, almost knocking her over again.

"Grace!" cried Ingrid. They clung to each other, laughing and hugging. Grace pulled back for a moment, and Ingrid saw her sister fully and completely in herself again. Her eyes shone with all the familiar spark. Ingrid hugged her close again, tears prickling her own eyes. "My God, Grace, you're back. You're safe."

"I knew you'd find me," said Grace. "Part of me was always trying to call to you, but, I couldn't make any noise. His voice . . ." She shuddered. "It was so loud."

"Shhhh." Ingrid stroked her fair hair. "Over and done with now. Now there's only Papa to fear."

"Tush," said Grace lightly. "I'll take care of that, don't you worry. We'll all be sitting around the table at breakfast, you'll see."

"All . . ." Ingrid found her head had cleared enough to admit more than one thought at a time, and she moved gently past Grace.

Avan stood at the very edge of the water. Ingrid could see nothing but his silhouette. She patted Grace's hands and got to her feet, pleased to find herself steady, if aching, and went to his side.

Another step and he'd have been in the water. Wavelets lapped around his boots. Both bandaged hands clenched the hemlock pole, and fresh blood stained the linen. In the faint glow from the remains of the fire she could see on his face the same straining look that had possessed Grace so recently.

"Avan?" she asked, although her throat had gone dry. "Can you hear me?"

"Yes." He shook himself and turned toward the shore, using the pole like a cane. "Fear not for me. Your sister?"

"We both owe you . . . I could never begin to repay. . . ."

Avan shook his head again, dismissing her words.

"Trust Ingrid to find me a genuine Finnish sorcerer." Grace laughed again, but in the next breath she pressed her hand against her head, swaying dangerously. "I don't think I'm well yet."

"You've been in bed a month solid. It would be a wonder if you were not weak." Ingrid took her arm, but she hesitated. Avan still hunched against his pole, staring across the water. She could not simply leave him. "I must get my sister home. Can you walk?"

Avan straightened his back, and his grip on the pole loosened, answering her question better than words. "I can," he assured her. "All is right."

"I will come and look in on you in the morning."

Avan opened his mouth, then closed it, seeming to think the better of his words, but then he did speak. "I would be glad of that."

With a shock, Ingrid realized she would too. "Then I will," was all she said before she turned and led Grace up the bluff.

Avanasy stood on the edge of the freshwater sea and stared out across the waves, doing nothing but lean on his makeshift staff and think over what had passed. He remembered the rush of freed power, the strangely savory struggle to raise power buried deep, and the unrelenting determination of one woman.

"She's brave that one," said a voice behind him.

"Yes." Avanasy knew the voice. Once a soul had heard the voice of a spirit power, they did not forget it. If he turned around, there would be a large rabbit sitting on the sand, probably combing its ears, or otherwise looking harmless.

"Strong, too," Nanabush went on. "Tell you true, magician, I did not think she'd manage."

"I believe she could manage anything she set her mind to."

"Pity about the family. They offer poor exchange to a giving heart."

Avanasy turned from the water. The rabbit sat on the silver sands, its nose whiskers twitching to take in the scent and feel of the night wind. If anyone else had been close enough to see, they would have wondered indeed how a rabbit could cast a shadow in the shape of a fat man. "She has a suitor. Why has she not accepted him?"

"The suitor isn't suited." The rabbit shrugged. "How much more reason can there be?" It cocked its head. "Will you give her better exchange?"

"I have nothing to give."

"Nothing you can give or nothing you will give?" inquired Nanabush. "What ghost calls you from the lake, sorcerer?"

Medeoan. Medeoan moved somewhere beyond those waters, having banished him from her future. Out in the vastness of the universe, Isavalta, his home, turned on its own wheel, he having banished himself from its future. It turned and did not stop for his urging, or his leaving. It turned and did not look back. Which was the proper way. Which, indeed, was the only way.

"None." Avanasy faced inland. His eyes easily found the track Ingrid had taken with her sister. Memory of her proud carriage, swift eyes, and soft and gentle hands rose warmly and effortlessly in his mind. "None at all."

Chapter Four

The rains had come to Hastinapura. They poured down in steady sheets of water, turning all the world silver and slick. Every window and door of the Palace of the Pearl Throne had been thrown open to welcome the cool and damp. The myriad sounds of rain wormed through all the carved screens of black wood and lacelike ivory. The dancers in the temple changed their songs and sacred steps to honor Chitrani who was the Mother of the Rains, and so the wheel turned within and without and the patterns were laid down afresh.

Chandra *tya* Achin Ireshpad knelt on a silken cushion in his private apartment. He stared out at the endless fall of the rain obscuring the usual view of the lush gardens and meditated on the nature of the palace and its patterns.

Those patterns served Hastinapura, keeping the land safe and in accord with the world shaped by the dances of the Seven Mothers. Those patterns served his brother Samudra even as Samudra served those patterns.

Those patterns should have served Chandra, had Samudra's greed not overwhelmed them both, had Samudra not distorted the flow of history.

Footsteps sounded lightly on the marble floor behind him. Chandra did not turn. He heard the rustle of cloth and a brief smacking sound as the floor was kissed.

"I am sent to say that the First of All Queens asks the Brother of her Heart to come sit beside her."

Chandra stayed still and silent for a moment longer. The rain had its own patterns, woven by the falling drops. If one could understand all that complexity, the thousands of millions of droplets and their paths, one could surely understand the whole world. One could see how to return to an earlier point and rectify one's mistakes.

"I am sent to say . . ."

"Yes, yes, I hear." Chandra sighed. "You may tell the First of All Queens the Brother of her Heart follows."

The slave kissed the floor again and scuttled away with a mouselike patter of sandals.

The First of All Queens. Chandra snorted as he rose smoothly, allowing his robe to fall neatly into place before he took his first step. Samudra kept only one true queen. Oh, there was a stable of concubines for appearances, girls and women taken on as part of treaties and to aid alliances with noble families. They lived well in the quarters, but it was known that Samudra visited them but rarely, choosing to prove his manhood in acts of destruction rather than generation.

By the time Chandra reached the corridor, the slave had long since vanished. The corridor's arches of black wood flew high overhead, contrasting with the walls of carved red sandstone and the white marble floors. It was said that when the palace was built each vein of the marble was scrutinized to make sure it would run in the correct direction to weave itself into the whole.

What few outsiders knew was that the palace itself formed a latticework of spells with the Pearl Throne at its heart. The order of the passages, the order of the day, the patrols of the soldiers, the dances of the worshipers, all combined to continuously renew the work of the thousand sorcerers who had built this edifice long centuries ago. Spells of protection, of wisdom, of peace, of prosperity, woven over and over again. His footsteps now, treading their way toward the throne room, worked their purpose to preserve the anointed emperor, to bring him wisdom and to bring his realm stability. All that for Samudra.

The throne room itself was a lofty chamber. The ceiling was a series of high, narrow domes banded with gold, coral and crystal. Those domes were linked by ivory arches minutely carved with friezes and hymns of praise to the Mothers. The Pearl Throne waited empty atop its broad dais of ten steps of polished black marble veined with ghost white. Black pearls made up its base so it seemed to grow out of the shining stone, and black gave way to silver, to rose, to pink, to the purest shimmering white rising to frame the occupant of the golden cushions in a shining halo. Behind it, carved in the same red stone as the floor, the Seven Mothers, each one four times the size of a man, danced in bas relief, their hands holding lotus, fruits, bowls and swords, the symbols of peace, progeny, plenty, and protection.

Chandra remembered the view from the throne. The vast chamber spread out at his feet, with all the ministers and their underlings kneeling patiently on the red stone. He remembered feeling the strength of the Mothers at his back and the strength of his dynasty rooted deep into the foundations of the palace. Nothing could touch him. Nothing could even reach him.

And so it had been, until Samudra had completed his plan. Now Chandra stood level with the secretaries and ministers, even the soldiers guarding the entrances to the rooms and the gates to the women's quarters, and he looked up, waiting for his turn to address the throne, to address his younger brother.

"The First of All Queens asks that you come sit near her now."

Without the emperor, the First of All Queens could not appear in public. So, a series of delicately carved sandalwood screens was erected next to the dais. A bench with red cushions had been placed beside the screens, along with a table arrayed with sherbet to drink and dainties to nibble.

As a member of the imperial family, Chandra had only to bow from the waist to properly acknowledge the First of All Queens whom he had to designate as the Sister of his Heart. He saw nothing of her but shadows on the other side of the screen, and the occasional flash of gold and crimson.

"As I am commanded, so am I come, First of All Queens," said Chandra smoothly.

"Such formality, Brother!" she exclaimed with mock surprise. "Had you business to complete, you could have sent word."

You know I have no business. Your husband, my brother, allows me none. "What business could I have more important than waiting on the words of the First of All Queens?"

The queen gave a sharp, impatient sigh, cut off short, and

replaced by soothing words. "I expect my Brother misses his son."

"Prince Kacha does well in the far north," he said. "He sends his duties and his felicitations."

"Which I am delighted to accept." Cloth rustled, and the queen's voice came closer. From the shadows, he thought she must have stepped nearer to the screen. "But, is it not true that you are often dull, my brother? My husband is much away and has left little business for your attention."

"I have all I need, First of All Queens." *My brother generously permits my lungs to breathe and my heart to beat. He values my flesh enough to barter it away for his treaties with the northern barbarians. What more could I expect?*

"I do not believe that to be the truth." The queen's voice was solemn, but without any note of accusation. Chandra felt curiosity rising in spite of himself. Could the woman be sincerely concerned about him? Was it possible Samudra had not completely drowned her sympathies? Perhaps there was room to work here.

"You have, I think, been too much alone since your wife died."

Anger swiftly replaced curiosity. How dared this woman speak of Bandhura? His first wife, his true confidant, his helpmate? How dare she speak of any woman to him when she was the one who deprived him of all his women? Bandhura had told him of the scene, of how this woman, who was just another woman then, had gone to the women's innermost quarters, where the ones who waited on the imperial pleasure were lodged and announced that Samudra, and Samudra's line, would ascend to the Pearl Throne, and that all who so desired could take their places waiting on her, and on him, now. And all of them had. All Chandra's wives proved themselves no better than the whores. All but Bandhura, who had stayed true and loyal, who had borne him his son to be vengeance for them both.

"There is a woman of my company, Abhilasha *ayka* Aditiela. Her dower is twelve towns in the south. She is young enough to bear many more children of your line. Further, she is fair and is skilled in all the sixty-four arts and sciences."

Chandra couldn't believe what he was hearing. Marry?

And marry one of the queen's spies? She could not possibly believe . . .

"I have communicated my desire for the match at length to my husband, and he is agreeable. It shall be accomplished when the First Rain is over and the moon is again favorable. Our wedding gift to you shall be a new household complete in your capital town."

Filled to brimming with your spies and lackeys so that I may not make any move without it being reported to you and my brother. You like not my presence in the shadow of the Pearl Throne to remind you of the wrong your husband did, so you must build me a coral prison with a wife for a jailer.

Chandra stood abruptly, unable to remain still any longer. "Then I should compose a letter of greeting to my new bride."

"Tell me this pleases you, Brother. I would not have it otherwise."

Chandra forced a smile into his voice. "It pleases me to do the will of the First of All Queens."

"It is hard, Brother, to break a mourning that has been carried for so long, but let your heart be softened toward your new wife. Let her bring you peace."

Chandra bowed. "The First of All Queens is great in her wisdom. I will do my best." *Probably you have found me some lowborn slut with the appetites of a cat in heat, thinking that, like my brother, I am counseled by the sheathe for my sword and will soon be lulled into complacency.*

Again the queen sighed. This time it was a reluctant, regretful sound. "You may go now, Brother, if that is your wish. We will sit together again soon and speak of these matters."

"I await the queen's word." Officially excused, he straightened up and turned politely away so that he might not catch even a glimpse of the queen's robe as she departed. He kept his pace even, his back straight, and his hands loose as he paced across the breadth of the throne room, following the ordained path to his apartment.

Inside, Yamuna waited for him. The brown skeleton of a man disdained the pillows and couches. Instead, he stood in front of the open window, his hands folded neatly in a position of patience and meditation. He could have stood so for hours, indeed for days, Chandra knew. He had more than once seen Yamuna do just that.

Chandra cursed futilely. He had hoped to have some time to himself, so that he might come to terms with what had just happened, and decide how to respond, and how to tell his *Agnidh*, his bound-sorcerer, what had occurred. But no, of course, Yamuna had heard of it the second it happened. It was part of his endless work.

"I dismissed the slaves," said Yamuna, lowering his hands. He wore only a white cloth wrapped about his hips. His skin stuck tight to bone and muscle, giving the impression that all of the humors had been long since drained from him. One only had to look into his eyes, however, to see all the dreadful vitality that smoldered within his shrunken frame. Ascetic practice had burned away Yamuna's youth, but it had concentrated his soul. His right hand only was the hand of a young man. Chandra tried not to look at it. Chandra had been present at the ceremony where Yamuna traded his hand for Kacha's, his eye for Kacha's eye, and the memory of it still could leave Chandra cold.

"I felt you would not want negligent ears to listen while we took council," Yamuna was saying.

"Thank you." Chandra sank onto his cushion. "You are correct, as ever."

"Do not speak to me as if I were your mindless brother or his strumpet wife," snapped Yamuna. "It is not seemly."

I am to be wed to a spy of the queen's, and now you are come to berate me. Chandra pressed his fingertips to his brow. *How did I fail to sever our bond when I had the Pearl Throne beneath me?*

"You did not think to argue with her, I suppose." Yamuna did not sit, or bow, as he should have. He simply stood with the whole world at his back and looked down at his charge. "Or suggest an alternate choice?"

"What choice is there? What woman could I name that she could not corrupt?"

"Then you should have told her you had decided to take an ascetic vow," snapped Yamuna. "In order to better purify your soul before the Mothers."

"Then I will do so now."

"Idiot!" The word slapped against Chandra. "She will know you have spoken to me, and that this is not a true vocation. She will not accept it."

"Then what does it profit me to speak of what I could have done? The order has been given. I am to be married and sent away, and that is the end of it." He shook his head. "It changes nothing. The plan proceeds. Your link with Ka-cha is not severed."

"So, you do remember that we are engaged in important work, and that the farther you are sent from the throne, the fainter your power grows." Yamuna snorted. "Your son is in truth the best of you. I am glad I did not waste my right hand on such stuff as I see before me now."

Which was finally too much to bear. Forgetting his robe and all his appearances, Chandra rose, meeting the sorcerer eye-to-eye. "You forget yourself, sorcerer, to chide me so."

Yamuna did not flinch, did not even hesitate. "All I forget is how you signed your throne over to your younger brother because you were afraid for your own skin," said Yamuna, and his words were as cold and hard as the marble under their feet. "Rather than face him in open battle, you sneak and skulk through the palace, looking for his bare buttock like a snake in the dark, and you force me to skulk beside you."

"Stop!"

"And abandon my office, as you have abandoned yours?"

"I command you!"

"Then do so." Yamuna dropped into a slave's obeisance in front of him. "I am, after all, yours to command. Tell me what to do, master. How shall we topple your brother? How shall we rule the three empires when they tumble into our laps?" Yamuna peered up at him from his mocking crouch, prepared, to all appearances, to wait all year long for his answer.

Chandra stared down at him. *I could strike your head off right now, old man. No one would question me. Not even Samudra. You are mine to do with as I will. I could rip your withered heart from your chest and hurl it into the rain.*

And what would he do if that heart, once ripped free,

crawled obediently back to its master, as his hand once had crawled away from him? What would Yamuna do to him then?

Chandra screamed inwardly at his own impotence. How much longer would he be ordered around by those who should have obeyed his least word? He gritted his teeth and stared at the ceaseless rain.

Not long, not long, he told himself, breathing the fresh damp deeply. *Soon, the three empires will be yours. Yamuna will require you to rule them. He thinks he sets a shadow on the Pearl Throne. But he will learn differently.*

"If the queen cannot be swayed, then this spy of hers must be convinced to turn. Her death would be too conspicuous."

"Very good, my lord." Yamuna rose from his mocking pose and faced Chandra with the light of approval in his burning eyes, one the eye of an ancient man, the other the eye of a hale youth. "You will permit yourself to be coaxed. The slaves and the lackeys will hear you rage and soften by turns. And then you will be turned by your bride, who shall be turned toward you. I will provide the means."

"And if they believe I am cowed, they will pay less attention to my doings."

"You show the beginnings of thought at last, Chandra."

You, old man, will one day be stunned by the depths of my thought. I will enjoy seeing your face then.

Yamuna bowed humbly and departed, backing from the chamber, not turning his face from a member of the imperial family, as if it was Prince Chandra who was finished with him, and not the other way around. When the slave closed the door between them, he straightened, turned silently on his heel and left, striding through the halls of ivory, coral and precious stone to his own chamber.

Chandra thought Yamuna did not see the hatred that blazed in his eyes, thought that Yamuna did not know the plans he harbored in his greedy and pathetic mind. Chandra thought he would one day humble Yamuna in truth. Perhaps he even thought to kill his *Agnidh*. Well, let him think it. It kept that mind occupied and let him believe he was cunning.

Chandra's vanity was as useful as his impotence.

Yamuna's private chamber waited at the summit of one of the palace's tall, narrow domes. A likeness of the summer sky with the phases of the moon inlaid in mother of pearl curved overhead. All the names of the Seven Mothers had been laid in ivory in the floor, so, it was said, that they might always pay attention to what happened within the chamber.

It was many years now since Yamuna had learned that was folly. The palace, so carefully designed and laid out to perpetuate its webwork of spells, was nothing more than a cage of lies. The gods were wily beings, extorting their worship. They were expert and immortal bargainers, no better than the demons who cowered under chains and treaties placed on them by the Ancients.

Well, soon the world would change. Soon, all the worlds would change.

For the moment, however, there were appearances to be maintained.

The smallest side chamber of Yamuna's apartment was lined with shelves, and the shelves were lined with jars of all shapes and sizes: tall, narrow jars of glass filled with smoky liquids; thick, squat alabaster jars that were impossibly cold to the touch; jars of red clay sealed in red wax; small obsidian jars the size of a child's hand that gleamed in the light; jars of cut crystal from the far north; jars of pure white porcelain from Hung Tse.

No slave tended these shelves. Yamuna had warned them all away years ago. No hand touched the jars save his own.

The jar he reached for today was on the middle shelf; a graceful carafe carved of cinnabar, corked tightly and sealed with beeswax imprinted with three sigils known only to a handful of living men. Yamuna carried the jar to the center of the chamber and set it on the floor. Beside it he set a piece of blank parchment. Then, he cracked the beeswax seal, breaking the sigils, and pulled the stopper.

Yamuna stepped back. "Your master calls you forth!"

There was no billow of smoke, nor any flash of light or peal of thunder. Such details were for children's tales. There was only silence, and cold, as the chill of death seeped from the jar where it had been confined. Slowly, it cocooned the room with cold. Only then did the dead man crawl forth.

Agnidh Harshul climbed painfully from his prison, cramped and crabbed, suffering from his cold confinement and having no choice but to suffer. In life, he had been a tall man, strong in his body and comfortable in his power. Pleased with his role as *Agnidh* to Prince Kacha, he had sought nothing beyond his service, a loyal son of the Mothers and a loyal scion of the Pearl Throne.

Kacha had killed him on the voyage to Isavalta, and Yamuna had supplied the poison and the locked box into which Kacha had placed his tongue, his seal, and one of his fingers to return to Yamuna so that Yamuna might conjure his soul into service, as he did now.

The dead man shivered before Yamuna, his raw hatred plain on his pained features. It meant nothing. He was bound and he must serve Yamuna's will. He had no choice.

"You will give me a letter," said Yamuna to the dead man. "A report of your activities in Isavalta. You will report on Kacha's satisfactory progress in his relations with the Imperial ministers. You will describe the coronation and how well he played his part in it."

Death should have severed Harshul's bond with Kacha, but Yamuna's sorceries had reestablished it. Even trapped as he was, Harshul touched Kacha, and he knew enough to compose what was needed, a false letter to lead the emperor to believe that Harshul was alive and keeping his watchful eye on Kacha. Emperor Samudra must have no cause to question what was happening in Isavalta. He must be kept in ignorance as long as possible. When the war finally erupted, he would have to admit to one of two things: that he had lost control of a mere boy, or that he had been party to a coup.

Either admission would badly damage the emperor's reputation, and make it that much harder for him to maintain his rule.

The dead man fought Yamuna's order, of course, but his struggle was as meaningless as his hatred. In the end, he knelt, as he must, and he shuddered with the effort of reaching across the veil that separated the solid and the ethereal. He breathed, if a dead man could be said to have breath, across the parchment, and the parchment filled with tight lines of words written in a precise hand the emperor would recognize as Harshul's.

The ghost straightened, trembling. Yamuna retrieved the parchment, glancing over it to be sure the missive seemed complete enough.

"You may speak," he told the ghost as he examined the missive. In life, Harshul had been gregarious. It pleased Yamuna to allow him speech now and again.

In death, Harshul's voice was as thick and cold as mist over the water. "When you die, the Mothers will give you to me. I will be a demon and I will feast on your soul for eternity."

Yamuna folded the false missive with care and let himself smile at his slave. "When I die you will be a shade, as impotent as you are now. You will never touch me. For I will never die."

"You are mad, old man." The bound spirit lacked the power to even name Yamuna's name. "All men return to the Mothers."

"But I shall not remain a man." Yamuna savored the words that he had so seldom spoken aloud. There was none to whom he could trust them. None but shades and slaves who could not utter a word unless it be by his own will. "When Chandra is bound to the Northern Empire, so will I be bound, and its earth will know me, and the creatures of that earth will know me, and they will reveal to me the secrets of that land's wild heart, and how those barbarians can rise to divinity on their own wings when we must remain in the mud and dust, groveling at the feet of the sluts who call themselves the Seven Mothers."

The shade said nothing, for Yamuna did not wish it to. But even dead and bound as it was, it recoiled from him, and Yamuna took pleasure in the sight. It was a foolish pleasure, he knew, like a little boy tormenting insects, but it was there all the same. He would have to retreat for a series of days and do sacrifice to worm this petty pride from his heart. It was unworthy of one who would soon become a god, and as an impurity it hampered his power and must be done away with.

But there were other matters to attend to first.

"Return to your prison, slave," said Yamuna. "I have no more need of you."

The dead man would have screamed if he could, but Yamuna held him silent. So, he turned, shaking violently, and crawled back into the jar. Yamuna returned the stopper to its place and, in his workroom, applied fresh beeswax and re-made the sigils before returning the jar to its place on the shelf. There also, he sealed the missive with red wax and Harshul's own seal.

According to the most ancient sagas, the Seven Mothers bound together the souls of sorcerers so that they might preserve the life and order of the lands in their care. In exchange for power, place, and extended life, sorcerers were guardians, protectors and advisers to all who might have need of them. Their very footsteps would weave spells of protection across Hastinapura. Still, they must forever remember they were servants, not rulers. They might strive for any earthly power they could reach in service of their magic, but power beyond that was forbidden. Royalty was forbidden them. Immortality, divinity, these were never to be theirs.

Most sages said that such a transference was impossible. It was outside the order of nature.

But, reasoned Yamuna, if it was impossible, why was it forbidden? Why forbid a thing that could not be done?

Did not the Nine Elders of Hung-Tse work transformations of their own, turning their members into spirit powers? Did not the barbarians of the north have ones of divided souls who could turn themselves into gods through sacrifice?

No, it could not be impossible, only difficult. Perhaps it could not be done here in Hastinapura where all powers were catalogued and treated with and for. But in the wild north, where the powers did as they would, where disorder and chaos swirled together, what power might he not harness? What might he not become? Worlds would come within his compass and not even the Mothers could forbid him anything his heart desired.

He smiled and tapped his fingers against his false letter. After dark, he would give the missive to one of his slaves, who would in turn go down to the city and find some Isa-

valtan captain or sailor who could be bribed to give the missive to one of the palace servants and say it had come from
Vyshtavos for the emperor. It would be delivered to the
mountains where the Emperor Samudra waged his latest war,
and Samudra would read the words and believe all was well
in Isavalta.

Yamuna smiled out at the rain. In truth, all was well, but
not in the manner which the emperor believed.

"And where are the Mothers in all their power to tell you
otherwise?" he asked the rain. When the rain had no answer,
Yamuna laughed softly, and set about his other works.

"I am beginning to believe," said Medeoan, rubbing her
eyes, "that either all my lords master are idiots, or they think
I'm one." She looked across the wide desk to Kacha who sat
behind a pile of his own letters and papers. "Listen to this."
She adjusted her voice to a fair imitation of an eastern accent.
"And I must further beg to inform Your Majesty Imperial
that due to the unusual number of spring lambs born this
year, additional pasturage has been allotted to nineteen shep-
herding families." She lowered the paper and sighed in exasperation. "Now why would I possibly need to know that?"

"Does Your Majesty Imperial wish to make any reply?"
inquired Senoi, her fussy, officious, but very efficient first
secretary. Even Kacha, who took such care in the appointment of her staff, agreed he was the very man for the job.

Medeoan opened her mouth, but Kacha spoke first. "Her
Majesty Imperial will answer that one in the morning," he
said, before he smiled across their desk at her. "You're exhausted, Medeoan. Why do you not retire? I will finish what
is needful here."

She shouldn't, she knew. Attention to detail was important, and she could not pay attention to details if she did not
know what they were. But even as she thought that, an enormous and undignified yawn forced its way out of her throat.

She stared at the mounds of paper still to be worked
through. "Perhaps I will retire," she said sheepishly. "But I'll
expect you to review the remaining business with me thoroughly in the morning," she added as she stood up.

"That I gladly will." Kacha gave a half-bow.

Medeoan rounded the desk and bent to kiss her husband good night. "And I expect you to attend me in my bed when you are finished," she whispered into his ear.

"That I gladly will," he replied just as softly and Medeoan smiled again at the mischievous light in his eyes.

Ladies and house guard behind her and pages scurrying before with lamps to light the way and herald her arrival, Medeoan traversed the corridors from her private study to her private apartments. She was tired, but cheerful. Another day successfully negotiated, thanks to Kacha's unflagging support and energy. As he promised, together they were the autocrat of Isavalta.

She had been so frightened! Medeoan smiled now to think of her dread. Before her, the page girls opened her chamber doors and her ladies hurried in to light the lamps and coax the fire into more vigorous life. Had it not been for Kacha, she was certain she would not have even managed the coronation. Hours of ceremony, hours of standing and sitting and bowing and having the heavy golden regalia handed to her, taken away, blessed, anointed, kissed and handed back, and all the time she could think of nothing except her parents watching her from the Land of Death and Shadows and frowning at their reluctant, trembling child. But there was Kacha, beside her, more solid and more real than her fears. Kacha to attend with grave dignity, and to breathe such salacious comments in her ears about the ceremony's other participants that she could barely keep her countenance. That night, he had held her close and whispered reassurances to her, stroking her hair until her fears eased and she could sleep in peace.

In the weeks that had followed, all continued as it had begun. Kacha remained always at her side, ever ready to help her plow through the endless petty work of empire. His counsel was always sober, and there was no point of her comfort, ease or service that he was not ready to oversee.

Medeoan sighed contentedly as she and her two head ladies moved behind the bed screens so that they could undress her for the night. She was happy. She had never imagined she would be happy as empress, but so it was, and it was because of Kacha.

Chekhania and Ragneda divested her of her outer coat and set to work on the laces of her dress and the catches of her jewels. They were competent, if inclined too much to giggle. She did miss Prathad and Vladka some days, but Prathad had been found in the hay barn with a sergeant of the house guard and had to be dismissed in disgrace, and Vladka had been found taking bribes from one of the court lords to bear him tales of Medeoan's doings. How could she keep such a one with her, no matter how many years she had served? Vladka did not even have the strength of character to own her guilt in the end. She had just cried and begged and tried to say it was not so, even when she knew Kacha and Chekhania had brought Medeoan all the proof.

Medeoan raised her arms so Chekhania and Ragneda could pull her nightdress over her head and lace it up. The covers on the bed were already turned down and the warming pans had been applied. Medeoan laid herself down and the ladies covered the braziers and drew the curtains, wishing her good night and departing to get themselves ready for bed.

Despite being tired, Medeoan found she was unable to compose herself to rest. She stared up at the shadowy canopy overhead, listening for Kacha's entrance into the chamber. But there were only the sounds of her ladies talking softly among themselves and making up their beds and changing into their own nightclothes. A restlessness to have her husband beside her took hold of Medeoan. It was becoming a familiar sensation, and a not wholly unpleasant one. She imagined him walking down the corridors, wishing good night to those whose business kept them up late. He would return to his own chamber, where his waiting gentlemen would ready him for bed, and then he would come through the connecting door, and pull back her bed curtains, and then, and then . . .

A thought struck Medeoan, a happy bit of mischief. Always, Kacha came to her. What if, this time, she went to him? He would come behind his bed screens, thinking he would need to come find her, and there she would already be.

The idea pleased her, making her smile in the darkness. She decided at once to put thought into action and slipped out of her bed. The floor was chilly under her stocking feet. She padded around the bedscreens, and the ladies immediately sprang to their feet and ceased their activities; plaiting and brushing their hair, laying out their clothes, gossiping. Chekhania ran up to her at once, pale in her nightdress, but Medeoan waved her away.

"I shall be in the emperor's chamber," she announced.

Chekhania's hand flew to her mouth to smother the giggle that surely must be coming, and Medeoan saw the slightly scandalized delight in her eyes. Lifting her chin in a mockery of imperial dignity, Medeoan turned and walked regally through the door and into Kacha's bedchamber.

The effect of her arrival there was as immediate as her unexpected appearance in her own room. The gentlemen were all still fully dressed, as their master had not yet retired for the night, but they too were engaged in their various activities; writing, reading, tending the fire, laying out wine and fruit, gossiping their own gossip. They stared for a moment at the sight of their empress in her nightdress, but swiftly remembered to drop their eyes, and drop into a reverence. Prithu, Kacha's head gentleman, a neat, dark-skinned man who had come with him from Hastinapura, approached Medeoan hesitantly, his eyes darting about the room, trying to look anywhere but at his partially dressed empress, and reverenced nervously before her.

"Is there any way I can assist Your Majesty Imperial?"

"I have decided to await my husband here," Medeoan said, amazed at how lofty her voice sounded. "And you will not say anything about it, as I wish it to be a surprise. Do you understand?"

A look of extreme consternation crossed Prithu's face, but he reverenced again. "I understand, Majesty Imperial."

Medeoan felt she ought to pity the man. After all, where he came from, the women lived separately from their men, even their husbands. This must be extremely shocking for him. Somehow, that idea gave her little plan a whole new relish.

"If one word is spoken, I will be most displeased," she

announced, loud enough for the room in general to hear. Then, she gathered up her hems and retreated behind Kacha's bed screens, and slipped under the covers of his bed. Settling herself in, she had to cover her mouth, as Chekhania had to smother her giggles.

Imagining Kacha's face, and his reaction to her mischief occupied Medeoan's mind pleasantly while she waited, listening to the muted, hesitant sounds of the gentlemen's voices and movements.

Then, at long last, she heard the outer door open, and the sounds of firm bootsteps, and the answering patter of quick steps from the gentlemen hurrying to meet their master.

"Mother's guts, Prithu, if I've had a more boring night, I don't know what it was," said Kacha gruffly. There was a sound after that, probably him drinking a cup of sweet wine offered to him by Prithu. "I've one matter to take care of first, then I must attend my lady wife."

Medeoan clapped her hand over her mouth again, and forced down her own giggles.

"Majesty . . ." began Prithu, and Medeoan froze. Was he going to give her away?

"What?" answered Kacha impatiently.

"Majesty, perhaps you should attend the empress directly. Perhaps your other business can wait . . ."

"Perhaps you should confine yourself to making sure my nightclothes are brushed and ready. My wife likes to see me at my best."

"But Majesty . . ."

If you do this, man, I will not be quick to forgive, thought Medeoan, quite miffed. He was going to spoil the whole joke.

The only answer was silence, and then Prithu saying "Yes, Majesty." Medeoan found herself wondering what look or gesture Kacha had made to his servant.

She lay back then, secure in her nest and delighted in her mischief. Kacha would finish this last business, he would come around the screens and see her there, and then, and then . . .

Firelight flickered beyond the bedcurtains. The noises of the servants settled to soft rustlings. Medeoan smiled in anticipation of the culmination of her jest. She smelled something sharp, not quite smoke, but not incense either.

Then, she felt it—the chilling of the air, the prickling in her skin that traveled deep into her bones. Magic. Nearby, someone was performing a working of will. She had given no orders, she knew of nothing needful . . .

Thoughts of danger shivered through Medeoan and she shot out of the bed.

"Kacha!" she cried as she dashed around the screens, and stopped in mid-stride.

She saw Kacha standing beside a brazier near his writing desk. He trembled hard, sweat pouring down his skin, his face in a wild grimace, torn between agony and ecstasy, and his hand, his withered right hand, thrust deep into the brazier's fire.

Shock froze Medeoan where she stood. As he gradually focused on Medeoan, a new emotion crept into his twisted visage—rage.

Medeoan couldn't think. Her vision blurred, refusing to see what was before her, she clutched at herself, seeking to still the sensation that told her against all reason that some strange magic was being worked here. Impossible, impossible. Kacha was no sorcerer. Kacha could not look at her with such hatred . . .

Medeoan fled. She turned and ran back to her room, slamming the door behind herself. Ignoring the startled flurry of questions from her ladies, she dashed toward the bed, like a child seeking safety from the night's terrors. She clambered through the curtains and huddled on the mattress, her hand pressed across her mouth, but now it was to suppress her screams.

It cannot have been . . . what did I see? Nothing, I cannot have . . . But it was a working. I felt it . . . I cannot . . . it was not . . . Fragments of thoughts, disjointed and purposeless, tumbled through her mind.

"Mistress . . ." came a tremulous voice beyond the curtain.

"Leave me be," whispered Medeoan, wrapping her arms tightly around herself. "Leave me be."

"Yes, Mistress."

She closed her eyes. Kacha's hand was in the fire. She

had seen it. She had felt the magic coursing through the ether. These things were true, but could not be true.

What happened? What happened?

"Beloved?"

Kacha. His voice sounded so tender, so like himself. How could he have been that creature who looked at her with such rage?

"Beloved, let me look upon you."

There was a rustle of cloth and the touch of flickering light upon her eyelids.

"Please, Medeoan. Look at me. Let me explain."

Slowly, Medeoan opened her eyes, and there stood Kacha, framed by the heavy curtains, a lamp in his good hand. His face was as soft, as tender as it ever was when he gazed at her.

Medeoan licked her lips. "What was that?" she whispered. "What were you doing in there?"

Gingerly, as if unsure of his welcome, Kacha sat on the edge of the bed. He pushed the curtain back so that he could set the lamp down on the bedside table before he spoke.

"What you saw, beloved, was what keeps my wounded hand," he held up his scarred and withered limb, "whole, if damaged, on my body."

"There was magic there," she said, her thoughts only reluctantly beginning to order themselves."

"The fire itself is magical. I must burn, each night, a series of sticks carved with runes, and give my hand over to the fire. This is the working of my father's sorcerer. If I did not do this, rot would have taken my hand long ago, and it would have been severed to save my life." He looked shamefacedly down at his shriveled fingers. "This is not a lovely thing, but it is better than no hand at all."

"Why did you not tell me of this?" Medeoan's voice was harsh.

"Because this treatment is painful, and I . . . I do not always bear it as a man should. I did not want you to see me that way. I did not want you to worry." His voice dropped to a whisper. "I did not want you to pity me."

She took his withered hand, and it was rough and crabbed as it always was. She had become well used to the touch of that hand. It wasn't even warm from the fire. The scars that ringed the wrist were as white and crooked against his dark skin as they had been before.

"This magic does not heal you," she said.

He shook his head. "It cannot. The damage was too severe by the time they were able to free me."

She held his hand, willing herself to believe, willing herself to accept, but at the same time, her blood prickled with the sensation of shaping magic, of the working of will. It came from Kacha, and from Kacha's wounded hand, and she did not know why. If all was as he said, why would she feel this now that the spell was over and done? If he lied . . . but how could she even think that Kacha might lie to her?

"I'm sorry if I startled you, beloved." Kacha's good hand tucked under her chin and lifted her face until she must look into Kacha's deep eyes. "I'm sorry I deceived you."

She kissed him, hard and suddenly, surprising herself at the force of her gesture. Kacha stiffened, but only for a bare instant. Then, he wrapped his arms tightly around her, answering her urgency with his own. She needed the urgency, needed the rush of it, to wipe away her doubts, the lingering feeling of a spell where there should not have been any, to restore the unclouded peace in her heart that had always occupied the place where Kacha dwelled.

Morning came. Medeoan opened her eyes to see Kacha sleeping beside her. She liked to watch him as he dreamed. She liked the peace in his face and his tousled hair and the gentle sound of his breathing. Their mornings together were never long, so, normally, she would watch him and then she would press herself against him, and he would sigh in his sleep and roll over to embrace her, and she would revel in that as well.

This morning, she did not move toward him. Her eyes felt dry and too hot, as if she had just finished crying. She had slept only fitfully, for she could not stop the thought tumbling through her head.

Why would any sorcerer impose such a healing, not even a healing, such a spell on a person? How could it be that this was the only way to keep Kacha's hand whole? She remembered too well the day Avanasy had called her from her studies and taken her out to the laundry sheds. Amidst the steam and the stench a woman lay on a pallet, screaming in her pain and writhing so her fellows were forced to hold her down. Her legs and both feet were a mass of burned and swollen flesh where a kettle had overturned and spilled a flood of boiling water over her. The stench from her roasted flesh sent Medeoan reeling.

Lord Sorcerer Iakush was already there. Avanasy ordered Medeoan to stand by the Mistress of the House, and the two men began to work. They had few tools at their disposal, and they had to work quickly, before the mere pain of her burns carried the woman away. Avanasy bound the woman's pain in a stone, the effort of it nearly making him swoon. Iakush plunged her legs into a basin of milk and herbs and then sprinkled more milk in a circle around her, weaving his spell as he made his circle. Perspiration sprang out on his forehead from the strength of his working and the heat of the room. Medeoan herself shivered from the waves of magic that rolled from the two men, cresting over the burned woman and crashing against Medeoan. No one else could feel anything. They could only stare and pray. Medeoan had been brought to watch and understand, and she tried to concentrate on the words Iakush spoke, on the touch of his working.

At last, at long last, a trembling Iakush knelt before the basin and drew out the woman's right leg. Even under the white film the milk left, Medeoan could see her flesh was whole and sound.

If an injury that should have killed a woman could be made whole by two Isavaltan sorcerers, how could the sorcerers of the Hastinapuran court, who were rumored to be among the most powerful and extensively learned in the world, fail to make her husband's wounded hand whole? Medeoan had never asked herself the question before, and now she hated herself for the asking. She wanted to accept what she had been told with all her strength and soul, and yet she could not.

Was there some neglect? Some lie, some secret, some incompetence on the part of the sorcerer? Could that be true? Medeoan stared up at the canopy. There had been a sorcerer at her grandmother's court, a dark and charismatic man. He had been given the care and treatment of her ailing great-uncle, and had, it was later found, been deliberately keeping him ill to prolong his appointment. He'd been beheaded in the courtyard.

Could this Hastinapuran sorcerer be doing something similar to Kacha? Was that what was happening? Was Kacha being deliberately kept in pain by a worthless servant? The thought clenched Medeoan's jaw in anger.

"Beloved?" murmured Kacha sleepily.

Medeoan turned toward her husband, and felt her love for him, unquestioning and unquestionable, well up in her. He was being wronged, but, unschooled in magic as he was, how could he know?

The fingers of his good hand brushed her cheek. "Your face was stern, beloved. What were you thinking of?"

"Your hand, my husband."

Kacha smoothed the coverlet over her stomach. "I wish you would not. What it is, it must remain. There is nothing to be done."

Medeoan pushed herself up on her elbows. "I'm not so certain, Kacha. I've seen miracles performed by Isavaltan sorcerers. It should not have been so impossible for a sorcerer to save your hand whole without this . . . treatment you must undergo."

Kacha shook his head ruefully. "Everything that could be done, Yamuna did. He is my father's *Agnidh*, his bound-sorcerer. The life and protection of our family is his charge."

Medeoan tried to choose her words with care. "Kacha, is it possible that Yamuna . . . did not do all that he might?"

"What do you mean, Medeoan?" Kacha frowned.

Carefully, Medeoan told him the story of her grandmother's court sorcerer. Kacha listened, his face remaining grave.

"That might be a thing that could happen in Isavalta," he said when she had finished. "But it is not possible in the court of the Pearl Throne. Yamuna is bound to my family, by oaths and ceremonies. He cannot act against us. It is impossible. He would call down the wrath of the Seven Mothers if he did." He tried to smile, and almost managed it. "I must ask you to accept what I myself had to accept years ago, beloved. My hand is ruined and its treatment is painful." He kissed her gently on the forehead. "Your concern speaks of love and I am glad of it, but try not to worry about it any more."

"I will do my best," promised Medeoan.

Her best, however, did not take her very far. The question gnawed at her through the breakfast with Lord Master Kagnimir and his men. It occupied her through the council meeting, and as she dictated her morning letters to her secretaries afterward and tried to concentrate as they read back to her a report from the legal advisors her father had assembled in an attempt to begin to codify the laws of the empire.

It stayed with her even after Kacha rode out to welcome the new convoy of ships arriving from Hastinapura, which carried the new ambassador from the Pearl Throne. Although Medeoan no longer had to watch him working with his weak and painful hand, the thought that he suffered repeatedly and needlessly would not leave her. But how could she make him believe that was so?

She would have to make sure he saw the proof with his own eyes. That would cause him pain, and she could not relish that thought, but the pain it would spare him would be much greater. After he saw how he had been wronged, he would allow her to bend her mind to the ways in which that wrong might be put right.

Medeoan left the papers and the laws and the blandly disapproving secretaries. Surrounded by her entourage, she returned to her private chamber. Through a series of audience chambers, sitting rooms and private studies, she came to a small, unadorned inner door. There, she took a silver key from the bundle she carried at her waist and opened it smoothly. The ladies took up lit candles in tall holders, placed them on either side of the door and retreated immediately. Here was the one room in the palace where Medeoan alone was permitted to walk. This room held the Portrait of Worlds.

The Portrait of Worlds was no mere carving or daubing

of paint on silk or canvas. It was a working clockwork model of all the worlds, mortal and immortal. Made of bronze, silver, copper, and gems, it was a conglomeration of delicate spheres formed of wires and jewels, each turning on its silver spindle and each swinging in its separate stately orbit, all part of a great dance, its steps regulated by the fantastic clockwork that had taken a century to execute.

Unbidden, Medeoan's mind unleashed a flood of memories, all of them filled with Avanasy. Avanasy's loving voice as he described the Portrait, making her learn the names of its parts, their functions, and the history of this immense and complex tool. Hours of study at Avanasy's side over the books written by the court sorcerers of the Portrait's various uses, and their discoveries concerning its nature and the further nature of the visions it might evoke and the barriers it might be used to bypass or uncover. Yet more hours of his patient, cautious tutelage so that she might work well and familiarly with the precious object Father had placed in her guardianship.

Now, as Medeoan stood before the Portrait, watching its intricate dance, she forced herself to consider, dispassionately, as Avanasy had always urged, the nature of her will, and how it might best be shaped. The sharpest knife was useless in a clumsy hand, he had always said.

Damn the man for all his words, for her being unable to set them aside no matter how hard she tried. Damn him for not staying beside her, especially now when she needed him.

Medeoan took a deep breath and pushed her anger aside. She must think now, and not waste her energies with useless curses or regret.

She would need something of Kacha's. That much was simple enough. She wore his ring on her hand. She would need a mirror in which to see the vision she hoped to call up. She would need something to represent Hastinapura. Ideally, it should represent the Pearl Throne itself, as that palace was where the wrong had been inflicted. She would also need something to stand for the wound that was made and something to bind all these parts into a whole.

Tightening her jaw, Medeoan set to work.

In less than an hour, Medeoan stood again before the Portrait of Worlds. At its base she had laid out a scarf of precious scarlet cloth from Hastinapura, its weave so fine the scarf was translucent. On the cloth she had laid a silver mirror, and at the quarter points of the mirror she had placed a pearl from one of her pendants, a china hand broken from an ancient childhood toy, a brass dish of blood from the slaughtering shed, and, last of all, slipped from her middle finger, Kacha's ring. Beside the mirror waited a small bag she had filled with fine earth from the gardens.

The worlds of the Portrait swung over the mirror, the brass, copper and jewels reflected in its depths. Medeoan closed her eyes, making herself breathe deeply and struggling to clear her mind. This was the true test of power, Avanasy had always said. It was one thing to perform a working that had been handed down the years, and carefully inscribed in books. It was quite another to meet the needs of the moment with only the materials on hand. There were those who never managed the strength or the discipline.

As ready as she could be, Medeoan opened her eyes. She shook a small pile of the black, damp-scented earth into her palm and began sprinkling it in a circle around her mirror.

"I stand before all the worlds," she said, drawing her magic from within and without. "I am rooted in earth, in blood, in flesh and love. My eyes are open and my heart is open to the turning of the worlds. This is my word and my word is firm. The turning worlds will show me how Kacha *tya* Achin Ejulinjapad was wounded by Yamuna *dva* Ikshu Chitranipad. This is my word and my word is firm. The turning worlds will show me how Kacha *tya* Achin Ejulinjapad was wounded by Yamuna *dva* Ikshu Chitranipad." She repeated the words again, and again, pouring her circle of earth through her fingers and pouring her working through her spirit, weaving it into the required shape with earth and breath and the dance of all the worlds in front of her. She stared into the silver mirror, and watched the worlds swing and dip, turn and turn again, rest, and turn, anti-clockwise, forward, backward, up when they should have been down, turn and turn, and turn . . .

For a moment, shadows swirled in the silver mirror, then those shadows reached up to meet the turning worlds and draw them close. The vision swallowed all of Medeoan's senses, until the present world vanished and she was wholly and completely part of the past.

It was hot here, unbearably, oppressively hot. Medeoan struggled to breathe. It was as if she had suddenly been wrapped in a wet woolen blanket at the height of a summer's day. She stood with three men in a circular chamber, inlaid with ivory and decorated in the elaborate Hastinapuran fashion. Despite the heat, a fire burned brightly on a carved altar at the center of the chamber. The first man was wizened, skeletally thin and dressed only in a white robe. The second man was soft of face and body, but his dark eyes were harsh and hard. His hands shook slightly. *He's afraid,* Medeoan realized.

The third man was barely a man at all. It was Kacha, young and fierce and proud, just as he had been when he had first arrived in Isavalta.

No, not just. His face was unscarred, and his hands—Medeoan swallowed against some emotion she could not yet name—his hands were perfect; the strong, unmarked hands of a prince.

The heat had hidden it from her at first, but now that she became more accustomed to it, she could feel that the room throbbed with magic. This was no mere prickling of some random spell. It thrummed through Medeoan's blood, making her stagger. She had never felt so much power. She would have thought a dozen sorcerers could not draw so much through themselves, and there was only one such here, and he held a black knife in his skinny hand.

"Are you ready, my prince?" he asked. His voice was soft but strong, like the first wind that hints at a storm.

Kacha squared his shoulders. Medeoan's heart melted to see him so strong, so proud, but at the same time fear chilled her. What was happening here, in this room as filled with magic as it was filled with air?

Kacha lifted his right hand and laid it on the altar. The

sorcerer, whom Medeoan was sure must be Yamuna, laid his own right hand beside Kacha's.

"Hold your son, my lord," said Yamuna.

The second man, who must have been Chandra, Kacha's father, stepped hesitantly forward. He took his son's shoulders in his hands, but even Medeoan could see he gripped without strength. He had gone pale, and the perspiration that stood out on his forehead did not come entirely from the heat.

Yamuna raised the black knife, and he spoke again. This time the words were in some mellifluous tongue that Medeoan could not understand. She could, however, understand their effect full well. The magic that pressed so hard against her senses flared like the flames on the altar, brightening, intensifying, becoming so impossibly strong that Medeoan felt certain the stone walls must burst because they could not contain it all.

The knife came down.

Yamuna did not scream. He did not even seem to flinch, not at the torrent of blood, not at the severed hand that had been his own lying curled and spasming like a dying insect on the altar.

Yamuna raised the knife again. Kacha lifted his chin.

Medeoan screamed, a high, hysterical, unbelieving scream, torn from her throat without thought of stopping. The shrill, wordless noise shattered her working, dropping the present and true world around her like a shroud.

"Mistress?" called a quavering voice. "Mistress? Are you well?"

Medeoan's breath left her and she could scream no more. Her eyes opened of their own accord and she gasped for more air. She had fallen to her knees, she realized, and she now groveled at the base of the Portrait like some serf before their icon. The voice had been Chekhania, who could not enter this room without permission, and who must stand and fret outside.

"Mistress?"

Medeoan could not answer. She could not even pick herself up. She could only remain as she was, huddled on the floor, tears streaming down at the memory of what she had just seen.

But what *had* she seen? She didn't know. Not clearly. She had some vague intuitions, but she did not *know*. Could there be some benign explanation? Some reason, some oath extracted by his father that kept Kacha from telling her the truth of what had happened to his hand.

His father, Chandra, who had trembled during the working, as his son had not. Medeoan hid her face in her hands. Blood, power and blood. The vision had been so filled with both. There had to be some explanation. There had to be some way this came out right.

"Mistress? Please! . . ."

She had to get up. She had to pull herself together and to think, to think of the way that made what she had seen come out right. But she could not. Her strength was gone, drained by her working and by what she had seen.

"Help me," she croaked. "Chekhania. Help me."

The waiting lady rushed into the Portrait room and lifted Medeoan to her feet. Medeoan had to put her hand on Checkhania's shoulder to steady herself. She had no strength in her legs at all.

"My bed," she whispered. "Get me to my bed."

"Yes, mistress." The lady's voice was breathy with her concern. "Shall I send for a surgeon, your sorcerer . . . ?"

Medeoan shook her head violently. "Just get me to my bed."

Chekhania supported her from the room to where Vladka waited. Together, they laid Medeoan on her bed. They loosened her laces and brought a cloth for her head. Medeoan waved them away.

"Let me sleep," she murmured. "Just let me sleep."

Unable to keep her eyes open a moment longer, Medeoan encased herself in a private darkness. She did not want to see her ladies, or her chamber, or anything but the answer she needed to understand what Kacha had done.

Help me, she prayed as her mind spiraled down into sleep. *Vyshemir, help me see what is true.*

But as she began to dream, it was not Vyshemir who came to her, it was her father. He appeared as she had known him in life; tall, distant, hawk-nosed and dark-bearded. His shroud draped around his shoulders like a cloak. He held out his hand to her and Medeoan took it without thought, in the manner of dreams, and without stopping to wonder how she had come again to be a little girl.

He held a finger to his lips, indicating a need for silence, and Medeoan nodded. Her father smiled approvingly and led her from her room, which had become her nursery, and down the corridors, which became stairways leading down, which became the antechamber for the treasury rooms, which became the treasury warehouse itself, with its chests and its bags and its piles of wealth.

Father gestured for her to stand where she was. Medeoan stood quietly with her hands folded in front of her. Father reached down a small, flat chest, and Medeoan saw the mark graven on the lock. She knew this box, and she knew what it contained. It should have been locked up tight, for what it contained was dangerous. But the box itself was not locked. Father opened it easily, and showed it to her, and it was empty.

In the moment she perceived it was empty, she also saw Kacha with his mismatched hands holding the silver girdle that had once been contained within, and she knew that Yamuna saw what he did through Kacha's right eye, his eye that was from Yamuna as his hand was from Yamuna, and Yamuna's voice whispered approvingly in the back of his mind.

With this you will be able to control your wife.

"No," whispered Medeoan. "No!"

And the dream was gone, and Medeoan was awake in her bed, her heart pounding with fear.

Calm yourself, she ordered her heart, even as she clutched at the covers. *Be calm!*

A dream after a vision working was not unusual, even a clear and powerful one. It did not mean it was a true dream. It did not mean her father had been here. It did not, it did not, mean that Kacha had robbed the treasury of a powerful magical artifact.

He did not mean to use it against her. He did not. He could not. Medeoan squeezed her eyes shut again.

Come back. Come to me. Tell me my dream lied. Tell me!

But all such pleading without a working was useless, and she was too tired to even begin to attempt any such. Yet, she knew she would not be able to rest anymore without an answer. Although she felt like a guilty traitor to Kacha's love, she had to know. She had to prove to herself that it was all a lie.

Medeoan threw back her covers and climbed to her feet. The ladies came running in a bunch to reorder her clothes and flutter anxiously about her, asking what their imperial mistress might require.

A surge of sudden anger washed through her. Anger at her father for not being here himself and leaving her only dreams. Anger, again, hot and fresh, at Avanasy for his betrayal and leaving her alone. Anger at herself for not being able to trust Kacha absolutely and without question, which was what she desperately wanted.

Medeoan said not a word to her ladies. She just stood impatiently while they made her decent, and then she marched out of the apartment. She would do this quickly. She would find her answer and then she would be done. Then, she would find a way to apologize to Kacha for doubting him, and for not being able to rid her mind of a dream.

The ladies, guards and pages scrambled to keep pace with her. Fortunately, they had enough sense to keep silent. She led the entourage down the North Stairs with its pink marble and graceful pillars, down the secretary's stairs which were plain, gray stone worn smooth by generations of feet, down into the earth where the vaults waited.

"Mistress," ventured Checkhania as the page girls hurried forward to announce her arrival to the soldiers guarding the treasure houses and the under-ministers of the treasury who kept count of it all. "Mistress, if you could perhaps tell us what you wanted . . ."

Medeoan did not answer her. She just gripped her hems more tightly and kept her eyes straight ahead.

She strode up to the members of the house guard who flanked the door of the main treasury. They needed no spoken command. They unbarred the door and stood back, giving her the soldier's reverence with their hands over their hearts.

The antechamber for the treasury was an undecorated stone room with two rows of copying desks, each manned by an under-minister with a huge ledger. As the door opened, all the servants of the storehouse leapt from their chairs and fell to their knees, properly respectful but obviously amazed at her presence.

"I require access to the treasury," she barked out. "Now."

The first under-minister, a little gnome of a man weighed down by his gold chain of office, sprang to his feet, but did not seem to consider it polite to stand up straight in the imperial presence. He fumbled with his bundle of keys that was almost as large as Medeoan's own, and unlocked the inner door. He reverenced as he stood aside, and Medeoan entered the dim storehouse.

Medeoan paused, trying to regain her composure, trying to calm her anger. She would do this swiftly. She would lay her doubts in their proper resting place. She would never again place more credence in dreams than she did in Kacha's word.

It was then she realized that her entire cluster of ladies had entered the storehouse behind her.

"Out of here," Medeoan ordered. "All of you. Out into the hallway." They stared at her, as baffled as a flock of startled hens. "Out!"

That got through to them. They grabbed up their skirts and scurried out the door, all their eyes wide in distress. Medeoan stared after them. How had she become surrounded by such a pack of fools?

You don't worry about Prathad? Beloved, you should, I've seen her with the guardsmen . . . Beloved, it grieves me to bring you this tale, but your lady, Vladka, has been carrying letters . . . Dismiss Chekhania? What for, beloved? She looks so well beside you . . .

Medeoan shook her head violently to interrupt these unwanted memories.

It was cold in the treasury. Guards hurried in to light the waiting lamps and braziers, but their illumination was too feeble to warm the great stone chamber. Medeoan shivered and gazed around her. Some treasures waited out in the open. Sacks of silver coins gaped between the rows of chests that ran the length of the room. Ropes of pearls hung on hooks. Slabs of precious amber were stacked as high as Medeoan's waist in the far corners.

These were baubles, Medeoan knew. They were there to impress visitors whom the emperors needed dazzled by the resources of Isavalta. Anything of true import waited safely locked in its chest and every chest was stacked in its appropriate place. Each chest was bound in metal, whether iron, copper, brass, or silver. Each had its separate lock, and each lock was graven with a symbol known only to the Lord Master Treasurer, or to members of the imperial family.

"Close the door," said Medeoan without looking behind her.

Someone obeyed. The clang reverberated against stone and metal, making the entire chamber ring. Medeoan hesitated where she was for a moment, her hand smoothing down the bundle of keys at her waist.

Come now, do what you must. You cannot stand here all day.

Down the years, her ancestors had collected, confiscated, commissioned, or been given many artifacts of powerful magic. These were locked in chests banded with silver and marked with Vyshemir's cup. Avanasy had spent many hours down here with her, teaching her the uses and histories of many of the objects. But there were some things that Avanasy was not allowed to know the use of. Some things about which even the lord sorcerer was kept in ignorance.

Medeoan paced up the left-hand aisle between the waiting boxes, each step carrying her farther from the lights. Her mind could not help but imagine that Father walked beside her. She could almost hear the rustle of his kaftan, and the heavy wheeze of his breath.

"Reach me down that small one, Daughter," he had said.

She had been twelve then, and had to stand on tiptoe. Now, she had only to stretch out her arm to grasp the long, flat box on top of the pile of teakwood chests. She set it down on top of a cedar casket that was bound in iron. The box she had retrieved was bound with silver and had a lock framed with a silver braid. She had a matching silver key on her ring. Her hand shook as she inserted the key into the lock.

"There are some things you must keep secret. You must whisper of them only in your own heart," Father's voice told her solemnly from memory. "This is one such. I pray you will never have to use it."

He took out a girdle that seemed to be woven of pure silver. A hundred tassels shimmered in the lantern light. As Medeoan peered at it, she could see a series of runes had been woven into the band, silver on silver. The power of the thing was meant to be hidden. It was made to look harmless.

"This girdle was made with the empire," her father said solemnly, laying the shimmering band back on its blue velvet lining. "Its magic is strong. Anyone who wears it is placed in thrall to the one who ties it onto them. Their minds are clouded for as long as they wear the girdle and they can only do as they are told." He closed the box. "When you are empress, should there ever be one you cannot act against openly, but whom you must silence and you have no other means, this is yours to use."

It will be there, insisted Medeoan to herself as she stared at the box and tried to still the trembling in her hands. *Of course it will be there.* The sorceress who had woven it was long dead. She had been old when she made it, and she had only told her mistress, Medeoan's grandmother, of its properties. How could Kacha, let alone Yamuna, even know of its existence? Her dream was false.

Medeoan inserted the key into the lock and turned it. The click of the lock seemed as loud as the clanging of the door that had shut her in here. She lifted the lid.

Medeoan stood amidst the wealth of her empire and stared at the one empty box with its blue velvet lining. Disbelief came first. It had to be the wrong chest. She had made a mistake. She had only seen it once, after all, and she had been little more than a child then.

But try as she might she could not make her heart to believe that. Then came denial. Kacha was being deceived. There were traitors in the court, and at the foot of the Pearl Throne. They were using him for their own ends. She would root them out. They would be hanged in chains over a slow fire. They would be torn apart by horses. They would die, slowly and bloodily. All of them who dared to betray her. She would tell Kacha . . .

What could she possibly tell him? That she had used her magic to spy on him? That it had shown her . . . that it had shown her . . .

Grief then. Silent tears pouring down her cheeks, all unnoticed as her heart shattered. She could find no more reasons. She could form no more questions. She had been taught to trust her powers even more than she trusted her heart and her reason, and her powers had shown her too much.

Kacha was the traitor. He did serve his father, and his father's sorcerer, and their cause. He had lied to her, from the beginning, about everything. Avanasy had tried to warn her.

Avanasy. Medeoan's hand flew to her mouth to stifle a sob. Avanasy had tried to warn her and she had turned on him, and now only the gods knew where he was. She had severed herself from her loyal servants and her truest friend. Now what would she do? Now that Kacha, her lover, her husband, meant to make her his slave?

It was that thought that finally brought fear crashing down on Medeoan. She swayed, pressing her palm against her mouth. She could not cry out. She could not let anyone hear. Too many people already knew she had come here. If Kacha heard . . .

No. No. No. This was not happening. It could not be. She was wrong. She had made a mistake. Kacha loved her. She loved him. This was wrong.

Wrong, yes, but this time she had not made a mistake. This knowledge was only the result of her mistakes.

Medeoan reached out and slammed the box lid shut. The sound echoed around the chamber for a long moment before it faded away. In the silence that followed, she turned away from the box and walked out. She could not see. The whole world was a great blur of color. She moved like a puppet, with some exterior force directing her. She could not even order her own thoughts. A jumble of images filled her mind, memories of her father, her mother, of Kacha, and all his bright promises, his whispered words of love, his warm touch.

"Imperial Majesty, did you find all in order?"

Medeoan blinked. Slowly, she forced her eyes to focus in the direction from which the voice came. The first under-minister of the treasury had unusually small eyes, she noted, round and dark like a rat's. His shoulders hunched up around his ears, probably from leaning over his ledgers. How much had he been given to allow Kacha into the place where only she should have gone? What account did they keep together? Did it even matter now? All that mattered was that he was Kacha's creature, which now made him her enemy. Her enemy, and Isavalta's.

"Imperial Majesty?" The under-minister blinked rapidly several times.

"Yes," said Medeoan. "I found all that I needed."

Chapter Five

Hours later, Medeoan slumped, exhausted, into the one chair that waited in the room with the Portrait of Worlds.

She couldn't find the stolen girdle. She had taxed her skill and strength to its limits. She had tried every symbol, every word, every prayer she could think of and she still could not find it. Kacha or Yamuna had hidden it from her most searching eye, and she could not even see how that had been accomplished.

Yet she knew Kacha had it in his possession and at any unguarded moment he might slip it around her waist, tie it tight, and then her mind would no longer be her own. She would belong only to him, unable to think or to act but as he bid.

She bowed her head into her hands, pressing the heels of her palms against her eyes.

Help me, she prayed. *Vyshemir, help me. You also found*

*your husband was your enemy, but I have no knife to use as
you did. What do I do?*

"Beloved?"

Medeoan's head jerked up. Kacha's voice sounded from
the other side of the door. Her heart hammered in her chest,
and for a long moment, she didn't dare move. How could
she face him? What could she say? She needed more time
to think.

But she had no time. Kacha was outside, and she could
not sit here with the locked door between them. If she did,
he would know something was wrong.

Trembling, Medeoan got to her feet and opened the door.

Kacha stood there, the man she had loved so much for the
past three years, and nothing about him had changed. He was
still tall and strong, his face handsome and caring. He was
so beautiful, despite his scars and his mismatched eyes. Even
now, knowing all that she did, she yearned to throw herself
into his arms and confess everything and ask what she should
do. In that moment, she hated herself more than she could
ever hate him. Despite all, Kacha was her friend as well as
husband, her sole trusted advisor since Avanasy had left her.

*Since I drove Avanasy away. Since I failed to believe in
the one I should have trusted above all others.*

"The ambassador from my uncle's court is safely here,
beloved," he said, not moving from his place in the doorway.
Even he would not come in here without an invitation. Not
when he could be seen, anyway. "I came to tell you so, and
to see how your preparations were progressing for his reception, but your ladies tell me you have locked yourself in here
all the day."

She had to answer him. She could not simply stand here
and stare. She must speak.

One art had she learned in all its perfection from her parents. Medeoan could lie, effortlessly and without any change
of demeanor. Now she found she could work that art against
Kacha, to whom she had sworn she would never lie, and
from whom she had believed she would never have to hide.

"I'm sorry, Kacha," she said, taking both his hands, the
one that belonged to him and the one that did not, lifting her
face to kiss him softly, and dying inside to find that the touch

of his kiss had not changed at all. "I had a working which could not be attended to by the court sorcerers." Which was true enough. "I wanted to see to things myself."

"And what working is this?" asked Kacha, his eyebrows rising.

She shook her head, smiling a little shyly. *Answer him, answer him,* she ordered herself desperately. Any doubt, any mystery and he would . . . he would . . .

She could not bring herself to think of the consequences directly, but the fear brought the lie she needed to her lips. "I have been thinking about what you were saying to me the other day." Medeoan smoothed her skirts down. "That we must be sure of the loyalty of the lords master. I may have found a means to help us in those determinations."

"Really?" Kacha sounded both impressed and wary. "How would it work?"

Medeoan shrugged. "I don't know that it can work yet, Kacha. I need some study in the library. Come to me tonight, and I will tell you all, I promise."

His fingertips brushed her chin. "I shall look forward to it." He raised one finger in admonishment. "But we must not neglect the ambassador. I will not have it reported back to my uncle that I have forgotten courtesy here in the north."

Then, slowly, as she gazed at him, the realization came over her that she did have a knife to use against him. She was the empress of Isavalta. She could have Kacha arrested and killed, or simply killed, and no one could question her. She could do it this instant, she could raise her voice to the men-at-arms who waited outside her door.

"What are you thinking, beloved?" asked Kacha suddenly.

"I'm thinking of you," said Medeoan honestly. "And how you have surely forgotten nothing so vital as courtesy."

His lips were warm, soft, and loving as he kissed her brow. She felt the smile in that kiss and closed her eyes, hoping he would not see the pain that racked her.

And if she had him killed, what would Hastinapura do? What would his uncle who sat on the Pearl Throne do? Emperor Samudra would surely declare war. He would have to. Could Isavalta withstand such a war? She did not know. She had not spoken with the Master of War in . . . How long? She could not remember.

"Let me see to my study and to my wardrobe, husband," said Medeoan, keeping her smile about her mouth. "We will speak again tonight."

"That we surely will." He reverenced to her with a wink and left then. Medeoan found she had to work hard for several moments just to continue breathing.

Fool, she cursed herself. *Fool! Now you have but a handful of hours, and what will you tell him at the end of them? What can you do?*

She looked around her chamber and the busy ladies, bent over their needlework or their books, pretending not to notice her until she gave an order. Any one of them might be a spy, or all of them. She did not truly know a single one. She was surrounded by strangers. She did not know her own council anymore. She had allowed them all to be taken from her.

She had to get away from here, from this pit of spies, before Kacha could steal her mind. She had to find a way to hide herself and a place where he could not reach.

A plan came to her then, formed from old learning and the fog of desperation. A way to escape, a way to hide and a place to go.

But she could not do it alone. She would at the very least need one other ally. But who? Who was there?

For the hundredth time, her heart reached out to Avanasy, wishing desperately she had let her anger cool, that she had known he had remained in Isavalta, even to the end, even to the day of her wedding. If she had known, perhaps in her joy on the day she could have forgiven him, and he would be with her now . . .

Another memory came to her. A memory of the commander of the House Guard standing before her, and telling her that Avanasy had not only defiantly stayed until the moment of her marriage, but that he had help leaving the palace. A guard named Peshek. Did Her Imperial Majesty wish the man put to death?

No, no, she had replied, regally. *Let him not be punished. Today is a day of amnesty to all.*

Kacha had not been pleased when he heard, but he had let the matter lie.

So where was this Peshek, this man who had risked death to help Avanasy?

"I am repairing to the Red Library," announced Medeoan to her ladies. "Let the commander of the House Guard attend me there."

She whisked out of her apartments in their untrustworthy company, silently planning her escape.

The Red Library was housed in a much smaller chamber than the Imperial Library that stood beside the god house. Its chamber was a blunt wedge lined with oaken shelves. Pillars of garnet-colored marble stood between them. Three arched windows overlooked the courtyard and let in the summer daylight. The ceiling had been painted with a replica of the astrologer's chart that was supposed to have predicted Medeoan's grandmother's rise to empress, and the floor was inlaid with stars in colored woods.

Like the room that held the Portrait, the Red Library was a place she could enter alone without arousing suspicion. Here she could study in private among the grimoires, the books of shadows, the manuals of necromancy, and the ancient scrolls that the Isavaltan court sorcerers had collected or captured down the years.

Medeoan lifted a particular volume from the shelves. It was bound in white leather edged in blue ink. She laid it gently on one of the oaken tables. She had studied this book for months, with Avanasy at her shoulder. It was a book of spells that might be worked in cloth and thread. She began to turn the vellum pages, scanning the thick black lettering and the precise drawings for the one she needed.

A knock sounded on the door.

"Come," called Medeoan, hastily shutting the book.

A man in the blue coat and gilded armor of the house guard marched into the room. One sweep of his eyes took in her solitary presence and at once he reverenced, not merely the soldier's bow from the waist, but the full reverence to the imperial presence, down on both knees, his head bowed before her.

Medeoan rose. This was the man she had ordered the commander to find. As he was, however, she could see nothing of him but a pair of broad shoulders under his uniform coat and his bowed back. "Captain Peshek," she said.

"Imperial Majesty," he replied in acknowledgment, but without looking up, as was proper.

It was a propriety that did not help her at all now. She needed to see this man's eyes. She needed some hint as to how to judge him. "Stand up, Captain. Look at me."

Captain Peshek hesitated, but only for a heartbeat, and then did as he was bidden. He had a good face under his helmet, Medeoan decided. It was lined by smiles as well as by wind and weather, and his eyes were open and cheerful. But handsome looks could blind the observer. She knew that too well now.

She did not have time to hedge or to engage in any sort of verbal dance. "You are a friend of Lord Avanasy's, I believe."

Would he admit it? His whole face went wary. "Yes, Imperial Majesty."

"Still? Despite his exile?"

He might well be answering for his position, if not his life, and the way he pulled himself to attention said he knew that. Would he deny the friendship in hopes of saving himself? Or would he acknowledge it and accept the consequences of his honesty?

"Yes, Imperial Majesty," said Captain Peshek.

He said it without flinching or hesitation. Medeoan felt at least some of her knotted muscles loosen. "I know he trusted you."

Peshek said nothing. He just stood at rigid attention, his eyes straight ahead, waiting for orders, like the soldier he was.

"Because of that, I also will trust you."

Peshek laid his hand over his heart. "I live to serve, Imperial Majesty."

Now she had to speak the words out loud, and once the words left her, it all became real and she could not explain away what had happened anymore. Medeoan clasped her hands in front of her to keep them from trembling.

"I am in danger, Captain Peshek."

That startled him. He stared at her, confusion giving way rapidly to anger in his eyes. "How, Majesty? From who? I'll have . . ."

Medeoan shook her head. "I can't tell you that. The less you know . . . it's my own fault . . . I . . ." She pulled herself together. "Do you know where Lord Avanasy is?"

For the first time, Peshek hesitated. Why would he not? She had decided to trust him, but who was she? The one who had exiled Avanasy, who would have had him killed if she had caught him. Peshek had to decide how far he trusted her.

In the end, Peshek shook his head. "No, Imperial Majesty. I don't know where he is. I'm sorry," he said and Medeoan judged his regret to be sincere.

Medeoan bit her lip. "He told you nothing of where he planned to go?"

"No, Imperial Majesty."

"I see." Medeoan circled the reading table. It had been a slim hope, but it had been all she had. The white grimoire lay on the table's polished surface, looking no more nor less dangerous than any other history or poem. Yet, in there lay her salvation, her promise of life. For that promise, however, she must ask for a sacrifice.

And you must do this now. You have only three days. In three days the household moved to the summer palace of Vaknevos. In three days she would be constantly in Kacha's company while they traveled, and her hopes for escape would come to nothing. That thought sent a chill through her bones.

Medeoan steeled herself. "Captain," she said as firmly as she could manage. "I need for you to bring me a girl, a drab, one newly brought into service, if possible. This must be done quietly. The Mistress of the House must not know." *No one must know. There must be no rumor, no gossip that can reach my husband's ears before I can have all my answers ready for him.*

Medeoan watched the question "Why?" form in Peshek's

eyes, but he did not speak it. Instead, it seemed to Medeoan that he turned his mind to the logistics of his assignment. Peshek, she knew, had lived in Vyshtavos for almost as long as she had. He was familiar with its ways, in some areas more familiar with them than she, whose provinces were only great apartments and grand halls.

"The Mistress of the House spends the first part of every day in her pantry reviewing the inventories," said Captain Peshek, again laying his hand again over his heart. "If that meets with Her Imperial Majesty's approval, I shall bring the girl then."

"In the morning, in two days' time," said Medeoan. "I will be walking by the canal. Bring her to me then. I remind you once more, this must be done quietly. No one must know."

"Imperial Majesty." Peshek pulled himself up to a posture of formal attention in acknowledgment of her orders.

Medeoan opened her mouth. She wanted to say something of her fear, of her fledgling plans. She wanted so much to have another heart beside her, as she thought she had with Kacha, and as she truly had with Avanasy. But Peshek, for all she must trust him, was not Avanasy, and would never be. So, all she said was, "Thank you, Captain Peshek. You may go."

This time, he gave her the soldier's reverence, a deep bow with his hand over his heart. But he did not leave at once. "Imperial Majesty?"

"Yes, Captain?" Medeoan rested her fingertips on the reading table, as if she might need to steady herself.

Peshek ventured a glance toward her face, but quickly recovered his discipline and dropped his gaze again. "You may also trust Keeper Bakhar. He too is a friend of Lord Avanasy's."

Bakhar. Thank goodness. I don't know if I could bear it if the attendant of the gods turned against me.

A thought struck her. Peshek would be a great help, but he could not provide all she needed. Nor could Keeper Bakhar. There would have to be a third. "What of the lord sorcerer?"

Captain Peshek shifted his weight. "Understand, Majesty, I am only a soldier, an unimportant member of the guard . . ."

"I understand, Captain." Medeoan felt tired. She did not want to have to ask these questions.

"I do know Keeper Bakhar believes him to be loyal to you," finished Peshek quickly.

"Thank you, Captain," she said again, and again he reverenced. This time, however, he turned smartly on his heel and left, as protocol dictated.

Just this once, let me have judged a man rightly. Medeoan bowed her head. *I cannot do this alone.*

Two days. Only two days, and yet all of two days. It was just one more space of time to endure, she tried to tell herself. She had endured more and for longer than this, playing her part as required. She could do anything for just two days.

Kacha held himself still while his waiting gentlemen stripped the heavy Isavaltan finery from him, replacing it with a linen nightshirt and a plain, if voluminous, indigo velvet robe. The formal reception and subsequent feast for the new ambassador had lasted until well after dark, but he was not yet tired, which was just as well. There was more work to be done tonight.

On the whole, the reception had gone well. As Yamuna had predicted, Uncle Samudra had sent Girilal to act as the new ambassador. Girilal was a concession to old wounds at court, as he was known to have disapproved of the disruption of the succession Samudra had initiated. This disapproval could be worked on much more easily than Tanmay's loyalties. It had been a constant struggle to keep Tanmay from realizing that Harshul, Kacha's bound-sorcerer and Uncle Samudra's spy, had not reached Isavalta alive. That was not a report which could be permitted to reach the Pearl Throne.

Soon Kacha would find time to be alone with Girilal. He would make the new ambassador understand the situation here in Isavalta, and show him all the benefit his plans would bring to Hastinapura, including restoring the rightful line of succession. Ambassador Girilal would see the truth, and Kacha felt sure it would not take him long to do so.

Despite Kacha's confidence in his new ambassador, worry still gnawed at him. Medeoan had been too quiet, too withdrawn, this evening, as if she had something on her mind. But she had confided nothing to him. He must have this matter, whatever it might be, out of her soon. If she was ceasing to speak her whole mind to him, it might be the first sign she was slipping from his control, as Yamuna had said she might. If that were so, he would need to make use of the artifact Yamuna's magic and his bribery had ferreted out. The best time for that would be during the change of households, a time at which the empress could become ill for so many different reasons, and during which the fewest number of people would have their eyes on her.

It must be done, Yamuna's voice had whispered to him. *It is better that it be done sooner. You have done well in cementing your alliances, my prince. The lies are in place, and her power wanes. It is better it be done before she realizes what she has lost and struggles to regain it.*

Kacha waved his man away and tied the sash on his night robe himself. He did not wish to dispute Yamuna, who had been so right about so much, but Kacha wondered if Yamuna realized how frequently the rulers of Isavalta appeared in the public eye. Matters here were not as they were at home, where that which was most precious was most carefully concealed and protected. Here, the reasons for the empress remaining confined were far fewer and would be examined much more closely. Here, many different sorcerers would be working to find the cure for any "illness" which struck, as opposed to just one bound-sorcerer. Kacha was not certain Yamuna believed how close they had come to failure with the old emperor and empress. The court sorcerers and Medeoan had almost saved them, even at the bitter end. He had felt Yamuna's workings strain to hold against all the efforts of the Isavaltan magicians.

They would have to tread very carefully with Medeoan, and haste would only make the path more difficult to navigate.

Kacha turned to his manservant. "I've a mind to visit my lady wife. You may retire. I doubt your services will be required again tonight."

The man was, of course, far too disciplined to so much as smile at that. He bowed low with his palms over his eyes, following the custom of Hastinapura. Kacha touched the man's head as he passed, giving his approval with that gesture for the man, and the other servants, to be about their business. He crossed the cold, stone apartment to the connecting door, knocked once and entered his wife's chamber.

The flock of ladies surrounding Medeoan was on its feet and performing deeply respectful reverences as soon as he appeared. Medeoan herself sat by the fire, her head bent and her hand busy at some task he could not see. She did not look up as he entered.

"Beloved?" he inquired, as he moved softly forward. The worry that had touched him earlier drew closer.

Then, he felt the tingling in his right hand, and behind his right eye. Fear settled over him. Whatever Medeoan did, there was magic to it. She sat deep in concentration over some spell. As he approached, he could see she worked with a pair of weaving cards; thin, square pieces of wood with holes in their corners through which threads could be strung to make a small hand loom. The threads in question were very fine and glittered silver and gold in the firelight. As her hands manipulated the threads, her breath labored in her throat. This working was taking its toll on her strength.

What are you doing, Medeoan? thought Kacha as he sank into the chair beside her. The ladies, receiving no orders, rose from their reverences and set to the night's business of readying their mistress's bed. Kacha caught the lady Chekhania's eye, questioning. She replied with a small shake of her head. Whatever Medeoan did, his best spy among the ladies knew nothing of it.

Medeoan must have become aware of his presence because her breathing gradually eased, as did the uncomfortable tingling in Kacha's hand and eye. At last, her hands stilled their weaving and she lowered her work, looking up to smile at him.

"Forgive me, beloved," she said, dabbing at the sheen of perspiration that covered her brow. "I am at a working here."

"I guessed as much." Kacha leaned close. His right hand twitched. She was weaving a golden band, about an inch across, shot through with silver. "What is this you are making, beloved?"

"Remember how I said I was thinking about how to be more certain of the loyalties of the lords master?" Medeoan fingered her work. She had not even completed four inches of whatever it was she labored over. "When it is done, this will be a girdle which will help us in those determinations."

"Really?" Kacha felt a stab of foreboding in the back of his right eye. "How will it work?"

"At midsummer, when the new appointments are named, the loyalty oaths are renewed. We will declare that each lord master who takes the oath must wear the girdle as he does." Medeoan touched the piece of weaving again, as if to check for flaws. "If one is not sincere, the girdle will slip off his waist." Her smile grew arch. "Am I not clever? Is it not a good notion?"

Clever enough to be truly dangerous, if only you knew it. "An excellent notion, beloved," he said, both surprised and pleased that she should have thought of such a thing. "But will not such an open display of your power make your lords master nervous? You have said to me that they are not pleased at the thought they will be ruled over by a sorcerer."

"They are not pleased that they will be ruled over by a man of Hastinapura either." An unfamiliar note crept into Medeoan's voice. For a moment, she sounded fierce. "But that is who has been set over them, and we must make sure that they know we are secure in our rule, and that there is no deceiving us."

Kacha found himself answering her smile easily. Perhaps his earlier fears had been unfounded. That would be as well. Despite Yamuna's counsel of the need to hold her harmless, having Medeoan whole and articulate at his side would cause much less gossip and speculation than having her mute and bewildered. "The midsummer appointments will thus allow us to take even better measure of our allies than I had thought."

"Yes. No one will be able to hide from us," she said firmly, laying her hand over his. "You always know what to say. You will be able to find us some way to explain this so the lords master will not be too disturbed."

"I will set my mind to it," he assured her, stroking her arm lightly. "But it is late. Shall we go to bed, you and I?

We could discuss that, and many other things."

Medeoan sighed and rubbed her eyes. "You must forgive me, beloved. This is a difficult sorcery. It will leave me profoundly weary. I wish to have it finished before we leave for Vaknevos, so that I am not overtaxed and a nuisance on the journey." She shook her head ruefully. "And if I am too often absent before the day itself, there will be talk we do not want."

"All of this is well thought of. I will leave you to your work." Kacha stood, and a new possibility occurred to him. "Shall I make your excuses to the ambassador tomorrow?"

At that, Medeoan looked deeply relieved. "Yes. Please. I am sure you can open whatever negotiations are required."

Excellent, thought Kacha to himself. This would mean he could easily interview Girilal in private, and ascertain how best to approach him concerning the ultimate plans for Isavalta.

And perhaps now would be a good time to return to another matter.

"Beloved," he said, letting his fingertips linger over hers. "While you are of mind to discuss the security of our rule, I would ask if you have reconsidered recalling Avanasy."

Medeoan turned her face away, her cheeks turning red. "Do you still believe . . ."

"I believe that while he is alive, he is a danger to you, my love. He knows your powers so well, he held your confidence for so long . . . who can say what he is doing with that knowledge? Beloved . . ." He touched her cheek, turning her back toward him. Her eyes were damp and her mouth was set in an unusually stern line. "It is only when he is secured under the hand of those we know are loyal that you will be safe from him."

And only when he is dead we will truly be sure of him, added Kacha to himself.

Medeoan took his hand, pressing it against her cheek. "Very well, husband," she whispered.

Kacha smiled broadly and drew her to him, kissing her long and deeply. She clung to him with the desperate strength that possessed her when she gave in to him on some matter that pained her.

He disengaged her gently, keeping hold of both her hands. "Shall I give the orders?" he asked gently.

She shook her head. "I will see to it. This was my doing, let mine be the undoing."

"I am as one of your guard." Kacha rose and gave her a soldier's reverence. "I live only to serve you."

"I thought you lived to love me." Medeoan pushed out her lower lip petulantly.

Knowing his part well, Kacha kissed that lip. "That as well. I shall seek my lonely bed this night, and let you get on with your good work." He kissed her forehead for good measure, and left.

So, wife, you have bought yourself some time. Kacha paused by the door and looked back at Medeoan, who had already reclaimed her weaving. *And you have bought it for me as well. I thank you for both.*

But watch her, cautioned the voice that never seemed to leave the back of his mind. *Now more than ever, watch her closely. That girdle she weaves might be used as easily against you as against any.*

I've thought of that, answered Kacha silently. *It could also easily be taken from her to be my own tool when I bind her thoughts forever.*

In the morning, the household of Vyshtavos began in earnest to prepare itself for the annual move to the summer palace. Legions of scullions and house servants were loaded onto wagons under the watchful eye of the aides to the Mistress of the House. They were then sent to assist the workers already there in opening and preparing Vaknevos. Half of Medeoan's ladies and half of Kacha's gentlemen were sent ahead in barges to make sure the imperial needs would be met without awkwardness or delay once the move was completed. Those who remained were doubly busy, not only in seeing to their masters, but in supervising the organizing and packing necessary for removing the imperial couple to the summer palace, and for securing the belongings, furnishings and necessaries that must be left behind over the summer.

Dispatches had to be written, inventories had to be reviewed, orders and letters had to be conveyed to various parties. There was almost none among the council and the high household who did not need to be spoken to.

A thing Medeoan was counting on. She was being watched, she was sure of it. Even when Kacha left her side to attend his own duties, she felt eyes staring at the back of her neck, reading over her shoulder, straining to catch every nuance of her work.

Could he tell what she truly did? Could Yamuna's hand and Yamuna's eye discern so much?

I am only tired, she tried to tell herself. *The working has been hard and slow, and that is what has me worried.*

The girdle was complete and lay in the basket with her sewing. Fatigue weighed Medeoan down. She had slept for only a handful of hours during the past two days, and it was only the thrumming of her nerves that kept her moving.

She had brought her entourage out onto the banks of the canal this morning by declaring that she and her ladies required some fresh air after all their time shut up indoors like bees trapped in their hive. Now, they sat in the willow grove, underneath the canopy that had been set up for them, their sewing on their laps and plates of white breads and fresh fruits before them. The birds sang and the wind blew fresh and strong across the grasses bringing them all the scents of early summer, and Medeoan could enjoy none of it.

Where is Peshek? she kept thinking as she stared at the linen in her lap. *Where is he?*

Unable to sit still any longer, Medeoan rose and began to stroll as calmly as she was able down the bank. The shadows of the willows played across her skin. Chekhania followed behind her in decorous silence. Beyond hearing the rustle of her skirts and her footsteps on the grass, Medeoan felt her there. She was watching Medeoan carefully, surely looking for something to report to Kacha.

Medeoan clenched her fists. She could not permit these fears to take over her mind. She had to be able to think clearly. She needed all her wits about her for tomorrow.

"Mistress?" said Chekhania.

Medeoan turned, and as she did, she saw Captain Peshek walking across the lawn with a thin, gray girl beside him.

"Chekhania," said Medeoan, despite her mouth becoming suddenly dry. "Bring me my basket."

"Mistress." Chekhania reverenced and hurried to do as she was bid. Medeoan did not watch her. She kept her gaze on Peshek, and on the young woman whom he brought with him.

That she was not a true Isavaltan was the first thing that Medeoan saw. Her hair, where it showed under her head-scarf, was coal black, as were her almond-shaped eyes. Her nose was long and straight and her skin had a dusky over-tones. Peshek had brought Medeoan a Tuukosov, a native of Tuukos, the dark island in the northern sea. That was well considered. The Tuukosov had few friends in Isavalta, so this girl would be missed less than even the lowest scullion of mainland birth.

"Drab" was a good term for the girl. She was bone-thin and the sleeves of her gray shirt had been rolled up to expose knobby wrists and elbows. Her headscarf had once been brightly and elaborately embroidered, but the colors had faded from many washings, and a number of threads had come loose, spoiling the symmetry of the design.

Peshek had a hand on the girl's shoulder for reassurance, but she trembled like a leaf in the wind. She stared mutely at Medeoan for a moment, and then recovered herself enough to drop to her knees.

"You may stand," said Medeoan as gently as she could.

The girl, eyes wide with terror, looked at Peshek. In turn, Peshek took her hand, lifted the girl to her feet. He had left his helmet behind for this duty, and for the first time Medeoan got a look at his full face and was surprised at how handsome he truly was. Surely, he had charmed this girl into coming with him.

"What is your name?" Medeoan asked.

Again, the girl stared at Peshek, who nodded and gestured for her to speak.

"Eliisa Hahl," the girl stammered. The name told Medeoan nothing. Had Eliisa been Isavaltan, her name would have said something of her heredity. But the Tuukosov took clan names instead of heredity names and kept their family histories as if they were a dangerous secret. Still, Medeoan could tell this much; this was a poor girl, possibly an illegitimate girl, and certainly one who had never before been prized for what she knew.

Chekhania arrived with the sewing basket. Medeoan took it from her and motioned Chekhania away. The waiting lady stepped back a polite distance, but not so far, Medeoan noted, that she could not see all that occurred.

"Now, Eliisa, your empress has a great favor to ask of you." The words came awkwardly to Medeoan. This girl, this drab, was about her own age, and her eyes were filled with fear. The empress gripped the rough handle of the basket. "I am going to tie a girdle about your waist. It will do you no harm, but as I work, I must ask you to think of your life as it has been so far. Will you do that for me?"

Eliisa thudded back down on to her knees, her face hidden in her hands. Medeoan looked to Peshek, and Peshek took the girl's elbow, whispering gently in her ear. Probably he was repeating Medeoan's promise that Eliisa would come to no harm. Of all the things she had said, Medeoan wished that one was not the lie.

Eliisa stood, visibly trembling. Medeoan set her basket down and drew out the shining girdle, taking a deep breath as she did. She ran the woven band through her fingers, breathing on its length, remembering the work of its making, and drawing up the magic in her soul. This was the completion of a spell that had been begun in those threads. She must concentrate. One silver girdle was to be her undoing. This one of gold would be her salvation.

Then, she had it, the connection between the girdle of her working, and the workings of her inner self. She felt it. This was a part of her, it had been shaped and was being shaped by her will, her desire, her soul. Medeoan opened her eyes.

"I made this girdle of my hand, of silver and gold I made it," she murmured as she walked around the girl, winding the waistband of the girdle twice around the drab's waist. The girl smelled of harsh soaps, strong grease, sweat, and fear. The wool of her skirt and overshirt prickled Medeoan's delicate skin. Her body shook under the empress's hands as Medeoan fastened the girdle about her. But the sorcery was stronger than Medeoan's senses and the current of it carried her past all other realizations. "With my own hands I bind Eliisa Hahl to the girdle, and the girdle to the earth, and the mind and the soul and the heart of Eliisa shall be known to the work of my hands, to the hands that performed the work, to the soul that guided the hands."

As Medeoan repeated the spell, Eliisa's trembling eased. She swayed side to side with the rhythm of words she could only barely have heard. Finally, gently, as Medeoan's quick fingers tied the final knot in the girdle, Eliisa's knees crumpled and she slid gently to the ground. Medeoan dropped with her, cradling the girl's fall.

Slowly, the stupor of the sorceries fell away from Medeoan. She looked down and saw Eliisa's face. The girl's eyes were closed and she seemed to be in a deep and peaceful sleep.

Vyshko and Vyshemir grant you rest, Eliisa, thought Medeoan, smoothing the girl's headscarf. *And may they grant you swift return of what I have just stolen.*

Medeoan laid the girl on the cool grass as tenderly as she could manage. Swiftly, she undid the knot holding the girdle and drew it from Eliisa's waist. She dropped it into her sewing basket and closed the lid. It would not do for her to handle the girdle for too long, not yet anyway.

"Captain Peshek," said Medeoan loud enough for Chekhania to clearly hear. "You will see that this girl is dismissed and returned to her home." Using her body as a shield, Medeoan slipped a small velvet bag from her sash and laid it on Eliisa's breast. Peshek knelt beside the prostrate girl and retrieved it. The gold inside clanked heavily as Peshek stowed the bag in his coat.

"Forgive me, Imperial Majesty, I . . ."

Medeoan did not let him finish his sentence. "It is the shock of discovery, nothing more." Another lie, but one Chekhania needed to hear.

Peshek reverenced as he was, on his knees, and this time asked no questions. Medeoan picked up her basket and turned her back on the girl and Peshek, using all her strength not to look back at them.

"Chekhania," said Medeoan as the waiting lady fell into step behind her. "I need you to take a message to the emperor for me. You are to say to him, I have tested my working and it has performed perfectly. Do you understand?"

"Yes, Mistress Imperial. At once." She reverenced quickly and hurried away over the lawn. Medeoan watched her leave, and from the corner of her eye she saw Peshek cradling Eliisa in his arms and slowly bearing her away.

Medeoan set her jaw and turned away. She must not dawdle. She must return to her ladies so they could sit and sew together for a respectable length of time, a pretty picture of idleness and unconcern. Hopefully, sending Chekhania with a message to Kacha would reinforce her lies to him and continue the fiction of what the girdle was meant to be used for.

Now, though, there was one more thing to be done, one more wheel to be set in motion. After that, all she could do was to wait for dark and what would come with it.

The morning passed slowly. Despite the myriad items demanding her attention once she and her ladies returned from their sojourn out of doors, Medeoan felt the time creep past. But, at last, the midday meal was laid in the blue parlor so that she might dine in private, and so that, afterward, she might have an audience with her lord sorcerer. Kacha was having his meal with Ambassador Girilal, and that gave her some freedom, although not much, for his eyes and ears were still with her.

Lord Iakush was prompt, as ever, arriving just as the meal was being cleared away. The lord sorcerer was a precise, dark man, well but plainly dressed in a burgundy kaftan sashed and embroidered in black. He looked to be only a few years older than she herself, but Medeoan knew he was older than her father had been.

Lord Iakush knelt before her.

"Please rise," she told him. "Sit with me." Iakush did as he was bidden, and took the chair the footman positioned for him.

"Thank you, Imperial Majesty," he said politely. Then, as was also polite, he waited for her to speak.

Medeoan glanced about. She was unaccustomed to taking

note of her ladies, or the other servants. They were engaged with their own tasks, her ladies with their needlework, the footmen with clearing the meal and rearranging the room. There was no way to tell how well they were listening. Medeoan swallowed. She needed to speak. She needed to trust in her plan and her understanding. She could do nothing else.

She rubbed her hands together. "I find myself in need of your counsel, Lord Sorcerer."

Iakush spread his hands. "I will be glad to offer what advice I can, Imperial Majesty."

Medeoan leaned forward. She wanted to shout at the company to go away, to leave her in peace, to stop watching her. She controlled herself. "I need to find Lord Avanasy, yet that seems to be beyond my power."

"Need to find . . . ?" Lord Iakush, began, startled, but he recovered quickly. "Her Imperial Majesty means to revoke the exile?"

Medeoan nodded and pressed her palms tightly together. "That is what I want Lord Avanasy to believe, for it is the only way he will return here easily."

Lord Iakush narrowed his eyes. "I do not understand, Imperial Majesty."

Why is this so hard? I lied to Kacha without effort. Why can I barely speak now?

Because I know who Kacha is now, and I do not know who this man is before me. In truth, she had avoided him as much as possible since her parents' funeral. She did not seem able to look at him without seeing him standing over her parents' biers, saying the rites to keep their bodies safe in the earth.

Yet she did not replace him, even though Kacha had suggested it more than once. Remembering that, Medeoan gained courage.

"I have recently found evidence that Lord Avanasy was guilty of much more serious crimes than I had initially believed. I want him back here to answer for them directly, with his life."

The lord sorcerer stiffened for a moment. She watched him attempting to relax himself, trying to think and assess what she might be leaving unsaid. "If I may ask, Imperial Majesty . . ."

Medeoan stopped him with a gesture. "No. You do not need to know what he has done, or has not done. You only need to tell me if you know where Lord Avanasy has taken himself."

Iakush dropped his gaze, but Medeoan could see that it was not a mere show of humility. "I only know rumors, Imperial Majesty."

Medeoan nodded. Well enough. He did not flatter, or make claim to knowledge he did not have. Such signs were no guarantee of loyalty, but they would have to be enough. All her energies were diverted to keeping Kacha's suspicions quiet. She had no strength left to search for Avanasy, even though it was Avanasy she most needed.

Medeoan reached down to the ring at her waist and unhooked the bronze key which wound the works of the Portrait of Worlds. "Find him, Lord Sorcerer," she said, holding out the key to him. "Even if he has gone beyond the borders of the Land of Death and Spirit, find him. Tell him I have forgiven him. Tell him I am in need of him. Tell him I am in danger, for that was what he tried to make me believe before he was banished. Tell him what you must, but bring him back here. He must answer for what he has done."

Medeoan watched Lord Iakush. His eyes were curious, he had questions he longed to ask, but he saw the key she held out to him. Handing such a key over was a sign of trust, and he was hungry for her trust. Her trust equaled power in the court and that key was a solid sign of that power. The position of a lord sorcerer under an emperor who was herself touched by magic was a precarious one. However, he would do as she asked because he would believe that her request proved she needed him.

She would have to hope that later he would do it because he understood the truth of this meeting.

"You will take him to Fortress Dalemar and await my representatives."

Iakush received the key and reverenced, almost more to the object than to his empress.

"I will do my best, Imperial Majesty," he said, tucking the key into the safety of his broad, black sash.

"Find him, Lord Sorcerer," she told him earnestly. "I require his return."

Iakush, recognizing the interview was at an end, knelt once more. She dismissed him and he left her there, alone with her servants and Kacha's spies.

One more day. Medeoan closed her eyes. *Only one more day. Then I will be free.*

Chapter Six

Summer deepened, and Sand Island grew warm and green. The mosquitoes rose in the marshes, making morning and evening into special times of torture. There were a thousand hot, tedious tasks to be done, and the boats were always out, taking advantage of the long, calm days and the huge runs of fish. Grace was sunny, and carelessly defiant as she had ever been, but her midnight wanderings were over, and no one in the house felt inclined to speak of them.

So far, it was a perfect match to all the other summers Ingrid had known. Nothing at all had changed.

And yet, everything had, because Avan had begun to call on her. The first time he came by at dusk, after the boats had come in and the evening meal had been cleared away. Ingrid had given him coffee in the back kitchen. There, they'd sat and talked about small things—Grace's health, how the fish were running, the nature and temperaments of the people on the island. The next time, he'd stopped by near dawn, just as the men were getting ready to go out. Papa and Leo had scowled when Ingrid invited him to sit down at the table and served out a portion of bread and porridge for his breakfast. But Avan had been unstintingly polite, asking their opinions on boats and nets, and the affairs of the town of Bayfield. Slowly, Avan found the thoughts Papa could not stand to keep to himself, and drew him out, word by word.

After that, his presence became part of the rhythm of her life. Mornings, he breakfasted with them. Evenings, when the work was done and the boats were back, he was there again, with her in the kitchen, talking in his low, strong voice of the events of the day, singing snatches of songs with her, telling stories, laughing when she teased him for his ignorance of local custom and history. He spoke no more of ghosts or of magic, and Ingrid was content enough to let the subject lie.

Then, at night when Grace snored softly beside her, Ingrid would lie awake and remember the touch of his hand against her skin. She wondered how it would be to have Avan beside her in the bed instead of her sister, and she both welcomed and feared the ache and restless anticipation that rose in her.

August came. The blueberries and raspberries were quickly stripped from their branches by birds and by questing fingers. Now the blackberries were coming into season and the women and children of the island were out in force, baskets on hips, and wearing their thickest clothes despite the heat. The men forsook the water for the day to help cut and clear brush for the fuel it provided and to help keep the island safe from the wildfires that plagued the mainland.

Ingrid worked side by side with Grace, keeping one eye on the berry canes and one on the little ones, making sure they put almost as much into the baskets as they stuffed in their faces. Mama was home by the stove, boiling the jams and syrups from the previous day's labors in field and garden.

She was not in the least surprised when a shadow fell across her and Avan's voice said, "Good afternoon, Ingrid."

She turned, smiling up at him. Summer had burned him brown as bark, making his dark gold hair shine even more brightly than usual. He carried a long-handled scythe on his shoulder.

"Hello, Avan. How are you today?"

"Well, thank you." He hesitated, looking hard at Grace and Ingrid's smallest siblings. "I saw a good patch of berries as I came past. I . . . would be happy to show you the way."

Which only caused Grace to giggle like a schoolgirl, without any attempt to hide it. Ingrid glowered at her.

"Oh, go on, Ingrid." Grace waved her away. "It's blackberries all the way through the marsh. If Papa asks, I'll swear on my life it is."

Ingrid felt her cheeks burn, but nonetheless she picked up the remaining empty basket. "Thank you, Avan," she said, giving Grace one last hard look. "We can use all we can find."

Avan tromped off through the thicket, and Ingrid followed. Gradually, the noise of chattering women and children and the distant calls of men's voices fell away. The thicket turned to forest as the huge, ancient pines laid claim to the ground. The underbrush thinned, replaced by an unbroken carpet of brown needles. The calls of crows and humans all seemed equally far away. Ingrid and Avan were truly alone for the first time since Grace's haunting ended.

Ingrid felt her heart begin to pound. Her mind raced off in a hundred directions, trying to guess what would happen next, and how she should prepare for it. At last, Avan leaned his scythe against a tree trunk. He stared at it for a moment, and turned to face her.

"Ingrid . . ." he began. Ingrid felt her throat tighten, and tried to tell herself she was being foolish. There was nothing to fear. This was what she had hoped for. The fear, however, would not leave. "I have some things I need to say to you," he went on. "I . . ." He stopped again, running a hand through his bright hair. "I am blundering very badly. I must ask you to have patience."

"Of course." Ingrid hoped he did not hear how her own nervousness choked her.

"Thank you." He looked around, saw nothing but tree roots and pine needles and shrugged irritably. "Will you sit awhile with me?"

In answer, Ingrid sat in the cleft formed by the roots of one of the ancient pines, smoothing her skirt down across her knees, and silently cursing her berry-blackened fingers and disordered hair. She wanted to be beautiful. She wanted to be calm and poised. Instead she was sweaty, disheveled and frightened to her core that Avan was about to ask her to marry him, and equally frightened that he would not.

Avan sat in front of her, crossing his legs tailor fashion. "Ingrid," he said, as much to the ground as to her. "Since we laid the ghost that troubled your sister, you have not asked me about my magics, or about how I came to possess them."

Ingrid swallowed hard, willing her throat to open so she could speak normally. "I thought you would tell me in your own good time."

"And I thank you for trusting me so far." The heel of his heavy boot scuffed the needles. "Will you hear a story?"

"Yes."

"Very well." He looked up at her and took a deep breath, like someone about to speak a parlor piece they had memorized with great effort. "Imagine if you will, that this whole world is like Sand Island, a single point of land in the midst of a vast sea. Imagine that it is not the only such island. There are others, an infinite number of others, each separate and complete in the sea, each alone without knowledge of its neighbors.

"Now imagine that one might sail that sea. If one had a chart and the proper knowledge of boats, one might travel from island to island. It would not be an easy journey, for that sea is cold and treacherous, and the way is very long, but it could be done by one who was trained in its ways."

Ingrid felt herself begin to stare. What was this? Was Avan mad after all? No, she could not believe it. This was a true thing he spoke of, like the ghost had been true, and the net he had made.

Ingrid cleared her throat. "And on one of these islands there is a place called Isa . . . Isav . . ."

"Isavalta." Avan's voice caressed the word, and Ingrid saw how loneliness dimmed his eye. "Yes. It is a vast and northern land. Bigger even, I think, than your United States. Some call it grim and wild, but it has its beauties." He bowed his head for a minute, remembering. It was that remembrance that wiped all thought of madness from Ingrid's mind. This was true. Every word of it.

"It is ruled by an emperor, and an empress. They had several children, but, as happens sometimes, two of them died, leaving only one, a girl, to inherit the throne.

"The girl, whose name was Medeoan, had been born a sorceress as well as a princess, and her parents wished her to be instructed in the ways of magic, and the powers of the spirits and the unseen folk. They summoned one of the masters of such knowledge to them, but he was an old man, even as sorcerers measured their years, and knew Grandfather Death waited nearby for him. So, he begged them to take his apprentice instead. It was thus the emperor and empress bound to their daughter a tutor who was a young man with more learning than wisdom. His name was Avanasy Finorasyn Goriainavin."

Ingrid felt herself grow very still. Avan wasn't looking at her. He stared at the needle-covered ground.

"The young man was proud of his new post, and did his best, studying as well as teaching, advising and making friends in the court whenever he could. Soon, however, he found that his student was gravely troubled by her destiny. She did not want to rule. She feared the responsibilities of her birth. He tried to be a friend as well as a teacher to her, and so the years passed." His voice dropped to a whisper. "She was most fair as she grew, and powerful in her magics, and the tutor came to realize that in his secret heart, he was in love with her."

Ingrid suddenly found it very hard to breathe.

"It was not a feeling to which he could give voice, nor even allow himself to think much about. So he buried it deeply, and things went on as they had always been.

"Then, the emperor and empress negotiated a marriage treaty for their daughter with the prince of a southern empire with which they sought alliance. Medeoan was distraught, but only because it was another thread binding her to the truth she disliked so. She had long known her marriage would be arranged to benefit Isavalta.

"The prince, Kacha, was brought to Isavalta so that he might learn its languages and customs before they married. He was handsome enough and he set himself to wooing his bride-to-be with great care and attention. They were both scions of powerful houses, both caught up in the political necessities of their realms. As such, they had much in common.

"At first, Avanasy was pleased to see friendship, and then love growing between them. He was sad at the loss of his special relationship with Medeoan, but he cheered himself with the thought that the one she must marry truly loved her.

"Then, he found, or thought he found, evidence that the prince was a spy, and a traitor. Kacha was being used by his father to conquer sovereign Isavalta, and possibly lead it into war. But when he tried to present his evidence to Medeoan, he found himself contradicted by the words and actions of the prince himself. Medeoan grew so angry with him for making accusations which in the end he could not prove, she ordered him banished from the boundaries of Isavalta."

Avan grew quiet then, remembering. Ingrid didn't know what to say. She herself could scarcely remember how to breathe. She had thought the ghost the end of the strangeness in her life, now she found it was only the beginning.

"Was he, Prince Kacha, betraying the princess?"

Avan tilted his head back so he could stare at the branches and the sky overhead. "I don't know."

"And the sorcerer, this Avanasy, what did he do?"

"Cursed himself for a fool," said Avan flatly. "And realized that he was further gone with his impossible sentiment than he had realized. Had he been thinking clearly, he would have gone straight to the emperor with what he knew, and the emperor could have ordered the prince watched over by all the court sorcerers. But he did not do this." A single muscle twitched in Avan's cheek. "Instead he tried to prove himself the better man to the princess, and so brought about his own ruin."

Ingrid opened her mouth, and closed it again. What on earth could she have possibly said?

"When Avanasy was certain he could not convince Medeoan to reverse the order of banishment, when he saw her finally married to Prince Kacha, he left," Avan went on. "Left Isavalta, and ultimately, left the world of his birth, because he could not stand to watch what he feared might be coming, and because he could not bear to face his foolishness and disgrace. He became a fisherman on an island in the middle of a lake a world away from anything that he knew." Avan lifted his gaze, and for the first time since he had begun his incredible story, he looked directly at Ingrid. "He never thought to speak of any of these matters again to another living soul, but he fell in love, this time with a gracious woman whom he could court with honesty and a fully open heart, and he wished the lady to know the truth before he declared as much."

Suddenly, Ingrid found she could not sit still. She rose to her feet and retreated a few steps. She might have run farther if she had not felt a tree right at her back. It was too much for her to take in, and yet she did not know which overwhelmed her more, Avan's story, or his confession that he did love her.

Then, she saw how he watched her, and how his face fell at her expression of bewilderment. Ingrid shook herself. She owed him better than this. She straightened her spine.

"Thank you for telling me," she said. "Thank you for trusting me."

"You believe me, then?"

She nodded. "Without the ghost and all that happened then, I might not. But having seen what I have, I cannot choose but to believe."

"There are not many who would do so." Avan stood. "And the rest?"

And the rest? Ingrid looked at him. She remembered how she first saw him clearly in the firelight. She remembered how generously he had helped her and Grace. She remembered all the bright weeks of his patience, his humor, and his company. She felt again the ache and the anticipation that she knew lying alone in the darkness. And the rest?

"I think I loved you the moment I first saw you beside the fire. I just was not free to say so until now."

Ingrid felt that with those words the whole world must change. Perhaps it did. Avan stood where he was, as if paralyzed by the sound of her voice. Then he took a step forward, one step, two steps, three steps until he stood right in front of her. He reached out one of his long, graceful hands and brushed it gently over her hair. Now it was Ingrid who found herself paralyzed. She felt as if she would never move again, unless he said that she should.

"I want to marry you, Ingrid," he said, his voice hoarse

with emotion. "I want to build a house, a proper house, and bring you to it. I want to work with you and for you to build a good life. I want to sit beside the fire with you and sing and tell stories. I want to lie down beside you at night and wake up beside you in the morning. No," he said as she opened her mouth and he held his fingertips just before her lips, not quite touching. "There are two more things you need to know before you answer me.

"You know that I am a sorcerer. In the world into which I was born, magic is not merely a skill one can learn. It is tied to one's nature. There is a great deal of argument as to why that should be so, and what it means. What is known is that there are two consequences that come with the gift. The first is that the getting of children is very difficult for a sorcerer. The second is that we live very long lives, sometimes four or five times the length of other men. I do not know if these things remain true on this shore of the Land of Death and Spirit, but you deserve to know of them." He stood back from her. "If you need some time, or if you wish to turn away, I understand."

Ingrid stayed where she was, trying to think. Life, life could end tomorrow or go on for a hundred years for either of them. There were a thousand accidents that could put an end to a person, and she had seen many of them one time or another in her life. Happiness in life was a matter of chance. The children . . . not to have children would be hard. Then again, that also was a matter of chance. There were women who brought four, five, six babies into the world and lost them all one by one. There were women who died trying to give birth to even one. It was all in God's hands, as was everything else. Had anything Avan told her really changed that?

But if Avan had told to the truth, she should repay him in kind.

Ingrid drew in a breath heavy with the scent of pine resin and all the heat of summer. "My father also came from a long ways off," she said. "From a place called Bavaria, as you may have heard. He traveled to Chicago and ended up working in the slaughterhouses. There, he met my mother, who was very beautiful, very young, and the daughter of a good family. They didn't approve of him. He was very poor, he was German, they were Irish." She hung her head. "That much I know for certain. The rest of this is only guesswork, letters, and gossip.

"My mother got in the family way without having married my father. Believing love would see them through, they ran away from her parent's anger and came up here to Bayfield, where no one knew them, and where no one was counting the days until she gave birth. I believe they worked hard at their lives, but something failed in the end. Maybe it happened when they began to have daughters, and they were afraid that those daughters might make the same mistakes that they had." She shook her head. "What I am trying to say is that I have no family who will speak to me, except for the ones you've met. I have no breeding or fortune, and I am in all likelihood a bastard." She squared her shoulders and met his gaze. Let him see her, let him look long and hard at her—rumpled, berry-stained, her hands coarsened by hard work, her clothes much mended, and her skin brown from the sun. "Can a man who has loved a princess settle for what he sees in front of him?"

But Avan only shook his head. "If I were to marry you, I would not be settling," he said, and his voice was as grave, as honest as it had been during the entire course of his narrative. "I would be reaching so high that I might grasp the stars themselves. I have seen your bravery, your honesty, your love, your joy. It is nothing but the purest selfishness that makes me wish to bind all that you are to my side."

Ingrid found she had no words. She could only cross the distance between them, stand on her toes and kiss him. He stiffened at her touch, startled, but in the next moment wrapped his strong arms around her, answering her kiss, her love, with his own.

When at last they pulled away from each other, Avan looked her up and down as if he had never seen so wonderful and precious a thing before. "I don't know what the customs are here," he said shyly, softly touching her hair, her cheek, her shoulder. "I don't know what is expected of me now. Should I make some gift . . . ?"

"You will have to speak to my father. He should give his consent."

"And if he withholds it?"

Ingrid shrugged a little. "I am of age, I'm free to marry who I wish. But, it will be easier on us both if he consents." She smiled. "As for a gift, it is traditional that you give me a ring."

He nodded with extreme seriousness. "A ring. I will remember that." He raised her right hand to his lips and kissed it gently. "And I shall come to the house to speak with your father tonight. Now," he added reluctantly, straightening up, "I think I had best return you to your sister."

"Yes." Then, she paused, an odd thought striking her. "I don't . . . I . . . what should I call you?"

He appeared to consider her question gravely, but she saw the merry light in his blue eyes. "In front of others, I think perhaps you should call me Avan, as that's how they know me. When we are alone, you may call me Avanasy, if you choose."

"I'd like that. You'll have to teach me to pronounce the rest later."

"Gladly. Come now." He shouldered his scythe easily. "Your berries are spoiling in the sun, and your little sister is beginning to despair of your reputation."

"Ha!" laughed Ingrid sharply. "Despair is not what Grace is beginning to do, I'll wager you."

But he was right otherwise, and Ingrid let him begin to walk her back. They made their way through the scrub and thickets silently, side by side, content for the moment just to be together. There would be time enough for everything else later.

When Grace saw them, she just grinned impishly and raised her brows. Ingrid made a show of cuffing her sister across the head, but Avan, Avanasy, did not even smile. He just gave them both a strange, formal bow, with one leg extended and both hands crossed over his breast. Then, he reclaimed his scythe and strolled easily away into the woods.

Ingrid stared after him, unable to take her eyes off the smooth motion of his body.

"Has something happened, Ingrid?" inquired Grace mildly.

"Not something," answered Ingrid. "Everything."

"Ingrid!" Grace shrieked, and leapt forward, hugging Ingrid so hard they both toppled over into the underbrush, barely missing the baskets of blackberries.

"Get off me, you idiot!" cried Ingrid, shoving her sister backward and making a great show of reordering her clothes and hair. "A little dignity would only improve your character, miss."

Grace just laughed at her and plucked a leaf from her hair. "I knew he would ask you. I knew it. When's it to be?"

"Would you keep your voice down!" snapped Ingrid, looking around. But little Thad and their sisters seemed to be out of earshot, and none of the neighbors had moved in. "No one knows yet. He's got to talk to Papa. He'll come by tonight."

"Perfect," declared Grace. For the look of the thing she began to pluck berries from the nearest bush, tossing them down into the basket without concern for whether they were crushed or not. "You can be married in the fall, and then we can all move to Bayfield for the winter and . . ."

" 'We?' " Now it was Ingrid's turn to arch her brows.

"Of course," said Grace blithely, popping a couple of berries into her mouth. "You can't set up housekeeping all on your own, you know. You're going to need my help."

Ingrid turned her attention to the blackberry canes, carefully moving aside thorny green branches to hide her surprise, and her irritation. "Mama is going to need help as well, you know."

"And I know you won't leave me in that house," said Grace with the blithe assurance that was so much a part of her. "With Papa and Leo breathing down my neck all the time, and no Ingrid to stand up for me? It's unthinkable."

Ingrid pulled a last few warm, sticky berries from the bush she worked and dropped them into the basket. The warm delight that had come to her when she accepted Avan's proposal had fled, replaced by an unfamiliar frustration with her younger sister. Did Grace only see Ingrid's happiness in terms of how it would help her?

"We'll talk about this later," said Ingrid, hefting her basket so she could move further into the thicket.

"Oh, Ingrid . . ." began Grace, but she did not finish her sentence, for at that moment, a man's horrible scream cut through the forest.

At once, Ingrid dropped her basket and hiked up her skirts to run for the trail and the direction from which the sound had come.

"Thad!" she shouted as she sprinted past her little brother. "Get the girls home! Now!"

"Yes, Ingrid!" he called behind her, but she did not look to see that he obeyed. Ahead in the woods, the man cried out again and sobbed in his pain.

On the edge of the true woods, a cluster of people had gathered, their backs bent, their voices raised into an incomprehensible gabble. As Ingrid came crashing forward to join the crowd, crabbed Vale Anderson turned and saw her, and pulled his wife aside, opening a small lane for Ingrid. Others turned and saw her, and they also drew away.

Her heart in her mouth, and her blood suddenly singing in her ears, Ingrid moved forward through the crowd of faces that she had known since birth but suddenly could not see.

In front of her, Leo lay on the ground, his face gone ashen and knotted and straining in pain. Papa squatted by Leo's outstretched leg, his hands red with blood. A scythe lay on the ground nearby. More blood stained its blade.

Ingrid took in all this in a single heartbeat. In the next, she was on her knees by Leo, cradling his head in her apron and putting a stick between his teeth for him to bite down on. Papa had a knife out and was cutting through Leo's boot and trousers. Each movement brought a fresh cry of pain from her brother's throat.

"What on earth . . ." Grace's voice, then Grace herself pushed through the crowd. Ingrid looked up at her mutely, and then followed her gaze down to their brother's injured leg.

It was bad. The gash was just above his ankle, and went clear to the gray-white bone. Blood poured out like it could never be stopped.

"Mary Mother of God!" cried Grace, and she went whiter even than Leo. She stuffed her fist in her mouth to stifle what might have been a scream or a sob, and, to Ingrid's shock, turned and fled.

Leo groaned again and his head pressed hard against her apron. Ingrid grabbed his shoulders to hold him steady. Papa did not look up. He used the cloth cut from the trousers to tie off Leo's leg below the knee. The red flood slowed a little and Leo moaned against the biting stick.

Ingrid glanced around at her anxious neighbors, but the only face she could see clearly now was Avan's. She looked at him, a silent plea in her eyes. He understood at once, but only shook his head. There was nothing he could do.

No. There was something. "Avan!" she cried. "Get to Bay-field. Fetch the doctor!"

"At once," said Avan, and he vanished from her sight.

Papa glanced at her sharply, but did not contradict, or even glower. "I need a hand here," was all he said. "We need to get him home."

Four men surged forward to help lift her brother between them. One of them was Everett Lederle. Of course it was. In her shock and confusion, Ingrid found time to think, *Oh, Everett, I am sorry . . .*

The men tried to be gentle, but they had to hurry and they all knew it. The bleeding had slowed, but it had to be stopped, and soon. Each jolt of their footsteps ripped a fresh cry from Leo. Ingrid was selfishly glad to be able to run ahead fast enough that she outpaced the sound of her brother's screams, up the track to their house.

She half-expected Grace to have preceded her, but Mama was alone in the kitchen wielding a huge ladle and presiding over the steaming kettles on the stove when Ingrid burst in.

"Jesus and Mary, what's happened?" she cried as she saw Ingrid.

Ingrid, gasping for breath and pressing the heel of her hand against her side, told Mama. Mama shrieked and threw up her hands. The ladle fell to the floor with a clang and a clatter. Mama just ran from the room to throw open the front door.

"Ingrid! Get a basin of hot water, and we'll need all the clean sheets!"

"Yes, Mama!"

Ingrid moved as swiftly as she was able through the clouds of blackberry steam, but she suddenly felt unbelievably clumsy. Her hands shook as she poured boiling water from one of the iron kettles into an ancient and chipped shaving basin. Thad appeared in the kitchen, peering around the door.

"Take this up to Mama," said Ingrid, shoving the basin into her little brother's hands. *Where's Grace?* she wondered desperately at the same time. Her two littlest sisters peeked around the door. "Girls, you stay in the yard, understand me?"

They vanished. Thad trotted out into the hallway, splashing little puddles of water as he moved. Ingrid ignored that. Instead, she hurried into the front room and threw open the cedar chest, one of the family's truly fine possessions. She scooped out an armful of fragrant, snow-white sheets, just as the men bearing Leo between them poured through the door.

"Upstairs," directed Ingrid. And there was too much jostling and too many cries of "Careful, there!" before they were able to maneuver him up the narrow stairway. Leo himself made no sound. He must have fainted, for which Ingrid was grateful.

Mama waited beside the bed in the bare room Leo shared with Thad. Her face was white as the sheets Ingrid carried, but she stayed steady as the men laid Leo on the bed. She shooed them all back and bent over her son, mopping away the blood and examining the gash. The men shuffled out of the room, murmuring their good wishes to Ingrid and Papa as they left. Everett brushed her arm in passing, and Ingrid, to her shame, found she could not look into his eyes.

"I need those sheets, Ingrid!" snapped Mama.

Then it was all blood and heat, and hot water and white sheets, and Mama stitching Leo's wound closed and Ingrid cradling his head, and hoping Thad would keep the little girls out of the way. They did not need to see this. Leo alternated between straining to hold still despite the pain and swooning from the same pain and loss of blood.

Then it was over and Leo was again in a faint and there was nothing to do but gather up the bloody sheets and the empty, rust-stained basin and lug the whole, stinking bundle down the stairs to the back kitchen.

The room was filled with the smell of burned blackberries. Ingrid nearly choked as she dumped the sheets into the tin washtub and hurried to throw open the stove to bank down the fire. Papa, seemingly oblivious to the stench, sat at the table, hunched over a cup that, from the smell, had probably held strong coffee not too long before.

"How's your brother?" he asked gruffly.

"I don't know," admitted Ingrid, surveying the disaster on the stove. A kettle of syrup and another of preserves had boiled down into identical thick, black, utterly inedible messes. A whole day's work gone. "He's lost a lot of blood. The doctor will be able to say more."

"You should not have involved that man Avan," Papa grunted to his empty mug. "It's none of his business."

Ingrid strangled a sigh, telling herself that was a reflexive remark from Papa and meant nothing. It needed no reply. She took the still-hot coffeepot off the stove and poured what was left of its contents into Papa's mug.

"I'll get supper started," she said, returning to the stove. She tried to give herself over to thoughts of the chore at hand. She'd set the kettles to soak and get at them with the wire brush after supper. There was still some stew from yesterday. A little water and it would stretch out just fine, with dumplings, and some of the fresh blackberries and what was left of the cream . . .

She wrapped a rag around the first kettle of burned blackberry essence and made ready to haul it out the back door.

"Your sister should have been here to tend to that," announced Papa, gulping some coffee. "Where is she?"

"I don't know." Ingrid set the kettle outside the door. "Thad!" she called to her younger brother. "Get this filled with water, won't you? Be careful, it's still hot. I'll have another out shortly."

She returned to the kitchen, only to find Papa glowering at her from under his heavy brows.

"Your sister's gone again and all you can say is you don't know where," he snarled. "Your brother can't keep his mind on his work and will probably have to have his foot off. By God, is there not one of my children who will do as they should?"

Ingrid set her jaw and concentrated on wrapping the dish-rag tightly around the handle on the old Dutch oven.

"You'll pay attention when I speak to you, girl!" The ex-clamation was followed fast by the crash of Papa's hand coming down hard on the tabletop.

Slowly, Ingrid turned. Her hands flexed, as if they wanted to curl into fists.

"You may be sure, Papa, I have heard every word you said."

Papa rose slowly and fear stiffened Ingrid's spine. He stalked forward until he was a bare six inches from her and Ingrid knew he meant to hit her. His heavy hand itched to lash out at something, and she was nearest. At the same time, in his eyes, she saw fear and disappointment, fear for Leo, disappointment at his life and his lot, and his children. Oh, most especially his children, and all that had become of them lately.

"You'll mind your place, Ingrid Loftfield," he said heavily. His breath was sour with coffee and worry. "And you'll not speak to me again in that tone."

Ingrid held her ground and her peace. There was nothing else she could do.

Papa's eyes searched hers for a long moment. What he found in her face, she could not tell. She could only see his anger growing cold and heavy, like a millstone around his neck. It seemed to be the only feeling he had left in him.

"Get about your work," he grunted at last. "It's time one of you did."

With those words he pushed past her. She heard the front door open and close, and she let out the breath she didn't realize she had been holding. *Let it pass,* she counseled her-self. *Let it pass. It does no one any good, and it will soon be over. Soon.*

Soon she would be married to Avan, and in a house of her own. She lugged the Dutch oven out to set beside the back door. Soon, she would be well out of this, and Mama might cry and Papa might carp and Leo might glower, and it would be nothing at all to her, because she would have her own home, and she would love and be loved.

And how will Grace manage? Ingrid returned to the stove

and squatted down in front of it. How will it be for her when there's no one to stand between her and Papa? She used the poker to uncover the embers and began laying tinder over them, watching the orange flames spring to life.

Grace will manage as she has managed everything else. Ingrid laid some larger sticks in the fire, and closed the stove door, letting them get on with the business of burning down to hot coals. *With a smile and wink. She'll be fine.* But even as she thought that, she glanced toward the back door. *But where is she?*

The sun slid slowly down behind the pines. Ingrid heated the stew and dropped in the fat, floury dumplings. She lit the lamp and took it upstairs to see if Mama needed anything. Leo still lay white and unconscious in his bed, the coverlets pulled up to his chin. Mama asked only for some fresh water to bathe his head, and Ingrid fetched it in a clean tin basin.

When she came back down to the kitchen, a shape stood in the shadows by the back door. Ingrid raised her lantern, and saw Grace standing there in the corner like a guilty child.

"Where have you *been*?" cried Ingrid. "I've been out of my mind . . ."

"I'm sorry," said Grace in a whisper. "Is Leo . . . is he . . . ?"

"We don't know yet." Ingrid set the lantern down on the table and turned back to the stove, picking up the worn wooden spoon. "Avan's gone to fetch the doctor." She peeked under the kettle lid to check the dumplings. "And you didn't answer my question."

"I'm sorry," said Grace again. "It was just . . . I was just upset, that's all."

"We could have used your help." Ingrid felt tired, tired, frightened and frustrated. "Mama lost two kettles of jam and syrup because there was no one here to take care of them."

"And don't you sound just like her," answered Grace saucily. "I've told you I'm sorry, and I am. I was just . . . sick."

Ingrid set the spoon down carefully. Unfamiliar and unbidden, anger rose in her at her sister's careless tone. How could she stand there, having run out on her family when they needed her, when *Ingrid* needed her, and now come back, without a word as to what had happened to her, and with only a breezy little apology when . . .

Before Ingrid could even begin to find the words she wanted to speak to Grace, a light moved beyond the door, and a moment later it swung open, pushed by a drenched Avan, who held a mineral oil lantern in his hand. Right behind him came Dr. Nicholson clutching his black bag, his round figure swaddled in an oilskin that was still shedding rainwater.

"Doctor," Ingrid greeted him with a rush of gratitude for his presence, both because it meant help for Leo, and because it kept her from having to voice her feelings to Grace. "I'm glad you've come. Has Avan . . ." She glanced at him.

"Aye, he's told me all," said the doctor, brushing water from his sleeves. "Where's the boy now?"

"I'll take you," volunteered Grace, just as Ingrid opened her mouth. "This way."

Grace ushered the doctor through to the front room, leaving Ingrid standing alone with Avan.

"You look tired," he said, setting his lantern down next to hers.

Ingrid wiped her hands on her apron, suddenly feeling awkward. "It's been a hard day," she answered. "Thank you for bringing Dr. Nicholson. Was it a hard sail?"

Avan shrugged. "There'll be a blow tonight. We got in before the worst of it."

Now that she listened, Ingrid could hear the wind rushing under the eves. She'd been so wrapped up in her own gloom she hadn't even noticed before, hadn't even spared a thought for Avan except for how he would rescue her from her own troubles.

"What is it, Ingrid?" Avan asked quietly. He wanted to move toward her, she knew he did, but he did not dare here. Not when her father might come in any second. Nor could she move toward him, so there they stood, awkward as schoolchildren on opposite sides of the kitchen table.

Ingrid shook her head, smoothing back her hair. It wasn't that she did not want to answer him, but she did not know how to begin. At the same time, she could not keep silent.

"Avan . . ." she began hesitantly. "What we talked about before . . ."

"I had best wait until your brother has somewhat recovered," he said for her. "We met your father on the road. He wasn't pleased. I think he is not as used to me in his house as I would have hoped."

Ingrid gave him a crooked smile. "No. I'm afraid not."

Avan reached out, and his fingertips brushed hers with fleeting warmth. "Try not to worry, my love," he whispered. "All will yet be right."

For the first time since he'd come in the door, Ingrid looked Avan fully in the eyes, and her heart melted once again with the love she saw there.

Grace chose just then to bustle back into the kitchen. "Good news!" she cheered. "The doctor says there's no reason for Leo to lose the leg. He says if we keep him warm and dry, and feed him on plenty of broth, he'll be sound again in no time."

"That is good news," said Avan, with a smile that was more for Ingrid than Grace.

"I knew it would all be well," announced Grace with unexpected force. "I *knew* it."

Ingrid could think of nothing to say to that, considering Grace's behavior that afternoon, so instead she turned back to Avan. "Will you stay for supper? We surely owe you that much."

Avan just shook his head. "Thank you, but I think not, considering all . . ."

"Oh, come now, Avan," laughed Grace. "Ingrid and I will manage Papa. You're welcome at the table."

"I thank you, but I must take my leave." He picked his lantern up. "Good night, Miss Loftfield. Miss Grace."

Ingrid followed him to the door. She could not have stopped herself. As she stood in the threshold, he turned, bent swiftly and kissed her, and then he turned and stumped down the path toward the gate, leaving Ingrid to stand there, her fingers touching her mouth and her heart brimming with warmth.

It would be all right. Leo would heal. Grace would come to see she must look after herself. Papa would relent, or he would not. It didn't matter. She was a grown woman. Avan loved her, truly loved her, and she loved him, and things would be all right. They would make them so, no matter what.

Chapter Seven

Kacha walked the moonlit gardens beside the imperial canal. It had become his custom on the few nights he was not attending Medeoan to take the air in this fashion. His men followed at a discreet distance with such lanterns and other accouterments as might be required. Tonight, however, the moon was full, and he scarcely needed any other light.

He liked these gardens underneath the moon. He liked the drooping willows shining with silver, and the soft grass and the scents of herbs and flowers. Here in the darkness, he could almost believe he was home again in Hastinapura, perhaps late in the wintertime when the air was dry and cool and the summer's blossoms had not yet woken. There was still the sound of water, and the trees seemed made of silver and shadow. Here, he could almost feel content.

"Majesty?" Prithu, his head waiting gentleman, gave a small cough. Kacha turned. A cloaked figure glided across the lawn. From this distance, it was impossible to make out any detail regarding the approaching person, but Kacha smiled to himself. He had no doubt as to who this was.

The figure paused, as if uncertain what welcome he would offer. Kacha beckoned it forward and it knelt in reverence at his feet. Kacha reached out and pushed the fur-and-velvet hood back to reveal Chekhania, Medeoan's first waiting lady, and his finest ally in Vyshtavos.

"Good evening, mistress," he said, raising her to her feet.

"Good evening, Imperial Majesty," She was a little breathless from hurrying, and even in the moonlight he could see that her cheeks were flushed.

"You have news for me?" he asked needlessly. Everything about her spoke of repressed excitement. Not only news, but important news, and Kacha had no doubt she was already anticipating how well she would be rewarded.

She did not answer, but glanced back at Kacha's men. They knew better than to come close during these meetings, but if Chekhania had a fault, it was that she enjoyed the drama of her position too much. Still, Kacha was inclined to humor her. He clasped her fingertips with his own, in the Isavaltan fashion, and walked her down the canal a little ways.

"Now, none can hear us," he breathed, stepping close enough to feel the heat of her skin. "Tell me what you've learned."

"Majesty, I would have come to you sooner than this, but this is so grave, and so strange, I had to make certain it was the truth . . ."

"Tell me," he said again. She smelled of musk and flowers, a scent, he was sure, she had chosen with care for this encounter, and he could not fault her choice.

She smiled, but still kept her eyes modestly turned down. "The empress plans to fly from Vyshtavos tomorrow."

"What!" Kacha jerked backwards. "When did you learn this?"

"Yesterday," she said, no longer so smiling. "I heard it when I was with the Right Hand of the Keeper. He and I . . ." She delicately waved the end of the sentence away. "Afterward, when I was waiting for a good time to take my leave, I saw Captain Peshek come into the house and make confession to the gods, and as Your Majesty Imperial knows, he did meet with the empress but lately."

Kacha felt his demeanor grow cold as stone. "Who else aids her in this plot?"

"I tremble to say that I don't know, yet."

Kacha whirled away from Chekhania, his hands tightening into fists. So, for all Medeoan's protestations, she had given him nothing but pretty lies. Yamuna had been right. He had been more than right. Kacha should have watched her, should have insisted he stay by her, should not have given her a moment's peace. . . .

I will hang Yamuna's spell about her neck for a noose, and pull her along behind me like a dog on a lead. I will teach her what it means to be a proper wife. I will . . .

Pain stabbed him from behind his right eye. Kacha grunted and slapped his hand over it. Slowly, with many deep breaths, he brought his anger under control. The pain eased, and he was able to lower his hand and think again.

This was not what he expected. Where he had thought Medeoan might betray him, yes, he had not even considered the idea that she might flee. He had expected her to try to win back her council and her lords, and to cut him off from the instruments of power as he had cut her off. But simply to run away . . . he never would have considered that. Well, courage had never been Medeoan's strength. The question was, what to do about this. Should he use the girdle on her tonight? Or should he wait and catch her in the act? Or . . .

The fingers of his right hand grew warm. Yes. Yes. There was a way. He could see it clearly now. Yamuna and his own heart showed him, and the picture pleased him well.

He faced Chekhania again, and found her a little pale, and a little anxious, properly afraid of her master's anger.

"You've done well, Chekhania," he said, and to make sure she knew how well, he kissed her roughly. She melted at once into his arms, answering the kiss with a pleasing ardor. He pulled her down to the ground with him, his hands fumbling with her skirts, even as hers expertly sought the knot of his sash that she might open his coat.

Kacha laughed as he took her then, laughed for the passion and the future, and for how little Medeoan had sealed her own doom and with her own hands had given him all he desired.

The morning that the imperial household was to move to its summer quarters dawned sweet and clear, full of the green scents of summer. Medeoan's waiting ladies pushed open what windows there were to let the warmth and sunshine wash through her stone room. A riot of noise rose from the courtyard as goods and people assembled to be borne down to the barges that Medeoan knew were waiting on the canal.

Her dressing screens cut her off from the rest of the world, confining her in a tiny space with two of her ladies, with no room to move and nowhere to go. As her ladies dressed her in her best traveling clothes of light wool and linen, and girdled her around with the imperial colors of blue and gold, she listened with a fluttering heart to the vibrant, busy sounds from outside.

Now was the time. All was in order. This morning she could make her escape, and, if she failed, then ... .

Then there was nothing to do but wait until Kacha decided to take away the last of her.

"Where is the emperor, Chekhania?" asked Medeoan as the woman tied the final neat love knot.

"I believe he is supervising the assembly of your entourage, Majesty Imperial." Chekhania stood back to inspect Medeoan and make sure that no piece of garment or ornamentation was missing. "Shall I tell him that you request his presence?"

"No." Medeoan's mouth had gone completely dry. Her words tasted thick with her own fear. "Send a page to say I give him my best greetings on this fine morning, and that I shall meet him in the god house so that we may receive the gods' blessing for our journey."

"Yes, Mistress Imperial." Chekhania gave the abbreviated reverence her position allowed and hurried out the door to alert the page girl who waited there with the men-at-arms. Medeoan had hoped that the lady's brief departure would allow her to breathe easier, but instead her whole chest tightened.

"Master Senoi," she called over the dressing screens to her head secretary. "Go down to the pantries and make sure the Mistress of the House has prepared a complete inventory for His Majesty Imperial. He was remarking on the need for it the other day."

"Mistress Imperial," her man said to acknowledge the order. She heard the sound of his footsteps, and the door opened and closed again. A moment later, Chekhania returned.

"Your message is being delivered, Mistress Imperial."

"Good." Medeoan stepped out from behind the dressing

screens, more so she would not have to look at Chekhania than anything else. "Chekhania, you'll stay here with Ragneda and see that the trunks are all packed and loaded properly. I do not trust some of these lackeys." That made Chekhania smile, and Medeoan swore she was going to start preening any second now. Chekhania enjoyed her position, and any opportunity to lord it over her fellows.

How did I miss that vanity for so long? Medeoan's fingers knotted themselves in her skirt. *Do not think of it now. You must think of what you will do next, and only that.*

"Ragneda, I want you to check the documents trunk off against the ledger. I do not wish any letters left behind. Report the results to His Majesty Imperial. Adeksii, come with me to the god house. We need to ask Vyshko and Vyshemir for a successful journey."

With only a single lady behind her, Medeoan swept out into the corridor. Her men-at-arms formed up, two in front of her, two behind, but if they noticed her abbreviated entourage, they said nothing. But then again, what could they say? They were only soldiers, and she was the empress. If she chose to wander the hallways stark naked, their duty would be to stay two in front and two behind and keep their eyes forward and their mouths silent.

All of Vyshtavos's grand corridors passed by her in a blur. The rhythmic tread of boots and the patter of shoes mixed together with the beating of her heart. Perhaps courtiers passed by and reverenced, perhaps a lord master moved forward to speak to her, she was not sure. Her sight strained past them, as if she were trying to see through the very walls of the palace to where Kacha was. She wanted to see if the loading of the barges kept him busy, or if he was even now on his way to the god house, and to her, to take her hand, and lead her down to the barge, to hold her prisoner with his constant gaze. He might already be there, waiting for her with his withered hand outstretched and his false smile. Medeoan swallowed as her stomach roiled. This was as cold as the hard frost of winter. She had never even considered that one day she might come to be afraid of Kacha, but so it was, for she now feared him worse than she had ever feared a living thing.

At long last, the gilt doors of the god house loomed before her. The two men-at-arms who walked in the lead stepped forward to push the doors open and then stood back, saluting her with their hands over their hearts. Medeoan, her heart filling her throat, strode past them. For a moment, the dazzle of gold and candlelight kept her from looking around the room. First, she saw the gods on their pedestal, then she saw Keeper Bakhar ready and humble beside them. She bit down on her tongue to keep herself silent, and her gaze swept the painted and gilded room. There was no one else there. She had been swift enough.

She approached the gods, her whole body trembling. With the deepest reverence, she kissed Vyshemir's robe.

"Help me," she breathed soundlessly. "Guide my steps and harden my heart. Lend me your courage, Vyshemir, for what I must now do."

She stepped back and turned to her servitors. "You may wait outside. I have matters to discuss with Keeper Bakhar."

The lady and the soldiers reverenced, and backed out the doors. The doors swung shut with a hollow thud, and Medeoan was alone with Bakhar. As simple as that.

"Quickly, Majesty," whispered Keeper Bakhar, hurrying toward the vestment room. Medeoan gathered up her skirts and ran after him, her ears all the time straining to hear the doors open behind her, to hear Kacha's voice say, "Beloved? What are you doing?"

"You must leave quickly once I am gone, Keeper," said Medeoan, gripping his hand. "Kacha will surely know you helped me."

The keeper's smile was grim and brief. "He will not dare do anything to me at once, Majesty. If it becomes necessary, I will have time to make good my own escape."

Keeper Bakhar threw open the vestment room door and Medeoan darted through. The door shut at once, plunging her into darkness so quickly she pulled up short and blinked rapidly. Her eyes adjusted to show her the long wall hung with the formal garments of the keeper and his underlings. Among them stood Captain Peshek.

"Majesty Imperial," he whispered, reverencing quickly.

"We must get you changed." He handed her a bundle of cloth.

"I can't alone," she said helplessly. She hadn't even stopped to think of this before. It took two women the better part of an hour to get her into these clothes. It was physically impossible for her to remove them alone.

Captain Peshek bit his lip, his gaze darting between the room's four doors. "I ask dispensation to commit a great liberty, Majesty."

"You have it, Captain."

"Then, Majesty, turn around." Captain Peshek drew his knife.

Realizing what he meant to do, Medeoan put her back to him. She heard him suck in his breath, and a moment later, she was buffeted by a series of jerks and tugs. Laces snapped, cloth ripped, and her girdle snaked off from around her waist and slithered to the floor. If Kacha came in now, Peshek would be dead before she could order him spared.

"Try now, Mistress Imperial."

Medeoan put her bundle on a nearby shelf and pushed the ruined finery from her shoulders. The cloth fell in a heap about her ankles, leaving her only her shift, stockings and shoes.

Trying not to think about the man in the room with her, Medeoan hopped over the crumpled cloth and undid the bundle she had been given. Inside was a rough woolen skirt, a gray blouse with sleeves that could be rolled up firmly past her elbows, a stained apron, and an embroidered headscarf that had seen many washings. With a start, she realized that the scarf was Eliisa's. She could not help but glance at Captain Peshek, but he had turned away from her and all she saw was his rigid back. Well, she had stolen much more from that girl than this, why should she now balk at a piece of cloth?

Nonetheless, her scalp shivered as she tied the scarf in place.

A pair of black, scratchy stockings and scuffed, badly sewn shoes completed the disguise. Medeoan caught sight of her reflection in the polished brass mirror that served the keepers and had to stand and stare. Was that her? That thin, pale, wide-eyed drab? That was a powerful sorceress, and empress of Eternal Isavalta?

"Mistress Imperial?" came Captain Peshek's urgent whisper.

Medeoan tore her eyes from her diminished reflection. "You may turn around, Captain. I'm ready."

Captain Peshek pivoted on his heel, saw her, and his eyes widened. In the next heartbeat, however, he recovered himself, and reverenced. "This way, please, Mistress Imperial."

He led her out the far door into an unadorned corridor where she, for all her life in the palace of Vyshtavos, had never walked. A skinny boy in rough, clean servant's clothes waited there, standing on one foot so that he could scratch his heel. When Peshek appeared, he lowered his foot hastily and reverenced.

"This is Sherosh," said Peshek. "He has no tongue, and cannot write, but he knows to show you out the servants' ways. I will meet you beside the stables."

Peshek did not reverence as he retreated, nor did Medeoan fail to notice that he had not used her title. The boy beside her probably did not even know who she was. He just faced her, as wide-eyed and curious as a puppy. Then he smiled, showing a row of ragged and dirty teeth, and took off running.

Suddenly a stranger in her home, Medeoan had no choice but to scurry after him. He led her down a bewildering array of windowless corridors that all seemed to be made of either aging plaster or dark wood. They passed other servants, some in livery, some in drab's clothes. No one stopped to notice her. Some cursed as she ran by, some bellowed, but no one stopped. No one knew her as their empress.

Sherosh lead her through the sculleries, where the air was thick with the stench of slops and garbage and ringing with the clash of pots and kettles. A door, black with age, stood propped open to let in what relief the summer's air could provide. Outside, it was only a little quieter, but it smelled even worse, if that were possible. This was the work yard. Sheds waited here for the tanners, the dyers, and the weavers. The smiths' great forges smoked in the shadow of the east wall. The butchers' yard and the brewers' hall stretched out along the west wall. All conceivable smells of animals, living and dead, mixed with the smells of hot metal and hot mash.

The stables waited upwind of the work yard, so the horses would not be disturbed by the smells of work and slaughter. Reaching the relatively clean scent of well-kept horses was a relief.

A man waited in the shadow of the stable's western wall holding the reins of a scrawny yellow mule. His boots were worn, but his rough pantaloons and undyed kaftan were clean, and the brown sash around his waist was broad and neat. A moment later, Medeoan realized this man was Captain Peshek. She had never seen him out of uniform, and she found him as much altered as she herself was, from imperial guardsman to peasant with a change of a costume.

"Good boy, Sherosh." Peshek flipped a copper coin into the dust at the boy's feet. Sherosh dived for the coin and scooped it up without even breaking stride. He slapped his fist against his heart in a child's imitation of the soldier's reverence and took off for the scullery again.

"Now, mistress," said Peshek hastily. "This mount is bad-tempered and inelegant, but it is inconspicuous. If you would . . ." He cupped his hands for her foot.

Medeoan allowed herself to be helped onto the mule's riding blanket. Peshek handed her the bundle she had entrusted to him the previous evening. It contained some money and the girdle she had woven of her magic and Eli-isa's memories. Even more importantly, it contained a plain wooden box in which she had secreted her signet ring. With that, she could still seal letters and decrees as the empress of Isavalta, no matter what clothes she wore.

The mule flapped its ears and snorted as Peshek grabbed hold of its bridle and urged it forward. Medeoan clutched the harness with one hand and her bundle with the other. The mule's backbone dug into her as the creature loped listlessly across the hardpacked yard.

The shout will go up any moment. They've seen me. The guardsmen have noticed. They'll have told Kacha. He's coming for me.

But no new voices shouted over the cacophony. The only people who came and went were the artisans and the bondsmen, and the apprentices with their baskets, bundles and barrows.

Now Medeoan could see the unadorned iron of the rear gates with their six men standing outside the guardhouse.

"Keep still and steady, mistress," murmured Peshek, halting the mule. "This will take but a moment."

He walked forward, arms outstretched, hailing the other men. They stiffened to attention, and then evidently recognized him, because they hailed him in return, slapping him on the arm and clasping his wrists. With a wave of his hand, he brought them close for some conference. Medeoan's ears rang. How much did Kacha know? How far had his search gone? What would he do when he found her? Who could she trust besides Peshek and Keeper Bakhar? Kacha would have them killed immediately, and she was not sure she could stop it. How would she keep herself whole until Iakush found Avanasy and brought him back?

The soldiers' conference continued, with several glances in her direction. Something, coins perhaps, passed between Peshek and the men on duty. Peshek then sauntered back to the mule. Behind him, the men swung the gates open.

"When you return, mistress, you may want to consider having those men taken up," he said quietly. "They are too easily bribed."

"What did you say to them?" she breathed as they passed between the gates and the soldiers. The men stared at her, measuring her with thin smiles on their faces.

"Nothing I would relish repeating to Your Reverence." Peshek ducked his head.

And they were through. No voice cried out. Kacha's shout did not drift to her through the thick, warm summer air. No column of guards came at the double to seize Captain Peshek. There was only the wide, rutted road cutting through the park and leading to the outer walls, and beyond that, the city, and beyond that the whole wide world.

In that moment, Medeoan knew there would be no pursuit. Peshek's arrangements had worked, and they would walk out of the grounds and into the city. She should have felt relief, but she felt only strangling anger. Was she worth that little? Kacha did not even consider pursuing her? He thought he

ruled so completely that he did not even have to consider
her presence anymore.

*You will learn differently, my false husband. And that pres-
ently.*

Isavalta was hers, and if she had neglected it before, she
would never do so again.

"Where is my Bride Imperial?"

Keeper Bakhar blinked down at him. The man who kept
house for Isavalta's little gods was barrel-like in stature, obviously fond of the good life his office afforded.

"The empress is not here, Imperial Majesty."

"I see that," said Kacha impatiently. The man was many
things, but not normally stupid. Suspicion formed in Kacha's
mind. "Where is she?"

The keeper reverenced, giving at least the appearance of
respect. "I do not know, Imperial Majesty. She came here to
await the blessing, but when you did not arrive, she left. I
assumed it was to go in search of you."

So, Kacha let out a sigh. *So. It has begun. The child has
run away from home, thinking by her actions to leave me in
disarray and confusion.*

Poor child.

"Very well," said Kacha mildly. "Should the empress or
any of her attendants come here, say that I will meet them
in the courtyard."

Again, the barrel-shaped keeper reverenced. "As you command, Imperial Majesty."

This time, Kacha caught the cold glitter in the man's eyes.
He said nothing of it, however, and simply turned away,
returning to the corridor where Medeoan's men-at-arms and
sole waiting lady stood, having been given, he was sure, no
orders to be elsewhere. They looked uncomfortable to say
the least. Doubtlessly they were wondering what was taking
their mistress so long. She was a pious lady, yes, but this
was excessive.

Kacha turned to his nearest man and said in the court
dialect of his home, "Run to the empress's chambers and
have her lady Chekhania meet me in my own apartments."

To Medeoan's servitors he said, "You may wait for your Mistress Imperial in the courtyard. We will be joining you there presently."

Medeoan had all her personal attendants very well trained. They did not question him. They only reverenced, each according to their station, and left as ordered. Kacha found himself smiling at their retreating backs. In many ways, this was going to be simplicity itself.

"Come," he said to Prithu and his men. "We will return to the private apartments."

The corridors of Vyshtavos were largely deserted now. Most of the servants and courtiers were already on their way to the summer palace. That household would be full and bustling, awaiting its imperial masters.

Well, we shall not keep you waiting long, thought Kacha with satisfaction.

As he had instructed, Chekhania waited inside his apartments, beside the empty fire pit. She reverenced as he entered, and he came forward at once to take her hand and raise her up. He saw in her eyes that the gesture had its intended effect and reminded her well of their previous night's sport.

"Now then, Chekhania," he said gravely, still holding her hand. "I must tell you, your Mistress Imperial has taken ill, but she must make the journey to Vaknevos, for there are none to care for her here. She must do so in complete quiet and seclusion. An enclosed litter, such that it can be made a bower for her on the imperial barge will be the answer, I believe. Can you arrange this?"

Chekhania did not quite lick her lips, but she wanted to, Kacha could see it in her eyes. She knew exactly what she was being asked to do, and how much it meant he trusted her. She reveled in that knowledge, and the sight of that pleased Kacha to his core. Such a one would do all he asked, and more to keep her place of power. Oh, yes, in her he had chosen well.

"All will be as his Majesty Imperial commands," said Chekhania solemnly.

"Excellent," he said, giving her hand a secret squeeze. "You may go."

She reverenced again and left him to stand and smile at the empty air.

Run away, Medeoan, he thought. *Run far, run fast. When the time comes, Yamuna will find you, and I will bring you home in chains, and none will be the wiser.*

"We'll spend the night in the lockhouse. The keeper knows how to keep secrets as well as his lock. Many's a man put themselves up here."

Medeoan nodded and clutched her bundle. Peshek led the skinny mule with great patience through Makashev's crowded streets. It was so strange, down here amid the jostling crowds. She had, after all, lived all her life amidst a crowd of people. She had thought traveling anonymously through the traffic of foot and cart would be liberating, or at least familiar. But the ones who had always surrounded her had been her people and there to serve her. Here, she was just another body, another obstruction. Carters hollered when Peshek could not hurry the stubborn mule along fast enough, and he shouted back. Gossiping women shouldered past her without a second glance. Herders screamed at them to make way for flocks of geese or drifts of sheep. Beggars spat and leered as she passed, holding up grubby palms. Several times, she barely escaped a deluge of filthy water dumped unceremoniously from an upper window.

So much noise and stench and mud. So many people, and not one of them knowing or caring who she was, and only Peshek to stand between her and the whole wide world of them.

I can't do this. Part of her shivered. *I don't know how.* She gripped the bundle tighter yet. *But I will.*

As bad as this was, the first part of their journey had been worse, for they had followed the imperial canal, and Medeoan had to bow her head and shut her eyes to keep from watching the barges, bright with pennants and heavy with the members and belongings of her household, row past. What if, despite all, someone recognized her? What if one of the guards Kacha had surely called out by now spied them on the bank? Fear had wrung tears from her eyes before

Peshek turned them away from the canal, and Medeoan could breathe again, if only a little.

Now the sun was going down, and Medeoan was torn between exhaustion and a sort of wretched excitement.

"Here, mistress," Peshek said. "Now we shall have some relief."

He nodded indicating the way in front of them, and Medeoan looked up. At last, they had almost reached the city wall, and she could see the great gate standing open. A fresh breeze cut through the miasma of the city and Medeoan felt her heart lift a little.

It sank again instantly as she saw the ranks of the house guard standing on either side of the gate. Of course, how foolish. The guards kept an eye on everyone leaving the city, as they did on all those entering. Surely they were looking out especially for her. Medeoan bowed her head and bit her lip.

The mule, however, never slowed. A shadow passed over her, and all the noise of their fellow travelers pulled together and concentrated for a moment. Then, the shadow passed, and all the sound spread out on the wind again. Medeoan raised her head.

They had passed through the gate. Ahead of them, the road spread out and branched. The carts and riders, the men and women under their yokes, the herders with their birds and beasts sprawled out, spilling like water from a stream into a pond.

"That simple," murmured Medeoan. "How can it be this simple?"

"It isn't, mistress," replied Peshek, thumping the mule's side to urge it onward at a better pace. "The Emp . . . your husband can hardly sound a general alarm to say to all the world you are missing. Any search for you will be done quietly, and it will be under the auspices of the commander of the House Guard, I promise you. We must take care to be in a safe house before dark."

"As you say." Medeoan shivered again. The sun was still high enough to give warmth, and indeed, the city streets had been stifling, but Medeoan remained cold. The countryside rolled gently away from the city walls, cut by the arrow-straight canals with their stone bridges. Suddenly profoundly tired, she longed for the comfort and ease of water travel, but she said nothing. Peshek had seen her safe so far. She must trust him just a little farther.

Only a few buildings dotted the landscape immediately beyond the city walls, so the lockkeeper's house was easy to spot. It was a two-storied, clapboard structure with a steeply pitched roof waiting beside a broad stone arch of a bridge. As they approached, Medeoan could hear the rush of the water through the lock's works.

She must have passed the place a hundred times during her life, but she did not think she had ever truly seen it before. The house and the yard around it seemed neatly kept. The pens for the chickens and goats looked sturdy, as far as she could judge such things. The whitewash on the fence and house was fresh, and the door to the home was gaily painted red with green knots and waves over all for protection and serenity.

As they approached the gate, a stout woman emerged, wiping her hands on her embroidered apron. Peshek halted the mule, and gestured for Medeoan to wait where she was. Accustomed now to doing as he said, Medeoan waited patiently while Peshek opened the gate and walked forward to greet the woman. They conversed for some minutes. Medeoan could hear none of it, but the woman's gaze kept darting from Peshek to Medeoan and back again.

At last, the stout lockkeeper's lady gave a harsh bark of laughter at something Peshek said and shouted inside the house. A little boy, as jug-shaped as his mother, came running out. She pointed him at Medeoan, and he trotted up to take the mule's reins while Peshek followed close behind and took Medeoan's hand to help her down.

"It will have to be one room, mistress," said Peshek apologetically as he accompanied her up the dirt path to the house. "They know me well here, so I cannot claim you as a sister."

"Good greeting, mistress," boomed the woman as she looked Medeoan keenly up and down. "You'll be tired after traveling all day with this ruffian, I'll be bound." She cuffed

Peshek affectionately. "I've a room ready for you to take your ease, now. Come along with me."

Without waiting for reply, she led them into the dim house. Medeoan had an impression of scrubbed wood, the smell of boiled vegetables and the rush of wind and water from outside. She climbed the narrow stairway that squeaked and creaked beneath her hostess. At the top, the woman stood aside and let Medeoan, followed by Peshek, enter the first room on the right.

There was not much to see. Medeoan turned around and took in the rough, whitewashed walls, the single bed with its lumpy pallet under the rough woolen blankets, the table and chair, the hearth and the stand for the chamber pot.

Peshek nodded to the hostess, who closed the door with a look that came very close to a leer.

"I'm sorry, mistress," said Peshek quickly. "If there was anything better to be had . . ."

Medeoan waved her hand to cut him off. "This will do very well, Captain," she murmured. "I owe you more than I can ever repay."

Peshek bowed, his hand over his heart. "I live to serve. We will wait here for a handful of days while I find us safe messengers to gather news and send out word to your loyal servitors."

"Yes. Thank you." Then, feeling utterly trivial and lost, she said, "Is there any chance of supper?"

There was. Turnip stew, hard bread and dark beer, but Medeoan ate gratefully while their hostess laid a fresh fire in the hearth. When they were done and the crockery cleared outside the door, Peshek laid his knife, sword and knout within easy reach, took one of the blankets from the bed and rolled himself up in it so his body blocked the threshold and he faced the wall. It was as much privacy as he could afford her. Peshek would never leave her alone, even in a house he knew.

Medeoan unwrapped her headscarf, undid her apron and took off her clumsy shoes. Except for that, she laid herself under the covers, stockings and all. She stared into the darkness, willing herself to stay awake. Despite the long, terrifying day, staying awake proved to be quite easy. All the sounds were strange; the night birds, the call of the distant watch on the city walls, the lapping water. Peshek's heavy breathing was nothing like her ladies', and even less like Kacha's. The pallet's straw bit into her skin even through her clothes, and she had an ugly suspicion that was not all that bit her. Without braziers to surround her bed, the room grew steadily colder, despite the fire, until Medeoan could see her own breath in the slices of moonlight the loose shutters allowed in.

The night deepened. Peshek's breathing grew slow and regular. The moonbeams lengthened on the floor. One by one, the birds outside silenced, and Medeoan judged her time was right.

Slowly, so as to rustle the straw as little as possible, Medeoan reached for her bundle. Pulling it toward her, she spat on her two fingers and rubbed them against the knot tying the cloth. It fell open at once. The tiny pile of belongings inside seemed pathetic. How could she get by with so little?

Medeoan did not permit herself to dwell on it. Instead she drew out the god's eye amulet she had woven against this night. It really should be tied around Peshek's neck, but she did not trust herself to be able to slip it over his head without waking him. Nearby would have to do.

Medeoan wrapped the amulet's blue thong around the bedstead. Raising her magic, she breathed across the knot as she tied it.

"Night and moon keep watch over Peshek Pachalkasyn Ursulvin and grant him sound sleep until you surrender the sky to Day and his sister Sun."

The knot finished, she spat on it to seal it shut. She paused to listen. Peshek's breathing deepened. For the first time, he began to snore.

Medeoan scrambled from her cold bed. Peshek did not stir. She took the sealed letter she had prepared for him and laid it on her pillow where he was sure to see it. Then, taking a deep breath, she lifted the gold-and-silver girdle out of the bundle.

Fixing her mind firmly on the need to reach the Heart of the World, Medeoan tied the girdle securely around her waist.

Eliisa Hahl cast a longing look around the room. It seemed a crime to abandon so stout a bed already paid for, and by a man who kept his hands to himself, of all the miracles! Still, there was no help for it. She reclaimed apron and scarf, and moved to tie up her bundle, and paused upon seeing her purse lying on the cloth. What fool had left so much money lying loose! As soon as she had time, she'd sew it into her waistband, but now there was nothing for it but to tie the purse up under her skirt and hope it would be safe enough.

The captain lay across the threshold, snoring in far too genteel a manner for a soldier. Well, he was an officer, after all. She leaned across him and pushed the door gently open. The captain did not stir. Hiking her skirts high, Eliisa stepped over him. She closed the door gently, and nimbly hurried down the stairs, making no more noise than a cat.

So far and all's well, Eliisa thought as she emerged into the night. Her gaze skimmed the length of the canal and she briefly considered making off with one of the boats, but decided against it. There was no point in theft when there was money to pay the way. So, instead, she fastened her bundle to her girdle like a peddler woman and strode back toward the town.

Peshek woke, rubbing his hand hard across his eyes and face. The first thing he noticed was that it was full light, which was strange because he was long accustomed to waking before dawn. The second thing he noticed was that the empress was not in her bed.

Peshek was beside the bed with his sword in his hand before he knew he had moved. His eye took in the tidy bedclothes, the flattened pillows, the unlatched door, the knotted amulet on the bedpost, and the folded paper, and his heart froze.

"Oh, no, Majesty. Please, no." Peshek had faced bandits, bears, and all manner of violent drunkards without fear, but now his hand shook as he picked up the folded paper and he found his mouth had gone completely dry.

Peshek broke the seal to open the letter. His breath catching in his throat, he read:

Loyal Captain Peshek,

Forgive the necessity of this ruse. It is the only way
to hide my escape from my husband and the magics he
has available to him. I may be found while I walk any
of Isavalta's roads as myself, and I may also be found
if I travel by sorcerous means through the Land of
Death and Spirit.

You must go to Fortress Dalemar and await Avanasy.
I have sent Lord Iakush to bring him home. Tell him
what has happened. If all goes well I will send you word
from the Heart of the World.

The letter was unsigned except for a crude sketch of a
spread-winged eagle, the imperial symbol.

Gods of my fathers, thought Peshek, clamping his fingers
around the letter so it would not tumble to the floor. *What
have I done?*

The autocrat, the embodiment of the imperial, was the life
and soul of Isavalta. When the keeper of the god house presented them to Vyshko and Vyshemir, they became Isavalta.
Protecting their health and life was protecting the health and
life of the land. Any order, all orders, no matter how incomprehensible, had to be followed, save one. Never was the
autocrat to be left unguarded. Peshek had been taught this
cardinal rule since he was ten years old and inducted into
the house guard by his father.

*I should have stayed awake. I should never have closed
my eyes.*

But he had not. Which left only the question of what he
should do next.

Carefully, Peshek refolded the missive. "I should slit my
own throat," he muttered to the empty room.

Answering for what he had done before his gods and his
ancestors certainly seemed a more attractive option right now
than watching Isavalta fall to the hands of a foreign emperor.
But he had orders. The question was, which should he dis-
regard—those orders he had just been given or the one order
that stood above all others? Should he chase after the empress, and be her guard, would she or no? Or did he obey
her and go wait for Avanasy?

Now, my son, I will tell you a great truth about dealing with the nobles. His father's voice echoed back to him across the years. *You do what they tell you, but you never, ever get involved in their schemes. They know what they are doing, and you don't. You are shelter for them, like the walls of the palace. Do the palace walls mix themselves in the doings of their inhabitants? They do not. And you, my son, are surely as smart as a pile of stone.*

So, he had his orders. He would go wait for Avanasy. Avanasy could find the empress in an instant if he needed to. Peshek had no magic in him, and knew no other sorcerer he trusted, and so had no choice.

Vyshko and Vyshemir watch out for her. Peshek buckled on his sword and knife, and sheathed his knout. He wanted a shave, and food, but what he needed was a canal boat to Biradost, and a fast horse from there.

Be there, Avanasy. Don't fail us, or I'll have to spend eternity haunting you for it.

Chapter Eight

Iakush, the Lord Sorcerer of Isavalta, stood on the balcony of his private apartments in the summer palace of Vaknevos and gazed down the cliffs to the lake. The view was stunning. The lake lay like a great sapphire in the midst of a landscape of emerald velvet. Its breeze freshened all the air, and as summer warmed it would prove to be lusciously cool in the torrid evenings. He always enjoyed the days here.

This day, however, he could not relax. Something was wrong, and he did not know what it was.

First, he had failed. Despite a full day closeted with the Portrait of Worlds, he had not been able to find Avanasy. Working with the Portrait was no easy matter, and required a deep familiarity with its ways, but still, he should have been able to find something. Even Avanasy, with all his cunning, could not have covered his tracks so completely. Now the Portrait was miles away from him, and he would have to find some other way to carry out the empress's orders.

Wrapping himself in his wounded pride, Iakush had meant to have a private word with Empress Medeoan as they journeyed, to assure her that he would find Avanasy and carry out her will. But he had not been able to see the empress. Emperor Kacha would let none near her curtained litter where it had been placed on the raised deck of the barge, saying she needed complete quiet until the physicians met her at Vaknevos.

"Respectfully, Majesty." Iakush had reverenced as best he could in the confined aisle of the rocking barge. "I do have knowledge in the healing arts. I may be able to bring her ease from whatever troubles her."

"I thank you for your concern," the emperor replied smoothly. "But I believe rest is what will be most beneficial."

"Majesty . . ." Iakush began again.

"I have said all I mean to, Lord Sorcerer."

He had spoken the words mildly, but Iakush had heard them before, and knew better than to pursue the matter any further. So, he reverenced again, and made his way back down to the common benches that he shared with the other members of the Council of Lords. The lords master eyed him, but said nothing, and Iakush was content to have it so.

As he took his place on the padded bench and watched the banks of the canal pass, he noticed who did not travel on the barge. Not one of the empress's waiting ladies was in evidence. Not even Chekhania, who traveled constantly at Empress Medeoan's side.

It was then that the first stirrings of disquiet settled into his blood. They stayed with him all the rest of the voyage, and even now, when his room was filled with the cheerful bustle of his servitors setting his chamber to rights and his eyes were filled with the beautiful and tranquil sight of the lake before him. Something was happening, something of which he was not being told, and it was happening too soon after the empress had petitioned him to find Avanasy again to be mere chance.

"Lord Sorcerer?" called his man Cestimir. "My lord, you are summoned."

Iakush turned. Beside Cestimir stood a boy in a kaftan of royal blue bound with a gold sash. The page boy reverenced and said, "Lord Sorcerer, I am sent to say that the Council of Lords is summoned by His Imperial Majesty, and that your attendance is required."

At those words, the disquiet that had filled Iakush turned still colder, and yet he could not have clearly said why. Perhaps it was because it was only the emperor who convened the council. That was a thing that had never happened before.

"Tell His Imperial Majesty I will not fail him."

Again, the boy reverenced, and he hurried away.

Iakush stared at the door as it closed behind the page. Unbidden, memory of Avanasy standing before him in his room in Vyshtavos rose up.

"Why will you not at least look?" Avanasy had demanded.

Iakush remembered how he had waved the imperial tutor's words away. "Because there is nothing to see."

"My lord sorcerer." Avanasy's voice had strained to remain calm while pronouncing the title. "Clearly, there is something not right. Kacha's hand, his eyes, the fact that he brings no sorcerer with him, when we *know* . . ."

"His Highness," Iakush spoke the two words clearly, "was badly injured in his youth, and his bound-sorcerer will be arriving once the marriage has been made."

Avanasy had pulled back then. "I did not know this."

"Lord Avanasy, sometimes I wonder if you do not have an inflated opinion of how much you do know."

Perhaps Avanasy should have said those words to me. Iakush turned his slow gaze to Cestimir, who stood ready for any order he might give.

But what order could he give? What provision could he make when he had no idea what was to come? He dismissed Cestimir with a wave to return to the business of unpacking.

What provision could he make? Against he knew not what or whom? A thought came to him, and he almost dismissed it, but the same cold disquiet made him reconsider.

There was a clothing press that Iakush had taken charge of himself during the journey and that had been set down beside his bed. Iakush unlocked it with a silver key and lifted the lid. Leaving his men to continue their chores, he removed his kaftan and his shirt. From the press, he lifted a shirt of blinding white linen. He had woven its cloth with his own hands, then cut and stitched that cloth. He slipped the shirt on over his head, fastening the buttons. Then, he put his kaftan back on, also paying particular attention to how he tied his sash. Only then did he emerge from his chamber and stride down the corridor to the council chamber in answer to the emperor's summons.

The council chamber of Vaknevos was a long, narrow room with a heavy table placed in its center and chairs on either side. On the low dais at the far end waited two chairs of gilded wood for the emperor and empress. Iakush entered to find the lords master and the emperor already assembled. His cautious gaze swept the room and found it as he remembered it, with one change only. A new carpet spread across the floor. Iakush's eyes flickered to the other members of the council. Probably none of them noticed. But then, none of them was a sorcerer. They knew about knots and weaving, and all their power, but they didn't comprehend it in their hands and their souls the way a sorcerer had to. They did not train themselves to notice every piece of cloth, of jewelry or carving that came into their view. They did not automatically try to decipher the pattern they noted, to see if it was a danger, or a hindrance, or perhaps, a help.

This carpet was blue and gold, so it looked very much in place in the imperial council room. Its pattern was nothing so blatant as interlocking circles or diamonds. The gold lines snaked through the bright blue background like the outlines of a maze—seldom crossing, seldom touching, each line involved in its own swirls and waves, and yet all of them held together by the expanse of blue.

It could be magical. It could be complexly and powerfully magical. Iakush felt the soles of his feet begin to itch, and his knees protested the need to bend, to touch it even through the cloth of his pantaloons, as he made the imperial reverence.

"Thank you, Lord Sorcerer Iakush," said Emperor Kacha. "Sit with us."

"Thank you, Imperial Majesty." Iakush stood and backed into the waiting chair, sitting beside weathered, broad, Lord Master Seasta, Master of the Horse.

Emperor Kacha mounted the dais and took his own seat, facing them all, his hands, the strong hand and the weak hand, resting on the chair arms. Still, Iakush found his attention straying to the empty chair beside the emperor.

"I have two pieces of news for you, my lords master, and I desire your counsel," said Emperor Kacha in his clear, precise voice. "The first is great good news for all of us, indeed for all of Eternal Isavalta. Her Imperial Majesty is with child."

"But this is wonderful!" cried out Lord Master Tsepier. "Vyshko and Vyshemir themselves must rejoice!"

The other lords master raised their voices in a clamor to let sound their pious delight. Only Iakush sat still. His shirt cuffs had grown tight around his wrists, and the collar pressed close against his neck. Even his sash embraced him firmly.

Iakush struggled to keep his countenance. There was magic here. It was in place at this moment, seeping up from some prepared source to work its maker's will. That source most likely lay in the new carpet underfoot. Iakush could not help but feel a cold admiration for the sorcerer who sat before that carpet and tied knot after knot, securing his magic and his purpose in a thousand-thousand strands of wool.

But who could be behind this magic? Avanasy? Was this the crime to which the empress had alluded? No. Surely not. If she had known so much, the carpet would not be here . . .

Then who?

"Our lord sorcerer remains grave," said the emperor. "He understands the deeper significance of this news."

Iakush shook himself. Now was not the time for introspection. Now was the time to take careful stock of all the men around him, perhaps the emperor most of all.

"Yes, Imperial Majesty," Iakush said gravely. "It is not easy for a sorcerer, male or female, to bring forth a child. No part of a sorcerer's soul touches the Land of Death and Spirit, which is the source of life's beginning, as well as its end. This severance gives us our magic and our long lives, but it also denies us the ability to pass life on to another. Frequently the females die in the attempt." That silenced all the lords, and settled them all back into their chairs.

Emperor Kacha nodded, his dark face a very mirror of sober thought. "So Her Imperial Majesty has informed me, and that is the real reason I have called you here, instead of allowing the keeper of the god house to make the first announcement as is customary." His withered hand waved toward the door. "For the sake of her own health and that of her child, Her Imperial Majesty has chosen to go immediately into confinement. She will correspond closely with her court, of course, and read letters and petitions with great attention, as she has always done, but, she has asked me to say, there will be no more public appearances before she has been safely delivered of our child."

The laces of Iakush's shirt drew themselves tight against his chest. He imagined the room thick with magic like some invisible perfume, with all the lords master breathing it in deeply. To what end?

"You will of course deliver our immediate congratulations," announced fat Lord Master Goriain, Master of the Archives. "Are we to assume His Imperial Majesty will be coordinating the receipt of the petitions?"

"I will, with your able assistance of course, Lord Master Goriain. Your secretaries and scribes will be much required in the coming months."

"I am here to serve." His words were echoed by the other lords master, and Iakush knew what spell oozed from the carpet. Belief. Credulity. They would not question this sudden removal of the empress from the public scene, and probably they would not remember that they had not questioned it. In their own memories, they would each have behaved ideally. They would have closely questioned the emperor, satisfying themselves as to the truth and necessity of the situation. If the spell were thoroughly thought out, they might even remember having demanded to see her, and being escorted to her chamber. All that would build itself into their hearts and minds until no doubt remained.

Iakush felt his collar constrict until he had to suppress a cough. Oh, yes. The maker of this carpet was very good, very strong, and very careful. This spell would do at least that much to these men, and perhaps more.

And the purpose it served was Kacha's.

Iakush felt a burning rage rush through him. He wanted nothing more than to spring to his feet, his knife in his hand, to bring down this man who was doing this thing, who had done the gods only knew what to the anointed empress.

But he could do nothing. He could only sit where he was and continue to listen to every poisonous word.

"Which brings me to the other piece of news which I have," said the emperor. "We have recently received word through the House Guard of a sorceress abroad in the land. She is mad, they think, or perhaps she is merely bold. She is claiming to be the Empress Medeoan, and making pronouncements in her name. Now, normally, such a thing would be ignored. She'd be picked up soon enough for vagrancy or some fraud, but I like not the timing of this appearance, nor does your empress. She asks me to convey to you how urgently we wish this woman silenced. You will coordinate with the lords master of the magusates, and she will be found and brought here before the lord sorcerer for judgment." Emperor Kacha leveled his gaze fully on Iakush. "And it will be a stern judgment, my lord, will it not?"

Again Iakush shook himself. He felt as if his mind had been as tightly swaddled as his body. For all his protection, the spell leaked through, making concentration difficult. Of course what the emperor said was true. Iakush had read the empress's declaration. He knew her words and hand very well and . . .

No. That did not happen. That did not happen. We only sat and listened to the emperor speak. That is all.

"It is unlawful for a sorcerer to impersonate any person of name," Iakush said, choosing his words with care. He must not say too much, not now. His tongue might run away with him, clouding his mind yet further. He must speak only in absolutes. "Should any who is not utterly mad have the temerity to say that they are the empress herself, it must surely be judged an act of treason."

"Even if she be mad," growled Lord Master Seasta, the muscles on his thick neck standing out from the force of his feeling, "it were better she was killed on sight, than that she be allowed to spread lies and treason, especially at such a time."

"There is much wisdom in those words, Lord Master Seasta," mused the emperor with a nod. "What say you to that, Lord Sorcerer?"

Iakush could barely speak at all. His collar choked him, his own magic drawing close and trying to stave off the spell that permeated the air and wormed its way into his blood. "With respect to His Imperial Majesty, I say that a thorough and openly witnessed examination will spark fewer rumors during this delicate time." Delicate time, time of birthing, the empress lying in surrounded by her doctors and ladies, as they had seen her, looking up at him, trusting him, finally, as she had once trusted Avanasy . . .

No. No. No. I never left this room. I never saw her. I see only Kacha, I know only that we are bespelled.

"That is also a worthy thought, Lord Sorcerer," said the emperor approvingly. "I will relay this counsel to Her Imperial Majesty. In the meantime, my lords master, and my lord sorcerer, I ask you to spread word of these matters among your people, and take counsel with them. Tomorrow at this hour we will meet again. I will have Her Imperial Majesty's words, and we will together decide on the best plan of attack."

Tell him I am in danger, Medeoan had ordered Iakush. Now he understood. She had couched that message as a lie to convince him to lure back Avanasy. Now, though, Iakush knew it to be no less than the truth. Avanasy's impending death sentence was the lie. She had done this thing so he would not only obey her, but so that he could not betray her.

Iakush clenched his fist. She had not felt she could speak plainly to him, and whose fault was that? He had, after all, done nothing but stand by and watch as Avanasy was banished on a charge he had known could not be true. He'd been too bound up in his search for power. Too much love of power was a danger for any sorcerer, and Iakush had fallen to it without even noticing.

That is what he tried to tell me. Tell him I need him.

He'd told himself then that it was Avanasy who had been

greedy for power, that Medeoan would come to trust him, Iakush. She did trust him, she looked up to him, he'd seen her handwriting, heard her speak, weak but flushed with inner delight as women with child often became . . .

Iakush heaved himself awkwardly to his feet. Around him, the lords master made their reverences and departed in twos and threes, whispering urgently about what they had heard.

Vyshemir's knife, he told himself sternly, as he crossed his hands to reverence. *From here you will go retrieve Vyshemir's knife from Keeper Bakhar. Hold fast to that thought, Iakush, if no other.*

Vyshemir's knife was in the keeping of the keeper of the emperor's god house, but in the hands of a sorcerer who knew the proper words to say, it could be used to cut away illusion and bring truth to light. It could save him now.

"Lord Sorcerer," said the emperor. "Stay but a moment."

Wants to keep me here. The empress has some message . . . No. No. Vyshemir's knife. From here I must go get Vyshemir's knife.

"Imperial Majesty?" Iakush made himself turn, made himself stay on the carpet with its power that reached out its magic to poison his thoughts. With an extreme effort of will, he made himself see Kacha. Kacha, not Medeoan. Kacha of Hastinapura. Kacha son of Chandra. Kacha who had been bargained away for peace, and was secretly harboring thoughts of conquest.

The emperor had risen, and he walked casually down the dais to stand beside him. "Her Imperial Majesty particularly asked that you look deeply into this matter."

"I will do my best, Imperial Majesty."

Emperor Kacha clapped Iakush on his shoulder, and steered him toward the door, forcing him to walk down the carpet. "She knows well she is young in her power, and relies heavily on your judgment."

Vyshemir's knife. Vyshemir's knife will cure me of this affliction, will open my eyes.

"She regrets that she has not said so before now, but her old teacher wounded her grievously, and she has not yet recovered from that." Kacha paused in his stride and shook his head. "She asks you to forgive her this failing, and says that when she is able, she wishes to continue her instructions under your guidance. She assures you that none other will be named lord sorcerer while you remain true."

It would have been so easy to give in. With or without the enchantment, he could see that the emperor was giving him a chance for the prestige and responsibility that he had longed for. He now spoke the words Iakush had ached with his whole being to hear since the death of the old emperor and empress.

It was in hope of those words that he had kept silent during the capricious exile of one who should have been as a brother.

And now she was saying them. Now, she finally saw his worth and his position was secure. Now, he would be able to . . . to . . .

No. Kacha speaks, not my empress. The knife, the knife, the knife, I must go claim the knife.

"I am deeply honored, Imperial Majesty," was all Iakush could make himself say.

Kacha faced him squarely, looking Iakush straight in his eyes, laying his hand again on Iakush's shoulder. "I also am trusting you, Lord Sorcerer. Once my lineage is secure, there will be numerous preferments and titles to be awarded. The empress needs no mere magical advisor. The duties, and the rewards of the office of lord sorcerer needs must become much greater during our reign."

The pressure of the spell was almost unbearable. Iakush fought to keep himself from shuddering as his mind and soul were squeezed as if by an invisible hand. "I live to serve."

"To serve your master and mistress, the emperor and empress of Isavalta," said Kacha. The emperor did not blink as he watched Iakush.

Iakush forced his shoulders to straighten. "I live, as we all do, to serve Eternal Isavalta."

"As we all do, Lord Sorcerer," said the emperor. "You may go now. I will expect you here tomorrow with your fellows."

Iakush reverenced. Relief washed through him. He could get away from this. Vyshemir's knife would save him. It would cut away this enchantment and restore his right memories.

A cold pressure touched his side, and Iakush straightened, startled to see the emperor right beside him.

"Did you think I would not know?" sneered Kacha. "Did you think I would be sent here if I could not see?"

The emperor stepped back, and Iakush felt something warm and wet against his shirt. His hand sought it automatically, and came away covered with something red. He stared at his stained hand mutely. What could this be? No wine had been served. He had spilled nothing. What could be so red?

The knot of his sash almost completely obscured the dagger's hilt.

"I should slit your throat," said the emperor casually. "But you will be much easier to bury with a hidden wound. Far fewer people will have to be bemused. Now then, while you die, I will fetch you a physic. Perhaps you will live long enough to succumb to a fever."

Blood. Still staring at his hand, Iakush dropped to his knees. But his knees would not hold him, and he sprawled against the carpet. Blood. His blood. Stabbed by the emperor. Dying. He was dying in the thick puddle of his own blood.

Why? What had happened? He couldn't remember. He had been obeying the empress. She had wanted him to go get Vyshemir's knife . . .

Vyshemir's knife. Proof against enchantment. The pain began now, lancing up his side, clenching jaw and throat, burning hotter than the blood that spilled. Enchantment. Emperor. Treason and greed, and blood, everywhere so much blood. He couldn't move, couldn't stop the pain or the blood. He was dying for his foolishness, dying for his empress . . .

No, not for her. She was not here. She was elsewhere, and she had asked him to take word to Avanasy.

But he had no words, only blood.

With one trembling hand, Iakush reached out and drove his finger into the blood. Haltingly, he tried to spit, and managed to drool a little spittle into the redness. He stirred them together. He coughed for breath. Mortal blood, mortal breath. These were the sources of the greatest power a single sorcerer could give. It would be enough. It would have to be.

"Beyond life there is a forest," he whispered, forcing his finger to move through the blood, drawing a wave that was the river, was a snake, was a ray of light, was all his hope borne on all his pain, was his last act, and he would complete this last act. "Within the forest there is a river. At the end of the river is another shore. On the other shore, there walks Avanasy Finorasyn Goriainavin. Breath and blood, carry me to the river. Vyshko and Vyshemir carry me to the river's end. My heart's blood, my breath, my life, carry me to Avanasy." He retched. Pain burned hotter than his blood, but he was so cold. His hand shook, and he could not feel it anymore, let alone make it move. The room was going gray. "My heart's blood, my breath, my life carry me to Avanasy Finorasyn Goriainavin. My heart's blood carry me . . ."

The room around him darkened, and vanished.

The Land of Death and Spirit is a land of eyes. This is the first thing taught to any sorcerer of Isavalta. It is not possible to pass through it unobserved. There is no true distance there, no true shadow and no true light. Anything may be shown to those who wish to see. The places that do not shift and change are few, and they offer nowhere to hide beyond the boundaries of the mortal world.

Inside a fence mended with bones, there stood a cottage on crooked, scaled, taloned legs. The cottage was called Ishbushka, and in it, an ancient witch with iron teeth sat at her loom of bones and spoke to her cat.

"What do you see?"

The cat sat on the windowsill, staring unblinking out the window. "I see another sorcerer walking from Isavalta." The cat twitched its tail. "If this continues, soon Isavalta will have none of them left."

The witch stilled her shuttle, which was made of an ancient jawbone. She perused the pattern of her weaving, reading what was written there in a language only she herself knew. "What else do you see?"

"His blood flows red." The cat turned and began to clean its shoulder nonchalantly. "He has come early to the land of

Death, but the grandfather waits for him. He will not reach the far shore."

The witch grunted and laid her long, bony finger a moment on her weaving. She nodded, satisfied with what she saw. "You will go to the grandfather, cat. You will send my greeting. You will ask him in my name to let the sorcerer pass."

The cat used its paw to smooth down its ears. "Grandfather Death will not be pleased to neglect one of his grandchildren so."

"Say it is a delay only," said the witch. "This one has an important message that must be delivered. Say that in my name."

The cat turned to groom its shoulder.

"There will be those who say you do this to protect the right and the order of things."

"They will be wrong. His message will bring the woman here. I have need of her."

The cat narrowed its emerald eyes as it gazed at her mistress. But the witch offered no explanation, and the cat asked no questions. She only leapt from the perch and silently padded out the cottage door.

The morning after Leo Loftfield was injured, Avanasy returned gladly to his work. It was something to occupy him until the sun set, for there was still plenty of brushwood to be cut and cleared. Even so, his mind was distracted enough that he abandoned the scythe as too dangerous and contented himself with bundling the cut brush and stacking wood. The news from Ingrid's home had been good. Leo would keep his leg, and was in fact awake, though he was still weak. He had stopped by the kitchen door this morning to speak a moment with Ingrid and say he would be back tonight. Perhaps it would be a good time to speak with her father, perhaps it would not, but he meant to sound the man out, so Ingrid's parents would know without a doubt that his intentions were honorable.

He would need to change his shirt, before he went to visit the Loftfields, and wash, and shave. Should he bring the ring with him? Ingrid had not said. He would have it, in case.

The ring waited at the bottom of his chest. His mother had given it to him when he had gone to be apprenticed. It was a golden band, set with coral and rubies. Perhaps it was too much for a fisherman's wife, but she would have it anyway. He would pass it off somehow, perhaps as an heirloom, or as paste, but he would tell Ingrid that it was real, and what its origins were. It would become one more tie between them. She'd smile when she saw it.

Or would she? It was beautiful, but in the Isavaltan fashion. Even riches were much plainer here. Perhaps she would only find it garish.

Avanasy had to laugh at himself. He was as nervous as a plowboy sending a bride gift to a milkmaid's mother. It was ridiculous. Of course, Ingrid would smile, because it was a gift freely given, and that was her way.

"You're quiet," said Everett Lederle, breaking in on his thoughts. Lederle worked beside him, gathering up newly trimmed branches and stacking them together to be bundled up and hauled away.

"Things on my mind," answered Avanasy. He stepped on the pile of branches in front of him so he could more easily loop the twine around it and tie the bundle securely.

"Like Ingrid?"

Avanasy paid careful attention to the knot he was tying. "And if it was?"

Everett said nothing to that. He just wrapped some twine around another bundle of brush and tied off his own knot. He pulled the clasp knife from his pocket and slit the twine. Then, he straightened to face Avanasy, the knife still held in his hand. "She loves you," he said flatly. "Use her badly and I will hunt you down like a dog. Understand me?"

"Very well," replied Avanasy, looking Everett in his face. The knife was nothing. Everett was not a man to use it without cause. Perhaps later, when some time had passed and wounds had healed, they could become friends. "Maybe you should know I mean to go to her father tonight and ask for her hand."

Everett drew in a long, low breath. He snapped the knife blade closed and returned it to his pocket. "That's good then."

Everett returned to his work without another word, and Avanasy bent to his own. The sun continued its long, slow trek across the sky, finally settling into Lake Superior and leaving no light left to work by. Avanasy shouldered his scythe once more and trooped back to the shore with the other itinerant fishers, his heart riding high with the memory of Ingrid's kiss. Part of him was greedy to know much more of her, but he was not that plowboy, and he could wait. Knowing what he did of her own birth, he could most definitely wait until they had been joined by the proper rites. There would be no shame for them. He would build her a proper house. They would wed and be feasted according to the expected custom. But then, ah, then, when once they were alone . . .

Savoring his imaginings, Avan pushed open the door of his shack. He smelled salt and copper, and for a moment did not realize how wrong that scent was. It smelled of the sea shore. He froze. Lake Superior was freshwater, what was the scent of the sea doing here?

Something dark crouched in the center of his dirt floor. Avan instantly took his scythe from his shoulder and hefted it.

"What are you?" he demanded.

"Avanasy," grated a harsh voice. "Please. Avanasy."

The scythe thudded from Avanasy's suddenly numb hands. The voice spoke to him in the court language of Isavalta, and it belonged to Iakush, the lord sorcerer.

"My lord sorcerer." He dropped to his knees. His eyes adjusted to the dimness and saw the dark stain spreading across Iakush's white shirt. Blood. It could not be anything else. Then he became aware of something else by the pricking of skin and soul. The Grandfather, Death, had walked into the room behind him, and he came for Iakush.

"Avanasy," croaked Iakush again.

"What has happened?" Avanasy laid his hand against the wound, but pressure would do no good. Too much blood had already been lost. "Tell me, Iakush."

"Kacha. You were right, from the first. Medeoan, Isavalta . . . all are in danger. Medeoan has fled, Kacha lies. He . . ." Iakush coughed. A stream of blood trickled from his slack mouth. "He has magics at his command, Avanasy. I don't know how, but they are strong." Death leaned closer. Avanasy felt the chill. "Medeoan sent . . . Medeoan . . ." Another cough racked him. "Ah, Grandfather, Grandfather, I hurt."

"Medeoan sent you?" Avanasy grasped his shoulders. "What of the emperor? The empress? Why have you left them?"

But Iakush just shuddered. Death was too close. Avanasy made a decision. He lifted his bloody hand to his mouth and breathed on it, then he pressed it against Iakush's lips.

"Blood to breath, Lord Iakush Vtoroisyn Gabravin," he whispered, steeling himself. "Yours to mine. My words, my breath, your blood, your words."

Avanasy reached inside himself to find the magic he needed to shape the weaving of breath and blood, but it would not rise. He strained himself, reaching deep with all his strength, reaching out as far as he could for the last vestige of the magics that had brought Iakush this far. He shook to his core and feared he was not strong enough to reach so far, but at last the magic rose, and the words wove it into shape.

Pain. Blinding, searing, strength-robbing pain. Avanasy doubled across the lord sorcerer's body. The cold of loss and death shot through him, along with all the fear in Iakush's mind. But below that, he touched the lord sorcerer himself, and he felt recognition, and then relief.

The old emperor and empress are dead, Avanasy. I truly thought it was fever then, but now I think it was poison. Medeoan is empress. She is fled. She sent me for you. She needs you, Avanasy. The rest of us have failed her. Kacha will kill her or worse, I fear. Then Hastinapura will rule us all. You must meet her at Fortress Dalemar.

They spasmed together, and Avanasy felt his heart squeezing itself to wring another drop of blood into his veins.

Let me go, Avanasy. I'm done and I cannot bear this anymore.

Avanasy lifted his hands away, and fell into darkness.

Eventually, Avanasy woke to night's cold and yet more darkness. A single shaft of silver moonlight squeezed through the plank boards of his walls and lit up his stack of kindling. Iakush lay beside him. The acrid stench of death filled the cabin until Avanasy could taste it. He struggled to his feet, weak as a kitten, and staggered out his doorway and down the shore.

"Hey, Avan! You all right?"

Avanasy only waved in response. Let whoever shouted think he was drunk. Let them think anything they wanted. He knelt, still shaking, at the edge of the lake and vomited into the water until his stomach was shriveled and empty and his whole mouth bitter with gall. He pushed himself sideways to cleaner waters and drank, and washed his face.

Medeoan had fled. Medeoan was in danger, from Kacha. He'd known it. He'd known it and he'd left her, abandoned his trust because he could not bear to face his own shame. Now, the emperor and empress were dead and Medeoan gone, and where was he? He stared out across the black lake. Playing fisherman in a village of drudges and rude mechanicals. Playing at a life to which he had no claim.

Oh, in Vyshko's name. Ingrid.

The moon was well up. It was late. He could not call on her tonight. She would think he had forgotten. She would think something had happened to him. That thought pulled him to his feet. She would think something had happened to him, and she would throw a shawl around her shoulders and she would . . .

Cursing his weakness, Avanasy stumbled back to his cabin. He threw open the door, nearly fell again but caught himself against the stove. Ingrid knelt beside Iakush's corpse. Even night's darkness could not disguise her from him. She lifted her head at his clumsy entrance and her face was as white as the moon.

"What happened?" she whispered fiercely. "Who is this? I came . . . I thought . . . I thought crazy things when you didn't come. I thought maybe the ghost . . ."

Avanasy summoned all the strength that remained to him. He pushed himself upright and walked to the bed. He pulled off the single blanket and laid it across Iakush's body for a poor shroud. Ingrid rose slowly to her feet. Even in the faint moonlight he could see how her eyes glittered hard. He wanted to stand to face her, but his legs were already weakening. As slowly as he could manage, he sat in the rickety chair.

Ingrid said nothing. He ran both hands through his hair. She was waiting for him. She had waited for him all night to fulfill a promise he had no right to make.

"His name is Iakush," said Avanasy. "He was the lord sorcerer to the imperial court of Isavalta. He . . . Medeoan sent him to find me."

"Why?"

"It seems I was right."

She left the corpse and walked over to him, kneeling down so that they were eye to eye. "Tell me."

He did. He told her about coming back to find Iakush, and how he had delivered his message, and how Medeoan was gone, and his master and patron, the emperor was dead. His strength failed him then, and to his shame, Avanasy found that all he could do was bow his head and begin to weep. He wept for his exile, and for his acceptance of it. He wept for his belief that he could begin a new life. He wept for the good man dead on the floor at his feet whom he lacked the strength to save. He pounded the chair with his fist and even the pain of it could not stop the tears.

Somewhere in the midst of this shameful weeping, Ingrid wrapped her arms around he shoulders and pulled him close, holding him while he poured out his grief.

"Jesus, Avan, what the hell's happened . . ." came a man's voice from the doorway.

"This is none of your business, Jan Iverksson," snapped Ingrid. "Go home."

The sound of her harsh words reminded him where he truly was. Avanasy found his strength again and was able to force himself back into some semblance of composure.

"You should not be here." He pushed himself back from her. "Your family, they'll think . . ."

Ingrid sat on her heels and shrugged irritably. "I'm here now, and there's nothing to be done about it. What are you going to do?"

Avanasy spread his hands hopelessly. "I'm going back to Isavalta. I have to, Ingrid. My homeland is in danger. Medeoan . . . she sent for me. She needs my help, and she is my empress."

"Of course," said Ingrid, but he heard how hollow her voice was.

He slipped from the chair to kneel beside her and he took both her hands. They were so cold. He could not help but remember how warm they had been the previous afternoon, from the sun and from her delight at his proposal. "I had no right to speak to you as I did," he said. As he spoke, sudden, hard anger filled him. Why had this happened tonight? Why had Medeoan not sent for him yesterday? Or a month ago? Or a month before that? Why now?

"Did you mean it?" she asked steadily. "That you wanted to marry me?"

"I did."

"Do you mean it still?"

"With all my heart, Ingrid, I do."

She was silent than for a long moment, and he saw her bite her lip. "Then let me come with you."

"Ingrid, no."

"Yesterday, I agreed to become your wife, and when I said yes, I knew who you were and what your past was. I accepted it."

"But not this, Ingrid." He swept his hand out toward Iakush's corpse under its rough blanket. Iakush should have had a shroud of white linen and gold, and all he had was gray wool. "You never accepted this."

She stood, turning from him as she did, and walked away a few steps, her arms wrapped tightly around herself. Avanasy stood as well, but swayed on his feet. He realized that the fear that filled him was the fear that she would say he was right, that she would walk out of his house and leave him alone.

But she did not. She just turned around again to face him.

"Avan . . ." she began, but then she stopped, and started over. "Avanasy, I never questioned how my life would be. I would help care for my family until one day I married someone from the island, or perhaps, if fate was especially bold, I would marry someone from Bayfield. Then, I would keep my own house and raise my own children." Ingrid kicked at the dirt floor. "And that would be that. It would be a good life, hard, but life always is."

"You can do so still," said Avanasy quietly. "Nothing prevents you."

Ingrid met his eyes. "Do you honestly believe that?"

For a long moment, Avanasy did nothing but look into her moonlit gaze. He felt all the waves of his feeling swirl around them both—sorrow, regret, determination, fear, but all these rushed away and left only love.

"No," he said at last. "I do not believe that."

"Well then?"

Avanasy folded his arms around her, pulling her into a hard embrace. He felt the thrill as Ingrid fell into it willingly, lifting her face to his kiss. She kissed back with a strength that left him dizzy with its heat. Avanasy kissed her cheek, her eyes, and buried his face against her shoulder, breathing her deeply. He held on, feeling the strength rushing between them—the strength of her body and the strength of his own heart which opened to her, and which he knew would never close to her again.

"I don't know what dangers there will be, Ingrid," he said when he could speak again. "I am exiled, and to return is to court death. If High Princess Medeoan . . . if the empress is indeed fled her capital, very few will know that exile is rescinded. I am long months away, and much has changed. I may no longer have friends where I go to look for them."

"When must we go?" asked Ingrid, pulling back just far enough to see his face.

"I must go at first light, as soon as I can raise my sails."

Her eyebrows lifted in astonishment. "You have a boat of your own? Then why . . ."

"Do I work for others?" The corner of Avanasy's mouth twitched into a weak smile. "It is not a boat for normal seas, at least, not entirely. I did not want to risk its sails being damaged in rough work while there was still a chance . . ." He paused, and then remembered himself and who he spoke to. "While there was still a chance I might be summoned home again."

Ingrid nodded and stepped back from him. "But you're tired. You should get some rest."

"I am, and it will get worse," he admitted. "This is no easy journey we undertake. But delay, even a few hours, may cost lives and loyalties." He caught her gaze. "Understand, Ingrid, this is not some squabble over fence lines that can be resolved in the court over in Bayfield. This is the game of kings we are entering."

Ingrid drew herself up. "My father fought in a very bloody war, sir. I know something of it. I have seen the dead myself, and fought for lives. You will not find me missish, or a fainting fool."

Avanasy allowed himself a brief, real smile. "That would be impossible."

"I'll go back and get a few things together," said Ingrid, picking up the shawl she had at some point discarded by the bed and wrapping it over her head.

There was, Avanasy realized, one other thing that had to be said. "Ingrid, your family, they'll believe you've run off with me."

"They'll be right," she said flatly. "I am running off with you. We are just going a little farther than is customary."

Knowing what this meant to her, and what it might cost, Avanasy held up his hand. "Wait."

He drew the iron key out from under his shirt and unlocked his chest. From the very bottom, he drew out a small linen bag.

"Everett would marry you in an instant, Ingrid," he said as he straightened. "There would be no need for you to be alone should you choose to stay."

"Stop it, Avanasy." She gripped his hand hard. "You say we go to somewhere life is difficult, and dangerous. What is life on this island?" She stabbed her finger toward the door. "I could die tomorrow from a wave swamping a boat, from the cut of a knife, or from a fever, or when old Johnny Keeter gets drunk and takes it into his head to go on another of his tears. If I stay here without you, the only difference is the kind of danger I would be in, and that I would be alone for the rest of my life." She released him. "I am not romantic. Whatever this is we do together, it is not a fairy tale, but we will see it through."

"Then, accept this, my pledge." He took the ring from the

bag. Its gold and tiny rubies sparkled in the silver moonlight. "I love you, Ingrid Loftfield. Let that be the one enduring truth between us, and let this be the sign of it." He slipped the ring onto her third finger, as he had observed was the way such things were worn here.

She kissed him, the only pledge she had and far more dear to him than any scattering of rubies. Then, she threw her shawl over her head and hurried out the door to do what she must and swiftly return.

Avanasy ran his hand through his hair again, trying to bring order to his thoughts. He was beyond wondering what he was doing. All was set in motion, and now he must ride the tide of it.

Chapter Nine

So, the little imperial cow has caught wind of her doom and strayed. Yamuna stared down at the parchment before him, pulled from the fire now and covered with Kacha's writing. He had to admit, the boy had done well. His plan was sound, and the beginning of it well executed. The council of lords, for the moment, believed what they had been told.

So, that much was done. Now, Medeoan must be found. Her lords were not powerless yet, and she might still rally them to her cause if she were not found and dealt with at once.

Yamuna's chamber possessed four balconies, one facing each of the cardinal points of the compass. Yamuna stepped out onto the one which faced the north. The rain fell hard against his leathery skin, but Yamuna ignored it. He pulled his knife from his belt and stabbed the tip of it into the index finger of his right hand. The pain was nothing; he had done himself much greater injuries, and would again. The blood was needed, so he released it, that was all. Then, he undid one of the hundred spell braids that bound his long, white hair and from it pulled out three white hairs. He twirled them in the fingers of his right hand, spinning them into a single thread, bound tightly with his blood, in the hand he had taken from Kacha.

"Kacha *tya* Achin Ejulinjapad, your blood calls, your flesh calls, my will calls, you will answer me," said Yamuna clearly to the north. "Kacha *tya* Achin Ejulinjapad, your blood calls, your flesh calls, my will calls. You will answer me."

Yamuna closed his left eye, and through his right eye, which once had been Kacha's as his hand had been, he stared out past the rain, past the gray of the sky, past the veil of air and the curve of the earth, and he saw . . .

A silver wine cup, a rug, a stone floor, a pit with a fire burning brightly. He knew cold and night, and a young man's gnawing worry.

Where is she? The thought took up the whole of Kacha's mind. *What is she up to?* She had sworn him vows, and now she deserted him and her kingdom. A coward as well as a foolish child.

At least the carpet had worked. The palace was at the moment under his control, but that might not last. Kacha slammed down the wine cup. His servants jumped, but he waved them back as he rose to pace around the fire pit. His plan was good, it was sound, but she was out there, and who knew where. There was so much that might still go wrong . . .

All the secretaries were busy with announcements of the empress's confinement, and missives about the false sorceress claiming her title. The council lords were preparing their own missives to the various magusates. There was nothing for him to do now but wait until Yamuna chose to, Yamuna chose to, Yamuna chose . . .

Come now, my prince, the Sun's Own Son, walk with me. Say you go to see your wife.

The reflection of Kacha's face in a night-blackened window showed Yamuna the prince's sharp smile. The boy might be somewhat prone to his father's hysteria, but he knew the worth of his advisers, and he relished his role. He saw a single empire under the sway of the Pearl Throne stretching across the length of the continent, with himself as ruler as soon as his father might be gotten out of the way, and Yamuna was happy to give him that toy.

"I am going to consult with the empress," he announced. "I need no company."

Despite that, a ruler was seldom alone. The house guard and footmen and waiting gentlemen all had to make sure doors were opened, lights lit or extinguished, movements announced, even if he did no more than walk through a door to the empress's apartments, which adjoined his own.

Medeoan's outer apartment was an ideal of feminine tranquillity and gentle activity. The minor ladies-in-waiting sat by the fire conscientiously bent over their needlework, if they were not engaged with books or letters. Every one of them duly laid aside their amusements and labors to kneel before their emperor as he passed into the inner rooms. Some observed him slyly, covetously, or nervously, according to their own petty natures. Kacha made note of all such expressions against the time when they might prove useful.

The chief of Kacha's footmen knocked his staff against the carved door that led to the inner apartments that had been hastily converted from audience rooms to confinement rooms. After a moment, the door opened and Chekhania, whom he had caused to be raised to the position of head lady-in-waiting, appeared. She reverenced politely to the footman.

"His Imperial Majesty requests an audience with the empress Medeoan."

"If His Imperial Majesty would deign to step within, I shall announce him at once to my mistress imperial." Chekhania kept her gaze modestly on the floor as she spoke.

The males all stood aside then, allowing the emperor to enter the inner chamber. Chekhania shut the door at once.

Such an excellent custom, confinement, Kacha thought, knowing Yamuna would hear him. *So useful in so many ways.*

In Isavalta, once a woman entered confinement, no man could come into her presence, save her husband or her father. That meant none of the multitude of servants and gentlemen surrounding Kacha had to be bemused or bound, and only a few of the ladies around the empress did, and then only those who, unlike Chekhania, could not be bribed.

Here too there was gentle activity on every side, the endless round of reading, sewing and writing, tending to the chamber and to themselves, but if one looked into the ladies' faces, one could see a hollowness behind their eyes and a distance in their manner. These were divided souls in truth. Through Yamuna's patient magic, each had been severed from that half of their vitality that waited in the Land of Death and Spirit. Now, they could only wander lost in both worlds, ready to answer any order or command.

Which would all be given by Chekhania, and were limited indeed, as none of the ladies would be expected to appear in public until the empress did.

So, Chekhania told them Medeoan lay in her bed, and they tended the empty bed as if she did. They brought it food, they changed its sheets, they brought braziers to warm it, read poetry to amuse it, and reverenced in its presence. All this they did gladly, for it gave them the purpose in living which Yamuna's work had deprived them of.

"Does my Master Imperial wish to visit his wife or her works?" inquired Chekhania. She was a pale, plump woman, round of hip and bosom, and beautiful in the Isavaltan fashion. It was a fashion Kacha had grown to enjoy a great deal and his gaze lingered on her full breasts. He would enjoy the work of ensuring that she produced the infant that would be passed off as Medeoan's when the time came.

But now, you must see your wife's works, directed Yamuna, and Kacha told Chekhania so.

Chekhania reverenced again and, although there was no need, she led Kacha to the small door that waited past the inner apartments. The door should have been locked, but only Medeoan could touch the key, so of necessity it remained open. It did not matter. Chekhania was as good as any key in these guarded surroundings, now that the lord sorcerer had been disposed of.

To remind Chekhania of the various ways in which he appreciated her, Kacha paused before the inner door, wrapped his left hand around her neck, and kissed her hard. Yamuna permitted this for a long moment, for to keep Chekhania properly in her place, she needed to believe the emperor's lusts controlled him, and that by her treachery she was gaining real power.

Enough, said Yamuna at last, and Kacha released the woman and left her to mind the door.

Inside the chamber, Kacha had to light the braziers himself. No servant, even under normal circumstances, would be permitted in this room. As the firelight brightened, Yamuna, even from his great distance, found a moment to stop and admire the map table that dominated the chamber.

The Portrait of Worlds could not be duplicated, and it certainly could not be transported. So, a different tool had been created at the behest of the Isavaltan emperors. It was a table the length of the one that sat the council of lords, which had been covered with a brass sheet. The brass was then etched with carefully drawn and divined lines and symbols that represented the worlds and relationships sketched out in the dance performed by the mechanisms of the Portrait. Because the brass did not move, this tool was not as delicate or precise as the Portrait, but it was here and it would serve.

It was said a sorcerer from the island of Tuukos had been smuggled in by Medeoan's grandmother to make this table. They were known for drawing accurate and detailed astrological charts, and had, since their complete conquest by Isavalta, been forbidden to do so. Kacha, however, could well believe that such a canny woman would have had little trouble putting forbidden sorceries to work for the benefit of her new empire.

Seeing it through Kacha's eye, Yamuna regretted the necessity of killing the lord sorcerer. He would have liked to have the man's secrets from him first, the secrets of this shining, engraved table, and most especially of the Portrait. Well, no matter. Avanasy would be found before all was done, that was not in doubt, and Avanasy could be made to tell the deeper spells concerning the detailed map and the exquisite mechanism. Until then, Yamuna's own skills could well answer.

Normally, some possession of Medeoan's would be required, but as Kacha was her husband, bound to her through the tightest of all bonds save that of birth, he himself would serve as the token around which the spell could be woven.

Kacha was used to stilling himself so Yamuna could work. He did so now, positioning himself directly in front of the center of the etched map of Isavalta. He relaxed himself, emptying his mind, making himself into the tool the sorcerer required.

Yamuna caused Kacha's right hand to take his left and place it palm down over the map of Isavalta. He reached inside himself, and pulled down his abundant magic, sending it outward across the bond of blood and flesh that tied him to Kacha. The power burned the young man, but he bore the pain proudly. Oh, it would be a pleasure to set him on the throne his father so coveted.

The spell itself had to be worked in the Isavaltan fashion to be most effective, but Yamuna had made a great study of their forms.

"This is my word." Yamuna funneled the words to Kacha through the thoughts they shared, and Kacha, holding still under the burning that filled him inside, chanted them in time to his own heartbeat, weaving the words and the pain and the magic all into the pattern of the room. "Upon the island of the sun there grows a tree, and upon that tree grows a branch, upon that branch sits a bird of gold and that bird has two eyes of silver. As those two eyes of silver see the whole of the world, so may I, Yamuna *dva* Ikshu Chitranipad who is Kacha *tya* Achin Ejulinjapad see Medeoan Edemskoidoch Nacheradavosh. May I see where she walks in all the worlds mortal and immortal, speaking and silent, waking and sleeping. This is my wish and this is my word, and my word is firm."

Kacha burned, but he struggled against it, and he said the words again, and again. Yamuna stared, pushing the power through his resistant blood, willing their eye to see. For they must see. Alive or dead, the map must show them. The spell commanded, there was no will here to resist. There must be a sign or signal, and it must come soon.

But Kacha cried out and his knees buckled, unable to stand against the pain, and Yamuna stilled the spell. Kacha dropped to the floor, panting, on hands and knees.

"How?" Kacha demanded through gritted teeth. "She could not hide from you, you swore it. How then?"

Yamuna considered. The little cow obviously knew secrets he did not. She was powerful, and she was well taught.

Which gave him a new thought. It would take magic to vanish from the sight of the map. Her teacher would surely know which spell she used, and where she might go.

Up. We must find Avanasy.

For a moment, Yamuna thought the prince was going to try to refuse. But Kacha gritted his teeth and heaved himself to his feet, held his palms outstretched over the map, his whole body clenched to keep them there.

Yamuna would have preferred to have a possession of Avanasy's for this. It would have made things easier on Kacha. He did not wish the boy damaged. But there was no time to go casting about the palace for something that might remain of Medeoan's former tutor.

This is my word. Upon the island of the sun there grows a tree, and upon that tree grows a branch, upon that branch sits a bird of gold . . .

Kacha screamed. Pain coursed through him, and more pain as the magic flowed through flesh that could not stand it and yet could not resist. Yamuna forced their right eye open and looked down upon the Map of Worlds, and he saw how the air shimmered and shone. Each beautifully rendered symbol that represented the myriad realms of the Silent Lands lit up in its turn—the Wheel, the Cup, the Wing, the Skull, the Fox—showing a passage through Death and Spirit. Here, the domain of the *lokai* had been passed by, here the fey, here the realm of Baba Yaga, and all had fetched up on a place marked with an etching of waves encased in two concentric circles. A nameless, mortal place, but now Yamuna knew its whereabouts, and Avanasy . . .

Hold just a little longer, my prince, directed Yamuna as Kacha's scream forced itself out through clenched teeth. The fey lights hummed, a strange, hinting resonance, and lit upon the map of Isavalta, and Yamuna's eye marked the spot, and in Hastinapura he threw back his head and laughed.

That laughter broke the spell, and Kacha reeled against the wall, barely missing a brazier as he slumped there, sweating and shaking, but standing upright nonetheless.

"What did you see?" he gasped.

The teacher is planning to return. Yamuna laughed again. *Poor fool. He will be most surprised to find his mistress fled and his country turned against him.*

But Kacha could not laugh. Anger shot through him, as white-hot as the lingering pain. "He will not be surprised at all."

What is your meaning, my prince? inquired Yamuna, indulgently. Kacha set his jaw.

"I knew the man for three years before Medeoan exiled him. He was not only completely loyal and half-blind with love for his student, he was as stubborn as a stone. There is only one reason he would come back now. Medeoan has somehow sent for him."

Yamuna's voice fell silent. Kacha collapsed into the nearest chair. He felt as if his hand were back in the fire. A single, involuntary tear of pain trickled down his cheek. He waited for Yamuna's anger and blame.

But instead, the sorcerer's voice came to him thoughtfully. *If this is so, would she have told him where she was going?*

Kacha's eyes widened ever so slightly. The strength of his realization muted the intensity of the pain for a bare instant. "She might. She might even meet him herself. At the very least, she would send this Peshek to bring him to her or her allies."

Then he will do us immeasurable good service, said Yamuna. *For all we need do is be there to welcome him home and persuade him to lead us in the direction your wife has run.*

Despite his pain, Kacha too began to laugh.

It was full dark by the time Peshek reached his father's gates. He'd been half-afraid he would have to stop on the road somewhere, spending another night out in the open, but the moonlight had made it possible for him and his exhausted hired horse to pick out the way.

After a few minutes of shouting, the sleepy porter opened

the window and squinted out at him without seeing him at all.

"Come, Labko, you know me," he said impatiently. The hired horse danced uneasily under him. Peshek patted its neck. This was the most spirit the beast had shown since he'd mounted its sagging back.

Belated recognition widened the porter's eyes. "Master Peshek."

Labko's face vanished, and he shouted something indistinct. The shout was followed swiftly by a great creaking and sliding as the crank was turned and the great bolt was lifted so the gates could be cautiously pushed open. Peshek rode through as soon as there was room enough. A pair of boys wearing nothing but sandals and long-tailed shirts stared resentfully at him from under tousled hair. Peshek swung himself down onto the cobbles. He handed one of the boys his horse's reins and took the lantern the other held.

When his father had retired from service in the house guard, he had been gifted with a thousand acres of land and twenty serfs by the emperor. By that time, Peshek himself was already in the guard, and consequently he had only visited the estate a handful of times, but he still knew his way across the yard and up the steps to the main door. Apparently his shouting had roused more than the porter, for the door opened as he approached and a rumpled servant looked at him like a startled rabbit before remembering to reverence.

"Is my father awake yet?" Peshek asked.

"He is in his room, sir," the man stammered. It was more than suddenly being roused from sleep that unnerved him so, Peshek was sure, but he did not want to take the time to inquire. He needed to speak with his father at once.

He did take the time to stop at the gilded alcove that served as the god house and reverence to Ywane, who had gained his godhood when he hid the family from a warlord by burying them all and drawing them alive again from the earth. It would be wrong, now of all times, not to acknowledge his protection.

His father's house was a place of dark wood, well fitted and beautifully carved, although he could only catch glimpses of the fine decorations as he marched through the narrow halls and up the zigzagging staircase with his flickering lantern. It was a new house with fireplaces and chimneys rather than fire pits, and windows in every room. He could hear some vague noises of the servants stirring, but mostly the house was quiet and dark. He knew his father's door by the thin line of light that showed underneath it. Peshek knocked and did not wait for a reply before he pushed open the door.

Pachalka Ursulsyn Rzhovyn sat close to the low fire in an elaborately carved chair. Peshek had a brief moment to regard his father and think that he had not changed much from when they had last met. His long face was a bit leaner under its gray beard and his hair was a bit whiter, but his body was still powerful as he pulled himself to his feet and crossed the room to the door in three strides.

And swung his fist against Peshek's jaw so hard that Peshek reeled backward and slammed hard against the wall.

"How dare you!" shouted Colonel Pachalka. "How dare you come here after what you have done!"

"Father . . ." gasped Peshek when he could speak again. He tasted blood.

But Pachalka's fist came down again, and Peshek's head cracked back against the wooden panel.

"Traitor!" spat Pachalka. "You betray your empress, your family, your very gods! There are no words low enough for what you have become!"

"No, Father!" Peshek held up his hands. He could feel the warm thread of blood trickling down from his rapidly swelling lip. "I swear . . ."

Pachalka lashed out again, but this time Peshek was ready for it and managed to block the blow with his forearm and shove his father backward, just far enough so he could dodge aside and put half the length of the room between himself and the old man.

Pachalka panted hard in his rage and Peshek seized the moment. "Father, listen to me. I swear, all I have done, I have done in the empress's name and at her command. I don't know who told you it was otherwise . . ."

"They came here looking for you not two days ago. Your own men. If I could have told them where you'd gone, I would have." The words grated against Peshek's skin, all the more painful because his father spoke them. Pachalka's fists opened and closed at his sides, seizing on the empty air and strangling it, over and again.

"What did they tell you?" His lip was thickening and his words slurring, but at least father was talking, not raining down more blows.

"That you left your post and your duty without leave." Which was surely sin enough in the old soldier's eyes, and Pachalka all but spat as he said it. "That you've been carrying messages for a band of traitors in their fine castles who would use the words of this madwoman roaming the countryside saying she's the true empress to throw our rightful ruler down from her throne." His breathing was harsh in the room and Peshek could see nothing of his face but shadows and the firelight gleaming in his eyes, and for that moment he was glad. He did not want to see the fury twisting his father's visage as he looked at his son.

"Honored Father," said Peshek, holding out his open hand. "I swear on my mother's grave that it is not true. It is part of a web of lies being woven over Isavalta by Kacha and his allies here and in Hastinapura. I came here to tell you all. I beg you to hear me."

Pachalka stood like a statue where he was, and for long, agonizing series of heartbeats, Peshek thought his father would call down the servants to hold him fast. But then, Pachalka said softly and sternly, "I am listening."

Peshek could not hold back his sigh of relief. Ignoring the pain in his mouth and the iron taste of blood, Peshek told his father how the empress had come to him in her need and what she had ordered him to do, and how he had done his best although he had agonized over it, but how he had seen where his duty lay, and how she had slipped from his charge, leaving him to spread word of her plight, and of Isavalta's, against her return.

Through it all, his father simply stood where he was. The shadows that veiled his face flickered as the fire danced in the hearth.

"Can you prove what you say?" he asked finally.

For an answer, Peshek untied his sash. With his knife, he

slit the end of the cloth open and then he drew out the folded and wrinkled letter written in the empress's hand, signed and sealed with the soaring eagle that was the imperial crest. He watched as his father unfolded the letter and slowly, carefully read its contents.

At last, Pachalka lifted his eyes from the paper, but did not look at Peshek. Instead, he stared for a long moment into emptiness. Then, with trembling hands, he handed it back to his son. Peshek found he could breathe again. If his father had not believed the letter to be genuine, he would have kept it to be used as evidence against Peshek at the martial tribunal.

His father's hands were still trembling, something, Peshek realized with a shock, he'd never seen before, as Pachalka turned and retreated to the chair he'd occupied when Peshek first came in. A silver mug of something, probably beer, waited on a side table and Pachalka downed its contents in a single draft. When he set it down again, his hands no longer shook.

He turned to face Peshek again, hands and eyes steady and his shoulders straight and square.

"Forgive me, my son. I should have thought better of you."

Peshek shook his head. "There is nothing to forgive, Father. How could you doubt such honorable men? Especially when they told the truth. I did desert my post."

"Will you sit, Peshek?" His father gestured to another chair.

"Gladly, Father." Peshek dropped into the offered seat. In another moment he would have been the one trembling. He had not known he was so tired until this moment.

Pachalka returned to his chair. He was composed, but also more grave.

"I don't know how long I'll be able to shelter you, Peshek," he said, his hand curling into a fist on the arm of his chair. "It is known there is a reward for you, and one of the servants is sure to talk."

"I thought as much." Peshek sighed. "In truth, it was one of the reasons I used the front door. I was hoping, when I've said my piece, you might throw me out that same way."

A knowing gleam lit his father's eye. "And send Kabak to meet you and bring you back in secret."

"As you say, sir."

"And what is this piece you wish to say to me?"

Peshek leaned forward, pitching his voice very low. "The empress will come back. The House Guard must be ready when she does."

Pachalka did not flinch. "But not before."

"Unless other orders come, no."

Silence settled over the room. The fire crackled and sparked in the hearth, but Peshek and his father remained silent, considering strategies, searching for possibilities, divining the difficulties, and there were many.

"You had best go," said Pachalka softly. "It would not do for you to be here too long." He stood. "Ywane will guide you, my son, and after the moon has set, Kabak will meet you by the goose pond."

And I will drag my father into a plot that could mean his death, thought Peshek as he embraced Pachalka, receiving the old man's kiss on his cheek. *And if I did any less, I truly would be guilty of betrayal.*

The house was dark when Ingrid stole back up the path to the front door. Fortunately, there was more than enough moonlight to see by, so she did not have to be bothered with a lantern. As softly as she could, she crept up the stairs to her bedroom, closing the door lightly behind herself.

"Ingrid, are you out of your mind?" came Grace's furious whisper. "Where have you been?"

Ingrid nearly jumped out of her skin. She whirled around to see Grace sitting up in their bed, the covers drawn up around her chin against the chill. Even in the dim silver light, Ingrid could see the anger on her face.

Ingrid put her hand over her heart, as if the pressure could slow its beating. "Grace," she began, hurrying to the bedside so she did not have to speak above a whisper. "I've been to see Avana . . . Avan."

Grace's eyes grew round. "You are out of your mind," she

snapped. "You almost have Papa won over. Are you going to throw it all away now?"

Ingrid lowered herself to sit on the edge of the bed. The springs creaked under her. "Grace, listen to me. I'm going to ask you to believe something very difficult."

"More difficult than a ghost?" asked Grace lightly.

"Yes." She told her sister then, everything that Avanasy had told her. Grace sat as still as a statue, listening.

"You can't mean it," whispered Grace when Ingrid had finally finished. "You can't truly mean to go with him."

Ingrid nodded. "I do." Those two words made it all real, and Ingrid felt an unexpected rush of freedom wash through her. This was her decision. For the first time in her whole life, she had made a choice for herself alone, and it felt . . . fine. "I've promised. I only came back to get some things, and to tell you. You will have to find something to tell Mama and Papa . . ."

"No, Ingrid." Grace seized her hand. "You can't leave me like this."

Ingrid smiled sympathetically at her sister, patting her hand and setting it down on the quilts. "If I married, I would leave you anyway," she said reasonably.

"But not like this. You cannot leave me alone here. What am I going to do without you?"

"I know this is sudden, Grace, and I know it is strange, but I have given Avanasy my promise, and he has given me this." She held out her hand so that Grace could see the ring.

Grace just struck her hand away. "I'm supposed to be the flighty one. I'm the one who is supposed to get into trouble with men, not you, Ingrid. We need you. I need you. Everything will fall apart if you're not here." She wrapped her arms around her knees and looked away, her jaw working back and forth.

Ingrid could not believe what she was hearing. After all this time, after all they had been through together. They were sisters. They had always stood together, against Papa, against everything . . .

"Grace, I thought you would be happy for me."

"How was I supposed to be happy with you running away in the middle of the night and leaving me here?"

"Grace . . ." Ingrid reached for her, but Grace jerked her whole body away.

"You don't even care what they're going to do to me when they wake up and find out you're gone," she muttered.

Which was too much, even if she had upset Grace with the suddenness of her plans. That was just too much. "How can you of all people, after everything that has happened, say I don't care?"

Grace wasn't looking at her. She just stared at the blank, dark wall and snapped, "If you cared, you would persuade this Avan, or Avanasy, whatever he calls himself, to stay here."

Bitter understanding crept into Ingrid's veins. She stood and turned away from her sister, rounding the foot of the bed to the linen press. "I don't have time to sit here and argue with you, Grace." She pulled out a clean sheet and laid it on the foot of the bed. Her clean dress and petticoats came off their hooks, and fresh linens and the thickest wool stockings she owned came out of the dresser drawers.

"I can scream," announced Grace. "I can wake up everybody, and Papa will lock you in here."

Ingrid couldn't bear to look at her sister. "All my life," she said, tying her bundle closed. "All my life, I have looked after you. I have stood between Mama and Papa for you more times that I can count. I have asked for nothing from you until now. Why are you doing this?"

Grace crawled across the bed to Ingrid. She looked like a little child, kneeling there on the covers, wisps of hair coming loose from her fair braids. "Because I can't lose you. Because I don't know how to live without you to lean on."

"Then that is my fault," breathed Ingrid, pressing both hands against her bundle. "And I'm sorry. But I'm going. You're a good girl, Grace. You're smart. You'll manage."

She lifted the bundle up and started for the door, biting her lip hard to keep back the tears. This was not the parting she had wanted from Grace. She had known it would be hard to say good-bye, but this reproach, this bitterness. It was too much, and she had to leave at once.

"Ingrid, I'm seeing things."

Ingrid froze, her hand on the doorknob. "What?"

"I'm seeing things. Since the night with the ghost. I've been seeing things, and I've been having dreams. Sometimes they come true." She paused and her voice dropped even lower. "I saw Leo's accident before it happened. I saw the scythe slip. That's why I was so upset when it happened. I think he . . . I think the ghost did something to me."

Ingrid pivoted on her heel and stared at her sister, who still crouched at the foot of their bed. "Why didn't you tell me this before?"

Grace huddled in on herself again. "I didn't want you to think I was going mad."

"Grace, you should have told me." Ingrid rushed to her and seized her shoulder. She could not help it. She had protected Grace for too many years to stay distant from her at this moment. "We could have asked Avanasy. He would know."

"We can go now. You can tell him . . ."

Ingrid saw the sudden light, the sudden hope that filled Grace's face as she said that, and she realized what was truly happening here. Grace was trying to work on her. Anger sparked inside her. "I don't believe this," she said, pressing her hand against her forehead. "I knew you would say anything to Papa and Mama, but I did not believe you would try this nonsense with me."

"It's the truth. I swear."

"Then it's too late," Ingrid told her. "I'm leaving. Now. This minute." She turned away. She couldn't look at Grace anymore. Not like this. Not with all that was hanging in the air between them.

"They'll never let you in the house again," said Grace desperately.

"Then you'll have to remember me in your prayers, as I'll remember you in mine."

"You promised me, Ingrid." Real anger touched Grace's voice, and it wrung Ingrid's heart. "You promised you would always be here for me."

Now. You must leave now, or you never will. Ingrid gripped her bundle more tightly. "You promised me too," she said without turning around. "You promised me we would always be best friends. This is not how a friend talks."

She left the house without pausing to close the door. Grace would see to it, or she would not. Ingrid ran down the track to the road, dashing the tears from her eyes.

She is only startled. When she has time to think it over, she will regret her words. She truly understands, she just does not want me to go. Later I will find some way to get word to her. Perhaps, when the troubles are over in this Isavalta it will be possible to send for her.

Clutching those thoughts like she clutched her bundle, Ingrid ran through the dying night to the docks.

The light of a single lantern guided her down the pier to Avanasy's boat. Avanasy himself was nothing but a silhouette in the false dawn, crouched on the deck coiling a rope. At the sound of her hurrying footsteps and her ragged breathing, he straightened up. Ingrid saw him fully in the lantern light and froze.

This was not Avan the fisherman who had sat so many evenings at her mother's kitchen table, drinking coffee and passing the time. This was a Cossack, this was a prince. He wore a wide-skirted coat of rich black. Two dozen silver buttons fastened the front of it. Elaborate silver embroidery adorned the high collar and wide cuffs. A cloth of silver sash circled his waist. There must have been a knife belt underneath that, because she could see the sheath with the dagger's handle protruding from the top of the sash. The coat's hems brushed the tops of polished leather boots and worked leather gloves encased his hands. A peaked black cap with yet more silver embroidery covered his hair.

Ingrid stared, and for an awful moment felt every inch the poor, pale, country girl.

But the loving eyes were all Avanasy's, as was the welcoming hand that reached up to help her step into the boat.

"Is all well?" he asked.

"No," she admitted. "I had a scene with Grace. She is angry at me for leaving."

Avanasy touched her shoulder. "I'm sorry."

"So am I." *But I am glad you are not asking if I would rather stay.* Even as she thought that, she knew in her heart they were already well beyond such questions. "Is there a hold? Let me stow my things."

Avanasy nodded toward the hatch. "Take the lamp. I must get us ready to cast off. The men will be coming soon, and we must be away before then."

The men, and Papa with them, if Papa is not already on the way.

She climbed down the stout ladder. Ingrid had lived all her life around boats, and she knew a well-made craft when she saw it. Avanasy's boat was clinker-built, but stout and strong. The cordage, casks and extra canvas were all neatly stowed. The chests from his cabin had been tied into place below one of the two bunks. Ingrid hung the lantern on a peg and stowed her own meager bundle in one of the cabinets built into the bow. This was a boat meant for fairly long journeys. Ingrid closed her mind against the idea of how long a journey she had just embarked on. She reclaimed the lantern and returned to the deck.

Avanasy stood in the bow waiting for her. As she emerged he smiled, but still managed to look grave. "Now there is one last thing I must require of you for this journey."

"And that is?" Ingrid tried to keep her voice light, but was not sure how well she succeeded. This night had already asked a great deal from her, and she was beginning to feel weary with all her trying.

He paused for a moment, as if searching for the right words. "The Land of Death and Spirit is a dangerous place, especially for those with divided souls, those with no magic in them. There are dangerous and jealous powers in that place, and there are some who are just mischievous. They will be attracted by the strength of your soul. They will try to lead you astray. You will see many things which are untrue."

"Then I will have to keep my eyes closed," said Ingrid simply.

Avanasy fumbled for a moment in the pocket of his beautiful black coat. "That will not be enough. They will still find ways to reach you, and I will not be able to protect you, for I must concentrate on keeping us on course." He brought out a small, stoppered vial. "This will send you to sleep. That way, all you encounter will be as dreams, and will have no more power to hurt you than ordinary dreams do."

Ingrid took the bottle from him, pulled out the stopper and inhaled the scent. It was sharp, clean and medicinal, a strong smell of laudanum and alcohol, and things she could not name.

"If that's how it must be." She tucked the vial into the pocket of her skirt. "But let me stay awake as long as possible."

"As long as possible," agreed Avanasy. "Now, we must away."

Avanasy hopped down onto the pier and cast the ropes off. Ingrid coiled then stowed them as he did. They were away. Avanasy climbed back onto the deck, grasped the mainsheet, and raised the canvas. The wind caught the dark sail a moment later, and they were off. Ingrid faced the shore as they pulled away. The docks remained empty and still. Papa had not come to fetch her back; neither had Grace.

Angry, although she could not have clearly said why, Ingrid stalked to the bow and faced the wind. It blew hard and cold in her face, setting her eyes stinging with tears. She welcomed it. This way she would not have to explain why she was crying. Behind her, she heard Avanasy working the ropes. A second sail rose over the first, and below her the deck creaked as they picked up speed.

She would not look back. Sand Island was not her home anymore. She stood steadily on the gently swaying deck and wrapped her arms around herself. She would not look back.

"Ingrid!" called Avanasy over the wind. "I fear it is time."

Ingrid took one last look at the gray waters of Lake Superior, which had cradled her since her birth. Then, she turned on her heel and, with the rocking gait of an experienced sailor, she strode to the stern. Avanasy stood at the tiller, one hand keeping it steady, the other feeling the tension in the mainsheet. She took his face in both hands and kissed him, drinking in the promise as he returned her kiss and embraced her with one arm.

"When you wake, it will be to see the land of my birth," he said.

"I look forward to the sight." Ingrid smiled at him, and went below.

Neither of the bunks seemed to be claimed, so Ingrid sat

herself down on the right-hand bed. She pulled the little bottle from her apron pocket and stared at it for a moment, ashamed of the nervousness that fluttered in her breast.

Then, she pulled out the stopper and swallowed the thick liquid in one draft.

She had time enough to taste sweet honey and strong brandy before a wave of dizziness swept over her. She managed to lie back and swing her legs up, but a second wave overcame her and all the strength left her limbs. She was distantly aware of the clatter as the vial fell from her fingers to the deck, but she could do nothing about it. Sleep already wrapped her in an embrace as warm as any Avanasy could offer and it pulled her close into its comforting darkness.

She lay oblivious for a time. Then, it seemed to her that she sat up, wide awake, although she did not know why.

"Come out," called a stranger's voice. "Come out. You are summoned."

The Land of Death and Spirit bloomed around Avanasy like a dream. Lake Superior and its wide gray waters were gone without a trace. Instead, he sailed up a broad brown river. The sails bellied full in a wind his skin did not feel. No sound came from his boat's timbers, nor did any come from the flowing waters, or the dark pines that towered on the mossy banks. These were the Silent Lands, the Shifting Lands, the homes of ghosts, the unborn, the never born, and the eternal. No sorcerer crossed them in the flesh unless he was desperate. No sorcerer carried an unprotected, ordinary human through them unless they were insane.

Avanasy could not afford to think of that now. He had to keep all his mind fixed on his destination. In the mortal world, a sorcerer had to reach for their magic and use their will to shape it. Here, the magic reached for the sorcerer and tried to shape him. Here, the need was to hold one's soul steady, to be a rock in the stream of the Shifting Lands. A divided soul would feel the yearning, lonely tug of the half of itself that resided here and would travel far to ease that ache.

Small memories, his master had told him. *It is the tiniest, most intimate details of life that will make the links in the chain to pull you through the Silent Lands.*

So, Avanasy remembered. He remembered the smell of the coal fire in his master Valerii's house late at night as Avanasy took down his instruction in the great vellum book. He remembered the taste of broth and dumplings in winter when he was a boy and had come back in from helping his father supervise the brewing sheds, and how the warmth of the good soup could be felt through and through. He remembered the day the *zhagravor*, the telling sorcerer, had wrapped the red sash around his waist and looked hard in his eyes and declared him sorcerer.

He remembered walking into the great hall at Vyshtavos, and how the keeper of the emperor's god house had barred his way, ceremonially challenging him, until Master Valerii gave his name and the keeper stood aside so that Avanasy might kneel before the emperor and hear his charge.

"The high princess, my beloved daughter Medeoan Edemshoidoch Nacheradavosh, has been declared sorcerer. It is my express wish that she be trained in arts magical and the meaning of sorcery. Your master, Valerii Adrisyn Rhasovin, has said you are most suited to this charge. Will you accept the task?"

Protocol forbid him to look up at the monarch's face until invited to stand and give counsel, so he gave his promise to the blue-and-gold carpeting and the tips of the emperor's black velvet slippers. He remembered how his heart sang as he spoke of his loyalty and honor.

He remembered Medeoan as he first saw her. Twelve years old, pale-skinned and pale-haired, with too little flesh for her rapidly growing frame. "Pinched" was the unflattering word that first came to his mind. She stood in the middle of the schoolroom flanked by her graceful music tutor and fat mathematics tutor. He had time enough to see that much before he had to kneel and study the parquet floor. He remembered the patterns of pale stars laid out in the darker wood. He had a long time to become familiar with them before she bid him stand.

But then came the summer days in the gardens, and the winters by the fire, and discovering Medeoan's voracious mind and troubled heart. Hours in the Red Library poring over the volumes kept there, increasing his own knowledge and opening his mind to the vastness of the world's possibilities that even his master could not teach him.

Memory on top of memory, long locked in the back of his own mind, all tumbling out in a flood, creating a current to draw them forward into Isavalta. He held his hand on the tiller to steady himself, but the tiller had no force in this river. There was only his heart and his concentration now, but after all those long months in a world where the magic was so stifled, even this amount of work felt like freedom.

Movement caught his eye, and despite Avanasy's deep concentration, his gaze flickered momentarily, and he saw Ingrid climb out of the hold.

"What!" he exclaimed, and his hold on the course and memory loosened dangerously.

Ingrid did not even pause at the sound of his voice. She continued across the deck with a slow, steady motion that was almost a glide.

"Ingrid!" Avanasy called desperately and he reached out as she passed him, unblinking. He saw his hand touch the cloth of her sleeve, but he felt nothing, nothing at all.

Illusion? Spirit? Avanasy's mind reeled, and he felt his hold on the course slip that much further.

Ingrid, or the seeming of Ingrid, did not pause when she reached the rail. She continued on, her stride unbroken, and then she was on the bank.

Avanasy could not believe what he was seeing. This must be a trick. Some fey spirit was trying to throw them off, trap them forever here in the Land of Death and Spirit. But as Ingrid vanished into the pine forest, his heart constricted, and he knew he could not hold his mind to the task without certainty.

He had to hurry, before his hold was gone, before he was awash in the unbroken and shifting sea that was the world around him.

Steeling himself, Avanasy lifted his hand from the tiller.

Remember Isavalta, he told himself as he crossed the deck. *Remember the hours at the loom weaving these sails. Remember how the threads cut even your toughened fingers.*

Remember the touch of the cotton dust in your throat. Remember.

He started down the ladder. The boat rocked under him, gliding forward still on the current of his thoughts.

Remember the summer day you spent painting this boat. Remember how the sun beat down on your back and the strong smell of the paints in the heat. Remember how tired you were when you were done, but how proud. Your masterpiece. Remember how Master Valerii smiled and clapped you on the shoulder and you knew you'd done well.

It took a moment for his eyes to adjust to the gloom of the hold, but when they did, he saw Ingrid lying still in her bunk and he wanted to shout with relief. He had almost been taken in by an illusion of the Silent Lands, but there she was, safe and whole.

Safe yes, but whole? nagged a little voice in the back of his head. *Are you certain?*

But how could she be otherwise? She had a divided soul. She was safely anchored, one foot in the mortal world and one in the Silent Lands. Asleep as she was, her spirit could not be moved. That was the law.

Despite this, Avanasy moved forward. He had to be sure. He could take no chances with Ingrid. In this place, she depended utterly on him.

Remember the first day in Master Valerii's house. Remember how you started at shadows, your boy's head filled with thoughts of ghosts and house goblins. Remember how you were so afraid to open the big cupboard in the attic, and when you did you found it full of nothing more terrifying than the winter's linens . . .

Avanasy reached for Ingrid's hand, and found it cold. Fear rooted him to the deck. She breathed, he could see the rise and fall of her chest clearly, but she had gone cold as a corpse, and her sun-browned cheeks had lost all their color. Her white skin seemed to glow in the darkness.

She was not dead, but nor was she alive. Her vitality, her spirit, against all he knew to be possible, was gone, and he had seen it walk into the Land of Death and Spirit.

How? he wanted to howl. *How has this happened? Who has done this to you?*

No. No. He must stop. He must think, he must remember. He must hold their course, and he must let go. It was too much. Avanasy threw his head back, his jaw and fists clenched to hold in his screams, to try to keep his thoughts together.

He must find her. She would die left like this. He must follow her spirit somehow. There must be a way.

Must be a way. Remember. Remember. Remember Isavalta. Ah, gods, gods, Ingrid, what have I brought you to? Stop. Remember. Remember your master's house. Remember his teaching, remember your study. It is all you both have now. Remember . . .

He had it. The ring. His promise given to her. He could follow that through the shifting lands. It would be a thin thread, but it would be enough. It would have to be.

His grip on his memories slid away just thinking about it. Too much to concentrate on. He could not guide the boat and walk the Silent Lands at the same time. He would have to let the boat slide into the mortal world, and it would have to take their bodies with it while their spirits both walked.

It was a grave risk. They could be so easily led astray. Ingrid might already be beyond him, in the grip of whatever great power could hail a divided soul from its body.

No. No, he could not believe that. There would still be something he could do. Some way to save her.

But even as he thought that, he felt his hold on the boat loosen yet further. The air around him seem to thicken and grow warm, turning into a comfortable blanket into which it would be so easy to fall, fall and sleep, and let what would come bring itself and never worry about any of it . . .

Clamping down hard on his feelings, Avanasy pulled the ring from Ingrid's cold, unresisting hand. Then, as quickly as he could, Avanasy climbed the ladder and crossed the deck to the tiller.

Remember. Remember Medeoan's wedding, if you can remember nothing else. Remember the touch of the door under your hands. Remember the anger. Remember how you prayed.

Keeping tight rein on his thoughts, Avanasy sliced a length

of rope from one of the coils. He wound it around his left wrist, and bound his wrist to the tiller.

Remember how Medeoan's eyes blazed when she spoke the words of banishment. Remember how Kacha stood beside her, and how coldly he smiled. Remember the triumph you saw glittering in his unmatched eyes.

He pulled the knot closed as tightly as he could with his one free hand. Then, he laid his iron-bladed knife aside. He could not hold such a thing and do what he must. Instead, he clasped Ingrid's ring.

Avanasy closed his eyes and willed himself to relax. He let the warm vapors of the Shifting Land enfold him. He abandoned will and memory, fear and anger. He must be a feather in the wind now. He must be light and air. No part of earth must he be. He must be free, a shadow, a thought, a dream, nothing at all.

Although he did not open his eyes, still Avanasy saw. He saw the wide brown river. He saw the small red boat with its white sails bellied in a wind he could not feel sailing with the current. He saw himself slumped over the tiller, but only for a moment. Boat and abandoned body vanished like mist at the touch of the sun. Back to Isavalta, if all was well, to drift upon the ocean, until he could make his way back.

Until we can make our way back, he told himself firmly.

He opened his shadow of a hand and in it found the memory of a ring. He let himself go further yet, unbound spirit, dream, vapor that he was, and he began to drift. Now it was the ring that provided the current. The ring would search out its mirror self in the Shifting Lands. The ring, his promise, would bring him to Ingrid.

All around Avanasy, the lands swayed and blurred. He had no true eyes to close in this form, but still, all turned to darkness, and he felt himself begin to fall.

Ingrid stepped onto the shore. All her clothing was perfectly dry. She did not remember having left the boat. She looked back, but all she saw behind her were the dark trunks of pine trees.

It's only a dream, she told herself. *There's nothing to fear.*

In the manner of dreams, Ingrid seemed to know exactly where she needed to go. She felt as if there were an invisible string tied to her waist and pulling her easily forward through the dark, pine woods. Her feet made no sound as she walked over moss and fallen needles. She could not see sun or sky. She cast no shadow before or behind her. But none of that worried her. She knew which way she must go, and she was content to walk until she found her destination.

Ingrid did not know how long it was before the woods opened before her. She stepped easily from the thick forest into an open meadow lit by a pale, green light for which she could discern no source. The grass bent and waved in a wind she could not feel, but it made no noise at all as it moved. A round green hill rose before her like a bubble from a pot of boiling water. On top of the hill stood a bright red fox.

Ingrid hesitated. She had seen no other living creature since she had entered the wood. Her way, however, lay past the hill. She knew that, as she knew she must continue walking. She could not linger here. She turned from the hill and started toward the woods again.

But the fox was in front of her, and it was enormous.

Ingrid stopped short. Her heart thumped once. She distantly knew she was afraid, but she could do nothing. The fox stood before her, its head level with her own, its ears pricked up and alert, its whiskers twitching interestedly.

"Well now," it said. "What have we here?"

The sound of the fox's voice sent a cold thrill through her, as if it were a knife blade that touched her bare skin. She was still pulled forward, but at the same time she was rooted to the spot.

"I said." The fox's, the Vixen's, tail swished back and forth. "What have we here?"

"I . . . I don't know," stammered Ingrid. "I . . . I'm supposed to go that way." She waved tremulously in the direction she was pulled. Without sun, without shadow, she had no way to give the direction a name. The pull, though, was becoming more insistent, almost a pain.

"Yes." The Vixen narrowed her green eyes. "Yes, you are. But, perhaps I should not let you pass." The Vixen whisked around Ingrid, more like a great cat than a fox. "Perhaps I should keep you for myself." She paused a moment, considering. "But no. Then I would never know what she meant to do with you herself, you see. The Old Witch has hidden in her house for so long, none understand it. She has so many to serve her, what needs she with one more? What can you do that they cannot?" The Vixen lifted her muzzle, gazing closely at Ingrid's eyes, and Ingrid felt herself begin to tremble although she did not know why. "Your eyes are sharp, but how sharp? Your sight may be your trouble, always showing you what you should not see." She stepped away, contemplating Ingrid now with a sort of cool disinterest. "Such eyes can plague a family down the generations. Such eyes can ruin kings and yet save kingdoms." The Vixen sat back, her mouth hanging open so that she appeared to be laughing. "But then, greed was ever a part of her nature. She may want you simply because she wants. Yes, I'm minded to let you go about her business for now, little woman. Perhaps she thinks you can bring back what she's lost."

The Vixen was gone, as suddenly as she appeared, and Ingrid was alone in the meadow under the pale green light, utterly bewildered, except for the pulling that led her down a path she could not measure toward an end she could not guess.

It is a dream. I was promised. It is only a dream.

Because she could no longer bear to stand still, Ingrid continued on into the dark trees again. The woods continued on for some time. Ingrid could not even feel the ground beneath her feet now. She might as well have been standing still while the woods flowed about her.

But slowly, gradually, the trees began to change. Maples and oaks intruded on the pines. A small creek ran silently between mossy banks. Ingrid stepped across it. On the other side, a birch tree pulled its branches back to let her pass. As it did, Ingrid saw a house swim into her vision as if from a fog.

It was a low, thatched building of gray stone. It looked as if it could be a cliff side, formed by wind and weather wearing away the soil rather than an edifice built by human hands. A low stone fence surrounded it, and a winding stone path led to its low door.

There was nothing in the least alarming about the place. It was an old homestead, well tended and sturdy. Yet, Ingrid found herself hesitating beside the gate. The pull had released her. She was where she was supposed to be.

"Ingrid," said a voice within the dark doorway. It was the same voice that had called her from the boat. "Come in to me."

Ingrid did not even think to disobey. She stepped across the threshold, and was suddenly dizzy, as if she had been swept up and carried some distance.

The inside of the cottage was as neat, and as solid, as the outside. The dim light that filtered through the doorway gave Ingrid the impression of heavy furniture carved of dark wood, a stone hearth without a fire, a broom, a dirt floor and, in the far corner, an angular shadow that it took a moment for Ingrid to realize was a loom.

A shadow emerged from the darkness of the cottage and stepped into the square of pale, green light that fell through the cottage's single window. Dizziness took hold of Ingrid again, but it cleared swiftly and she saw the shadow had become a tall, slender woman. Years had etched themselves into her face, but each line held both beauty and strength. Her eyes were clear and filled with purpose. A waterfall of white hair, unbound like a girl's, hung down past her shoulders. She wore a simple black dress and held her capable hands folded neatly over a white apron.

Ingrid had never known either of her grandmothers, but what she felt now was a mix of longing and comfortable love that surely must be what she would have felt for them.

"You are a good child," said the woman, nodding her approval. Her voice was melodious, nothing at all like the wild voice of the Vixen.

"Who are you?" asked Ingrid, her voice faltering. It seemed strange to speak after so much silence, and she sounded so clumsy to herself.

"I am grandmother and I am crone," said the old woman. "I am the one who sent for you and the one whom you heeded."

"Yes," said Ingrid, although she did not know why. Had

she truly been expecting a name? That seemed presumptuous somehow.

"I called you here because I have a task that needs doing. I need you to hear me and to complete it."

Ingrid hesitated. She yearned to do as she was told. She felt the gentle authority of this woman and, again like a child, she wished for her approval.

It's only a dream, she told herself. *What's wrong with giving a promise in a dream?*

"Ingrid."

Ingrid turned to the window. Avanasy stood in the yard. The world seemed to ripple unpleasantly where he stood. The neat fence was at the same time pickets and bones. The gray stones were simultaneously skulls. The house rocked where it stood.

"Ingrid!" he called again. "Come out to me!"

"Granddaughter, stay yet awhile," said the woman behind her. "Let the man cool his ardor for you while you attend your elders, as you should."

"Yes, Grandmother." But Ingrid's words had no force. Even as she spoke them, she felt herself drifting toward the door. The floor shifted and shuddered under her feet. Bones, she thought again. Why were there bones in the roof beams and bones underfoot? She could not see them, but she knew they were there.

"Ingrid!" called Avanasy again.

"Bind you by the threshold, bind you by the word," said the old woman behind her. "Bind you by your promise to me."

"But there was no promise," said Ingrid vaguely, and the door fell open in front of her.

The house seemed to have grown stilts, for now she looked down a long stair at Avanasy.

He seemed insubstantial, somehow, as if he were nothing more than a shadow among shadows. Yet, she felt drawn to him, as she had been drawn to this house.

"Come away, Ingrid." He held out his hand, beseeching. "Come to me."

"I will," she assured him. "But there is an old woman inside who needs my help."

"No, Ingrid, she means to harm you." Why could she not see clearly? This place had seemed so solid, such a part of the earth. Now it rocked under her like a restless boat, and all that was dark seemed to be bleached and white.

"How can she hurt me? This is only a dream. You told me so."

Distress creased Avanasy's face. "I was wrong."

"Only a dream, Granddaughter," said the old woman. "Say you will help me and you will soon wake to your lover."

"No!" cried Avanasy, starting forward. He stopped short, as if something blocked his way. "Ingrid, promise her nothing until she tells you her name."

"Name?" The world swam again. Avanasy drew further away, although he did not move. The doorway tipped and tilted, and Ingrid gripped the frame to steady herself, but the rocking would not cease.

"You go too far, sorcerer," said the old woman behind her, her voice suddenly stern and hard as stone, as bone. "Leave her now and you will have her again when I am finished."

"She has not told you her name, has she?" said Avanasy doggedly, oblivious to the distress he caused. "Shall I tell you what it is?"

"Take care, sorcerer." The Grandmother's voice grew shrill and strange, and Ingrid shivered to hear it. "Your flesh and your iron are far away. You may be compelled to stay here."

"Then you will deal with me, Baba Yaga."

At those words, the world split in two. The stone house and its gardens fell away on either side of Ingrid, leaving behind a room built of bones. Skulls and skeletons of a hundred different animals hung from rafter beams that curved like gigantic ribs. Human skulls framed the fireplace, gaping and grinning. Even the loom in the corner was built of the gruesome ivory. Where the Grandmother had stood so tall and strong now hunched a withered crone who was little more than a skeleton herself under her tattered black robe. Her lips drew back in a grimace of anger, exposing teeth of black iron, and she leaned on a stained and begrimed pestle.

Ingrid opened her mouth to scream but no sound came.

Baba Yaga pointed one bony finger at her, and Ingrid felt the touch of it as if it pressed against her heart.

"Ingrid! Come to me!" cried Avanasy. "Wish it so! Ingrid!"

Ingrid backed away even as Baba Yaga's hand curled shut. Ingrid knew the ancient witch meant to cradle her heart in that hand. As impossible as that was, it was also true, and fervently, desperately, she wished she was on Avanasy's boat, standing beside him, looking out across the banks.

And she knew the way. She felt it in her fingertips, a faint but certain tugging, and all she had to do was follow. Now she cried out as she turned and ran, and in a minute she was flying. All the world around her was a blur of blacks, browns and greens. She felt a pain in her side as if claws raked her, but it was brief, and she ran on, flying and running all at once.

And she saw herself, lying limp and corpse white in the little wooden bunk, and then there was darkness, and then she opened her eyes.

The boat rocked hard underneath her and, for a dizzying moment, Ingrid thought she was still in the bone-framed house. But her hand gripped honest wood on the side of her bunk. Her stomach heaved hard with the motion of the vessel for the first time since she was a tiny child, and she had to swallow hard to keep it from spilling out.

What happened? Strange dreams. No, not dreams. Avanasy.

That thought rallied her sea legs and Ingrid threw back the blanket and ran to the ladder. Brisk wind smacked her face as soon as she emerged onto the deck. She had the vague impression of an iron-gray sea and a horizon that might have been the hazy coast or a bank of clouds.

Avanasy slouched beside the rudder, slack-jawed and staring. Ingrid hurried to his side and saw the cord binding his hand to the tiller.

"Avanasy?" she called, but his eyes did not blink. She reached immediately for the cord, but hesitated. What if this was one of his spells? What would happen to him if she broke it? He had saved her from the bony-legged witch, whether that had been a strange dream or a stranger reality, but what would she do if she now had to save him?

Ingrid sat back on her heels. Only the rise and fall of Avanasy's chest told her he still lived. She could not hear his breathing over the sounds of the wind and water. She brushed back her hair where it whipped into her face. The wind was rising. The ropes creaked.

That she could do. She could trim the sails. She could keep the boat upright. She could pray.

The rigging was unfamiliar to her, but it was all neatly done, and it did not take her much looking to understand how the lines ran. She left the mainsail alone, but brought in the stemsail, lashing it tightly. The horizon had darkened. There was land out there, growing closer. That meant shoals, and coves and currents, none of which she knew. Ingrid bit her lip.

Here I am in this new world, and I am useless. Tears stung her eyes. *What do I do, Avanasy?*

She yearned hard for her answer, and in response came an unaccountable sensation of floating, of drifting far too free, like a boat without mooring. There was danger in this, she knew that too, but still she reached. There was so much out there, the answers, Avanasy.

No, Ingrid.

Ingrid's eyes snapped open. She had not even realized she had closed them. She had leaned out over the gunwale, and she did not remember that either.

Had that been Avanasy? Or the wind? What was happening?

She wanted to reach out again, but realized that in another moment she would have fallen right over the side.

She remembered the last time she had seen Avanasy so incapacitated. He'd asked her to sit by him, to sing, to bring him back into the world.

Ingrid pushed aside all thought of feeling foolish and steeled herself. She put her arms around him, laying her hands over his slack hands.

> *"Here I sit on Buttermilk hill*
> *Who could blame me cry my fill?*

> *Every tear would turn a mill,*
> *Johnny's gone for a soldier . . ."*

She sang of loss, and of sorrow, of a woman who had given everything and was left alone, and she felt whole, rooted impossibly through the deck to the surging ocean, and she felt Avanasy stir.

> *"Oh my baby, oh my love,*
> *Gone the rainbow, gone the dove,*
> *Your father was my only love . . ."*

"Ah!" Avanasy cried out. His head snapped up and for a terrible instant his whole body went rigid with pain. His spasm swung the tiller wildly and Ingrid tightened her hands over his automatically to bring it around again.

Avanasy cried out again, but Ingrid could make nothing of his words. She could only hold him close. In a moment he subsided, and blinked slowly.

"Ingrid?"

She opened her mouth to answer him, but before she could speak, he seized her face with his free hand, bringing her forward to kiss her hard and desperately on the mouth.

"I'm sorry," he whispered as he released her. "I'm so sorry, Ingrid. I didn't know."

"Know what, Avanasy? What happened?"

"I can't tell you. Not yet. We need earth and stone under us for those words, not shifting water."

"What . . ."

"Trust me in this, Ingrid. Please."

Ingrid closed her mouth, her spine stiffening. Avanasy did not look at her. He instead lifted his knife from where it lay and cut himself free. In another moment, he was busy with line, canvas and tiller. Ingrid sat on the stern bench, scant inches from him, but she felt as if she were suddenly miles away.

The wind blew through her shawl and dress, and she shivered from the cold. She did not clearly know what had happened, but this much she did know. In the space of this moment, all had somehow changed.

The house of bones that bore the name Ishbushka turned on its great, scarred legs. Its windows opened like blank and bleary eyes on the shifting world around it. Beyond the ragged fence of bones that marked its territory, the Vixen sat on her haunches and watched.

"So, you will send another to do your work for you?" The Vixen's tail swished back and forth. She spoke softly, but she knew Ishbushka's mistress heard every word. "She is an unnatural thing, to be sure, but did you really think you could hide her from me?"

The house stopped its restless motion and bent its monstrous legs to kneel on the ground. The rotted door fell open toward the Vixen, who did not even blink. In the doorway stood Baba Yaga, leaning on her pestle, her tattered black robes clinging to her bony frame.

"You have stolen what is mine," rasped the Old Witch. "I will have it back."

The Vixen yawned. "Prove that I have stolen it then. Call me out according to the law." She let her mouth hang open in a wide grin. "But then, you would have to leave your house, wouldn't you?"

Baba Yaga bared her iron teeth. "You think you've won this game. You do not even see the next move, let alone the end of it. You have no idea how far my power reaches."

"At the moment, I'd say it reaches to the edge of your charming yard." The Vixen flicked her tail again. "As I'm sitting here quite undisturbed."

"Think that, then," sneered Baba Yaga. "You've thought many a more foolish thing."

Ishbushka's door shut and the house heaved itself back to its taloned feet to resume its alert and watchful turning. The Vixen gazed at it awhile longer, her own lips drawn back to show just a gleam of her sharp, yellow teeth.

You think I do not see the end of this? she thought. *Are you certain you know which game I am playing?*

And she was gone.

Chapter Ten

Avanasy would not look at her.

For her own part, Ingrid found herself remaining determinedly silent. She wrapped her arms around herself and concentrated on the approaching shoreline. It was a rocky coast, as gray as the ocean and about as inviting. A thin border of stunted and twisted trees surmounted the cliffs. As they sailed closer, Ingrid could see the shore was ragged, with countless tiny coves and points. An excellent place for catching shellfish, or for smuggling, but an awful place for boats.

Still, Avanasy seemed to know the shore well. He adjusted the sails with precision for the erratic wind and was an expert hand with the tiller. No wonder Papa had found him such a good sailor, if these were the waters he learned on.

But he still would not look at her.

The land curved around to the port side. Gradually, Ingrid saw that one of the broader cliffs was topped with a mass of stone that had a more regular shape than the tumbled boulders they had been seeing. It was a fortress, squat and massive, with fat turrets obviously meant for keeping watch over the ocean.

"That is Fortress Dalemar," said Avanasy, shouting to be heard over the wind of the water. "When we have landed, I hope to gain us news from there."

Ingrid did not answer him, and she found herself wondering what reason there could be for her own black mood. A whole new world spread out before her. Avanasy sat beside her and she once again wore his ring on her finger. Whatever had happened during their strange crossing, it was over. They were safe on a sea that was obviously familiar to Avanasy, who was an excellent sailor. He had promised her an explanation soon enough. Where was her patience? What was the matter with her?

The truth was, she felt torn. Not between excitement and fear, or any other two emotions she could name. Rather, she felt as if some physical force was literally tugging at her insides, separating out some vitality from the core of her, and it was wrong, this feeling. She knew it. Yet, who was she to say that it was not just the sensation of being taken to a new world? There was no way to tell, until she could ask Avanasy, and Avanasy would not answer until they reached land, and he showed no signs of steering them to harbor just yet.

They sailed around another sharp point, close enough for Ingrid to see the breakers rolling against the rocky beach. In the tiny cove sheltered by the point worked a cluster of people. Some sorted through heaps of seaweed, some cast nets into pools, confirming her thoughts about shellfish. The workers all straightened up as the boat came into view, raising their hands.

"Do they know you?" asked Ingrid.

"I hope not," answered Avanasy. "It is custom, and good luck, to bless any sail that is sighted."

"Ah."

They lapsed into silence again.

At last, Avanasy sailed them through a channel between the rocky shore and, judging from the way the waves broke against them, what must have been some ragged shallows. The cove here was wider than the other, and some sand actually showed between the stones, but the cliffs behind it were high and unbroken, and the way in was narrow. The piles of seaweed on the beach told Ingrid that this was low tide. Yet, this inviting cove was deserted, probably because of the risky entry.

Avanasy sailed them up close to the shore, and finally tossed out the anchor. Without being asked, Ingrid took in the mainsail and lashed it down. Avanasy climbed out into the shallows and gave her his hand. Ingrid pulled off shoes and stockings, knotted the laces so they could be slung about her neck, stuffed the stockings into the shoes, hiked her skirts up around her knees and took his hand. Together they waded to shore.

"I am sorry this is all the welcome I can give you to my home," said Avanasy.

Ingrid looked about her. Now at least somewhat sheltered from the driving wind, Ingrid felt the warm sun on her face and shoulders. Seabirds wheeled overhead, giving calls to each other that were as familiar to her as the feel of the sand under her boots and the bright summer blue of the sky overhead. Unaccountably, the feeling of being pulled apart vanished, and Ingrid found herself able to smile.

"I like the view," she said. "But I believe you must speak to your carpenter about that draft."

Solemnly, Avanasy bowed to her, stretching out one leg and folding his hands over his breast. "As my lady wishes."

They laughed together then, and that laugh was as welcome as the warmth of the sun on her shoulders.

"Can you tell me what happened now?" she asked.

Avanasy sighed and rested his foot against a stone. "Yes, and no."

Ingrid swallowed another burst of impatience. "How is that?"

He stared over the gray waters for a moment, ordering his thoughts. "One of the dangers of the passage through the Land of Death and Spirit is that the powers that live there may take . . . notice. They may have use for mortal life, or they may simply desire trouble or blessing. I had thought, asleep as you were, you were safe from interference. A sleeping mind moves more swiftly and more lightly than a waking one, and is far less likely to be noticed, or to be of interest if it is noticed." He ran one hand through his dark gold hair. "But perhaps you did not sleep deeply enough, or, perhaps the Old Witch was looking for someone . . ." He shook his head, anger creasing his brow. "I cannot say more clearly, and I wish I could. Whatever the case, she was able to lure you from the safety of the boat." His frown grew sharper. "What I do not understand is how she was able to make you walk as spirit. She should not have been able to separate soul from flesh."

"I should hope not," said Ingrid, growing chill despite the warm sun.

"There exists natural law, even in the Silent Lands. There are things which cannot be done."

"And you know all those laws?"

"No, Ingrid. I don't."

"Ah."

He knelt in front of her, taking her left hand in his. "Should I have turned you away, Ingrid? Left you on the shores of your own world?"

She touched his lovely cheek. "No. I would not have let you in any case." She squared her shoulders. "Assuming there is no more immediate danger from that witch, what do we do now?"

"We secure the boat more firmly and walk to the nearest village. There I should be able to barter for news from the fortress. I may even still have friends there."

"A sensible plan," said Ingrid, getting to her feet. "Shall we begin?"

"You are not tired? Or hungry?"

"No. I feel remarkably well."

Again, Avanasy frowned.

"I should not feel so well, should I?"

"In truth, Ingrid, I do not know."

His words sent a thrill of fear through Ingrid, but she pushed it aside. What would come would come. She was past caution now. Her decision had been made back on Sand Island, a whole wide world away.

So, Ingrid knotted her skirts into her waistband and together they returned to the boat, unshipped the mast, gathered their belongings, such as they were, into bundles that could be slung over their shoulders. Finally, they drew a canvas over the hatch. As he tightened the lashings, Avanasy breathed out some words Ingrid could not understand and spat on the last knot. For a moment, he closed his eyes, and Ingrid saw a look of peace steal over him. When he opened his eyes and saw her staring, he actually blushed.

"It has been a long time since magic came easily to me," he said by way of explanation. "There is . . . joy in it."

"You did . . . you made a spell, just then?"

He nodded. "A small protection on the boat. Nothing complex or truly secure. We do not have the time. But if the boat is meddled with in any way, I will know."

Remember the ghost, said Ingrid, as she felt her face wrinkle. *Remember all you have seen.*

"You want to know if there is truth in what I say. Despite all, you cannot quite believe that it is magic which you have seen."

"I'm sorry, Avanasy."

"There is no need. For all you know this is dreams and superstition, and the habits of a lifetime are hard to loosen. But I may give you proof yet, as soon as we are back on shore."

Once more they clambered over the side and splashed through the chilly ocean waters to the shore. Ingrid put down her things so she could wring out her hems. She glanced up and saw the sun was high in the sky. She hoped it would give enough warmth to dry out her skirts, or she would be far too cold, far too quickly.

While Ingrid drew her shoes and stockings back on, Avanasy set his pack on a stone and from it brought out a strip of brightly braided cloth.

"I made this when I reached Sand Island, and kept it afterward, because the making was so hard." He ran the braid through his fingers. "With it, I can grant you an understanding of the language of Isavalta."

"What will you need to do?"

"Give me your hand, and I will show you."

So, Ingrid held out her hand, and Avanasy began to speak. His words were rhythmic and rich, all clipped, hard consonants and round vowels. The sound of the chant made Ingrid feel absolutely still inside. Still chanting, Avanasy wrapped the end of the braid around her right wrist, once, twice, three times. Then, he wrapped the other around his own wrist. His voice reached into her, and through her, it pulled her close, even as his hand pulled her close, and yet at the same time left her feeling incredibly distant.

Then, he kissed her full and openly on the mouth. For a startling moment, she felt his warm breath filling her lungs.

In the next moment, he released her and stepped back. Ingrid pressed her hand hard against her chest.

"How does my lady?"

"Well, I thank you." Her hand flew to her mouth. Those syllables that had tumbled out of her bore no relation to English. They were, well, they were all hard consonants and round vowels.

She stared at him, both amazed and a little frightened.

"Can I still speak . . ."

"As surely as I can speak both languages," he said, this time in English.

"That's a mercy," she said, and then hastened to reassure him. "Not that I thought you had taken anything from me . . ." She hesitated. "I am simply not used . . ."

But Avanasy only smiled and shook his head. "Give yourself time, Ingrid. I must ask for time as well. I have worked very hard to put my old life behind me." He looked ruefully down at the embroidered cuff of his black coat. "I will need time to find my way again."

Ingrid took his arm. "Then we will find it together."

He smiled the bright smile that she had come to love, and arm in arm they began to pick their way up the rocky beach. Their wet boots skidded and tripped over the round stones, but they only laughed and clung more tightly to each other for balance. Ingrid felt an unfamiliar warmth creep over her. She had not realized it could be enough to just *be* with Avanasy; that love could, for a time, be satisfied by simply being in the presence of the one who was beloved. Every lover, she supposed, found out this truth, and every lover, she supposed, found it a great surprise.

Eventually, the cliffs broke, and Ingrid could see that someone had wedged stones and branches in the break to make a kind of rough trail leading upward. Despite this, it was still a scramble to reach the top. When they emerged again onto level ground, Ingrid was breathless, soaked with perspiration and salt spray, and her back had begun to ache.

Without the cliffs, the world opened around her, an undulating plain under the misty bowl of the sky. A single crabbed and crooked tree stood sentry on the cliffs' edge. The land around them was covered with thin grasses and dotted here and there with bright red flowers. At their feet, a faint track wound through the grass toward a series of shadowed mounds that Ingrid took to be some sort of village. Toward the right, she saw a dark rise that looked like a distant forest. To the left, she thought she could just barely make out the outlines of the fortress they had seen from the sea.

Avanasy inhaled the salt-scented air deeply. Then, he bent and plucked up one of the blossoms and presented it to Ingrid with a courtly bow.

"It is called heartsfoil," he said as she took it. "It is said to awaken passion." Now his smile reminded her of all that they had not yet done, and she felt a different warmth grow inside her.

Without a word, Ingrid tucked the blossom behind her ear and took his arm again. Together, they started down the track, their gaits easy and long, despite their recent climb. It felt good to be in the open air and on level ground again.

Might as well be on our way back from a picnic, thought Ingrid absurdly.

But the thought gave her a moment's pause. "Isn't it a risk to travel this openly? You said you were an exile."

Avanasy scanned the land around them as well, picking out landmarks he recognized, Ingrid supposed, and regaining a feel for the place. The ceaseless breeze blew his hair back from his brow. "It is, but it is less of a risk than acting furtively, and I have the best disguise I might at this time."

"What is that?"

"You, Ingrid." He rubbed her hand where it lay in the crook of his arm. "If any are watching for my return, they will be watching for a single traveler."

"Ah, so that's why you brought me." Ingrid pushed her lip out into a pout. "And here I'm thinking it's my feminine wiles."

"My grasp of your language is not complete," Avanasy said with an air of complete sobriety. "I believe you will have to explain that phrase to me."

Ingrid tossed her hair back. "Ha! You wish that I would."

"I do."

They laughed again. Ingrid felt light, and free, traveling a strange track in a strange country with a man she knew so little of, and yet it was a marvel, all of it. For the first time in her life, she was not watched. Neither Mama nor Papa could catch word of what she did. There would be no shouts, no tears, no dreaded guilt and threats of blows. There was only the wind and the cries of seabirds in the distance. Her family was, quite literally, a world away, and she was free to do exactly as she would. She did not even have to think of looking after Grace, although thoughts of Grace stirred some of the old guilt that lay slumbering in the back of her mind.

Still, something pricked at her.

"Avanasy? This village, will there . . . will there be someone, a minister, or a magistrate, or some such . . ."

"To marry us?" he finished for her.

Ingrid nodded, blushing furiously. "It's a fool thing to bring up now, I know, but, I, you promised, and I trust you, of course, but I . . ."

He squeezed her arm gently. "The village will have a god house, and the house will have a keeper. The keeper will be able to see us married."

"I know it must seem ludicrous to you, Avanasy. I've come this far, but . . ."

"It is my wish to take you to wife, Ingrid, before man and the gods, and the law as well. I wish there to be no bar between us. Not ever."

"I don't think there ever could be."

Silence seemed enough after that.

The village that was their destination approached only slowly. By the time they reached it, Ingrid's skirt had dried itself completely and fresh perspiration trickled down her back. She began to hope sincerely that a long, cool drink of fresh water would be available when they found human company again.

A wall of stone screened the settlement from the ceaseless winds that scoured the grasslands. No guard kept the gate, however, and they were able to pass through without impediment. Ingrid felt suddenly nervous, and she had to stop herself from pulling closer to Avanasy. This would be, after all, her first meeting with other people in this strange land, and she had no idea what would be considered polite. The fear of making herself or Avanasy ridiculous seemed to loom very large indeed.

Still, not everything was strange. The round, stone houses with their grass roofs were silent and empty. This was, after all, a fishing village and it was a fine day. Everyone who could walk would be at work in some fashion.

The smell of smoke drifted on the wind. In silent accord, they disengaged their arms from each other, and they followed the scent to the rear of the village. There, old women tended huge iron kettles full of something steaming that smelled of the sea. Brown-skinned, fair-haired children ran between the kettles. They were of various ages, although none older than eight at the most, Ingrid guessed. Some played, some attempted to sort heaps of drying seaweed into piles under the eyes of the stooped old grandmothers.

The first grandmother to see them approach hissed a warning to the others and all chatter, all motion stopped. Avanasy and Ingrid approached under the silent stare of a dozen strangers, and inside Ingrid felt her stomach tighten. The steam from the kettles seemed to flicker and shimmer in air gone suddenly still.

Avanasy gave them all his courtly bow. "A good greeting to you all on this good day," he said.

One of the women put down the huge wooden paddle she had been using to stir the kettle. She had a face like a dried apple, but blue eyes that were bright and sharp. A worn scarf covered in faded embroidery hid her hair.

"A good greeting and a good welcome to you, stranger," she replied, wiping her hand on an apron that had long ago been embroidered to match her scarf. "And to your lady."

"Thank you," said Ingrid, bobbing a curtsy. She hoped it would be appropriate. The steam flickered strangely before her eyes again. She blinked.

"We were hoping we might find a roof to shelter us for the night," Avanasy went on. "We've come a long way, and have a long way to go yet."

The wrinkled woman wiped her hands again. Her face had gone sour, but she glanced at her fellows, looking for what?

Approval? Or the opposite? It was hard to tell with all the steam . . .

Something's wrong. Ingrid wiped her eyes. *Why can't I see?*

"We are a poor village," the woman was saying. "We have little comfort to offer such folk as yourself."

"We do not have any wish to impose," Avanasy replied as Ingrid lifted her gaze again. "And will gladly lend our hands to what we can while we are here. I have some skills . . ."

Ingrid did not hear the end of Avanasy's polite speech. A man had appeared behind the children who all clustered together to stare at the strangers. His tunic and pantaloons hung loosely on his bony frame, and he reached out to gently stroke the hair of the tallest of the boys.

He had no eyes. Like the ghost that had tried to drown Grace, his eyes were only empty sockets staring down at the young boy.

Ingrid's hand went to her throat which had suddenly closed itself up tight.

"Ingrid?"

"Is something wrong, mistress?" inquired the leader of the women, in an icily polite voice.

The ghost laid its hand on the boy's shoulder. The child, who was all of seven years old at the very most, didn't seem to notice anything as he drew closer to the others, staring uneasily at Ingrid.

What do I do? What do I say? It's a ghost. Oh, God, what does it want?

"Ingrid, tell me what is happening," said Avanasy. In English. Oh, of course, of course. This way they could speak in private even in front of this whole assemblage.

"There's a ghost," she said quickly. "With the tall boy."

"A ghost?" Avanasy repeated, stunned. "You see a ghost? You're sure?"

"It's got no eyes. It's like the one who tried to take Grace." She knuckled her eyes, uncertain if she wished she could see the thing more clearly, or if she could make it vanish. "It's standing right behind him. It's got both hands on his shoulders."

"I think we've nothing for you here," said the head woman edgily. "You two had best be going."

Avanasy swung around to face her. "Forgive me, Mother," he said. "Has there been fever in your village? Any mortal illness?"

The headwoman frowned. "And what business is that of yours?"

"Because it has not left you yet." Avanasy strode into the crowd of children, who scattered like a flock of sparrows. He dropped to one knee in front of the tall boy. One of the grandmothers came instantly to stand behind the boy, laying both hands on his shoulders, just as the ghost had. Ingrid could still see the ghost, its features superimposed over those of the ancient living woman, turning her eyes hollow and her skin deathly gray. Ingrid shuddered.

"There's nothing to fear, lad," Avanasy tried to reassure the boy, who just shrank backward against the grandmother's apron. "I just wish to . . ."

"Leave him," snapped the headwoman. She hefted the great wooden paddle in her hand, and Ingrid saw what an excellent club it would make. "You've no business . . ."

But Avanasy cocked his head up toward her. "His father died of fever recently, didn't he?"

The headwoman opened her mouth and closed it again. "How did you know that?"

"His ghost is here," said Avanasy simply, flatly. "It may mean the boy is to be dealt the same fate."

The grandmother gave out a shriek and hugged the boy tightly to her. The ghost had moved to her right, and was now staring at Ingrid with its black and empty eyes. Pleading? Warning? Ingrid couldn't tell.

The headwoman did not put her paddle down. "If you're some mountebank . . ."

"I promise you, Mother, I am not. I am a sorcerer, and I can furnish proof of that, if you require. I also promise that if this boy is ill, I can help him."

The headwoman set her jaw and laid aside the paddle, balancing it on the kettle's rim. She marched forward and grabbed the boy by the shoulder. Startled, the boy squeaked but the grandmother—his grandmother? Probably—let him go. The headwoman turned the boy roughly to face her while she crouched down in front of him. She seized his pointed chin and turned his face sharply this way and that. She reached up under his hair and felt the back of his neck, and then she thrust her wrinkled, calloused hand down his shirt and felt about under his arms, ignoring the way he squirmed. Whatever she felt made her blanch, and she shoved the boy's tunic up to expose his bony ribs and sunken stomach, and even at a distance, Ingrid could see splotches of red making a rough circle on his summer brown skin.

"Dimska's tears, no!" cried the grandmother. One of the little girls shrieked and darted away behind the kettles; soon all the children were screaming and running away, leaving the little boy dazed in his grandmother's embrace and the old women shouting for the children to stop that nonsense!

"Take him home, Edka," said the headwoman to the grandmother. "We'll send for his mother."

"But I'm not sick!" protested the boy. "I promise I'm not. I feel fine!"

"Of course you do," murmured his grandmother. "This is nothing. It will pass." But she was looking up at the headwoman as she spoke and her eyes were bright with tears. "Come, help me home, Iakhnor," she said to the boy. "I need my tea."

Dutifully, but with a rebellious, frightened frown, the boy took his grandmother's arm and let her lean on him as she shuffled toward the cluster of huts. The ghost, its head and shoulders drooped in what Ingrid could only believe was an attitude of misery, moved to follow them.

The women had drawn the children back, clustering around them like so many birds around their chicks, as if their bodies alone could ward off what they had just seen. The headwoman, however, rounded on Avanasy.

"What are you? What do you know of this?"

"I told you, Mother," said Avanasy without even blinking. "I am a sorcerer. I can help you, I promise it. It is possible that the boy need not die, nor anyone else."

Two bright pink spots appeared on the woman's wrinkled cheeks. "Last winter, we had a man come here. He said he was a sorcerer too. Had plenty of fine tricks to prove what he said. Said he could dose all the goats against the winter dropsy, and he did too, and took plenty of pennies for his trouble, and this spring, what do we have? Not a kid born alive, and no milk fit to drink."

Avanasy's face hardened. It looked to Ingrid as if he wanted to curse, but he controlled himself. "I ask no fee for my work," he said doggedly. "I ask only that you let me do what I can for the boy, and for your people."

The woman's face darkened with her internal struggle. The other women huddled together, whispering and darting glances at Ingrid and Avanasy. She scanned them and their children, seeking for other traces of ghost or smoke, and saw none, much to her relief.

"And her?" said the headwoman suddenly, pointing at Ingrid. "What will she take?"

Pride drew Ingrid's shoulders back. "Nothing I am not freely given, I promise you, Mother," she said.

That silenced the headwoman, but did not lighten her expression at all. "Well, I don't know," she said flatly. "It'll have to be talked over. You can stay 'til it's decided."

"Thank you, Mother," said Avanasy gravely.

"Ara!" snapped the headwoman to another of the grandmothers. "Stop fussing, old woman, and take these two to the god house."

A particularly ancient woman bent almost double under her dowager's hump broke away from the others and hobbled past them without a word. Avanasy bowed once more to the headwoman. Taking this as her cue, Ingrid curtseyed again. Together they followed the ancient dame toward the center of the village.

Ingrid found she could not tell one of the round, stone huts from the other, until Ara led them around to a threshold that had been painted red. She stood aside, gazing at them sourly as Avanasy thanked her. She did not wait about as he and Ingrid entered the gloomy hut.

When Ingrid's eyes adjusted to the dim interior, she saw a single round room with an altar in its center. The altar was a simple affair; carefully piled stones surmounted by a polished wooden plinth holding a plaque that looked to be worked brass or bronze on which the figure of a weeping woman had been painted. She stood ankle-deep in the foaming tide and a pair of gray seals raised their heads to her.

There was little else to see; some bales, baskets and folded blankets, a table and two chairs, a hearth built against one wall with a stack of firewood beside it.

"This, I imagine, is Dimska of the Tears," said Avanasy. He bent and kissed the icon. "We should leave some gift as well." He drew his pouch from his sash and brought out a pair of copper coins which he laid at the icon's base.

Ingrid realized she was staring. She blinked and looked away, but not soon enough. Avanasy smiled at her.

"This is very strange for you, isn't it?"

Ingrid nodded. "Although I'm not certain what my trouble is. My family was never one for church, not really. Mother had us all baptized, and she read the Bible on Easter and on Christmas, but that was the end of it."

"To honor the divine in one form, Ingrid, is to honor all its forms. Here, the divine is Dimska," he gestured toward the icon, "who performed some great miracle that helped her people."

Ingrid nodded. "It's just one more thing to get used to, I suppose." She shook herself. "Avanasy, what happened out there? What did I really see? What's happening to me?" She shivered again. She couldn't help it. It was wrong, what she had seen, where she was, everything that was happening. It was all wrong, although she could not have said why.

Avanasy was beside her at once, wrapping his arms around her and pulling her close. "Ingrid, I'm sorry. I did not foresee anything of this kind, and I should have." He held her for a moment, and Ingrid let herself be held, letting his warmth enfold her and ease the shivering that crawled up and down her skin.

"Magic in your world is buried deeply. For it to make an appearance at all, it must be strong, but I had, I have, no good measure for how strong. What plagued your sister on your shores was in your world nothing more than a restless spirit. On this shore, it would have been a monster, a lord of the storms and hurricane. There, it touched you and left no effect. Here . . ."

"Here I'm beginning to see things." She pulled away from

him and stared out the door, looking at the tiny slice of the village it showed her; gray walls, pale roofs, gray sky, gray and stony ground. "Oh God, and Grace tried to warn me."

"What?"

"Before I left . . . as I was leaving actually. I thought . . . I did not take her seriously. Not really. I thought she was trying to trick me into staying, which she was . . ." Ingrid shook her head. "Grace told me she was beginning to see things, that she'd had a premonition of Leo's accident." She drew in a long, shaky breath. "She thought the ghost might have done something to her."

In the distance, she could hear the faint sound of women's voices calling and children answering. Other than that, the world was hushed.

"Probably it was not done deliberately," said Avanasy. "The touch of the immortal can affect the mortal being. It can bring . . . changes."

"Changes, like the second sight?" Ingrid clutched the doorframe more tightly. She could not bring herself to turn around, but she also could not say why.

"Yes."

"Is that all that's happened to me?"

"I don't know," said Avanasy softly. "I don't even know that I have correctly interpreted what has happened. I am far from my books and my tools."

Ingrid nodded and bit her lip. She felt him move close behind her, but she still did not turn to look at him. She continued to stare out at the tiny piece of gray world. By straining her ears, she could just hear the sea, an eternal rushing sound that would never silence. She could smell its salt on the wind.

Something was happening inside her. She could feel it stirring in her blood and her bones. She had no name for it and no way to perceive what she might be at its finish. Fear gripped her, and anger at her willingness to come so far in such ignorance; for all she knew her love for Avanasy was real and to let him leave alone would have broken her heart, and yet, and yet . . .

"You can't see ghosts?"

"Not without a great deal of preparation, no."

"But you can help that boy?"

"Yes, if they let me." Avanasy was very close behind her. She could feel him, close enough to touch, but not willing to do so. He would not want to feel her pull away from him. She knew that.

"And if I hadn't seen what I saw?"

"We might have been gone before he was ill enough for them to ask for help from a stranger, especially since they've been so robbed before."

Ingrid let out a long, slow sigh. "Well, that's something then."

"Is it enough?"

Ingrid turned to face the man whose ring she wore. Even in the dim light she could see the worry and hope warring with each other in his face. "For now," she said honestly. "You will have to give me time, Avanasy. This is . . . unexpected is far too faint a word."

He took her hand then and kissed it softly. "Just remember, my heart, that you are not alone. Tell me always how it is with you, and we will come to understand this new thing together."

"I promise," she assured him.

He leaned forward to kiss her and she tilted her mouth up to meet his, but all at once, the world seemed filled with the sound of tromping boots and the shouting of coarse voices.

"I believe our hosts are coming home."

As Ingrid watched the fishers flowing into their village, she was struck by the familiarity of the scene. Oh, the clothes and the faces were strange, but the attitudes, the combination of dour weariness and neighborly joviality was a thing she had witnessed all her life. Men and women called out to each other, split up to enter into their homes, joked with their fellows, greeted or scolded their children, or simply stretched their backs and shoulders before stooping to enter their own doorways.

Eventually, an older man with a gray beard that now had only a few threads of what must have been its original golden color made his way to the god house. He glanced at Ingrid and Avanasy with one appraising blue eye.

"So. I was told you'd be here."

Avanasy made his bow and Ingrid curtsied, but the man ignored both gestures, instead moving straight to the altar and the icon. He bowed first, laying down a small cache of shells and what Ingrid was sure were pearls. Then he kissed the icon, his eyes reverently closed. Only then did he turn to face the strangers.

"I fear you've had a thin welcome," he said, cocking his head toward Avanasy.

"I have heard of your troubles, Keeper . . ."

"Hajek Ragdoksyn Kraichinivin," he said, tucking his thumbs into his sash. "And who are you, sorcerer?"

Avanasy hesitated for a moment, and then evidently decided that the risk of the truth was less than the risk of a lie. "I am Avanasy Finorasyn Goriainavin, and with me is Ingrid Loftfield." Ingrid nodded to the keeper, who looked her up and down with a face gone suddenly hostile.

"A Tuukosov?" he demanded.

Avanasy touched Ingrid's arm to reassure her and shook his head. "No, good keeper. She is from an island much further away than that."

The keeper's expression relaxed at once. "Malan'ia's calling for a parley about the pair of you. I think she's hoping you'll be run out for a pair of frauds." He pursed his lips. "She's even muttering you brought the fever on young Iakhnor."

"Then he has got the first flush of it?" asked Avanasy quietly.

Hajek nodded. "So she says. I must go there now and offer Dimska's words of blessing." He plucked one of the pearls off the altar and tucked it into his sash.

As the man turned, Avanasy said, "And what do you think of us, Keeper?"

"Ah." Hajek held up one thick finger. "I think you have to be who you say, or you're a great fool to be giving out that name." His grin showed a scattering of crooked teeth clinging to his pink gums. "Yes, I know it well, and you thought I might. But we're loyal to the true empress here." His voice went suddenly grim. "We are her people, and none others, especially not that Hastinapuran bull who calls himself emperor." For a moment, Ingrid thought Hajek might spit, but he refrained, probably because of the house he was in. Instead, he just shook his head, his bearded face gone sour. "If it's the fire and snow with Iakhnor, I'll have you sent for, and then we'll see."

He left them there, striding out into the fading daylight, calling to people they could not see and receiving their hails in return.

"What has happened?" murmured Avanasy to his retreating back. "What have they said? What are they doing?" His fist clenched.

"Can't you find out?" ventured Ingrid. "Some spell . . ." It felt odd to say the word in perfect seriousness.

Avanasy shook his head, pacing to the far side of the hut. "Scrying without the proper tools is an uncertain business. You might see the past, or the future, or, more likely, nothing at all." He tapped the wall with his fist. "And the proper tools can take months to create. The best take years. There was so much I could not bring with me, and so little I believed I'd need." He added absently and Ingrid knew he was talking because he could not bear the thoughts silence would bring, "At least part of me believed she would call me back within a few weeks, when her anger had passed. When that call did not come . . ." He shrugged. "I did not believe I would have any need for such divinations again."

They were silent for a moment, then Ingrid rubbed her arms. The evening was turning chill, as was only to be expected with the ocean wind blowing so constantly. "Why did the keeper say the boy had fire and snow?" she asked, changing the subject and feeling something of a coward for doing so. She knew who Avanasy was, and what had brought him to her. She could surely stand to hear him speak about it when he needed to. Surely.

"It's the local name for the fever," he answered, circling the hut to the hearth. "The victim turns red and white from the fever, spots and swelling." He crouched down next to the woodpile. "I think Dimska will not begrudge us some warmth in her house." He reached for some kindling, but before he could lay it in the hearth, Hajek's voice sounded from outside the house.

"Sorcerer!" he called. "Sorcerer, come quick!"

Avanasy was on his feet and out the door in the next heartbeat and Ingrid hiked up her skirts to follow fast behind him. Keeper Hajek swung around as soon as he saw them, stumping off between the scattering of round huts to one bright with flickering light and full of murmuring voices.

Hajek, Avanasy and Ingrid had to push their way through the mass of people to get inside. It seemed as if the entire village had crammed itself into the hut to stare. The boy, Iakhnor, lay on a pallet in front of the hearth, where the fire had been built up so high Ingrid feared the chimney might catch fire.

It could not have been more than two hours since they had seen the boy, as wide-eyed and spry as the other young children. The change was terrifying. He lay wrapped in a blanket in front of the fire, his skin as white as paper except for fist-sized blotches of red on his cheeks and neck. Sweat poured in rivers from his face and yet he shivered constantly as if from some awful ague. A stout woman, her hair covered by an embroidered cloth, knelt beside him and buried her face in her hands, rocking back and forth while all her neighbors stood about solemn-faced and watched the boy perspiring his life away.

The ghost was there too. He stood beside the woman, but all his attention was on the boy, waiting for that last moment when the child would depart with him, Ingrid was sure of it.

"Ingrid," murmured Avanasy, and Ingrid knelt beside the woman, wrapping her arms around her.

"Shhh," she said, stroking the woman's head. "Shhh, it will be all right. It will be all right." Useless words. This woman's child was dying and it would not be all right, but the woman buried her face in Ingrid's shoulder, and sobbed, and Ingrid held her, and that was all that could be done. Avanasy laid his hand on the Iakhnor's head, and then his heart. He looked at the red weals, the blazing fire, and the whole village crowded in to see the contagion.

"I will need a birch pole with the bark still on it," he said to Hajek. "And a strip of red cloth, and salt. As much as you can bring me."

"For what?" snapped the old woman whom they had spoken to when they first arrived. Malan'ia, Keeper Hajek had said her name was. She pushed her way to the front of the crowd. "What will that do, sorcerer?"

"Of itself, nothing, mistress," said Avanasy, working to keep his voice even. His hand still lay on the Iakhnor's chest, and even over his mother's cries, Ingrid heard that the boy's breath was becoming ragged. Jesus and Mary, it was taking his tiny body so fast. And they were all in here, breathing the bad air. Oh, God, this was going to be a disaster.

"If I can begin before sundown," said Avanasy firmly, "it can allow me to drive this illness from the whole village."

"Lies," Malan'ia snorted. "The boy wants sweating and beating with birch branches to stir the fever from his blood. That's all."

Avanasy rose. Ingrid saw how hard and still he held his face as he towered over the shrunken woman. "Mistress Malan'ia," he said softly, but his words stilled all other voices in the hut. Even the woman Ingrid cradled fell silent. "I grieve for your losses and if I could find the one who lied so to you and yours, believe me, I would make him regret his works more than you ever could. But if I do not work quickly, by morning the boy will be dead and half your people will be ill. If I fail, you may deliver my bones to Dimska for judgment if you choose, but if I am to have any chance at success, I must begin now."

"Burnah, you've some untrimmed birch waiting in your shed, haven't you?" asked Keeper Hajek mildly. "And Daliunda, didn't your good man bring you home a red petticoat from the market at Musetsk?"

"He did," said a woman's voice from the back of the crowd.

"Good," said Hajek firmly. "The rest of you, you will bring all the salt in your homes to the god house, and if any grain is left behind, Dimska will know it." With that, he marched from the house.

His words might have been a spell in and of themselves, for all at once the crowd poured out the door, each person rushing to their own home to search out what was needed. Only one wizened woman stayed behind to kneel carefully next to Ingrid and Iakhnor's mother.

"I'll take her now," she said kindly. "I'm old, and if I'm to be cursed, I can be spared."

It was doubtful the mother even knew she was being passed from one set of arms to the other. She simply sagged against the old woman, insensible in her grief.

Avanasy bowed over the boy for one more moment, his lips moving in prayer, or perhaps in promise before he rose. "Ingrid, I'll need your help."

"What did she mean?" asked Ingrid as she followed him out into the sharpening night wind. "If she's to be cursed?"

"It is believed that the mother of a dying child can pass the curse on," he said, weaving a path back toward the god house. "That was why no one would stand by her, lest in her frenzy, she say their name and strike them down with the illness."

Ingrid wanted to proclaim that for superstitious nonsense, but here, who was she to say?

"Ingrid, I have a delicate question to ask you." Avanasy halted and turned toward her.

"What is it?"

He dropped his voice to the lightest whisper. "Are you virgin?"

Ingrid felt all her blood rush to her face. "Avanasy!"

"Forgive me, but it is important. As part of the spell, a ring of salt must be sowed around the village, and the salt must be dropped from the hands of a virgin woman."

Ingrid tried to swallow her discomfort, but it was difficult. Speaking directly of such matters was not something she was accustomed to. "Yes," she said finally. "I could do it."

"Thank you."

The god house now had a steady stream of people trickling in and out through its low doorway. Each person carried a covered dish or little cloth bundle. These they laid on the altar before kissing the icon and receiving a nod of approval from the keeper. As they departed, the villagers still glanced sideways at Avanasy and Ingrid. The suspicion Ingrid saw there tightened her throat. Avanasy did not seem to notice. He frowned up at the sky, which was fading from pale gray to the color of slate with the coming night.

"Time enough, but barely," he muttered. "Ingrid, see if the

keeper has a container that can hold all the salt and fill it. No one must touch it but you from now on."

"I understand," she said, but in truth she did not. This was Avanasy's world, and his work, and that would have to be enough for right now.

Once inside the god house, they found a birch branch leaning beside the hearth with the red petticoat laid beside it. Avanasy claimed them at once, drawing his knife to trim the branch into a pole and to slice the petticoat to ribbons. At Ingrid's query, Keeper Hajek produced an earthen soup pot and Ingrid began pouring the coarse and lumpy salt into it as fast as she could open bundles and empty dishes. The light was fading rapidly, and she could feel the tension thickening in the air.

She caught glimpses of Avanasy as she worked. He sat cross-legged, his eyes distant, his hands busy wrapping strips of red cloth around the birch pole so that they crossed each other, and crossed again, making a complex pattern, bright red against the white bark. She could have sworn he did not see what he did. His lips moved the entire time, working on some pattern of their own with breath and word that she could not hear.

At last, Avanasy stood. "Come," he said to her. His voice was hollow. He was not there, not truly. His magic, his working, had laid hold of him and he was in a place beyond. Perhaps he was in the Land of Death and Spirit. Ingrid had no way to know.

She rested the pot of salt against her hip and followed him.

The entire village lined the rough path toward the cliff. This time, however, Ingrid was ready for their stares, and only lifted her chin. Avanasy paid no notice to them at all. His eyes were locked rigidly ahead of him, and his hand clutched the birch pole.

When they passed through the gate and stood just outside the rough wall, Avanasy rested the birch pole on the ground. He had sharpened one end, Ingrid now saw, so that it dug into the dirt.

"Sow the salt into the line I draw," he said in his pale, hollow voice. "We must go twelve times around the village.

We must not stop or falter, no matter what you see or hear, or the working will not hold."

"Yes," said Ingrid. It was all she could say. This was so strange, so incomprehensible, all she could do was agree, and keep following.

Slowly, Avanasy began to drag the sharpened birch pole through the dirt. "I call out Triaseia, who is the maiden with the unbound hair, who is the daughter of the red *rusalki*, who is the one who has taken hold in Dimska's place. I call out Triaseia who makes Iakhnor shake, by my heart and by my breath, by Dimska, Vyshko and Vyshemir. I call her out and I forbid her entry, by the transparent line I draw, by white birch and red cloth and salt sown by maiden's hands."

Avanasy's words were hollow no more. They were heavy with purpose and fell like stones through air that had suddenly and inexplicably stilled. Ingrid forced herself to concentrate on her strange task. She scooped up a fistful of salt, allowing the grains to trickle in a tiny snowfall into the furrow Avanasy's staff plowed. They settled all but invisible into the dark earth. She could not look up to see how far she and Avanasy had traveled in their circuit, or what would be coming next. She had to keep her eyes on the furrow stretching out before her and let her salt fall carefully down. In all the world there was only the salt, Avanasy's heavy, droning words, and the furrow, fading from her sight in the gathering dark.

Suddenly, she heard a rushing wail, as if all the sounds of sea and wind had suddenly returned, and her eyes rose to see a woman, like a ghost but more solid, pale as death. The ends of her hair swept the ground unhindered by any ribbon and her dress, without any sash to bind it, fluttered in a wind Ingrid could not feel. Her fingers raked the air, reaching for Avanasy. Ingrid's chest tightened as the wraith reached for her.

The woman vanished, and Ingrid saw they were again at the gates of the town.

"I call out Ogneia," said Avanasy, without pause, without any change to his tone or the weight of his words. "Who is the maiden with the unbound hair, who is the daughter of the red *rusalki*, who is the one who has taken hold in Dimska's place. I call out Ogneia who makes Iakhnor burn, by my heart and by my breath, by Dimska, Vyshko and Vyshemir. I call her out and I forbid her entry, by the transparent line I draw, by white birch and red cloth and salt sown by maiden's hands."

Time vanished, sense of place and self vanished. The moon must have risen, because she could see the furrow black against the silver ground. The salt glowed white as it showered down from her fist. She should have been cold. She should have been tired, but she was aware of these things only dimly. The words carried her forward, the words and her task. Salt was lifted from bowl to hand to be poured into the dark line of the soil. The salt rubbed her hand until it was so tender she imagined she could feel every grain that spilled through her fingers. The pale maidens—Ledia, Gneteia, Grynusha, Glukheia, and all their sisters—with their ghost-locks, and with their wails that sounded like the sea, appeared one by one. They hooked their clawed fingers into the wind itself in their fury, only to vanish, dragged into the earth by the weight of Avanasy's working.

After a time that might have been a few hours or a few hundred years for all Ingrid could tell, they came again to the gates. One more pale maiden rose and choked on the air and drowned in earth, and Avanasy did not move on. He stood, leaning on the birch staff, and Ingrid blinked stupidly up at him, dazed by her efforts, by all she had seen and by the magic.

Together their knees buckled and, slowly, almost carefully, they fell to the ground, slumping forward to lean against each other. As the darkness took hold of her, Ingrid was aware of Avanasy's breathing and of three words. "It is done."

After that, for a time, there was nothing else. Then, it seemed to Ingrid she must be dreaming, for she stood at the edge of the village, just beyond the salted furrow, and saw herself and Avanasy lying on the ground. She watched while the fishers flowed out of their huts. Under the direction of Keeper Hajek, they lifted Avanasy and her empty, distant body and carefully bore them away, leaving her alone there in the night.

Then, she heard a noise. She turned and saw a man on horseback. He wore chain mail and a thick coat and carried a pennant in his right hand, and all about him was as red as blood or sunset. He looked down on her for a long moment, but she could not distinctly see his face. She opened her mouth to speak, but she could form no words.

The man wheeled his horse around and urged it into a trot until they were both lost in the darkness. Curiosity washed through Ingrid to know where he had gone, and she moved to follow, but then, just as strong, she felt a tugging in her heart, calling her back to the village, back across the salt furrow, back to sleep and herself, and the world swam and was dark again.

Baba Yaga stood at the door of her house, Ishbushka. Two huge black dogs flanked her. Ishbushka's taloned legs rested for the moment as its mistress watched the lands out beyond her mended fence of bone.

Eventually, the thin and dying birch tree that stood beyond her gate drew back its branches. From behind it rode a blood-red horse guided by a rider who himself was dressed in the same red and who carried a plain red pennant in his gloved fist.

The gate in the bone fence swung open to admit him. The rider walked his horse up to Ishbushka's ragged and splintered steps. He stood in his stirrups and bowed low to the witch. In turn, she bared her iron teeth to speak.

"What did you see?" she asked.

"The woman's spirit is housed secure enough by her flesh when the sun is in the sky," he replied. "But at night, its will is to fly free."

"Good," said the witch, laying one crabbed hand on her dog's head. "Very good."

"Shall I fetch her to you, mistress?" inquired the rider.

Baba Yaga looked out past her rider, past her fence, past her lands. Currents flowed and changed. The taste of the world was changing, and there were those who thought she could no longer demand her share. They would learn of their error before much longer.

"You shall not fetch her yet, but soon, my Red Sun. Soon."

Chapter Eleven

"You are certain, old woman?"

Garrison Commander Mareshka was in a black mood. The dispatches coming out of Vaknevos spelled nothing good. The empress in confinement. The border patrols being stepped up. The garrison forts all being ordered to inspect and repair their walls, and to prepare to receive new levies of men. Something was in the wind, and it did not bode well for what had, so far, been his quiet command.

Pirates and smugglers did not as a rule favor these waters. There were too few people to help shelter them, or to buy what they brought. Those who came were ready to pay for safe passage. His men were in general surly, but he'd never met a crew of bored soldiers that weren't. He kept them as busy as he could with regular patrols and drills, and made sure the rotations for supply duty out to Musetsk, the nearest town big enough to have both liquor and women freely available, were regular.

He was not in the least pleased to have been roused from his bed by his over-lieutenant, saying there was a fisher-woman in the keep swearing up and down that the traitor Avanasy was asleep in her village.

"He gave his name to the keeper of our god house," she said. She, withered old creature that she was, did not seem in the least tired. She held her chin high and her back straight with the force of her righteousness. "He has given a display of his power. It is the sorcerer. I will swear to it."

"No need." Mareshka waved his hand, ending the gesture

by clapping it over his mouth to stifle a yawn. "Who did you tell before coming here?"

The woman's wrinkled chin rose a little bit higher. "No one. I am here alone."

"Then if we bring him in, and it is him, yours alone is the reward." Mareshka tried to brush a few of the wrinkles out of his uniform coat.

"Keep it," spat the old woman, and the force of her tone made Mareshka look up in surprise. "Just get him away from us."

Curiosity narrowed Mareshka's eyes. "What's he done to you, old woman?"

"He is a sorcerer." Anger burned in her words. "That is enough."

As you please. Mareshka shrugged and turned in his chair toward his over-lieutenant, who had stood at ease beside the door during the entire conversation. "Over-Lieutenant Dajik, you will pick four men. Make sure they carry cold iron. Mistress Malan'ia will guide you to her village . . ."

"Not I." The old woman stepped away. "I must get back before light. There are fools who will turn on me if they know what I have done here."

Mareshka shrugged again. "You will take her directions to her village," he amended. "You will arrest Lord Avanasy, and you will bring him back here."

"He has a woman with him," Malan'ia warned. "She's clever and glib as he is."

"And you bring any companions he has as well," Mareshka said smoothly to his over-lieutenant. "Is there anything else I should know, Mother?" He let his voice take on an edge, hoping the vindictive creature would realized this was her one chance to give him complete information, or things might not be so pleasant for her.

In response, the woman folded her arms across her breast and bent her knees in a peasant's reverence. "That's all, master," she said.

It had better be. "Very well. Over-Lieutenant, you have your orders, and you will see that Mother Malan'ia is escorted to the gate."

"Sir." Dajik put his hand over his heart and bowed. Then

he stepped smartly back, pushing open the door to allow Malan'ia to stride through with remarkable speed for one so old.

When they were gone, Mareshka yawned hugely and knuckled his eyes. Out past the door, he heard the rumble of Dajik's voice, probably giving orders to his under-lieutenant to get Malan'ia out of the fort. So, he waited.

As he suspected, a moment later Dajik knocked and walked back into the office.

"Yes, Over-Lieutenant?" inquired Mareshka, folding his hands across his stomach.

"Sir." Dajik reverenced again. "Sir, I just wanted . . ." Mareshka raised his eyebrows and waited. "Do you honestly believe we will catch Avanasy napping in some fishing village?"

Mareshka lifted one corner of his mouth in a slight smile. "I believe if we do, you and I will find ourselves with commendations and bonuses for our trouble. If not, it will let us see how some of your men do going into a village to drag out someone who may be more popular there than they are."

"Do you think he's being willingly harbored, sir?" Dajik's brow wrinkled.

"I think our fishwife did not want her neighbors to know what she was doing for a reason," Mareshka replied. "You have your orders, Over-Lieutenant."

"Sir."

Dajik left, and this time Mareshka heard his boots marching down the hallway. Mareshka sighed and rubbed his eyes again. With all that was ringing around his head, it probably wasn't worth returning to bed to toss and turn for the few hours of darkness that remained. Instead, he took himself out into the stone hallway, up a narrow, curving stairway and out onto the battlements. The salt wind from off the ocean hit him on the back of his neck, making him shiver, and at the same time bringing him instantly awake. The night's patrol saluted him smartly with their pikes as they marched by, and Mareshka answered the gesture with his hand over his heart.

Mareshka turned inland. The stars still shone brightly overhead, but the moon had long since set. Dawn was a thin, white line on the horizon. Mareshka leaned his hands on the parapet and gazed across the dark carpet of the land, trying to guess what was happening. It smelled strongly like war. But war against who? And what was it that brought Avanasy back into Isavalta just when the empress had retired from public view? Mareshka shivered again, this time more from his thoughts than from the wind. It smelled strongly like war, and that war stank.

In a little while, he heard the rumble and creak of the gates cranking open. A cluster of men on horseback, four of them bearing lanterns, rode out, heading due east along the rutted road. As their hoofbeats faded, the gates cranked shut, and quiet fell again.

Mareshka stared out into the coming dawn for a while longer, turning his uncomfortable thoughts over in his head. Then, because there was nothing else to do, he turned and went back down the stairs.

As a result, he did not see the single rider emerge from the rubble by the cliff's edge and slowly and carefully follow his men.

Ingrid woke alone to a dim room, raging thirst and utter confusion. For a long, tense moment she recognized nothing around her. The shadows were all the wrong shape and why was she wrapped in blankets on the floor instead of in bed with Grace?

Fragments of memory surfaced gradually. The voyage and its dreams, which were not dreams, the village, Avanasy and the magic.

Where is Avanasy?

Ingrid disentangled herself from the rough blankets and got to her feet, appalled to find her knees weak enough to tremble underneath her.

"Good morning, mistress." Keeper Hajek ducked through the doorway, toting a bucket in his gnarled hands. "I have brought us water."

Ingrid thought she might fall to her knees in gratitude as Hajek handed her a clay dipper. She drank ladle after ladle from the bucket before she felt her thirst begin to ebb.

"Thank you, Keeper Hajek," she was finally able to say. "Do you know where Avanasy is?"

"He is with Iakhnor." Hajek took a deep draft from the dipper.

"How is the boy this morning?"

Hajek lowered the dipper to reveal a large grin. "The boy is complaining because his mother is keeping him in bed another day. The fever's tokens have vanished."

Relief and unexpected pride washed through Ingrid. "That's wonderful."

"You and Lord Avanasy have surely saved us all, mistress," he told her, setting the bucket aside and wiping the water from his beard. "It was Dimska herself who sent you to us."

Lord Avanasy? thought Ingrid absurdly. *There is something he neglected to tell me.*

Even as that thought spread another smile on her face, Avanasy entered the god house. The dim light did not hide his own pleased grin.

"Lord Avanasy?" she inquired, in English.

"It is only an honorary title," he replied with a dismissiveness Ingrid found a bit too lofty to be entirely trusted.

Before Ingrid could make any further remark on the subject, Hajek said, "Will you break bread with me before Dimska today, Lord Avanasy? The village will wish to thank you publicly tonight, I am certain."

Avanasy looked to Ingrid, but Ingrid just raised her eyebrows to indicate this was his decision. "I do thank you, Keeper," he said, "but I fear we must be gone before the evening falls."

"I am sorry for it," said the keeper. "But not surprised to hear it. Still, let me help you break your fast."

Breakfast turned out to be thick black bread toasted on the hearth, spread with a potted paste made of dried and salted fish. All this was washed down with drafts of cool water. The meal tasted strange to Ingrid, but she was now as hungry as she had been thirsty before, and was not in the mood to decline any food, even if she could have done so without giving offense.

After they had eaten for a time in polite silence, Avanasy

turned to Hajek. "Good keeper, you recognized my name when I gave it . . ."

"The garrison sends men down here every so often." Hajek jerked his chin in the general direction of the coast and the fortress. "They buy our catch and salt. Sometimes they drop a bit of news. More often they grumble in our hearing and we take our news that way."

"Have you had any news from Vyshtavos?" He was doing his best to keep the strain of worry out of his voice, and not entirely succeeding.

Keeper Hajek made a face around his current mouthful as if he was keeping down a laugh. After a moment, he swallowed and regained his countenance. "Precious little of that sort reaches this far, Lord. We were, of course, commanded to pray for the empress and the new heir . . ."

"What!" cried Avanasy.

Hajek blinked. "The empress is with child. She has gone into her confinement."

Avanasy's whole face tightened, and Ingrid knew he did not believe what he had just been told. She remembered what he said about the difficulty for sorcerers to get children.

"Is there any other news?" Avanasy went on, his voice hard.

"There's been some . . ."

Before Hajek could finish what he meant to say, a boy rushed through the door. He bowed hastily to the icon and ran up to the keeper.

"What is it?" asked Hajek.

"Soldiers," panted the boy. "Riding fast."

Hajek wiped the crumbs from his beard. "It's too soon for this to be for our fish . . ." He stood. "Perhaps, master, mistress, you should stay here. We will meet them at the wall."

Hajek put a hand on the boy's shoulder and steered him out the door.

Ingrid rose together with Avanasy and they followed the keeper as far as the door.

"You believe this will be for us then?" she asked him softly in English as they waited in the shadows.

Avanasy nodded. "But what that means depends on who it is."

Which was no sort of reassurance, but Ingrid was certain Avanasy knew that.

Outside the low arch of the doorway, the morning was bright and cloudless. It might even have been hot, if it were not for the constant ocean wind. Only a few voices drifted through the village. Ingrid realized she must have been very soundly asleep, for she had not heard what must have been the considerable noise of the village rising early to go work their nets.

In the far distance, she could just make out the rhythmic thudding of hoofbeats on turf. If they had been riding fast as the child reported, they did not do so now. There was more horse than one, but they moved at a steady walk.

Perspiration prickled the back of Ingrid's neck.

Keeper Hajek's voice raised itself on the wind, possibly in greeting. Ingrid could not make out the words. Another man's voice answered. Avanasy pressed his hands against the wall as if that could help him hear better.

"Three of them, at least," he murmured. "I cannot hear the names."

Ingrid strained her own ears. The men's voices lifted and lowered, as if in easy conversation.

"They don't sound as if they're making demands," she ventured.

"Yet." Avanasy's jaw worked back and forth. "If only there was some way . . ."

But he was not allowed to finish his wish.

"Will you come out then, my lord?" inquired a man's polite voice. "And whoever's in there with you. I charge you in the empress's name."

Ingrid's heart leapt into her throat, choking her. She could see at once what had happened. While some of the soldiers had kept Hajek busy talking at the gate, others had circled around the back of the village, crept between the houses, and found the place where the strangers were most likely to be sheltered. Overhearing their whispered conversation, the soldiers ordered the strangers out.

For all the anger and self-reproach in Avanasy's eyes, there was nothing to be done. The god house had only one door and no windows at all.

Shoulder to shoulder, they walked out into the daylight.

Three soldiers met them with swords drawn. They had taken care to stand so their shadows would not cross into the line of sight of the threshold and give away their presence. They were all brown from sun and wind. Two had golden hair showing underneath their helmets and heavy beards concealing their faces. The third was younger and slighter. His beard was neatly trimmed along the line of his pointed chin and his eyes glittered as he looked Avanasy and Ingrid over.

Uniform seemed to be woolen coats with chain mail over all and breastplates over that. The rows of braid and brass buttons on cuffs and collars were probably indications of rank. Leather gloves covered their hands, and worn leather boots their legs, just below the round steel caps that protected their knees. Their swords were clean and straight, and glinted in the sun, and Ingrid suddenly felt very keenly that her neck was quite bare.

"Thank you, my lord," said the one with the trimmed beard. "It is best to do these things quietly, don't you agree?"

In reply, Avanasy drew himself up to his full height. "Over-Lieutenant, I have been summoned back to Isavalta by imperial order. The errand is urgent, and must not be hindered."

"And my commander will be happy to examine any documents you carry to prove your assertions," said the over-lieutenant, sounding like the soul of reason. "In the meantime, my orders are to return you and any companions you may have," his eyes raked Ingrid over, "to our fortress. So, if you will be so good as to walk with us, and to remain quiet." He gestured with his free hand, indicating that they should start toward the rear of the village.

Avanasy's fists opened and closed, but they were unarmed, and the soldiers surrounded them. He brushed his fingertips against the back of Ingrid's hand, as if to reassure himself that she remained solid, and they turned and walked as they were ordered. One soldier took up position on either side of them, and the over-lieutenant brought up the rear.

Avanasy held his head and shoulders proudly as they were marched through the village, but his eyes were never still. They darted this way and that, looking for a way out of this,

Ingrid was certain. She tried to do the same, but all she seemed able to see were the glinting swords in the hands of the armored men that flanked them. Her mouth had gone as dry as dust and her brains seemed to have fled.

But if they were unarmed, they were not unnoticed. Their escort led them around another hut, and straight into the grandmothers. Two of them carried the big wooden bats used for stirring the kettles. Another pair carried a kettle between them full of something that steamed and smelled strongly of the sea. The others, maybe half a dozen old women just stood like stones, blocking the way and making no noise at all.

Which left Ingrid wondering where the children were.

"Good morning, honored Grandmother," said the over-lieutenant. "How do I find you on this fine morning?"

"You've two guests of ours there," said one of the old women, a squat creature, wrinkled and brown as the stump of a tree. It was then Ingrid noticed that Malan'ia was also nowhere to be seen. "We're here to say you'd best leave them be."

"Grandmother, I honor your respect for the laws of hospitality," the over-lieutenant replied seriously. Beside Ingrid, the nearest soldier shifted uneasily. His eyes seemed to be counting the old women, and taking in the long wooden bats, and the steaming iron kettle. "But these two are wanted for questioning. If they've done nothing, they'll be back with you soon, you may be sure of it."

"You'd best leave them be," repeated the old woman. "There's no trouble wanted here."

"You old fools!" cried a different voice.

Ingrid began to realize what a warren this village really was. A place of dark doorways and careful ears, where anyone might appear from anywhere. Apparently the soldiers did too, because the new voice made them all jump.

Malan'ia stormed out from one of the doorways. "What are you doing?" she shrilled. "Do you want to see the entire village burned to the ground?" She planted herself squarely between the villagers and the soldiers. "Burned for a sorcerer?" she sneered. "Have your brains all turned to sea foam? Do we need that much more trouble? Let them pass!"

The squat woman narrowed her eyes. "Malan'ia, it may be you'd better stand back too."

"Stand back and what?" demanded Malan'ia, hands planted on hips. "Let you kill us all? Let you wipe our home away into memory? Get along with you, all you old fools! This has nothing to do with us!"

"Be advised by your good friend here, Grandmother. We're taking our leave, and our prisoners now."

The over-lieutenant tried to start forward. The squat woman stepped into his path. The flanking soldiers drew in closer to Avanasy and Ingrid. Ingrid heard the blood singing in her ears. Malan'ia, with a snort of derision, raised the back of her hand to the squat woman and slapped her full across the face.

At the same time, Avanasy grabbed the soldier beside him, and using his sword arm as a lever, swung the man around and sent him careening into the over-lieutenant.

"Run!" he shouted to Ingrid.

But Ingrid had no intention of doing such a thing. The soldier flanking her lunged for her, and Ingrid dove forward, measuring her length on the ground and rolling sideways. As she did, the two old women with the kettle hefted it in one motion and flung its contents straight in the soldier's face. He reeled back screaming as the boiling water drenched him and the weed wrapped his hands and face. He fell, clawing at the green mass that clung to his face, searing his skin and blinding him.

Ingrid scrambled to her feet. For an instant, she saw Avanasy facing the over-lieutenant with one of the paddles in his hands. In the next heartbeat, Malan'ia was on her, pushing and pinching, with sharp elbows and sharp fingers. Ingrid staggered backward, and tried to shove the old woman aside, but she was tougher and more wiry than Ingrid had given her credit for, and she just pushed back, sending Ingrid stumbling toward the remaining soldier, before the other woman reached her, and pulled her cursing back.

"Let them go, damn you! You'll have us all put to the sword for a *sorcerer*!"

The second soldier wrapped one brawny arm around Ingrid from behind. She kicked back, but her shoes found nothing but armor and leather. She would have bit down, but there was nothing but leather and armor holding her pinned.

Avanasy parried the over-lieutenant's blows with the stout paddle, but splinters flew with each cut. Only the length of the thing kept the over-lieutenant back, and it would not hold much longer.

"Sorcerer!" the soldier bellowed. "I've got your woman!"

Avanasy swung around, and the over-lieutenant pulled his sword back to aim a fresh blow. Ingrid cried out in warning, but at the same moment, she heard the sound of galloping hooves.

The soldier wrenched Ingrid around toward the sound. The over-lieutenant hesitated just long enough and Avanasy dodged the blow. The old women screamed, scattering like leaves, and another soldier on horseback plunged between the huts.

He held no sword, but a pike, and he bore down on Avanasy. Ingrid screamed. She could not help it. But the blow did not catch Avanasy. Instead, it sent the over-lieutenant spinning and crying out, dropping into the dust, his sword falling from his hand.

The rider wheeled his roan horse around in a tight and expert circle. The soldier behind Ingrid tightened his grip until she could barely breathe, dragging her back from the rider. The edge of his sword pressed against her belly.

"Let her go," said Avanasy, his voice low and dangerous as he picked up the sword dropped by the fallen over-lieutenant. His eyes never left the soldier. "Where will you go and how will you get there?"

The rider closed in beside Avanasy, his pike lowered and ready. Ingrid could make out nothing of his face in the shadow of his helmet, but his coat was bright blue and its trimmings were gold.

The wind carried yet another new roar, over the perpetual sound of the ocean. The sound of men's angry voices, and there were a lot of them, and Ingrid knew where the children had gone. Their grandmothers had sent them scampering down the cliffs to call back the fishermen, the young men with strong backs and arms, nets and hooks and perhaps even spears for their work. Horses neighed and voices cursed, and yet more voices roared, and the soldier holding Ingrid swung her around yet again, and she felt his grip slacken.

Ingrid threw herself sideways, lunging with all her weight, and trusting desperately to her woolen petticoats to keep the edge of the sword from her flesh. She fell again into the dust, skinning her palms and banging her chin so hard it rattled her teeth. Hooves started behind her and she rolled again in time to see the soldier trying to flee from the horseman, and taking the blow from the pike straight in his back so he too went sprawling in the dust. This time the old women got him, falling on him, rolling him over, kicking and beating wherever there was enough bare flesh to make a target. The over-lieutenant staggered to his feet, but the horseman wheeled around again and charged back. This time he took the blow on his helmet, fell backward, and stayed down.

Evidently satisfied with his work, the rider stilled his horse, and patted its neck as he dismounted. His free hand worked the straps on his helmet and he pulled it free.

As soon as the sunlight touched he face, Avanasy gave a delighted shout.

"Peshek!" Avanasy ran forward and clasped the man's shoulder.

"Avanasy!" The rider grinned in return. "Still don't know when to run, do you?"

"It would seem not." Avanasy laughed with him, sounding happier than he had since they arrived in the village.

"And who is this good lady?" The man, Peshek, turned toward her.

Ingrid had never seen a man as straightforwardly handsome as Peshek. His hair was a rich chestnut, his eyes were summer blue. His face was strong and open and his shoulders broad. All about him hung an air of easy confidence. Despite herself, Ingrid felt her cheeks begin to redden as he regarded her.

"She is Ingrid Loftfield of Sand Island in the United States of America, and she is to be my wife, Peshek. So, you may keep those rogue's eyes to yourself," he added with a mock growl.

"Wife!" Peshek exclaimed, genuinely startled. "What . . ." He stopped himself. "Well," he amended. "I knew there was no woman of Isavalta good enough for Avanasy. My greetings and my duty, mistress." Peshek bowed to her with his hand over his heart.

"Thank you, sir," said Ingrid, curtsying. "Your timing is excellent."

"And you are not the first woman to tell him so." Avanasy laughed again. "Quick, Peshek, come stand here by me. I think a second rescue is coming."

Sure enough, the tide of village men boiled around the houses, coming from all directions to cut off any retreat, and what they found was Ingrid, Avanasy, Peshek, the horse, which danced back nervously, the old women, and the fallen soldiers. Peshek grabbed his horse's reins and patted the animal's nose to soothe it.

Two of the fishers with wicked-looking iron hooks in their hands started forward from the crowd.

"I beg you, put up your arms," said Avanasy, stepping into their path. "This man is a friend and helped us in our need." Grumbling, the fishers fell back, but their suspicious eyes did not leave Peshek.

All of which was too much for Malan'ia.

"You've slain us all!" she cried, shedding tears even as she glared around at her neighbors. "Just see if you haven't! How long do you think it will be before the garrison sends out a search for this lot!" She swept out her hands to indicate the fallen soldiers. The over-lieutenant lay still as death. The other two gazed around them with wide and nervous eyes, but did not seem to think it wise to move.

Malan'ia spat on the ground and stumped back into her house.

"I think you will not need to look far to see how the garrison knew you were here," murmured Peshek very softly, stroking his horse's nose again. Then, he raised his voice. "I fear she is right. I saw their horses making straight back to the fort. If they are found without their riders, a search party will go out immediately."

Keeper Hajek made his way to the head of the crowd of fishers. "If we send some men out now, we might still be able to catch them."

"That will help for a while," agreed Peshek. "But not for

long. The best course for the three of us is to be gone from here."

Hajek nodded. He pointed to one cluster of fishers who all carried stout ropes over their shoulders. "Get you out and find those horses if you can." To another group he said, "Take these three out of sight, and then you'd better see to the others by the gate." The men growled their affirmation, and with three of them to a soldier, they hauled them out of sight. The rest of the village parted to let the men through, and muttered uneasily among themselves. Ingrid caught Malan'ia's name spoken several times, and the tone used was not friendly.

Apparently, Hajek heard it too. "Friends, friends," he called. "There's work to be done, and if we're missed from the cliffs, suspicions will rise fast and high."

Hajek stepped smartly up to Avanasy and Ingrid and bowed in front of them, adding a nod for Peshek, who returned it gravely. The rest of the village followed suit, all of them bowing with great solemnity, leaving Ingrid feeling like the guest of honor at a huge country wedding. As Hajek led his people away, their voices lifted high in song.

> *"Let the waves roll, let the wind roar,*
> *You've brought me home, from many's the shore.*
> *Your eyes light the moon, your tears fill the sea,*
> *Your hands hold my heart, your voice calls to me."*

A question filled Ingrid as the villagers departed to their tasks. She was sure she did not want to know the answer, but she could not stop herself from asking. "What will they do with the soldiers?"

"They will make sure the men do not follow us," said Avanasy flatly, and his cold voice told Ingrid all she needed to know. "Come, Ingrid. Let us get our things. We'll take shelter beneath the cliffs. There'll be a moon tonight and we can sail out after dark."

Ingrid tried to catch Avanasy's eye, to get some reassurance from his voice or his manner, but there was none. He was distant from her, although they walked side by side, with Peshek leading his horse behind them. His mind was on his empress and thoughts of the danger to the empire, and she would have to try to wait until his thoughts turned, with as much patience as she could muster. But she did not feel content to wait. Something pulled at her, some restlessness like the sensation left over from a bad dream made her uneasy inside, and she could not give it a name.

Avanasy watched Ingrid sink into her own silence, and he regretted it. He wanted to speak comfort to her, but he had no words. A day and a night in Isavalta; already six men were condemned to death for no more than looking on his face. The first casualties of the war to come.

No, Iakush came before them, and I'll lay all I own down that even he was not the first.

Peshek waited outside the god house with his horse while Avanasy and Ingrid went inside to pick up their bundles and sling them over their shoulders again. Avanasy took this moment of privacy to touch Ingrid's arm and look into her eyes. She returned a small smile that held no more than a spark of warmth, but there was no time now to inquire as to just what troubled her. He would have to trust to her patience just a little longer.

There was no question of Peshek's horse being able to negotiate the path that had brought Avanasy and Ingrid up to the village, so they were forced to head eastward along the coastline, until the cliffs gentled into hills, and then trek back over sand and stone, following the waterline as the waves ebbed and surged at their right hand.

At last, with much coaxing of the skittish, tired horse, they made their way around the rocky point to the cove that sheltered Avanasy's boat. Salt stung his lips and sand grated against his skin. Ingrid looked wan, and even Peshek's banter had ceased to make her smile.

Peshek already seemed to have forgotten the men left behind, but that was ever his way. He lived for now and what was to come. The past was over and done with as soon as it happened. He did as he must, loved as he would, and never labored under any shadow. Avanasy sometimes envied him, and sometimes grew exasperated with his carelessness.

Added to all that, he suspected that the nagging that teased at his insides as he watched Peshek coax Ingrid with his light words—telling her of the pleasant sights that Isavalta held—was the first mild stirring of jealousy.

Which was so ridiculous he had to laugh, grimly and silently, at himself.

"Well," announced Peshek, gazing at the narrow cove about him. "Not so fine as your other country home, Avanasy, but I'm sure all the fresh air is most healthful."

"It wants a woman's touch," replied Ingrid. "And a fire. I'll see if there's driftwood to be found. I'm sure you two need to talk." Before Avanasy could offer advice or caution, she plunked her bundle onto a boulder and started down the shoreline again, pausing here and there to pick up what driftwood she found.

While Ingrid wandered farther afield, Peshek busied himself with his horse, uncinching the animal's tack and laying it aside. Relieved of its bridle, the horse began to nose among the rocks, in case there was some shred of edible greenery to be found.

"She's a fair one, Avanasy," he said cheerfully as he bent down to take up the horse's near hoof and check for stones. "But I'd stay on the right side of her tongue if I were in your shoes."

"If you were in my shoes, you'd have wedded her and bedded her months since, rascal that you are," joked Avanasy in answer, but his humor did not last long. "Peshek, what has happened? Is the empress truly with child? The lord sorcerer said nothing of it."

Peshek shook his head, and straightened up. "Nothing so simple. Where is Lord Iakush? I cannot believe he stayed away when all is falling apart."

"He's dead, Peshek. Kacha killed him."

Peshek's face turned thunderous, and he spat. "Not the first and not the last by a long chalk," he muttered in grim prophecy. "The empress is not with child. She is fled her palace, and all that comes out of there are Kacha's lies."

Avanasy's cheeks paled as Peshek told him how he had taken the disguised empress from the Vaknevos, and how he had been charmed to sleep and how she had escaped his custody.

"She bids you meet her at the Heart of the World. I know no more than that." Peshek turned away again, laying both hands on his horse's mane. The creature snorted and stamped one hoof. Despite his attempt to hide it, Avanasy clearly saw the shame that filled Peshek's face. "I am glad you are back with us, Avanasy," he said.

"But how!" Avanasy thumped his fist with his thigh. "How is he able to do this! Kacha is no sorcerer, yet magic comes under his hands. Only through magic could he deceive the entire council and put Medeoan to flight."

"And it is not possible all the council lords are traitors," added Peshek. "Fools, perhaps, treacherous, perhaps, but most of them believe in the empire."

"Which is why they are council lords." Avanasy stared past his friend toward the rushing gray ocean. The foam-crested waves spoke in their wordless, unceasing voices and gave him no answers at all. "This is a deep plot, Peshek, and it was set in motion well before Kacha was sent to wed Medeoan. Why did I let her send me away?"

"Because you are of more use to her alive than dead, wherever you might be, and you knew that." He shook his head. "Still, the news is not all bad." Peshek went on to tell Avanasy of his meeting with his father, and how word was spreading to find the truly loyal.

Avanasy blew out a sigh to the dimming air. "I should have known you would not be idle. This will be good news to give to the empress when I reach her."

"So I hoped." Peshek pulled on the fingers of his gloves for a moment. Then, he said in a low voice. "A wife, Avanasy? In truth?"

"We have not been prayed over yet, but, yes, I have given her my pledge."

"Was that wise? The empress . . . now that Kacha has betrayed her, she's going to turn back to you, and . . ."

Avanasy held up his hand. "No more, Peshek."

"Avanasy, you are not a fool."

"No. But there are things that may not be spoken of. Not even here in the middle of nowhere. I fell in love. I made a promise. I did not believe I would ever be welcomed back, and when I was sent for, I could not abandon her." His eyes instantly searched the mouth of the cove for Ingrid, but did not see her. It was just as well. This was not a conversation he wanted her to hear.

"And what will you do when you face our mistress imperial again?" inquired Peshek mildly.

"What I must, but I will not desert Ingrid, Peshek. She holds my heart."

Peshek simply shrugged at this, and changed the subject. "Can you get us to the Heart of the World?"

Avanasy nodded once. "I can, but I won't be taking you, Friend Peshek."

"And why not?" Peshek's voice filled with mock indignation.

"Because we need to know the true state of things among the lords master and at the court, and there must be someone utterly trustworthy who can carry that news between those who join with your father. I cannot find out so much and still reach the empress, but you can."

For the first time, hesitation crept into Peshek's manner. "You cannot believe they do not know what I have done."

"I'm counting on it," Avanasy told him, making sure Peshek could see his whole face, so that the soldier would know Avanasy was not asking this of him lightly. "It is how you will know friend from foe."

"So, I am to walk into the wasps' nest and count their numbers for you?"

"Yes."

Peshek sighed. "Are there any other miracles you wish me to perform?"

"No, that should be sufficient, and I thank you."

Neither man laughed, but neither did they look away from each other.

"For what it is worth, and in spite of what you've just asked of me," Peshek smiled wryly, "I am glad you have come back."

"It is worth more than you know." Avanasy leaned one foot against a stone. "I had scarce hoped to find so good a friend so soon upon my return."

They clasped hands then, but only for a moment before Peshek turned his eyes to the sky. "There's little enough daylight left. I'd best be getting on."

Without another word, Peshek picked up his saddle and settled it back onto his horse. The rangy beast snorted and danced in annoyance at being encumbered again so soon, but Peshek went about the business of cinching girth and harness with a practiced hand.

"How will I get word to you, all the way out there in the Heart of the World?" he asked.

"I'll send a bird to you. Speak your message to it, and that message will be carried to me."

Peshek turned, one foot in the stirrup and both hands on the saddle, ready to hoist himself onto the chestnut horse's back. "You are in earnest, aren't you?"

Avanasy nodded, and Peshek just whistled as he mounted and gathered up his reins. "What a marvelous thing to be a sorcerer. Good luck to you, Avanasy. Send your bird soon."

With the slightest touch of the reins and a soft click of Peshek's tongue, the horse started forward, careful of the loose stones. As Avanasy watched horse and rider pick their cautious way along the waterline, leaving footprints on the darkened sand, his heart lifted a little, despite all. If there was anyone he could have hoped to find upon his return, other than Medeoan herself, Peshek was that one.

Be strong, Medeoan, Avanasy thought, gazing out across the ocean, which had dimmed to charcoal gray in the shadows of the cliffs. *Wherever you are, I will be with you soon, and together we will restore you to your place.*

Through his spell of protection he felt the boat rather than saw it clearly. They should get aboard. Once the moon rose, they could be on their way.

And Ingrid should have been back ages ago with whatever firewood she found. With that thought, Avanasy realized how cold the wind off the water had become. His cheeks and hands tingled, and for a moment, his breath drew sharply.

He clambered over boulders and stones that were little more than lumps of shadow in the deepening night, following the direction Ingrid had taken and cursing himself for forgetting her, even for an instant. He pulled himself over the outcropping that protruded from the cliff, and stood for a moment, taking the measure of the rocky land and dark water, all under a sky that had dimmed to indigo.

In the distance he saw a figure, and realized that not even in the darkness could he mistake Ingrid's silhouette. She stood with her arms folded and her head tilted upward to gaze at the cloudless heavens.

Relief as much as exertion warmed Avanasy as he picked his way to her side.

"And how fares my lady?"

"I shall have to learn a whole new sky full of stars," she answered him without looking down. "Otherwise, how will I know which way I'm going?"

Worry stirred inside Avanasy. "Do you feel lost already?"

"I feel useless." She rubbed her arms. "You were there talking strategy and politics and . . ." She broke her words off. "I am wondering if, after all, I should have imitated a fisherman's wife and simply waited for you to come home from the sea."

Avanasy stroked her arms, seeking to bring her both warmth and reassurance as he pulled her close to his chest. "Does it mean anything to you if I say that I'm glad you did not wait?"

"It does," she said, but her shoulders did not relax. "Something is wrong, Avanasy."

"Many things are wrong, Ingrid," he said, brushing his fingertips across her hair. "Which thing do you mean in particular?"

"Something is wrong with me."

"How do you mean?" He turned her around to face him so that he might look in her eyes. The falling night had become cold again. "Are you ill?"

"I wish I knew." She pressed her fist against her stomach. "Something is gnawing at me, Avanasy. It is not worry, it is not regret, it is not loneliness. It is something physical. I first felt it out on the water. Now it has come back, and I cannot make it go away."

Avanasy laid his hand on her forehead. "No fever. I feel no magic at work here, and yet, there is something, you're right." He frowned. "Ingrid, think. When you were with the

Bony-Legged Witch, did you take anything from her, or did you give her anything? It does not matter how ineffable it was. Did you exchange anything other than words?"

Ingrid shook her head, but even as she did, she winced. "I thought that it might be my time of month, but . . ." She winced again and grasped his hand. "Avanasy, what is happening?"

Ingrid's knees collapsed. Avanasy caught her as she fell, suddenly unconscious as a stone. He had to bite back his cry. Swiftly, he scooped her up in his arms and carried her back away from the waterline. As he did, he saw Ingrid's silhouette, quite separate from her body, standing out against the darkness. In the next moment, it dissolved into nothingness.

"No. Oh, no." He laid Ingrid tenderly on a bare patch of sand, and felt for pulse, and felt for breath, but he could find neither. The blush remained on her cheeks, and her eyes moved underneath her lids, but she did not breathe and she was now cold from much more than the wild ocean wind.

Somehow, something had pulled her soul from her body.

It should not have been possible. Ingrid was a divided soul. Her flesh could be led astray, but her spirit was rooted firmly in both worlds and could not be moved. Or, so he had always been taught, and so it was written in every tome he had read. In the Land of Death and Spirit it was just barely conceivable for her to be so separated, especially by as strong a power as Baba Yaga, but from the world of flesh? Avanasy had never even heard legend of such a thing. It was the mortal's body that was vulnerable, and the sorcerer's soul. That was the way of it.

"No time, no time," rasped Avanasy to himself. However it had been done, it had been done, and he had to call her back. But he had so little to work with. A promise might be enough to bind them when in the Silent Lands, but not here.

Avanasy drew his knife. Blood was the first and last resource of any sorcerer, his master had told him. His blood, and hers, his breath, and his magic, those would reach her however far away she had been taken.

He rested the blade against his arm, and in front of him the darkness shifted. It rippled, bowed, distorted and reformed. Avanasy rose slowly so that he stood over Ingrid's still form, shifting his grip on the knife, ready to strike out instead of down.

A horse and rider stood in front of him now. Both were as black as the darkness from which they had been shaped. Avanasy could see no face under the rider's obsidian helmet. He rested a black javelin against his black stirrup, and from it a black pennant flapped in the salt wind.

"Sorcerer," said the rider. "I bring you a message from my mistress."

Avanasy felt his heart constrict as he realized who faced him. Baba Yaga, the Witch with the Iron Teeth, commanded the service of three knights. She called them her Black Night, her Red Sun, and her Bright Day. They were her spies, and her messengers.

"What does your mistress want with this woman?" There could have been no other reason for this creature to be here. Baba Yaga had taken her away. Again.

Ingrid, Ingrid, I was too slow and too stupid. What have I done?

The faceless knight spoke. "She bids me say that as long as you do not interfere, and as long as the woman does her bidding, neither of you will be harmed, and she will be returned to you."

"Your mistress has no right to interfere with the soul of this woman."

"She does not interfere. The woman was broken in twain before she ever came here. My mistress merely waited for her spirit to work itself free." The horse stood unnaturally still under its rider, more akin to a carved statue than a living beast. "You should be grateful to my mistress, sorcerer," said the rider in a tone that was both arrogant and casual. "Without her, the woman's spirit would have simply drifted away."

But what could have done this? Avanasy clenched his teeth to keep the question from bursting forth. *It is against all the laws of nature.*

Except that in Ingrid's world, the magic was buried so deeply that only the greatest effort called it forth. What, then, would a tiny spell, or the lightest brush of a spirit power in that other world be in Isavalta where the magic hung heavy in the air? He had not stopped to think. Heedless in his own need for her, desperate in his need to return to Medeoan, he had not even considered that some hurt from that encounter would be harmless in her world and yet would show as a gaping wound in Isavalta.

Fool, fool, fool! Avanasy's teeth ground together. With an effort of will he managed set all that aside. At his feet, Ingrid's skin glowed white in the darkness. He could not let anger at himself cloud his mind.

"It is a grand statement," he told the knight. "By what does your mistress swear?"

The knight's helmet tipped back, just a little, as if he lifted his head to look down his nose at Avanasy's presumption. "She swears by nothing. Who are you to require an oath from the Old Witch?"

"No one," he admitted. "But if she does not swear, how may I trust her?"

The pennant snapped once, sharply in the wind. It was a sound like a branch breaking. "She has sent her messenger, man. Let that be enough for you."

"Then," said Avanasy, feeling the weight of his iron knife in his hand, "let her messenger stay until my wife is returned to me."

"This woman is not your wife."

Avanasy should have been afraid, and he knew it. This was the servant of a true power. This was no boggle or spirit of the roof tree to be bribed with a bowl of milk and pretty compliments. This one could kill him if it would. Its mistress could haunt his dreams and ride him mad in the darkness.

But Ingrid lay still as death at his feet, and no other fear could touch him. "I say that she is my wife, and I say you will stay until she is returned to me."

"You are arrogant, sorcerer. You forget yourself."

"Forgive me." He inclined his head without taking his eyes off the shadowy presence. "Perhaps it is only that I have been too long from Isavalta. Nonetheless, you will stay. If your mistress will not swear, you will stay."

"I have no more words for you." The rider wheeled his horse around.

Avanasy charged. Knife-first, he leapt for the horse's reins. The animal reared and a heavy hoof struck Avanasy's shoulder, felling him to the ground, but his grip held and he swung down his blade. The iron cut through the fabulous cloth the rider wore and stuck fast. The horse reared again, but the rider could not be ripped free from the iron blade and he fell, heavy and silent, to the ground beside Avanasy.

Avanasy, pain burning through his shoulder, ground the knife in deeper until the rider hissed like a snake. He struck out, but his blows had no force. The cold iron that impaled him drained him of strength. The horse, acting for all the world like a mortal beast, bolted into the darkness and was lost to his sight. Perhaps it had gone home to its mistress. Good. Then he would not have to waste attention crafting a message for her.

"Now," he said to his prisoner. "We will wait together, you and I, and when your mistress returns what is mine, I will return what is hers."

"You are a fool, man." The rider's voice was thick with unaccustomed pain. "You will pay for this, and pay again."

"I know it well," answered Avanasy. "In the meantime, we will wait."

Overhead, the night turned and Avanasy held his grip on the iron knife. Beside him, Ingrid lay cold and motionless, and all of Avanasy's soul cried out to her.

Come home, my love. Come back to me.

Ingrid watched herself fall unconscious into Avanasy's arms. She watched his eyes widen with alarm as he caught her.

Avanasy! cried Ingrid. *Avanasy!*

But she could make no sound, and, all unbidden, she felt herself drift away like smoke.

No! No! She tried to scream, tried to dig in her heels, but she had no sense of place. No touch of the world seemed to reach her. She was air and vapor, and the wind blew her away into the night, out over the seas, faster than thought, until she could not see land, until she could not see stars.

Avanasy!

But for all the force of will in it, her cry was soundless. Darkness of earth and darkness of sky merged, and Ingrid was nowhere. From blackness thick as sleep, dreams emerged, strange flashes of images. She saw a young man and woman wearing clothes stained and wrinkled from long travel. They shouted at each other with heartbreaking fury. She saw herself as a child, holding onto the waistband of Grace's skirt so Grace could lean out over the edge of a bluff and spread her arms into the wind coming off the lake, pretending she could fly. She saw herself as she was, standing on the deck of an unfamiliar ship, leaning far too far over the gunwale and reaching down for Avanasy, who stood on the shore.

And she saw a stranger, a young woman with auburn hair and strong features that reminded her sharply of Avanasy. The woman stood beside a trio of gravestones and struggled not to weep. Ingrid's heart went out instantly to the stranger, but she could not tell why.

The images all faded, and instead a formless light shone from the darkness. Ingrid started and tried with all her strength to reach it. She found she could move, but it was like wading through syrup. The light was bright as the sun and slowly it took shape. Now it was a horse and rider, both shining so brightly Ingrid felt she should not have been able to look at them. They trotted away from her. Unable to bear the idea of being left alone in the darkness any longer, Ingrid strained forward, reaching with all the force she possessed, and the light grew brighter, and brighter yet, until the darkness retreated, and Ingrid could see.

She stood under the branches of an ancient birch tree, its branches tossing this way and that, although Ingrid could feel no breeze. A brook ran fresh and free at her feet, but it made no sound. On the other side stood a woman in working clothes and thick boots. Ingrid looked into her brown eyes and saw . . . herself.

The woman on the other side of the brook was Ingrid's double. Hair for hair, thread for thread. Ingrid realized she should have been afraid, but she could not be. All she felt was anger radiating at her from her twin, or, was this more than twin? Avanasy had spoken of Ingrid as a divided soul, with a portion of herself in the Land of Death and Spirit. Was this that place again? Was this her other self?

If it was, then this other Ingrid was steeped in fury, but not at Ingrid—at the force that brought her here. It was violation, it was wrong. Her other self lifted her hand, in greeting, in warning or in blessing, Ingrid could not tell. The other did not speak, and Ingrid could find no voice in her throat.

"You'd better go in," said someone behind her.

Ingrid jerked her head around. Behind her, a cat sat on a fence of ancient pickets much mended with human bones. The cat washed its paw and smoothed down its ears, and looked up at Ingrid with an expression of impossible intelligence.

Behind the cat waited another impossibility. A house, a thatched cottage, ancient and covered with the stains of years, but it turned on a pair of taloned and scaled legs, each as thick around as Ingrid's own waist. It was a thing out of nightmare, and Ingrid shrank away from it. At the same time, she recognized it. This was what Avanasy had shown her when she thought she stood in a pleasant stone cottage with an old woman who might have been her grandmother.

This was Baba Yaga's house.

Ingrid felt her other self at her back, straining to reach her, but the brook ran between them, and she could not cross. She pressed her fist against her forehead. She wanted no more of this—this unaccountable knowledge drifting into her head from outside. She wanted her voice, she wanted to understand in the normal way. She wanted herself, alone and solid. She wanted to weep, but she could not cry any more than she could speak.

"You'd better go inside," said the cat, tucking its legs underneath itself as it settled down on the gatepost. "You would not like what she sends out to fetch you."

Ingrid's anger drowned out all other feeling. What was happening? How dare she . . . interfere like this?

But I will not find out here.

Knife-edged warning reached Ingrid from her other self. If she went inside she would be trapped. This was different from last time. The other's knowledge filled her. Avanasy's ring would not pull her out again.

Ingrid tightened her will and strode up to the gate of bones. With painful slowness, as if its hinges were rusted past redemption, it opened for her. The cat watched her with disinterested eyes as she moved as close as she dared to the house, turning on its monstrous, crooked legs, its talons gouging the ground.

She stood there, watching it turn slowly and silently, impossible, ridiculous and terrifying all at once.

You know I'm here, she thought toward its owner. *I will not come into your parlor, spider. If you want me, you must come out.*

A wave of contempt as palpable as a raw wind engulfed Ingrid, and she withered under the force of it, but not completely, for her other self made a wall for her back. She was supported and sheltered by that other. Not much, but enough, just enough so that she could stay where she was and resist.

After a long moment, the house ceased its restless turning. Carefully, the scarred and scaled legs bent until its steps touched the ground, and the door fell open toward Ingrid. She felt as if she were looking into some terrible open maw.

Baba Yaga squatted in the threshold, as gaunt and tattered as the spirit of famine. She leaned on her filthy pestle that was as thick around as both of Ingrid's arms. Two huge, black mastiffs waited at her side. Both bared their yellow fangs, and Ingrid could feel their growls, low and sullen, vibrating through the air.

"I have need of you, woman," she said, and Ingrid could see the black iron of her teeth as she spoke.

Ingrid stiffened. This place was all bone and blood, and she was in danger. She knew that. But she also knew boundaries had been crossed here, and wrong had been done. It made a difference.

"So I gathered," she said simply, and tried to hold back her relief at being able to speak. The witch's regard seemed to have made her more solid, more real in this place of horrors and fancies, and that idea sent a tremor of fear through Ingrid.

"I will not be brooked." The witch thumped her pestle on the floor, and the whole house shuddered. "Aid me and you will have aid in return. Cross me and you will be held until you yield. There is nothing else."

"What could you possibly need me for?" Ingrid spread her hands.

"You will find me the Vixen and bring back what she has stolen from me. When that is done, you may depart."

"I don't even know what you're talking about."

"Nonetheless. You will do this thing I ask."

The words fell against Ingrid like a weight, pressing her down until it was a struggle to think of anything else. Images of foxes and meadows, and a round green hill flashed unbidden through her mind, and she remembered with crystal clarity the creature who had spoken to her when she was here before, who had sent her off to the Old Witch, just to see what would happen. She knew all at once that her other half could lead her to the Vixen again, and she would do this thing because the Old Witch bade her, and because she could do nothing else.

But there was the crossing of boundaries, that bit of wrong, that bit of freedom.

"No," said Ingrid.

Baba Yaga pointed one long, crooked finger at Ingrid. On either side of her, the mastiffs raised their hackles. "I give you this last warning, woman. I know your name, I know your future and your past. I see the warp and weft of your tapestry life. Without me, your death is sure. Think carefully before you wake my anger."

It was too much, it was too strange and the fear of it too great. Despite that, she would not place herself in the power of this creature, this hag. She could not. But she could not move.

Then the witch's head went up as if she had caught some strange scent. She bared her iron teeth in a death's head grin.

"So, your man thinks to take a hostage. Thinks to have and keep what is mine in exchange for you."

Avanasy? Some caution outside herself kept Ingrid from saying his name out loud.

Baba Yaga snapped her teeth and they came together with a hollow clang.

"You try my patience, you two. This is the second time you have refused me and he has tried to pull you from me. Very well." She turned her black, black gaze on Ingrid, and for a moment Ingrid felt she would burn to a cinder from the heat of it. "There will be a third time, and you will beg to do my bidding, because only I know how the Firebird may be caged. Go freely. I am done with you. Now, you may see if you can find your own way home."

At those words, Ingrid found she could not stay still. The dogs advanced, snarling. The house lifted itself up onto its legs, and without feeling her own movement, she was outside the gate, which swung shut with the slow straining of dry and rusted hinges.

And they all faded away, leaving her alone beside a brook in a piney wood staring at her own double.

Avanasy? she choked. Her voice was gone again. What substance she had possessed had dissolved, leaving behind only vapor and desperate sensibility.

What am I to do? she thought toward her double, and knew that other self was consumed with anxiety. *Why can't you speak to me?*

For a moment, she thought to cross the brook that separated them, but as soon as it entered her mind, the thought filled her with loathing. It was more wrong to go closer to her reflection than it was her being here in the first place. She did not know why this was so, only that it was.

Ingrid wished she could cry. She wished she could scream, but all releases seemed denied her. Already, she was drifting, pulled by some current she could not feel. It was as if the bank flowed and the brook stayed still.

No! She steeled herself again. *No!*

That act seemed to root her in place, at least for a moment. It occurred to Ingrid that if she failed to will herself to some destination, her destination might be chosen for her, and who knew what else was out here. It might even be worse than Baba Yaga.

Ingrid lifted her eyes to her other self, and wrapped her determination around herself. She willed herself to turn, to follow the current of the brook at her feet. Her other self turned with her, and together, side by side in the silence that this spirit land enforced, they began to travel downstream.

Avanasy ached. His hand ached from holding his knife. His shoulder burned from the blow it had taken. His soul ached from seeing Ingrid still and lifeless on the sands.

His prisoner's body pulled against the iron knife that held him pinned, and his encased spirit pulled against Avanasy's command enforced by that iron. He pulled toward his mistress, and his mistress would know it soon, if she did not already. Grimly, Avanasy held on, because to let go would be to leave Ingrid alone. Overhead, the stars wheeled toward morning, and his pain settled into his bones, and he still held on.

Then, the rider lifted his head as if he heard a distant sound.

"Your woman is free," he said. "You may not hold me any longer."

"But she has not returned," croaked Avanasy. His hand had begun to go numb with cold and effort. All he could feel now was the pain that throbbed in time to his heartbeat.

"My mistress did not take her," sneered the knight. "And now my mistress does not hold her. You have no more right to me, and even your iron cannot claim me."

The pull which Avanasy had fought all night turned into a sudden wrench, and Avanasy cried out, but he could not hold on and the rider tore himself free. Before Avanasy could stumble to his feet to try to strike out again, the rider snatched his black javelin up from the ground where it had fallen, and was gone.

For a moment, Avanasy only stared at the suddenly empty night. Then, he roared out in wordless frustration and stabbed his knife deep into the ground. But it changed nothing. Ingrid's body still lay abandoned.

He crawled to her side and cradled her head against his chest. He had to think. He must think clearly. Where could she be now? What path could she have taken? The Rider said Baba Yaga had not to pulled her forth. This must be true or by the laws that governed bargains between the mortal world and the Land of Death and Spirit he would not have been able to break the hold Avanasy placed on him. All the magics Avanasy knew were for binding that which was already together. He knew no spell to call a spirit back into its body. Not a divided spirit. Even if he could go in search of her, could he find her in the vastness of the Silent Lands? Did he have the strength to walk that road now?

"Oh, Ingrid," he breathed as he held her yet more tightly. "I will try. I must. But, love, help me to find you."

Ingrid felt the current again, a gentle undertow to her awareness. At first, she tried to steel herself against it, but then she realized this current had a familiar touch. She looked across to her other self and that other self nodded once.

Avanasy.

Ingrid pushed forward. The world around her had grown thick and sluggish again. She was no longer vapor as she had been, but nor was she yet solid. Movement was difficult, even with the current. She had weight now, but not flesh. Will, but not strength, and she was growing tired.

Help me. Love, reach for me. Please, I'm here.

Soft, so soft Avanasy almost did not feel it, Ingrid's breath blew across his hand. He froze, his heart pounding, but no other breath came. He chafed her wrist gently. "Here, love. Here, please, I am here."

He pressed two fingers against her wrist, and felt the tiniest trace of living warmth. Beyond that, there was the flutter of a heartbeat, and another. But that was all.

"Yes. Here." He drew her even closer. "Here."

Her breath touched his cheek again, and her chest rose and fell, once, and again.

"Yes." He kissed her mouth, breathing into her with his breath, and willing her with all his strength to find her way home.

Weight and form, distant but real. Ingrid felt her sluggish blood in the netting of her veins, the frame of her bones and the binding of her sinews. But it was all too far away, and she was so tired. What had she done to become so tired? She could not reach out, but she knew where her hands were. She could not cry out, even though now she knew where her voice lay. She was weighted down with weariness and fear, struggling through a world that grew thicker with each passing instant.

But then, then, she felt Avanasy's kiss, and she felt her being, flesh and spirit, yearn to respond, but she did not know how.

But the weight was hers, and the will was hers, and she could feel her hand. She would raise her hand, she would touch him. She would hold him. She would.

Avanasy, almost not believing what he saw, watched, filled with hope and fear, as Ingrid's hand struggled to lift itself.

"Yes." He kissed her again. "Yes, love. Come back to me."

Ingrid felt herself sinking into the ground, into the weight of her flesh, into the sluggish flow of her own blood, and into Avanasy's embrace. She was still so cold, so far away, and yet, too, she felt the warmth of her bones gathering around her. She could raise her hand now, could touch his cheek, and feel its warmth and roughness underneath her palm as her hand traced its way down his back to his shoulder to his arm to his hand where he held her. She kissed him and held him close, for if he let her go now she would fly away again.

"Hold me, hold me," she said and she knew she spoke with her true voice. Avanasy gathered her close in his arms, kissing her endlessly, taking her breath, breathing again into her. She felt him weary, and in pain, yet she also knew his desire quickened his blood, as her desire quickened hers, growing insistent, pulling her home, and she embraced him, wrapping his hands around her so he might caress her, the warmth and strength of his touch bringing her closer to him still.

She had no other thought—no care for propriety, or fear

of abandonment. She wished him close, wished no barrier between them, and he knew her need and he laid her down and covered her and she was able to wrap herself around him so that they could lie close, and closer yet, and she knew nothing but joy, and she opened her eyes and she saw Avanasy and she was whole and alive and for that one moment they were together in life and love, and the morning star shone down from a brightening sky, and Ingrid knew this was all the blessing that they would ever need. This was their true marriage, whatever ceremony might come afterward.

For a while after that she slept. She woke at last to the dawn, and the feel of Avanasy stroking her hair. She turned to look up at him, and found him gazing down at her, and his cheeks were wet with tears.

"You found me," she rasped, her voice dry in her throat.

Avanasy shook his head. "No, you found your own way. I think it must be ever so with you."

She took his hand to still it and also to pull herself up. She was covered in sand, and hungry as a bear, but she didn't care. "Do you know what happened?"

"I think I do. I think that touch of the ghost that troubled your sister loosened your soul from your body."

Not even reflex made her say that was impossible. She was far beyond doubting any word he spoke of sorceries and spirit. "But . . . why now? It's been months."

"Until now you have not been in a place where magic and spirit dwelt openly, and I brought you here without thought."

"Can you . . . undo this?"

"No," he said simply and bitterly. "Not yet. I do not understand it. It should not be possible. I would have to consult with . . . others. A way may be found. Until then, though, I think I can bind you together so that the danger is at least lessened."

"Then we had better do that. I do not want to see that . . . old witch again anytime soon, thank you very much." She wondered if she should tell him what Baba Yaga had said, about seeing her future and her past, but she looked in his eyes and saw how much he already blamed himself for what was happening, and how real his pain, physical and spiritual, was. She decided to wait. The witch sought to discomfort her, and him. She thought to frighten Ingrid into doing her bidding.

Ingrid set her jaw. *Well, I for one will not play into your hands.*

But those thoughts made Ingrid shiver, and a small voice in the back of her mind wondered if somehow they had been overheard.

Chapter Twelve

The house guard captain gave his horse its head, guiding the animal only with his knees while he raised his javelin. As the horse raced by the posts that had been set up on Vaknevos's great, green lawn, the captain neatly spitted the small brass rings hanging from their threads—one, two, three, four. He missed the fifth, but wheeled the horse tightly around and sent it galloping back to capture the fifth ring. Holding his javelin high for the roar of approval from the assembled nobles and courtiers, he walked his sweating horse up to the dais with the imperial canopy, reverenced from the saddle, and dropped the rings into a heap of similar trinkets at the emperor's feet.

Kacha acknowledged the gesture with a bow of his head. At his back, the lords master laughed over their various wagers. Ambassador Girilal, for whose benefit this display ostensibly had been arranged, applauded politely before reaching again for the tiny cup of clear, peppery liquor set out on the refreshment tray for him. Girilal was developing quite a taste for the stuff, Kacha noted. It was a taste that perhaps should be nurtured.

Out on the lawn, the servants had hung fresh rings from the waiting posts. The invited guests who did not merit a spot on the dais milled about behind the temporary fences of blue-and-gold ribbons while other servitors dispensed drinks and dainties among them. When all was ready, Nausha, the commander of the Imperial House Guard, raised his hand, sending the next officer charging out.

"These seem a well-trained and disciplined group," remarked Girilal. "I confess, I am quite impressed."

"I was myself when I first saw them," Kacha acknowledged. The officer on the field had tossed aside his pike with its catch of rings and drawn his sword. Riding back down the lawn at full tilt, he clove a spitted apple neatly in twain as he thundered past.

Kacha lifted his cup to the officer as he wheeled the horse again to take aim at another set of apples already stuck into place. "We have taken great care to keep them actively employed so that they will be ready for whatever may come."

"A wise policy," said Girilal blandly. "Especially in a land known for its fractious provinces."

Kacha pursed his lips. On the field, the officer slashed left and right, never once missing his mark. The cheers rose up to shake the day. "Not so fractious as you might believe. This empire offers great advantages in peace and security for those who accept their part in her."

"And, of course, they nurture great love for their empress." Girilal nodded toward the empty chair that stood at Kacha's left side. "And her soon-to-be heir."

"Of course," acknowledged Kacha, and his right hand twitched. Girilal was probing, but for what?

The officer on the field finished his run and rode his sweating horse sedately past the imperial dais to make his reverence and receive the nod of approval in return. Behind them, there was more laughter, and more wagers proposed and accepted. They were content, his council lords. Regular meetings in the room fitted out with Yamuna's carpet kept their minds calm. The ranks of the House Guard swelled, and the newer officers could be safely charged with keeping order among the *oblasts* and the cities. Eventually, they could be trusted with more extensive duties, should such be necessary. There where whispers, here and there, of potential difficulties that would have to be dealt with, if what was to come could not sufficiently distract the troublemakers.

On the lawn, the setup for the next run was complete. The council lords finished their current round of betting to watch the next officer. Girilal reached again for his liquor cup.

In that moment of relative stillness, a very different cry rang out across the lawn. This was no soldier's bellow as he charged, no shout of triumph from a betting noble. This was a harsh, rattling cry torn from a worn throat desperate to be heard.

"News! News!"

Hoofbeats thudded across the lawn. Exclamations rose from the assembled crowd. Commander Nausha barked two orders and a rank of mounted officers assembled themselves in front of the dais while the armed guard that flanked the emperor and the council came at once to attention, their hands slapping onto the pommels of their swords.

A single rider careened across the lawn. Foam flew from the horse's mouth, and the rider slumped low across its neck as if he lacked the ability to hold himself upright. Yet, he mustered the strength to cry again.

"News! Imperial Majesty! News!"

Commander Nausha rapped out another order and the front rank of horsemen moved forward to intercept the rider, but Kacha got to his feet.

"Hold!" he called. "Let him approach!"

Another order rang out. Smartly, the mounted ranks parted to let the stranger enter the Imperial presence, but none of the soldiers on the dais removed their hands from their swords, nor did Commander Nausha relax at all.

As the rider drew nearer, it could be seen he wore the black coat and green trim of the Sol'uyche oblast, one of the most southern provinces. His boots were caked with mud, and more mud spattered his coat and helmet. He had lost one glove and that hand, where it clenched the reins, had been slashed and battered and fresh blood oozed out between the scabs.

The crowd on the lawn had gone completely still. Only the horses stamped and shifted restlessly, jingling their harnesses and snorting out their disapproval.

The rider halted his trembling, sweating horse and lifted a paper white face to Kacha and the assemblage on the dais. He tried to lift his naked hand to make the reverence, but Kacha waved the gesture away.

"Imperial Majesty," the man gasped. "I am come from the border. From Miateshcha. My commander sent me across into Hung Tse to see . . ." He tried to draw a deep breath and it ended in a rattling cough. "Hung Tse is sending its troops on the border. I overheard a band of raiders. They said . . ." Again, his words were lost in a wracking cough. "They said there would soon be no work for them to do, because the soldiers of the Heart of the World would level all before them." He managed to take one shaky breath. "I have ridden many days to bring you word, Imperial Majesty . . ."

The man's strength gave out at last, and he slumped forward over his horse's neck. Commander Nausha glanced at Kacha for permission, which Kacha gave with a sharp nod. Nausha ordered forward a clutch of soldiers who gently slipped the rider off his horse and bore him away. Another took charge of the trembling beast and led it after its master. Its head hung so low that its mane all but brushed the ground.

But Kacha had no time to think more on the fallen rider. Behind him, the voices of the council were rising from murmurs to demands for explanation. The crowd on the field sounded like the surging of the ocean.

He lifted his voice to carry across the field. "This is grave news indeed. The empress must be alerted at once. But be sure," he raised his hands, "no threat to Isavalta will go unanswered!"

"Strike them down!" shouted someone from the crowd.

Kacha suppressed a smile. "All enemies to Isavalta will be struck down and they will never rise!"

A cheer started, softly at first, but it rose and gathered strength and broke upon the summer air. "Strike!" cried a voice. "Strike them down!" shouted another.

"Let them die!"

"Kill them all!"

The cheer turned into an ugly thunder of voices and Kacha made no move to be heard over it. Instead he spoke to Commander Nausha. "Disperse the crowd gently, and call your men back to the barracks. You will be summoned to the council room shortly. My Lords Master." He turned to the men behind him. "Meet us in the council room within the hour. I must go to the empress." He looked to Girilal. "Be so good as to walk with me, Ambassador. There are things we must speak of at once."

He took the ambassador's elbow. The council lords, their faces ranging from worried to furious stood back and reverenced while Kacha led Girilal down the dais's steps.

Once they were away from the council and striding across the grass toward Vaknevos with the honor guards a prudent distance away, Girilal drew close to Kacha and whispered low in Kacha's ear.

"I will ask you plainly, Son of the Throne. What are you doing?" Girilal used the court language of Hastinapura, and the first title Kacha was given at his birth.

"With all reverence, Learned Sir," replied Kacha, just as softly and in the same tongue, "your meaning is not plain to me."

"That man came at a time too convenient for it to be a coincidence of nature," replied Girilal in the same, even whisper. He might have been speaking of some rare and beautiful bird he did not wish to frighten away. "And at a time when you were displaying the military prowess of your new realm. I ask you again, Son of the Throne, by all the names of the Seven Mothers, what are you doing?"

"Ridding Isavalta and Hastinapura of a common enemy." Kacha had to work to keep his smile from his face. He had not meant to tell Girilal of this so soon, but the man had forced the issue. It was best he hear the bones of it, and that Kacha could see how he would respond, now, before a communiqué indicating unease could be written to the Pearl Throne.

"Think on it," he went on, folding his hands behind his back. His right hand twitched again. The part of him that was Yamuna did not like this course, but neither did it actively interfere. "If Isavalta goes to war, the resources of Hung Tse will be sorely taxed. They will no longer be able to support the invaders my uncle battles against. He will then be able to harry their southern borders as we take the north. The central lands will be ours to divide, and there will be no bar to the peace and prosperity between us."

Girilal narrowed his eyes, as if seeking to see beneath

Kacha's skin to find what truth lay there. "And has your uncle approved of this plan?"

Here came the risk. "Not my uncle, no."

Despite his wish to appear casual, Kacha found himself watching the ambassador intently. Girilal did not know it, but what he said next might determine the length of his life. Sweat prickled Kacha's scalp. The ambassador would make an excellent and useful ally, but if he could not see . . . well, one additional death would not be that much more difficult to hide, especially as a war was about to begin.

"No, it is not something of which your uncle would approve." Girilal fastened his gaze on the approaching walls of Vaknevos. "There are many important things to which he has given no credence."

Kacha felt himself relax. "Fortunately, we are discussing the affairs of Isavalta, and not of Hastinapura. It is not the Pearl Throne which decides actions here."

"So, the empress agrees with your plan?"

"The empress has left all in my hands." Which was the truth, at least in part.

Girilal walked beside him in silence for a time, digesting his thoughts with care. Kacha tried not to watch him too closely, to give him some room in which to think. To frighten him now would be to lose all. If Girilal decided his duty was to the one on the throne, then their alliance was over before it had begun, and he would have to ask Yamuna how best to deal with a man who had seemed to hold so much promise. But, if his alliance was to the throne itself, and the proper order . . .

"Then, I suppose," said Girilal at last, "it remains for me to ask the Son of the Throne how my office may assist in this hopeful plan."

Now Kacha could smile with ease, as he felt the future Yamuna had taught him to dream of come that much closer.

Yamuna arrived in Devang on foot, the only proper way to approach such a place. Although he had been there a hundred times or more, he leaned upon his staff and took a moment to simply stare.

Once, Devang had been the greatest of all temples. Every bit of it had been carved from the living rock of the cliffs that towered high on all sides—the obelisks, the reliefs, the altars under their stone canopies, and the niches where the acolytes had trained and worshiped. All were the same shiny red stone. All were of a single piece growing out of the smooth red stone floor. It had been seven generations in the making, and now none even came here. It was a place of ghosts and demons, a place of old gods and goddesses conquered and cast down by the Seven Mothers before Ajitabh bowed down before them and rose up again in their names to lead the founding of the Pearl Throne.

Now the conquered received their sacrifice only when the Mothers were done, and no one came to this temple but tribes of monkeys to house themselves in the niches. And Yamuna.

The red stone reflected all the heat of the sun, turning the ancient temple into an oven. Yamuna walked unhesitatingly into the blazing heat. All around him, the squawks and calls of the monkey tribes filled the air. One sat on the central obelisk, gazing down at him. A family groomed each other on the eastern altar and on its canopy. Another pair squabbled by the lone fountain that still bubbled from the earth to spill across the barren stone. The place smelled strongly of heat and animals.

But for all that, the place had been made for power, and power simmered here, even now. Great things could still be accomplished here by one who knew the proper rites.

Monkeys screamed at each other in alarm as Yamuna strode into their midst. They scattered like leaves in the wind to the mouths of their niches, where they might squeal their insults at him in safety. For a moment, they reminded him very much of Chandra.

"I will not permit this!" Chandra had shouted at him, red-faced and shaking in his anger. "Your place is with me!"

"It is your wedding night," replied Yamuna coolly. "I cannot see how you would need my help for what must be done."

"You would send me alone to my exile and a house of spies," he sulked.

"You have your work to do there." Yamuna produced an

amber bracelet carved with serpents, symbols of wisdom and fidelity twined around each other. "When you arrive, you will give your bride this for her wrist, and you will put this," he held up a small clay vial stoppered tightly with wax, "in her tea as soon as you are able. Take care that you do not yourself inhale any steam from that tea. When all is done, she will not be able to keep any secret from us." *From me.* Chandra grasped the trinkets as greedily as the monkeys around him now grasped their fruit rinds. "The preparations I go to make now will help ensure that while Samudra and his queen may believe they spy on us, their eyes will be clouded while ours see clearly."

All of which had been more than enough to satisfy Chandra. Escaping Samudra's subtle traps was not so easy.

He had been summoned to the emperor's balcony the morning after the wedding rites. A dainty breakfast had been spread on low tables beside the bathing pool. The emperor, the Father of the Throne, Samudra the Usurper, sat on cushions of rose-and-gold silk, indecently close to his queen, who had been draped in silks and linens in all the colors of flame. Servants clad in white paced silently back and forth, filling goblets and removing plates. All the while Samudra's bound-sorcerer, the woman Hamsa, stood as still as the pillar that shaded her, one hand resting lightly on her staff. The queen's bound-sorcerer was nowhere to be seen, a fact Samudra noted with disquiet as he knelt and bowed his head to the tiled floor.

"*Agnidh* Yamuna," said the emperor in a perfectly friendly fashion. "Rise. Sit with us. There are matters we would discuss with you."

Hoping his silence would be taken for respectful humility, Yamuna lifted himself from the obeisance and knelt on the sky blue cushion the servant set down for him. A few slices of bread, thick with candied fruit, and a goblet of tangerine juice were placed in front of him, for it was known that as part of his asceticism, Yamuna ate only the simplest and plainest of foods. He was not one like *Agnidh* Hamsa, to gorge himself whenever the opportunity arose.

"We wanted to take this opportunity before you leave with

Chandra to thank you, Yamuna, for your loyal service to our
family," Samudra went on.

Yamuna bowed his head. What was running through the
usurper's mind? What did he want?

"I did not succeed the throne under favorable circumstances," Samudra went on. "I do not deny it. I have since
tried my best to make peace within the palace as well as
without."

Samudra was a soldier. His mind worked at all problems
as if they were campaigns. Yet, he had convinced more than
one enemy to surrender without bloodshed using the promise
of a liberal treaty in place of a long siege. He knew well
how to flatter, and when to use a soft word while laying his
naked sword across his lap for the enemy to see. It was
Samudra who left his brother, and Yamuna, alive, when all
around him, including the queen, urged that they be killed.

"The wisdom of the Father of the Throne is well known,"
murmured Yamuna piously.

The queen's eyes flashed, seeing the platitude plainly for
what it was. Yamuna did not care. Whatever plan they had
concocted between them, Samudra would not permit her to
disrupt it through something so trifling as anger.

"Yamuna, I have known you as long as I have known any.
You have been with my brother his whole life, as Hamsa has
been with me. I know your service does not come easily to
you, and it comes less so now that *Agnidh* Hamsa has taken
your place beside the throne to do the rites of empire and
sacrifice in your place."

Yamuna glanced sharply at Hamsa, who did not even raise
an eyebrow to indicate that she saw him. Not that Hamsa
had ever deigned to take much note of him since her part in
Samudra's . . . ascension.

"I accept my place." Yamuna told the lie smoothly and
without inflection. He had, after all, said it often enough. "I
do the office the Mothers have given me."

"I can break your bond with Chandra."

Yamuna's head jerked up. Samudra's face was perfectly
open, and perfectly frank. The queen raised a gilded goblet
in a slight toast to Yamuna before she drank, watching him
carefully over the bejeweled rim.

"I am bound to the life of Chandra *tya* Achin Ireshpad," said Yamuna firmly. "It is a thing fixed and cannot be broken."

"Yes, it can."

Samudra was too much of a soldier to recline on his pillows, but he did lean back a little, letting Yamuna get a good look at the full length of him. He sat, straight, cross-legged and calm, with an imperial bearing Chandra could never have managed. His hands rested on his knees. It did not take much work for Yamuna to imagine the sword lying under them.

"*Agnidh* Hamsa has found the way. There are bonds that my word as emperor, Father of the Throne, the one who is joined to the land, may break. This is one of them."

To his shame, Yamuna felt his mouth go dry as he realized what Samudra was truly offering him. Freedom. Were his bond broken, he could walk away from Chandra, from the Pearl Throne, and from all the petty cares that clustered in its shadows. He could step into the sunlight and go where he would. He could even walk into the northern lands on his own, and seek out his destiny there without having to coax and crawl before Chandra and his son.

Freedom.

Yamuna had to swallow before he could make himself speak clearly. "But such a thing could not come without price."

"There will be no further price." Samudra shook his head. "You are dissatisfied with your service. You do not like your place in the shadow of the throne, and you will like the southlands even less. That is enough. You have proven true when your master most needed you, and I am willing to reward that fidelity by releasing you now."

Yamuna's heart beat hard within his chest. Samudra was not lying. Not he. Oh, he was not above a ruse and deep deception when it suited him, but not like this. Not a bald lie to an enemy's face.

What do you want? Yamuna thought, working to keep his expression bland. He added another thought. *What do you know?*

Then, he saw it. *You know your brother to be harmless and ineffectual. That is why you let him live when you could*

*have killed him. For all you would do, you would not shed
family blood without true need. You will get him out of the
court, you will give him women to keep him watched and
sated, and you will send me away. You know he has ideas
of regaining the throne.* Despite all, Yamuna felt his eyes
narrow. *And you know where they come from.*

*If my bond is broken, if I leave him, the last true danger
to your rule is gone for good.*

But what did Yamuna care for any of that? The politics
of empire meant nothing to him. They were but the means
to an end, and Samudra had just offered to remove all need
for them.

Freedom.

Yamuna laid his staff down at the fountain's edge. The
monkeys there proved reluctant to desert their territory and
splashed and scrambled to the far side, shrieking insults at
him as he stripped off his loincloth and sandals. The water
ran clean and pure into the red stone basin, warmed by sun
above and stone below. Yamuna scooped the clear water into
his hands and used it to wash the dust of walking from his
body. He poured more water over his head and combed his
fingers through his hair and beard to clean them as well. He
rinsed his mouth and spat, startling the monkeys again and
making them leap and scream in frustration, waving their
arms at him, plainly saying "go away, go away!" The male
leaned across the edge of the fountain, baring his teeth and
growling low in his throat, but he made no move to attack.

Very like Chandra. Yamuna rewrapped his cloth and
picked his staff back up. *His fall was not undeserved.*

Well, Yamuna, what will you do?

Those were the words the queen had spoken to him on the
sun-drenched balcony. The break in the rains was quite welcome, and all were enjoying it. To all appearances she was
a leisurely lady, stretched across a suite of pillows, picking
at the dainties before her with her right hand and listening
without too much attention to the business of her husband.

It was a ruse, and those who believed her wits were not
as sharp as her husband's swords often learned of their mistake far too late.

"Father of the Throne," said Yamuna, stalling for time.

"You ask me to break the oath of a lifetime with the words of a moment."

"It is not breaking an oath to be lawfully released from it." Samudra nodded toward Hamsa. "Tell him what you have found, *Agnidh*."

Hamsa turned her head toward Yamuna, as if she were just becoming aware that any conversation was taking place before her.

"When the Mothers came to bless the Pearl Throne built by Madher, first of the emperors, they brought with them Laws that the emperor must obey, and the Laws in which the emperor must be obeyed."

I know this as well as you, woman. But Yamuna sat silently.

"Among these laws is the prescription that, as the emperor is father over all born in the shadow of the Pearl Throne, his alone are the hands that finally hold all oaths and contracts made to the throne and the imperial family." Her eyes glittered amber in the sunlight. "All oaths."

Was it true then? Was there no bar to his leaving Chandra to fend for himself, to walking away, to devoting himself to study and asceticism until his ends were reached, until he could stand in the north lands and call down the Mothers, god to god?

"I beg you, Father." Yamuna bowed down and covered his face with his hands. "Give me time to think, and leave to seek solitude to take my heart's council."

"Of course," said Samudra amiably. "You may give us your answer tomorrow."

So, Yamuna had come here, to this place of old power and chittering monkeys to seek his answers and understand what he must do. If he needed the bond Chandra and Kacha's formal conquest would bring in order to find his divinity, then he could not free himself. But if he did not . . .

Past the fountain, Devang became a plaza with curving walls that were the towering red cliffs, carved with reliefs of the gods; playing games, calling down storms, healing the sick, sitting in judgment over the demons. The only other decoration had been carved into the smooth floor.

It was a sun wheel, a pattern of concentric circles and

radiating arms. Each circle was filled with meticulously carved planets and stars along with their ruling gods and elements. It was so large it was difficult to take in all at once down here in the plaza. One had to scale the cliffs and look down on it to see its true sweep.

It was also what Yamuna had come here to find. Years of study and searching through the oldest texts and tablets had led him to believe that this was part of a weaving, one that could allow the skilled to see into the future, one of the most difficult of the sorcerous arts. He had traced a trail of hints and possibilities, from ancient acolytes to worn carvings on pillars that marked ancient cities and shrines to one great, black pillar of iron that was supposed to mark the spot where the gods stood to create Hastinapura from the surrounding ocean.

From his small travel bag, Yamuna pulled a tiny vial made of obsidian. In it was a liquid it had taken him a lifetime's work to distill. Patient skill and patient magic had been woven into this liquor to bring it properly into being, and now he would use what was left to make this last, most important decision.

The stone wheel spread out before him, its carvings as elaborate as the pattern woven into the finest carpet. Yamuna cracked the seal on the vial and pulled out the stopper.

Gently, reverently, he stepped onto the first circle of the wheel. He held the vial before him, and tipped one drop of the golden distillation onto the burning red stone. Its rich, heady scent rose up at once.

"I give you to drink of the fruits of the trees," he said, walking forward so that the soles of his feet pressed the liquor into the stone. It was slick and hot underfoot and its perfume wafted about him. Another careful drop, another careful step. "I give you to drink of the flowers of the field and the blood of life." Yamuna kept his words steady, matching them in time to his steps, and his offering of the sacred liquor. It was not easy. The scent soaked into his mind as the strong liquor soaked into his skin, turning him dizzy and making him feel far too light. The heat began to burn his much-toughened soles, but he held himself firmly. This was a weaving of the most delicate kind. Although it was built on a foundation of stone, all was done in air, the least solid of all the elements. He must not miss a single step or syllable.

"I give you to drink of fire and water, of earth and air. I give you to drink of the world, of all that is present and past. I give you to drink of myself. I walk the paths of stone and I pour out all I have that you might drink. Only show me, show me what is yet to come. Show me, show me if I may accept what is offered and gain what it is I seek."

Heat beat down. The air felt strangely dry for this season of rains. It seemed to grate against every pore. The scent of the liquor was too thick to be mere vapor. It was a tactile curtain, thick and binding, pressing against him, smothering his breath and making his footsteps unsteady. But he did not feel afraid. He felt buoyant, as if any step might lift him off the ground and allow him to fly freely away. The sensation made it difficult to see. His own hands and voice felt far away. The scented curtain surrounded him and supported him. It was a rich veil between him and the world, removing all care, all responsibility, lifting him into the air, dissolving him from flesh and the cares of the flesh, the world of the flesh, winding and binding him into a new world, where he himself was nothing but a vapor.

In this new world, the wheels that had been beneath his feet turned freely in the golden light of the sun. All that drove mortal destiny was visible. Each of the figures danced within its own sphere, the gods at their wars and their justice, the symbols turning like the wheels themselves, pausing to point this way, then that, to bestow fortune or tragedy to the immortal dramas unfolding around them.

As a vapor, Yamuna wafted calmly over the turning wheels, until one of the turning symbols stilled before him. It was an empty throne. It pulled at him, airy being that he was, and he saw himself sitting in it. The gods crowded around his feet, ready to greet him as great among them. His left hand held a lotus, his right held a sword, and he knew himself to be powerful, even as the immortal reckon power. He tossed up the lotus and as it fell, he sliced it neatly in two with his sword and the petals rained down upon the old gods who lifted their hands to catch them, accepting his bounty, and he knew that beyond the range of his golden vision, the Seven Mothers saw all this, and grew unquiet.

Yamuna drifted closer to this vision, this turn of the wheel that promised him all he sought, and he saw that around his neck was a golden collar, and from the collar dangled the severed end of a golden chain. His broken oath, his freedom from Chandra brought him to this throne. Yamuna saw all this and rejoiced.

But the wheels kept turning. The throne turned under Yamuna, the sword turned, the severed lotus turned, and all the dances moved, but Yamuna did not move, and their turning toppled him from his seat, and lotus and sword fell, and pierced his side. Yamuna saw himself sprawled at the feet of the gods, impaled upon his own sword, covered in the petals of the lotus, his hand stretching out toward the other end of his chain as if seeking to join the two together again.

The wheels turned and the world turned, and their current caught up the vapor that was Yamuna and spun it wildly around until all became a blur of red and gold, heat and heady perfume, senseless, swirling, spinning ever faster until the force of its fury cast Yamuna out, back into his flesh, falling hard against the unmoving stone wheel where he had begun.

Yamuna tasted blood where he had bitten his tongue. More blood trickled down his split chin onto the carved wheels where he sprawled, darkening and hardening quickly in the baking sun. He felt as parched as a stone himself, but he could not move. All force of will and strength of body had been wrung from him, and he had no choice but to lie unsheltered in the sun until they returned to him.

But he had seen what he needed to see. If he severed his chain, if he allowed his vow to be annulled, it would bring his destruction.

So, my little Prince Chandra, it would appear I need you yet awhile longer.

At last, burning from the heat of the sun above and the heat of the stone below, Yamuna made himself move. He crawled one painful inch at a time back toward the fountain. The sound of the cool, trickling water sent tremors through his frame. The monkeys, chased away by his magics, had returned now, and they hooted and screamed at him. Aware that he was much weakened, perhaps even dying, they grew bold and scampered close to shriek at him before running back to the safety of their niches. He crawled forward, concentrating only on moving arms and legs. At last, he fell into the fountain's shallow trough. Water cascaded over him like the blessings of paradise. He lay in the fresh water, drinking with his mouth and with his pores, until the burning lessened and he was able to stand without shaking, and reclaim the meager clothes that he had laid beside his pouch and staff.

Dressed again, but feeling only a little stronger, Yamuna knelt in the shadow cast by the nearby temple. He opened his pouch and took a little bread to eat with fresh drafts from the fountain. Then, he brought out another bottle. This one was a squat, ungainly jar of red clay, the exact color of the stone around him. Yamuna had made the vessel from clay from a spring close to Devang, and with his own hands he had carved the weaving patterns that covered its sides. More red clay, carved with a representation of the sun wheel at his feet, sealed the jar tightly.

Yamuna took a deep breath. This would not take much strength, which was fortunate, as he did not have much to give, but it would require a show of strength. He crossed his legs, stiffened his spine so that he sat up straight and fixed his face in a stern attitude.

Then, he swiftly cracked the seal and cast the jar away.

The air above the jar blurred and warped. Opaque figures formed slowly, as if they pulled their constituent elements from the surrounding ether. They grew red and gold, like the surrounding sun-baked stone. They lengthened and separated into a crowd of four, all standing on sinewy legs, with taloned feet. Torsos, armored and chained, thickened and sprouted terrible arms that ended in clawed hands clutching spears and curved swords. Fangs as curved as those blades protruded from gaping lips. Sail-shaped ears hung with gold turned in Yamuna's direction, as did the terribly alert, round, yellow eyes. Wings, heavy with feathers the color of old blood, spread from their shoulders.

The first among them, the tallest, with the most terrible eyes, roared out a wordless challenge and rushed toward Yamuna, shaking his weapons and raising his wings to blot out the sun so that all Yamuna could see was a shadow in the shape of a nightmare. He did not permit himself to flinch, even as the demon stabbed his spear down at his heart and his eyes, at his hands and his private parts. The demon could not harm him. The invisible bonds that restrained it were too well forged.

At last, the demon seemed to have vented its immediate rage and it retired, snarling, to its fellows.

"Why have you called us?" demanded the demon, its voice heavy with hatred.

"Because I have need of your eyes and your wings," Yamuna replied calmly. "I need you to see Avanasy Finorasyn Goriainavin."

"What if we do see?" growled the first of the demons.

"Then you will tell me what you see."

"And if we do not see?"

Yamuna narrowed his eyes just a little. "You will see." *You will see because I can't find the little straying cow. But she will have recalled her teacher, and where he is, she will be.*

The first of the demons snarled. He turned west, away from Yamuna and his fellows. His wide, yellow eyes stared steadily out through Devang's gate, searching, Yamuna knew, the whole world beyond.

"The man Avanasy Finorasyn Goriainavin sails south down the coast of Isavalta," said the demon slowly. "He stands on the deck of a small boat. There is a woman at the tiller."

"Who is the woman?" snapped Yamuna.

The demon squinted. "She has no name in this world. I know her not."

"What else?"

"He is waiting for something. He speaks to the woman of it." The demon's sail-shaped ear twitched. "He waits for a crow. The bird is a messenger for him to his man in Isavalta. He hopes it will find them before they reach the Heart of the World." The demon's wings shook themselves restlessly. "That is what I see."

The Heart of the World! The little cow had taken shelter with the Nine Elders? Yamuna considered. It was not so foolish a move as it might first appear. The Heart of the World was well protected against both force and magic. She could not be readily reached there, and she could warn the Nine Elders and their emperor somewhat at least of what came toward them, removing the advantage of surprise. It might, in fact, be a swifter way to gain aid for her cause than sending her messengers hither and thither about her provinces trying to determine who was still loyal to her, especially if she had trusted spies still in Isavalta who could do that for her.

Well, well, there is a brain in that head after all. Yamuna permitted a small nod in deference to the child's scramblings. She would fail in the end, but at least she would put up a fight.

"You will allow that crow to meet with this man in Isavalta, and then you will bring it to me along with whatever message it carries," said Yamuna to the demons. "You will also find the sorcerer Avanasy, and kill him and all who are with him." There would be little Medeoan could do if she were cut off from her aides and information, and now that they knew where she was, they could watch movement down the coast all the more carefully. As soon as his strength was restored, he must send a message to Kacha.

The demons growled, a long, low noise that he felt trembling through his torso.

"You ask too much of us, man," said the first of them. "Take what we have seen and be content."

Worry rippled through Yamuna's blood. If the demons challenged him now, it was possible they might break free from his grip. The spell was strong, but he was weak, and he did not know how much of the working he could call on. He could not let it come to that.

"I still hold your chains," he said coldly. "I could at this moment bury you deep in the earth and you would not be able to move until I so ordered. But I am not such a master. You will do as I say because if you do not, you will suffer, and you know this." His mouth twitched, as though he were about to smile. "You remember other times you have suffered."

The first of the demons shrank back. Yamuna held himself

very still. Like most of their kind, these four were inherently cowards. Terrible, powerful cowards, but cowards all the same. When Yamuna had first bound them to him, he had not done so out of immediate need, but because need might arise. He had driven them deep into the earth first, and left them there, snarling and howling. When he had finally pulled them forth, they were firmly his, cowed by fear of imprisonment in an element that was no part of their being, and so gave them no succor, only pain.

They remembered that imprisonment now. He saw it in their eyes, and in the way they pulled their heavy wings close about themselves.

"We will do as you say," the first demon told him.

"Good." Yamuna nodded. "Then go."

The four demons raised their arms, and rose from the ground in a rattling flurry of wings and hot wind. In a heartbeat, they were gone and Yamuna was left alone with his exhaustion and a stark sense of relief.

It had almost been too much. He had almost failed.

It does not matter, he told himself, taking a long breath to purge the tremors beginning again in his limbs. *I did not fail, and now I know not only that I must stay bound to Chandra for this little while longer. I know where the Isavaltan empress has hidden herself, and I can turn her shelter into her prison.*

Yamuna moved his gaze to the stone wheel again. *What does it matter that I am bound for a while longer? Only the gods are truly free, and once I have that freedom for myself, nothing else will matter. Nothing at all.*

Eliisa paid off the canal boat's pilot with the three copper coins she had carefully counted out from her stash the night before. Thankfully, he took them without comment, slipping them into his sash, and nodding her farewell. The night before he'd suggested a way she might save the fee, and she'd been afraid she'd have to fight him off before the trip was over. But it had not come to that, and now she was safe in Camaracost.

If safe was the word for it. Even thinking the name

brought a sour taste to her mouth. Camaracost was a market town, a port town. Anything could be bought here, be it a passage to Hung Tse, or a girl for the kitchens of a fine house.

She wondered for a moment if Mother or Father still lived inside the city walls. She dismissed the idea. She could not idle here. If she was lucky it was a market day, and she could see who was about doing the buying and the selling.

The streets by the canals were warrens of warehouses and storage barns. The best could be told the by the hired guards standing alert at the doors in their clean kaftans and broad sashes. The worst slouched in the shadows near the open drains, either unattended, or watched over by greasy men with greasy eyes that glided over her as she strode past.

Noise and distant memory guided Eliisa's feet. Soon, she found herself in better, if more crowded, streets. Wooden houses, some two and three stories high, with brightly painted doors and roofs, crowded up to the cobbles. They left barely enough room for three grown men to walk abreast, let alone for the carts and mule trains that tried to squeeze through the streets.

Finally, the narrow thoroughfares opened onto the public square. The city's gilded god house shined in its center, and around it flocked all the crowds, noise, and smell of a bustling market. Stalls and tents filled the square the way the merchant's voices filled the air. Eliisa plunged into the crowd without hesitation. Housewives and husbandmen jostled shoulders with servants and agents for the noble houses. Men in the bright silks of Hastinapura haggled over baskets of nuts and bags of spices. Moneychangers weighed and counted. Scribes recorded bargains and set the lord master's seal upon bills of goods and sales to show that the taxes had been duly paid. There were even men of Hung Tse here, in long coats of plain, undyed cotton with jet buttons, pacing quietly through the throng, their sharp eyes darting this way and that.

They might be just who she wanted. If they were not, perhaps they could lead her to the ones she did.

As in all other transactions, however, appearing eager was a sure way to get cheated. Eliisa wished she had a basket so that she would look more like she was on an errand for some mistress. But, as it was, she kept most of her attention on the stalls she passed, fingering grains and dried beans. Sniffing suspiciously at the summer's first fruits, she was able to see the two men of Hung Tse arguing with a seller from Hastinapura over sacks of cinnamon and peppercorns, judging by the smell the wind brought her. Eliisa bought herself a portion of black bread and liver sausage from a sharp-eyed biddy and squeezed into a corner between a stall and a house to eat it. The foreigners argued, haggled, and dickered in a mix of languages, with much waving of hands and beating of breasts. At last, though, they bowed to each other, each in the fashion of his own country, and the shorter of the two men from Hung Tse left his partner to write up the contract of sale and see to the proper seals while he stepped back into the stream of the crowd.

Eliisa smiled. Now, it only remained to see which ship was his. The captain, whoever he might be, would surely not be averse to a little extra money, and another pair of hands in the galley.

Munching the last of her meal, Eliisa followed the foreigner through the crowds. He knew well the ways of below-market, and crossed the center of the square nearest the god house where the crowds were thinner. On market days, beggars with their bowls were permitted to cluster around the sides of the god house to see what charity was to be had. They smelled even more strongly than the stalls of the spice merchants in the heat. As she passed, Eliisa caught the eye of one of the god house keeper's assistants, who frowned at her. Ducking her head, Eliisa fished one of her remaining pennies out of her girdle and tossed it into one of the brass bowls that waited at the foot of the stairs. Supposedly, it not only garnered the good will of the gods as a charitable act, but it was good luck. Eliisa was not so sure of herself that she was ready to turn down a little extra luck.

Eliisa followed her guide to the edge of town where the canals emptied into the bay. The world took on the smell of fish. Because it was summer, the docks were a forest of masts and sails. Tiny fishing boats bobbed between huge, sharp-keeled, oceangoing vessels. It was to one of these that her guide went. Eliisa marked the ship. It had a scratched, black hull, but the knotwork paint was bright and the wind nets hanging from its sides were whole and stout, and might even have been woven by an actual sorcerer. It was a prosperous ship, and Eliisa smiled. The voyage aboard that craft might even be fun, or at least comfortable.

"Now, then, my girl," said a voice behind her. "You're going to come along and explain yourself. I've many a question to put to you."

Eliisa's throat closed and she turned. Behind her stood a soldier. He did not wear the gray-and-red livery of Cameracost's lord master. He wore the bright blue and gold of the Imperial House Guard.

"I don't have to go anywhere with you," she snapped, trying to keep the tremor from her voice. "I have my papers. I am free."

"You're not, and you do," replied the soldier, darting his eyes sideways so that Eliisa could not help but turn her head to see the two other guards waiting at the end of the dock. "Come, my girl. You're wanted."

"But why? They let me go!"

"That's not for me to say or you to ask." His hand closed lightly around her elbow, with the clear implication that he could hold her much harder should she decide to struggle.

Eliisa's mouth hardened, and she knew there was something she could do about this, but she did not move. Instead, she remained quiet while the soldier, an over sergeant, by the braid on his cuffs and the brass buttons on his kaftan, walked her back to the pair of under sergeants that waited for them.

"Next time, my girl, if you want to stay hidden, do not pay off the local gods in imperial coin."

Eliisa's mouth went dry. "What do they want me for?" she asked. The over sergeant had not released her and she had to step smartly to keep up as the under sergeants marched them over the bridge and between the long tables where the fishermen unloaded and scaled their catch. The cobbles were slick with blood and the smell made Eliisa's head spin even worse than her sudden capture did. Despite that, she could not help but note the dark hair and features of the fishers, which told her they were probably all from the island of Tuukos, as her mother had been.

A bent man struggling under a yoke of buckets filled with fish heads and guts staggered into the road. One of the under sergeants reached out to cuff the old man and the blow knocked him off balance. The man sprawled onto the street, pouring guts and scales all across the soldiers' boots. He mumbled his apologies, and tried to scramble out of the way, but slipped in his own mess so that one of the under sergeants tripped over the yoke and hit the ground beside him, cursing.

"Under Sergeant!" shouted the soldier beside her, and his grip on Eliisa loosened, just a little.

Eliisa twisted hard and threw herself sideways. The sudden motion startled the soldier and Eliisa yanked herself free and ran, skidding on the slick cobbles but keeping her feet. She had more experience on wet slates than the house guard. They must not catch her. They must not. She only barely knew why, but they must not.

Eliisa dodged between the tables, tossing one over as she passed, earning shouts and curses from the fishers working there as she splashed fish all across the muddy street.

Then, a fresh set of hands grabbed her. Before she could think to struggle, they shoved her into a pile of empty pickling barrels. A fishy-smelling tarp dropped over Eliisa and the barrels, cutting off all light. But by then she was recovered enough to think to hold quite still. Outside, something was piled atop her shelter, pressing the canvas down until it rested against her skull.

Boots ran by. Voices shouted and argued. Someone brushed her canvas and Eliisa bit down hard on her lip. She tried to breathe quietly in the choking, fish-scented darkness. The sounds outside faded away, but she still did not move. The heat sent rivulets of sweat trickling down her cheeks and neck, but she didn't dare shift herself to wipe them away. Her right foot went to sleep.

Just as she thought she would surely faint from the heat and lack of air, a corner of the canvas peeled back to let in painfully bright light and the silhouette of a human head.

"Come out, Daughter," said a man's voice, and Eliisa

started. He was speaking in the language of Tuukos. No one had spoken that to her since she was five or six. Since her mother had signed her into service. It was like hearing a voice from a dream.

Stiff, and blinking hard, Eliisa crawled out of her stinking shelter. As she straightened up, she saw how badly she had lost track of time. The sun had already sunk behind the tallest houses, and the shadows lengthened across the water, turning the bright green bay to somber gray. Eliisa's hand flew to her mouth as her eyes sought out the water level as measured against the dock pilings. The tide had turned. Her ship might have already sailed.

"Calm yourself, Daughter," said a lithe little man at her side. It was only by the bright red cuffs on his rough, woolen smock that she recognized him as the man with the yoke who had tripped up the soldiers. She had thought him old, but now that he stood upright she saw he had not yet even reached his middle years. He added something more which she could not understand.

"I'm sorry, Father." She tried to answer him in Tuukosov, but her tongue fumbled the words badly. "I don't understand anymore."

A woman nearby with a face like an old apricot spat and muttered something angrily. The only word Eliisa caught was "Isavaltans."

"Never mind, Daughter." The man spoke slowly, as to a child, and patted her arm with his thick, calloused hand. "What did your parents name you?"

"Eliisa."

"Well, Eliisa, and it's no good you standing here in the street. You had best come along with us."

"Thank you, Father, but I must . . ."

"That ship you were so intent on is still there," he said kindly, but firmly. "You'd best come with us."

Eliisa swallowed her next words. The stubby woman frowned hard at her, and she remembered she should not be questioning her elders. So, she just nodded. She was too tired to do otherwise. Besides, she had to get somewhere she could be alone, and take her girdle off. It was important, but she couldn't remember why. Thinking in Tuukosov seemed to push the Isavaltan words out of her head.

"Good," said the little man. "And I am Finon. The woman there is Ilta. We'll see you safe, stowed among your own for the night."

"Then, my girl," said Ilta, taking her arm even more firmly than the over sergeant had and steering her toward the docks, "you can tell us what the House Guard wanted with you."

"I don't know," answered Eliisa stubbornly. "I was let go. I've got the paper. It's sealed. I can go anywhere in the oblast."

"And where in the oblast would you be going on that tall ship?" mused Finon.

"That's my business," snapped Eliisa in Isavaltan. Ilta pinched her elbow hard. "Hey!"

"Mind your manners, girl. You've Isavaltan blood in you by the look of you. If it shows stronger than your clean blood, we may just hand you back to them."

Eliisa swallowed. Here it came. Half-blood. Mother wouldn't have given her over else.

"Now, then, Ilta," said Finon, his dark eyes glittering. "She's still wearing the patterns, isn't she? Still knows her name, doesn't she? Give her time to remember herself. How long have you been with them, Daughter?"

Them. The Isavaltans, with their bright hair and pale eyes. Demons who came out to the Holy Island and slaughtered the people and tried to drive out the True Ways by killing every sorcerer of the pure blood they could find. She'd heard all the stories when she was a child, and had held them close, even after Mother signed her away. "I was six when I was sold."

"Huh. Your Blood Father should have starved himself first," said Ilta.

"He was a soldier, Mother said," muttered Eliisa to the cobbles. "Isavaltan."

She didn't have to say any more. They understood how she had come into the world. Ilta spat again.

The warm summer darkness swiftly enclosed the bay. Ilta and Finon walked her past the tall ships and the tugs and the Isavaltan fishing boats, to a cluster of boats the like of which she hadn't seen in years. They had square sterns and dark, square sails. Each was painted red, black and green with lettering stretched out and run together until it looked like knotwork, but each pattern was really a spell written out for the individual craft, taken from its name and blessed, if not painted, by a sorcerer.

Guttering lanterns hung from spars. The boats had been tied together in a cluster, and Eliisa knew there would be planks stretched between them to make walking from one to the other easier. The tiny fleet was, for the time being, a tiny village huddled in the shadows and hoping the Isavaltans would not take notice of it tonight.

Finon led them to one of the boats. By the lantern light, Eliisa could see that it was painted bright green all over. That meant this was the headman's boat. Eliisa swallowed and hoped she could remember her manners. It would not do to anger these people. They knew knives and darkness. She could vanish so easily down here. Why had she agreed to come?

Because you had no choice, she reminded herself sharply as she tried to reassemble her nerve.

Eliisa had lost the trick of the boats along with most of her blood's tongue, so she was forced to scramble clumsily over the side, even though Finon extended his hands to help her. The boat's deck was wide and its gear tidily stowed. Voices drifted down from the bow. Up by the galley, a pair of lanterns showed a gathering of solemn men and women, their heads together as they conferred. Finon removed his round cap and stepped forward, not seeming to notice the rocking motion of the deck. The gathering parted to reveal a young man sitting on a carved bench. Eliisa sucked in a breath. There was only one reason so young a man would be sitting when so many elders were standing. He was not a headman. He was a sorcerer.

Her heart sank within her and Eliisa tried to hang back, but it was far too late. Ilta was already pulling her forward, and Finon had raised his hand in salute to the sorcerer.

"We've rescued this daughter of the Holy Island from the guard," he said, speaking slowly for Eliisa's benefit. "With your blessing, I'll take her to my boat for sanctuary."

Ilta pushed Eliisa forward. The sorcerer looked young, but he could have been any age. Sorcerers lived two and three times as long as a normal man. His thick black hair swept back from his high forehead, and his black eyes glittered in the lamplight. Here was one who knew his own power. As his gaze raked her from head to foot, Eliisa also knew that his power, at least here among these people, was considerable.

"Who taught you to tie your girdle in such a fashion, Little Sister?" the sorcerer asked. He had a smooth voice. It was easier to understand him than either Finon or Ilta.

Eliisa started to shrug, but caught herself. "My mother, I suppose, Honored Brother," she said, remembering to speak softly and keep her eyes cast down. Looking too long upon a sorcerer was bad luck, they said. They could draw your soul out through your eyes.

"Did your mother have power then?"

"No, Honored Brother."

"Strange she should know that knot to teach you. It is a spell knot. Much in favor among the Isavaltans."

Reflexively, Eliisa covered the knot with her hand, shrinking back as she did. "I did not know, Honored Brother. Perhaps I learned it in the scullery. I was there a long time."

"That could very well be," said the sorcerer. "There's many a scrap of knowledge in such a place." He put his hand under her chin and tilted it up so she could see he smiled at her, and Eliisa felt herself relax a little.

A moment later, she heard fabric tearing, and her girdle thudded to the deck. Pain stabbed her heart and the whole world swam in front of her eyes as the spell snapped in two, and Eliisa vanished.

Medeoan stared at the knife in the sorcerer's hand. All around her, the Tuukosov had gone completely silent. The sorcerer stepped back, but made no move to sheathe his knife.

"Or perhaps, that knowledge has been too well remembered."

There were no shouts, only mutters in the language she could not understand now that Eliisa had left her. Ilta, the woman who had been just barely willing to give one of her own the benefit of the doubt, raised her hand and would have brought it down against Medeoan's face, but the sorcerer stopped her with a sharp gesture.

"Who are you?" he asked in Isavaltan.

Medeoan lifted her chin. "I thank you for saving me from the guard. I wish no quarrel, or trouble. I want only to be on my way."

"That was not a question I asked," said the sorcerer. He still had the knife out, and yet he also held back his countrymen with his word. "Answer me truthfully, for you know that I can have the truth at any time."

"I am taking myself away from my husband's home," said Medeoan. "He wants me back. Surely you do not need to know any more than that. You do not want to be able to give answers to the guard."

The sorcerer nodded thoughtfully. "That is a reasonable thought, especially for an Isavaltan woman. It is still, however, not what I asked."

Then, Finon, who had been standing very still, moved over to the sorcerer. He murmured something, and the sorcerer's eyes widened. He touched Finon's hand and whispered back in his own language. Medeoan felt her throat tighten. An attempt to run would be useless; she would just have to bargain for time, until she was left alone and could contrive some weaving to help her escape. They were on the water; that would help with any magic of motion and uncertainty.

"Ilta," the sorcerer said. Then he added something in his own language. Ilta's face went grim, and she grabbed Medeoan's elbow, with no pretense at gentleness this time.

"Come," she barked and dragged Medeoan toward the boat's hatch. Medeoan saw the sorcerer watching her carefully while Finon murmured in his ear.

She had no opportunity to see anything else, for Ilta was stuffing her down into the boat's dark, fish-scented hold. At least there was somewhat more air to breathe here than there had been under the canvas. She heard Ilta moving about and then saw the spark and soft glow as a tin lantern was lit.

"Sit," growled Ilta, stationing herself at the ladder leading to the deck. "Make any other move and I will give you reason to regret it."

Medeoan could not make out any benches or bunks in the shadows, so she picked a small cask and sat, folding her hands on her knees. Overhead she heard the sounds of many voices, rising and falling. They were all of them stern, and angry. That much she needed no language to understand. One glance at Ilta showed that she had no intention of leaving Medeoan alone. Probably that was on orders of the sorcerer. Medeoan bridled at her confinement. There were so many things in this hold she could use to free herself, if she had the chance. There were ropes, and cloths, there was fire and there was water. Nothing would be easy, but so much could be done.

Once again, she found herself missing Avanasy. Not that she believed he would have automatically known what to do in this bizarre situation, but because she did not wish to be alone here. It was to Avanasy she had always turned when she did not want to be alone. Until Kacha had come, of course. Until Kacha had filled her heart with his lies and driven her to this. She could die here tonight, her throat slit by a crowd of peasants and dark sorcerers, and no one would ever know, and Kacha would rule Isavalta, and she would have failed her parents and her land.

Anger shifted her weight and straightened her spine. Ilta straightened up instantly in warning. Medeoan forced herself to subside. Her fingers idly smoothed down her apron. Her apron, her headscarf. Medeoan swallowed. Her headscarf with its bands of embroidery. Ilta stood in the lantern light, and Medeoan was surely lost in shadow. The embroidered threads she wore were faded, and worn, and surely some of them were loosened. Anything she could make from such threads would only be a small weaving, but if she could make herself concentrate, it might be enough.

Sighing heavily, Medeoan pulled off her scarf and ran her hand through her hair.

Ilta made no move. Above her the voices continued on, now louder, now softer, debating her fate.

"I truly do not mean you any harm," said Medeoan, drawing the scarf through her fingers. "I just want to be on my way."

Ilta only glared at her. Under her searching thumb, Medeoan found the crinkled end of a knot that had come loose. Overhead, someone pounded the deck to emphasize their point.

"I have no family who would pay for my return." Medeoan plucked the thread. It came blessedly loose from the fabric. She plucked at it again, and a little more unraveled from the patterns woven to keep Eliisa safe.

"You think we are bandits then?" sneered Ilta. "You think we have no pride? That shame is for your people, not mine."

"Then what do you want from me?" A bit more thread unraveled under her restless fingers. "I'm worth nothing, I know nothing."

"To begin with," said the sorcerer's voice, "we want to know what happened to the girl whose life you used."

The sorcerer climbed down the ladder. He was tall and, for a Tuukosov, he was slender, but that was all Medeoan could see. She crumpled her scarf in both hands.

"She was returned to the home from which she came, with enough gold to keep her in comfort for many years."

The sorcerer looked frankly surprised. Medeoan was not sure he believed her.

"Ilta," said the sorcerer, and added a string of words. The woman ducked her head in acquiescence, and made her way up the ladder while the sorcerer strode forward.

"Now, then," he said, taking a seat on another cask. "Let us not mince words you and I. You are a sorceress. No other hand wove that girdle or bound it to you."

Medeoan said nothing. The sorcerer reached out and took the scarf from her hands. It did not take him long to find the loosened thread and hold it up for inspection.

"Finon tells me the Isavaltan soldiers are all running about like rats looking for an insane sorceress who is claiming to be the Empress Medeoan, and that she is to be brought in for high treason and sowing dissent."

He looked down his long nose at Medeoan, who felt herself go still as stone. Was that their plan? They had her own people, her own soldiers, sworn to her until death, planning to drag her in as a madwoman to be put to the question? How *dare* they!

Medeoan wanted to hang her head and cry, but she did

not move. Of course, how could they dare leave her free? But what had they done to hide her absence? What lie had Kacha dreamed up for this one?

"You do not act like one who has lost their wits to the moon," said the sorcerer, toying with the loosened thread. "But, so Finon tells me, you do look like the Empress Medeoan. Who is, as chance would have it, also a sorceress, and a powerful one at that."

Medeoan turned her face to the darkness. She was out of lies. Her disguise was broken and her own people were in search of her. How could she convince soldiers, common soldiers who had never been to court, who she was? Could she take shelter with the Lord Master? Where did his loyalties lie? All this assumed she could even find a way to leave this tiny boat.

"But how could the Empress Medeoan be here?" went on the sorcerer, winding the loose thread around his finger. "When all know she is in her confinement waiting to give birth to an heir for the glory of Eternal Isavalta."

Medeoan's head snapped up. Confinement! That was their lie! Who assisted them? That treacherous crowd of hens Kacha had surrounded her with? Oh, she was a fool, a *fool* and she almost deserved to die for what she had allowed to happen.

"So." The thread snapped abruptly in the sorcerer's hand. "So," he said again, and the soft whisper was like a laugh. "They say the world moves in patterns woven on fate's own loom, but I had not truly believed that before this moment." He stood up, and reverenced to her. "Majesty, you must forgive me if I take some time to decide what should be done now. There are many among my people who would like to see you dead, and would be only to glad to do the deed." He looked down at the scarf he held. "No more of spells, Majesty, please. I will not be far away, and I will feel any such workings. I have no wish to bind your hands."

He left her then, and she heard the hatch close. She stood at once, and in the dim lantern light, began to search the hold. It was packed with casks and crates, cages and nets, but there were no portals, and no other hatch. Medeoan looked around at all the lengths of cord, and thought that the boots she heard pacing the deck must be the sorcerer's. He had not even told her his name, damn the arrogance of him. The Tuukosov were ever arrogant. It was their nature, Father said, and why they had to be watched so closely. Yet, when Kacha's murderous plans had come to fruition, Father had been at work negotiating with the Tuukosov nobility, such as they were, with an eye to increasing the freedom of the island. Perhaps that had been a mistake. Medeoan sat back down and rested her head in her hand. Or perhaps not. That mercy might be what now kept her alive.

A swift spell could be finished before the sorcerer came down the hatch, which was surely battened down. But a swift spell would carry little power. A powerful spell would take time. There had to be a way. Whole nets were made of single knots. There had to be a way, a way to build on small bindings, windings and entanglements. There had to be a way . . .

In the darkness of the hold, alone and exhausted, Medeoan fell asleep.

"Empress." A hand shook her roughly. Medeoan started awake, instantly ashamed and afraid. The face of the man Finon looked down at her.

"Come on. Hush." He beckoned to her and began climbing the ladder.

Medeoan gathered up her skirts to follow. "What are you . . ."

"Getting you out of here, Empress." He lifted the hatch and peered into the darkness. "Come, quietly."

Medeoan closed her mouth and followed him up the ladder, setting her boots lightly on the rungs. Out in the moonlight and the fresh wind, she could see the deck cluttered with sleeping bodies. Finon stepped nimbly between them, moving toward the bow. Medeoan followed as best she could. Fortunately, the sleepers seemed used to people walking among them, and none woke.

Finon slipped over the rail, down into a dinghy with its broad oars neatly shipped. He reached up for Medeoan and she allowed him to help her down onto the bench beside him. She knew enough to scramble out of Finon's way so that he could grasp the oars and push off from the sorcerer's boat, dipping one oar and then the other silently into the gentle waves, steering them deftly through the larger craft.

"I've seen the master of the *Gull's Wing*," Finon whispered as they pulled away from the docks. "He's willing to take you aboard and quietly, provided you've money to pay. Have you money, Empress?"

Medeoan nodded.

"Good."

Finon said nothing else. The oars clacked and splashed as he worked them, and their boat pulled past the end of the dock. Finon turned them parallel to the shore and pulled harder, heading for the berth of the *Gull's Wing*.

"Why . . ." she began.

"Do not ask that question, Empress," said Finon through his teeth. "You might not want the answer."

Medeoan held her peace. She did not wish for this man to change his mind. After another moment's silence, however, Finon said, "I have seen my cousins, my blood kin, beaten in the streets for failing to bow to the imperial flag. I have seen friends burned out of their houses under suspicion of harboring rebels." He did not look at her, he kept his gaze on the water past her shoulder. "What will be done to us if it is found we murdered the empress of Isavalta?" He sucked on his teeth for a moment as he worked the oars in steady strokes. "Though there are those who say it would be justice."

"Such as your sorcerer?"

Finon chuckled. "Do you really believe I could have taken you out of there with such ease without Valin Kalami's permission?" He shook his head. "Kalami knows the reality of our place in the world. He knows that we must bow before we break."

Medeoan was silent for a moment. Who was the Lord Master of Tuukosov? Direshk, wasn't it? When had she last seen a letter from him? Had she ever? She had never asked the secretaries for any such thing, she was sure of that. How well did he carry out her father's new policies?

Medeoan suppressed a laugh. Here she was, a peasant in a peasant's boat, wondering about matters of high policy.

She didn't even know if she'd live to reach the next shore, let alone to take her place under the imperial canopy again.

Nonetheless, she said, "I will not forget this."

"See that you don't, Empress."

There was nothing she could say to that. Finon steered the boat to the end of a dock and shipped the oars again. "This is as far as I go. The *Gull's Wing* has the third berth. The night watch knows to listen for your hail. They know you by the name Eliisa."

Medeoan hesitated for a moment and then reached into her waistband, bringing out a silver coin. "Take this coin to the fortress of Dalemar," she said. "Ask for Captain Peshek. Tell him what has passed. He will see you safe in some new position. Tell him it is my order."

But Finon just waved the coin away. "Save your favors, Empress. But do not forget them."

"But those others . . ."

"Are my people. I'll deal with them. I just ask you remember what happened here today." He sucked on his teeth again. "It may be one day I turn up at your high palace, and it may be I have someone with me who needs a place as badly as you needed shelter. Then I'll take my empress's boon, and be glad of it."

Medeoan nodded. "Tell me your full name then, so I can remember."

"Finon Pasi," he replied, staring intently at her with his dark eyes. "I will hold your promise, Empress."

Of all the things that had happened in the long, hard day, that one stung her pride. "You will not have to," she said, drawing herself up. "For I hold it myself, and Vyshko and Vyshemir have heard me speak."

Finon made no answer, he only bowed where he sat. Medeoan accepted the gesture with a nod. Then, she turned and clambered up the ladder to the dock, hurrying toward the ship that would take her to Hung Tse and the Heart of the World.

I must succeed now, she told herself. *I have made promises in the name of the rule Imperial. I cannot fail now. Vyshko and Vyshemir have heard me speak in their stead.*

There, alone in the darkness, surrounded by tall ships and

fleeing from her own soldiers, Medeoan at last felt them, the bonds of empire of which her father had spoken. Shackle and support, he'd called them, and he'd been right.

Medeoan felt her shoulders square themselves as she hurried forward into the night.

Chapter Thirteen

T'ien, the great city that held the Heart of the World, was a city of walls. Walls sheltered it from the outside world. Walls separated its quarters from each other. Walls lined its streets and hid its gardens. Walls sheltered its garrisons, and their broad tops provided pathways for its soldiers. Walls cradled its markets and squares.

Medeoan sat hunched in the shadow of one of the beige stone walls, nursing her sore feet and trying to feel fortunate. Her ship had arrived without incident. No one on board had questioned or molested her. She had been able to perform the tasks assigned, not as well as Eliisa could have, but she got by, and she was safe and sound in the city that held the Heart of the World.

All that was left was the question of how she was to approach the Heart's gate. She could not simply walk up, tattered and unattended, and announce she was the empress of Isavalta. She did not have enough money left in her waistband to buy even a decent wardrobe, let alone the regal one she should have worn. She could not even hire a single bodyguard.

But neither could she appear weak before the Nine Elders. She could not be seen to beg.

"I am so tired," she whispered. "Vyshemir, help me, I am so tired."

Tired of moving, tired of wondering what was being whispered behind her, tired of being so constantly afraid. Even if she could have acquired the proper materials to weave herself another disguise, Medeoan did not believe she could have concentrated long enough to complete the spell.

Medeoan lowered her head into her hands and scrubbed her scalp to try to wake herself up. This was useless. She had to try. She had to find some way. She could not simply sit here and wait for some spy of Kacha's to find her, if he could even be bothered. She leaned her head against the wall. The empress of Isavalta, lost in a foreign land in a servant's clothes. Why go looking for her? She had put herself out of the way most efficiently. Kacha could consolidate his power over her empire and birthright without hindrance.

That thought rekindled Medeoan's anger. If for no other reason, if not for duty of birth or the gods or her parent's deaths, she would see Kacha crawl to prove she was not to be taken lightly, to prove she was no longer lulled by his warm words or warmer touch, that she would not forgive him, even if he begged. She would only spit on him and order him put to death . . .

So why can I not stop missing him?

She did miss him. She missed his touch, his scent, looking into his eyes and seeing the light within them. Part of her knew that she would miss those things until the day she died, and that part wept.

"Now then, here's a pretty lady all alone."

Medeoan jerked her chin down. A man stood in front of her. His robe was plain, black cotton with wide cuffs of deep blue that no one but the imperial family would be allowed to wear in Isavalta. His burlap pack made a hump for his left shoulder. He wore his hair in a long ponytail, as was the fashion for the men of Hung-Tse, and his eyes twinkled as he smiled at her.

Medeoan mustered what she hoped was a haughty stare. Evidently it was close enough, for the man shrank backward in a pose of mock cowardice.

"Such ice! Such power! I shall surely be struck to pieces with another such glance!" He peered at her from behind his hands. "Perhaps the pretty lady will accept a gift? To show that we are indeed friends?" When Medeoan did not move or answer, he lowered his hand. "A poor sorcerer am I," he said, waving his left hand about in the air. "A poor sorcerer of packs and the roads under the shadows of walls, but even such a poor sorcerer as I may give a gift to a pretty lady." He opened his hand to show a fold of silk. Deftly, he knotted the silk, and pulled the knot close, and through, and opened the silk again, and inside lay a delicate summer flower with petals the color of ripe peaches.

With a flourish, the man made the silk vanish, and handed Medeoan the flower. To her surprise, she felt herself smile.

"Thank you," she said, inhaling the sweet scent. "But I have nothing to give you."

"Ah, but perhaps you do." He smiled. "Perhaps the pretty lady will allow me to ply my arts on her behalf. A horoscope? To tally the lovers that will surely be lining up before her door? An amulet of good luck? My powers are humble, to be sure, but they will serve, they will serve."

"They will serve to make a pretty trick for a sad day," Medeoan answered. "But no further."

"The pretty lady assumes because my workings are humble, they are not sound," said the man, his voice for the first time growing peevish.

"There was no true working made here," Medeoan said sternly. During the moment of creation, a sorcerer could feel a spell being created, especially if it was being completed nearby. "You know that, as do I. Thank you for the flower, man. I have no coin to spare."

"Then may someone teach you what it is to give your best for nothing," he spat and stalked away, hitching his lumpy pack up higher on his shoulder.

"It's already happened," she whispered to his back and his flower.

Still, it was a pleasant trick. Even as she thought that, a fresh idea tickled at the back of her mind. A trick. Could such a trick get her into the palace? She was already in disguise. Eliisa was gone from her, but she still remembered some things that the girl's presence had left in her mind. If she could just get inside the walls, then she would be able to find her way. She knew the ways of palaces, and of servants as well as of nobles. All she had to do was get herself inside.

Medeoan, hope and energy restored, climbed to her feet

and strode briskly down the street, following the path the trickster had taken.

The walls guarding the five palaces that were the Heart of the World were, at first glance, painted a bright, solid yellow. Only after staring at them for a long time could Medeoan discern the patterns made with delicate brush strokes and enormous skill. Dragons, whiskered unicorns, phoenixes, tortoises, horses, oxen and cranes all had been woven together, layer upon layer, picture upon picture, to create a net of protective spells that stretched out on all sides, sealing the emperor away from any dangers.

But such walls must have gates, for the servants as well as for the nobles, and although she knew the Heart of the World held orchards, gardens and fish ponds as well as palaces, what could be grown, herded or hunted on its extensive grounds was not enough to feed all its occupants. Food, at the very least, had to be procured.

Medeoan bought herself a scrub brush and a bucket, and now she knelt outside the tall, yellow walls, slowly scrubbing at the bricks in the street, keeping one eye on the western gate, the servants' small gate. It had a complement of six guards, which was changed regularly, for no one charged with the emperor's safety was foolish enough to believe that a servant could not bring harm to their master. But still, she could see that in the steady stream of traffic flowing in and out some carts and some pack animals were searched more thoroughly than others and fresh plans came into Medeoan's mind. Could she follow such a servant, and be smuggled inside in a bag or a basket? She shook her head. She was beginning to think like a tale in an opera, but still, it might work, and it might be less risky than an attempt at bribery. Medeoan dunked her brush in her bucket and turned her attention briefly to her bricks, so as not to be caught staring too long at the imperial gate.

A mule tender, an empty hay cart and a detachment of soldiers all paraded out from the gate. Medeoan squinted up at the driver. He was a pudgy man in a good green coat, and a broad-brimmed straw hat to protect himself from the sun.

Follow him, she told herself. *See where he goes, how he is regarded. See where your chance is.*

She dropped her brush into the bucket with a splash and a thunk and staggered to her feet. Her entire right leg had gone numb from spending the entire morning kneeling on bricks. She would have thought her shipboard labors would have hardened her to such tasks, but not yet, evidently.

She shook her leg, and tried to rub some feeling back into it, when a shadow fell across her.

"Well, here's a pretty lady all alone."

Medeoan could not stop herself from looking up. In front of her stood the mountebank, the false sorcerer. He still wore his black coat with its blue cuffs, but his pack was gone and he carried himself straight and proud, all trace of mischievous twinkle gone from his black eyes. Around him stood six soldiers, the saffron sashes around their waists and gold trim around their helmets marking them as members of the Heart's guard.

"Take her," ordered the false sorcerer.

One of the soldiers reached for her. Medeoan swung her bucket, a pathetic weapon at best, and doused him with muddy water, but the bucket itself only clanked against his armored coat, and he swatted it angrily away. Before she could run, another of them caught her from behind, seizing both her wrists. She twisted, trying to kick out, but he held her fast. Another of them moved forward, and Medeoan screamed as she saw the iron shackles ready to close about her wrists.

"No!"

But her cries did no more good than her struggles, and the soldier snapped the shackles shut, twisting the iron key in the lock that sealed them, and then turned with a bow to present the key to the false sorcerer.

"Who are you?" demanded Medeoan. "How dare you!"

"I am the one who has found a foreign sorceress," he replied mildly. "And I dare for I serve the Nine Elders and through them the Emperor Himself. If she speaks again, you may strike her," he said to the soldier to Medeoan's left.

"Sir." He bowed.

"Bring her."

The soldier pushed Medeoan, who stumbled forward, too startled to protest. The shackles weighted her hands down in front of her. The short chain that held them together rattled. The false sorcerer, the imperial official, walked ahead of her without a backward glance.

The yellow walls with their iron-studded gates passed by, and Medeoan had her wish. She almost laughed. She was inside the Heart of the World.

All she saw before her, though, was another yellow wall, as cunningly and delicately painted as the first. It was thicker though, and held its own garrison she guessed by the narrow slits of windows in its sides, and the sentries on its top. The two made a narrow lane that her nightmarish escort now marched her along. Her hair had come loose and wisps fluttered into her face, but she didn't dare raise her hands to brush them aside.

After what seemed an age, they came to a portcullis in the inner wall. Six guards raised their spears and swords in salute to her party. Medeoan had to stop herself from giving a reflexive and regal nod in return. Again she almost laughed. This was indeed becoming a bad dream.

Medeoan only caught a glimpse of the great tiled courtyard that lay beyond the inner wall. The imperial official unlocked a door on the right side of the passage and the soldiers marched Medeoan into the wall.

The world at once became cool and dim. Single beams of light filtered through the slit windows, and a pair of lanterns hung on either side of an iron-banded door that the official unlocked with a key he drew out of his robe. Medeoan blinked hard, trying to will her eyes to adjust, and she succeeded well enough to see the beginnings of a stairway leading down into the earth and darkness.

"No," she said, hanging back. "You don't . . ."

A heavy hand came down, and pain exploded in Medeoan's head, making her see stars. Reeling, she barely felt herself shoved forward. She stumbled and would have fallen, had someone not caught her up under her arm and, pinching her painfully, hauled her forward.

Slowly, the dizzying pain receded and Medeoan realized she was once again on level ground. Her vision stilled and cleared enough for her to see she was being led down a stone corridor lit at intervals by copper lanterns hung from the ceiling. Ahead, the corridor opened into a square room dominated by a table of chipped black wood behind which waited a crooked stick of an old man who wore a black coat that matched that of the imperial official who led Medeoan's escort. The two men bowed to one another and spoke together, too fast and too soft for Medeoan to follow. The stick figure official sniffed and wrote something down on the paper scroll that was spread out before him. Another soldier came forward and grabbed Medeoan's chain, jerking her forward. She opened her mouth, to try to protest or explain, but the memory of the last blow was too fresh and she shut it again.

The new soldier dragged her into another square corridor, lit by more lamps, but this one was lined by iron doors. An eerie silence filled Medeoan's ears. The guard's square-toed shoes did not even make any noise against the dusty stone floor. One door in the left-hand wall stood open. The soldier tweaked the chain, causing Medeoan to stumble inside. The door swung shut without even a whisper from the hinges, cutting off all light. As if from a great distance, Medeoan heard a lock click shut.

Then there was only silence, and the sound of her own shallow breathing in the absolute darkness.

A tear trickled from her eye, tickling her cheek with its slow descent. It was followed by another, and another, until a stream of them ran down her face. But she could not raise her hands. The chains were too heavy. All she could do was stand and weep until her strength failed her and she fell to her knees, weeping still, until, at last, the darkness wrapped itself tight around her mind and she knew no more.

The god house of Vaceta was seldom empty during the summer. Much of the prosperity of the town came from the fact that the court was in residence, and its merchants as well as those who tended its fields trooped in and out to ask their god that their sons, their daughters or themselves might be noticed by some member of the household staff and signed to indenture for the summer, earning a year's wages in a few months, and a reputation as having served the imperial household, which would last for a good deal longer than a year. Courtiers not housed in Vaknevos itself also had need of their houses, their staffs, their artisans and servants. While not as good as an imperial appointment, appointment with a courtier was more secure than the hit-and-miss life of one bound to no house, and therefore much sought after. It seemed that the entire town was more engaged in offering prayers or giving thanks than they were in the business of the day.

Peshek found it easy to settle in under the shadow of one of the carved pillars and wait without being noticed or re-marked upon.

Vaceta did not have anything like the imperial budget for gilding their god house, but they had made up for it by employing the best of their woodworkers to carve the interior into a haven of bounty. The supporting pillars were trees laden with apples and pears. The arched roof held friezes of all manner of artisans at their trades. The walls showed reliefs of farmers reaping and gathering in plentiful fields, accompanied by fat-cheeked children lifting sheaves of grain or baskets of vegetables to the sky.

Cezta, the god of the city, stood on his pillar, a fresh, green branch in one hand and the other raised in blessing. Supposedly, he had gained his divinity during a famine by going out into a field and feeding his own blood to the soil. The next day, the grain waved fresh and green in the summer sun, and Cezta was gone.

But it was not of Cezta that Peshek had come to beg aid. Once every ten days or so while the court was in its summer home, the keeper of the emperor's god house would come to Cezta's god house, to call on the keeper and extend the courtesies and the blessings of Vyshko and Vyshemir. Peshek had been hanging about the doorways and market-places for days waiting to overhear when the visit might be expected. Now that the day had finally arrived, all that was left was to wait and see if Keeper Bakhar had managed to survive at his post.

Peshek forced himself to exercise again the patience he had spent the recent days practicing. Since leaving his father's house, he had traveled on foot, mostly at night, pausing here and there to work a day in a field or barn for a meal or a night's lodging, so that he might be taken for nothing but an unattached laborer, no one to rouse suspicion, or even comment, except from maids, and, not infrequently, matrons with good eyes and lively minds.

He had tried to plan for what to do if Bakhar was no longer the keeper, but his mind could not seemed to address the problem. He could only wonder what could have been done to the keeper, and what the keeper would have said before Kacha's people were finished with him.

The doors to the god house opened again. Peshek let his eyes flicker up from their reverent attitude, and his heart leapt. Bakhar strode into the dim house, accompanied by the men who bore the titles of Right Hand and Left Hand. All three were dressed in the simple, belted blue robes Bakhar favored for non-ceremonial occasions. Bakhar's only adornments were the small gold symbols on his belt's end: a cup, a knife and a pike.

Peshek pushed past a knot of worshipers, hurrying toward the central aisle. Bakhar walked forward toward Cezta to pay his respects. The local keeper came out of the back, and opened his arms wide in a gesture of welcome. Bakhar lifted his hand in return. Peshek hurried forward, and collided straight into the Left Hand, who in turn collided with Bakhar.

"Clumsy . . . !" began the Left Hand, but a glance from the keeper checked his exclamation.

"I'm so sorry!" gasped Peshek, stepping back just a little and folding his hands to reverence to the keeper. "Forgive me, sir, please . . ."

"That's perfectly all right . . ." began Bakhar. Peshek lifted his head and met the keeper's eyes. Recognition and surprise flickered swiftly across the other man's visage. ". . . my son," Bakhar went on, smoothing down his robe. "No harm."

Reverencing humbly, and keeping his head ducked lest the Left Hand and Right Hand should chance to recognize him, Peshek retreated down the aisle and out the doors. The summer sun was painfully bright after spending the better part of a day inside the dim god house, but the fresh breeze was more than welcome.

Fortunately, there were not many loiterers around the god house steps to notice him cross the street and settle himself into the shadowy niche between two houses across the way. This time, though, he found it hard to make himself wait. The man he needed was but a couple of dozen feet away, separated by from him by a few wooden walls. The keeper had seen him. If he couldn't get back in there quietly, his best chance at good information would shortly be beyond his reach, again, and there would be nothing for it but more delay and yet more waiting in shadows. Peshek's palms began to itch with impatience.

At last, a small troop of men with muddy boots and undyed kaftans strode up the street and turned toward the god house. Peshek ducked out of his hiding place and joined their number, affording himself an anonymous entry back into the holy place after his rather public exit.

Peshek queued up with the farmers to kiss the hem of the god's robe, as was proper. As he put his lips to the bright green fabric, he glanced toward the back of the house. There stood Bakhar in quiet conference with the local keeper, a far slighter man with a mournful face and stubby hands.

But did Bakhar see him? Peshek bit his lip and stepped sideways to make way for the other worshipers. After a bad moment wondering what to do, he dropped to one knee toward Cezta's image and bowed his head, making himself the picture of a poor man with many cares, praying for succor from this most prosperous god, and at the same time, putting himself directly in Keeper Bakhar's line of sight.

The move had its intended effect. After only a few heartbeats, a hand touched his shoulder, and Peshek looked up to see Bakhar standing over him.

"I see your heart is heavy, my son," Bakhar said. "Would you care to come and talk a little? Perhaps together we can understand how Cezta, under the hands of Vyshko and Vyshemir, touches your life."

"Thank you, good keeper," said Peshek, keeping his voice low and his face solemn.

"Come with me."

Peshek rose and followed Bakhar into the niche that each god house in Isavalta kept for Vyshko and Vyshemir. Their representations were carved into an alcove above a curving shelf meant for offerings. Two low stools had been placed there to accommodate any who needed to stay and meditate for a long period.

Bakhar kissed his fingers and laid them on the carved folds of the gods' robes, and then reverenced. Peshek did the same. As he did, he stole a quick glance at the keeper. The man had aged since Peshek had last seen him. Tired lines ran down his cheeks and his normally serene eyes had grown uneasy.

"You take a chance being here," whispered Bakhar as Peshek straightened up. "But I am glad beyond words to see you. Tell me quickly, how fares the empress?"

"I wish I could tell you," muttered Peshek, his gaze darting around the niche and the greater house, just to make sure no one had strayed too near. "She has fled to the Heart of the World, and, as much as it pains me, I have other orders. I can tell you she has help on the way. Avanasy has returned."

Bakhar closed his eyes and let out a long sigh. "I had not dared to hope, but I could not believe he would stay away at such a time."

"Avanasy says that Lord Iakush gave his life to warn him as to what was happening." Peshek rubbed his hands together.

This time, Bakhar's sigh was heavy. "I wondered. It's been given out that the lord sorcerer died of a hemorrhage in his spleen. No one will speculate though on what might have caused that hemorrhage, and his body was not allowed to lie in state before burial." Bakhar's hand strayed to the golden icons on his belt. "You've heard what happened at the games for the Hastinapuran ambassador?"

Peshek sat himself on one of the padded stools, scrubbing his scalp and face. "I've heard something dramatic happened, but the rumors in the streets have doubtlessly improved greatly on reality."

Peshek listened grimly while Bakhar told him of the arrival of the lone, tattered soldier right in the middle of the martial display, and his declaration of Hung Tse's treachery.

"Is what this man said true?" he asked when the keeper's soft voice fell silent.

Bakhar shook his head. "I have not been able to learn for certain, but I doubt it." His whole face hardened. "Kacha has already orchestrated far more difficult displays."

"And where stand the council? Do they all accept Kacha's story of early confinement and an impending heir?"

"To a man. Kacha has done something to them. I smell magics here, but I cannot find the source. Kacha is no sorcerer himself, nor did he bring one from Hastinapura. He barely holds any conference with the sorcerers who remain at court, so who is aiding him and how?" Bakhar's gaze rested on the images of Vyshko and Vyshemir for a long moment. "Avanasy might be able to tell us, but Avanasy is needed elsewhere."

"Except that Avanasy was asking the same questions." Peshek's fist tightened. "So, the empress has no friend left at court?"

"None I am certain could be trusted with the truth."

For the first time, Peshek heard the strain in the keeper's voice, and he realized suddenly that since the empress's flight, Bakhar had been even more alone than he himself had. He reached out and touched the other man's arm.

"How is it you remain above suspicion?"

Bakhar's mouth twisted into a humorless smile. "By pretending to be a foolish old man concerned with nothing outside my god house. Kacha is juggling so many intrigues right now, I believe he is content to let that facade stand." Again, he looked to the gods, reaching out from their alcove, their weapons held high. "But what luck have you had?"

"My father is sounding out the lords he believes will hear the truth and keep it close to themselves. I am to meet his messenger shortly. If all goes well, we will soon have arms to back our answer to Kacha's declarations."

"You have brought me the first good news I've had in many days." Bakhar smoothed his beard down. He looked as tired as Peshek felt. *We are not either of us meant for intrigue,* thought Peshek. *Not truly.* "I will begin to move beyond the house as much as I am able. Perhaps I can find the source of what has blinded so many shrewd men."

"Do your best, good keeper," said Peshek, getting to his feet. "Send what word you can to my father. If any know where to find me, he will." Remembering his role, Peshek reverenced in the peasant fashion. "I will send your news to Avanasy. Perhaps he can puzzle this out from a distance, or at least tell us where to begin looking."

Bakhar touched Peshek's brow in blessing. "Vyshko walks strong beside you, my son."

There was nothing more to be said. Head ducked, shoulders rounded, Peshek left the house for the broad, cobbled street and the summer sun. As soon as his eyes had adjusted again to the brightness, he set off down the street, heading for the city's wooden walls and the south gates. He wound his way quickly and confidently through the crowded streets, the carts and mules, the goose-herders and the men toiling under heavy sacks.

Then, faintly, he heard a rhythmic sound that made him pause, causing a woman struggling along with a huge basket to curse and shoulder her way past him. Peshek listened. Under all the thousand sounds of the busy city, he heard it again. A steady, rhythmic tramping that could have but one source; the boots of many soldiers.

No sooner had Peshek identified the sound, than a faint, but imperious voice from a man as yet unseen called out, "Clear the way! Clear the way for the House Guard Imperial!"

Groans and cursing broke out from the crowds. Carters whipped their animals, trying to get them off to one side. All around, beasts and people jostled one another, noisy with their complaints, seeking some side street or alley that would get them away from the crush. But Peshek heard another noise as he strove to keep the pressure of the crowd from pushing him down the alley at his back. Cheers swelled up ahead, growing louder with each heartbeat, as did the sound of marching feet.

Up ahead, the street bent in a broad curve. Peshek craned his neck along with the rest to try to see who was coming. At last, a broad shadow filled the bend, and then the ranks of the House Guard marched into view.

They were decked out as brightly as for any imperial review. Gilded armor shined in the sun, as did the tips of the pikes. Blue coats were flawless. They marched in stride, rank on rank, their armor and arms jingling in metallic counter-point.

Officers on horseback flanked the foot soldiers, and Peshek stared in dismay at faces he knew. Habat, whose nose was as crooked as an old man's back from the number of times it had been broken. Maccek, who he'd fought with over one of the weaver girls in the sheds and gotten far too drunk with an hour afterwards when they both found out she preferred Over-Lieutenant Oal. Rzhova, who still owed him two days' pay from their last game of dice.

Stop! he wanted to shout at him. *Stop! You don't know what you're doing! Come with me! I'll show you the enemy!*

But he was alone in the cheering crowd. They'd heard the stories come down from Vaknevos, and they believed. Why shouldn't they?

"Cut the heart right out of them!" shouted a man to Peshek's right.

"Captain! Captain!" cried another man with a sack of charcoal on his back. "Give 'em two for me!"

Rzhova turned his head and began to reverence genially to the crowd, and then he froze, and Peshek had a single heartbeat to realize he'd been a fool.

Here he stood, at least half a head taller than those around him, close enough to the grand parade to recognize the faces of old comrades.

Close enough to be recognized by them.

He had only enough time to turn to run before Rzhova shouted, "Peshek, you traitor!"

The press of bodies before him suddenly became a solid wall. Peshek swore and tore at shoulders and coats, shoving people sideways as far as he could. He could feel the crowd stirring behind him to try to let Rzhova ride through. He was sure he heard the rasp of a sword being drawn. Peshek slammed his shoulder against a portly man who tried to grab his arms. That broke the wall of bodies just far enough and Peshek fled down the stinking alley. In the space of another breath, hoofbeats clattered after him.

Peshek didn't dare look back. He pelted ahead as fast as he could, but his boots skittered on the garbage that littered the cobbles. Twice he stumbled and almost fell. He slammed his shoulder against a door, seeking to find a way into one of the houses, only to find it solidly barred.

"Coward!" shouted Rzhova. "Make your stand!"

Clutching his shoulder, Peshek turned. Rzhova, tall and terrible on horseback, bore down on him, standing in the stirrups, sword held high. Peshek bit back a cry of terror and got ready to duck if he could.

All at once, another harsh scream cut the air. Peshek jerked around, thinking it was another soldier. Instead, a black bird dove down, making him duck his head. Rzhova hollered and flung up his arm to protect his eyes as the bird went straight for him, cawing fiercely.

Peshek did not wait to see what would happen next. He took off running down the alley again, praying that Vyshko really did walk strong beside him, and that He had made it hard enough for the other officers to get their horses through the crowds that there would be no one waiting for Peshek at the end of the alley. Behind him, the crow squawked angrily and Rzhova cursed, and the horse's hooves clopped as the animal danced, but none of those sounds grew closer.

Several sacks of chaff and straw waited by the alley's mouth. Peshek snatched a pair up as he ran past, hoisting one onto each shoulder and plunging straight for the middle of the crowd. The continuous roll of voices, the brays and snorts of animals, and the creaking of overburdened carts filled up the world and Peshek could make out no other noise. Flanked by his sacks, he could only see a narrow slice of what was ahead of him. The sacks itched his cheeks, and their must and dust tickled his nose. But he heard no shouts for him to halt, and the only clopping of hooves came from reluctant mules and flocks of sheep.

At last, Peshek spied another alley. He slowly worked his way to the edge of the crowd, tossed down his sacks and slumped momentarily against the corner of a house. From the cool and dirty smell coming up from the narrow way, this one led to the canals. Good. From there he could get his bearings again and maybe find a boatman for hire. It would be the quickest way out of the city.

While all this flashed through his mind, two sharp caws sounded overhead. A glossy black crow perched on the eves of the house Peshek leaned against. With a clatter of wings, the bird dropped onto the sack he had just discarded.

There was absolutely no doubt in Peshek's mind that this bold creature was the same one that had saved him from Rzhova. Pushing aside all feelings of foolishness, Peshek crouched down until his head was level with the crow's. It regarded him first with one round eye, then the other, then it cawed again.

"I owe you my thanks, Master Crow," murmured Peshek, reaching out with one finger to stroke the shining feathers. The bird cawed again, outraged at the familiarity, and hopped backward.

"Your pardon, your pardon," Peshek murmured, drawing his hand back at once. "And may I assume you are the messenger my friend Avanasy promised to send?"

The bird cawed once more and puffed its feathers out proudly.

"Your timing, sir, is impeccable." Peshek rested his forearms on his knees. "You may tell our friend . . ."

It was only then that the enormity of what he had seen and heard engulfed him. Until this instant, he'd had no time to consider what it meant. But now he grew cold as his thoughts ordered themselves. Isavalta was going to war against Hung Tse, and the empress was in the Heart of the World. She'd be taken hostage at once and held for ransom, and Kacha would never pay such a ransom, because that would mean he would have to admit that she was not in confinement in Vaknevos after all. If she could not be ransomed . . . Peshek closed his eyes. Hung Tse would not waste their time on her.

"Tell him urgently that the empress must not go to the Heart of the World. Kacha has mobilized for war against Hung Tse, and she is sure to be taken hostage by the Nine Elders."

The crow bobbed its head several times, as if to reassure Peshek that it understood. Then, it shook itself once and leapt into the sky, spreading its wings and flying off over the rooftops. Peshek watched, wishing for a long, vain moment that he could do the same.

"And if I've been here talking to someone's tame crow,

what a complete ass I'll have made of myself," he muttered as he straightened up. He pushed the thought aside at once. That was Avanasy's messenger. He would reach the empress in time. Peshek had done his part there. He would have to trust to Avanasy's skill to manage affairs in the Heart of the World. His whole purpose must be to raise what troops he could to stop the unlawful war that Kacha sought to start.

Resuming his soldier's bearing for the first time in days, Peshek marched down the alleyway.

Cai Yun leapt from the sedan that had carried her to her uncle's house with no thought to decorum. She left it to her bodyguard to pay the bearers who had brought her and instead hurried through the gate and up the garden path to the verandah. There, her two old servants bowed to her, but this once she passed them by without a word. She had news that could not wait.

Fortunately, Uncle was in his study, sitting calmly at the low table that served as his desk, working on a letter. Her abrupt and undignified entrance made him pause, the ink brush poised in mid-stroke, and look up at her with raised eyebrows.

"I have come from meeting Zhang Sung, Uncle," said Cai Yun breathlessly, kneeling down in front of him. "You were right. He was worth every coin, and all my flirtations. He . . ."

Uncle raised his free hand and set down his ink brush before it could drip on his carefully written letter. "Pause for breath, beloved niece. You will be fainting on the mat before you finish this tale."

Cai Yun did pause, and struggled to slow her breathing and regain her calm. When she was no longer panting like a horse, she bowed to Uncle, who bowed in return. Thus composed, she said, more slowly and more properly, "He tells me there is an Isavaltan prisoner in the cells below the Heart of the World."

"An Isavaltan?" Uncle savored the word, as Cai Yun knew he would. "This is indeed interesting. Does Zhang Sung know who this Isavaltan is?"

Cai Yun limited her triumph to a flash of her eyes. "A woman. A sorceress."

"So?" Uncle's eyebrows lifted again. "Well, well, a sorceress, at a time when we have word that the Isavaltans are chasing a mad sorceress about the countryside for impersonating their empress. This is indeed interesting news."

Cai Yun searched her uncle's face, even though by now she knew well he would show her nothing he did not wish her to see. Still, the lilt in his words made her believe that this news was more than interesting. It was welcome.

Uncle moved the brush to the shallow dish of water beside the stone and grinder so that the ink would not harden and ruin the bristles. "Niece, I have a task for you."

She was not surprised. "How can I assist my uncle?"

"I believe someone will soon be coming to retrieve this Isavaltan sorceress. I would speak with them when they do." Uncle stood and lifted a casket down from the shelf behind him. It opened easily under his hands, although, Cai Yun knew from the painful experience of childhood, if she had tried to lift that same lid, her fingers would have smarted for a week.

From the casket, Uncle drew a silken bag, and from the bag he took an amulet of jade carved in the shape of a dragon with a fox's head and cunning eyes.

"I suggest you go to the river docks. This amulet will help bring you and such as seek the sorceress together." Uncle handed the precious object to Cai Yun, who took it with a bow and concealed it in her sleeve.

"I will do my best."

"I know you will," Uncle replied, a hint of pride in his placid voice. His eyes shone and Cai Yun felt an answering warmth run through her. "Understand this, this may be the beginning of something much greater. If we act swiftly and with good information, you and I, Niece, will strike such a blow against the Nine Elders that they will never recover."

Chapter Fourteen

A sharp, swift pain in her stomach woke Medeoan. She cried out and rolled over, clutching her side. Light flared in the darkness and she shrank from it. Gradually, she could see the soldiers had carried in a table and chair, and the little stick of a man who had ordered her put in this cell sat before her, a fresh scroll laid out before him. Two guards flanked him. A third stood beside Medeoan, and she realized his square-toed shoe must be the source of the pain in her side. Her anger flared, but she kept her mouth shut.

"Can you understand me?" asked the stick figure official.

"Very well, thank you," croaked Medeoan. Her throat burned, her head spun. Despite the pain from the kick, her stomach cramped up with hunger. How long had she been left here in this hole?

The official noted something down. "Stand."

Medeoan gritted her teeth and made herself get to her feet. Her knees shook, but she remained upright. They would not see her grovel. They had already seen too much of her weakness.

"Who are you?" the official asked, without even looking up at her. His pen was busy on the scroll, but from this distance Medeoan could not make out what he wrote.

Medeoan drew herself up as straight as she could. This brief moment, at least, she was going to enjoy.

"I am the empress of Isavalta."

She expected a blow, and steeled herself for it, but none came. The skinny official just tightened his mouth into a smirk.

"It is at least a creative lie," he said. "Who are you?"

Let him see it. Medeoan let her anger blaze in her eyes. She remembered standing before the throne, she remembered the coronation and the oaths of loyalty. She remembered looking out the window of Vyshtavos and seeing her lands spread out before her. "I am Medeoan Edemskoidoch Nacheradovosh, the Empress of Eternal Isavalta, the Heir of Vyshemir, the Prince of the Northern Marches, and the Autocrat of Tuukos," she said in her own tongue. "And you will address me properly, or the Heart of Heaven and Earth will know why."

The skinny official blinked slowly. How much did he understand? Was she just speaking gibberish to him? Did they now believe her to be a madwoman?

Slowly, the skinny official set down his pen. He stood, and then he bowed, not deeply, but he did bow. Medeoan inclined her head in response.

"I must look into this matter," he said, gathering up his scroll. "Stay with Her Majesty."

He left then, and two of the guards went with him. They closed the door behind themselves, leaving Medeoan in the cell with the third guard, who positioned himself by the door and assumed an attitude of attention.

Medeoan did not bother to try to speak to him. She claimed the official's chair. Her guard made no remark. He did not even look at her. So, she got ready to wait.

Hunger thinned Medeoan's blood. She tried to be grateful for the light and the chair, but that did not last long. What was the skinny man doing? How could he look into this matter? She had arrived in secret, at least she hoped she had. He either believed her or he did not. If he did not, her trouble deepened. If he did, he should have her taken out of here. Immediately. She should at least be provided with food and clean clothes. Whatever else she was, she had declared herself to be an empress, and there were rules of treatment.

After an unendurably long time, the cell door swung open again. Medeoan started at the sudden, silent movement, but forced herself to remain seated and simply look up.

As expected, the skinny official stepped back into the cell. This time, in addition to the soldiers, he was accompanied by a second, taller man in a long scarlet coat. His black hair was rolled into a bun rather than hanging down as a braid. A serpentine green dragon had been tattooed onto his right cheek. The loops and twists of its body probably wove some permanent protection or silence into his being.

A sorcerer then, probably of the outer court, or he also would have been wearing a cap to match his coat, and would have had more than one visible tattoo.

"You are the one who claims to be the empress of Isavalta?" he said in the language of Medeoan's home.

"I claim nothing," replied Medeoan. "I speak the truth."

He blinked. "You will, however, agree it is a truth that must be verified."

"That depends entirely on the means of verification."

The sorcerer stepped forward and held out his hand. His palm had also been tattooed, this time with a brown snake twisting itself into a pattern that, Medeoan was sure, matched that of the dragon on his face.

"You will take my hand."

Medeoan hesitated. Avanasy had required her to become familiar with the common symbols and patterns of magic in Hung Tse and Hastinapura. The snake was wisdom, but it was also cleverness, and truthfulness. She had no protection about her. What could he compel her to say?

Still, she had little choice. Medeoan lifted her chained wrists. She grasped the sorcerer's hand, and found it cold and calloused from his workings. With his free hand, the sorcerer raised her chin so that he could look into her eyes. Medeoan bit back the rebuke that rose at this familiarity.

The sorcerer began to chant. It was a high, tonal language, like the tongue she knew, but not the same. Some ancient dialect or some sorcerer's secret, she did not know. All she knew was she felt the cold prickling of a spell being worked. It traveled down her skin from her scalp and reached inside her, through flesh to her veins and her blood and crawled along her bones. She felt the sorcerer draw toward her, although her outward senses told her neither he nor she had moved.

Who are you? he asked, although she heard no words. *Who are you?*

Unbidden, a hundred images rose in Medeoan's mind. Her mother holding her hand and telling her a great prince never cries, looking up and up the high dais to where her father sat, a god enthroned in gold, her parents dead under their shrouds, looking into Kacha's eyes on her wedding day, looking into Avanasy's eyes as she banished him from her land. Too many, too fast, the images tumbled over each other: Kacha in her arms, her coronation, her parents in their grave, Kacha in her bed, Avanasy staring at her, his whole face full of betrayal . . .

"Enough!" shouted Medeoan. With all the strength she had left, she tore free of the sorcerer's grip. The prickling faded instantly, but Medeoan was seized with an icy trembling that she could not control.

The sorcerer too was shaking, and Medeoan was secretly glad she had been able to cause him some discomfort as repayment for what he had just done to her. It was a long moment before he was able to harden his face and regain control. None of the other men said a word. Medeoan could not even hear them breathe.

"Yes," said the sorcerer at last. "It is enough." He turned to the skinny official. "Release Her Imperial Majesty."

The skinny official bowed immediately and deeply. He pulled out his ring of keys and unlocked Medeoan's shackles. She stood, letting the chains fall rattling to the floor without looking at them. They were beneath her notice, as was the raw chafing on her wrists.

"If Her Imperial Majesty will follow me." The sorcerer bowed, although not as deeply as the skinny official.

Medeoan nodded. She hoped her face was strong, for she did not trust her voice. Her body felt weak, weak from hunger and thirst, from fear and relief, and from the working that had passed through her.

The sorcerer straightened up and paced through the door. Medeoan followed, and the soldiers formed up at her back.

Medeoan knew from childhood lessons that the Heart of the World was laid out in a pattern of nine squares containing five palaces. Each of the four outer palaces was surrounded by four walls, and had two adjoining gardens. One palace was for the imperial women, one was for the high-level administrators and bureaucrats. Another was for foreign ambassadors and hostage guests. The fourth was for the Dowager Empress and her family.

The fifth palace waited at the center of the great complex.

This was the true Heart, the home of the emperor, who was "the Heart of Heaven and Earth," and the Imperial Protectors, the Nine Elders. It was toward this palace that the sorcerer led her. The final yellow gate opened for them and they stepped out into a courtyard so huge that Medeoan was willing to swear it could have held all of Vyshtavos and still had room left over. Across the expanse of pale sandstone, Medeoan saw the scarlet-and-emerald wings of the Heart spreading out so far she could not take them in with a single glance. In the center rose a great, gilded tower with more windows than she could easily count looking out across the land of Hung Tse.

Medeoan tried to keep her composure. She worked hard not to gape at the pillars of carnelian and jade that flanked the palace's entranceway. More pillars, these scarlet with gilded tops and bases, held up the soaring golden roof. Instead of tapestries, the broad hall was hung with silken banners. Some had been painted with images of the four protectors: the dragon, the phoenix, the unicorn and the tortoise. Others carried pictograms woven together so fancifully they could not be anything but spells. More silk covered the polished floor they walked. Beneath the silk, the wood was so dark it could not have been anything but lacquered mahogany.

They did not stop at any of the doors they passed. None of the guards in their shimmering black armor made any move as they passed.

The hall ended at a gate of carved wood that had been polished until it shone like silk. Medeoan's eyes automatically traced the carving. She found the spells woven into the carving and knew that despite its delicate appearance, this gate was stronger than any she had yet passed through.

Before the gate stood a single figure. Medeoan thought it was a man, but it was difficult to tell. The figure wore a long, enveloping robe of deep blue embroidered all over with sinuous dragons of so many colors that they dazzled Medeoan's eyes. More dragons covered his folded hands. Curving lines and graceful clouds had been tattooed all across his face, turning his skin into a living mask. It was by these signs that Medeoan knew she stood before the Minister of Air.

Her escort knelt, pressing their hands and their foreheads against the floor. Medeoan remained standing. Properly, the minister should have knelt to her. The fact he remained standing sent a shiver of warning through her. All was not going smoothly yet.

"If Her Imperial Majesty will consent to come with me," said the minister in perfect High Isavaltan. He had a rich, mellifluous voice that nonetheless set Medeoan's skin to pricking. Even in his words there was an undercurrent of power, and he was but one of nine.

"Lead on," said Medeoan stiffly. Hunger and uncertainty both gnawed at her. What manner of reception would she have beyond this deceptive gate? How would she be able to stand up to it?

The Minister of Air turned and bowed to the gate, holding his hands out so his left hand covered his right fist. At this gesture, the gate pulled open of its own accord. The minister stepped through, without looking back to see if Medeoan followed. Medeoan straightened her shoulders and walked past her still-kneeling escort into the audience chamber.

Like everything else about the Heart of the World, the audience chamber had been built on a grand scale. Life-sized statues of the gods and the powers with their swords and spears raised, or their arms lifted to bar the entrance of any unwelcome thing, stood guard between elaborately carved pillars of cinnabar. At the center of the chamber rose a dais with ten stone steps. The emperor himself sat on a simple platform of lacquered wood. His robe was unadorned saffron and his hair was rolled high on his head and lacquered until it shone like the platform on which he sat. His skin was clear brown and his eyes black, and he was younger than Medeoan had thought he would be, almost as young as she. Beside him stood a man in white with his hands neatly folded. This was the Imperial Voice, Medeoan knew. The emperor could never be heard to speak by any other, lest his words be captured and used to weave a spell against him.

Five steps below the emperor stood the remaining eight of the Nine Elders.

Medeoan swallowed the temptation to giggle nervously. At least they took her seriously. Avanasy had told her that the way one measured how seriously Hung Tse regarded a threat was to see how many of the Nine Elders stood between the emperor and any ambassador or messenger. All nine were seldom present at once.

One minister for each of the five elements, Medeoan remembered; earth, air, fire, water and metal. One for each of the directions; north, south, east and west. The emperor himself was the fifth direction; center.

So, as the Minister of Air mounted the dais to stand with his colleagues and turn toward her, the whole world faced Medeoan.

Mindful of her position as an unwelcome guest, Medeoan folded her hands over her breast and reverenced deeply to the assemblage in front of her.

"I am most grateful to my Brother Emperor for receiving me into his Heart," she said in her best court manner. Her words echoed briefly around the still chamber, and were quickly swallowed by the vast space.

The emperor nodded and gestured to his Voice.

"I greet my Sister Empress, and I ask her to accept my sorrow and deep respect for her departed parents."

Medeoan reverenced again. "My thanks to my Brother Emperor."

"Your refreshment has been arranged for. Please, take your ease and eat and drink."

At those words, Medeoan almost collapsed with relief. But she forced herself to remain standing while silent servitors in black robes with white hems and cuffs swept forward, bringing with them a chair and table of carved wood. Still others laid out a tray covered with small bowls of cold dainties, and a ceramic beaker of clear wine and another of water, and a pair of small cups to accompany the drinks. A maid bowed before Medeoan, offering a bowl of steaming water and a clean towel.

All this was done under the eyes of the emperor and the Nine Elders. Medeoan's eyes narrowed. This had the feel of a subtle insult somehow, but she could not unearth its meaning. So, she rinsed her hands and dabbed them dry. She sat in the presented chair, and ate from each of the bowls. It was all she could do not to fall upon the food like a dog, but a lifetime of training helped her keep her dignity.

"Again, I thank my Brother Emperor," she said when she could make herself stop eating. "The courtesies of the Heart of the World are as legendary as its wealth. Now I see those legends spoke nothing but the purest truth."

The emperor nodded briefly and turned to his Voice again. Medeoan saw his hand move swiftly, making some sign or signal that the Voice might interpret.

"I wonder what grave circumstances have occurred that cause one of my Sister Empress's station to be wandering alone and in common garb in the open streets of the city."

Here it was. Here was where she had to pull her mind together. She'd had plenty of time on the voyage and wandering the streets to think of what to say, and now was her time to speak.

Medeoan rose to her feet. The eyes of all Nine of the Elders tracked her as she did.

"It has been said, and wisely, that the enemy of my enemy is my friend," said Medeoan, pitching her voice to carry. The room would hear her, the emperor would hear her. She would make them listen. "I do not pretend that there has not long been great trouble between Isavalta and Hung Tse. My Brother feels we have wronged him, and we feel that my Brother has wronged us. This is ever the way of Empire." Father had spoken those words, but he had said them to the ambassador from Hastinapura. Medeoan had sat at his side that day, still and quiet, and wishing she was somewhere else. "But when a common threat arises, it is also the way of the wise in the empire to set aside reckoning for those wrongs and attend to the business of survival."

The emperor's eyes narrowed, and he gestured to his Voice.

"Do you say there is a threat to Hung Tse?"

"I do."

"And the name of this threat?"

"Hastinapura."

Much to Medeoan's consternation, the Nine Elders all laughed. Even the emperor smiled.

"That there is danger to the south of our borders is not

news," said the Voice. "Perhaps it is because our Sister Empress is so young she finds it noteworthy."

Medeoan forced herself to wait until the last of the laughter had died away. "The danger of a bear sleeping in its den is far different from the danger of a bear hunting and hungry."

"You say that Hastinapura plans to attack us?"

"They seek to use treachery to overthrow Isavalta, with whom they have a treaty. If this is accomplished, will they leave at peace Hung Tse with whom they have an active quarrel? Kacha . . ." She stumbled over the name. ". . . has broken the treaty my father entered into with the bonds of our marriage. He is supported by powerful magics and more powerful lies. Because of them, my own lords may not be trusted. But," she raised her finger, "long is the memory of Hung Tse, and subtle are the ways of my Brother Emperor and his Protectors. If we together end this ignoble and unclean overthrow of the right order, the benefits to both our lands will be manifold."

The emperor and the Nine Elders were silent for a long time. Medeoan's heart beat hard in her chest, driven by uncertainty. Did they believe? Did they hear the promise in that last statement?

At last, the emperor waved his hand to his Voice.

"But none of this explains why my sister has come here alone and in such disguise."

For which there was no choice but to lie. She could not have them know that Isavalta had already fallen. "There are some matters that may be spoken of only between princes. What messenger could I now trust with such a letter? Who else's magics could I safely employ? The efficiency and perception of the Heart of the World are known to all; I knew I would be brought before my Brother Emperor before it was too late."

Silence again, and she and the emperor looking across a gulf into each other's eyes. She felt a sudden stab of envy for her "brother," comfortable on his dais surrounded by advisors he could trust. *One day*, she tried to tell herself. *One day, it shall be so with me.*

Then, the emperor turned away, making signs to his Voice.

Medeoan wished fervently her tutors had thought to teach her this language of the emperor's hand, so that she might know for certain what was being said.

The Voice spoke. "I hear the words of my Sister Empress of Isavalta and they are grave and worthy of much thought. I ask that she accept the hospitality of the Heart of the World while I take council with the Nine Elders so that I may give to her a worthy answer."

Hospitality. A bed, a bath, a true meal. Medeoan kept her face still and solemn. "I accept willingly. I only ask that my Brother Emperor understand that this matter is most urgent, and delay for leisurely debate only allows the treacherous to further their plans."

"I assure my sister that I am quite aware of the urgency of her words, and she will not have to wait long for my answer."

Medeoan reverenced, and the emperor bowed in acknowledgment. The Minister of Air left his fellows and walked her back to the inner gate. All the time, she felt the eyes of the others on her, and she could almost hear the air whispering around her. What were they thinking? What were they planning? Medeoan's jaw tightened. She needed to find out.

Medeoan expected to be conducted to the foreigners' palace, but instead, she was taken to the Palace of the Autumn, and there was greeted by the dowager empress, Dieu Han, as soon as she stepped through the gilded doors.

"Ah! My Daughter, how pale you look! It is a shame upon my son and my house that he left you talking so long!" She wagged her head to express the strength of her emotion. "Come, come, let me show you your rooms. Let me summon your attendants. You must be faint from all your trials!"

Or, at least, that was what Medeoan could make out from her speech. The woman talked fast and moved constantly, and if she was old enough to have mothered the emperor, she did not look it. Her face appeared only gently lined and her hair was as black as his. She looked more like his sister than his mother, and Medeoan found herself wondering if the woman was a sorceress. She did not know. She could not remember her father, or anyone else, talking about the dowager.

Dieu Han took Medeoan's arm with comfortable familiarity and steered her through the scarlet-and-sienna corridors, sending servants scurrying in every direction with rapid-fire orders, so that by the time they reached the "poor, very poor," as she called it, chamber set aside for Medeoan, the room was open to the warm sun and fresh air of the early afternoon. Fresh flowers bloomed in the basins, a cold meal of roasted meats and chilled rice was waiting along with tea and wine, and even a small pot of coffee. "It is much favored in your country, is it not?" asked the dowager anxiously. "There is so little comfort here to offer such a visitor."

In truth, her activity and her orders left Medeoan a little dizzy. But, at last, she was satisfied that Medeoan had all the food she could possibly desire beside her, and that the water for washing was just the right temperature, and the robes laid out were of sufficiently good quality. Medeoan was used to being waited on, but not like this. Her hair and body were washed for her. She was swiftly dressed in rich silken robes. Her plates were prepared and served to her by servants who knelt with each offering. Even her cups were held for her so that she could sip from them.

The dowager sat beside her, supervising the service, and making small talk about the weather, the history of the palace and the silliness of waiting ladies, but Medeoan soon found herself less and less able to answer without suppressing progressively energetic yawns.

"But there, you are tired," said Dieu Han at last. "I am as guilty as the emperor of keeping you talking." And she sent the women running to ready the teakwood bed with its smooth sheets and coverlets, and herself escorted Medeoan to its side. Medeoan lay down, and her eyes closed at once. She was asleep so fast, she did not even hear Dieu Han order the ladies out, nor did she see the woman searching her clothing before it was handed over to the serving women to be stored away.

————

Medeoan woke to an oddly familiar scene. Around her hung the curtains of a great, carved bed. Beyond them she could see a peaceful and well-organized apartment with the waiting ladies bowed over their sewing and their letters. So much the same, and so much utterly different. Medeoan had grown up with stone and darkness. This place, palace though it was, was so airy and filled with light she wondered briefly how it did not fly away when the winds were strong. The light had reddened to evening, and Medeoan realized she had been asleep for hours.

"Ah, good, you are awake." Medeoan sat up as Dieu Han rose from her place by a low rosewood table and bustled to the bedside. "First, you must eat, then we must talk."

Medeoan's stomach grumbled, despite its also tightening at the tone the dowager gave her final words, but she only nodded her agreement.

More tea and wine, and another light meal of rice, cured fruit and fish was laid out by the silent, efficient ladies, with many orders by the dowager. Medeoan ate and drank hungrily, learning quickly that she was not to reach for the dishes or the cups, but indicate with a flick of her finger what she wanted. It seemed excessive to her, but she was not going to show herself to be any less sophisticated than this silk-clad and lacquered woman in front of her.

"Now then, my dear child," said the dowager. "I must tell you, the emperor has taken me much into his confidence on matters concerning you, quizzing me most closely on your behavior and demeanor."

Medeoan felt the muscles in the back of her neck begin to knot up. "As to be expected. I should surely do the same if my guards brought my Brother Emperor into my great hall, alone and dressed in a peasant's clothes."

"To be sure, to be sure." The dowager patted her hand. "But there is more to it than that. He does not like Isavaltans, and never has, and looks on you with suspicion, be your face and heart ever so open."

Now Medeoan's eyes narrowed. "And what would he say to you if he knew you were telling me these things?"

The dowager waved Medeoan's words away. "What could he say? He has given me charge of you, to house as I see fit. I may hold such conversation with you as I choose, and I choose to advise you that undue discretion may jeopardize all you would accomplish here. You must be open, and confident. The emperor will in no way support a usurper unseating his Sister Empress, but he must be convinced yet that that is what has happened here."

"I assure you, Mother, I mean to be nothing but honest with my Brother Emperor."

"Good." She pronounced the word with firm satisfaction. "I told him it would be so."

Medeoan picked up her porcelain wine cup again, and studied the letters written in red and gold on its side. They had been cleverly drawn to resemble a field of waving grasses. She couldn't read them all, she only saw the occasional character that made sense, such as "truth," or "peace," or "heart."

"Forgive me for asking such a question, Mother," she said. "But if the emperor has these reservations, why do you not share them?"

The dowager sighed. "Perhaps I should. Perhaps I would be wiser if I did, but I will tell you, in the last year, my daughter, Mei Lin, was given in marriage to a king in the southern states. It was a good match for Hung Tse, but less so, I fear, for my daughter. I can do very little to help her, but in her place, my mother's heart urges me to help you."

The older woman spoke with such feeling that Medeoan's tired heart longed to reach out to her, but she held it in check. She had no proof, no reason to believe anything Dieu Han said, and she had lived too long among sycophants to immediately accept protestations of sympathy. Most of the time. Once upon a time.

A plan formed in Medeoan's mind.

"Mother," she said, setting her cup down. "It grieves me to hear of your daughter parted from you. You have been very good to me, and perhaps I can now return your courtesy."

Was that wariness that flashed past her dark eyes. "In what way, Daughter?"

Medeoan chose her words with care. "I am sure you know that I have some humble gifts of spirit." Medeoan used Hung

Tse's phrase for sorcery. "If you can give me something of your daughter's, and a mirror, I can show you how she does at this moment. It may ease your worries for her."

The dowager hesitated. "Thank you, Daughter. Your offer is gracious. But you may put yourself in danger with the Nine Elders, who will surely be aware of any such casting within the Heart of the World . . ."

Now it was Medeoan's turn to wave words away. "Should they inquire, you will be able to reassure them. Indeed, they will be able to make their own examination of all I do. It is not a complex working, nor, in truth, a very subtle one."

Yes, she looked wary. She was not entirely the worried mother then. How far would she persist in that game?

The dowager reached her decision. "I will return in a few moments." She rose, and swept from the room, surrounded by her gaggle of ladies.

That surprised Medeoan; she had expected some of the ladies to be sent running. Did the dowager need to alert the Elders as to what was about to happen? Send a message to the emperor? Either of those things were possible. It was also possible there was some casket or drawer that needed to be unlocked by the dowager's own hand. Such things were not common in Vyshtavos, but they were not unknown either.

Medeoan forced herself to be patient. If she could just wait a little while longer, she would have her means for gaining real information that she could indeed trust. She wandered about the apartment, examining the blooming flowers in their bowls of water, the finely executed landscapes with their attendant poems painted on lengths of translucent paper. She exclaimed with approval over the work of the waiting ladies, who responded by clapping their hands over their faces in a way that made her think of Kacha, and caused her to turn away.

At last, the dowager returned. With a furtive expression, she handed over to Medeoan a circular mirror of polished silver and a hair comb that had been beautifully etched with a chain of blossoms.

"Thank you, Mother," said Medeoan as she accepted them. "These will do admirably." Especially since the comb still had one long, black hair entwined in its teeth. "I will need to borrow some of your ladies' sewing thread as well, and then we may begin."

The ladies worked exclusively with silk, which was perhaps too fine a thread for this spell, but it would certainly serve. Medeoan arrayed the cut threads in the lap of her robe and began to weave them into a net, with red threads knotted together to make the left half and blue to make the right. All the while she breathed deeply, drawing the magic out and calling it in.

"I stand on the isle of the world, and the sun shines down upon me. The sun sees all that is, all that has been and all that will be. Mei Lin stands on the isle of the world, and the sun shines down upon Mei Lin. The sun sees all that is, all that has been and all that will be." The spell flowed strongly from her, and the weaving caught the words and the magic and gave them the needed shape. It felt surprisingly good. In this, at least, she was sure of what she did. "I will see Mei Lin as the sun sees Mei Lin. I will see all that is, and all that is true for Mei Lin. This is my wish and this is my word, and my word is firm."

With the final word, she wove the net through the teeth of the comb, and laid the mirror down in the center. She breathed across the smooth silver, all her work done for now. Now, she had only to wait and watch, along with the dowager.

At first, the mirror reflected her face, and the dowager's where she leaned over to see. After a few brief heartbeats, the shining surface of the mirror clouded over, as if obscured by fog. Then, the fog cleared, and Medeoan no longer saw her own face. Instead, she saw a garden of willow trees with a carefully constructed stream trickling over rounded stones and golden roots. A young woman, Mei Lin, who appeared to be perhaps a year or two older than Medeoan, sat on a curved bench on the bank. A cluster of waiting ladies laid out a picnic in a silken pavilion nearby. It was a peaceful, busy scene, but, for some reason, it made the dowager frown.

Then, Mei Lin turned her head, probably at the sound of someone's approach. Her face lit up, and she rose gracefully to her feet. A man stepped into the mirror's view. He also was young, and, Medeoan supposed, handsome after the fashion of Hung Tse. His robe was of good green-and-white cloth and he smiled to see Mei Lin. Instead of bowing he folded his arms around her so they might embrace and kiss.

Oddly embarrassed, Medeoan turned her face away.

"The fool!" spat the dowager. "Oh, the little fool!"

Before Medeoan could move, the dowager snatched up the mirror and hurled it across the room. It clanged against one of the wooden pillars and clattered to the floor.

"I'm sorry, Mother," said Medeoan softly. "I did not know . . ." *But I do now. Your daughter has a lover, and this jeopardizes her position, and possibly yours.*

"No, you could not." The dowager bit off the words, plainly struggling to regain control of herself. "You will excuse me. There is something I must do."

The dowager and her ladies swept from the room, leaving Medeoan alone with her servants. Only when the door closed did Medeoan allow the smile she had been holding in to show itself. Vyshemir bless Mei Lin in her inconstancy, she thought. The shock that delivered to Dieu Han had meant the woman left comb, stray hair, and completed net with Medeoan. She had been wondering how she might keep hold of them without arousing attention.

Now, Dowager, we shall see in what regard you are held by your son, and in what regard he holds me.

What she was about to do was dangerous, but she could not leave herself without information. The lies that might cover it were many and easy, but might not be easily believed. Still, she must take the risk.

Around her, the ladies sewed or read passively. One rose to tend the small stove where the water heated for tea. By all appearances they were ignoring her, but Medeoan knew this could not be so. Like her ladies back home, they had to be ready for any soft summons. But unlike her ladies back home, Medeoan knew no way to get rid of them.

So, to screen herself as best she could, Medeoan got up and folded the items she had been left with into her robe's voluminous sleeves. Casually, as if she only meant to stretch her legs, she wandered out onto the apartment's sun porch. One of the ladies immediately responded by fetching a pillow for the low wooden bench. Another placed a steaming cup of tea within easy reach. Both retired at once to the company of their fellows.

Medeoan sat in the place that had been prepared and sipped the tea. The sun was pleasantly warm against her skin, and she would have loved to spend the day just dozing in this spot, bathed in the rich perfumes that wafted to her from the gardens beyond.

Instead, she spilled her booty into her lap. She picked up the comb and gently disentangled the single hair from its teeth. Then, gingerly, she began to twine it into the center of her net, calling up her magic as softly as she could.

"As daughter is bound to mother, so is my sight bound to Dieu Han," she whispered, winding the hair around the silken strands. "As daughter's heart is hidden from mother, so is my sight hidden from those in the Heart of the World." She spoke the spell again, and again, as she delicately knotted the hair to bind it firmly into her net.

Then, as she had before, she laid the silver mirror across the net in her lap and breathed across its smooth surface.

This time when the mirror cleared, Medeoan saw the throne room. The emperor sat on his dais as before, with the Nine Elders ranged before him. But this time, the Elders faced inward, and from Medeoan's view, it seemed she sat at their center in a chair made of some dark wood with elegantly carved arms, for she now saw through the eyes of the dowager empress, Dieu Han.

The emperor signed to his Voice. It seemed that he could not speak aloud even to his mother. Medeoan leaned close to her mirror. Very faintly, she heard the words, "What have you to tell us, Mother?"

Dieu Han dropped her eyes briefly. "Little, my son. I found no charms about her person, nor any one thing I could easily say was enchanted. There was no possession she seemed to cling to. I found only a few coins, and no jewels at all."

Medeoan repressed a spasm of anger. She had in truth expected to be searched.

The emperor nodded and his Voice said, "This is also the word of the jailer who held her." The Voice paused thoughtfully as the emperor did the same. "Did she speak at all of her hopes or fears?"

"Not yet, but I believe she may, if I am given time."

So, you are my hostess and my spy. Well, I cannot truly be surprised at that either. Medeoan bit her lip and bent closer.

Now one of the Elders spoke. This one wore robes that gleamed with threads of copper, silver and gold. Their tattoos were all squares and angles overlaid with serpents coiled together. This was the Minister of Metal. "Time is not something we have, if what she says is true," said the minister. From the depth of the voice, Medeoan decided this minister was male.

"It does not matter what truth she speaks," Dieu Han said with a dismissive wave. "What we know is that Isavalta is grown unstable and this must threaten us to the north."

"Must it?" inquired the Minister of Air, who had greeted Medeoan so politely when she arrived. "If Isavalta falls again into a pack of squabbling kingdoms, we may safely regard them with indifference."

The emperor tapped his fingers on his knee, the first stray movement Medeoan had seen him make. "Unless she speaks the truth and Hastinapura seeks to seize them all," said the Voice.

Another Elder spoke. This one was all in blue, as was the Minister of Air, and sparkling fishes chased the dragons on their robe and on their skin—the Minister of Water.

"Let Hastinapura try. What matter? We are still surrounded by enemies. What matter if there are one or two? While Hastinapura strengthens itself in Isavalta, we will be able to gather our own strength to meet whatever challenge may come."

"But how far along is this plan?" asked the Minister of Air. "It is possible that the Isavaltan empress did not leave as voluntarily as she claims. If they have already driven out their own empress . . ."

"That is a key point." Dieu Han raised her finger. "It may be Isavalta is already conquered. It may be Isavalta is but a prelude for greater conquests."

All looked toward the emperor, who signed to his Voice

with energy. "I am finding it difficult to believe so much of our Brother Emperor Samudra. All his letters have been crisp and direct, saying he wishes no quarrel, that he has quarrels enough of his own to contend with."

"There are more powers in Hastinapura than Emperor Samudra," Dieu Han reminded him.

"You do not believe Chandra may have a hand in this?"

Oh, believe that much, thought Medeoan as her grip tightened on the mirror. The scents of summer and the touch of the fresh wind seemed incongruous. She was in a closed chamber, surrounded by pillars of cinnabar and the statues of the gods.

Dieu Han turned her head a little so she could regard the emperor owlishly from one eye. "It is Chandra whose son was sent to bed the Isavaltan empress."

"You think he seeks to invade his own land from the north?"

"He spoke with great feeling of a single empire when he was a young prince," said the Minister of the North, whose robes were white as snow and embroidered over with broad-winged geese and beautifully stylized gulls. "Our reports on this matter are most reliable."

The emperor considered this for a moment. "But he does not hold the Pearl Throne."

"That may make him safer for this work," said the Minister of Metal slowly, as if testing a fresh idea. "All the blame must go to his brother Samudra, who does sit on the throne."

All in the chamber fell silent for a long moment. Medeoan felt sweat prickling the back of her neck, even though it was not that warm. Tension tightened her throat and snatched at her breath.

"There is another possibility," said Dieu Han finally.

The emperor cocked his head. "What is that?"

"It is all a trap."

No. Medeoan felt herself go cold. *No. That's not what is happening. You cannot believe that.*

The Elders did not stir. If she had spoken so in council in Isavalta, every lord master would have been shouting at once. As it was, the emperor just regarded her coolly and signed to his Voice. "How so, Mother?"

Dieu Han rubbed the chair arm with her palm as she put her thoughts in order. "This little girl, this sorceress, with her tale of woe and wrong. What if she seeks to trick us into committing our armies and our protection, and we lead them into the waiting arms of her forces? We are weak. We cannot here, in this room, pretend that we are not. What if the Isa-valtans have discovered that and seek to maneuver us into a war we cannot win?"

Vyshemir protect me. Medeoan licked her lips. *I spoke only the truth. You cannot believe I did any less.*

"It is an elaborate ruse, if ruse it is," said the Minister of Air.

"Of course it is." Dieu Han spread her hands. "Would a simple plan suffice?"

"Her father spoke of exchanging emissaries, and quelled the pirates in Hastinapura's waters," the Minister of the North reminded them.

"Her father is dead, and she may now be ruled by her husband. We also have reliable reports from Vyshtavos, about how she seldom conducts any business, how all her thoughts are given to her own pleasures and none to her rule. The emperor is Chandra's son. It may be he has persuaded his bride to yield her unwanted power to him."

No, no, no. Medeoan wanted to shout out her frustration. *I told you the truth!*

"But why come alone?" asked the Minister of Metal. "Why in this state?"

"Because there is a limit to what one may safely carry through the Land of Death and Spirit," replied the Minister of Fire, whose scarlet robes and tattooed skin were covered with representations of the phoenix. "Could she sail through with an escort of mortal soldiers? It would be dangerous. Could she take her court sorcerers into her confidence? It is not likely. We would know if her escort consisted only of magicians, and be alerted."

Again the emperor tapped his knee. "These thoughts are unwelcome, but they are worthy. They must be given careful consideration."

"Thoughts will only scatter us like leaves in autumn," said Dieu Han firmly. "We must have facts."

The Minister of the North bowed her head. "Vyshtavos is well protected. Even we may not see within its walls."

"There are other places, and other eyes than our own that may be trusted," said the Minister of Metal. His heavy robes glinted in the light, rivaling the draperies of the gods around them. "We must know how the ships and soldiers move in Isavalta. If there is to be danger in this year, they cannot now be idle, for their summer is short and their winter is long, and they must strike quickly before the ice comes so that they may have secure garrisons for the winter. Whether or not Medeoan is involved in the plan, if they mean to attack, they will now be on the move."

At these words, the emperor frowned. "Minister of Earth, if the Isavaltans do mean to attack, how well may we withstand them?"

The Minister of Earth was robed in green. Tortoises adorned his robes and skin, picked out in sienna and sparkling gold. "Not well, Your Majesty. Our dealings with Hastinapura and the pirate fleets have left us drained, as the Isavaltans surely knew. If we now must face war from the north . . ." He shook his head.

As the Isavaltans surely knew? Tears pricked the corners of Medeoan's eyes. *As Kacha surely knew. Oh, Vyshko, Vyshemir. What if this is true? What if this is his plan?*

The emperor nodded. "Very well. If it cannot be open conflict, what means can we employ?"

There was silence for a long moment before the Minister of the North said, "We must invoke one of the great protectors."

"Not yet," said the Minister of the South. Her robes were scarlet as were the Minister of Fire's, and her phoenixes pursued white cranes across the cloth and her skin. "We must try to treat first with our enemies. The pirates may be turned to war on Isavalta."

"For what payment?" countered the Minister of Air. "Will you return the islands of K'ien and Shai to their mercy, which is their capital demand? Will you hand them those bases and fortifications, those walls over which they may look with greed at the Heart of the World?"

Again the Elders fell into their profound silence. Medeoan

found herself wishing they would shout, would argue, would *do* something, not just stand there like ciphers believing she came as the pawn of their enemy.

Oh, but you do come as that pawn, whispered a treacherous little voice in the back of her head. *If Kacha's moving troops to the southern border, what else could you be doing here?*

Furrows creased the emperor's brow. At length, a tiny smile appeared on his face. "Perhaps you should have chosen another for the throne, Mother. Look where I have led the Heart of the World."

"I do not regret my choice, my son." Dieu Han drew herself up straight. "If danger threatens from many directions, then it must be met at each turning. If there is conflict at the foot of the Pearl Throne, expose it. If Isavalta threatens the north, break it. If the child Medeoan is a treasure, keep her."

"There is wisdom in what you say, Mother. Very well." The Voice hardened, growing even more imperious. "Let our eyes be turned toward Isavalta to see what there is to be seen. As we strive for that understanding, let a letter be drafted to the emperor of Hastinapura protesting this attack by his representative in Isavalta. If we cannot muster mortal protection, we will summon the immortal."

"And Medeoan?" inquired Dieu Han.

"Will be moved into the Heart where she may be kept more closely."

Medeoan could not stand to listen anymore. She tossed the mirror and her spell net aside, burying her face in her hands for a moment before she remembered the watchful, silent ladies behind her. She straightened up at once, but did not turn to look into her chamber. She did not want them to see her face, for she could feel that her chin trembled as badly as her hands as the full weight of her folly tumbled down on Medeoan's head.

Since her second brother had died of his fever, Medeoan had wanted to run away from her destiny. She had imagined a free life, one where she lived separate from politics, free to enjoy her days and her companions without worrying whether it was her rank that made them stay beside her. Her parents had worked hard to train her for her appointed role, and she had responded by isolating herself from all those around her. All except Avanasy, and then Kacha.

So, what did I do when danger truly threatened? Medeoan ground her teeth together until the pain ran through her jaw. *I thought of nothing but to run away. I did not think to find a counter to the spell Kacha would place on me. I did not think to gather my own loyal followers, no. I ran, and now I will be put under lock and key as strong as any Kacha could have devised for me, and I have left Isavalta without friend or protector under the hand of a bloody usurper!*

She knotted all the muscles in her neck to keep her head from falling forward as the tears began to trickle down her cheeks. *What have I done? Oh, Vyshemir, what have I done?*

But there was no time for despair. She wiped her eyes quickly. She was about to be placed under arrest. They would be on their way shortly. They would take from her every means they could to work her will. Without sorcery, she would never be let out until Kacha paid a ransom for her, or until whatever conflict might come between Isavalta and Hung Tse had reached a resolution, and that might take years. She could not leave Isavalta alone under a false power for years. She could never leave Isavalta alone again.

Medeoan cast quickly about, but saw nothing to help. There was only the carved balcony rail, the sun-drenched garden beyond, the wooden verandah beneath her feet, the bench, the cup of tea, and the mirror, net and comb lying where she had discarded them. An idea came to her all at once and she snatched up the net. The spell woven into it would not be of much use should she need to escape, but the silken threads could be reknotted to provide the base for some more elaborate working. She wadded the net up into a fine ball, and then tucked it as deeply under the elaborate braid that held her hair in place as she could. A quick glance in the mirror showed her no trace of colored silk showing under her golden hair.

A breeze at her back and the rustle of cloth told her the chamber door had opened. Medeoan rose and turned, as calmly and smoothly as she could manage.

Dieu Han entered the room, with the Minister of Air standing impassively beside her. With them came six guards with their long-handled axes and their black, lacquered armor trimmed in Imperial saffron.

"What is this?" demanded Medeoan. "What has happened?"

"Oh, Daughter," sighed Dieu Han, shaking her head. "I told you to be open with my son."

The Minister of Air gestured once, and the soldiers moved forward to surround Medeoan.

She feared they might return her to the cells she had been held in before, but instead they took her into the very center of the Heart, placing her in a small chamber in the gilded tower. The room was bare stone with only a leather mattress resting on the floor. There was a window, low enough for her to look out of, so she could see the expanse of stone walls that surrounded her and the constant patrols of guards that traversed their battlements.

They took her clothes away and left her a shift of leather. They cut her hair. Medeoan almost cried out as they did. But they seized her braid and sheared it off right at the base of her skull. Her heart rose to the base of her throat, but the maids had done their work too well and the hidden netting did not fall.

Then they left her, taking her shorn braid with them.

Alone, Medeoan's first thought was to undo her few remaining pins and pull her netting free. She clutched it in her hands. As little as it was, it was her only weapon, her only chance. They had left her nothing else but her ragged hair and the blood in her veins.

The leather shift chafed her skin as she moved to the window. She looked out on the neat walls and their guards, moving as precisely spaced as if they were driven by clockwork. She saw the splendid gardens and the majestic gates and beyond them the teeming city dissected by its own walls.

Loneliness settled like a stone into her heart. All she had in the world to aid her was a tangle of silken threads. And Avanasy. If Avanasy were here. If Iakush had found him. If, if, if . . .

Medeoan bowed her head. She would not weep. Even as she was, she was a great prince, and she would not weep anymore.

Avanasy, you will find me. You have never let me down. You will find me and we will be free, and together we will return to free Isavalta. My land. I have been shown the error of my ways, and I will never flee from my land again.

Chapter Fifteen

The time on the water acquired its own rhythm, and Ingrid found herself coming to relish it. She and Avanasy shared the work of canvas and tiller, fishing with drag lines for whatever the ocean felt like offering. She liked his boat and soon learned its strange rigging and its easy ways. In the evening, they would anchor off the coast. While they remained in Isavalta, if one of his maps showed there to be a village nearby, one or the other of them would hike inland to hear the news and barter for bread and other provisions. Although Ingrid found herself missing any number of things—sugar, coffee, white flour, more than one change of linen—the days still felt sweet.

Nights were spent cradled in each others' arms and that was the sweetest of all.

Only two things kept the time from being perfect. The first was Avanasy's growing anxiety to reach their destination. Every day he would scan the skies, looking for the messenger from Peshek. Every day his face would grow just a little more grave as the messenger failed to appear.

The second flaw was Ingrid's dreams.

As soon as they had left the cove below Hajek's village and reached the open water, Avanasy had given her the tiller and sail and gone below. Ingrid sailed them across calm seas in a steady wind, and wished that there was a little more for her to do so she would not have to wonder so much about what had happened to her, what would happen next, and how Avanasy was going to do what he needed to if he was going to have to keep worrying about her.

An hour or so later, Avanasy returned to the deck, looking tired but satisfied. In his hand he held a delicate, complex braid made of colored cloth, canvas threads and several strands of his hair, and hers. He tied his creation securely around her right wrist, and kissed the knot when he was finished.

"It should be a girdle, or a sash, but I have no time to weave you such before dark." He met her eyes anxiously. "How do you feel?"

Ingrid considered, searching inside herself for an honest answer. "As if something has eased," she said. "At least for now."

"Good." Avanasy kissed her. "Good."

She knew he did not sleep that night for watching over her, and, in truth, she was hard pressed to give herself over to oblivion, but at last fatigue won out. She slept, and she stayed within herself, but she was seized with a straining and stretching, as if she were struggling against the bond that held body and soul together. It was the same every night after that. She would see things, fleeting as shadows in the darkness, and would feel them pausing to stare at her: a knight all dressed in red; the Vixen, who was the size of a cart horse; a snake, a tortoise, a huge chestnut horse, a dragon, a beautiful bird with trailing wings.

She would tell Avanasy of her dreams, and he would frown and reconsecrate her wristlet.

"They are spirit powers," he told her. "You are seeing into the Land of Death and Spirit, and it is looking back at you. I don't like it."

Neither did Ingrid, in truth, but there was nothing to be done. Avanasy said there would be help in Hung Tse, perhaps even from the Nine Elders, depending on what Medeoan had been able to accomplish. Ingrid would be whole again, he swore, and with that, Ingrid worked hard to let herself to be content.

It was their tenth day on the water. Ingrid was taking her turn at the tiller. It was a good day, with a clear sky and only a few hazy clouds. The sea was blue and the swells were high, but regular, and the wind stiff and steady and smelling only of warm salt. The seabirds sported lazily over the low green coast.

Avanasy stood by the mast, one hand shading his eyes as he stared toward land. Then, he pointed toward an oddly cleft rise, where it looked like a single hill had been split open with a giant axe.

"Ngar-Chen," he said. "That puts us about a day out from the mouth of the Sze-Leng River. From there we will be able to find our way to the Heart of the World. There may even be a riverboat, if we are lucky." He came to stand beside her, one hand wrapping itself around the gunwale, the other touching the line, as if testing its tension. "Grant that we have not been too long."

"Whatever we find, we'll deal with it then," said Ingrid. "Your empress arrived safely, you know that much."

Avanasy nodded absently. He had tried several times over the past days to work a spell which would allow him to see Empress Medeoan, and possibly to pass a message to her, but there had been little success, even though his efforts would leave him drained and shaking. He had nothing of hers to create a bond between them, he told Ingrid when he had recovered from his first attempt, and working with the unshaped elements was chancy at best. He had been able to find traces that led him to believe she had reached the Heart of the World in safety, but beyond that he could see nothing.

"The Nine Elders will not permit prying eyes near their emperor," he had said ruefully.

The wind shifted, tugging at line and canvas. Ingrid, in response, shifted her grip on the tiller and checked the ropes. All seemed well to her, but Avanasy had straightened up, and turned his gaze from the shore to the open sea.

"What is it?" she asked.

"I don't know. Something . . ." He lifted his head, as if he had caught a sudden sound, or scent. "Something new . . ."

Ingrid stared in the same direction, but saw nothing. All the sounds of sea and wind seemed the same.

"Ingrid, take us in to shore," said Avanasy. "I do not like this."

Ingrid did not question or protest. She trimmed the sail and swung the tiller around, steering them toward the green land. She badly wanted to see what Avanasy was staring at as he watched the open water past her shoulder, but her business was the boat, and she needed to keep a sharp eye out for breakers that would mark any shoals or other shallows.

Then it seemed to Ingrid that the day grew dimmer, and something was lost. In another minute she knew what it was. The seabirds had fallen silent.

"Vyshemir defend!" Avanasy leapt over benches and gear to reach the port rail.

Ingrid risked a look back, and her grip slipped from the tiller.

They flew behind the boat, faster than the wind for they were gaining. They were huge and ungainly, shaped more like apes than men. Their wings blocked out the sun, and they were armed. What light there was outlined spears and swords in their huge fists.

"God in Heaven," was all she could breathe.

"Get us in, Ingrid," cried Avanasy, drawing his knife. "I'll hold them off, but we must get to land!"

Ingrid forced her eyes back down. *Work the ropes, raise the sail, steer the tiller, watch the shore, watch for breakers. Don't look back, don't look back.* She forced these words through her, although her mind was awash in panic. What were those things? What did they want? Oh, God, how could Avanasy face them all down with just a knife?

Shadows swooped over the boat, and despite all her resolve, Ingrid had to look.

Avanasy did not hold his knife now. Both his palms were cut and the blood ran red down his hands as he lifted them to the wind. He cried aloud, harsh words Ingrid could not understand and the demon—what else could it be?—responded with a laugh like the low roll of thunder and swooped closer. Light glinted on red skin and black armor and cruel yellow fangs. Fear left Ingrid dizzy, but Avanasy didn't move.

All at once, the wind blew hard, making the boat buck against the waves. It scattered the demons. The nearest shouted in his frustration and dove down on them again, and again the wind blew him back. But it also strained the canvas and made the ropes creak dangerously. A wave rolled over the rail, and Ingrid leaned all her weight against the tiller. The boat fought her, torn between Avanasy's wind and the natural actions of the waves.

Avanasy, pale as death in the bright sun, snatched up a length of rope in his bloody hands. Shouting again, he tied a knot in its length. One of the demons arched its back, screeching in what Ingrid could only believe was pain. It plummeted into the sea, tossing up a fountain of brine. For a moment, the wind stilled, and Ingrid was able to haul hard on the tiller and swing the boat about, aiming the prow for a cleft in the shore that she prayed would make a harbor.

Avanasy staggered, the motion of the boat sending him reeling against the rail. The chief of the demons laughed again and whirled his sword over his head, bringing it flashing down as if it meant to cleave rope and sail. Ingrid hauled hard on the line and the boat heeled over, its rail skimming the water, and the sword missed by a bare inch. Avanasy slid to the deck, but braced himself against the bench.

"This is my wish," Ingrid heard him grate, his hand curling around one of the belaying pins. "This is my word, and my word is firm, my word is firm, my word is firm!"

He lifted the pin high, raising himself to his feet, and in his hand it was a pin no more. It was an axe on a long pole, and the demon swooped close again and he swung it out and their weapons rang together with a mighty clash. The demon shrieked and fell back, beating the air with its wings. It dove again, and again Avanasy parried, and it was all Ingrid could do to keep her seat and make herself watch the water, but when her eyes dropped again, she saw what she feared more than any impossible monster.

Breakers.

Rocks, shallows, shoals, it didn't matter, the safe cove she had steered them toward had no safe entrance. Immediately, Ingrid leaned forward to bring in the canvas, to swing the boom and bring them about, but the demons had seen, and they dropped low behind the boat, their great wings fanning the wind and driving the little boat forward, toward the breakers.

"Avanasy!"

Avanasy saw, and swung his axe through the air, cutting

at wind and wings. The demons shrieked and fell back, giving Ingrid a moment's respite to haul the sail down, but the boat still surged forward, and the breakers were far too close. She searched the pattern of them desperately, watching for a clear space, or at least a strong wave to carry them over whatever lay beneath.

She spied their chance, or what she hoped was their chance, a place in the swell where the waves seemed to surge through rather than smash against the shallows. She leaned hard on the tiller, aiming the boat and praying hard to whatever gods watched over sailors here.

One of the demons dropped in front of the boat. Ingrid did not let herself flinch. The way was too narrow, she had to hold steady. Avanasy gripped the rail with one hand and raised his axe, shouting to the sky. The demon shook as if buffeted by heavy blow, and it fell back.

At that moment the boat shuddered, and the tiller ripped itself momentarily from Ingrid's hands, but it was enough. The other two demons rose grinning from the side, and she had just time enough to realize they had battered themselves against the boat before the surge drove them onto the rocks.

The world filled with a hideous splintering, crashing and roaring. Thrown backward, Ingrid tumbled into the surf, dragged instantly into the swell by her heavy skirts. Her hands clamped around the stern rail, barely able to hang on. A demon dove grinning toward her. She screamed and dropped down into the water, and the world was suddenly blue gray and silent and her lungs strained and salt water stung her eyes. Waves shoved her forward hard and she struggled to swim, expecting any second to be snatched into the air. But no grip seized her, other than the water, relentlessly surging, weighting her down too heavily. She thought of Grace and, for a moment, despaired.

But her foot found the ragged bottom and she kicked upward at the same time a wave tumbled her forward, dashing her against a shelf of rock and knocking all the air from her lungs just as her head broke the surface, allowing her to scream for her pain and fear.

The waves rolled her over again, driving her into the pebbly shoal and then dragging her back out again. Scrabbling with hands and knees, Ingrid managed to gain a little purchase and forced her head and shoulders above water. Salt water burned in her eyes as she struggled upright so she could see.

And she saw Avanasy. He stood up to his waist in the surging water, his axe over his head. The demons wheeled above him, but they did not come close. Avanasy slashed the air with his axe, again, and again. With each slash, the demons pulled closer together, as if bound by invisible ropes. Avanasy cried once more, and the demons fell. Not in a straight line, not into the sea, but in an impossible arc, to vanish into the forest that covered the coast.

At that same moment, Avanasy's arms dropped, and he fell forward into the surf. With a cry of her own, Ingrid launched herself to his side to try to catch him, but her own strength was failing her, and she could only prop him up against her shoulder. But his eyes were open, and he was breathing, and it was enough.

"Come, come," she croaked, her throat harsh with salt and sand. "We must get to shore."

Avanasy mustered a nod and, together, leaning on each other, they labored to the shore, half swimming at times, sometimes Ingrid dragging Avanasy forward, sometimes Avanasy dragging her. At last, the waves pushed them forward and left them stranded on the stony beach, collapsed and panting, bleeding and bruised, two lost creatures of the sea left upon land to die.

The sun was hot and the water she had escaped from was harsh. Eventually, thirst became a stronger force than exhaustion, and Ingrid was able to push herself upright. Avanasy already sat up, hunched over his own knees, facing inland. He had been white before. He was gray now, and his breath was a sickening rattle.

"We need to find water," rasped Ingrid.

Avanasy just shook his head. "We need to find the demons."

"Why?" was all the answer Ingrid could make.

"I've bound them. They pull at me. If I don't transfer the bond . . . If I don't make some bargain, or bind them to some element, they'll break free, and they'll set on us again. I've not much strength left, and they'll know it."

The thought of facing those monsters again made Ingrid shudder, but she would not leave Avanasy alone, not while he was shivering despite the bright sun.

She made herself swallow and say, "Do you know where they are?"

"All too well." He tightened his sinews and stood, and Ingrid stood with him.

This coast was as different from the place they had first come ashore in Isavalta as it was possible to be. That place had been all gray stones and gray cliffs. Here, there rose a thick forest beyond the stretch of sand. Salt wind twisted the trees, making them stooped and kinked like arthritic old men. From inside the forest, she could hear the demons, their thrashing and their shrieking like the sound of tortured metal. Beads of sweat stood out on Avanasy's forehead as they entered the wood, but he walked with determination.

The farther they ventured from the shore, the straighter the trees became, and sand gave way to loam, dead leaves, ferns and rich moss. The noise did not pause or abate. If anything it grew more riotous. Avanasy staggered, and Ingrid caught him by the arm, lending what little strength she had to his support. He squeezed her hand, and they went on through the green dimness toward the unearthly clamor.

"You will be bound," said Avanasy through his clenched teeth. "I will it so, you will be bound."

At last, the trees pulled away from a stony clearing. The last two demons waited there, shaking their weapons and straining their wings at the sky. Their leader, or so Ingrid thought of him, had rings of gold in his ears. He beat the ground with his spear as if he could force it to let them go.

"Be still!" ordered Avanasy.

And they were still, but even so, Ingrid could see them quivering as they strained against the order. Even restrained as they were, they were terrifying. Fangs curled from their mouths and talons from their hands and feet. The constant wind rattled the scales of their armor like the leaves of the trees. Their yellow eyes were the size of saucers, and a rotted, burning smell clung to them that went straight to the back of Ingrid's throat and choked off her breath.

The chief of the monsters snarled at Avanasy. "You transgress, man. We may not be twice bound."

"You may be bound until the end of time if I so declare it," answered Avanasy. "The roots in the earth beneath us can be called on to bind you tightly. The air can weave a net to hold you close."

"Such boasts, such brags. You have not the strength."

"You are bound to me with bloodshed between us. If I transfer that bond, what can you do?" Avanasy's voice turned dangerous. "You are creatures of fire, air and metal. I will bind you here with earth and water, by earth and water, under earth and water, between earth and water, I will bind, and my binding will be as firm as my word, as strong as my blood . . ."

Beneath the demons, the earth began to move. Runnels of dirt ran up their legs like reaching fingers, swaddling their skin and exposing the bare tree roots. The roots themselves writhed and parted, revealing dark holes beneath the trees. Ingrid smelled a sudden gust of sea wind from the opened hole. Avanasy had gone freshly white with effort, but his voice did not falter. The demons screamed, their cries of pain shuddering the wood and filling the air with heat and the scent of burning. It did them no good, and terror joined pain in their screams. Avanasy put out one hand to steady himself against a tree, but he grimly worked on, his spell never faltering, although his voice began to soften. The demons looked like living statues of sand now, and the weight of the earth heaping itself over them began to bear them down, into the opening caves and the scent of the sea.

"No!" cried one of the demons. "Please, master, no!"

"Mercy!" cried the leader, and its cry now was as heartbreaking as it had been horrible before.

Only then did Avanasy cease his slow chant, and for a moment, all the world held still.

"Mercy?" said Avanasy, softly, dangerously. "Why should I show mercy to the ones who sought my blood and the blood of my wife?"

"We were ordered, master," wailed the leader of them all.

"We bear you no ill. Set us free, bind us no more, and we will leave you and yours in peace."

"Ordered by who?"

"We know no name."

"Do not lie to me. What is his name?"

"Yamuna, Yamuna, master, now let us go! Let us leave each other in peace!"

Slowly, Avanasy shook his head. "It is not enough. Not for the hurt you would have dealt us." He began his chant again, and, relentlessly, the weight of the earth pressed the demons to the ground.

"Please!" gasped the leader, forced to his knees. "Master, please. What is your price?"

Again, Avanasy halted the spell, and the whole world was still for a single moment. "You will never again plague any under my protection, and you will carry us safely to the Heart of the World."

"We cannot, we cannot."

"Then be you buried," said Avanasy implacably. "For I cannot leave you free."

The demon nearest the pit began to howl, struggling against the earth that bound him like a shroud, to no avail. The hole simply widened, yawning like a mouth to receive a morsel.

"Mercy, mercy!" cried the chief demon. "It shall be as you say!"

"Swear it," said Avanasy.

"I swear, I swear!" gibbered the demon. "Spare us the earth!"

"By what do you swear?"

"By my own eyes, by the fire that birthed me!" screamed the demon.

At that, Avanasy nodded. "It is enough." He knelt, laying his bloodstained hands flat upon the ground. He murmured something Ingrid could not hear, and all at once the earthen shrouds fell from the demons, the grains scattering like the dust they were. The ground heaved once more, and the tree roots closed over the pit again, lacing themselves into a tight, natural net.

Avanasy did not get to his feet. Rather than have to look

at the creatures that faced her, with their fangs and their wild yellow eyes, Ingrid crouched beside him. "Are you all right?"

"No," he answered flatly. "But it does not matter. Help me up."

Ingrid tightened her jaw around all her questions and helped Avanasy to stand. The chief of the demons did not seem able to look him in the eyes. It bowed its head and its great wings slumped until they dragged the ground.

"You have doomed us, man," he growled. "When would you have us fulfill our bond?"

"Now," said Avanasy. He looked toward Ingrid, and Ingrid could not keep her trepidation from her eyes.

"How can we do this? How can we trust them?"

"They are bound to me now. They cannot harm or disobey," he said with utter conviction. Avanasy moved close to her and gripped Ingrid's forearms. "Hold tight to me, Ingrid, and do not be afraid."

"Come now, master," growled the chief.

Freed from Avanasy's spell, the demons showed no further sign of weakness. In a single moment, they embraced Ingrid and Avanasy, and their wings raised up until the sun was blocked by the bloodred feathers. Ingrid bit her tongue to keep silent. Then there came a great rush of air, and the ground fell away from underneath her feet.

Ingrid had little time to imagine what such a flight would be like, but if she had a thousand years, she never would have anticipated the reality of it. She could not see anything. The world was the rushing of wind, red, gold and black shadows, the stench of burning and Avanasy's hands gripping her arms. The heat was stifling. Her feet dangled loosely, and she had to fight to keep from kicking out in a vain attempt to find some footing.

Then, it was over, and it was only she and Avanasy, their backs against a sandstone wall, and busy river docks spreading out before them. It was only then that Ingrid realized she was soaked with sweat and stench and her hands had gone completely numb. Avanasy looked like death itself, but at the same time, his limbs seemed steady while Ingrid's felt weak as water.

"Come," his voice rasped in his throat. "Let us sit for a moment, here."

Still holding tightly to each other, they settled themselves stiffly at the base of the wall. Avanasy gently extricated himself from Ingrid's grip and laid her hands in her own lap. For a while, she was content just to sit, and feel the warmth that was no more than sunlight touch her skin, and draw some sensibility back into her hands, even if it was only pins and needles. Indeed, it seemed as if she might never will herself to movement again. But, gradually, as the world stayed steady and the familiar sensation of wind in her hair and on her face proved it would not change suddenly into the breath of a demon in black-and-gold armor, Ingrid found thoughts once again beginning to coalesce inside her battered mind.

"Where are the . . . demons?" she asked.

Avanasy let his head fall back to rest against the wall so that he stared up at the summer blue sky with its drifting clouds.

"Perhaps back in their home in the Silent Lands. But, more likely, they have fled to try to avoid the summons from their other master, which will surely come." He watched the clouds slowly shifting their shapes overhead. "I cannot imagine Yamuna will be pleased."

"Who is Yamuna?"

"Each member of the royal family in Hastinapura is assigned a sorcerer as a protector and advisor. Yamuna serves Chandra, who is father to Kacha, the one who was married to the empress of Isavalta."

"They know you have returned then."

Avanasy bowed his head and ran his hand through his hair. "So it would seem. I have not been as subtle as I thought."

"But these will not come again."

"Not these. They are bound by their oaths to me now."

"Can't they break those oaths?"

Avanasy shook his head. "They cannot. It would put them in my power again."

"How so?"

Avanasy's smile was thin. "It is one of the mysteries between this world and the Land of Death and Spirit. An oath between a mortal and a spirit or a power is not as an oath between mortal and mortal. Words between us have powers of their own. They can wound, they can tie, they can break. The arguments about why this is so are extensive. They fill books and scrolls of great antiquity. The only point which cannot be argued is that this is the truth."

Ingrid stared out across the docks. She had not imagined a river could be so broad. It must be to rivers as Superior was to lesser lakes. The ships waiting at the piers came in all sizes. There were huge galleons with four masts and three tiers of portholes. There were lean three-masted cutters with knife-sharp prows for slicing through the waves with all speed. Sloops and smacks and dories of all descriptions crowded in the shadows of the larger vessels. Bare-chested men in broad, peaked hats worked in and around their vessels, singing, swearing and shouting by turns. These were surely the common sailors, decided Ingrid. They carried huge bundles on their backs, or tightly packed baskets on shoulder yokes. The air was full of the smells of tar, sweat and spices. Despite the strangeness of dress and the sight of so many sails, the place felt strangely familiar to Ingrid. It reminded her sharply of the port at Bayfield.

Between the shirtless men worked men in short coats and wide trousers, mostly white or unbleached cloth with colored bands around the cuffs and hems for trimming, but here and there was one dressed in solid black or bright green or sapphire blue. These men stood in groups, talking, or supervised the unloading of ships and the loading of carts, or sat at trestle tables beside ships' gangways weighing samples of goods or reviewing what Ingrid supposed were bills of goods.

But all these sights and sounds were not enough to drive the question that had formed inside her out of her mind. "So, if I had promised that . . . Baba Yaga that I would carry out the task she gave me . . ."

"You would have been bound to her by that promise until the task had been completed, yes. If you had tried to break that promise, your life itself could have been forfeit to her."

"Oh."

Ingrid was silent for a time, breathing in air that smelt of spices, fish and garbage. Then, another thought occurred to her. "But surely those demons were sent to murder us."

"They were."

"Did they not break a promise then by failing to do so?"

"They did. Which is why they have fled. At the time, they feared me more than they feared Yamuna." He rubbed his forehead. "I was gambling, I confess, that they were of those breeds not noted for their courage, and that they might indeed have been coerced." He lifted his eyes again. "If they had given their oaths freely, there would have been nothing short of their annihilation that would have saved us."

To that, Ingrid made no reply. At her silence, Avanasy's face fell. "It is a dangerous place I have brought you to, Ingrid. But these are dangers beyond what I anticipated. I am sorry."

She shook her head. "It was my decision." She tried to smooth down her filthy dress. "Now, where are we and how are we to make ourselves decent enough to be seen here?"

He smiled at her sudden turn to practicality. The expression brought a more healthy color to his cheeks, which her heart lifted to see.

"I have some gold," he said. "Not much, but some. We can change it for local coin easily enough, which in turn will buy us a bath and whatever else is needful. As for where we are . . ." With a grunt, Avanasy got himself to his feet, and extended his hand to Ingrid to help her do the same. "We are in T'ien, the city that holds the Heart of the World."

Together they waded into the busy crowd surrounding the river docks. The warm damp air was only made heavier by the presence of so many bodies surrounding them. Although Avanasy said he had only been to Hung Tse three times in his life on errands for the emperor of Isavalta, he spoke the language well. So too, apparently, did Ingrid, for he had imparted that understanding to her through his enchantment. She could understand the language of the sailors and the wharfmen in all its rough color as they worked their way down past the piers and the warehouses.

Finally, Avanasy found what he was looking for. He touched Ingrid's forearm and gestured for her to wait by the seawall. She nodded and backed away while he strolled onto the docks toward a man in a white coat with narrow green lapels and deep cuffs who sat behind his table weighing out what looked from Ingrid's vantage point like thimbles of tarnished silver. He looked up at the sound of Avanasy's voice, and from the men's expressions, Ingrid became confident that a period of pleasantries and bargaining was about to begin.

She let her attention wander to the business of the port. A rhythmic song rang out as sailors hoisted heavy loads aboard one of the galleons. A cart loaded with live chickens in their coops turned a corner in a flurry of feathers and frantic clucking. A drunken man wove his way unsteadily through the throng clutching a wineskin to his bosom. Ingrid rolled her eyes. There was a recipe for disaster in this crowd.

Disaster was not long in coming. The drunk, rather than choosing the path of least resistance, seemed determined to force his way through the thickest part of the traffic. He was shouldered off to one side, and then the other, but before he had gone many yards he collided straight into one of the few women who walked near the docks, sending up a spurt of clear liquor between them, which drew a laugh from the passersby. The woman drew back in an obvious attempt to regain both distance and dignity. The drunkard himself batted at the woman's robe, in either an assault, or an attempt to wipe away the dampness. Angrily, the woman pushed him away, shouting something that was lost in the general laughter and noise of the crowd. But, even as she did, traffic began to flow around her again, one man brushed against her, and Ingrid saw his hand reach quickly into her sash and secret something in his own sleeve.

"Thief!" shouted Ingrid, before she even had time to think. She jerked herself upright and leveled an accusing finger at the man. "Thief!"

A general shout rose from the crowd. Some drew back and others surged forward, and the thief himself tried to dart into the crowd. Ingrid leapt forward, putting herself squarely in his path, and grabbing his sleeve as he tried to push past her

"Let me go!" he shouted. "Are you mad? Let go!"

But the assaulted woman reached into her sash, and found her property missing.

"Thief!" she echoed Ingrid's cry. "Thief! That man has my purse!"

Then it was not just Ingrid who held him. Two of the passing sailors seized the thief roughly by the shoulders, pulling him from Ingrid's grip. Avanasy was beside her all at once, urging her back. A third sailor, with a moth tattooed in blue on his shoulder, searched the thief roughly, coming up with a bag of scarlet leather.

"My purse!" cried the woman, running forward to snatch it from the sailor's hand.

The crowd did not take this declaration well, and the shouts turned ugly. The thief was shoved from hand to hand and his pleas were lost under the general roar. But someone's grip must have slipped, because the thief darted through a cluster of sailors and pelted up the alleyway between two warehouses, the mob in hot pursuit behind him.

"Are you all right?" Avanasy asked Ingrid.

Before she could answer, the assaulted woman stepped up to them and bowed deeply, holding both hands before her, palms pressed together as if for prayer.

"May your sharp eyes be blessed," she said breathlessly. "I and my family are in your debt."

Ingrid glanced sideways at Avanasy, her eyebrows raised, but she quickly recovered herself and curtseyed to the woman. "You're welcome. Anyone would have done the same."

"But anyone did not," replied the woman, straightening up. She was a slender woman, a few inches shorter than Ingrid. Her eyes were almond-shaped, and a rich almond brown hue in her round face. Her black hair had been piled high on her head and bound with peach-colored ribbon that exactly matched the skirts and cuffs of her robe. "I am Cai Yun Shen. May I have the honor of knowing to whom I owe the return of my property?"

Caution nibbled at the edge of Ingrid's mind. "I am Ingrid," she said. "And this is my husband Avan."

Cai Yun looked from one of them to the other, but did

not ask about their abbreviated names. "And you are strangers to this province?"

"Travelers only," said Avanasy.

"Then please allow me to extend to you the hospitality of my family's house. My uncle will be pleased to personally thank you both."

Ingrid felt her face begin to warm, and opened her mouth to protest she had not done so much, but felt Avanasy's gently warning touch on her shoulder.

"The honor would be ours," he said to Cai Yun. Then, to Ingrid, in English he added, "Hospitality is not something we can lightly refuse here. It would be a grave insult."

Ingrid nodded her understanding. At that same moment, she thought she saw Cai Yun's eyes narrow ever so slightly. What disconcerted her? Was it the language? Why would that be?

But all Cai Yun said was, "Then, if you will please follow me."

"Gladly," said Ingrid, despite her troubled propriety. They were still filthy, covered with the residue of their travels. The idea of entering a decent home in this condition did not leave her at ease.

But Cai Yun did not seem to notice, and Avanasy walked with his head up, apparently unconcerned. Ingrid tried to put it out of her own mind and pay attention to the city passing around them. She soon came to realize she was in a city far larger than any she had ever been in. For all she knew, the place might be as big as Chicago. The narrow streets were filled with people and lined with houses of stone and wood with tiled roofs, some as much as three stories high. The tallest and the richest rose behind walls of carved and painted stone, and Ingrid saw the tops of rich green trees, leading her to believe the walls enclosed gardens as well as homes.

They had not been walking many minutes before Cai Yun stopped before one of these private walls. The opening in it was a narrow, dark wooden door carved all over with patterns that might have been swirls of wind, or might have been winding ribbons. She would not have given them a second thought, except she heard Avanasy's sharp intake of breath at the sight of them.

Inside the gate, as Ingrid had thought, there was a garden. It was a lush, green lawn overshadowed by drooping trees with leaves of all shades of green and red. Rich ferns and reeds clustered about still, brown ponds blooming with lilies and purple flags.

Beyond the garden waited a house Ingrid could only describe as grand, which made her shabbiness feel even more apparent. Two stories tall and far broader than it was high, it was a beautiful building of painted wood with wide, red-lacquered eaves, covered with flowing decorations of green and gold. Rather than windows, it seemed that whole panels of the walls folded back like screens to open the rooms to the sea breezes that drifted over the walls.

Avanasy's eyes looked about ready to fall from his head, he was staring so hard as they walked up the flagstone path. "I have never seen a house so elaborately protected," he murmured. "If these sigils are real, this place is protected by more magics than the Imperial winter home in Isavalta."

Ingrid wanted to ask him why anyone would protect their home so heavily, but Cai Yun was watching them again with her narrowed eyes, so Ingrid responded with a smile.

"What beautiful gardens you have," she said. "My husband was just remarking on them."

Cai Yun smiled, apparently satisfied. "They are indeed lovely. I have spent many peaceful hours here, and am always glad to return when I have been away."

"You travel a great deal then, Lady?" inquired Avanasy.

"My family makes its living by ships," answered Cai Yun, a trifle coolly, Ingrid thought. "I have sailed some distance with them."

They had reached the verandah now. Two servants, a man and a woman in identical coats and trousers of unbleached cotton with black cuffs, opened the doors and bowed deeply.

"Welcome, mistress," said the woman to Cai Yun. "Your uncle has been awaiting your return and asks that you join him in his library at once."

"Gladly, Shien. Now, these two travelers are my honored guests. You and Jiu will show them to a good apartment and see that they are brought clean clothes and all that they will need to refresh themselves." She spoke with the casual ease of one used to command. "As they are northerners, you will see them housed together." She blinked up at Avanasy. "That is customary for a husband and wife in your land, is it not?"

Avanasy did not frown, not quite, but a flicker of suspicion crossed his face. "It is," he acknowledged, and Ingrid wondered what he was thinking.

"Welcome to this house, master, mistress," said Jiu. "If you will come with us please."

"I will relate the full story to my uncle," said Cai Yun. "He will be anxious to meet you and thank you for your vigilance."

"I'm just glad I could help," murmured Ingrid, and she was glad to be able to turn quickly away to follow the old servants.

The inside of the house, at least on the first floor, seemed to be composed of only a few separate rooms. The rest of the space seemed to be broken by gleaming wooden pillars and screens of carved wood or painted silk. Ingrid felt as if she was in some grand pavilion rather than a true house.

Up the broad, shallow stairs the rooms were smaller, with solid walls and doors. Jiu and Shien led them down a corridor to the far corner of the house, opening a pair of doors to reveal a room of rose-colored wood and water blue silk. The two servants bustled about, opening the broad windows and sheltering them with intricately carved screens. Jiu hurried to fetch water while Shien opened a rosewood press and laid out two sets of robes, one white and green, one white and blue. Black sashes accompanied each robe. As Jiu returned with water for the porcelain ewers, Shien also laid out towels, soaps, combs and brushes in such profusion that Ingrid was not sure she could decipher uses for them all.

It took some doing to convince the pair that she really wanted them to wait outside during their ablutions, but Ingrid was firm. She apologized repeatedly for her coarse and foreign ways, but she shooed them out just the same. She wanted a moment to think, and to catch her breath with Avanasy. She did not want to be fussed over by a stranger.

At last, however, Shien closed the door behind herself murmuring that she would see to their meal, and bowing to Ingrid's thanks. The door shut, Ingrid let out a sigh of relief

and set about stripping her filthy dress off down to her petticoats. She had peeled off her outer layer and tossed it aside,
only to look up and see Avanasy smiling at her.

"What is that for?" she inquired with mock stiffness.

"You. A world away from your home, and you are stopping thieves, graciously smoothing our entrance into the
homes of the wealthy, and ordering servants about, and yet
I believe you think nothing of it."

Ingrid shrugged, pouring water from an ewer into a basin.
The faint scent of jasmine rose from the cascade. "Compared
to what I have seen you do today, it's a small thing."

"No." He came to stand next to her, his hands resting on
her shoulders. "It is a great thing indeed." As if to prove
what he said, he kissed her lingeringly, a gesture Ingrid willingly accepted.

"Do you have any idea where we might be?" she asked
when they parted. With towel and soap, she set about scrubbing her face, neck and arms. The water turned from clear
to gray with distressing speed.

"If I am not mistaken," said Avanasy, filling his own basin, "this house belongs to a pirate."

"A pirate?" repeated Ingrid, lifting her dripping face in
surprise.

Avanasy nodded, stripping off his shirt and laying it aside
with Ingrid's dress. "They are a plague on Hung Tse, and
most embarrassingly on T'ien and the Heart of the World,
but they flourish, well paid and well protected."

"You don't sound as if you believe we are in much danger."

"I don't. They have their own honor in many ways, and
judging from our Lady Cai Yun's reaction, whatever was in
that purse was valuable to the master of this house. I think
we will be safer here than we could have been in hired rooms
and public baths, and much less observed."

"It is no worse than demons, I suppose," admitted Ingrid,
bending once again to her wash.

But she heard no indication that Avanasy was doing the
same. "Ingrid, what is wrong?" he asked softly.

For a time, Ingrid did not answer. She washed her neck
and arms, wrung out the towel, folded it onto the side of the

basin, picked up a fresh towel and began to dry herself.

"I don't know," she admitted. "I . . . It's all so strange. As soon as I think I know what to expect, everything seems to change, and I know nothing. I even find . . . I wonder . . ." She bit her lip. She had not meant to say so much.

"What?" asked Avanasy, drawing close. "Wondering perhaps how much you know of your husband?"

She could not look at him. "I don't want to feel this way, I swear to you, Avanasy . . ."

He just shook his head to silence her. "It would be strange indeed if you did not. You have seen me threaten torture and murder against my enemies. You have been swept from one land to another with barely a word, and you have been torn in two since you came here." He ran his fingers lightly over the braided wristlet. "What sane woman would not have doubts about what she had done?"

"And what do we do about it, then?"

"We trust," said Avanasy. "We hold each other close. We hold close the hope that this chaos must end and the world will be righted again."

Ingrid knew her smile was wan. "I will do my best."

"As will I." Avanasy picked up his own towel. "And we will speak more tonight, but I think now we must finish our washing. I fear poor Shien and Jiu will be fretting outside the door for not being allowed to do their jobs."

Ingrid set her hair in order and Avanasy finished his wash. Then they attempted to help each other on with the robes, which had looked so tidy when Shien laid them out, but proved to be absolute acres of cloth that had to be carefully folded, wrapped, and tied. After several laughing attempts to get them on, they retired to opposite sides of the room behind separate screens and called for the servants. As Avanasy suspected, they were just outside the door. Shien bustled in behind Ingrid's changing area and in moments had her wrapped and tied neatly in the thick, clean cloth so that the robe fell in graceful folds from her shoulders and her waist.

Now that her charge was dressed to her satisfaction, Shien busied herself with setting out the numerous diminutive bowls and cups that were evidently required for their meal. Each dish held just a taste of some delicacy; a few pieces of fresh melon, a piquant vegetable pickle, cold rice flavored with jasmine, some shelled nuts, a few small steamed rolls. The cups held various teas and liquors. It all seemed incredibly exotic to Ingrid, as she sat at the low table and allowed Shien to help her to various samplings and Jiu helped Avanasy, and yet at the same time was an undeniably refreshing way to eat on an afternoon that was becoming increasingly sweltering.

When the last dish was emptied and cleared away, and Ingrid had sipped the last of the orange-blossom water, Shien bowed low again and said she had been instructed to take them down to the study to meet their host.

The food and wine had mellowed Ingrid, but not enough to ease her apprehension. What sort of hospitality had they accepted? Avanasy's reassurances notwithstanding, she knew something of banditry and even piracy, and such men might have honor, but it was of a notably expedient sort.

The study was in a well-shaded corner of the house on the lower floor. Cai Yun stood outside its screened entrance, and dismissed Shien with brief thanks and a wave as they arrived to stand in front of her. Cai Yun, in turn, led them around the screen into a spacious and beautiful room. Its many low tables were spread with maps or piled with scrolls or folios of thin paper. In the midst of these tools of scholarship sat a man whom Ingrid assumed must be the master of the house. He appeared to be a man just entering middle age, with sharp cheekbones and keen eyes. His black hair had been bound into a neat braid at the back of his head, and, unlike most of the other men of this country, he wore a thin beard that outlined his jaw. His robe was solid black with white cuffs and sash.

Cai Yun bowed to the seated scholar. "Uncle, may I introduce to you Ingrid and her husband, Avan. It was Ingrid who saved our family property and my honor this morning. Mistress Ingrid, Master Avan, may I introduce my uncle, Lien Jinn."

Lien Jinn bowed without rising. "Please accept my thanks. My niece was on an errand for me, to meet a ship of mine that had come in. What you saved was much more than a maiden's pocket money." He gestured toward two chairs that looked to Ingrid to be little more than low platforms with thin pillows on them. "Will you sit with me?"

"Gladly, sir," answered Avanasy. He was holding his face oddly, as if trying to keep some unwanted expression at bay. He and Ingrid settled themselves tailor-fashion on the seats while Cai Yun stationed herself at her uncle's right hand. "I have only rarely had occasion to enjoy the fabled hospitality of T'ien, and my wife not at all. I am humbled by its extent."

"Your words warm my poor heart," answered Lien solemnly.

"I was most struck by the beauty of your home," Avanasy went on. "Great care has been taken in its construction, and its protection."

"What peace can there be if a man's family is not safe?" Now it was Lien who narrowed his eyes, and it was easy to see the family resemblance between him and Cai Yun.

"This is wisdom." Avanasy nodded. "Your own children are grown then?"

"My ancestors deemed my role should be to look after the health and well-being of my brothers' families."

"Having seen how you provide for strangers, I have no doubt your family is in excellent hands," said Ingrid, beginning to get a feel for the rhythm of this conversation.

"It is a blessing to be able to help those who are far from their homes." Lien's face grew shrewd. "And I cannot help but believe you are both very far from your home."

"Not so far as I have been," answered Avanasy. "But not so near as I would be."

"You did not wish to travel then?" Lien inquired mildly. Ingrid noted that although she sat silently, Cai Yun was watching both her and Avanasy, like a cat might watch a mousehole, not blinking, missing nothing. Looking for lies under the pleasantries, Ingrid was sure of it. Looking for what might be hidden by words.

Avanasy sighed. "In truth, no. We find we have become seekers, my wife and I."

"And what is it you seek?"

"Something valuable, which was removed from its rightful place."

"Ah." Lien nodded sagely, as if Avanasy had spoken with

perfect clarity. "This is a common problem. It must be very valuable for you to have traveled so far."

"It is unique."

"I thought it must be. It may be I am in a position to help you."

"Indeed?" Avanasy's eyebrows shot up in mock surprise. "We would be most grateful for any help that could be offered."

"It happens in the course of trade that I occasionally hear of valued moveables, and may be able to bend my humble skills toward negotiating its retrieval."

"I fear it is not only retrieval which we must concern ourselves with, but return. While I hope those who have it will return it willingly once certain conditions can be met, I fear they may not, in which case they may pursue it."

Cai Yun frowned openly at this, but the light of curiosity sparked in her uncle's eyes. "This enterprise could lead you to some expense, I think, my friend, as well as trouble."

Avanasy bowed his head. "It can, and it has, but I am under obligation."

"Ah, yes. I thought as much. Isavalta is noted for its dedication to duty."

"And you, mistress, what are your people noted for?" asked Cai Yun lightly.

"Stubbornness, mistress," answered Ingrid, which earned her a laugh. "And an inability to keep our opinions to ourselves."

"Have you an opinion on this matter then, mistress?"

Ingrid decided to risk it. "It is my opinion that the Master of the House already knows who we are, and has some idea of what it is we seek. I believe he is taking our measure, for which I cannot fault him, but I think it would be beneath all our dignities to begin bargaining over the fate of nations like a fishwife over fish."

Lien laughed out loud. "Well spoken, mistress. Well spoken. What do you say, Avan? Do we bargain thus? Or do we open our books each to the other and show what we know?"

"I would not presume to tell the master what to do in his

own home. But I do find myself reminded of a legend they tell in my homeland."

Lien's eyes glittered. "I would be most interested to hear it."

"I was trained by the sorcerer Valerii. When it came time for me to leave my master, he gave me many gifts. The most precious of these was the secret of making sailcloth that could catch the wind that blows between the worlds and enable a boat to sail between mortal shores and the Land of Death and Spirit. He told me the secret of its making had been won by a sorcerer from south of our home. This sorcerer, it seems, loved a young woman who was chosen to enter the Heart of the World as a concubine. But she continued to write to him, so the story goes, and he to her, swearing he would find a way to spirit them both away without even the Nine Elders being able to follow.

"My master went on to say that this sorcerer walked across the Land of Death and Spirit and, through immense patience and cleverness, won the secret of making the sailcloth from the Old Witch herself. But when he returned to his home, it was only to find that his love had been discovered and made to drink poison for her transgressions. The sorcerer vowed vengeance upon the emperor and all his heirs, and he has ever since been taking that vengeance, as slowly and as patiently as he took the secret he needed from the Old Witch."

Lien's eyes glittered. "So. You know rather more than I would have told you left to my own devices, Master Avan."

"Avanasy," Avanasy corrected him, and there was no look of surprise on Lien's face. "I believe Mistress Ingrid is correct. The time has come for us to call things by their proper names."

"And while we are so doing, what would you have of me?"

"Beyond a night's shelter, nothing, if all is well."

"And if it is not?"

"Safe transport for myself, my wife and one other to a destination of our choosing, safe transport that the Nine Elders cannot follow."

"This item you seek, it is valuable to the Nine Elders."

Avanasy nodded. "If they are so inclined, they will find it

a treasure great enough to buy the peace of an empire."

The smile on Lien's face then was thin, and filled with greed, but his words were cautious. "I shall consider your words carefully. We shall speak again at the evening meal. In the meantime, I invite you to treat my house as if it was your own. Niece, show them the gardens."

"Gladly, Uncle." She bowed to him even as she rose.

"The peace of an empire?" inquired Lien as they turned to go.

"Perhaps," said Avanasy. "If they have chosen safety over honor."

At those words, Lien's face turned utterly bitter. "That has ever been their choice in the past. I think we may easily rely on them to do so again."

Chapter Sixteen

The temple city of Durah was normally a place of solemn monks, prayer fires, and the smells and smokes of sacrifice. Pilgrims filed up the narrow way to pay what coins they had to the priests and pray at the feet of the Mothers for guidance or deliverance. Today, however, the way was blocked by vigilant soldiers and those pilgrims who did not wish to return home waited in a makeshift camp at the bottom of the cliff. More soldiers crowded the alleys and twisted walkways between the temples and dormitories, pitching their own tents and adding the smoke of their cooking fires to the sacred smoke rising in tribute to the gods and the Mothers.

Emperor Samudra *tya* Achin Hariamapad, Father of the Pearl Throne, Beloved of the Seven Mothers, Warrior of the Gods, the Uniter and the Deliverer, having prostrated himself for a suitable time in the highest temple and having in addition paid for a seven-fold sacrifice and added a gift for the high priest, was given a priest's house to use as his headquarters, and not too grudgingly either.

The house's great room had been cleared of most of its furniture and appointments. In their place, great maps had been unrolled and laid on the floor, decked out with copper markers indicating where the enemy troops were last known to be stationed. The latest news from the scouts was not good. The Huni had dug themselves into the mountain fastnesses, and showed no sign of being willing to come out for a fight. Indeed, why should they? All they needed to do was wait for winter to descend upon the mountains and fill the passes with snow and ice. It was still early enough in the year to start a siege, but a siege would have costs, and not all of them would be paid on the battlefield.

The true problem lay in not having an accurate count of the enemy, nor a good idea of the state of their supplies. His generals were questioning some of the local villagers even now in other, quieter rooms, but so far they were not getting good answers. Shepherds could count rams and ewes accurately, but to them five soldiers were the same as five thousand: too many for safety.

"We could parley, Majesty," suggested General Makul, seeing Samudra frowning at the delicately drawn maps and the copper coins. "Draw them out and take their measure across the negotiating table."

"And have them think we are weak," growled Samudra.

"The better to know how weak they are," replied Makul calmly. He knew the growl to be purely reflexive, a mark of Samudra's disappointment more than anything else. This had been meant to be a brief campaign. The march from the Pearl Throne had been accomplished quickly. He had believed that the rout of the Huni here might be the same. The Huni in these mountains were known to be fat and careless, convinced Samudra's attentions lay elsewhere. It should have been a quick fight, with Samudra and his men home in time to supervise the tallies from the harvests and deal with Chandra, Yamuna and their antics, all the time having let Hung Tse know that their days of holding the land that belonged to the Seven Mothers were almost done.

But the Huni had been warned, and when Samudra arrived they were long gone.

"Would they parley, do you think?" he mused, rubbing his chin.

"I think they would sneer. I think they would bluster," Makul replied. "And I think they would be glad of a chance to do so to Your Majesty's face."

"I think that some of our scouts led by a well-paid shepherd might keep watch at such a time in a hidden place, to observe their comings and goings so we might better know how they can be winkled out of their shells."

"Your Majesty thinks wisely and well," replied the general gravely.

Samudra let the flattery pass with a smile. "What do you think, Hamsa?" He lifted his head to his sorceress.

Hamsa stood in the corner of the room in front of a fire of smoldering sandalwood and incense. She balanced herself neatly on one foot, with one hand raised above her head, her fingers cupped in the sign of supplication to Jalaja, first of the Seven Mothers. She had been standing so for three days and three nights using prayer, smoke, strength and sacrifice, binding her magic into shape. She sought to see into the warp and weft of time, to see what was possible and what was not, at least as far—as she would have been the first to remind him—as the Mothers would permit. Despite her fierce concentration on matters beyond the flesh, he knew she heard him, for it was the consequences of what was said in this room that she was meant to see.

"I think . . ." she murmured, her voice slurred with trance and fatigue. "I think I see a ravine in the foothills where a tributary to the river Harsha cuts sharp through the rocks." She swayed just a little on her one leg. "I think I see a man's broken body at the bottom. His horse lies beside him for the ravens and the wolves. He came fast and far, that man, and he had a message."

"What message?" demanded Samudra. Inside he cursed. What this ill-starred expedition did not need was more complexity.

"Gone," said Hamsa thickly. She did not look at him, but stared straight ahead, seeing further than any untouched human might. "Consigned to the fire, blocked, blotted, ashes . . ." She swayed again, like a young willow in the wind, bending so that Samudra sucked in his breath, but still she remained upright. "For that message could not reach the emperor, or all would be lost, lost . . ."

"Do you see the message, *Agnidh* Hamsa?" asked Samudra quietly, uncertain whether she would even hear him where she had gone.

"In the fire," she whispered, her words swaying in rhythm with her body. "In the fire, first and last, beginning and ending. It was in the fire, it is in the fire, it will be in the fire, ever in the fire . . ." She shuddered violently, and Makul started forward, but Samudra stopped him with a touch on the arm. Samudra disliked magic. He shied away from it when possible. But he knew enough to know Hamsa had gone from a trance to an active working, and to interrupt could be perilous, to the sorcerer and the mortal attempting the intervention.

"In the fire," Hamsa said again, bending forward from her waist, still balanced on only one leg, breathing the scented smoke deeply, weaving her spell of breath, smoke, sacrifice and words. "Fire, flame, ash, smoke, message to the mighty, message in the fire, in the flame, in the ash, in the smoke, in the fire, in the fire, in the fire . . ."

Hamsa lowered the hand she had held cupped over her head for three days and reached it unhesitating into the bright flames. When she drew it out again, she held a piece of sealed paper in her fingers.

"There," she whispered, and let it fall to the floor. Immediately, she herself sank down to sit on the flagstones, arms and legs folded, eyes closed, and lungs laboring to keep breathing. This too was the way of things. Samudra motioned to the waiting servants. They knew what to do. Water, bread and fruit would be placed beside her so that she could regain her strength as soon as she was ready to rejoin the human world, but first, there was the message, which Makul had already retrieved from the floor.

What he had taken for paper was in fact white silk, tied with a saffron ribbon and sealed with saffron wax, the sort that was only used by one source: the emperor of Hung Tse.

Samudra slit the ribbon with his knife and unrolled the silk. The characters had been painted in red and black ink

with a minute brush, and the whole of it was finished with
the yellow dragon seal of the Heart of Heaven and Earth.
Samudra allowed himself to sit and spread the letter out before him. He could read the language of Hung Tse, but not
as quickly as he would have liked. For such a letter, however,
no translator could properly be called, not yet. However it
came to him, this message was from ruler to ruler and must
be treated with respect.

So, slowly, he read:

> *To the Emperor Samudra* tya *Achin Ireshpad, Revered*
> *and Respected, Father of the Pearl Throne and Beloved*
> *of the Seven Mothers, we send greeting.*
>
> *It is not our wish to speak to you with anger, but for*
> *the care we hold our sacred lands, our borders allotted*
> *to us by the will of Heaven and of men, we must protest*
> *the injustices that have their origin in the blood of the*
> *Pearl Throne.*
>
> *The northern border of Hung Tse is assaulted, the*
> *leader of the assault is the nephew of the Pearl Throne,*
> *Kacha* tya *Achin Ejulinjapad. He moves to attack with-*
> *out provocation, without warning and without lawful*
> *reason. We would appeal to the lawful Empress of Is-*
> *avalta and bring forth our suit to her, but it has come*
> *to our ears that she has been driven from her own court.*
>
> *We ask you to appeal to the filial responsibility of*
> *your nephew to stop this unwarranted and unjust attack*
> *on our lands and peoples. Whatever are the lawful*
> *quarrels of our empires one to one, to break and reform*
> *the power of the North must lead to a war so complete*
> *that powers will fall and be broken under its wheel. As*
> *a man of prudence and martial wisdom, you surely see*
> *this and will not desire such an outcome.*

Samudra felt the blood draining drop by drop from his
cheeks.

"What is this?" he whispered. "What is this!" he shouted,
staring at the letter as if it had burst back into flames. "War,
war with Hung Tse, and Isavalta and Kacha at its head! What
is this!"

"The truth," said Hamsa before Makul could even open his mouth. The sorceress lifted her head. Even across the room, Samudra could hear her breath wheezing in her lungs. "The Mothers forefend, Majesty, but it is the truth."

"How did we not know? Why did Kacha's bound-sorcerer not write to me or to the queen?"

Hamsa had to take several rattling breaths before she was able to answer. "I don't know. The *Agnidh* Harshul may have been corrupted."

"Or he may have been killed," said Makul grimly.

"And the letters forged?" demanded Samudra. "How? By who? I know Harshul, and Kacha does not have the mind for this, let alone the skill." *At least I believed he did not, I believed he was safe to send as pledge and prize. Oh, Mothers, what have I done?*

"Those are questions that should be put to Prince Chandra," said Makul. "I cannot believe that the son acts without his father's blessing."

"Yamuna," breathed Hamsa. She coughed, and reached a trembling hand toward the water bowl that had been placed out for her. She dipped her fingertips in the water and sucked them dry. "I saw . . . as I saw the history of the missive, I saw . . . Ah, forgive me, Majesty." Coughs wracked her, shuddering her bony frame. A servant knelt beside her, lifting the bowl to her lips that she might drink. Samudra waited. He had seldom seen Hamsa so drained. The effort it was costing her to speak was as great as if she had been wounded to the heart in battle. As much as his blood wanted immediate answers, he held himself in check.

"The missive came from the Heart of the World to the Pearl Throne," rasped Hamsa. Her head drooped. The wheezing in her chest did not lessen. "The First of All Queens saw the seal and sent it on, unopened, with a courier. But Yamuna's spies . . . Yamuna saw . . ." She shuddered again, and again the servant held up the bowl, and Hamsa drank deeply. "Yamuna laid a curse on the pass, and his servants hurried to the spot to find the courier dead and they burned the missive. They should not have." She smiled weakly. "They should have left it whole. If it had remained separate from the element of fire, I would not have been able to call it forth."

Yamuna's spies? Yamuna saw? Samudra stared at the sorceress. Not Chandra? Yamuna was but a servant in this matter, and a foolishly loyal one at that. He detested his service, and yet would not take freedom when it was offered in a sanctioned bargain. Samudra had to admit himself completely unable to understand why the sorcerer's answer had been no.

Yamuna's spies. Yamuna saw.

An almost unthinkable, and certainly unwelcome idea stole slowly into Samudra's mind. Could it be that Yamuna already had such freedom as he desired?

Could it be that Chandra had come to allow himself to be ruled by the one who was bound to serve him? Could this plot be Yamuna's rather than Chandra's?

It went wholly against the order of the world. It was worse than treason, it was sacrilege, a defiance of the patterns laid down by the Seven Mothers. Jalaja herself declared it was only by observance of the sacred dance of life that Hastinapura would remain safe. Such reversal, such removal . . .

And yet there were those who said that Samudra himself had done exactly the same thing. He was the younger brother. It was not his place to rule, not while Chandra lived. Had he not removed himself from his proper place in the dance in search of a higher position?

No. Hastinapura would have been nibbled away by the Huni under Chandra. The Mothers meant this for me. All the signs portend . . .

This was Samudra's private agony. He feared that in badgering Chandra into relinquishing the Pearl Throne he had truly saved Hastinapura for the Mothers, but that he himself had truly violated the order of the world. What could this be but another consequence of his transgression?

"Rest now, *Agnidh* Hamsa. Surely you have earned it," said Samudra aloud.

"Thank you, Majesty." Hamsa's head sunk onto her breast as she fell into her meditations again, or perhaps it was only that she fell into simple exhaustion.

"Make up a pallet for the *Agnidh* that she does not have

to be moved," Samudra ordered the servants. "And stay by her in case she wakes and has need." Beside him, Makul opened his mouth. Samudra held up his hand to keep the general silent. "Have your scribe craft a message to the Huni asking for a parley. Choose us a reliable courier, a reliable scout and the most reliable shepherd you can buy. If you have need of me, I will be out walking in the night for a while."

"Majesty." Makul bowed with his palms pressed over his eyes, and then hurried away to carry out his orders, shouting for his scribe Ikshu as he went.

Samudra did not stay long after Makul had gone. He left the servants scuttling to take care of Hamsa, left the soldiers standing at attention waiting for any orders he or Makul might give, left the maps and the copper counters, and emerged into the dry, chilly air of the mountain evening. The sky blazed orange and copper, and the land falling away from the cliff where the temple city perched was nothing but a carpet of shadows.

This was one of the luxuries when he was campaigning. There were times he could be alone, as he never could when he was only the emperor. Samudra stood for a moment on the steps of his borrowed house and breathed in the thin mountain air and the smoke from both profane and holy fires. He listened to the shouts and clatter that were as much a part of a soldier's camp as the patrols and the tents. Then, he strode up the narrow way to the temple of the Seven Mothers.

The temple stood at the highest point of the city. Seven narrow, tiered domes surmounted the building, stretching like searching fingers toward heaven. Seven broad, shallow steps led up to arched doors carved all over with scenes from the great epics, scenes of gods and heroes and the Mothers' intervention in their deeds. As this was not the hour for any rite or observance, the doors were closed. Samudra pushed them open and entered the temple.

The way to the sanctuary was not straight. The progressively larger chambers and the narrow corridors that connected them were precisely measured and laid out according to the ancient formulas. As the paths in the Palace of the

Pearl Throne caused all to constantly reweave the patterns of protection and prosperity, here the pilgrims and the priests alike walked the patterns of generation that were the mortal representation of the Mother's eternal dance.

The sanctuary opened before him. Its chamber stood under the largest dome, creating a ceiling that rose tier upon tier over the circular chamber. Dominating all the carvings, and all the altars to lesser gods and their many aspects, were the statues of the Seven. Carved four times a man's size, they danced eternally around a central fire that smelled of the heady herbs that might set a man to dreaming if he stayed too long in his meditations. Summer blossoms in many colors draped and crowned the Mothers, and petals lay scattered around their feet.

Samudra dropped to his knees, prostrating himself before the images.

I am sorry. I am sorry. I truly believed I was only doing what you desired.

Chandra had played at ruling as if it was a garden sport. He had ordered lavish palaces built. He had filled the women's quarters with skilled and exotic beauties and opened them freely to his favorites. He had feasted himself and them liberally, and had ordered the ministers and administrators about like a petulant child giving orders to slaves. Through it all, Samudra had stood by and watched. It was not his place, he told those who came to him to speak of taking the throne. His place was to be a soldier, to defend Hastinapura. That was his role.

He had held to that, until the day the Huni moved. They marched unimpeded down from their holds in the northern mountains, occupying first a few valleys, then a few cities, then three whole provinces, and Chandra refused to let Samudra take his armies north to meet them. They would not be able to hold such vast tracts, Chandra said with a wave of his scented hand. They would soon withdraw.

But they did not, and at last Chandra was forced to act. But he still did not send Samudra, who had trained all his life for this fight, and who was adept in the arts of war. No, he himself would be carried to the fight, an umbrella over his head and a naked sword at his side.

He was captured three days after the ridiculous, limping battle was joined, and immediately sent word back to the Pearl Throne that he should be ransomed, whatever the cost.

Samudra could not stand it anymore. He consulted the best astrologers; he spent long hours with Hamsa, making her draw him out fortune after fortune. All said the same thing; if Chandra were allowed to rule, Hastinapura would collapse. The thought of the Pearl Throne falling to ruin inflamed him. It could not be permitted.

Samudra traveled in secret to Chandra's camp. He dressed himself in women's clothes and went to the Huni commander, begging to be allowed to see Chandra, "my dear husband." His plea was granted, and Samudra killed the Huni duke with a hidden dagger and escaped, slinging Chandra over his saddle bow when Chandra would not move quickly enough.

When he had Chandra safely back in the camp, and had made sure the story of the rescue was spreading fast, he presented Chandra with his demands. Chandra would leave the camp, Samudra would pursue the war. When Samudra returned to the Pearl Throne, Chandra would turn over the rule over to Samudra. In return, Samudra would not rise up against him, and he would grant Chandra his life.

Chandra snarled, Chandra barked, Chandra threatened. Samudra stood silently before him while the shouts of praise bearing his name, not Chandra's, rang through the camp, more than loud enough to be heard in the imperial pavilion. In the end, Chandra tried to bribe, and then he begged, and Yamuna stood to one side in the pavilion and watched it all. Chandra finally agreed and Samudra marched away to his own quarters. Hamsa did not sleep that night, nor for many nights afterwards, waiting, wary, for whatever attack Chandra might order Yamuna to launch.

But from that quarter, no attack came.

Or so he had thought then.

After a time, Samudra sat back on his heels, gazing up at the Mothers whose images had been before him all his life. Jalaja, Queen of Heaven; Daya, Queen of Earth; Ela, Queen of Mercy; Harsha, Fertility; Indu, War; Chitrani, the Rains and Waters; Vimala, Destruction.

"Yamuna," he whispered to them. "I did not look for him. I looked long and hard at my brother, but Yamuna is a servant. He vowed to serve you, and us. How could I believe he had come to rule? Even Chandra could not permit himself to be so ruled. It never even crossed my mind." He bowed his head. "And I believed myself to be such a fine soldier, a great planner, and I failed to take the true measure of the traitor in my own house, and now his son has begun a war I do not know if I can stop." He lifted his eyes. "We cannot have chaos in the north. We cannot have Hung Tse uncontained. My brother is days away with his master, I am committed here, and his son is out of reach in the north. So many pieces so far away. Mothers, how do I guide the patterns on this board where all the players are out of my reach?"

Samudra sat in the silence of the temple, alone with the Mothers and the heat and scent of the sacred fire. If the priests came and went, he did not hear them, sunken as he was in his own thoughts. At last, slowly, the layers of anger, worry and reproach peeled themselves away, and he saw into his own memories, and found the answer waiting there.

Samudra prostrated himself once more to the Mothers, and got stiffly to his feet. He had no idea how long he had sat in his meditations. But it was cold now, and when he stepped outside, the moon was well up. He breathed in the air made chill by the deepening night and returned to his borrowed residence.

Hamsa had been carried to a side chamber and laid on a pallet of blankets. A fire smoldered in the hearth, and her body servant slept beside her. Samudra looked down on his sorceress and noted how drawn her face was from the day's exertions. Still, he was not surprised when her eyes fluttered slowly open. She had ever known when he needed her.

"Majesty," she croaked, and reached for her staff to help her stand.

Both Hamsa and the servant, who was also now wide awake, struggled to rise. He waved his hand to keep them both down on their beds. Hamsa obeyed, lying back on her pillows, but her servant scuttled backward, moving herself off to a polite distance so her presence might not intrude on their conference.

"Hamsa." Samudra settled down cross-legged next to her. "You have done me good service today."

She bowed her head humbly, but he saw the deprecating twinkle in her tired eyes.

"I am afraid I will have to ask yet more of you."

"I stand, or lie," she gestured toward her pallet ruefully, "ready to serve however I can."

"I was taking council with the Mothers," he said, rubbing his hands slowly together. "And they reminded me of my coronation, when you told me certain things. You told me that you could curse an enemy of Hastinapura, no matter how great the distance."

Hamsa shook her head. "I cannot," she said. "But you can, Majesty."

"I am no sorcerer."

"No, but you are lord, bound to the land and the heavens through your anointing and your sacrifices. I can make a working that will give your will force and weight in the ethereal realms, but it must be your will, and your words must form part of that working."

Samudra considered this in silence for a long moment. "It is a difficult undertaking then?"

Hamsa nodded.

"Will there be a price?"

Again, the sorceress nodded. "Normally, it would be mine, but, in this case, my price will only be partial payment." She met his eyes, her face set and serious, an expression he knew well from his childhood, when she was trying to drum in some particularly difficult lesson. "Because it is your will that sets this thing in motion, you too must pay. Some day, in the future, you may lose what you hold dear because of what this curse sets in motion."

Again, Samudra turned over her words silently. "Will it be Hastinapura I lose?"

"I cannot say, Majesty. I think not. But it could be a child, or your queen, or your life. It will be a high price, that much I can be certain of."

Samudra continued to rub his palms slowly together, as if he could feel the shape of the truth between them. "I do not like magic," he said at last.

Hamsa smiled. "I know."

"It is imprecise, and it has too many hidden costs, and the powers play their own games in the Silent Lands, and no man may know how their dice are cast."

"These are true things, Majesty," Hamsa agreed soberly, but he could still see a ghost of a smile on her face. These were matters they had spoken of often before.

"But even if I sent a missive to the queen this instant and bid her act against Yamuna, even if I sent to Kacha in the north and bid him stop this nonsense, it would be tens of days before any action could be taken."

"Even with my help, yes, Majesty."

He was talking himself into an unpleasant task, and he knew it. Hamsa knew it as well, and she, as usual, simply let him do it.

"Hastinapura itself is at stake," he said. "If Isavalta is fractured, the Huni and Hung Tse will begin seizing territory in the north. With new men and new resources, the Huni will be bolstered and we will never root them out, and they will expand again, like the poisonous weeds they are." He growled the last words, letting anger shore up his resolve. "I do not have time to deal with Chandra myself, yet he must be dealt with, and now, and your magics are all I have to cross such distances in such times."

"I can have all ready in two days, Majesty," was all Hamsa said. Her voice held no tremor or hesitation, but all Samudra had to do was look at her to see how close to utter exhaustion she was. Neither of them spoke of that. Neither of them ever would.

"Thank you, Hamsa." Samudra stood and bowed to her, giving her the salute of trust, with his palms over his eyes. She returned the gesture, and he left her to go seek his own bed, although it was a long time before he found sleep there.

Two days later, Samudra received a message from the Huni saying they would deign to meet him, and an additional message from Makul's chosen spy saying there was a break in the mountain pass that might be exploited by a small force of men as part of a larger attack. Both missives were highly welcome and allowed Samudra to spend time with his maps and his generals, deep in thoughts and plans that he understood well. This, in turn, kept his thoughts diverted from the Temple of the Mothers. Hamsa had disappeared in there the morning after he had laid out her task, and he had not seen her since.

Hamsa had been a part of his life since he was an infant. She had been chosen by the most learned sorcerers and astrologers his father's court held as the one who would best be able to serve and support him in his life, as it was thought, as high prince. She had cared for him alongside his nurses. She had taught him alongside his other tutors. She had saved his life more than once with her art when he was a young and reckless warrior, chafing at watching Chandra, spoilt, spineless and careless on his father's throne. She, even more than the priests, had presided over the horse sacrifice that had bound him to throne and land, and set the seal on his rightful claim to the throne.

He had set old and dear friends to tasks that might take their lives before, but not like this. Never like this.

It was evening again, with the dim, orange sun just balanced on the rim of the world when Hamsa's woman servant knelt in the map room and said, "It is time, Majesty."

Without a word, Samudra rose from his place at the table and left the house while his generals and servants bowed around him. He followed Hamsa's servant up to the Temple of the Mothers and through the winding corridors to the sanctuary.

Inside, heat struck Samudra even before the light did. All seven of the dedicated fires leapt up waist high from the fire pits. The central fire burned just as fiercely. Even over the incense and sandalwood, he could smell the sweat of the priests, two for each Mother. A hump-shouldered bullock stood beside the central fire, its tether held by three acolytes in pure white tunics. In the center of it all, her skin glistening in the light and heat of the sacred fires, stood Hamsa. One hand clutched her staff. The other clutched a curved, bronze knife.

Samudra knelt, prostrating himself to both the Mothers and Hamsa. When he rose again, Hamsa nodded once and drew back her shoulders. Samudra recognized the gesture. Hamsa was calling on her magic.

Hamsa lifted her staff from the ground. An acolyte ran forward to take it from her. Unsupported, on legs as thin as twigs, she walked to the bullock, which bellowed nervously. Samudra saw how glassy the sorceress's eyes were. Wherever her mind was, it was a great distance away.

Hamsa laid her free hand of the bullock's shoulder. With one swift, clean gesture, she slashed the knife against its neck. Blood, dark and fresh from the vein, poured freely into the great stone bowl that waited for it. The bullock bellowed and the acolytes tightened their hold, patting its neck and murmuring to it soothingly as it fell to its knees, breathing in the steam from its own swiftly draining blood.

Hamsa gave her knife to an acolyte, and held her cupped hands under the flowing blood. She anointed herself: head, hands, and the soles of her feet. When she arose again, her face was terrible and her eyes as bright and hard as diamonds, and Samudra knew that by her working Hamsa had become an aspect of Vimala, the Mother of Destruction.

Hamsa began to dance. Slowly, she circled the central fire, leaving bloody footprints behind her. Her arms waved high over her head, weaving new patterns in the air as if she were painting the stars with her stained hands. Gradually, her steps grew quicker, wilder. She touched each Mother, each priest, bringing them all, heartbeats, breath, pulse of life into her dance. She laid both hands on the bullock, gathering up even its death into her working. All was done in silence, with no sound but the slap of her feet against the stones, the ragged breathing of the witnesses, the dying of the bull, the crackle of the fires, and yet, as Samudra's ears strained against the near-silence, he seemed to hear a deeper music—a rushing that was neither the wind outside, nor the blood in his veins, although he heard both. This was a deeper pulse, a rhythm more strange and more compelling, and yet more terrifying. It was too great, too strong, too wild, like Hamsa's blood-stained dance in front of his eyes. It called to the depths of his heart, and his heart knew it would swallow him whole.

But all at once, Hamsa stopped stock-still before him. She lifted his hands, pressing them between hers, and her eyes were wild with that rhythm they both felt to their cores.

"Speak, Lord of Men," she cried. "Speak, Son of the Land. I will hear your words."

But the voice was not Hamsa's. Samudra knew this and dropped to his knees before the goddess. "Curse him, Mother," he whispered. His breath did not wish to leave his body, lest it be pulled free and drowned by the rhythm pulsing through him. "Let the works of Yamuna *dva* Ikshu Chitranipad turn in his hand and cut him to the heart. Make his greatest weakness his only support. Blind him with his own sight, drive him out with his own folly."

"It is heard, and all is accepted," said the voice that spoke through Hamsa. She let go of his hands and rose to her feet, her arms stretched over her head. "It is spoken and may not now be undone."

Again, the dance took her, tracing its bloody trail on the stones, around the fires, around the priests and their acolytes, and the Mothers in their watchfulness, around the dying bullock and its spilled blood. Over and over the pattern repeated, filling Samudra with its wild rhythm until he felt he must burst. It was too strange, too strong. It surrounded him, bound him, called him through the stones of the temple and the stones of the cliff beneath them. He could not move, could not think, could not breathe, there was only the rhythm and the dance and it was inside him and outside him, it was everything and all, and he was everything and all.

Without a sound, Hamsa stepped into the central fire, her arms raised, her face ecstatic, and the flames enfolded her in a lover's embrace, and she was gone.

The spell broke like a string snapping. Samudra shuddered, his strength failing, and pitched over onto his face. Gasping from pain and shock, he pushed himself upright. He saw the room, the blazing fires, the bemused priests, the dead bull, and Hamsa's staff in the hands of a dazed acolyte.

She was gone. Samudra passed a shaking hand in front of his eyes. Of course. He should have seen this was how it must end. How could she remain part of the mortal world once she had danced with the Mothers? She had surely known this, even though she had not told him.

And I did not ask. Samudra pushed himself shaking to his

feet. Every person in the sanctuary stared at him, none of them fully themselves yet.

"Let the funerary rites be prepared for *Agnidh* Hamsa," Samudra said to the priests, a little amazed that his voice had returned to him. "Call me when all is in readiness."

"Majesty." All bowed, but Samudra did not stay to acknowledge their obeisance. He teetered around and staggered for the door.

Out on the broad steps, he breathed deeply of the night air, his fists clenching and unclenching, trying to find something to grasp for support. But there was nothing. His support had gone, burned alive in the Mothers' fire. Gone because his need had used her up.

"Brother," he whispered to the night. "Chandra, I would have let you live. I gave your son position and power. I gave you land and freedom when my advisors said I should have you trampled to death. But the Mothers say we must bear our brother's burdens, and I tried, Brother, I tried." He swallowed. The servants would remember their duty and be behind him in another moment. "But you would break apart the realm like a child's toy, and for that you will pay. For that, and for Hamsa, you will pay."

There, in the darkness, where none could see, the emperor of Hastinapura wept for his loss.

The Vixen sat on a wooden throne on the crest of her green hill underneath the spreading thorn tree. She was not currently a fox, but a woman of sleek and strong build, red-haired and green-eyed, wearing a garment of gray fur belted with black. A cluster of foxes, red, white and gray, lay at her feet. Thus, she prepared to greet her visitor.

The second woman came on foot. Brown-skinned, black-eyed. She wore little besides the ropes of pearls around her neck and the sword belt at her waist. More pearls bound her black hair high on her head. Her footsteps left behind bloody prints on the grass.

The Vixen made no move to hinder the woman as she climbed the green hill and came to stand in the shadow of the thorn tree. They looked into each other's eyes for a moment, before the woman bowed courteously, and the Vixen nodded to receive the gesture.

"Welcome, Mother," said the Vixen mildly. "How is it I have come to merit a visit from so illustrious a personage?"

"I am come with a message from my sisters." The Vixen's voice had held the wild tones of the green wood. This woman spoke coldly, like the winds of autumn.

"I am most interested to hear it." The Vixen gestured with one hand, indicating the woman might sit if she felt so inclined.

The woman sat cross-legged upon the ground, drawing her sword from her belt and laying it across her knees. The blade was black and had an edge so keen, even the Vixen's eyes could scarcely see it. One of the red foxes at her feet pricked up its ears and lifted its head, alert to the warning of that drawn blade.

"It has been seen that soon the Old Witch will send an ambassador to you to reclaim that which you stole."

The corner of the Vixen's mouth quirked up in a crooked smile. "Yet I insist I stole nothing. The Old Witch wounds me to the heart." She laid her long white hand on her bosom. "To think that she believes I would wrong her in that fashion."

The woman did not blink at these words. "My sisters and I say that we would be grateful if the ambassador were able to find what she will seek."

"Would you?" The Vixen raised her eyebrows. "And how would this gratitude be expressed?"

"Your help would be remembered," said the woman, her words as solid as stones. "We would swear it so."

"Hmmmm . . ." The Vixen leaned her chin in her hand. "Gratitude from you seven. You who seek to bring permanent order to your lands being grateful to me. Tempting," she admitted. Then she straightened and shook her head. "No. It is too much. I cannot give what I do not have."

The woman's dark eyes glowed. "What then, pray, can you give?"

The Vixen considered. Her gaze lingered for a moment on the naked sword with its keen edge. A gray fox lifted its head and drew its lip back, showing a gleam of fang. She reached down idly and scratched its ears, soothing it so that it once again curled up calmly.

"Why would you wish to do a favor for the Old Witch?" she asked. "She has no claim on you, or your sisters."

"Our lands are troubled by a little man who walks too tall." The woman gripped the hilt of her sword. A dangerous light sparked in the Vixen's green gaze, but the woman moved no further. "He has begun a chain of dangers that will crash down over that which is ours. If the ambassador returns to the Old Witch what has been lost, the little man will fall."

"May fall," the Vixen corrected her. "Nothing is set. Not where I can see. Your little man is most resourceful."

The woman bridled at those words, but did not move to contradict them. "Will you do this thing we ask?"

"No," said the Vixen. The woman lifted the sword a fraction of an inch from her lap. One white fox rose to its feet, its tail bristling.

The Vixen just smiled. "But I will give this ambassador a chance. One chance, for a price. If she succeeds, she may have what she wants. If she fails . . ." The Vixen shrugged. "Then you too will have to be resourceful."

The woman laid her sword back down. As she did, the white fox lowered its hackles, but did not sit.

"What price?" asked the woman.

"A favor, from your oldest sister. A favor of my choosing, to be granted without questions or restrictions."

"You ask a great thing." The woman's voice rasped in the still air.

"As do you," replied the Vixen calmly. "Especially for one who has come to my place of power to call me a thief."

The Vixen watched the woman bridle at this, and smiled as she struggled to hold back her rage. But need and, more likely, the warnings of her sisters, kept her hand from her sword.

"Very well. A favor, without questions or restrictions. It shall be so."

"Then this ambassador from the Old Witch will have her one chance," replied the Vixen. Her smile spread so that all her shining teeth showed. "Then we will see what may happen, Mother Vimala. Then we will most certainly see."

"Well?" said Chandra, looking up from the pile of pillows where he lounged on the balcony. "What news have you?"

The rains poured down in solid sheets outside, obscuring the gardens with a curtain of silver and filling the world with the scent of fresh water. This was the beginning of the Second Rains. Samudra had timed Chandra's wedding, and the beginning of his campaign, nicely. The brief respite that separated the First Rains from the Second had given the emperor enough time to march his army inland, beyond the floods. It had also given him enough time to see his elder brother sent to the far south with his new bride and household of spies.

Chandra had never been able to wait well. Every day he summoned Yamuna to him and demanded to know how things proceeded in the north. Not even a full month had passed, and already his exile seemed to chafe at him beyond endurance.

Yamuna looked down his nose at his master, and considered lying. No, he decided. It would be more humiliating should he have to retract his words later.

"The quest did not succeed," he said blandly.

Chandra stared at him, as if he could not believe what he heard. For a time, the drumming of the rain on the balcony's arched roof sounded very loud.

"My servants who failed me have been punished," said Yamuna, his memory filling with the sound of the demons' screams as the earth pulled them down. "They will have no further opportunity to make such mistakes."

"In the meantime, Avanasy is still alive, and the empress is still out of our control, and has her best advisor hurrying toward her," sneered Chandra. "Excellently managed, *Agnidh* Yamuna. For all your machinations, you have accomplished exactly nothing." Disgusted, he turned back toward the rain.

Yamuna held himself very still. They were not truly alone. Slaves still moved about the interior apartment. If any of those were ears for Samudra, they had already heard too much. It was very like Chandra to have forgotten such a salient fact at this moment.

"Son of the Throne," said Yamuna, slowly and deliberately, so that Chandra turned one eye to look at him. "I must beg your leave to undertake a quest of my own." *I must, for I must remain bound to you, whether I wish it or no. The gods have declared that your success is the determinant for my own.*

Chandra narrowed his eyes at Yamuna. His gaze flickered left, looking through the archways to the apartments beyond, this time noting the slaves who were there, and actually remembering which master they might truly serve. As he did, an unexpected smile flitted across his face, before his bland mask of disinterest and disdain settled back in place.

"Yes," he said. "Undertake your quest. You have good leave."

He settled himself back down to watch the steady fall of rain, and did not even look as Yamuna knelt to him and rose again to take his leave.

That flicker of a smile haunted Yamuna's thoughts as he returned to his own apartments. It was a strange expression, sly and unfamiliar, and indicative of hidden thoughts.

Was it possible Chandra would attempt to plot his own coup while Yamuna was gone? It would be a disaster. It would ruin all. Chandra had no mind for subtlety. He was merely a petulant child who wanted his brother's pretty toy. When the plot was discovered, which it would surely be, Samudra would have no choice but to execute his brother, and without Chandra, weak support that he was, Yamuna's own plans would crumble.

But Avanasy must be stopped. The little empress could not be allowed to regain power in Isavalta. Alone, she was helpless, she had proven that often enough. But with a powerful and subtle sorcerer to aid her . . . Yamuna knew full well how that could make the weakest of men an enemy to be feared.

No. Without a servant he could trust, he himself must take care of Avanasy. There was no choice. He must go swiftly and swiftly return.

Yamuna proceeded through his outer apartments, paying no heed to the servants there, still putting them in order for their master. The innermost door he unlocked with a key and a word. He closed the door carefully behind himself.

This chamber was much less fine than the one where he worked in the Palace of the Pearl Throne. Arches and domes with their inlays of coral and ivory were here replaced by simple carvings of gray-and-red stone surmounted by a wooden dome with seven tiers, each tier, of course, dedicated to one of the Mothers. Yamuna did not spare them a thought.

The only furnishings in the chamber thus far were four chests which Yamuna had carried there himself. No other hand would touch them, as no other foot would tread in this place that was his alone. For the bare moment he stopped to think on it, he did not believe those who served him were sorry to obey this order.

Yamuna's touch and five more words opened the first chest. There, packed in straw, were one quarter of his precious vials and bottles. Some glinted dully in the watery daylight. The most delicate, however, had been wrapped first in white linen.

Yamuna lifted one of the linen bundles out, brushing a few wisps of straw from the cloth. Inside lay a small faceted bottle, the color of garnet. If he peered closely through the translucent crystal, he could see the contents swirling and blurring like contained smoke.

Despite its wrapping and despite the warmth of the day, the sides of the bottle were cold to the touch.

A curse waited in that bottle, a curse made into a solid thing so that it did not have to be woven again, no more blood had to be shed, no detection had to be risked. The bottle simply had to be opened with the name of the one for whom the curse was intended. The closer one came, the more quickly this solid, pulsating thing would envelop them and suck away their fortunes, their good destiny, their love and, at last, their life. Applied to Avanasy, it would not kill at once. It would allow him to live, hobbled and increasingly impaired. His advice would sour, as would his commitments. If he reached Medeoan, he would do her more harm than good.

Yamuna reached for the bottle. As his fingers came within a hairsbreadth of its surface, he paused. Was it possible he had misinterpreted the scrying he saw in the sun wheel? What if it was the road he traveled, the violation of his sworn place and purpose, that would bring about his doom? The symbol of the broken chain could be intepreted in many ways. What if . . .

Yamuna sighed sharply. He had thought himself immune to such cowardly doubts. His sight was clear and his purpose was right. He knew well what he had seen, and there was no other interpretation of its meaning. It was only the old teachings of his youth that made him afraid now that he was so close to his goal.

Yamuna laid the bottle carefully inside a pouch of soft deerskin leather that he tied firmly about his neck. The pouch hung against the hollow of his throat. Already, he could feel its intense chill seeping through the leather wrapping. It was not a thing that was healthy to hold for long, but he must endure for the present.

He lifted out another jar. This one was alabaster, opaque and milk white. The stone was smooth to his eye, but strangely rough under his hands. It seemed almost wasteful to reach into his hoard twice like this, but this was the time against which he had laid by this stock of workings. He would spend it all in pursuit of his destiny. After that, it would no longer matter. He would, when his godhood was achieved, see what an infinitesimally small effort it had been.

Unlike the vial at his throat, the jar of alabaster was warm. He had bargained heavily for this jar when he was still a young man, giving away a small fortune and a large secret to possess it. The seal was of white clay engraved with symbols Yamuna could not read. Once it was opened, he would not be able to close it again, or duplicate what lay within. This jar was made by priests in the farthest of the southern islands who worshiped gods they would not name. Not even Yamuna could squeeze their secrets from them.

Setting the jar on the floor, Yamuna drew his knife and cracked the seal. Again, he hesitated. Was there something he had forgotten?

Yamuna shook his head angrily. What were these doubts that assailed him? Nothing had been forgotten. All preparations were complete.

He lifted the heavy lid. An odor of iron and old copper wafted up. He laid the lid aside. The jar brimmed with deep, red blood, still fresh and liquid, even though the jar had been sealed over two hundred years before.

Yamuna reached into the warm blood, and after a moment, his fingers found the soft treasure it concealed and nourished. He drew out a small bird, just barely fledged. It struggled hard against the clutch of his fingers to stretch its wings and gain its freedom.

It smelled of flesh, of blood and of heat. Its heart beat frantically against his hand.

Yamuna took the frightened nestling into his mouth and swallowed it whole.

A shock of pain ran through him so strong that he saw darkness and stars. Even Yamuna could not stand against the fire and doubled over, clutching his stomach. His bones snapped within him, the jagged ends rearranging. Yamuna clamped his jaw down to keep from crying out, and felt his teeth shatter and sink into his gums as his jaw lengthened and the flesh around it peeled away. His joints popped as they dislocated and reformed. Too many changes, too much pain. Yamuna roared in agony, even as he felt the first of the feathers pushed through his skin.

After that, he lost track of all but pain.

When the pain ended, Yamuna was gone. There was only a white crane huddled on the polished floor beside an alabaster jar, empty except for a thin coating of red-brown dust on its inner surface. The crane blinked and flopped its wings clumsily so it could stand on its slender legs. Strutting delicately, as was the nature of its kind, it stepped out onto the broad balcony. Heedless of the rain, the crane launched itself into the air. Wheeling on the wind, it flapped its great wings and turned toward the north.

Kacha reviewed the lists showing the levies of men with growing satisfaction. Barbarians these northerners might be, but that turned out to have its advantages. They were ever ready when it came to a fight. As they marched south, the army grew stronger. More lords arrived at the heads of columns of men, many of them trained, with letters and lists from their Lords Master, pledging their allegiance to the empress in this "great and long-overdue action." All were placed under the command of officers of the House Guard, and the ranks swelled.

He had thought long and hard before deciding to lead the campaign himself. So much required careful control at the summer palace. But, he reasoned, if he hoped to continue to rule in his own name, he must prove his manhood. He could not be seen to be sitting idle while Isavaltan men went out to fight. So, he had crafted his permission from the empress to go and lead the troops, and had ridden out at their head.

Now he sat in a stone room in one of Isavalta's many coastline fortresses. On the fields outside had sprung acres of tents like summer wheat. When he went out into the fresh air, the world was filled with shouts, the ring of the armorer's hammer, the sounds of horses and the tramp of boots. He imagined the noise reaching down the peninsula and across the sea to Hung Tse and making their own border guards quake. Kacha smiled at the image.

This had proved to be the right decision. He was able here to gain the trust of the truly powerful men of the empire, and the news from Vaknevos was all good. Chekhania reported that the status of the "empress" continued healthful, and that her belly swelled daily and she glowed with health, meaning their child was alive and lively in her womb, readying himself to be born and take his place in the world. Ambassador Girilal held a number of conferences with the Council Lords who were jointly acting in regency until the empress would finish her confinement. The bemusements held. Yamuna's magics and Chekhania's cooperation allowed him to see still into the palace. She had developed a real talent for imitating Medeoan's style in her messages to the council.

A dull ache began behind Kacha's right eye, surely a reminder that despite all, Yamuna was not at ease. Yamuna believed that Medeoan had taken refuge in the Heart of the World, but no word of confirmation had been received, nor had definite news that her ally Avanasy had died. Several popular and prominent landlords had not sent their levies yet, and their reasons for the delay were slow in coming and vague when they arrived. Most notable among these was Pachalka Ursulsyn Rzhovyn, father of the house guard captain Peshek who had disappeared with Medeoan. Peshek had also not been found.

These were little things against the might of the army in the camp surrounding him, but little things might be enough to change the course of empires. Kacha had studied enough history to know that much.

The head secretary coughed politely. "Imperial Majesty? Did you wish to continue?"

Kacha rubbed his eye, but it did nothing to lessen his ache. No voice whispered to him from the back of his mind, no compulsion radiated to him from his withered right hand. He felt alone for the first time in years, and the sensation frightened him.

"No," he said abruptly to the secretaries. "I do not wish to continue. Take what you have and get the documents fair copied as soon as possible. Send someone to find General Adka."

"Imperial Majesty." The four secretaries reverenced and gathered up their sheaves of paper, scuttling out the door like the flock of old women that they were. The ache behind his eye deepened, but it remained only an ache.

If you want something, Yamuna, you are going to have to give me a better sign than this. Kacha lifted his silver tankard from the tray and found it empty, likewise the pitcher beside it. Only the smell of beer remained.

"Boy!" he shouted and the waiting page ran in. Kacha stuffed the pitcher into the boy's hands. No other order was needed. The child reverenced and ran out again, nearly colliding with General Adka as the man reached the door.

Adka sidestepped the page and let the door close behind him. He gave the soldier's reverence. "You sent for me, Imperial Majesty?"

"I am concerned about the levies, General," said Kacha as he beckoned Adka to take a chair. "Specifically, I am concerned about who has not delivered them yet."

"We do have men enough for the actions we have planned before winter." Adka sat stiffly, unwilling to relax his formal posture even for a moment. Adka was a square man, not overly tall, but broad and solid with thick hands, hardened from their life's work. His caftan of imperial blue strained at the seams, giving Kacha the impression that the man had not worn it much before he was called up on these actions. He preferred, doubtlessly, some less cumbersome, more well-worn coat when not in the presence of his autocrat. He also firmly believed that Hung Tse was a constant danger to Eternal Isavalta, and so had been more than ready to answer when Kacha called.

"That is not the point, General," said Kacha, pushing himself fully upright in his chair. The ache continued, becoming a low throb in his bones. "I am concerned that a traitor's father has not yielded up his men, as is his duty."

"Lord Pachalka was a member of the house guard. He knows his duty." Adka spoke the words as if saying someone knew the sun would rise tomorrow. Duty was an unalterable fact with him.

"Captain Peshek was also a member of the guard," answered Kacha evenly. "Despite that, he ran off with some scullery maid in complete breach of that same duty." That reminder made the stalwart man drop his gaze.

The page boy chose that moment to return with the pitcher of beer. With a child's extra care, he filled Kacha's tankard. Kacha gave him a nod, and he filled another for the general. Adka accepted the beer, but did not drink. Kacha took several swallows of the black brew, only to find it did nothing for his ache.

"Now." Kacha leaned forward. The movement sharpened the pain in his eye. "I do not wish to trouble her imperial majesty with this. You will select a detail of men, and I will grant them police powers. They will go investigate the reasons for Pachalka's lateness. If necessary, they will make an example of him and his, and they will collect the levies after that. Is this clear?"

Adka set down his untouched tankard and laid his thick hand over his heart. "Yes, Imperial Majesty."

Kacha meant to nod and dismiss the man, but at that moment pain stabbed hard behind hand and eye. He felt his finger twist, crabbing up like old roots. His eye swelled until it pressed against the bones of its socket. Long practiced at enduring pain, Kacha did not cry out, but neither could he speak: His bones writhed under his skin and his eye twisted in answer. But throughout all this torture, Yamuna's voice remained silent. No hint of why this was happening touched his mind. Unfamiliar, dizzying fear worsened the pain.

"Majesty?" Adka held out his hand. "Majesty, is something . . ."

"Get out!" cried Kacha. "Get out of my sight!"

Adka blanched white and retreated at once. Alone, Kacha ground his teeth together and fought to master the pain. Through his right eye now, he only saw a blur of meaningless color that swam and shifted like oil poured on water. And his hand . . . Kacha looked down at his hand with his good eye, and bit his tongue to stop the scream.

His skin had tightened against his bones and his fingers had grown long and brittle. The hand Yamuna had given Kacha to work his will now resembled nothing so much as the claw of some great bird. Trembling, he moved a plate of dainties from a silver tray and strained to see the wavering relection in its etched surface.

And he saw how Yamuna's eye had become round and black, and how it bulged grotesquely in its orbit, and how it was in no way a human eye any longer.

It was a spell, it must be. Some working of Yamuna's, for who else could have done this? What other power could have touched them? Kacha's heart froze. That Yamuna could use a spell of such power that it transformed the hand that was no longer completely the sorcerer's own, from a distance of a thousand miles . . . that he would do it without thought or warning of how it would effect Kacha. . . .

Kacha threw the tray aside, because he could not bear to see. *What have you done to us? Mothers All! Yamuna, what have you done!*

But Yamuna did not answer.

Chapter Seventeen

Medeoan had lost track of days. She only knew there had been too many of them. The leather shift which was her only clothing had chafed welts under her arms. Some of them were beginning to bleed. The silent women who were sent in to search her every day saw the weals, and did nothing. Not even ointment was permitted her. She was brought regular meals of fairly good food—fresh meats, pastries, rice and vegetables—well, if plainly, prepared, but she ate under their watchful gaze, and all that was brought in was removed again as soon as she was finished. A chamber pot was provided at these times so she could do what was needful, but not even that was left to her when she was alone.

With the first meal each morning came the search. Her shift was removed and inspected. The leather mattress was turned over and examined closely for any irregularity in the stitching, in case she had managed to use her fingers to loosen the gut to get at the ticking or to conceal something inside. The bare room was inspected. Medeoan's cropped hair was rifled. Only when all was found to be in order did they permit Medeoan to sit and break her fast.

After her guards departed, it had become Medeoan's custom to sit in the window for a time, looking down at the gardens and across the walls to the city. She watched the green sea of trees waving below her and the flights of distant birds. After the first few days, she realized that it was becoming increasingly unlikely that she would be released alive. True, she was not being treated quite as a common prisoner. She was not in chains, but would the Nine Elders really want their honor impugned by stories of how they treated the lawful empress of another realm? No. They meant to make her a prisoner for life, and they were the ones who would determine how long her life would be.

When she was sure her guards were going to stay outside, when she heard no footsteps coming or going in the narrow hallway just beyond her door, she would leave her window and push her mattress away from its corner.

To her eye, it was easy to see the circle of braided silk plastered to the floor with a mixture of blood and less pleasant things. Inside the circle lay a delicately formed weaving of blond hairs. It looked like a short chain of flowers, their stems wound and knotted together to hold them in place.

Sitting cross-legged on the floor, Medeoan pulled three more hairs from her head. She had ceased to wince at this small pain. She wet them with her spittle and twirled them together to make a slender thread. Then, she took a deep breath and carefully, tentatively, she drew up her magic. She did not seek to release a river of power, which she normally would, especially for so complex a spell as she created now, but only a soft trickle. If her power rose too strongly, the Nine Elders would feel it. They would come and search her chamber with magic and find this working, her one chance at escape.

Concentrating, and attempting to relax at the same time, she spun the single new thread into the weaving, and that was all. To do more than that at one sitting was to invite detection. She laid her working back in its circle of protection, repeating the spell that caused it to be overlooked.

"I, Medeoan, servant of Vyshko and Vyshemir, place my working with a stone barrier about it, closed with a stone door, locked with three times nine locks and three times nine keys, with one key and one lock let no one cross this barrier, no bird fly over it, no eye light on it."

She replaced the mattress. Then, there was nothing to do but return to her window to wait and watch until the next meal. She had so often wished to be left alone, to not be princess or empress. Now, she had that wish, and she was locked up in a single room without any sort of help. Her captors attempted to make her nothing and nobody. But even they had not succeeded. She was still the empress of Isavalta. She was still Medeoan the sorceress, and she would make them remember that before the end.

And Avanasy will come for me.

She held fast to that hope most of all. As the sun crept across the sky, her only measure of the hours, she would picture him coming to the Heart of the World, and to her. Sometimes, in her dreams, he arrived at night, alone and stealth, and they eluded the guards and their magics flew them over the walls. Sometimes he arrived with Peshek and a legion of loyal soldiers, leading a proud horse, and she would mount it in broad daylight and ride in triumph back to Isavalta, where Kacha would kneel at her feet and beg for mercy. He would find none. She might, she thought sometimes, choose to keep him in the dungeons long enough for a public trial, but then he would die. She would have him beheaded in the courtyard as befitted his rank and crimes.

Each day, she found it a little easier to think of Kacha without longing, and with a clearer view to who he was and what he had truly done to her. It was his fault she was prisoner here, locked away and struggling for her freedom. She would see this added to the list of crimes that would be read out at his trial. If she chose to give him a trial. If she did not simply choose to have Peshek, or some other loyal guard, run him through the moment she saw him again. That would prevent him from using his honeyed words to try to soften her heart toward him again, not that it would work, but she was not certain she wished to hear him try.

Then there would only be her and Avanasy. She would make him lord sorcerer for his loyal service to her. She would have it published and proclaimed that it was only Kacha's treachery that had caused him to be banished. She would rule Isavalta wisely and well, just as her father had wished, and he would be chief among her advisors, and she would never turn him away again.

And perhaps, in time, he would become more than advisor, more than teacher and friend.

This dream she permitted herself to dwell on only occasionally, even though she found it warmed her the way no other plan could. She had to remind herself that she did not know what state Avanasy would be in when he returned. He might be angry with her for a time for not valuing his loyalty more highly, for throwing him aside for a traitor. It might take time for him to forgive her so much, but they would have that time. There would be so much to do. Starting with renewing the loyalty oaths of all the lords master. Then it would probably be necessary to appoint a new council, as Kacha could not be acting alone at this point. The traitors would have to be tried and sentenced before any other work could be done. Then . . . then . . . then . . .

Dreaming her unfamiliar dreams of empire, Medeoan smiled out across the walls of the Heart of the World, worked her magics and learned to bide her time.

In the end, Ingrid and Avanasy traveled to the Heart of the World in fine style. Lien hired them a troop of guards, and saw that both Ingrid and Avanasy were properly outfitted with silk robes and riding in a sedan chair carried by six bearers. Avanasy had thought they should ride horseback to the gates in Isavaltan fashion, but Ingrid had to admit she had never been on a horse in her life, so it was the sedan.

They did not go unannounced. Three days before, a hired messenger had accompanied the hired guards into the Heart of the World bearing a courteous message written on translucent rice paper naming Avanasy, and Ingrid, as messengers from the empress of Isavalta who begged an audience with the emperor of Hung Tse so that they might deliver the empress's "sagacious and urgent words." Two days ago, a message sealed in saffron ribbons had been returned, fixing the time for their arrival.

Avanasy was barely able to sleep the night before. Ingrid, awake with her own worries, had seen him pacing the gardens and gone down to join him. They said nothing to each other, only walked side by side across lawns silvered by moonlight. They had not been able to discover any news of Medeoan. Lien had consulted his numerous sources carefully. Cai Yun had taken Ingrid with her, visiting the ladies of several rich and possibly noble families, all of whom had relatives serving or living in the palaces of the Heart, but her discreet questions of these ladies yielded nothing.

Was Medeoan here, incognito? It was possible, but there should be servant's gossip if that was true. Had she yet to arrive? What could have held her up? Her route should have been more direct than theirs, even with their magical aid.

Had she died? Had she been captured? Was Isavalta now truly in the hands of the Usurper? Ingrid knew the thoughts rang around Avanasy's head, and she had no answers for him. But first and foremost among them was, is my charge, my student, safe?

To make matters even worse, there was still no word from Peshek.

So they walked, and they held hands, and they looked at the moon reflected in the still garden pools. They held each other close as the night wore away, parting at dawn with a soft kiss to prepare for the day ahead.

Now, the eastern gates of the Heart of the World stood open before them. Soldiers in black lacquered armor with saffron sashes stood rank on rank, some holding colorful pennants, some holding poles tipped by wicked-looking hooked blades or spears. In the center of the martial display stood two ... people. Ingrid could not readily identify whether they were male or female, their features were so obscured by a myriad of garish tattoos. The person on the right seemed marked mostly in veins of green and brown. The person on the left had been decorated in sharply angled stripes of silver, gold and copper. They both wore heavy robes of an identical cut and style of wrapping, save that the right-hand person wore a rich emerald robe covered all over with embroidered tortoises, and the left was in what appeared to be cloth of silver with copper trimming.

"The Minister of Earth and the Minister of Metal," murmured Avanasy to Ingrid. "Two of the Nine Elders. We are indeed honored, and the Heart is indeed suspicious of us."

The sedan's bearers halted inside the gate, set their conveyance upon the ground and bowed to the ministers who stood solemnly before them. The ministers did not even nod to acknowledge this gesture, but kept their gazes fixed steadily on Avanasy as he helped Ingrid out of the chair so that they in their turn could stand before these representatives of the emperor and bow. Ingrid held her hands before her as Avanasy had instructed, and bowed no lower than he did, such gestures being serious matters of etiquette here. The ministers bowed in return, in perfect unison with the soldiers who stood guard behind them.

"We have been instructed by the most elevated, the Heart of the Sun and Earth, to say that you are welcome to the Heart of the World on behalf of your Mistress and his Sister Empress, Medeoan Edemskoidoch Nacheradovosh," said the Minister of Metal.

"Please return our thanks to his Reverent Majesty," returned Avanasy. They had not yet straightened up and Ingrid was beginning to feel the strain in her back. "For the grace of this welcome and his willingness to receive these humble messengers."

The pleasantries having been delivered, it was all right to stand straight again. The two ministers turned gracefully and the guards parted for them. In perfect step, they walked through the great gates. Ingrid glanced at Avanasy with raised brows. He just gestured for her to walk beside him and together they entered the Heart of the World.

Until that moment, Ingrid had been feeling fairly comfortable with what was happening to her. Now, with the great palace spread before her and the impassive soldiers in their black-and-saffron armor escorting them up the expanse of stone, she suddenly a fraud; a rough, country girl done up in borrowed silks, a caricature in a bad pantomime. Her mouth had gone dry and she had the unaccountable desire to hike up her skirts and run. It occurred to her that this was exactly the effect this splendid vista was supposed to inspire. The thought did nothing to put the strength back in her spine.

After what seemed an age of walking and watching the spreading scarlet-and-emerald palace with its great golden tower approach, they reached the beautifully lacquered doors. Yet more soldiers bowed before the two ministers who led them, and then drew the doors open to allow them admittance to a great pillared hallway hung with elegant paintings executed on pale paper.

Ingrid worked hard to keep her mouth closed before the splendor that opened before her as she stepped across the threshold. As soon as her thin-soled shoes touched the polished floor, however, the air swam in front of Ingrid's eyes, and the whole world changed.

The palace was full of ghosts.

Gaunt and gray, they lined the corridor, watching all the passersby with their blank eyes. Some were bloody, some held their mouths slack, some bore burns or brands on their shadowy flesh. Some were blank-eyed maidens who wept bloody tears and wiped them away with their long, black hair. If she could have heard their wailing, Ingrid was certain she would have been deaf in an instant.

Ingrid felt she could not breathe for the press of them. If the ministers could see them, they gave no sign as they continued serenely down the wide hall. The ghosts reached out to them as they passed, some beseeching, some cursing and crying, others kneeling in respect or desperate humility; Ingrid could not tell.

Avanasy's hand brushed hers, and Ingrid jerked her gaze sideways to look at him. His face was straight ahead, but his eyes flickered.

What is it? he was asking. She must have hesitated without being aware of it, or her distress must show in her features.

"Ghosts." She breathed the word in English, hoping no one heard her speak.

Avanasy sucked in a breath, but did not look at her. They could not afford any conversation right now, especially not any that could be perceived as secret. Ingrid struggled to school her features into a calm blank, but she could not tell if she succeeded at all.

In truth, she could barely see her way because her gaze kept getting caught by the lonely, empty eyes of the dead. They seemed barely aware of her, and relief at this realization almost buckled her knees. All their attention was on the ministers. Watching them in their shuddering, pitiful crying, mouthing their pain in an attempt to shout it, Ingrid suddenly understood what had moved Grace to make her promises to the drowned sailor lost in the grip of Lake Superior, and this was worse, hundreds of times worse, because there were so many more dead.

All Ingrid's attention being taken up by the crowds of dead, she barely noticed that they had reached the end of the corridor, or that the interior gates had opened onto a grand room that was even more opulent than the corridor they had just passed down, with pillars of semiprecious stone and elaborately enameled statues of stern and beautiful beings she could not take for anything but gods standing guard with their weapons raised. But again, these were all things she barely noticed, for the dead were here too. Some of these were soldiers standing around the base of the dais, rank on rank of ghostly troops ready, it seemed, to defend the young man in the saffron robe who sat at the top of the curving steps next to an older man robed completely in white. Others of the dead were old men, young men and boys, some as young as three or four, each of whom wore a robe identical to that of the young man sitting on the dais. In attendance with them were dozens of women, their robes and elaborately done hair heavy with ornamentation. None of these cried as did the ghosts in the corridor. These whispered among themselves, pointing to the ministers, and to Avanasy, and to Ingrid. Some looked concerned. Some merely shook their heads.

The two ministers mounted the steps halfway up the dais and turned to face Ingrid and Avanasy. It was only then that she saw there was another minister already there. This one was robed and marked in white with gulls, and snow geese the prominent motif for the decoration. This, Ingrid assumed, must be the Minister of the North.

She only had a bare moment to note all this before she remembered what she was supposed to be doing at this time. Both she and Avanasy knelt and pressed their hands and foreheads against the cool, silky-smooth floor. Under her breath, Ingrid counted to thirty. Part of her was sorry the time was so short. Huddled facedown like this, she could not see a single one of the pale, attentive dead.

But, beside her she heard the rustle of silk as Avanasy stood, and so she had to stand herself. The ghosts around them all looked stern or disdainful, and Ingrid felt herself withering under their blank-eyed attention.

As she had been told would happen, the emperor made a series of elaborate signs to the old man in white who was the Imperial Voice. As he did, all the ghosts filling the great chamber stilled themselves and seemed to strain to listen.

"We extend our welcome and hospitality to the messengers who have come at the word of my Sister Empress, Medeoan Edemskoidoch Nacheradovosh of Eternal Isavalta, and I am now well disposed to hear the missive they carry."

Avanasy had considered long and hard what he would need to say at this moment. Even so, Ingrid saw the flicker of uncertainty in his eyes. Fear took her, because the ghosts saw it too, and they whispered to each other, pointing and smiling cruelly behind their hands.

Despite that flicker, and despite what Ingrid knew he would have to say next, Avanasy's voice rang out clear and steady.

"Esteemed and Reverent Majesty, I must speak to you with slow and reluctant words. I must speak of treachery and the usurpation of rightful power. I must also speak of a danger to both the Heart of the World and Eternal Isavalta."

None of the audience, living or dead, moved for a moment. Then the emperor made his signs to the Voice.

"This prologue is indeed grave. Let us hear your words."

So, Avanasy told them. He told them what he knew about Kacha's treachery and his plans for war. He told them rather more than he knew about the rallying of the loyal Lords Master, raising their own armies to fight the usurper. With an utterly straight face, he told them about the empress being escorted across the borders by her loyal followers to take council with her brother emperor and how she desired to speak with him about how their powers could be combined for the protection and prosperity of not only their realms, but of the right order of the world.

All this time, Ingrid watched the ghosts. They stood still as he spoke of Kacha. At first, Ingrid thought they were listening attentively, but then, she saw how their pale faces were set. Bored. The dead heard Avanasy's dire warnings, and they were bored. When he spoke of the loyal nobles of Isavalta rallying to the cause of their mistress, the dead smirked and whispered back and forth to each other. Ingrid imagined she heard the rustle of ethereal voices. When Avanasy spoke of the empress being escorted by her followers, the ghosts began to laugh. They were not merry laughs, for their faces were hard and cruel. Their hollow eyes squinted, and would have rolled, she was sure, if they had orbs still in their sockets. They pointed at Avanasy, and they mouthed silent jeers. It was all Ingrid could do to stand rigid among the crowd of taunting dead, their hands waving in gestures of mockery, the jibes she could not hear passing back and forth between them. Her ears burned with anger, shame, and the reflexive effort of straining to hear what could never become audible to her.

Her fists and jaw clenched; she could not help it. She forced her eyes to look ahead of her, to focus on the living who stood on the dais, the one place in the great room that was free of the jeering ghosts. It was only then she noticed that the Minister of Earth was staring straight at her.

Ingrid, unable to endure another searching presence, dropped her own gaze to the floor, studying the polished boards at her feet. But she knew they were there, the ghosts, the ministers, the emperor, the Voice. They knew something was wrong with her, and by extension with Avanasy. She could not stand steady in the face of the mockery of the dead and the inquiry of the living, and her failure was ruining all of Avanasy's careful planning.

Ingrid forced her head up in time to see that the ghosts had sobered, and were again straining toward their emperor, who was, in turn, signaling his Voice as to what was to be said next. The Minister of Earth, however, still had his (her?) gaze pinned to Ingrid. She made herself watch the emperor and his Voice.

"We are most concerned by what you have told us. You may be assured that we will be at once deploying members of our personal guard to watch the roads down the peninsula so that the empress may be properly greeted and escorted when she arrives in Hung Tse. In the meantime, you will be given quarters where you may rest and take refreshment while we consider what else may be done regarding these most serious tidings."

Avanasy bowed, and barely in time, Ingrid remembered to do the same. Four servants who had gone unnoticed by Ingrid, the living lost among the dead, stepped sedately forward and bowed to them. Avanasy nodded in acknowledgment, and they followed the quartet out of the throne room. All the way, Ingrid could feel the eyes of the living and the dead staring at her back.

Returning to the hallways was agony. At least the haunts in the throne room had seemed composed, as if they accepted their fate. The dead who lingered in the corridors were in torment. Tears and blood both streaked their faces and hands. They wailed to heavens that seemed to have long ago ceased to hear them, and reached out to the living who never could. Some, to Ingrid's horror, seemed to realize she could see them, and they fell on their knees, reaching up to her, mouthing their pleas. She wanted so much to shrink against Avanasy, to have him shield her from the desperate, tortured spirits, but she could not. There were living beings in the corridor. Men, mostly, in fine robes, or soldiers in armor, going to and fro about their own business, but most definitely taking note of the two foreigners and their escort. She could not show such overt weakness yet, but neither could she repress the tremors seizing hold of her.

The corridors seemed endless, an interminable stretch of painted pillars, gilding and works of art Ingrid could barely discern for the press of the dead. Her resolve ebbed with every step. She wanted to throw herself on the floor with her eyes shut and her hands pressed over her ears. She wanted to scream and scream until someone made these hideous visions vanish.

Then at last, at *last*, the servants stopped in front of a green door painted over with gilded sigils.

"Honored Sir, Honored Lady, in deference to the customs of your nation." There seemed to be a small deprecative sneer in the voice, but Ingrid could not be sure, her head was reeling so badly. Next to the servant, the ghost of a crone reached out her crabbed hand, trying to pluck at his sleeve, her mouth shaping one word over and over. "We have been instructed to see you housed together," he was saying. Bowing low, he pushed the door open.

The first thing Ingrid saw about the room was that no ghosts stood within. She practically ran across the threshold before she remembered she was still watched, and recovered herself enough to stand up straight and look about with something like detachment.

Thankfully, this chamber seemed to be designed with comfort more than grandeur in mind. The low, carved benches were laden with pillows. The hangings on the walls were pleasant landscapes of lakes and mountains. Feather mattresses had been piled high on the beautiful bedframe. Curtains of sapphire silk hung from the canopy. A fresh breeze and the scents of flowers and ripening fruit told her that the lacelike wooden screens against the far wall concealed open windows, or possibly doors to a verandah. Ingrid found she could breathe normally again.

Avanasy stepped up beside her, his own gaze sweeping the room, and nodding with approval at what he saw, particularly the plates of dainties laid out on one of the tables.

"This will be quite satisfactory," he said in the same utterly confident tone he had used before the emperor. "We will send for you if we have need."

The chief among the servants blinked in surprise. Ingrid knew enough now to understand how strange the dismissal would sound to him. Nonetheless, he and his fellows simply bowed without other comment and slipped out the door.

No sooner did the door close behind them than Ingrid collapsed onto the nearest bench, pressing her palms against her eyes.

"Vyshemir's knife!" exclaimed Avanasy, coming at once to sit beside her. "What is it, Ingrid?"

"Ghosts," she said. She couldn't look up, not even at him. She had seen too much and needed to be in darkness for awhile. "This place is full of them. Hundreds of them. They're . . . they're in pain, Avanasy. They're crying, and they're begging, and I can't hear them. I can't ask them what they want."

Avanasy's arms wrapped tightly around her and drew her close to his chest, holding her safe from all that she had seen. She relaxed into his embrace. She had thought she might cry when this moment came, but she did not. Fear and pity had drained her dry for the moment, and she needed no more than Avanasy's warmth to sustain her.

When at last she was able to push herself away and look Avanasy in the face, she said, "I wanted to tell you, there were ghosts in the throne room. I think some of them were old emperors, and there were soldiers, and some women. I don't know who they were, but when you started talking about Medeoan being escorted here, they all started laughing. Not kindly either." She shuddered remembering their mocking gestures and pointing fingers. "It was as if they were making fun of us."

Avanasy let out a long, slow breath. He pushed his hair back from his forehead. "So, I did feel it. Medeoan is already here."

Ingrid felt her brow furrow with perplexity. "Surely not. They would have told us."

"Not if they are keeping her prisoner." Avanasy rose swiftly and crossed the room. He folded back one of the elaborately carved screens and revealed a stretch of lawn trimmed with drooping trees and brightly colored blossoms. It ended in a high wall painted with saffron and bordered in black. Several wooden gates had been set into the stone, all of them solidly closed. Avanasy's shoulders slumped and then stiffened as he gazed at that well-built wall. "When a spell is being worked, a sorcerer nearby can feel the making of it. I know the touch of Medeoan's working quite well." Ingrid could hear the soft smile in his voice, but it faded quickly. "While we stood before the emperor, I thought, for just the briefest instant, I felt that touch. This place is such a warren of spells and workings being constantly employed to protect the people within . . . I thought I must have imagined it among all the other currents, but no, I did not." He turned and his face was grim. "The empress came here before us, and the emperor and the Nine Elders are holding her captive until they can decide what to do with her."

"What should we do?" asked Ingrid softly.

Avanasy looked over his shoulder at the high wall and the closed gates. "I don't know," he murmured. "Yet."

Pa K'un, the Heart of Heaven and Earth, sat in the summer garden, to all appearances contemplating the small waterfall where it ran over the perfectly rounded gray stones. The sound of it was pleasant, especially when mixed with the rustle of the leaves around him and the warmth of the summer sun on his skin. The servants, secretaries, soldiers and elders had retired to various discreet distances, which gave him rare and welcome room to think for himself.

His thoughts, however, were far more troubled than the chattering water in front of him. Counts of troops, of supplies, of moneys, of stores whirled through his head, and they were far from enough to repel a determined invasion. He held what would be a valuable hostage under normal circumstances, but if the goal of the enemy's game was conquest, even the anointed empress would not be hostage enough.

Now there came these two "messengers," also with tales of usurpation. They came in the name of the empress of Isavalta, but obviously had no idea where she was. The first of them, Lord Avanasy, was a known name, and was a close advisor and tutor to the empress before her marriage, but then was sent into exile. Which led to the question, did he truly come in the empress's name, or did he secretly serve the usurper?

The silent woman who accompanied him in the station of his wife was a complete unknown, but the elders felt an oddness about her, as of someone who might not be a power, but who had most certainly been touched by power.

There had been no answer yet from his missive to Hastinapura, and Pa K'un found himself beginning to fear what that answer might hold. For the first time in several years, he felt himself too young for his sacred office.

Movement off to the right caught his eye. He turned and saw Dieu Han, the dowager empress, kneel on the grass before him. She performed the obeisance carefully, conscious of the fall of her silken sleeves and of the gold and jade ornaments adorning her lacquered hair.

"Please rise, Honored Mother," said Pa K'un, torn between relief, as she was the one person to whom he could speak of these matters freely, and annoyance, as he wanted to think more, and knew she would have her own firm opinions on what should be done next. "Sit with me." Here in the garden, he could speak without the Voice. This earth was sacred, and plowed deep with spells of peace and protection long before the first stone of the Heart of the World was laid. Even the

Minister of Air acknowledged that no malevolent magic could be brought to bear here.

Dieu Han rose as gracefully as she had knelt, giving her robes time to settle back into their proper lines. A pair of servants instantly slipped forward with a low chair for her and placed it behind her where she might sit without having to rudely glance away from the emperor.

Pa K'un contemplated the dowager. She was not his blood mother. She had not been the mother of the two emperors before him, both of whom had died when they were still boys. Her blood son had been Jian Ayd Cao, whom she bore to Emperor Seong Kyung Cao when she still bore the more humble title of Beloved Companion, and was only the first among the concubines in the women's palace. Emperor Seong had at once raised her to be empress, and she bore the change, they said, with all appropriate dignity. But Emperor Seong had died in battle against feuding overlords, and Emperor Jian had died of a fall in the arms of a careless nurse when he was only three. That left Dieu Han as dowager, with the responsibility to choose the next emperor, with the guidance of the gods and the Nine Elders, of course. Should such advice lead her to one who was under the age of manhood, then she also had the ruling of Hung Tse as regent until the imperial boy could rule in his own name.

Pa K'un was not so foolish as to believe it was mere coincidence or divine will that had led Dieu Han to choose three boys in a row. Nor was it accidental that he was the first to have survived past sixteen. He had ever been diligent about making sure his "mother's" wishes were attended to, and that her voice was always heard in council. Never forgetting other facts, Dieu Han could be an excellent advisor on certain matters. This might well be one of them.

"So, Honored Mother," said Pa K'un. "How do you think we should dispose of these northern visitors?"

The set of Dieu Han's jaw and the glint in her dark eyes told Pa K'un that she was not in the mood to waste words on ceremony. "My son, you must let them escape."

Pa K'un blinked. He had been expecting an audacious answer, but nothing like this. "And why should I do this thing, Honored Mother?"

"Because," replied Dieu Han in a voice that was little more than a whisper, "when the empress of Isavalta is gone, it will force the Nine Elders to do what they will not do otherwise—summon one of the four guardians to protect us all."

Pa K'un took a moment to let the implications of that suggestion settle in. The possibility had been raised before, when last he had spoken with Dieu Han in the throne room, as a matter of fact. He had given it lip service then, but now he forced himself to consider it seriously.

None of the immortal guardians had been summoned in three hundred years. To do so was to demand the sacrifice of one of the Nine Elders. If that was not reason enough to give one pause, there was also the well-documented fact that such a summoning could be a two-edged sword. The four guardians would indeed protect Hung Tse from her enemies, but once summoned, they had been known to decide that one of those enemies was a rash and careless emperor.

A fact which Dieu Han was as aware of as he.

"I may not order such a thing," he said, reminding the dowager of another fact which she also knew perfectly well. "The Nine Elders are preeminent in the magical defense of Hung Tse. In this area, even I may not interfere."

"Which is why the northerners must escape," murmured Dieu Han without even the show of demure deference to her emperor. "We may be honest here, you and I, my son. Hung Tse is weak. We know this. Hastinapura, the pirates, the rebels in the east and our own lords. There has been too much for too long and we are a hollow land. Our enemies will know this soon. We cannot wait for them to make this discovery."

"You are very sure of this, Honored Mother."

"I have outlived three emperors to choose you for the throne, my son. I may outlive you. We cannot know what the future holds, but I am growing old, and I have seen the way of things for a long time."

The emperor regarded her steadily, understanding full well what she had said, and what she had not said. Around them, the wind blew in the leaves, the waterfall chattered, and the warmth and scents of summer wafted on the breeze, yet it seemed to Pa K'un he sat in the middle of a profound stillness.

"It would be a thing which must be most carefully accomplished," he said slowly.

"As you say, my son." Dieu Han finally let some deference creep into her tone, if only because she knew she must not push him too boldly now that he appeared to be leaning toward agreement. "The orders must be given only to those whose loyalty is absolute."

"Do you know of any such?"

"I do." The confidence in her voice was absolute.

She played a dangerous game. There were so many possibilities, and once the guardian was summoned, they were in no one's control, not even the gods. The guardian would surely defeat the invaders on the northern border, but what else would it do? It might decide Pa K'un was weak and unfit, and devour him, leaving Dieu Han to choose yet another emperor and regain the rule of Hung Tse.

But it might also decide that Dieu Han had played one too many games with the sacred rule, and there would be no more dowager in Hung Tse.

If this was a gamble, it was one of legendary proportions. Pa K'un carefully considered the state of readiness his generals had outlined to him again, and again he saw how badly short it fell. He had inherited a much-weakened empire, and he could not be the only one to see that much of that weakness was attributable to the woman who sat across from him, and all her cleverness. How long had she planned this? Why should she desire it? Or was it that she finally realized that she had brought Hung Tse to the brink by all her years of surreptitious rule?

Pa K'un gazed at the woman who had adopted him as her son. It was not possible that her face paint had been poorly applied, so the shadows under her eyes must be real. Perhaps she was afraid. They were weak. He knew that, and she might know it better than he.

He would have to accept her wager, and pray hard to be granted a pure heart as he did.

"Then, Honored Mother," he said, forcing his voice to stay

steady as he did. "I will trust you to see this thing properly done."

The dowager empress slipped from her chair to her knees, making the departing obeisance. Her gold, jade and silk sparkled in the clear light. Holding herself still as she did, she might have been some beautifully carved statue. "You honor me, my son."

"But mother," he went on. "Have a care when you contemplate which of us will live the longest. My gratitude at you placing me upon the throne is great, but I am no longer a boy. I have held the seat for some years now, and there is every sign I may hold it for many years yet."

"That is my only wish for you, my son," she murmured piously.

"I thank you, Honored Mother," he replied. "You may now go. I wish to be alone awhile yet."

She rose and left him. Pa K'un watched her gliding away among the carefully tended willows and drooping lilies.

And thus the thing is set in motion, he thought, and permitted himself to shiver despite the warmth of the day. *We play with the dice of lives and empires, Honored Mother, and we know not what is truly stirring in the hearts of the Isavaltans or their kings. O gods, oh spirit of my father, let my throw be true.*

There is no such thing as a warm night on guard.

Ferin Zarnotasyn Ferinivin, Over-Lieutenant of the Imperial House Guard, tucked his poleax under his arm and clapped his hands together, trying to get some blood circulating through his fingers. His leather gloves seemed to be holding the cold in more than they were keeping it out. In the darkness, he could hear his fellow guards giving each other the watch word as they patrolled the edges of the encampment in the light of the campfires and the slender moon. Most of them worked in twos and threes. Ferin had the dubious distinction of a lonely outrider's post, gleefully assigned to him by his bull's ass of a captain who liked the southern emperor's ideas of camp discipline. What was a dice game to anyone? A man had to do *something* with his time. There was only so much sitting around a man could bear.

Make sure to tell Rasina he was lucky they didn't catch him with that woman. Probably had the balls off him for that. Ferin stripped off his right glove and blew on his fingers.

Damn, we're too far south for it to be this cold.

To his left, the woods rustled. Ferin broke off his train of thought, and lowered his poleax to a ready position. No need to get upset if it was just a fox, but no excuse not to be ready in case it wasn't.

The rustling continued. Whatever was out there, it was far to big for a fox, and too bold for a deer.

"Come out and be recognized," Ferin called into the darkness, straining his eyes to see further, but there was nothing but shadows.

After another moment's rustling, an indistinct figure emerged from the underbrush. It took Ferin a minute to realize what he was seeing was a thick kaftan with a hood pulled down low to disguise the face underneath it.

What Ferin did not see was any weapon. That, however, did not ease his mind at all.

"Friend or foe?" he demanded. *And you'd better speak your Isavaltan pure, friend. Any Hung accents and I'm having your head off here.*

"Friend," came back a man's voice, muffled badly by the deep hood.

"What's the word?"

The stranger hesitated and Ferin tightened his grip on his axe.

"The word is that the night you made over sergeant, Ferin Zarnotasyn Ferinivin, you decided you were going to celebrate in Voislava's house, no matter what anyone tried to tell you about that particular whore's den being a thieves' den as well. You got so drunk, you passed out and woke up to find out the women had stolen your purse, all your gear, stripped you naked and left you out in the street for the dawn patrol to find, and if you hadn't had good friends in the foot guard at the time, you would have lost your new rank as well."

Ferin choked. There were two men who knew that story. One of them was still guarding Vaknevos. The other . . .

"Peshek?" whispered Ferin despite the disbelief that filled him.

The hooded figure nodded.

"Vyshko's pike!" Ferin reached out to clasp his friend's hand, but stopped in the midst of the gesture. "What are you doing here?" he demanded in a harsh whisper. "Are you out of your mind? They'll kill you if they catch you!"

"You should kill me here and now, Ferin," replied Peshek steadily. He moved sideways just a little to let the moonlight filter under his hood. It was Peshek all right. There was no mistaking that face, or those blue eyes that held their spark of mischief even at such a time as this. "I'm a traitor after all."

Ferin spat. "Pah. Not a man believes that."

The corner of Peshek's mouth twisted into a smile. "Tell that to the ones that have been chasing me halfway across Isavalta."

"Not a man who knows you then." Ferin looked sharply left and right to make sure no one was approaching. "But what in the name of Vyshko's bones *are* you doing here?"

"Recruiting." Peshek's smile faded and his partly lit face became a mask of perfect seriousness. "Starting with you, I hope."

"Recruiting?" Ferin gaped at him. "Who? For what?"

"For the empress's army."

Ferin pulled back. He could see enough of Peshek's face to see the man was perfectly sober, and that he meant what he said. Could it be true after all? Could Peshek, Peshek of all men, son of one of the best commanders there ever was, truly have turned traitor?

"The empress's army is here." Ferin planted the butt of his poleax on the ground for emphasis.

"No," replied Peshek gravely. "This is Kacha's army. The empress's army is with me, and my father."

Again, Ferin's gaze shifted left, then right. The other patrols sounded reassuringly far away. If he were caught at this moment, what he'd be staring at would be a lot worse than a cold patrol. "Peshek, I think maybe you should get out of here, now."

Peshek didn't move. "Do you think I'd be here if I couldn't prove what I say?" he asked with his familiar, light confidence. "Will you hear me, Ferin?"

Vyshko's bones. I should be calling for the men. I should give you a count of three to get your fool self out of here. I should.

But he did not. "I'll hear you, but only if you talk fast."

"I'll do my best." Peshek reached into his sash, and despite all he knew of the man, Ferin automatically stiffened, ready to dodge sideways should metal flash in the moonlight. If Peshek noticed, he said nothing. He just pulled out a folded piece of paper and held it out for Ferin.

Ferin took the paper, squinting closely at it to decipher the broken seal. At last, he made out the spread wings of the imperial eagle.

"Where did you get this?"

"From the empress."

Ferin opened the letter and read the brief words it contained. As he did, Peshek began to speak in a steady whisper, telling him of being summoned to the Red Library, of the empress's fear for her life, of how he and the keeper of the empress's god house had helped her imperial majesty flee toward the Heart of the World, of how he had carried out his orders by meeting Lord Avanasy, whose treason was also a ruse, and sending him on after the empress. How he continued to serve by raising an army to stop the one now led by Emperor Kacha.

"He's nothing but a southern usurper," muttered Peshek. "I know not what he's done to the Council of Lords, but he has strong magics supporting him. This whole business of the confinement is a lie to explain why the empress does not appear in public anymore. I'll bet my head that they'll say she died suddenly in childbed, probably with the heir, when her time comes."

Ferin looked down at the letter again. The paper crackled between his fingers. "And that is why we could not find this madwoman sorceress, although we scoured the country for her."

Peshek nodded. "This war is not the empress's. This war is the southerner's."

Ferin looked away from Peshek toward the camp. The fires flickered between the trees. The noise of voices had abated as those not on watch took to their tents, if they were lucky enough to have such, or rolled themselves in blankets to get what sleep they could on the unforgiving ground.

"What's the mood of the camp?" asked Peshek.

Ferin shrugged. "Good enough. No one likes the southern emperor, that's certain, but they do like the idea of taking a bite out of the Hung."

Peshek fell silent. Ferin kept looking toward the fires. He did not want to think about this. This was not the sort of choice he should have to make. He knew where his orders came from and where his loyalties all lay. Before Peshek had come with this . . . story of his, Ferin would not have questioned any of that, any more than he would have questioned his need to breathe. But if what Peshek said was true, then it was Ferin himself who was the traitor right now, not Peshek. But if he was being led astray . . .

"Do you believe what I'm telling you, Ferin?" asked Peshek finally.

The night wind blew cold against his cheeks, and Ferin inhaled the scents of wood smoke and pine resin. "I don't know." It was the only answer he could give.

"I think you do." Ferin did not turn to look at him. He did not want to see Peshek's face right now. He did not want to hear these words anymore. But Peshek continued. "And I'm going to prove it to you. At the Padinogen passage, my men and I are going to attack the baggage trains. If you don't believe me, warn your commanders. Send out search parties. If you do believe . . . come away with us, and let it be known why you're going."

"Start a camp rumor for you," he snorted. "And then desert."

"Yes. Because it won't be desertion. It will be returning to the proper service of the empress."

Ferin said nothing. He did not know what reply to make. His head swam with the implications of what he had heard, and of the fact that he had been willing to stand here and listen.

"I'll take my letter back now."

Ferin turned, startled. He had forgotten he still held the thing. He stared at the pale paper. He could no longer make out the words. He should keep it. Show it to his commanders. It was a forgery. It must be. What Peshek told him was ridiculous. It would mean Isavalta had been conquered by Hastinapura, without anybody knowing the thing had happened.

Ferin folded the paper and handed it back to Peshek, who took it without a word and stowed it in his sash. The two men looked into each other's eyes for a long moment. Ferin knew Peshek saw all the disquiet inside him. Peshek, on the other hand, looked back at him with nothing but calm certainty.

The sound of tramping boots and crackling scrub broke the moment. Peshek drew his hood down and plunged back into the woods.

"Vyshko's balls," growled a familiar voice. S't'pan. His relief was here. The big man loomed in the darkness. "What was all that racket?"

Ferin blinked and straightened up. Peshek was already well out of sight. "A fox," he said. "Nothing more."

Chapter Eighteen

"The Revered Person of the Dowager Empress, Dieu Han, requests the company of the Lady Ingrid in the Autumn Garden."

Ingrid shook herself to avoid staring. She had not realized until they spoke that the person clad in black armor and sashed in saffron, bowing deeply before her, was a woman.

She glanced back at Avanasy, who sat at one of the room's low tables where he was, to all appearances, puzzling through a silken scroll recounting Hung Tse's recent history. Avanasy raised his brows, somewhat in surprise, and nodded, which was the gesture she expected.

"Of course I will come," Ingrid told the woman soldier. "When should I be ready?"

"Her Revered Personage requests that you accompany me as soon as is convenient."

Which, of course, could not mean anything but now. "Certainly," said Ingrid, self-consciously smoothing down the jade-and-black robe she wore. "I am ready."

Ingrid exchanged a parting glance with Avanasy. They had not spoken much during the past day. Avanasy had been absorbed in delicate magics, trying to find some way to reach out past the room they were in without alerting the Nine Elders. Ingrid, in an attempt to give him the freedom he needed to concentrate, had roamed the little space of garden outside their rooms, and watched the guards walk by on the walls, and tried hard not to feel trapped.

They had heard nothing from the emperor, or the Nine Elders.

Now, the woman soldier led Ingrid across the garden to one of the wall's arched doorways. She produced an iron key and unlocked the portal. The wall, it seemed, was actually a pair of walls that made a cool, dim tunnel. She could hear the footsteps of the patrols overhead. She stood back as Ingrid entered, locking the door behind them. Ingrid felt her heart speed up, and hoped her sudden attack of nerves did not show in her face.

"This way, Honored Lady."

The soldier led her off to the right, so they were following the sound of marching. Ingrid could see nothing except her escort's yellow sash. Even as her eyes adjusted, there was little to make out but beige stone and a dusty floor. The dust tickled her nose and she suppressed a sneeze. It seemed a strange way to take an honored guest, and Ingrid's unease grew stronger.

Nothing was made better by the occasional ghost standing beside this or that door. They drew to attention as her escort passed them, and saluted her with pale hands. Ingrid tried to keep her eyes on the living woman's heels.

At last, she stopped them in front of one of the doors in the left hand wall. Two ghosts stood on guard here, big and grim, pale and hollow-eyed, surrounded by the smell of old dust. Ingrid could discern nothing from them. Was this a trap? What truly lay beyond that door?

Her escort produced a second key, this one smaller and more highly polished than the first. She unlocked the new door smoothly, and a shaft of sunlight shot through. She stepped back and bowed again, and Ingrid, blinking, walked out into the welcome daylight.

When she could see clearly again, she knew why this place was called the Autumn Garden. The carefully trimmed trees had leaves the color of burgundy and rich brandy. Gold, orange and claret chrysanthemums bloomed in profusion. Tiny yellow flowers of a sort similar to those her mother called "eggs and butter" bloomed in the grass. White lace blooms and tall stalks tufted with purple swayed above beds of low red-leafed plants around the garden pools where herons and storks stood tall and graceful in the brown water. One blue heron looked at Ingrid and stretched its great wings, flapping them in the gentle breeze, but it did not fly, and Ingrid realized those wings must have been clipped.

There was no question as to where she was supposed to go. Toward the center of the garden, a great pavilion had been erected. In keeping with its surroundings, it was made of burnt orange cloth that Ingrid suspected of being silk.

The woman soldier accompanied her across the neat lawn to the pavilion. In its shade, a sienna cloth had been spread, and some of the low, dark furniture in which the people of Hung Tse seemed to delight had been set up. Serving women glided gracefully to and fro, laying out dishes, taking up cloths, brushing away the occasional leaf or insect that had strayed into the tent.

In the tallest carved chair sat the woman who must be the Revered Person of the Dowager Empress Dieu Han. She was thin and straight, like a willow wand, and something in her dark eyes told Ingrid she was just as tough. Saffron embroidery ornamented her white-and-sapphire robe. Combs of jade and gold decorated her lustrous black hair. Her face had been made up white and red, but Ingrid could see the faint wrinkles around her mouth and on her brow that no cosmetic could hide. The woman was not nearly so young as she was being made to appear.

As soon as she entered the pavilion's shadow, Ingrid began the deep bow with her hands held before her that she hoped was a polite and appropriate greeting, but she was not permitted to finish it. The dowager rose swiftly and grasped both Ingrid's hands, a familiar gesture that seemed so out of place among these formal people that Ingrid started.

"Honored Lady Ingrid, I am so glad you have come." The dowager drew Ingrid back with her and set her into a low, curving seat next to her own chair. "I apologize for the dirty route you had to take to come here, but I needed to speak to you at once, and I wanted as few eyes as possible to see you arrive."

Ingrid's gaze flickered to the serving women. The dowager did not miss the gesture.

"All my ladies are bound to silence by more than oaths," she said gravely. "They can say nothing without leave."

In many ways this was not a terribly reassuring statement, but Ingrid said nothing of it. "What is so urgent . . ." she groped for an appropriate title. "Majesty?"

The dowager had obviously heard the hesitation, but she nodded in what Ingrid hoped was approval of her choice of words. "I am afraid, Lady Ingrid."

"Afraid?" was all Ingrid could think to say. *Here? In this walled place surrounded by soldiers?*

"The emperor, my son, is speeding the doom of Hung Tse."

Is he? Ingrid knew her shock showed plainly on her face. "I don't understand, Majesty."

"He holds the empress of Isavalta in humiliating captivity." The dowager breathed the words as if afraid after all they might be overheard. "He will not give her up. He violates the order of nature and the laws of man by so treating a fellow monarch. No good can come of this." She trembled, just a little. "No good at all."

Ingrid licked her lips, trying to compose herself. She badly wished Avanasy were here instead. This was not the sort of conversation she was adept at.

"But, Majesty, why is he doing this?" she asked. "Surely the empress Medeoan told him what was happening in Isavalta."

The dowager ducked her head. "He is doing it because he can. It pleases him to be able to hold so powerful a person to his pleasure." She glanced up, shamefaced. "My son is new to the throne, and he is in love with his own power. I did not guide him well enough when he was young. I . . ." She glanced away, but not before Ingrid saw the tremor around her mouth. When she collected herself, she went on. "I want only what is right for Hung Tse. I fear that if Empress Medeoan is not released soon, she will have her own reasons for continuing the war against us when she regains the throne. Indeed, she has ample cause now." The dowager swallowed. "But if you and your lord tell her it was only the whim of a young man, that Hung Tse itself is not her enemy, then perhaps you may cool her blood and avert what can only bring disaster to both our countries."

Ingrid sat silently for a moment, trying to absorb all that had just been said. The scents of the Autumn Garden wafted around her. The gowns of the serving women rustled like the leaves of the trees as they moved about their tasks.

"But how can we tell her anything?" she asked at last. "We cannot even reach her."

The dowager leaned forward, clasping Ingrid's hand again. "Peik Shing, who brought you here, is one of my personal guard. She has found out where your empress is secreted. She can take you there. It will have to be done swiftly, tonight if possible. Rumors fly faster than wrens in the Heart. I have taken all the precautions I can, but they will not be enough. The whispers will begin soon, and then the guard will be changed, or the empress will be moved."

And if we're caught? Ingrid did not ask that question. She said. "Very well. I must speak to . . . Lord Avanasy." It was the first time she had used the title in something other than jest, and the words sounded strange to her ears. "How may we get a message to you?"

"You cannot," said the dowager flatly. "Peik Shing will come to your windows at midnight. If you are not ready then, this will not happen. There will be no second chance."

Ingrid nodded, and despite the heat of the day, goose pimples pricked her arms. "Thank you for this, Majesty."

Again, Dieu Han dipped her gaze. "I want only what is best for my land," she murmured to her hands where they lay in her lap. "And for my son." She looked up and around, but not at Ingrid. "Peik Shing will take you back now." The dowager gestured over Ingrid's head.

Peik Shing marched up smartly and bowed to her mistress. Ingrid got to her feet and she also bowed, both grateful for what the dowager had told her and frightened for what was to come. But there was truly no choice. Unless Avanasy had formed some other plan, this was their chance.

Ingrid found herself so thoroughly distracted as Peik Shing led her back through the walls, she barely noticed the soldiers' ghosts as she passed. Her mind was too busy turning over the conversation she had just had, turning it over and over, trying to find what might lie hidden beneath it.

She had made no progress on this task by the time Peik Shing opened the door that led to the bit of garden off which she and Avanasy had been housed. The woman bowed and shut the door before Ingrid could stammer her thanks. She heard the iron key turn in its lock, securing the door to what Ingrid could only think of now as their cage.

"What happened?" asked Avanasy behind her.

Ingrid whirled around to face him, opened her mouth, and closed it again. "I don't know."

"Tell me."

Ingrid did. They sat on one of the stone benches that had been set beneath the willows and she described her encounter with the empress, repeating the dialogue as accurately as she could. When she was finished, Avanasy's face remained quietly grave, but Ingrid could feel the tension humming through him.

"Could it be as she says?" Ingrid asked.

"It could be," Avanasy acknowledged. "But it could also be a trap of some kind. For who, and for what purpose, I cannot begin to guess."

She watched the way his fingers slowly curled into fists, quite sure he was not even conscious of the gesture. "But we have no choice, do we?" she said, knowing the words were true as she spoke them. "This is our single chance to find her, trap or no."

Avanasy turned his face away. "I should have left you with Lien."

"I would not have stayed," she answered him simply. "We are well past that sort of wishing, Avanasy."

That brought a smile to him. "I think I was past it when I first met you, despite all I knew."

"So then." Ingrid took his hand and smoothed his fingers out until they lay gently in hers. "We wait."

Time did not pass easily. Avanasy went back to his scrolls, and Ingrid joined him, listening to him read, and taking in some elementary lessons in deciphering the language. Despite this, it seemed an eternity until the servants carried in the evening meal. Still no message came from the emperor or his ministers. The dowager sent no fresh word, which Ingrid took to be a sign that their plan remained unchanged and, hopefully, undiscovered.

Gradually, the light outside dimmed and the servants returned to light the lamps, screen off the windows and ready them for bed. One fortunate consequence of Ingrid and Avanasy being lodged together was that the servants, men for Avanasy and women for Ingrid, chose to retire modestly to the outer rooms where they would not have to observe a custom they found uncomfortable.

Night deepened. The moon rose over the walls, highlighting the patrols that continued across the tops of the walls without stopping for so small a thing as darkness. Avanasy extinguished the lamps, and they lay in the bed, side by side, with no chance of sleep coming to either of them.

Then, as Ingrid was watching the moonbeams creep across the floor and wondering how much longer midnight could be in coming, something scratched softly at one of the wooden window screens. Avanasy was on his feet in an instant. He carefully folded back the screen and Peik Shing entered the room, little more than a shadow in her black armor.

She carried a bulky package in her arms. "You must put these on, Lord, Lady, and quickly."

Avanasy slit open the knot that tied the package and its cloth fell open to reveal two identical coats of plain black

cloth, with black sashes and round black caps. Ingrid wanted
to ask questions, but Peik Shing was already glancing about
anxiously, first at the door leading to the outer room where
the servants slept, with one ear alert for any call from within,
and then at the darkened wall where another patrol would
soon be passing by. Seeing this, Ingrid held her tongue and
managed to struggle into her coat. Avanasy tied off her sash
and she performed the same service for him. Fortunately, the
pillbox cap was large enough for Ingrid to bundle her hair
underneath it, allowing her to pass for a young man at a
casual glance, in bad light.

Peik Shing silently beckoned them to follow her. One by
one they slipped out into the garden. Avanasy took a minute
to fold the screen back into place behind them. Then, casually, they strolled across the lawn. Ingrid felt precious time
crawling like ants across her skin, but she knew that should
there be eyes watching now, hurrying figures were more
likely to raise suspicions that those that might simply be out
for a stroll due to sleeplessness.

Once again, Peik Shing opened the door in the wall. It
would have been pitch black inside, but every few yards had
been hung small lanterns which gave a dim light. This time,
she turned to the left, and in another few feet turned again,
leading them down an earthen staircase into a completely
different set of corridors. The air around them grew damp
and there was no smell but that of old earth. Peik Shing
walked rapidly, navigating the twists and turns of the place
without hesitation.

The place is a rabbit warren, Ingrid realized as she hurried
behind Avanasy. *If she means to lose us down here, she'll
have an easy job of it.*

Soon, however, they came to another, longer staircase, this
one of the same beige stone as the walls. They climbed its
length to reach yet another door. This one Peik Shing did
not unlock. Instead, she gave the same soft, scratching knock
as she had outside the window. Only silence followed and
Ingrid's heart hammered hard. Then came a muffled reply
that Ingrid could not make out.

"Friend," rasped Peik Shing. "Open up, Ayd."

There followed the sound of sliding bolts and heavy hinges.

The door swung open, and another soldier, this one a man, squinted at Peik Shing.

"What are you doing?" he demanded in a hoarse whisper. "Who are these?"

"Heart's business, I promise you, Ayd." Peik Shing held up her right hand to swear. "Let me through?"

Ayd looked at Ingrid and Avanasy, and then back at Peik Shing. "All right, as it's you," he growled. "But if aught of this comes back, I'm not giving up my ass for yours, understand?"

"Perfectly. Come, friends." Peik Shing slid past the other soldier, and Ingrid and Avanasy followed suit.

Open air touched them. They had come out on top of one of the walls. Ingrid could see the wonderful outlines of the Heart of the World clearly in the moonlight. Peik Shing did not give them time to stand and admire the view, however. She hustled them down an outer stair into the great stone courtyard.

As soon as her shoes touched the paving stones, Peik Shing's entire manner changed. She assumed a martial stance, with her back and shoulders ramrod straight. She did not walk swiftly before them now, she marched at a steady pace. Walking so openly sent fear to choke off Ingrid's breath. There was no place to hide here, no way to run should they be spotted, no one to turn to except Peik Shing, who might be on a mission of her own.

The guards at the main doors closed ranks as they approached. Ingrid was sure they were caught. But Peik Shing flashed them some sigil—Ingrid saw a graven gold disk in her palm—and the other guards drew back.

Inside, the ghosts watched them even more closely than the guards had. Hollow eyes weeping blood followed them, hands clawed for them, in beseeching and in warning, thought Ingrid, although that could have been her imagination. She made herself watch Peik Shing's back, but the movements of the dead kept catching at the corners of her eyes, and tears began to form from the effort of trying not to see.

The end of the corridor opened into a broad rotunda. A black spiral stair rose from the wooden floor, winding up around gilded walls hung with silk. Not one ghost stood upon those stairs.

"Cold iron," murmured Avanasy in wonder. "I've never seen so much in one place."

Peik Shing marched them up the steps. Their soft-soled shoes made each stair ring like faint and distant bells. Below them, the dead raised their hands up and mouthed incomprehensible words.

Ingrid counted four stories passing by them as their path spiraled higher and higher. She breathed more easily here, despite the height growing dizzying. It was easy here not to look down, not to see the ghosts below.

On the fifth story, Peik Shing led them onto the circular balcony with its fantastically carved rail. Ingrid thought she recognized a few of the signs Avanasy had showed her worked into the design. Corridors opened like spokes off the central hub. Still, here there were no ghosts. But Ingrid found no comfort in the cold and empty place. Peik Shing picked one corridor and led them down its dim length. The open window at the end let in some of the moonlight, but there was no other illumination. Still, Ingrid saw exactly where they were going. Doors opened on the left and the right at regular intervals, but only the left-hand door at the end was decorated by a pair of guards.

Peik Shing stopped in front of the guards, who might have been her sisters in their black armor and yellow sashes. She flashed the golden sigil she carried again.

"The dowager has sent these two doctors to inspect the prisoner," she declared.

The right-hand soldier frowned and squinted at Ingrid and Avanasy. "At this time of night?"

"She is concerned. There have been signs that the prisoner is not thriving well. These honored physicians have traveled far and are concerned enough by the reports they have heard they ask to see her at once."

The left-hand soldier glanced at her partner. "I've seen no such signs."

"You're not a doctor trained in northern medicine," snapped back Peik Shing. "Perhaps you'd care to go wake the Revered Person of the Dowager and tell that her in your opinion the prisoner is fine and her orders may be disregarded."

Right Hand looked at Left Hand for a long moment. Ingrid's heart rose to fill the base of her throat. Left Hand watched Peik Shing for some wavering in her expression. None came. Reluctantly, Left Hand turned and lifted first one, then the other heavy bar that blocked the door. She next unlocked it with a key taken from under her breastplate, pulling the door open and standing aside. Peik Shing also stood aside, and Ingrid and Avanasy walked alone into the bare room.

The door slammed shut behind them.

A single figure shot up from the mattress that lay in the corner. Avanasy stood where he was, amazed or bewildered. Then, he reached up one hand, pulled off his cap and walked into the patch of moonlight the room's open window allowed in.

"Avanasy?" the young woman breathed. She took a step forward, then another, trembling and staring as if she could not believe what she saw. Then, all at once, she ran forward and threw her arms around his neck, burying her face against his shoulder. "I knew you would find me!" Ingrid barely heard the muffled exclamation. "I knew it."

Gently, Avanasy extricated himself, stepping back just a little so the young woman had to stand on her own, but he did not let go of her hands. Then, slowly, and with dignity, he knelt before her.

She was slight, this young empress. Her fair hair had been cropped off and now stuck out wild and ragged in all directions. Dark circles ringed her blue eyes. Despite it all, Ingrid could see the bloom of her beauty, and saw easily how a man who spent much time in her confidence could come to be distracted as Avanasy had confessed to being. Nothing she could name as jealousy stirred in her though, as she watched the man she called her husband kneel, only an odd, straining sadness.

Remembering how custom here called for so many salutes and bows, Ingrid also knelt.

The empress Medeoan did not even seem to see her.

"You heard then?" she said to Avanasy, looking down at both their hands. "Iakush found you?"

"Yes, Imperial Majesty," Avanasy replied. "But he gave his life to do so."

Ingrid saw no flicker of emotion pass across the empress's face as she heard this. "Stand," she told Avanasy. "There is no time for ceremony here."

"No, Majesty." Avanasy rose quickly, and Ingrid stood with him. It was only then that the empress truly noticed her. Medeoan's expression was nonplused. Ingrid might have been a goat or a ghost, for all the sense the empress seemed to be able to make of her presence.

Avanasy licked his lips. "This is Ingrid Loftfield, Majesty. She returned with me from the far shore of the Silent Lands. She has been of great help to me in my quest to find you again."

He did not say "she is my wife," and Ingrid's sadness deepened, but she just bobbed a curtsey for the empress.

Medeoan's gaze raked her over, evidently still uncertain as to what this stranger was doing here.

"You are most welcome," she said quickly, and Ingrid tried to tell herself the lack of warmth was due to circumstances, which would be natural enough.

"Avanasy, have you a way out?" asked the empress.

"A guard outside says she'll guide us."

"I have a better way." The empress's blue eyes gleamed, and all at once she looked very young. She ran to the leather mattress that was the room's only furnishing and flipped it aside. Ingrid retreated to the door, listening. She heard no running feet, no cries or even conversation. Surely that must mean they were still undiscovered.

She glanced back. The empress held up something for Avanasy's inspection. At first, it seemed to be nothing more than a flat mat of hair, but as she stared, she saw it was a wreath of flowers, woven, obviously, from Medeoan's own shorn locks. Avanasy, as he gazed at it, seemed nothing short of stunned.

He took the thing from the empress's fingers and laid it flat on his palm. "Is it complete?" he asked in an awed whisper.

"No," the empress answered. "But it should serve, and it means we will not have to trust one of theirs."

As she spoke, a single knock sounded against the door, followed fast by the faint sound of boots against a wooden floor.

"Whatever it is," breathed Ingrid, "you'd best do it quickly. Our time is up."

"Let them see the mettle of the empress of Isavalta," said Avanasy. "Call for the place of Lien to receive us."

The young woman's shoulders straightened. She turned to the window. Ingrid caught just a glimpse of her expression, at once proud, mischievous and vengeful.

"The sky is held in place by twelve apple trees," she intoned. "The trees are held up by three pillars. Beneath each pillar is a green snake. The first is named Shkurapeia. The second is named Polikha. The third is Liukha. I beg you Liukha, Polikha, Shkurapeia, loan me the strength of your pillars to hold up the moonlight under my feet. I beg you Liukha, Polikha, Shkurapeia, let me and mine walk safely to the place of Lien under your ever-watchful gaze. I beg you in the name of divine Vyshemir, vengeful Vyshko and in the name of their daughter Medeoan Edemskoidoch Nacheradovosh!"

Medeoan tossed the woven wreath of hair out into the darkness. For a moment, Ingrid saw it, dark against the waning moonlight. Then, impossibly, the wreath began to unravel. The golden strands glowed, catching up the silver light in themselves, stretching out as if spun by fantastic spiders into arching, shining webwork that spanned from the windowsill to the dark distance.

Gasps of wonder from below. More shouts. Hammering at the door. All urged Ingrid to motion, but all she could do was stand and stare. With all she had seen so far, nothing equaled this bright miracle.

"Hurry, Majesty," said Avanasy. "Ingrid, come quickly."

There was no way she could brace the door against the hammering, so Ingrid ran to Avanasy's side. He cupped his hands and held them to help boost the empress onto the windowsill. The young woman bit her lip and murmured something, perhaps a prayer, perhaps another spell. She stepped onto the bridge of gossamer and moonlight. For a moment, Ingrid's lungs refused to draw air.

But it held. The shining span of fairy tales and impossibilities held as strong as mortared brick under the empress's bare feet. Eyes ahead, and lips still moving, Medeoan strode up the gentle arch, her shadow standing out stark and black on its glowing surface.

"Ingrid."

Behind her, the door splintered. She jumped hard at the sudden shock of noise, and scrambled up onto the sill. She could see the ground plainly through the thin veil of maiden's hair and moonlight, dozens of yards below. The door crashed open, wood cracking and iron bands slamming against stone.

Jesus, Mary and Joseph. Ingrid hiked up her skirts, fixed her gaze on the empress's back, and ran.

The moonlight bridge did not yield the least bit under her hurrying feet, nor did it make any sound. She ran in eerie silence, hearing only her own breathing and the diminishing shouts of the soldiers who had broken into the cell. The motion of her black shadow caught her eye, but she forced herself not to look. If she looked down now, she would be lost, and she knew it.

Something whistled past her ear, and Ingrid screamed and involuntarily jerked sideways. A familiar, welcome hand clapped onto her shoulder, righting her balance, and she saw an arrow arch past, falling to earth on the right of the glowing span.

Avanasy looked down at her, and his face was hard with strain. She said nothing, but took his hand, and together they ran. In a few strides they reached the empress, Avanasy catching her with his other hand. Another arrow whistled through the night. Ingrid ducked, but Avanasy didn't even flinch. He just strode on, holding them solidly anchored on either side of him.

Then she heard another voice call out. This was no soldier shouting orders or profanities. This was a voice like thunder, like storm wind. She could make out nothing of what it said, but around her the air shivered with sympathetic vibration.

The night exploded into a cloud of shrieks and battering,

clawing things. Ingrid screamed and threw up her hands, to beat the hundreds of tiny shadows off, to keep them from her eyes. They screamed back at her in a million tiny voices. Birds, she realized, as her hands flailed out. Birds, with beaks pecking and claws catching her flesh, scrapes and pinpoints of pain setting her blood flowing. Wings and feet snarled themselves in her hair, pulling on it from the roots. They battered at her clothing, tugging at it as if they sought to tear it from her body. She couldn't see, and she couldn't move for fear of putting a foot wrong and plunging to the ground. She crouched down, striking out feebly, only to have her fingers bitten over and again.

"Disperse!" roared Avanasy over the din and pain. "By blood and moon's fire, I order you be gone!"

The birds screamed again in one last wrenching chorus. Something wet touched Ingrid's cheek, but the birds were gone. She risked a look up. Avanasy stood tall in the moonlit darkness. Dark blood ran down his hand, and his chest heaved from trying to draw enough air. Ingrid realized it was blood spatter that had touched her. She pulled herself to her feet. She wanted to get away from here, she wanted to be on the ground again. She had enough of miracles, and she wanted this over. For that there was only one course. She caught Avanasy's sleeve again, and they ran once more, all three of them, across the gossamer road into darkness.

But the world below was not done with them yet. Another arrow, this one shining like the bridge beneath their feet, shot straight up, several yards ahead of them, arching high over their head. At first, Ingrid thought it trailed a rope that would ensnare them, but then she saw how the "rope" shimmered and gleamed. Then, she felt the heat of it.

Fire. A bow of fire arched across the moonlight bridge. A few seconds later, another arrow shot up, this one through the weaving of the bridge itself, and then down again. Medeoan balked, and Avanasy drew back, and a second bow of fire joined the first at a ninety degree angle.

"What are they doing?" demanded Medeoan. "I can feel heat . . ."

"Breaking the bridge?" Avanasy knuckled his eyes. "There's something but I cannot tell what."

"You can't see it?" cried Ingrid. Two more arrows whistled through the night, one more from below, trailing another rope of fire to arch across the bridge, the other from straight behind, making Medeoan leap sideways, coming down perilously close to the edge of the bridge.

"What is it, Ingrid?"

Before she could answer, something tugged at her skirt. Looking down automatically, Ingrid saw an arrow sticking from the billowing silk, and even as Avanasy yanked it free, another shining arrow shot up, adding another strand to the net of fire in front of them.

And she saw what they were doing. The arrows from behind and the net before. If they stayed where they were, they'd be picked off like birds on a branch. If they ran forward blindly, they'd be burned to death. If they jumped . . . they would be shattered on the ground.

"It's a net," said Ingrid, her words choking her. "Mary Mother of God, it's fire."

"I can't see it!" shouted Medeoan. Frustration and fear tore at her words.

"Nor can I," replied Avanasy calmly, and Ingrid could feel how much that calm was costing him. Another arrow whistled overhead, but barely. "But I feel the heat. Ingrid you'll have to lead us."

Ingrid bit the inside of her cheek and tasted blood. She snatched up her hems in one hand and Avanasy's hand in the other. Another arrow arched overhead, trailing its rope of fire behind it, adding another strand to the web. Moonlight and firelight blended starkly together, dazzling her eyes and making her skin shine red and white.

"Step exactly as I do."

Swallowing so much fear she felt heart and belly would split open from the pressure, Ingrid strode forward. Another arrow, another strand of fire, shot up straight in front of her, and she had to jump back. She could hear the sizzle of the magical flames now, and their heat licked at her skin, breaking sweat out on her brow. She dodged the fiery strand, and the next, and the next. Cloth ripped near her, and she knew another arrow had come too close. Behind her, Avanasy cursed, and Medeoan cursed. She did not look back. She dodged under the last arch and looked out and saw nothing but the unbroken bridge ahead. The impossible span of moonlight suddenly seemed the safest thing she had ever known and she ran, forgetting Avanasy's hand, forgetting the young woman they had come so far to save, forgetting everything but the need to get away from the arrows and the fire; she bolted into the darkness, her only guide the shining road at her feet.

Slowly, slowly, she realized the moonlight arch had begun to slope down. Her bedazzled eyes could make out some landmarks ahead of her; trees lifting from the darkness, and another light. A lantern held high by a man waiting at the foot of their bridge.

Lien. The man was Lien and the trees were in Lien's garden. They had made it.

The glow of moonlight gave way to the springy darkness of grass. Gasping with relief, Ingrid missed her step and tumbled to the ground. The cool dampness of night's dew bathed the hundred small wounds she had taken. She lay there panting for just a moment, not caring for the dampness soaking rapidly through her fine silken clothing, before Avanasy's arms scooped her up and pulled her close, pressing his body tightly against hers for a long moment.

Eventually, Ingrid and Avanasy were able to loosen their hold on each other, and turn toward the others. The first thing Ingrid saw was the utter shock on Medeoan's face. Suddenly ashamed she took another step back. She could not read the look on Avanasy's face, and did not at this time care to try. Instead, she looked up in the direction from which they had come.

The bridge of moonlight was already gone. No trace of it lingered to shine against the night sky.

"Was it a dream?"

Avanasy shook his head. "No dream, but a working of great skill." Pride filled his voice. "Imperial Majesty, may I make known to you our host, Lien Jinn, and his niece Cai Yun Shen."

Lien and Cai Yun bowed deeply. The empress blinked dazedly in the lantern light. She seemed reluctant to take her gaze from Avanasy's face. Her bewilderment tightened Ingrid's throat. But at last, she gestured to Lien and Cai Yun to stand.

Something was wrong with Lien, but it took Ingrid a moment to realize what it was. Instead of his silken robe, the old sorcerer wore only a short coat of unbleached cotton with dark cuffs and short trousers to match. A dark cap covered his hair and he wore sandals on his feet instead of his soft shoes.

"I thank you for your hospitality to my advisor . . . advisors," the empress was saying. "And now to myself. I am in your debt."

"Your Imperial Majesty honors my home with your presence." Lien bowed. "But I fear we may not stay. The Nine Elders have many ways to track such sorceries, and may already be on their way here. We must be gone as soon as possible."

Ingrid swayed on her feet. As bad as she felt, Medeoan looked close to collapse. Avanasy hurried to the empress's side and held out his arm so she could steady herself against him.

"Of course," said Medeoan. "Is conveyance ready?"

"This way, please."

He set off into the depths of the garden at a pace Ingrid felt she could not possibly match. She was damp, cold and filthy, she had been dragged through dark tunnels by soldiers, shot at by sorcerers, and now her husband was back together with the woman he . . . she could barely bring herself to think of it at this moment. She wanted to stamp her foot, to screech her disapproval, to refuse to move until she could get some sleep in a bed. Any bed.

She did none of these things. She gathered up the hems of her ridiculous silken robe and set off after Lien as best she could. Avanasy shot her a worried glance, but did not reach for her; both his hands were occupied in supporting the fainting empress and keeping her moving forward.

The garden passed them in a blur of shadows with flashes of lantern light on pale leaves and silver pools. They reached the back wall, and Lien paused at the arched gate. He laid his hand on the latch and spoke three words Ingrid could not understand. The latch snicked open, and Lien led them out into a tiny back lane. Moonlight and lantern light showed Ingrid a black canal and a sharp-prowed boat moored to an iron post.

Lien blew out the lantern, leaving them only moonlight to see by. It took Ingrid a moment to realize the old man standing at the long steering oar was Jiu, and Shien hunched by the high gunwale.

"Go below, please. Shien will show you where."

As Avanasy and Shien helped the unsteady empress aboard, Lien turned to Cai Yun and grasped both her hands, saying something soft and urgent that Ingrid could not make out. She had just time enough to see the young woman nod before Avanasy motioned to her, and she had to clamber over the rail and onto the deck. There was no time to survey the little craft. Shien was already leading them to the stern ladder and down belowdecks.

Only one covered lantern lit the hold. Ingrid could make out nothing but bundles and stacks of shadow. Shien stepped nimbly between them and beckoned that they should follow.

They obeyed, with considerably less grace. Ingrid barked her shins several times against unidentifiable objects, bit her tongue to keep from exclaiming, and wished for her usual thick skirts and petticoats.

"In here, please, master, mistresses," whispered Shien.

She gestured down. It took Ingrid a moment, but she realized the old woman was gesturing toward a hole in the lower deck. It was a smuggler's hold.

Ingrid saw at once what she was to do, and she balked. They had done enough, and all her nerve had left her. She felt hollow and her limbs began to shake. The idea of being shut up in the tiny, black hold, even with Avanasy's presence for support and comfort, filled her with revulsion.

But there was Avanasy, helping Shien to lower the empress, whose skin glowed white as a ghost in the faint light. Ingrid heard her bumping and shuffling below. Avanasy stretched his hand out to Ingrid.

What was there to do? She took his hand, and felt how warm it was, even though her own was so cold, and let herself be lowered into the smuggler's hold.

It was pitch black inside. She put up her hand and found

the upper deck barely three feet above the lower. She had to lie flat on her back in the straw that had been strewn on the hull boards in order to fit. She heard the empress's echoing breath off to the right, so she shifted herself to the left to make room for Avanasy to climb down and stretch himself out. Shien laid the planking back into place. Ingrid had just time enough to see the planks had padded backs, both to muffle any sound from below and so they would not sound unusually hollow if thumped, before Shien settled them down, cutting off all light.

Ingrid lay where she was. Overhead, she heard Shien's soft footsteps and the sound of something heavy being dragged and thumped into place. They were sealed in now. She swallowed against the panic that tried to rise in her throat. More soft footsteps crossed the upper deck. Then that sound was gone. The straw was rough against her back, and the cold and damp began to sink in, raising goose bumps across every inch of her. The hold smelled of old seawater and mildew. The breathing of all three of them sounded far too loud in the confined space.

"Well." Ingrid drew a deep but shaky breath to prove to herself that there was plenty of air, and to help pull her tattered nerves back together. "They do say there's nothing like traveling first class."

"And this is nothing like," answered Avanasy gravely. "Majesty? Are you well?"

"As well as I can be," the empress whispered in reply. "Although I am beginning to have second thoughts about Hung Tse's reputation for hospitality." The lightness of her tone quickly faded. "Avanasy, do you know where they will take us?"

As if her words were a signal, the boat rocked sharply under them, and began to slide through the water, in the direction of Ingrid's feet. She tried to remember which way that was, and failed. Little waves slapped the hull underneath them. The cold seemed to deepen, but perhaps that was only her imagination.

"We'll go down to the river docks, I think," murmured Avanasy. Their confinement seemed to forbid speaking in normal tones. "Lien has access to . . . grander ships there. It

is my hope he will be able to sail us directly back to Isavalta."

"Vyshemir grant your hope is correct."

There was no more to be said. They lay still in the darkness, packed like sardines in a strange, cold tin. The boat
rocked steadily, the waves and the slow creaking of the
boards making a gentle counterpoint to the steady splash of
the steering oar. Were it not for the fact that she was now
soaked to the skin from bilge water, Ingrid believed she
might have fallen asleep. As it was, she just fell into a kind
of waking doze, her mind trying to sense something of the
boat's speed, and trying in vain to measure time to guess
how far they had come, and how far they might have to go.

Avanasy's hand brushed hers, ice-cold now, but Ingrid
grasped it gratefully anyway. A small traitorous part of herself wondered if he held onto the empress with his other
hand, and then she wondered why it should matter, which
brought back the strange sadness she had felt in the tower
room.

Time must have passed, but how much of it, she could not
tell. Her skin went numb. She could barely feel Avanasy's
hand now. She tried to wriggle her toes to get some blood
flowing, but it was no good.

Then came the sounds of footsteps, and Ingrid almost cried
out in relief, but fast on the heels of the footsteps came the
tramp of boots. Ingrid choked herself off. She had enough
sensation left to her to feel Avanasy tense beside her. Her
bloodless fingers gripped his hand.

Scraps of sound filtered through the padded boards. A
woman's voice, high and querulous. That must have been
Shien. A man's baritone that might have been Lien, or Jiu,
or a stranger, answered. The boots clumped up and down the
decks, shoving heavy burdens this way and that. Something
that might have been a spear butt thumped against the deck
above Ingrid's right shoulder.

They were going to hear her heartbeat. They were going
to hear her breathing. She tried to hold her breath, tried to
quiet her heart, to be wood and stone here in the cold.

Something heavy was shoved aside directly overhead. Ingrid bit down on her lip until she tasted blood. The boots

clomped, the spear butt thumped. Shien spoke again, and a stranger's bass rumbled answered. The baritone that might have been Lien or Jiu spoke, and the bass barked out a sharp reply, and the spear butt came down right over Ingrid's face, making her whole body jolt. She squeezed her eyes shut like a child desperate not to be seen.

The baritone said something else, and the words were followed by a faint, new noise. After a moment, Ingrid recognized it—the chink of metal, possibly of coins. Was Lien paying a tax, or perhaps a bribe? Would it work? Her throat closed. All was silent for a moment. Then, the baritone rapped out some order, and more burdens were dragged across the deck. Tears leaked out of Ingrid's eyes and she began to shake again.

But then, miraculously, the boots all trooped away toward her head where the stern ladder was. Footsteps padded after them, and blessed, blessed silence fell around them again.

Tears of gratitude ran down Ingrid's cheeks to mix with the bilgewater, and she did not care. She wept in silence as the boat started to move again, and the steering oar splashed once more into the water.

It was too much. The sudden release from terror robbed Ingrid of consciousness. Whether she fainted or simply fell at last into sleep, she could not have said. For a time, however, the world went away.

Light struck Ingrid's eyes. She would have cringed but she could not move. Shadows moved overhead. They reached down long arms, grabbed Avanasy and hoisted him out of the smuggler's hold.

"Careful, you wastrels!" shrilled Shien's voice.

Then the arms reached out for Ingrid. Powerless to resist, or even to question, Ingrid was lifted like a sack of grain and set upright on the deck. She could not even feel her knees, let alone stiffen them to stand, but fortunately Shien seemed to guess her condition and the old woman was there beside her, wrapping an arm around Ingrid's shoulder to support her weight as she slumped down.

"Carefully!" Shien barked again.

Ingrid could see at least a little now. Two men in loose shirts and short trousers bent down and raised the empress up from the hold. Avanasy sat on a bench nearby. As she was lifted, he struggled to rise, and failed.

"Bring them with me," snapped Shien. "And *gently,* you louts, that lady is of quality."

One of the two men began to snigger, but his companion stopped him with a glower. Shien moved toward the ladder, and Ingrid had no choice but to stumble along with her.

Climbing onto the upper deck was a nightmare. Sensation came back to Ingrid as pins and needles stabbing her skin from the inside. Shien, stronger than she looked, hauled Ingrid bodily up the ladder to stand blinking stupidly in the first gray light of dawn.

They were back at the docks. There was no mistaking the noise or the smell of the place. Shadowy sailing ships rose up on either side of the small boat. Shien steered Ingrid toward the starboard rail, where Jiu was helping Avanasy to a rope ladder lowered from the side of one of the larger vessels. His hands shook badly, but he managed to hang on while sailors at the top hauled the ropes up, pulling Avanasy with them.

To her shame, Ingrid whispered, "I don't think I can."

"You will," said Shien with gentle practicality. "Because you must."

The sailors let the ladder slither back down over the side. Shien guided Ingrid up to it and folded her hands around the rungs. Ingrid made her left foot step up and rest on the rope, then her right. She dangled there for a moment, and her hands clamped down reflexively. The sailors began to pull, and she gasped, but did not scream.

In less time than she would have thought, she was on the deck of the ship, being helped over the rail, and stood next to Avanasy so the ladder could be let down once more for the empress.

Somewhat more composed, and at least able to stand on her own, although the pins and needles still plagued her, and the ruined, sodden silk clung to her back like a wet rag, Ingrid was able to look about her. The ship was a big one for its kind; a four-master, and elaborately rigged. The quarterdeck rose up proudly from the stern, and even in the dim light she could see the long arm of the tiller. Shouted orders filled the air. Men and boys swarmed up the rigging, loosening furled canvas, which came down like a snowfall. Others lashed it into place on the yardarms, plainly getting ready to sail as soon as the captain gave the order.

The sailors lifted the empress over the side, and set her swaying on the deck. Avanasy moved toward her, but Shien came over the rail under her own steam a moment later and caught the young woman before she could fall. She looked dazed. However bad the recent trip had been for Ingrid, for the empress it had obviously been worse, and Ingrid felt a stab of pity for her.

A man ran down from the quarterdeck, and as he approached, Ingrid recognized him as Lien, still in his short coat and sandals. The sorcerer bowed hastily.

"I apologize for the mode of bringing you here, but it was necessary. Let my men conduct you below. We will be under way in moments."

He signaled for a sailor, an officer in all probability. The man was slender and taller than most she had seen in Hung Tse. His coat was short and practical in cut, but brilliant green in color and its buttons sparkled silver. He bowed and led them all, with Shien supporting the empress, to a ladder beneath the quarterdeck, and down past the second deck to the third. By Ingrid's mental measure, they were only just down to the waterline, and she saw the ladder went farther down yet, so there must be at least one more deck beneath them, possibly two.

They went no lower, however. The officer conducted them toward the bow. They passed doors on both port and starboard. The officer opened one of the starboard doors, bowing to the empress. Shien led her through, and closed them in. Then, the officer opened a port door. Avanasy bowed his own thanks, and he and Ingrid filed into the cabin.

It was small, which Ingrid had expected, but it was also snug and dry. Two cozy bunks had been built into the wall. A gracefully carved table and high-backed bench stood under an unlit tin lantern. What illumination there was came from two portholes with glass so thick they turned the light watery.

Ingrid managed to take two steps toward the bench before the strength that had supported her this far failed and she collapsed. Avanasy caught her and they sank to the deck together. They knelt there for a time, doing nothing but holding onto each other, each reminding themself that the other was solid and real.

Eventually, by silent, mutual consent, they pulled themselves to their feet again. A carved chest had been lashed into one corner. Avanasy investigated the contents and pulled out Ingrid's ordinary clothes, the thick skirt, apron, petticoats and stockings she had missed so recently. Avanasy's black coat, trousers and boots were also inside.

Groaning with relief, Ingrid shucked her ruined silk and dressed in her clean, familiar clothing. Avanasy also reclaimed his traveling clothes, and when he turned to face her, he looked more comfortable than she had seen him in days. But at the same time, his face was troubled.

"Ingrid." He took her hand and sat them both down on the carved bench. "Lien will be sailing us through the Land of Death and Spirit. This . . ." he touched the spell braid on her wrist, "will only provide you with some protection. You must not be asleep when we cross the veil."

She nodded. "You'll warn me when that's to happen?"

"I will, but I must leave you for a time. I . . ."

He stood there for a moment, his hand against the smooth wood, as if looking for words in the pattern of the grain.

When he did not find them, Ingrid said, "If you want to go see the empress, you should."

That turned him around. "Ingrid . . ." He stopped and started again. "I don't wish you to have cause to doubt my love for you."

"I don't," she said, and she meant it, but she did not speak further. She did not say how she still felt the sadness she had known the moment she first saw Avanasy and his young empress together. For in that moment she had seen not how much Avanasy loved empress Medeoan, but how much love shone from the young woman for him.

Did Avanasy still love Medeoan as other than pupil and monarch? Looking at him now, she saw that he did, but she could not bring herself to fear that love. She was too numb to do anything but accept that it was so. Later, she knew, she would have to weep, or rage, or do some other thing that she might regret in time, but now, she could do nothing but look at the man who was her husband and see the truth.

"Go," she told him. "Say what you must."

Avanasy crossed the distance between them in three swift strides. He kissed her long and lingeringly on the mouth, and left her there. That kiss, that love, was as true as the other, and she knew that as well, but that knowledge did nothing to lift the numbness that had settled over her heart.

Sad, tired and still bewildered by all that had happened, Ingrid found she had no trouble at all creeping beneath the covers on the lower bunk and falling gratefully into oblivion.

Avanasy stood outside the door that led to Medeoan's cabin, trying to calm himself. He could scarcely number the emotions swirling through him. He felt like a nervous school-child. He felt like a courtier who knows he is out of favor. He felt like a parent who wanted desperately to comfort his child, but knew he had no comfort to offer. He told himself he was too tired for this, and surely Medeoan was as well. He wanted to run and take shelter in Ingrid's arms until they reached the shores of Isavalta. He wanted to know that Medeoan had already gone to sleep so that he would not have to do this thing.

He raised his hand and knocked softly.

Shien opened the door a moment later. Behind her he saw the soft glow of morning through thick glass.

"Has her imperial majesty retired?" he asked.

"Not yet," replied Shien. "I will see if she will grant you admittance."

She closed the door, leaving Avanasy alone with his inner turmoil for a seemingly endless moment. Above, the capstan ground as it turned to the rhythm of stamping feet. The ship around him strained as shouts rose from a variety of throats.

Shien returned to the doorway and beckoned him inside.

Medeoan sat on the lower of two bunks, wrapped in a woolen blanket. Underneath, he glimpsed a robe of bright blue cotton, a shade very close to the imperial blue she should have been wearing. Avanasy had no doubt Lien had specifically arranged for that. Her bright, cropped hair had been loosened and brushed. She looked far too thin, and too pale.

Shien ducked out the door and closed it again behind her. Medeoan did not look up at her departure. She just stared at the deck and rubbed her thin, wounded hands together.

What have you been through, Medeoan? Avanasy wanted to blurt out. He did not. He simply knelt, as was proper before his empress. The deck rocked under him and Avanasy swayed gracelessly as the ship slowly slipped forward.

The motion lifted Medeoan's head. She glanced toward the ceiling and the sounds of men's orders and creaking ropes. Then, she finally seemed to see him there, kneeling in reverence before her.

"There is no need for such between us, Avanasy," she said, running a hand through her badly shorn locks. "I would have thought that much you would remember."

"I've forgotten nothing," he said, getting to his feet again. "Including the fact that you are now empress of Eternal Isavalta."

"Such an empress as the world has never seen," she snorted. "Crop-headed, imprisoned, alone . . ."

"Never alone," he said, moving to her side.

"Oh, but I was." She gazed up at him, and he saw the dark circles under her eyes. "You will never know . . . I'm sorry, Avanasy. I should have known you would not betray me. This is my fault."

Hearing the dejection in her words, Avanasy knelt again, but this time it was so he could look directly into Medeoan's eyes. They were under way. The ship rocked with its own easy motion as they moved out into the bay. They were making good their escape. His heart should have been light, but guilt grown old weighed it down.

"No. The fault is mine. I should have gone to your father with what I suspected. I should have . . ."

She smiled and straightened up a little, shaking her head to stop his words. "There are so many things we both should have done." She ran both hands through her shorn hair again.

"I should have found a lady in the Heart of the World who knows how to cut hair!"

They laughed a little at that, but too soon Medeoan grew serious again. "He did not take the crown," she said, staring out of the tiny porthole. "I gave it to him."

"No, Medeoan."

"Yes, Avanasy." Her face hardened. "All I could think to do was run, and I did. I left Isavalta in his hands. I *gave* it to him." She spat the words. "Because I was such a child, I couldn't understand, I couldn't accept who I truly was. I stood at the foot of my father's throne and I swore to Vyshemir and Vyshko I would protect Isavalta, that I would be a true daughter, and at the first opportunity, I abandoned them."

"The gods forgive, Medeoan," he said, laying a hand on the edge of her bunk, as close as he dared come to touching her. "They know it was not them you ran from. They will welcome your return."

"Yes." She was not looking at him. She looked out the portal at the green-brown river and the brightening sky. Avanasy was not sure what she saw there, but it turned her expression to stone. "We will return together, and together we will make Kacha rue what he has done to Isavalta, and to me."

It was then Avanasy saw the depths of the bitterness that had taken hold in Medeoan. Imprisonment had only fostered it. It had begun with Kacha, whom she had truly loved, and who had committed betrayal on top of betrayal. She had a right to her anger, he could not say otherwise, but it chilled him to the heart to see the hard light it sparked in her eyes.

"Medeoan, thinking too much on blame will not help you do what must be done," he ventured.

She smiled mirthlessly. "I am sure you are right. But it is past time I opened my eyes . . ." She shook herself, and did not finish the phrase. "So, tell me, Avanasy, where have you been, and who is this woman you are traveling with?"

All that Avanasy had thought of saying crowded into his mind at that moment—the evasions, the careful words, the partial and more easy truths—but he pushed the babble of it aside. Instead, he settled into the cabin's one chair and told her, fully and deliberately, of his time on Sand Island, of his life as a fisher, which at least made her smile, of the ghost and of Ingrid and her sister. He told her how, dying, Iakush found him there, and how he determined at once to return, but could not leave Ingrid behind.

"She is worthy of you then, Avanasy?" asked Medeoan softly.

"More than I am of her, I sometimes think." He could not help but smile as he thought of Ingrid's warmth and courage again.

Avanasy looked again into Medeoan's eyes, and saw fresh pain there. His throat tightened. Vyshemir's knife, what was she thinking? Cut off, alone, frightened, waiting for him to come to her, as she had been, what had happened in her heart? She was still so very young. Had a dream of love come to her, as it had once to him? He had found the truth of love in Ingrid, but Medeoan had only lost that love she thought she had. Had she hoped to turn to him?

While he looked into those eyes, he saw that this was true, and for a moment he was afraid that he might feel his old, reluctantly acknowledged love stirring. But he thought of Ingrid waiting for him, and he knew that other wistful, unformed love was now no more than tender memory.

He could only hope that he would find the words to make Medeoan understand.

But Medeoan only touched his hand and said, "What else?"

Relieved that the moment he had dreaded had passed so easily, Avanasy spun the tale to the end, bringing her news of Peshek's continued bravery and his quest to raise a loyal army in Isavalta, of the certainty that Kacha meant to war with Hung Tse, and how that war had probably already begun, and how he was certain they had been permitted to escape.

Medeoan's jaw worked itself back and forth. "He plays this game with my land?" she rasped. "With my people now? In my name?" She spat the final word. "And then, after all, he would blame me for his wars! I won't leave enough of him left for his mother to mourn!"

The force of her words rocked Avanasy back.

"We need to be home," she announced. "We need to find Peshek, and then Kacha."

"Lien speeds us on the way. There is no one better able to sail through the Land of Death and Spirit."

An unfamiliar, calculating expression crossed her face. "Avanasy, could he raise more than one crew of men?"

"I believe he can."

"Good. We will speak to him as soon as we are safe in Isavalta. His men could come in useful to whatever force Peshek has managed to raise." She stood, and as the morning's watery light flickered across her, Avanasy saw how very much she looked like her father. "You will stand beside me then."

"As ever, Imperial Majesty." He bowed his head, and this time she did not reject the gesture.

"Thank you." Even those words sounded stern. "There is nothing to be done at this moment. You should try to sleep. I'll need you awake when we arrive."

Avanasy rose and gave a formal reverence. "You should also sleep."

"I'll try, I promise," she said, sounding a little more like the child he remembered. Avanasy let himself be content with that and showed himself out the door.

In the passage, he lifted his eyes to the gods. *Vyshko, Vyshemir, protect your daughter. She is ready to become what she must be, but I beg you, do not let her forget what she should be.*

"They are gone. We have failed." Anh Thao, the Minister of the North, spoke the words. She, with the other Nine Elders, knelt on the dais, a gesture of apology and an admission of guilt all at once.

"We have searched the house of the pirate Lien, but they have already been taken away," added Shaiming, the Minister of Metal. "Nothing has been learned from questioning his niece."

Pa K'un held himself still and silent, letting the Nine Elders bask for a moment in his disapproval. Then, when he judged that moment had lasted long enough, he signed swiftly to his Voice. Seeing him ready to speak, the Nine Elders stood.

"We must turn our minds to what may be done about this invasion," the Voice intoned solemnly. "And we must do so now. We have information that tells us the Isavaltans hasten toward Erh Huan. They mean to attack there, and if they do not have plans to attack soon by sea, they are fools."

"If the story the three from Isavalta told is true . . ." began the Minister of the North, but Pa K'un cut her off with a gesture.

"If it is true, then the security of Hung Tse will be the Isavaltans' last consideration. The empress will return with her advisors to try to take her own land back. It may be she will be able to do so swiftly, but can we rely on that? Their winter comes early and hard. If she must stage a pitched campaign, she will not be able to do so until the spring thaw. That will give the usurper time to dig in on our borders, and prepare at home for her assault, if he has not already begun to do so." The Voice spoke sternly, in good reflection of the emperor's mood. "And if she has lied to us, and works with her Hastinapuran husband rather than against him, she has escaped with whatever information or advantage her magics were able to procure. No, Ministers, we have no choice. We must act swiftly."

He did not say it. He was not permitted to say it. But as he gazed at the nine solemn faces before him, he knew they saw the direction in which his words led.

Xuan, the Minister of Fire, walked up a single step of the dais and knelt.

"I am ready," he said.

The other eight said nothing at first. Xuan remained where he was, bent in obeisance and offering, ready to sacrifice all to make good his failure and to protect the Heart of the World.

"Let it be done," whispered Chi Tahn, the Minister of Water.

"Let it be done," whispered En Lai, the Minister of Earth.

"Let it be done," whispered Shaiming, the Minister of Metal.

Eight times the words echoed around the throne room. As

the ministers spoke, the air seemed to thicken with the force of their resolve, until the hairs on the back of Pa K'un's head stood up, and it seemed that the very images of the gods must shiver from the strength of it.

Pa K'un signed to his Voice. "Can it be done now?"

"It can," answered the Minister of Air. "It has been prepared for these many years."

The Voice looked to the emperor, and Pa K'un nodded.

"Then I also say, let it be done."

The eight of the elders who still stood all bowed in unison. "Will Your Majesty deign to come with us?"

Again, Pa K'un inclined his head. With this as the signal, the Voice beckoned to the bearers with their black coats and saffron caps. They mounted the dais from the rear, carrying the poles which were their badge of office. The poles were fitted into slots on the sides of his throne and the emperor was lifted onto the shoulders of his servants. Already, the soldiers were assembled at the foot of the dais that he might have a proper escort.

The Nine Elders stood aside so that Pa K'un preceded them down the dais steps. As a result, the emperor had no opportunity to see how bravely the Minister of Fire walked toward his destiny.

There was only one place for such magic as this. The ministers and the imperial escort proceeded up the winding stairs of the Heart's central tower, the Heart's Spear. Only those who had the privilege of mounting the final stair could tell that the last chamber was open to the moon and stars. Silver light flooded down and filled the circular room with its polished floor inlaid in gold and ivory with maps of the heavens and ringed round with signs of protection for Hung Tse.

In the center of the chamber waited a stone altar the size and shape of a millstone, its top blackened by years of fires and its sides carved with prayers to the gods and the imperial ancestors. As his bearers lowered him, Pa K'un read those prayers, and wondered if either of the two boys who sat here before him would hear if he spoke those prayers aloud. He wondered if they would bless or curse him if they could.

The Minister of Fire stepped forward and knelt before the

altar. He bowed and kissed the ground before it, remaining in the position of obeisance to pray. Then, at last, he stood straight, and stepped into the center of the altar. He stood there, still and seemingly unafraid, but Pa K'un could not believe that was so. He remembered his investiture as emperor. He had schooled himself to sit perfectly still through the hours of chants and formal declarations. He had appeared calm and strong, or so he had been told, but inside he had felt weak as water, even though he knew it was a glorious thing that was happening to him

Even in the moonlight, Xuan's tattoos shimmered brightly as if he were living flame himself rather than just flesh and blood.

The Minister of Earth and the Minister of the South joined their fellows in the circle. Each carried a shining bundle reverently in their arms. Xuan lifted his chin just a little higher. Then, he inclined his head once.

The Nine Elders bowed in return. Then, they lifted their voices and, together, they began to sing.

Pa K'un had studied many languages, but the spell tongue of the Nine Elders was known to them alone. It was never written down, and was only passed on when a new elder was chosen and invested with the robes, markings and name of the previous sorcerer who had held the office, and then it was passed on by magic. That particular ceremony had not been required, the emperor knew, for three hundred years. But then, neither had this one.

The nine voices rose higher, became more commanding. Even Pa K'un could feel the air shiver as the song wove the elders' will into corporeal form. It grew bitterly cold for a moment, then, slowly, it began to warm, as if the song reached up to the stars themselves and pulled down their fire.

En Lai, the Minister of Earth, broke the circle, still singing high, ringing harmonies that soared above the other tones. He stepped onto the altar. The Minister of Fire did not move, did not look at him. En Lai lifted the burden he carried and draped it around Xuan's shoulders.

It was a robe, stiff with golden embroidery. Phoenixes soared across scarlet cloth. They raised their trailing wings in triumph. They stretched their necks out in song. They spread their long tails out to wrap around Xuan's body so that they encompassed him completely.

En Lai bowed again, and slowly, Pa K'un thought lovingly, tied the golden sash and returned to the circle.

The song deepened, strengthened, drawing its power from the stones beneath as well as the stars above. The night grew warmer. Pa K'un felt sweat begin to prickle his scalp and the back of his neck.

On the altar, Xuan sagged under the weight of the song of power and the robe that bound him. The song did not cease, but grew louder and stronger yet. Pa K'un, for all his years of training, could barely hold himself still. He had ordered this thing, but now he wanted to flee it. This was wrong. This tore at the fabric of what was and what must be. This power was too great, this song too loud. The gods heard this sound, and they answered, and their answers were not kind.

The Minister of the South stepped onto the altar with her burden. Xuan, no longer able to stand on his own, sagged against her. She bore his weight sturdily, singing her thread of this terrible, powerful web, and laid her burden across Xuan's face. It was a mask, made of gold and etched with delicate feathers. It was a bird's face she bound with scarlet ribbons over Xuan's own. He arched his back from the weight and the pain and the burden of the song that pressed against him, but he made no sound. The Minister of the South returned to the circle, and Xuan collapsed in a heap of gold and beauty onto the stone.

The elders' song grew louder yet. Pa K'un felt he could not stand it a moment longer. He must clap his hands over his ears, he must scream, he must leap up and break the circle. He must stop this. It was wrong, wrong. The song would tear the world open. It would shatter night and day around them. It was too huge, too loud, too terrible to be contained.

The emperor shot to his feet, and in that exact moment, the Phoenix rose from the altar.

It was dazzling. It shone like the sun as it lifted its wings, each feather a tongue of flame. The blue of the heart of the flame burned in its eyes. Pa K'un felt he would be blinded

if he looked too long, but he could not turn his face away
from the power and the unearthly beauty of this creature that
rose, graceful as smoke, into the night sky, dimming the stars
themselves with its blaze. It uttered one cry that pierced Pa
K'un's ears through to his heart, and it flew, a star of impossible proportions rising from earth instead of falling from
the heavens, toward the north.

Only when its blaze had faded could Pa K'un breathe
again. He fell back on his chair, his strength gone. The af-
terimages of the Phoenix flickered brightly across his vision.
Sometime, he could not have said when, the elders had
ceased to sing. They clasped hands now, bowing toward the
empty altar. There were only eight of them in that circle.
Xuan, the Minister of Fire, was gone.

Pa K'un gathered himself back into the approved position
of calm reflection, then, he too bowed toward the empty altar.

*Thank you, Xuan, for your sacrifice. Thank you, immortal
one, for answering our call. If there is a price, I will pay,
but I beg you, burn these invaders from our door.*

As his prayer winged skyward, a fierce cry echoed in the
distance. Pa K'un knew then he had been heard, and he could
not help but tremble.

Chapter Nineteen

The white crane soared through the sky. The long plains
passed beneath it, giving way to rolling hills and ragged
mountains. Inside the crane's shape, the man, Yamuna, reveled in the freedom of his flight. Despite the cold of the
bottled curse he carried around his neck, his heart was warm.

He remembered the day he took his oath to the Pearl
Throne, and how heavily the words fell from his tongue. He
remembered watching the sullen, petulent boy he was bound
to serve and wondering how the old emperor could bear to
call that his son.

Soon. Soon I will be transformed forever. Soon the Mothers will answer for my fate.

Avanasy sought his friend Peshek. So too did Yamuna. Last night, as he rested, his scrying showed him Peshek lurking in the woods of a mountain pass, getting ready to commit his own treasons. Avanasy would find him there. So too would Yamuna.

When they all met, it would be the beginning of the end.

"Majesty?" General Adka stepped into the dim imperial tent and knelt. Dawn was still too far off to bring any warmth to the air and his breath steamed in front of him, a white cloud in the flickering light of a single brazier. No servants were present. The emperor himself was nothing more than a shadow beside the dark lump of the bed.

"Adka. Is the decamp proceeding?" The emperor's voice was harsh with fatigue, and something else Adka could not fathom.

"Yes, Majesty. We should be able to move before full light." The order had come hours ago, delivered by the emperor's chief secretary. Over Colonel Gavren, Adka's second-in-command, had gone to the imperial tent to make sure his majesty was informed as to what the coming day would bring, and had returned with a surprising and disturbing order.

Emperor Kacha wanted no scouts sent forward. The army would move out without hesitation, and without information.

So, here Adka knelt, perplexed, and more than a little concerned. No one had seen the emperor in days. He had taken to traveling in a curtained litter and barking out his orders in a strangled voice. Worry was growing among the men, and among the officers as well.

Adka understood the caprice of emperors. His imperial majesty was a young man at his first command. A nonsensical order or two was to be expected. But his absence from camp and council was spreading unease, and the desertions continued, despite the increased patrols on the perimeters of the camps and the marching columns. It was time to get some solid reassurance he could take to his officers and set percolating through the camp as a counter to the rumors that had been building since they left Ontipin.

Adka kept his voice low and humble. "Imperial Majesty, we will be entering the Pass of Padinogen today."

"You wish to give me a lesson in geography, General?" The shadow that was the emperor moved in the darkness, but Adka saw nothing he could clearly identify as a gesture to stand, so he remained on his knees.

"No, Majesty. I only wished to confirm the order to proceed without the scouts."

"They will only delay us." The emperor's voice shook a little as he spoke. "We must make all speed to the plains. Hung Tse is surely on the move. We are still in Isavalta. No one opposes us here."

"No, Majesty," Adka said. He did not ask if the emperor had forgotten those lords and lords master who had failed to send their levies to join the troops. "But there is an additional possibility . . ."

"I am not interested in possibilities, General, only speed."

"Yes, Majesty. However . . ."

With three deliberate steps, the emperor strode out of the shadows, and Adka saw him fully for the first time in days. He saw the round black eye that should not have looked out of any human face, and the skinny hand so grotesquely twisted into a parody of a bird's skinny claw.

"What are you gawking at, General?"

He had thought it might be drink that slurred the emperor's voice, but now that Adka saw his face, he realized it must be pain.

"Is something wrong with my coutenance?" the emperor demanded.

As a soldier, Adka had looked on horror before, and knew how to keep his voice steady. "No, Imperial Majesty."

"I am glad to hear it." The emperor half-turned, hiding his ghastly right side in the shadows again. "March the men on as soon as they can hoist their packs. Nothing is going to delay our victory, do you understand me? Nothing."

Adka drew himself up. He served the imperial house. He had his orders. But he also served Eternal Isavalta. He swore to protect the land with blood and bone, as Vyshko and Vyshemir had. That oath necessitated he try just once more.

"We have made good time. Our best estimates put us a week ahead of the Hung. If His Imperial Majesty wished to . . . rest for a day or two, it would lose us no more than . . ."

"You will not question me!" The emperor swung around, raking the air with his twisted hand.

Now, Adka saw beyond the pain to something else. The young man who was emperor of Eterna Isavalta was terrified. The smooth, calculating assurance that had been his since he came as a boy to Isavalta had vanished. He had no idea what he was going to do or how he was going to do it. His only thought was to push forward and hope he broke through. But to what?

Cold inside, Adka drew himself up and gave the soldier's reverence.

"All will be as His Imperial Majesty commands."

"You may go." The emperor shrank back to the shadows again.

Adka left the tent before he had to look again on the emperor's transformed face. He walked through the chaos of the camp—the shouts, the clatter, the men scurrying about like ants—without seeing any of it. His mind instead ran back and forth over the encounter with the emperor, and what he had just seen.

"Well, General, what do we do?"

Over Colonel Gavren had come up beside him, and Adka hadn't even noticed. He thought on the rocky pass that waited ahead of him. He thought on the black, birdlike eye, on the twisted hand, the pain and the terror, and the fact that the emperor could have him killed instantly for disobeying his orders, and in pain and panic as he was, he just might. Something had happened, something bad that stank to the sky of magic. He needed a sorcerer and he had none to ask. The emperor did not permit any to be brought on the campaign. Once again, Adka found himself wondering why.

Adka made his decision. "Get the baggage train moving immediately. Put the lightest possible guard on it. Bring the imperial litter right behind, again, lightest possible guard. Keep as many of the men back as you can for as long as you can. Make sure the runners are ready to keep communication with the head of the train."

He watched Gavron's eyes flick back and forth as he absorbed the order. He saw the questions rise in the man's mind, and knew that the over-colonel was far too good and disciplined a soldier to voice any of them.

Adka gripped the man's shoulder briefly. "Let us work toward seeing the sun down today. Tonight, we will talk further."

Gavren laid his hand over his heart and without another word turned to march back toward the baggage carts.

Adka struggled to muster his own discipline, but part of his mind was heavily occupied with an old prayer he had learned when he first came into the service.

The child came from the womb. It had no mind, no eyes, no will, no wicked heart. So may the fates of war have no mind, no eyes, no will, no wicked heart against me, Adka, faithful servant of Vyshko, Vyshemir and Eternal Isavalta.

But the prayer brought no comfort, and Adka shivered as he set himself to his work.

Peshek watched the columns of blue-coated men marching east, and swore. He had been right in many ways. As it was, Isavalta's navy could not seriously challenge Hung Tse's, at least not at first. Kacha meant to start this war on land. He was hurrying his troops to the place the Isavaltans called Miateshcha and the people of Hung Tse called Erh Huan. It was a narrow peninsula of land that stood between the two empires. Mostly flat plain, with few difficult mountain ranges, it had been in Isavaltan hands, or in Hung Tse's hands, or in the hands of its own people on and off since time immemorial, fought over, invaded, taken, re-taken, laid waste again and again. Its advantage to Kacha at this moment was that he could get Isavaltans to march there faster than the Hung Tse emperor could. Now the emperor could surely sail troopships up the coast, but if Kacha had not already started hiring pirates to harass any such attempts, he was an utter fool, which, unfortunately, he was not.

Put that together with what Peshek knew of the reinforcement of the garrisons on the coast, and the strategy became clear.

Kacha would attack the peninsula defenses swiftly, making short inroads and digging in before winter came. The Hung Tse, unable to maintain a winter siege, would get what they could through the pirate harassment and attack the Isavaltan coast. Having thus tied up and weakened Hung Tse's navy, which was their true strength, Kacha would, come spring, start the real press, on land, down the Miateshcha peninsula, and up from the south. Because, by next year, his father in Hastinapura would be brought into the battle, and Hung Tse would be facing its worst nightmare. They would be besieged from north and south, and for all the size of their lands, they would not be able to survive that for long.

The only question truly was, did the Heart of the World realize yet what was happening to them? And if they did, what would they do? The armies of Hung Tse, Peshek did not fear overmuch. He was a soldier, and he had faced them. Isavalta could match them, not easily, perhaps, but it could be done, but the Nine Elders would not be idle, and their powers . . . Isavalta had nothing to match that, and how then would those men down there suffer? The Nine Elders were said to be able to call down armies of demons from the clear blue sky, or to be able to open the earth at your feet and swallow you whole.

It was this thought that steeled Peshek toward what must be done. They had to attack the army on the march, and inflict heavy damage doing it. The only place they could do that was while the marching men were confined within the pass, because this was the only place where he and his followers could create advance preparations unseen. On the other side of the pass waited Raichik's plains, and they would have to move to much more dangerous night raids, swift hit-and-run efforts. That would harry and annoy, but would inflict minimal actual damage, even though Lord D'rno was promising them help in the form of two score of his famous horses. If they were going to strike a true blow, here and now was when it must happen.

Peshek squinted toward the east. The masses of men were

thinning, giving way to the slower and more cumbersome supply and baggage carts.

This was wrong. These were Isavaltans. These were members of the house guard, whose only crime was obeying the orders that had come down from the imperial hand.

Peshek crawled backward from his perch to where Ferin waited for him. Ferin's raised eyebrows asked the only question there could be, and Peshek's nod gave the only answer needed.

They had chosen this overlook because it was heavily forested. It gave them cover for when Kacha's advance scouts rode through, and it gave them the raw materials for their work. Ferin raised his hand in signal to the nearest crew of men, and that signal traveled all down the ridgeline. The men crouched behind the great piles of pitch-and-resin-soaked brush that they had spent the past few days gathering. Each team set to work with their flint and steel, starting up a tiny fire, little more than a spark on the end of a taper.

Peshek raised his hand. Ferin raised his. Peshek flattened himself down, and scanned the pass. The first of the baggage carts passed under the first of the waiting brush piles. He could hear the faint echo of the driver cursing the mules as they struggled with the stony ground. At last, the beasts pulled him clear of the obstacles. A knot of boys ran up and began clearing the stones away for the next cart. Peshek swallowed. He had forgotten the boys. How could he have done so? The second cart entered the pass, and the third, and the fourth.

Now. It had to happen now. Peshek closed his eyes, and swung his arm down.

He smelled the smoke instantly as the nurtured sparks were applied to the brush, with the pitch-soaked logs underneath. The crewmen scrambled back instantly and took up the long-handled pushes they had fashioned. The dry brush caught clean, clear and fast, the flames rising up and the heat reaching down.

The smell of it was strong, and reached the bottom of the pass quickly. Heads rose, and spied the fire, and voices shouted out, but the carts could not be quickly turned, and no archers were in position, and Peshek gave the signal to Ferin, and Ferin gave it to the men.

They pushed the piles of tarred and burning brush down onto Kacha's baggage train. The burning bundles fell like stars, trails of sparks shining in their wakes. For a moment, it was beautiful.

Then the burning mass landed at the feet of the mules, who reared and stamped, struggling at their traces and screaming in their mindless, animal voices. Horses bucked and ran, beyond the control of any rider. The fire fell onto the carts, which erupted with fresh flame at once. It fell on the heads and backs of the men, who screamed even louder than the animals and threw themselves to the ground trying to smother the flames, and then it spread to the boys, who, lacking any experience or discipline, simply ran, and took the fire with them down the train. The stench soon grew worse than the screams.

But there was no time to wait. Already the fire crews had retired, making their retreat to the rendezvous. A man had Peshek's horse and he mounted swiftly, charging down the ridgeline to join the other raiders cascading down the shallower pass toward the far end of the train. Someone among Kacha's men had organized a response, and arrows flew up toward the raiders, and were met with an answering volley from Peshek's own men. Lit torches flared in their hands, and pikes and swords were held at the ready.

He noted that absently, as the majority of his concentration was occupied trying to keep his horse and himself upright as they charged down a slope that was still steeper than he would have liked to see. The arrows whistled overhead, and the shouts of the hale and ready mixed with the screams of the burning.

"Medeoan!" shouted Peshek, and his men, as agreed, took up the cry. "Medeoan! Empress Medeoan!"

The litter rocked and tipped under him. Kacha pushed himself up on his good hand. Pain from the eye that strained to see coupled with the pain from the too-much wine he had drunk so he could find rest in the bottom of his cups.

"What is it!"

No answer came, only chaotic shouts and the maddened cries of men and animals. The litter swung this way and that and the horses neighed and balked. The smell of burning wood, and burning flesh, drifted through the curtains.

"What is happening!"

"Attack, Majesty!" answered some man. "Peshek and his deserters!"

Peshek. He dared.

Kacha curled his twisted hand. "Get me my sword!"

"Get His Majesty back!" barked someone else.

Voices shouted, men whistled and a whip cracked. The litter tipped again as the handlers attempted to back and turn the horses.

"Stop!" Kacha thrust open the curtains. "You will bring me my sword!"

Servants and handlers stood and stared, despite the rain of arrows, the rising flames, and the rush of men and beasts all around them.

Kacha climbed out of the litter, landing heavily on the rocky ground. "My sword, and if I have to ask again it will be over your corpse!" he bellowed at the nearest servant. *I will not cower in here. I am Emperor!*

The man ran. Kacha did not bother to watch him go.

"Medeoan!" the wind brought the cry along with all the sounds and scents of burning, "Empress Medeoan!"

Damn them. Damn her. "Where is General Adka?" he demanded of the nearest soldier. "What is the situation?" *I will take command. I am the Emperor. Yamuna be damned as well, wherever he has gone.*

The man opened and closed his mouth several times as he gaped at Kacha's ruined eye, but endeavored to pull himself together.

But before he could speak, there came a new sound overhead—a scream the size of the whole world, as if the heavens themselves had been wounded.

Kacha looked up in time to see his own death streaking down from the sky.

———

They poured down the slope into the baggage train. The flames roared high in the narrow pass, cutting the baggage train off from the majority of the army. Peshek rode hard down the line, swinging his sword at those who challenged him, knocking them off balance or out of the way, long enough for the men behind him to thrust their torches into the baggage carts and spread the fire further yet.

"Medeoan! Empress Medeoan!"

Shouts, flames, screams of horse and man, all blurred into one incomprehensible roar. The smells of tar, wood and flesh assailed his nostrils, and the smoke stung his eyes and wrung tears out to trail along his face. Heat pounded at his back and right side. The guards in the train managed to assemble themselves for their own charge. Screaming their own battle cries, they rode head-on into Peshek's company.

Peshek could spare no thought for what was happening behind him. Men reared up before him, swords or pikes jabbing and slashing, and it was heat and noise, and only instinct and reflex to keep him alive.

Fight through, fight through, fight through. The words sang in his mind as he slashed at the men he should have been fighting beside. He pushed his horse forward, wading through the fray. *Fight through!* That was the order, that was the plan. Fight through and get out the other side, and run for it. Ignore the screams, ignore the way your arm is beginning to ache, don't see the faces, see the weapons, knock them aside, thrust, parry, hit hard, take down the horse and the man goes with it, ignore the arrows, ignore the flames, ignore the screams . . .

All at once the way in front of him opened to the sloping and stony apron that was the mouth of the pass, and Peshek drove his knees into his horse's sides. The animal launched itself forward, streaking free down the remaining slope, galloping hard to leave the smells of smoke and battle far behind.

Peshek found himself grinning. He sheathed his sword and gripped the reins with both hands, hearing the other hoofbeats behind him.

They'd done it, they'd done it. They'd done serious damage to the baggage train; they'd slowed the march while the fire was dealt with and the damage assessed. They had maybe weakened Kacha's force, not just by the dead and wounded they'd left behind, but by the men who might be sent out to find them.

If they were pursued, let it be so. They could deal with any such, especially if they were given a moment to talk, to show their proofs and make their pursuers believe. Then they would be that much stronger, and Kacha that much weaker.

"Vyshko's name! What is it!"

A heartbeat after he heard that shout, the whole world changed. The light turned orange. A rush like the roar of the sea filled the sky, accompanied by a scream that grated Peshek's bones and left him deaf. Then all was heat and a light of blood and brass overhead. Peshek tried to rein in his horse, but the animal bucked and fought, and it was all Peshek could do to keep his seat. He looked up, and the heat beating down from the sky felt as if it would singe his face.

And he saw the Firebird swoop down low over the pass. His jaw hung loose and his hands went slack around the reins. His horse lost no time. It charged, and Peshek was on his back on the ground before he knew what had happened. He pushed himself upright, and not even the pain of his fall could make him look away. The whole of his mind was filled with the sight of the creature of living flame. Even as it flew away, he could feel its heat against his skin. Fear and wonder left him paralyzed. It was coming for him now. He was vaguely aware he ought to run, ought to warn, but he could not do anything but stare at the wonder and deadly beauty that filled the sky.

Kacha's army began to scream.

Peshek didn't think. He scrambled to his feet and stumbled into a run. The world around him shivered with heat, and his lungs protested the need to breathe the burning air. The last of his men galloped past, in the other direction. A few saw him, and shouted. A few more turned around, and he heard the hoofbeats as they raced on with him, until he topped the stony rise.

The heat sent him reeling backward, both hands held up in a futile attempt to ward it off. The whole world was on fire, a blazing, roaring curtain of red, gold, and white. It boiled up the mountainsides; not even the stone could stop it. Men and animals screamed and were silenced. Smoke black as tar poured into the sky, and the Firebird, magnificent and terrible, rode it high, shrieking in its triumph. Peshek could see nothing but its fire, feel nothing but its heat. Pain seeped into his skin, his throat, his eyes. He turned and he ran.

He had no conscious thought, he could only run, away from the fire, away from its cause. He could not even pray, he could only run.

A hot wind blew over him, and Peshek's gaze lifted without his willing it to. The Firebird streaked above him, and dove again.

"No!" screamed Peshek. "No!"

But more men began to scream, and more smoke rose ahead of him, and more heat and more deadly red light leapt into being.

Fire raging ahead and fire raging behind, Peshek threw himself at the hillside, scrambling for purchase on the stones that were already growing hot from the Firebird's blaze. He had to get above the fire. That was his only hope. Had to get above, had to get away, had to find a way to help his men, his men who were screaming and dying, whose deaths he could smell and taste as burning flesh in his mouth.

No, no, no, Vyshko, Vyshemir, no!

He couldn't see. He couldn't hear. Heat burned his hands, but fear was stronger than pain, and he lunged forward again and again, a wild animal acting only on the desperation of instinct.

Impossibly, the ground under him grew level. Peshek drew another lungful of burning air, and turned to run again, but a thin bush in front of him burst into fresh flame. Shock took his balance and he fell, and he saw yet more fire on his coat. Peshek screamed and rolled, beating at the flames, the smoke and the stench of his own burning filling his lungs now. He burned inside, he burned outside and pain engulfed him utterly, and all the world went black.

The wind blew hot from the west and Yamuna turned into it, despite the instinct of his muscles to wheel about and fly away. His crane's eyes saw the smoke welling thick and black from the cleft in the mountains. The battle had been joined. Peshek's treason against his annointed emperor moved across the face of the land.

Yamuna flapped his wings, lifting himself above the hot wind, seeking still air that would allow him to speed on his way. Then, the world before him changed.

The black clouds of smoke parted, and a great bird formed of living flame rose from the ground with a terrible cry of triumph welling from its throat.

Phoenix. Yamuna's flight faltered as, for a moment, fear drowned out all other thought. He dove for the ground, with no other aim than to find a hiding place. He landed, clumsy and terrified, beside a small stream and ducked beneath a drooping willow, cowering as the sky above glowed orange and gold. If he was seen . . . if he was known to those immortal eyes . . . He was not strong enough yet. This bane came too soon. Yamuna shivered.

But the light faded and the sky turned to blue again, streaked with white clouds and the gray of distant smoke.

Yamuna lifted his crane's head. The bottled curse burned cold against his throat. He needed to be rid of it, and that soon. But if Peshek were dead in the charred field under the Phoenix's wings, where would Avanasy go then? And how long would it take to reach him?

Crying in frustration, Yamuna launched himself again into the wind.

Pain. There was nothing in the whole of Peshek's world but pain. His throat whimpered and gasped, but he could not open his mouth for fear he would crumble to ashes then and there. Yet, with each faltering heartbeat, the pain grew worse.

Grandfather Death, your hands are said to be cool, Peshek moaned. *But I've failed. I've failed . . .*

"So, the Nine Elders have played their highest card," said a voice. "We must have scared them badly."

Like a child that will reach out to whatever help may be

at hand, Peshek lifted his head and tried to open his eyes. He could, but only barely, and the attempt was agony.

For a second, he saw a thin brown man. He seemed to have a blaze of red at his throat. Then he had to drop his head again, and there was only darkness and pain.

"Yet, he will still come back to you. You reek of him, Man," said the voice. "And where he is, she will be, and once this fire is burnt out, we still cannot have them trying to make whole what has been broken, can we?" There was a smile in the voice, Peshek realized. He wanted to move, to beg for water, or for a knife, if that was the only way to end his pain.

"So, we will wait."

"Ingrid."

The gentle voice dragged Ingrid reluctantly back from the deep place she had gone. She peeled open her eyes. Avanasy sat on the edge of her bunk, his hand warm against her arm. She had not thought it possible to see him looking any more tired than he had when he had left her to go speak with the empress, but he did now. The dark circles under his eyes made his face look hollow.

Ingrid pushed herself up onto her elbows and brushed her tousled hair back. She had gone to sleep without braiding it, she noted ruefully, and would be brushing the tangles out for days.

Odd how it's the little things that bother one at such a time . . .

"How is the empress?" she asked.

Avanasy shook his head, and his face grew just a little more pinched. "She is . . . much changed. Kacha has wounded her deeply, and I think her confinement has not been good for her." His eyes grew distant for a moment, but then he shook himself. "But, it is time for you to be awake. Lien readies us for the crossing."

"I'd like to see it." Ingrid pushed back the covers.

"Very well." Avanasy gave her his hand and helped her out of the bunk. She brushed down her skirts and apron and together they climbed to the upper deck.

Up top, the wind was stiff and sharp, and whipped her hair into her eyes. Medeoan stood at the port rail, watching them. Ingrid pushed her hair back and followed Avanasy's gaze with her own up to the quarterdeck. Lien stood tall and alone, staring out ahead into the misty morning. The ship sailed easily with the current, the rush of water blending with the rush of the wind. The banks with their burdens of buildings and walls slipped past on either side. She could see a few other vessels in the distance, both before and behind, their sails blending with the morning mists. Overhead, the taut canvas of their own sails bellied in the wind, giving the ship wings.

Now Ingrid saw that those sails were more than the plain white canvas she was used to. Each had been painted with complex red sigils, woven together into rings and knots. She could make nothing of them other than that they seemed well done, but the expression on Avanasy's face as he took them in was something close to awe.

"He's going to take them in awake," he murmured. "This ship must have a crew of a hundred men, and he's going to take them all through the Land of Death and Spirit wide awake. I would have said impossible, but this . . ." He gestured toward the sigils. "No wonder he has been able to defy the Nine Elders for so long."

On the quarterdeck, Lien raised his hand. He might have shouted something; Ingrid thought she heard his voice, but the wind snatched his words away. Ahead of them, the green river and the bright sky seemed dimmed and she wondered if they were sailing into a genuine fog. The edges of the world blurred and whitened. The wind dropped, but the sails stayed impossibly full.

The whiteness brightened and, at the same time, all sound dimmed. The pitch and roll of the ship eased, changing into an even glide, as if they sailed across a garden pond, and all the river turned to flat white mist. There was no more wind.

Ingrid sucked in a breath of air suddenly grown chill and thin. The silence pressed against her ears, making them ring as she strained to hear some sound beyond the beating of her heart. The men in the rigging and on the deck did not seem to have noticed a thing. They went obliviously about their business, but as one shirtless sailor passed Ingrid she saw his eyes as fixed as glass. Whatever Lien did, it blinded them. They could see nothing of the strangeness beyond the ship, and so, in these Silent Lands, could not be seduced or frightened by any of it.

Avanasy fingered the braid Ingrid wore on her wrist, as if to reassure himself that it was still sound.

This time Ingrid felt no tugging, no strange separation of self. She felt whole and sound, almost as if she were stone in this world of mist. Was this how Avanasy felt? Was this what it was to be a sorcerer here? Or was this something else? A spell-wrought rooting that kept her severed soul tied to the deck, like a water cask or a bundle of cotton.

That thought chafed at her, although she could not have said why. She did not want to leave, to roam in the white mists that swirled before and behind, where she would surely lose herself and all that she was. She could not possibly want that. She wanted to stay beside Avanasy, to see this business she had helped start through to the end, and then . . . and then . . .

She wanted to see whatever came next, of course. She did not want to vanish into the mists. Whatever it was. Avanasy loved her. Truly. The empress was an old love from other days. She was his wife.

Her fist closed around her ring.

Around them, the mists parted enough for her to make out patches of green beyond the whiteness. Round, green islands rose from the shifting snow white fog. Each had a single tree growing from it, and each seemed to Ingrid more beautiful than any garden she had ever seen. She meant to take a step toward the rail, but Avanasy gripped her arm and shook his head, and she stayed where she was, her fingers still wrapped hard around her ring.

From the quarterdeck, Lien waved to them, gesturing for them to come join him. Avanasy moved aside so that Medeoan, and then Ingrid, could precede him up the ladder to stand with Lien on a far-too-steady deck.

"Who is it you seek to meet?" asked the sorcerer captain. "Is there a name?"

Medeoan looked to Avanasy. "Peshek Pachalkasyn Ursulvin," he answered. "And Vyshko grant that he has lived long enough," Ingrid heard him add under his breath.

Still with one hand on the rail, Lien stared out past the prow of the great ship. The mists and the green hills moved around them. Here and there, a dark tree floated in the whiteness. Ingrid forced herself not to look. She did not wish to see what birds nested in such trees.

"I sense him," said Lien softly, his gaze distant and clouded. "Yes, I sense him. But we may not sail where he is."

"You promised . . ." began Medeoan.

With painful slowness, Lien turned to focus on her. "We must walk," he said reasonably.

"But your ship . . ." began Avanasy. The sailors went placidly about their duties, unseeing, uncaring. Even Ingrid understood his concern. How long would that last without their master's will to follow?

"Will act as if becalmed until I call them forth again," replied Lien placidly.

Avanasy had to struggle to keep his jaw from falling open. "You can do such a thing?"

Lien smiled faintly. "How is it you think I've eluded the emperor's navy and the Nine Elders all these years? This has been all my study, the full focus of my art." His eyes were calm as he spoke, but his voice was grim. "I pay, and I pay heavily, but I have what I want."

"Master Lien," said Avanasy, and Ingrid heard the awe in his voice, "you should be one of the Nine Elders."

"You would not wish such a fate on me if you knew what you spoke of." He wearily waved Avanasy's words away.

A tremor of uncertainty ran through Ingrid. Whatever it was he did, it clearly cost him some effort. How much more did Lien have to give? Would they be able to make it out of these twisting mists?

But if Lien felt any such doubts, he did not show them. He only faced forward, and began to chant. It was a high, thin sound, oddly loud in the silent world that surrounded them. It chilled Ingrid, and filled her with disquiet, although she could not have said why.

Then, faintly, blessedly, a sound touched her ear. A distant rushing, like the sound of the sea, or a crowd of voices heard from a long way off.

The sound of the living world. It could not be anything else.

Slowly, the mist darkened. The single rushing noise separated into distinct sounds. Ingrid could make out the sound of wind in the trees, a crackle, like dust falling, and the sharp sound of fires burning.

Lien held out his hand to Medeoan. She took it, and held out hers to Avanasy. Avanasy caught up Ingrid's hand in his firm, familiar grip, and took the empress's hand.

Lien walked forward. Disdainful of the wooden sides of the ship, he strode straight ahead. Ingrid closed her eyes and let herself be pulled along, following the tug of Avanasy's hand.

Ingrid's shoes touched solid ground, and the cool air around her turned warm. She breathed out a sigh of relief, and opened her eyes.

And she looked out to see the charred remains of a scraggly forest and a rocky hillside that looked down onto a ravine filled with blackened stone and plumes of gray smoke. The myriad, terrible scents of burning assailed her nose. She clapped her hand against her mouth and stumbled backward, and fell.

A man groaned, and Ingrid suppressed a scream. A mound of ash moved, and was not ash, but a man, a man burnt black and red who looked up at her with startlingly blue eyes.

"Vyshemir's knife! Peshek!" cried Avanasy, falling to his knees and raising a cloud of ash.

Peshek? Ingrid's mind refused to compass it for a moment. This ruined man was Peshek?

The ruined man reached out to Avanasy, his ravaged throat struggling to croak out a few sounds.

"No, Peshek, no." Avanasy's own voice cracked. "Lie still, lie still. I'll help you, but you must . . ."

"There you are," said a new voice. "I've been waiting."

Ingrid scrambled to her feet. Avanasy rose more slowly, as a man's form emerged from the shadows.

He was lean and brown. Ashes turned his bare feet gray, and more ash settled in his braided hair.

Avanasy moved at once to stand in front of Medeoan and Ingrid.

"Who are you?" he demanded.

Medeoan stepped around him, her eyes wide. "Yamuna."

The lean man bowed, palms over his eyes, with an air of complete mockery made more terrible by the destruction around them, and by Peshek still as death at their feet. Ingrid saw that his hands were mismatched. One of them was smooth and strong, the hand of a much younger man.

"I am flattered so illustrious a one would recognize so humble a servant as myself." Yamuna straightened up. "Your husband has sought long and hard for you, Majesty, but I fear you are a little late in returning." He smiled toward the cloud of smoke that hung in the distance. Ingrid could smell nothing but burning, and her throat itched from the smoke and ash they had to breathe even here.

Medeoan went white. She swayed for a bare instant, and murmured a single word. "Kacha."

Yamuna smiled. "Yes, poor young Kacha. The Nine Elders were more frightened by his maneuvers than he realized, and played their highest card against him."

"Highest . . ."

"No," croaked Lien. "No."

"Yes, old man," said Yamuna with mock solemnity. They chose to summon one of the four immortal guardians, and the one they selected was the Phoenix."

"The Phoenix?" stammered Medeoan. "They brought the Firebird into the world?"

"And it is not pleased with your realm." Yamuna pursed his lips and shook his head at the smoke, even as his dark eyes gleamed.

"You did this." Medeoan clenched her fists. "Your magic allowed all this!"

"So it did," agreed Yamuna. "And now, my magic will allow me to make an end of you, as well as your man here." He held up a bottle of scarlet glass, and a chill swept across Medeoan's skin. She glanced at Avanasy's face, and saw how he groped for a spell, for a defense against whatever magic was to come. Yamuna raised his arm. Medeoan lifted her hands, as did Lien.

Ingrid leapt. She tackled Yamuna with all her weight and they fell together. She rolled over, coming up on top of the skinny old man, clutching the wrist of his impossibly young hand in both of hers. He snarled and struggled, but she hung grimly on. His fingers loosened from around the bottle, and it fell.

It dropped into Avanasy's outstretched hand. Avanasy stumbled forward, handing it to Lien, who received it quickly. Yamuna screamed and Ingrid screamed, but she had been distracted and he threw her off, causing her to hit the ground hard and take in a lungful of ash. Choking and sputtering, she forced herself to her feet. Yamuna was already standing. Avanasy snatched up a pike that lay beside a dead man. Ingrid heard the hiss as the hot metal touched his flesh, and now he too screamed, but he wheeled around. Avanasy charged forward, and the pike spit flesh and bone and heart.

Yamuna fell without a sound.

Avanasy dropped the pike and stood over the body, panting for a long moment. Ingrid moved to his side, as did Medeoan, but he did not seem aware of them. Ingrid's lungs and eyes burned, and she knew he felt the same, but she also knew that his heat did not only come from outside. It came from the rage that would not be quieted by the death of this enemy. This man's whole world should burn, for what he had done, was doing to Peshek, and Medeoan, and himself, and Isavalta, and to her, to Ingrid.

"There is no time for this, Master Avanasy," said Lien's voice, sounding far sharper than Ingrid had yet heard it.

They all turned, and Ingrid saw thunder and fear in Lien's face.

"The Phoenix has been unleashed. We must get away from here at once."

"No!" cried Medeoan before Avanasy could speak a word. "Master Lien, if this is the Firebird, it flies in Isavalta. I cannot leave my people . . ."

"There is nothing you can do!" Lien shouted in reply. "It is one of the four immortal guardians. It will fly until it has destroyed Hung Tse's enemies." He swallowed hard. His face had gone deathly pale. "I must return home. I must warn Cai Yun . . ."

"Master." Avanasy's wounded hand curled up.. "Do not lose your way."

"You don't understand." Lien pulled himself roughly from Avanasy's grasp. "The Phoenix will seek out Hung Tse's enemies. After Isavalta, who is a greater enemy than myself? Than my niece who aids my vengeance out of loyalty? I must get her to safety . . ."

What little color she had faded from the empress's cheeks. "No," whispered Medeoan. She knotted her fists and gritted her teeth hard.

Avanasy turned to say something to the empress, but Ingrid did not hear it. Her ears were ringing and her eyes were filled up with memory—the house of bones on its taloned legs, the famine-thin hag with her black iron teeth, the growling dogs, the watching cat. Ingrid's hand flew to her mouth. She began to tremble. Despite the golden heat radiating from overhead, the world about her had gone suddenly cold, and she could do nothing but shiver.

"Ingrid, what is it?" Avanasy stretched his hand out toward her.

"The . . . Old Witch," gasped Ingrid from between her fingers. "Oh, God, oh, Mary, she told me. She told me she knew how to cage the Firebird."

Avanasy gaped. "She said this?"

Ingrid nodded, pressing her hand against her mouth as if she were about to be sick. Gently, Avanasy urged her to sit. She thumped clumsily onto the ground, raising up a cloud of soot, unable to look anywhere but straight ahead, unable to see anything but Baba Yaga.

"You have spoken with the Bony-Legged Witch?" said Medeoan, sounding half angry, half disbelieving.

Again, Ingrid nodded. "She . . . called me to her. She has something she wants me to do. She said . . . she said that I would come to her a third time, that I would beg to be allowed to do this thing, because only she knew how to cage the Firebird."

"Is this true?" the empress demanded of Avanasy.

"Yes." Avanasy dropped to one knee at Ingrid's side. "Oh, Ingrid, why did you not tell me?"

Ingrid let her hand fall into her lap. "I meant to. At first,

I didn't want to add to your worries. Then, so much was happening . . ." She gestured vaguely at Lien and the empress. "As foolish as it sounds, I forgot."

"No. It is not foolish. It is easy to forget what happens in the Land of Death and Spirit. It is as when we walk in dreams." He took her hand. "Do not reproach yourself."

"What did the Old Witch want of you?" asked Medeoan flatly.

Ingrid shook her head. "I'm not sure. I can't remember clearly. Something that had been stolen from her . . ." She tried to concentrate, but the memories slipped through her mind's fingers like water. "I don't know anymore. I'm sorry."

"It doesn't matter," said Avanasy. "We know the knowledge exists. We will seek it out."

"None of this matters," said Lien, his cold voice cutting across whatever else might be said. "It is too late. The Phoenix has flown ahead of us. It has already burned the army of Isavalta."

Ingrid thought Medeoan was going to faint. The empress swayed on her feet, as white as the mists around their ship.

Avanasy gripped the empress's hand. "We can still save Isavalta. We will . . ."

"You will stay to die!" shouted Lien. "Do you not hear me? The Phoenix will not permit your empire to survive. Your capital may already be on fire, you can't know. We cannot wait here for you to come to your senses. I will not leave my child . . . my niece to its judgment."

"How do I find the Old Witch?" Ingrid asked, putting out one hand to push herself to her feet.

Avanasy covered her hand with his free one. "Ingrid, no. I can't let you do this. I don't know what going alone into the Silent Lands will do to you. I have not had time to understand the whole of your . . . divided state. If you attempt this," Avanasy's voice dropped to an urgent whisper, "you may not be able to return to the mortal world. I will go and bargain with the Old Witch."

"With what?" said Ingrid. "I'm the one she wants. What else do you have to give her?"

She knew nothing of Isavalta, except for some coastline

and one fishing village. She had no obligations there, no family, except Avanasy, and Avanasy said she did not need to do this thing, that another way could be found. She could let that happen. She did not need to go back to that place, to face that . . . hag again. She did not need to acknowledge the split in herself before Avanasy could heal her. It did not have to happen.

Yet, even as she told herself that as firmly as she could, she knew she lied. She knew what wildfires were. She had seen them on the mainland, the aftereffects of the loggers' efforts. She had seen smoke blackening the sky and smelled the choking stench. She had heard the screams.

No, she knew nothing of Isavalta, but she knew very well what had been visited upon the Isavaltans.

"There is no other way, Avanasy," said the empress.

Avanasy's face creased, at first, Ingrid thought, from anger, but then she knew it was from the effort to hold that anger back. "You would order this from one who is not even subject to you?"

The empress did not flinch at this question. "I am not ordering her, she is freely offering."

"Do I have to take this off?" Ingrid asked, touching the braid on her wrist. "Or can I just . . . go as I am?"

Avanasy wanted to protest. He wanted to rage, Ingrid was sure of it, but she also saw how terribly he knew that there was no other choice. Whatever must be done to cage the Firebird, it would surely involve magic, and strong magic at that. Even she could see that much. If he drained himself white to gain the secret of this working, the empress would be left alone to do what must be done afterward, and that could not be allowed either.

"No," he said sorrowfully. "If the Old Witch wants you, she will take you. All you need to do is speak her name. Do not remove the braid. It will, I think, lessen the disorientation and difficulty you will have as you move through the Silent Lands." His fingers trailed gently around her wrist. "And as with the ring, the binding of the spell will help bring you back to me."

"I will set vigil for you myself," announced Lien. "If you can do this thing, you will be saving my family's lives."

"Well, then." Ingrid faced Avanasy and smoothed down her apron. "I'd best get on with it, hadn't I?"

But Avanasy's eyes glistened brightly. He grasped both of Ingrid's hands and drew them up close to his chest. She could feel his heart beating hard and frightened, even underneath his woolen coat. "Listen to me, Ingrid. Courtesy is all where you are going. Do not fail to be polite, to anyone or anything. Accept nothing until you know the conditions under which it is given. Refuse nothing that is freely given, and trust your heart over your eyes."

"I'll remember," she told him gravely.

"I love you."

"I'll remember that as well." She kissed him softly, feeling afresh how the warmth of his mouth was like no other heat there could be. Not even the fire still smoldering around her could burn her so deeply.

Then, she let go of his hands and walked forward three short steps. She faced the blackened forest. The sooty wind teased at her disheveled hair.

"Baba Yaga!" she cried out, as if she stood at the back door of her father's house calling one of her little siblings in for supper. "I know you're out there! I'll do what you want if you'll tell me how to cage the Firebird. Do you hear me, Baba Yaga?"

There was no transition. Ingrid was simply elsewhere and she did not understand how it could be so. Bewildered, she stared about her, and her confusion only deepened.

This was not the Land of Death and Spirit as she had seen it before. These were not the dense pine forests lit by the directionless glow. These were ordinary pine trees hedged by fern and bramble. Birds called to one another overhead and mosquitoes whined uncomfortably near. High summer had passed, and the green leaves of the underbrush paled toward autumn's yellow. The wind smelled of pine resin and fresh water, and she knew where she was.

She was home. This was Sand Island. She was sure of it. If she headed south, she would come to her family's house.

How had she come to be home so suddenly? What had gone wrong?

Ingrid didn't know what to do. She had expected the fairy land, and the insistent tugging telling her where to go. Not to be home, not to be alone.

Because no other idea came to her, she hiked up her skirts and trudged southward. She moved only because she could not stand still in the middle of the woods. Her mind was so awhirl with astonishment, she had no clear idea whether she thought movement itself could bring her answers, or whether it was merely an instinctual reaction to get clear of the mosquitoes the frost had not yet come to kill.

In the distance, she heard someone humming a familiar tune. Ingrid broke into a run, shoving aside the brush and brambles with her elbows. There, in a small clearing, stood Grace, smiling her sunny smile and breaking dead branches into kindling.

"Grace!" cried Ingrid, running up to her sister's side.

Grace turned and looked at her mildly, with no surprise or ruffling of her expression at all. "Hello, Ingrid. What are you doing here?"

"Grace, I'm home," Ingrid panted. "I'm back."

"Why?"

"Wh . . . why?" Ingrid could only stammer in surprise.

"Yes, why?"

Ingrid stared at her sister. Grace just smiled, the careless smile that Ingrid knew so well.

Why am I here? Ingrid rubbed her forehead. The sun warmed her shoulders. The scents and sights she had known all her life surrounded her. She had been away, she knew that, and there had been good reason, but now . . . now . . .

"I came home," she said uncertainly.

"Well, good," said Grace. "You can help me carry this." She handed Ingrid a bundle of kindling wood.

"Yes, all right." Ingrid's hands closed around the deadwood. It smelled of earth and bark and pricked her hands. She tucked the bundle under one arm. Grace hoisted her own bundle on her shoulder and took Ingrid's hand. She had forgotten what her sister's touch felt like, that warm, light palm. She was a grown woman, but walking with Grace still felt like walking with a child, cheerful, careless, enjoying the moment.

Grace swung their arms, and began to sing.

> *"An old man come courtin' me, fa-la-la-loodle!*
> *An old man come courtin' me, hi-derry-down!"*

Ingrid grinned. They had sung this one together so often, she joined in instantly.

> *"An old man come a-courtin' me, all for to marry me,*
> *Maids when you're young, never wed an old man!"*

Grace began to giggle, and Ingrid could not help herself. She began to laugh as well. It was so good here, so simple, walking with her sister, all forgiven, heading for home and hearth with nothing more complicated than a bundle of firewood to carry.

> *"It's when that we went to church, fa-la-la-loodle . . ."*

Ingrid faltered for a moment. What had needed to be forgiven? What had she done?

"Look." Grace broke off the song. "There's Leo."

Leo stood beneath a birch tree, his scythe raised. Fresh-cut brush lay in heaps at his feet.

"Be careful!" Ingrid cried at once, although she didn't know why.

Leo swung the scythe down, it tore through the tangle of brush and saplings, laying them flat on the ground.

"So, you've turned up at last, have you?" he said, bringing the scythe around again. "I don't suppose you remembered to think of your family while you were gone?"

No, she hadn't. She had been too busy, with . . . all that needed doing. She had been . . . on the mainland? In Bayfield? Farther? Had she gone to Chicago? Ingrid shook her head. It was wrong to return without a gift, that much was clear. But what did she have? She had left so much behind already.

She groped in her apron pocket, and brought out a spear tip. She did not remember placing it there, but it didn't matter. Leo would like this.

"Here, Leo," she said, extending it. "This is for you."

He shouldered the scythe and took the spear tip. He held it up to the light as if it was a coin of dubious quality.

"Well, all right then," he said, pocketing the shining piece of metal. "Better get on, the both of you. Mama's waiting." He jerked his thumb over his shoulder in the direction of home.

Grace took Ingrid's hand again. "That was a good gift, sister."

"Yes." Ingrid fell into step beside her. She felt lighter and emptier at the same time. But she was happy. She was walking and singing with her sister. She was going home.

"It's when we were walkin' home, fa-la-la-loodle!
It's when we were walkin' home, hi-derry-down!
It's when we were walkin' home, he let me walk alone.
Maids when you're young, never wed an old man!"

"Look," said Grace suddenly. "There's Papa."

Ingrid looked, and there was Papa standing in the clearing with his gun. A rustling filled the long, blanched grasses and Papa aimed and shot, the gun sounding horribly loud in the still afternoon.

What a strange time to be hunting rabbits, thought Ingrid, perplexed. *Rabbits are all underground in the middle of the day.*

"What are you hunting, Papa?" she asked.

Papa cracked open his shot gun and reloaded the breech. "What's been lost," he said tersely. "What are you hunting, young woman?"

"What's been stolen," answered Ingrid promptly. *But why? What does that mean?*

Papa just grunted and sighted along the barrel of his shotgun again. "And what have you brought home for your father?"

Ingrid dug in her other apron pocket. This time, she brought out a tiny golden statue of a long-tailed bird in flight.

"Here, Papa." She handed it to him carefully, suddenly afraid she might drop the precious thing. She could not lose this. It was precious, but she didn't know why, or where it had come from, or how it had come to be part of her.

Part of me? This is part of me?

Papa snatched the golden icon off her palm and turned it over, examining its workmanship before he tucked it into his shirt pocket. "I suppose that'll do," he grunted, not looking at them, but staring off across the clearing. "Get along, both of you. Mama's waiting."

Grace took her hand and led her away, even as the grasses began to rustle again, and another shot exploded through the warm air.

"Grace," said Ingrid as her sister took her hand again, "what's happening?"

"We're going to see Mama," said Grace with a grin. This time, her teeth, bared as she smiled, seemed unaccountably sharp.

"Its when that we went to bed, fa-la-la-loodle!
It's when that we went to bed, hi-derry-down!
It's when that we went to bed, he lay as if he were dead.
Maids when you're young, never wed an old man!"

But this time Ingrid did not join in. She felt too hollow for singing. Where was she? She was with Leo, and with Papa, and with Grace, but what was with herself? She hunted what had been stolen, but she was led away to Mama. How was she to look for it if she was being led to Mama?

"Look," said Grace. "There's Mama."

Ingrid looked. She saw the back of their house, with the outbuildings and the chicken coop. Mama stood beside the big, iron laundry kettle, stirring it with the long, well-worn paddle. But no steam rose from the kettle. In the next moment, Ingrid saw why. No fire burned underneath the pot.

"Well, you're here at last," said Mama grimly. "Lay the fire, you two."

Ingrid knelt beside the kettle and laid down her bundle of wood. "Mama, why are you stirring before the fire's lit?"

"I'm keeping fresh a past that's gone missing," she answered. "Why are you wandering loose in the woods?"

"I'm looking for a heart that's been stolen," said Ingrid, laying out the wood to be ready for the fire. *Why? Why? I don't understand. Why am I saying these things? Why am I here?* She stared at the pile of sticks. *What is happening?*

"Light the fire, Ingrid," said Grace, sitting back on her haunches and grinning at Ingrid with her oddly pointed teeth.

Ingrid automatically reached in her pocket for matches, but her pocket was empty. "I can't," she said muzzily. "I must have given it away."

Grace shook her head and clucked her tongue. Above them, Mama stirred the kettle relentlessly. The liquid inside sloshed, making the sides of the great kettle ring.

"You should not have given so much," Mama grumbled. "I dare say you didn't even bring anything for your poor mother."

Ingrid searched her pockets, unaccountably frightened, but there was nothing to be found.

"I'm sorry," she stammered. "Really. I didn't mean . . ."

"Oh, Ingrid," sighed Grace. "Whatever are we going to do with you? You have so much, and know so little of anything you carry. You'll waste it all on trivialities, and never know what you could have been."

"Nothing else for it, then," muttered Mama.

"No, I'm afraid not." Grace's eyes glinted. She snapped her fingers, and a fire sprang to life underneath the kettle. But the fire wasn't . . . right. It should have burned red and gold. Ingrid was sure of it. Grace's fire burned bright green. She had seen such light elsewhere. Where? It was important. Where had she seen that light?

"In you get," said Grace cheerfully.

"What?" Ingrid scrambled to her feet, her heart pounding hard.

"If you've nothing else to give, you must give yourself." Mama's paddle stirred the thick, black liquid in steady, even strokes. It had already begun to steam. "In you get." She nodded toward the kettle.

"No! Mama, Grace, no!" Ingrid backed away. She'd die in that darkness, she'd drown. She'd lose what little of herself she had left, the tiny spark inside her would be snuffed out. She knew it, and she didn't know what else to do.

"Nothing else for it," rumbled Papa's voice behind her. Ingrid swung around. Papa emerged from the woods, his gun tucked casually under his arm, and a brace of birds slung over his shoulder. Leo walked beside him, his scythe held in both hands ready to swing up. "You didn't bring enough."

"You never did," said Mama to the black liquid. "Tries, and tries, and it's never enough for her, is it? Would have been enough for anyone else, but not for her, oh no. Can't let go, can't let it be enough, ever. Well, now you're called on to give the last, my girl."

"You've always offered that much, but no one's ever taken you up on it, have they?" Grace's eyes were very green, and slanted in her face.

Not right. Too much wrong here. She stared around at Mama, at Papa, at Leo. Then she saw the blade of Leo's scythe wasn't steel. It was stone, stained dark with something that was not tree resin.

"Why are you doing this?" she cried. "*Why?*"

"Because you won't stop," said Leo, stepping closer.

"Because you can't be stopped." Papa stepped away from Leo, blocking Ingrid's path.

"Because there are limits to any power," said Mama without breaking the pace of her endless stirring.

"Because you've been divided and remade into something new," said Grace pleasantly. "Unnatural thing that you are, you cannot be held back in any of the usual ways, as you fall under none of the usual provinces. She knew that. Now." Grace's eyes shone green with the same light that came from the strange fire under Mama's kettle. "In you get."

She? She? Ingrid backed away, but there was nowhere to go. Grace, strangely altered as she was, stood behind her. The rest of her family surrounded her, pressed against her, herding her toward the great, dark steaming kettle.

"Still afraid."

"In the end always afraid. So ready to give, until the end, then there is only fear."

"No!" shouted a new voice. Ingrid jerked her head around.

Everett Lederle, his blue Union Army cap askew on his head and his clasp knife open in his hand. "Ingrid, here! Run!"

"Everett!" Ingrid cried, and leapt toward him, pushing past her family in one burst of speed until she was beside him, her arms thrown around his neck in gratitude. "Mary Mother of God, Everett. How did you know?"

"Don't worry about it." Everett wrapped one arm around her waist. He brandished his knife at her family, who stood clustered around Mama's kettle. The green light gleamed in their eyes and caught the smooth stone of Leo's scythe blade. "I've got you safe now. None of them will touch you while you're with me."

But why should they stay back? Ingrid swallowed and pulled away just a little. Leo had his scythe, and Papa had a gun. All Everett had was his tiny knife. *Why stay away?*

"Everett, what's happening?"

"I don't know. We just need to get out of here. We'll figure it out later." He grasped her hand and tugged her toward the house. "Come on."

But Ingrid held her ground. "Everett, I have to find . . . There's something stolen and I have to find it."

"I know, I know." He patted her hand. "But not here, Ingrid. You're not safe. We have to get away."

Grace's eyes glowed and she stepped forward. "Yes, run away, Ingrid. Do." Her teeth, yellow now, and shining like her eyes, snapped.

"Take her away from here, ungrateful girl," muttered Mama, stirring, constantly stirring. "Get her out of my sight."

"Yes. Do." Now Leo took a step forward, hefting his strange, stained, stone scythe.

"Ingrid, please," said Everett, retreating before Leo's fierce grin, pulling her back toward the safety of the house. "Let's go!"

Papa lifted his gun.

She should run, she knew it. The ones who faced her were dangerous. She knew that with all her heart. Everett was safe. He would protect her and keep her close, as he had always sought to do. Why didn't she run? What held her here?

Trust your heart over your eyes, said a voice in her memory. Whose voice? What memory? She didn't know. Her head swam. Papa put his gun to his shoulder. Everett yanked on her hand, almost pulling her off her feet. He wanted to save her, to keep her close, to keep her from drowning in Mama's kettle, that was somehow the source of all this danger. She had been led here, and now she was being torn away from here by these people who were not quite her family. But Everett was Everett still. Wasn't he?

Ingrid looked up into Everett's eyes. They were blue as she remembered. His grip was as strong as she had always known it would be.

The knife he carried had a blade of stone like Leo's scythe.

"Please, Ingrid," he said desperately. "There's no more time! Let me get you out of here!"

"No more time," repeated Ingrid.

And she ran.

She tore herself from Everett's grip and she charged toward her family. She knocked Papa's gun away. Leo's scythe swished past her. Grace stretched out clawed hands, and Mama lifted her paddle, but Ingrid did not break her stride. She dove forward, flinging herself headlong into the steaming kettle.

Ingrid fell into darkness. Nothing touched her, no heat, no cold, no air, no light. She fell, flailing her limbs, and there was no light above or below, only emptiness and falling as in a nightmare, but she did not wake. She screamed, but the sound went nowhere, and still she fell.

Just as she thought for sure she must faint, the fall was done. There was no sensation of landing, just of ceasing to fall. She stood, she thought. There seemed to be some uneven surface underfoot, and she seemed to be whole and unhurt, but she could see nothing. Blackness as thick as blindness surrounded her.

"So," said a voice Ingrid was sure she should have known. "Not afraid enough."

Two eyes opened in the darkness. They were huge and green and slanted. Animal's eyes, feral and cunning. Grace's eyes as Ingrid had last seen them in the face of the apparition who had been Grace and yet could not have been.

Her throat closed, and Ingrid swallowed hard.

"You cannot see, little woman?" inquired the voice. "How very rude of me."

There was a soft pop, as if someone had snapped their fingers. Green fire sprang up before Ingrid. She blinked hard and stumbled backward.

When she could look again, she saw a gigantic fox loung-ing on the other side of the fire. The light in her eyes was the same light that filled the green flames that burned without fuel between them. All of Ingrid's memories came back in a single wave, of where she had seen this green light before, of who she was and why she had come to this strange place, and how this must be the Silent Lands, and who waited on the other shore for her.

"I beg your pardon." Ingrid's voice shook. The Vixen's mouth fell open, laughing. Her rank scent filled the place where Ingrid stood. The green fire illuminated only a small space around them. She thought this might be a cave, but she could not be sure. "I did not mean to intrude, I only . . ."

"I know what you want, little woman." The Vixen nodded her head toward Ingrid's feet. "And you have won it. I give it to you freely."

Ingrid looked down. At her feet, in a small hollow of rough stone, gleamed a golden ball about the size of Ingrid's fist. She picked it up, marveling at its great weight and cool smooth skin as it lay in her hand.

She was looking for what had been stolen. She was look-ing for a heart that had been taken. She knew that, although she did not fully understand how. In that same way of un-derstanding, she knew this golden ball held what she needed.

"Why . . ." she began, and then she stopped. Questions might be dangerous here. They might be considered rude. The answers might have conditions she could not meet.

"Why did I take it?" The Vixen cocked her head. "Why do I give it back now?" She lifted one great paw and scratched her chin thoughtfully. "Perhaps one day when the Old Witch had gone about some errand, she left her heart behind, as she is wont to do from time to time. Perhaps someone crept into her window and stole it then. Perhaps they meant it as a joke, or perhaps they meant it in earnest, for without her heart, without knowing who held it or what they might do with it, how could the Old Witch go about her business? How could she even dare to leave the safety of her house?" The Vixen's eyes gleamed dangerously. "For she has much power and many enemies, the Old Witch does."

Ingrid swallowed again, and clutched the golden ball close to her chest.

"But perhaps there was a little man who aspired to divinity and I was asked by one whom I'm glad to have owe me a favor to stop his plans." The Vixen grinned. "Perhaps I saw the future and it amused me to help it come about. Perhaps I just saw an opportunity to anger the Old Witch. It could be all these things, or none of them." Her teeth were white, and very sharp. "What would you give to know the answer to that riddle, little woman?"

Courtesy is all where you are going. Avanasy had said that to her. How could she have forgotten, even for an instant? Ingrid pushed the guilt away. This was not the time.

"Thank you for your hospitality," she said, dropping a curtsey to the Vixen. "I am very much afraid that it is time for me to go."

"Perhaps," laughed the Vixen, swishing her tail back and forth. "Take care of what you've been given, little woman, and take care of your daughter while you can."

"I . . ." began Ingrid. But she stopped. She meant to say, "I have no daughter," but standing knee-deep in memories freshly brought back to her, she realized she could not remember when her time had last come. So much had been happening, she had completely lost track of her days.

Was she carrying Avanasy's child? She could well be. One hand went automatically to her belly.

The Vixen threw back her head and let out a snarling, growling laugh that went straight through to Ingrid's bones. "Go, little woman, get away with you, before I decide perhaps I'd like to keep you here." Eyes and teeth flashed in the light of the green flames. "Or your daughter."

Grabbing up her hems, Ingrid turned and ran. The Vixen's growling laugh followed fast behind her, and she had no thought but to get away from it. She stumbled through the darkness, the golden ball held tight to her bosom. Gradually, she saw light up ahead; it was strange and diffuse, and certainly not daylight, but she followed it anyway, because she had no other guide.

At last, Ingrid stumbled out into the odd, pale light of the Land of Death and Spirit. Ahead of her lay a green meadow surrounded by the dark piney woods she remembered. Behind her rose a smooth green hill like a bubble from a pot of water. A single thorn tree grew from its crown, spreading its branches up to the sunless sky. She knew this place. She had been here before.

Ingrid saw no movement from the dark cave mouth from which she emerged, but she hurried on toward the piney woods anyway.

The only question being, which way do I go? She looked around for the river, for her other self, and saw only the dark tree trunks in every direction.

Something pushed at her palm. Ingrid stared at her hand where it held the golden ball. The ball stirred against her and pushed outward, as if seeking release.

Slowly, uncertainly, Ingrid set the ball onto the grass. It glinted for a moment in the pale, greenish light, and then it began to roll toward the woods. With nothing else to do, Ingrid followed.

She followed the ball into the darkness that gathered under the pine trees. The thick carpet of needles should have crunched underfoot, but did not. She followed the ball across the narrow brook that ran silently over the rounded stones that lined its bed. The water did not wet her shoes or the trailing hem of her skirt.

She followed until the trees turned from pine to oaks and maples, and she saw the lone, crooked birch tree that spread its branches as if to bar her way. The golden ball rolled unhesitatingly beneath it, and the branches sagged, defeated, to let Ingrid past.

Ahead stood the fence mended with bones. The cat perched on top of it, ears alert. The bone gate swung open for the golden ball, and Ingrid followed. She was owed for this and that knowledge removed her fear as she stood in the torn and savaged yard before the house on its scarred and taloned legs, turning and with each step gouging up great chunks of mud.

The golden ball stopped and Ingrid waited, her hands folded neatly over her apron. Slowly, the house stopped its restless turning and knelt so that its splintered steps touched the ground and its door could fall open.

Baba Yaga stood in the doorway, leaning on her stained pestle. Eagerly, the golden ball skipped up the steps and hopped into her hand. Baba Yaga caught it firmly in one skinny claw. With the other, she rapped on it with her knuckles. The gold cracked open and fell away. Inside lay an egg, smooth and white and gleaming. Baba Yaga cracked that too. The white spilled away leaving something red and blue and pulsing in her crabbed hand. Baba Yaga looked at the thing hungrily for a moment, then tucked it inside her tattered black robe, as if she were tucking away a full purse or a precious locket.

When she drew out her hand again, Baba Yaga smiled, a rictus grin that exposed all her black iron teeth. Ingrid shuddered but held her ground. The Old Witch set aside her pestle, and did a thing Ingrid had never seen her do before. She walked down the steps of her house.

As she came nearer, bone-thin and bent, her eyes nearly as hollow as a ghost's, Ingrid felt her nerve fail her. Her knees began to shake and she wanted more than anything to run away, but she could not. Baba Yaga held her pinned with her dark gaze.

The Old Witch stood before her now. Ingrid should have been able to feel her breath, but could not. She smelled a dry, musty scent, like old dust, like bones.

In a single, swift motion, Baba Yaga kissed Ingrid on the mouth. Ingrid staggered back, only just keeping her balance. Her mouth filled with the tang of cold iron.

And she knew how to cage the Firebird. She knew it like she knew her own name. She could forget everything else, and she would remember this, she was sure of it.

Ingrid thought to stammer out her thanks, but one glance from Baba Yaga silenced her utterly.

"You have been paid your price, now go. I have business to which I must attend." There was a quality in those words that made Ingrid shiver. She was about to speak up to say she did not know which way to go, but the world around her was already fading. She did not feel herself being dragged, so much as all that was around her seemed to be rushing away, wrinkling, like a cloth pulled from a table. She screamed, because she feared another long fall into darkness.

Ingrid woke.

Chapter Twenty

She might not have moved at all. She was in the burned forest on the hillside. Lien knelt beside Peshek's wracked body, but . . . Ingrid blinked and looked again. Peshek was ruined no more. His skin was red and blistered, but no longer blackened. His breath did not rattle in his chest as he lay on the scant bed of coats that had been spread for him. He would live. She could tell that in an instant. Her first sight returned to the world was that Peshek would live.

"Magic."

"And neatly done," replied Lien. Ingrid jumped. She had not realized she had spoken aloud. "She is powerful, your empress."

Ingrid's first instinct was to say, "She's not mine," but she stopped those words. "Where are they?"

"I sent them down," he nodded toward the pass where the smoke still hung heavy in the air, "to see if any lived yet there."

Ingrid swallowed hard. "I must find them." Her blood rushed in her veins, and she knew the sensation to be from the knowledge the Old Witch had given her. She must pass it on and quickly. This was not a secret she was meant to hold.

"Then we will go." Lien stood. "You have your answers?"

"I do." Despite the need for movement that sang inside her, she glanced down at Peshek where he lay, dead to the world. "Shouldn't you stay . . ."

"All that can be done for him has been. We will return." His voice was stone. He was making his choice. He could not worry about Peshek, because his niece was in a danger he knew better than any of them. Ingrid wanted to berate him, but could not. She just tucked up her hems in her waistband and started down the hillside toward the center of the devastation.

It was a long walk. The wind blew hot and heavy with ash. It was difficult to breathe without coughing. The stones were black with ash. Ingrid's eyes and lungs burned, but she kept slogging forward, the strength of the secret she carried urging her onward. Lien paced quietly beside her, and she was very glad for the presence of another being.

Then, at last, they crested the rise, and looked down on the real horror.

The army had been caught in the blaze with nowhere to flee. Men and beasts had died where they stood, and now were nothing but char and black sticks that once were bones. The stench was unspeakable. Ingrid's hand went immediately to her face, and she had to choke down her bile.

"Come, mistress," said Lien, but even his voice shook. "Come. We must keep going."

And they did. They waded through the ash and ruin. Ingrid blocked her mouth and nose with her apron held crumpled in both hands. It brought only a small measure of relief. Heat nibbled at her skin and horror nibbled at her mind.

After what felt like hours, they were at last able to see Avanasy and the empress, the only bits of color in a world gone black and gray with death. They stood near the far edge of the worst of the destruction. This must have been the head of the procession. Medeoan looked down at something, frozen, unmoving. As they came closer, Ingrid could make out a hand, an arm, sticking grotesquely out of the soot and char that had once been a man. It was as burnt and as black as all the rest of the dead Ingrid had tried not to see, but Medeoan seemed transfixed. She did not look up as Ingrid and Lien drew near enough to see the gleam of a golden ring on the dead hand, which must have been what attracted Medeoan's eye to it in the first place.

"I believe," murmured Lien, "the empress has found her husband."

"So." Medeoan spoke to the blackened limb, and her voice was as cold and brittle as glass. "This is where you've ended. Your plan worked and brought war to Isavalta. Are you happy? Are you pleased with how well you've succeeded?"

Her skin showed white where tears had washed the ash and grime away from her face. "Did you know where I was? Did you even care? Did you spare me a single thought once I was no longer an obstacle?" Her voice rose and sharpened, becoming at last a scream. "I loved you! I gave over an empire to you and you gave me nothing but vicious, vicious lies!"

Medeoan lifted her robe of blackened silk and aimed a swift and vicious kick at the pathetic remains, shattering them into flakes of ash. Then she turned away, and Avanasy put his hand on her shoulder.

Ingrid found a small piece of herself that had not been numbed by her smoldering surroundings and felt pity for the young woman. To be so betrayed . . . could even what she saw now be worse than that?

At last, the sound of their approach reached Avanasy. He looked around quickly, and when he saw Ingrid his face lit up with a joy incongruous to see in the midst of this burned world, but even so, her heart answered with an equal joy.

"I knew you would find your way!" he cried as he wrapped his arms around her, covering her soot-smudged face with his kisses. "I knew, I always knew. Oh, Ingrid . . ." They kissed, long and deep then, and when he pulled away, Avanasy looked startled.

"Did the Old Witch give you what we need?"

Medeoan had come up behind Avanasy, her face cold as stone. Whether it was from the devastation of her people, or from what she had just seen between Ingrid and Avanasy, Ingrid could not tell.

"Yes," Avanasy answered for her, his voice thick with wonder. "Yes, she did, and Ingrid has given it to me."

"I would have warned you, if you had given me a moment," she said, an odd gaiety taking hold in her now that her burden was lifted and Avanasy was before her, whole and sound.

"What must we do?" demanded the empress. "How do we begin?"

Avanasy's eyes flicked back and forth, as if he were drawing out some deep memory. "We need a forge, or a crucible. We need gold and blood to shape the cage, and . . ." He froze and, under his coating of grime, he paled. "Mortal breath."

Medeoan bowed her head. "Of course," she sighed. "It would be so, for such a thing, it would be so."

Despite the heat, Ingrid shivered. "I don't understand." She had carried the knowledge inside her, yes, but she had been a vessel only. It was Avanasy who knew what these things brought from the Silent Lands meant.

"Mortal breath." Avanasy was not looking at her. He was looking at Medeoan where she stood, turned away, her arms wrapped around herself. "Is the last breath. The dying breath."

Whatever Ingrid had thought to say died in her throat. Avanasy turned back toward her, his eyes soft.

"Oh, no, Avanasy. You won't . . . you wouldn't . . ."

He took both her hands. "Ingrid, I'm going to ask you to leave."

"No." She gripped him, hard. "No. Avanasy, listen to me. I'm with child. We're going to have a baby."

Avanasy's face went completely blank for a moment, as if he could not understand a word that she said. Then, he swept her into his arms and held her so closely she could scarcely breathe.

"Oh, Ingrid," he breathed against her shoulder. "Oh, my heart."

"You can't send me away now. You can't die." Because he would do it. She had no doubts. He would not let the empress be the one to sacrifice herself. He would never do such a thing.

"I will only do what I must, Ingrid," he said, but the soft words had all the force of an oath. Then he drew away, and looked her steadily in the eyes. "But you must be safe. That is what will sustain me. If I can think on you and our child without fear, I will live. But I cannot do that while this battle may touch you. I beg you, go home. Let Master Lien return you to Sand Island. Wait for me there. I will come for you as soon as I can."

"But the Firebird may be finished," she said, grasping at straws. "Perhaps this is all it was sent to do . . ."

"No, mistress," said Lien. Ingrid started. She had forgotten him entirely. "The Phoenix will not stop at so little when the whole of an empire has been arrayed against Hung Tse."

So little? Ingrid wanted to cry and sweep her hands out to encompass the devastation, but she could only stand and tremble for a moment while the implications of Lien's words sank into her.

"I cannot abandon this now," she said stubbornly. "I cannot abandon you now, Avanasy. I also have a stake in what happens here."

"Think of our child, Ingrid," whispered Avanasy. "Take our child to safety."

Ingrid's throat closed. "I came here to stay," she said, laying her hand across her belly. "This child belongs in Isavalta, with its father."

"Ingrid." Avanasy took both her hands and led her a little ways from the others. "Ingrid, listen to me," he whispered. "I never thought to father a child. I was told from the moment it became known I was a sorcerer that such a thing was difficult, that it had only happened a handful of times. I feel as if a star has been placed in my keeping. I . . ." His fingertips brushed her cheeks. "Isavalta may burn, Ingrid, if we are not successful. How can I let this star, this love, fall into that inferno? I am begging you, my love, take yourself, take our child, into safety. Let me be sure of that."

Ingrid kissed Avanasy then, all other doubts, all other fears drowned in the terrible knowledge that she might never see him again.

When she drew back, he wrapped his arms still more tightly around her and pulled her against him again. "I will come back to you," he said, and she felt his breath warm against her cheek as he spoke. "I swear it, by all that is in me, I swear it."

She nodded. She did not trust her voice. Avanasy released her and turned to Lien.

"Lien, will you return her to her home? You can then go back to Hung Tse and take your niece to safety, in case we fail."

"If you fail, there will in truth be no safety for us," replied Lien, looking stooped and aged. "But for what she has tried, I will carry Mistress Ingrid to her home."

"Can we go now?" asked Ingrid, her voice breaking, as

she had known it would. "I can't . . . I don't want . . ."

"Go, Ingrid," said Avanasy. "Go and let me know that you are safe."

She did not say good-bye. She did not look back. She turned on her heel and marched away through the ruin of what had been an army. Lien was beside her, and he took her hand. She did not resist him. He began to chant, to draw on his power, but all she could feel was the touch of Avanasy's lips against hers. All she could think of was the sound of his voice.

She barely noticed when the world faded away from around her.

Medeoan stood at Avanasy's side and tried not to be impatient. One moment, Ingrid and Lien walked through the ruins. The next moment, they were gone. It was not until the wind blew again and raised a whorl of hot ash where they had stood that Avanasy was able to turn away.

She saw the pain in his eyes, and had to resist the urge to shout at him. *What of Isavalta?* she wanted to cry. *What of me?*

But she saw the ravage his emotions had wrought on his face and held her tongue.

"Come, Majesty," said Avanasy roughly. "We must see what we can salvage."

The work was as grim, as hard and as filthy as she imagined it would be. The ash was greasy with grisly fat, making what debris there was slick. The stench filled her to the brim. She wrapped her sleeves around her hands to try to stave off the smoldering heat, but it did not work well. She would have blisters soon.

But she went on. All the ruination around her reminded her of Lien's words. This could be Vyshtavos. It could be Camaracost, or Biradost. It could be the whole of Isavalta from Tuukos to Miateshcha, wherever the Firebird decided to fly. She glanced at the horizon, again and again, terrified at the thought that she would see fresh plumes of smoke.

At last, she and Avanasy, filthy, wheezing, and burning with heat and with thirst, assembled what they had been able to find. Avanasy had ranged back along where they thought the baggage train had been and found the smith's cart with its small forge and anvil. They righted it as best they could, but could not move it, so they would perform their working beside it. Medeoan had guessed that Kacha would not be far from the war chest his army carried, and she was right. Some of the gold was only partially melted, and she was able to retrieve the misshapen bits of still-hot metal in the skirts of her robe.

They would need blood as well, but there was no shortage of ways to let that flow.

Behind them, the last rays of the sun shone over the hills. Medeoan imagined she could hear the distant rush of wings that was the Firebird.

Stop! she wanted to cry out. *If you want to fight Isavalta, you will come to me!*

She wiped her brow and tried to calm such thoughts. They would call the Firebird to them soon enough. Avanasy, his voice rough with thirst and ash, had told her what they must do. Pain made his face haggard, but he held himself still and strong.

He had split open a blackened cart rail and found that its center still burned red. Carefully, he took those coals and applied them to the heap of charcoal underneath the iron brazier that was what was left of the portable forge. Medeoan held her breath, and concentrated, and pushed the ruined world, the world where the Firebird roamed at will, away. In this world, her world, there was only Avanasy and the spreading flames, lapping at the half-burned splinters they used for kindling, and the charcoaled wood they had laid on top. In this world there was only the fire and Avanasy's injured hands.

Avanasy's hands that had held Ingrid's face so gently before he kissed her farewell.

Stop that. There is no place for that here. You are not a child. You are Empress, and he serves you. That is all you require.

"Now, Medeoan."

Relief washed over her at those words. As Avanasy stood and stepped back, Medeoan knelt in front of the fire. Indi-

vidual flames danced in front of her eyes, in all their shades
of gold. Each one could be a feather in the Firebird's plumage, or each one a bar in its cage. It was up to her. This, at
last, was one thing she could do for her people, her empire,
and for herself.

Medeoan steeled herself. She reached out until the heat of
the flames became too much for her already seared and
tender skin. With a supreme effort she shut out the sensations
of the world one by one—the hot wind, the scents of smoke
and burning, the crackle as yet another bone or bracing broke
and fell—until all that remained was the pounding of her
own heart. She reached down deep, past that familiar rhythm,
past the surge of her breath, past the current of her blood
and into her spirit. There she drew up the magic cradled there
until it flowed freely down her fingertips and into the fire.
The barrier of their heat dissolved, and she pushed past it as
easily as if it had been cool well water, until she cupped the
flames in her hands.

They were soft to hold, and smooth and delicate as the
petals of the rarest flower. Her fingers stroked them lovingly
and her magic willed them to grow, to spread, to become
white with heat and life. The flames responded to her urg-
ings, turning from individual petals into silken sheets of pure
white light. She was aware of the heat in some distant part
of her mind but it was of no significance. This fire was hers
and could do her no harm. It could only serve. Not even the
Phoenix could wrest this fire from her.

She felt the touch of Avanasy's magic even before she
glimpsed him kneeling beside her. He was cool and strong,
as he ever had been, earth and metal to her fire and air. She
welcomed the touch of him, the solid, familiar and loved,
yes, loved, presence beside her. The manifestation of her
spirit that was her magic opened and made room for his, the
pair of them twining together even as he lifted the charred
board where they had laid the lumps of gold and emptied
them into her fire.

Magic, fire and hands caught the gold. Guided by her will
and her work, the flames encircled the gold, claiming its
shape, softening it to the texture of molten glass. Avanasy
drizzled their pitiful store of water, claimed from a stream

nearby, into the crucible, sending up great clouds of steam, and only increasing the greed of Medeoan's fire, and then he bent close, so close his mouth almost touched her fingers, and he breathed out, long and cool across the molten gold.

Medeoan caught the gold and their magic up and her fingers began to spin it into threads, long, hair-fine and pure, as strong as steel and pliable as flax. In her mind, she fixed the image of the cage, a filigree thing of shining gold, made of all these threads, woven together by sorcery, skill and need. It would be made of all the elements of the world summoned together, and the work of her hands. Her fingers moved, and her mind moved and the gold took shape.

All at once, she saw the Firebird. Burning bright and deadly, she saw it streaking across the pale blue sky on its own mission. She gasped and her fingers snapped the thread they held in two. The heat bit hard into her skin and her magic faltered.

But there was Avanasy, to catch the broken thread and cup her hands again. He breathed across her fingertips and the heat receded. His power swirled around her, supporting her like bones, like the bars of a golden cage, their cage, the Firebird's cage.

Together, they spun the molten gold. Together they wove the bars of her fire and Avanasy's breath and their mingled blood and in the midst of raging war and the flood of magics, Medeoan felt she at last knew the meaning of her own love.

The mind of the Phoenix burned bright with thoughts of vengeance. The invaders dared to wake its anger, dared to approach the threshold of its home and flail at its people. They would know the fire and they would know a generation of fear. The Phoenix opened its mouth and cried aloud to let its people know they were not abandoned.

Fire gripped Avanasy. Its spirit dragged his down into the flames, spinning it with the gold flames, weaving it into bars. He was the cage, was the fire, was the spell, reaching up and out to find the Firebird. It burned bright. He hungered after it, longed to hold it close. It was his purpose, his need for being. He would give his all to encompass that wildness.

Ingrid. Think also of Ingrid and your child. She waits for you, and you must hold on.

But, oh, how the bird soared free in its beauty, and how brightly it burned, how the gold shimmered with its own fire, and it pulled him, pulled breath from his body, pulled will from his soul.

And Medeoan needed him, and Isavalta needed him.

The cage rose before him, impossibly balanced on the crucible, open like a filigree flower, reaching, waiting.

"Now," whispered Medeoan. "Now."

She plunged her hands and her magic deep into the fire.

Vyshemir, I never knew her true strength. She caught him up as easily as a handful of chaff and flung him into the air. He soared free on the gout of flame, his own power the connection between flame and cage, and the flame sought its living avatar, and flashed toward the Phoenix, and touched the bird, and merged as it must, for that was the nature of the world.

And Avanasy, suspended between earth and sky, began to pull.

I can't breathe. I can't breathe. I am stretched too far. There is too much heat. I can't breathe.

I must breathe. I must live.

Ingrid waited for him. He had to live to cross to her, to carry her home. She carried their child.

Avanasy breathed, and Avanasy, with all the strength of purely human need, pulled.

The Firebird was impossibly huge. The sun never burned so brightly, nor in so many colors of flame. Its cry was sharper than the screams of the dying, more thunderous than the wood that exploded at the merest brush of its wings. It was vengeance, it was protection. It was fire in all its forms set loose. It cast no shadow, for it was nothing but light.

It surely must consume the world.

But then, the Firebird paused in its flight, hovering over the darkening plains. Then it spread its wings and loosed a strange, new cry. Fire leapt up from the ranges it had left, fresh fire, strange fire. The new flame stretched out and it and the bird's fiery plumage melted into one.

Then the Firebird began to sink.

No! screamed the Firebird.

Medeoan started, and almost dropped the weaving again. She had not expected the creature to have a voice.

The heat of it was volcanic. It seared the skin on her face and scalp. Medeoan felt she must burst into flame at any second. Her fire seemed such a slender thread by comparison, but it held, and it dragged the great Phoenix down to her cage.

Their cage. Avanasy clung tightly to the delicate bars, holding the weaving together with magic and will as the bird fell closer, pulled by her fire.

Stop! You have no right to interfere! screamed the bird inside her mind.

"I am the Empress of Isavalta!" cried out Medeoan. "I will protect my own!"

The Firebird shrank and shriveled, its fire fading as her flame bound it ever more tightly. Now it was the size of a swan, then a crane, a heron, a great golden eagle. Now, it was the size of a hawk, and Medeoan's flame pulled it down into the waiting cage that balanced atop the crucible.

It was then Medeoan felt it. The real burning. Not the physical fire that blistered her skin and singed her hair. She felt the burning inside, the fire that stretched from the center of the earth to the stars and the sun, the single flame at the heart of all fire. It lanced through her like pain and elation, and she knew all at once what she was trying to bind.

She caught sight of Avanasy beside her, gripping the cage. His skin cracked with heat and his face was blistered. His brows were a single smear of ash and pain turned him gray, but he held. His knees buckled under him, but still he held, and still he breathed out, a single long exhalation into the smoke and steam of her fire, swirling around the immortal bird, penetrating it, and binding it fast.

The Firebird was only the size of a raven now, and Medeoan grasped the woven gold and bent the bars over its head. It flailed, striking out with wings and beak, and her hands burned where it touched and she screamed with the pain, but Avanasy cooled her flesh with his breath and she held her flames in control, and the cage began to weave itself closed under her fingers.

You will pay for this, screamed the Firebird. *Life and blood and realm I will have from you. You will pay with your whole life for this act!*

Medeoan shaped the gold and fire together, weaving them into a ring to hold the bars, to suspend the cage. But in the flicker of the flame she thought she saw images. She saw a young man, and she saw herself, impossibly aged, holding the tasseled girdle up before him. She saw Ingrid, no, not Ingrid, the girl had Avanasy's face, standing before her, her expression full of bitter gall. She saw herself dying on a couch, alone, in the cold, and the Firebird soaring free over a stone tower.

It doesn't matter. Nothing matters but what I do now. Medeoan drew on the last of her strength. Pain and blood and breath and magic, she drew out all she had, and sealed the ring, and the cage closed and the fire winked out.

For one heartbeat, triumph raged through Medeoan's blood. Then, Avanasy, still bound to her by all the strength of their working, crumpled to the ground.

"Avanasy!" shrieked Medeoan, falling to her knees on the scorched earth beside him. Avanasy lay in the midst of the destruction, his skin white against the black ash, his golden hair filthy with char. He couldn't seem to breathe. He could only choke and gasp.

"No." She seized his hand. "No, you cannot leave me. Not now."

But she was so tired. Weariness dragged at every muscle. Her throat cried out with a thirst that could never be slaked, and behind her, the bird and its miraculous cage burned so brightly, she could feel it pulsing in her blood, sapping what little strength remained to her.

But Avanasy could not die. Not now. Now that she knew where her heart lay, now that he had saved her and all of Isavalta.

Slowly, Avanasy reached out with his free hand. "Please," he whispered. "Medeoan, help me."

Medeoan leaned across him. She looked in his eyes and she saw the love that was there even as their light died. She kissed him, open-mouthed, breathing her life, her magic into him. Bound as they were, this they could share. Source to source, spirit to spirit, she could give this to him, and she would, for their work, their need, their love, she pushed her magic hard into his heart, willing it strength to beat.

And she found Ingrid there. Not herself, the stranger.

Shock and rage threw Medeoan backward, all but severing the connection between them. Avanasy's whole frame convulsed, and his throat gasped hard for air. His whole back arched as he struggled to breathe. She stared at him, heart beating hard, skin burning from what waited behind her, unable to believe that now, when they had been heart to heart, now when she had been willing to share with him her mortal breath, he still loved a stranger, a peasant, a nothing.

Avanasy collapsed, the struggle finally becoming too much. Only his hand clenched itself. He was dying. She felt him ebbing, his spirit pulled away from his body by Grandfather Death, even as their cage had pulled the Firebird down.

She saw then, in one blinding instant, how she could make all right. If Avanasy lived, if she gave her future to him, the Firebird's hideous prophecy could not come true. Isavalta could stand free and strong. She could do as Vyshemir herself did and give her life for her realm, and go to the Land of Death and Spirit in Avanasy's place.

She could give him back to his lover.

The thought made her hesitate, and she watched Avanasy's hand curl tight once more, and then the fingers loosened, and his head rolled sideways. Medeoan cried out and threw herself forward, but she was too weak. His strength had been sustaining her, and she could only fall beside him. She pushed herself up, and tried to reach him, to kiss him, to breathe into him, to say she was sorry, that he must forgive her, that she was not thinking of herself, not really, that she loved him, that she needed him beside her.

"Don't go," she breathed the words into his mouth, reaching inside herself for the last of her strength, searching her sorcery for the barest thread of their connection. "Don't leave me." She pressed her mouth against his, and breathed out the last of herself.

Blackness swirled around her then, and Medeoan slipped forward to meet it.

Ingrid dozed on the deck of Lien's ship, surrounded by the white mists of the Land of Death and Spirit. Mindful of the warnings and dangers, she had tried hard to stay awake, but the day and the parting had been too much, and her mind and soul sought a relief that she had no strength left to deny.

"Ingrid."

Ingrid was dreaming. She knew it. The cabin deck was warm with sunlight and she could see waves sparkling over the side, but there was no sun here. She sailed no real ocean. She dreamed and she should wake herself.

But it was a wonderful dream, for Avanasy knelt beside her, gazing at her with eyes full of love.

She reached out to take his hand, but although he was there, and she could see him, she could not touch him.

"Come closer," she said, in the manner of dreams.

"I'm here beside you," he told her. "Where I'll be forever."

"But I can't touch you."

"No. Not yet."

"Soon."

"Not for years to come, Ingrid. For you must live now."

Cold dread seized her, and she tried to tell herself this was only a dream. Nothing more, but part of her knew that was a lie.

"No, Avanasy. Be here. You can't . . . you can't . . ."

Avanasy was silent. He reached out to stroke her hair, but she felt nothing at all.

"You promised."

"It was not for lack of love, Ingrid, I swear."

"No," she said, with a rock-hard certainty. "Not alone. Not without you." Her fingers found the wristlet he had made for her, and began tearing at the knot.

"Stop, Ingrid. Don't do this."

"I am not going to live without you," she said doggedly. "You're all I have."

"And you are all our babe has now."

Ingrid stilled her hand.

"You must live for her, and for yourself, Ingrid. You must see her living into the world, for all our sakes."

"Say you'll be beside me. Say you will be there with us."

"As close as I can be, Ingrid. As close as I am allowed."

"Don't leave me," she whispered, reaching again, and failing to touch him, yet again.

"I love you, Ingrid. Carry that with you always. Tell our daughter that."

He was fading like a ghost, like a dream, he was pulling away from her.

"No! Avanasy! No!"

And she was awake and on her feet, staring out at the swirling mists and green islands, and strange dark trees, and the whole empty world between worlds.

Ingrid bowed her head and began to weep. Her tears fell into the mist, and were gone.

Epilogue

Lien's men rowed her ashore in the early morning, and left her on the sand of Eastbay. As soon as their boat returned, the ship raised sail and vanished from her sight.

It was cold, and the trees were bare. November already maybe. Maybe only October. It didn't matter. It was cold and the wind bit hard at her bones.

Ingrid entered Avanasy's shack and sat in his chair. She could not think. She was numb. All she could do was sit and stare at the empty stove, and remember how he had lain in the now empty bed and let her sing him back to the world.

Eventually, cold overcame even numbness, and Ingrid found matches in a tin can, and some tinder, and some kindling, and with only a little trouble, managed to light the stove. On a shelf, there was coffee, and tins of beans, and some others of beef. She ate some of the beans, and returned to Avanasy's chair, and curled up in it, watching the fire through the grate in the old stove.

She lived for two or three days that way, doing no more than absolutely necessary to keep body and soul together. She did not weep. She could not seem to remember how.

Then, one morning, she had lost count of the mornings, as she knelt to light the stove, she heard a footstep outside, and the door swung open.

"Ingrid?"

Still on her knees, Ingrid turned, and saw Everett Lederle standing in the doorway.

She rose, but could find nothing to say.

Everett pulled off his cap and stepped inside. "I heard you'd been seen."

"Did you?" Ingrid smoothed down her worn and filthy dress.

Everett took another tentative step toward her. "Your family is saying they won't have you back."

"I'm not surprised." It was hard, but she made herself think of her family, of how she had come to be in this place. "Did you speak with Grace?"

Everett shook his head. "She's gone to Bayfield."

Ingrid laid her hand on the edge of the warming stove. "She's better off there."

Silence hung between them while Ingrid stared past Everett to the doorway, wondering if her paralysis was because she wanted Everett to go, or because she wanted Avanasy to come for her.

"Ingrid, you can't stay here."

Ingrid shrugged. "It's only for a few days," she lied, "until I can convince the tug to take me across to Bayfield. I'll find work."

"Where?" asked Everett. "It's all over how you ran off."

"If no one will have me in Bayfield, then I'll just have to go further." She couldn't meet his eyes. She did not want to see how earnestly he looked at her. She did not want to see love on another man's face.

"You could come with me," he said.

Now it was Ingrid's turn to shake her head. "You don't want me, Everett."

"I've never wanted anyone else." He did not move closer to her. He relied on his words to reach her. He had no idea how far they had to travel.

Better to end this now. Ingrid laid her hand against her belly. "I'm pregnant, Everett."

"I don't care."

Those soft words caused Ingrid to finally raise her eyes and look directly at him. A good man. He had always been such a good man. Even now, as he stood ready to forgive her so much, she could feel only regret, only grief, and love for another.

"Come with me," urged Everett. "If not for your own sake, then for the baby's."

The baby. Yes, she had to think of the baby, her baby, Avanasy's baby. What would life be like for it, born a bastard, even more of an outcast than it needed to be?

Everett held out his hand.

"I don't know if I will ever love you, Everett."

"But you don't know that you won't," Everett answered.

His faith was warming, like a fire at her back. He believed. He believed if he loved her enough that the dry tinder of her heart would catch fire. Maybe he was right. They could hope. Even now, they could still hope. If there was hope, then what she did was not a lie. Her child would be born healthy and alive to a loving mother and father, and then one day, one day she would find a way to return to Isavalta, just a little while, just so the child would know that part of its heritage, would at least know the land of its father. Then, she would return to Everett whom she would have learned to love. If she could hold tight to that hope, then this was not a lie. If she could hold tight to that hope she could find some corner of her heart that could hold love for Everett as well as for Avanasy.

Ingrid gave Everett her hand, answering his soft smile with her own as he took her arm and led her to his home.

Medeoan entered the long pavilion with her entourage behind her. A gleaming trestle table had been placed in the center. At either side sat the representatives of Hung Tse—generals in lacquered armor, scholars in modest black-and-white coats, and, at the far end, two of the Nine Elders; the Minister of Earth and the Minister of the North.

They had left the carved chair at the foot of the table for her. Prathad pulled it out for her and Medeoan sat, letting her ladies adjust her trains and sleeves, while the Council Lords and secretaries arrayed themselves behind her with their caskets and scrolls and other small burdens.

Captain Peshek, in his crisp coat and gleaming breastplate, stood at Medeoan's right hand.

Peasants had found them both. Peshek had been carried from the ruin. Medeoan, they had not dared touch because of the Firebird caged beside her. When she had woken, with the ones who had found her and the keeper of their village god house as a ragged escort, she had carried cage and captive to their lord's estate. He had not doubted who she was, and, no matter who he had followed before, he knelt to her and her cage now and sent instant word to the lord master, who knelt himself, and proclaimed his fealty.

Later, she would sort out who had remained true, who had been bemused by Kacha and Yamuna, and who had truly betrayed. For now, it was enough that they obeyed and gave her what men were left to march in procession to the next fortress, the next manor, the next lord and lord master. Word flew ahead of her, the tale of betrayal and duplicity, and the countryside turned out to cheer her return at the head of her growing guard.

She kept the cage covered.

By the time they reached Vaknevos, the whole of the palace turned out to greet her. With Yamuna's death, the spells he had laid with Kacha's help had broken and the newly freed seized the traitors, or the supposed traitors, and offered them up to her in exchange for forgiveness. They waited in the cells for her judgment, all except one.

The woman Chekhania sailed in chains to Hastinapura, her belly big with Kacha's bastard. The Hastinapuran ambassador's head in a jar of honey was her accompaniment.

That left Hung Tse's army massing at Miateshcha, and their navy gathering its strength in the southern sea. So, she had made her arrangements, and had ridden here to meet with the representatives of Hung Tse. She'd had to come herself, as until she'd had time to investigate what had happened in her absence, there was still no way to know who she could really trust.

The Minister of the North bowed her head in acknowledgment of Medeoan's arrival. "We thank Your Majesty Imperial for appearing before us. We are certain that this recent misunderstanding between yourself and the Heart of Heaven and Earth can be quickly resolved and appropriate reparation made."

She looked from one of the ministers to the other. Their faces behind their tattoos were bland, but their eyes were not easy. They were wondering, she knew, why she lived. She should have been dead. She should have been ash and char.

"Ministers of the Heart of the World," she replied evenly. "I am not here to speak of reparations. I am here to confirm

that Isavalta has no lawful quarrel with Hung Tse. Our armies have been removed and disbanded and we hope soon
to exchange ambassadors with the Heart of the World. We
expect that our Brother Emperor will give similar orders as
soon as you carry my word back to him." She gestured to
her chief secretary, who walked to the ministers and handed
over a scroll bound with sapphire ribbons and sealed with
red wax.

The Minister of the North received the missive in silence.

"We are of course delighted to hear that Your Majesty
Imperial has understood that this quarrel previously standing
between our empires has no basis in the laws of earth or
heaven," said the Minister of Earth. "But, it is Hung Tse that
was attacked and . . ."

Medeoan did not let him finish. "We will not speak of
attacks, Minister. We will not speak of damages or reparations. We have withdrawn. You will withdraw. That is all."

"It is Hung Tse that was attacked," the Minister of Earth
repeated. "You have acknowledged that this attack was unlawful. That entitles Hung Tse to reparations from Isavalta."

Medeoan looked to Peshek. Peshek turned to the commander of the House Guard, who handed him the object
covered with black cloth that he carried. Peshek set the object
in front of Medeoan.

All the representatives of Hung Tse shifted uneasily at
their end of the table.

Medeoan pulled away the black cloth, revealing a curved
jar of purest crystal. Inside lay a single feather that at first
glance appeared to be perfectly formed of shining gold, but
if one looked longer and more closely, one saw how lights
of orange, red and white played along its length.

She lifted the curved jar from its base. The air touched the
feather, and it burst at once into a single gout of flame that
burned for an instant, and was gone.

The two sorcerers of Hung Tse let their gaze linger on the
now empty jar, and then, slowly lifted their gaze to meet
Medeoan's.

Medeoan replaced the crystal jar on its base, and Peshek
lifted it away.

"We will not speak of attacks," she said. "We will not

speak of reparations. We have withdrawn our forces. Hung Tse will also withdraw. That is all."

Medeoan left the pavilion. Her grooms had her horse waiting for her, and she mounted. Without looking behind even to see if her escort followed, she mounted and rode back across the plain to the encampment that had been made around her banner with the golden imperial eagle on its bright blue field.

At one time, she might have found her tent cramped and uncomfortable, for all its carpets and finely made furniture. No longer. She had known far rougher accommodation. Prathad hurried about, directing the other ladies, all new, and all chosen by her, to take her outer coat, to fetch small beer and refreshment, and to do all else that was needful for the maintenance of their empress.

A shadow crossed the entrance of the tent. Medeoan glanced back and saw Captain Peshek waiting to be acknowledged.

"Come in, Peshek."

Peshek entered and knelt. She nodded and waved him to a chair, which he did not accept as she still stood.

"Majesty, I do not mean to question your judgment, but was that . . ."

"Wise?" she finished for him. "Perhaps not, but it will do. They will spend this night trying to understand what has happened to the Firebird and how we came to possess any fragment of it. When they understand that their guardian is no longer free to protect their borders, they will withdraw, and we will have peace." She sat, slumping as far into her chair as her layers of clothing permitted. She closed her eyes briefly. "That is enough."

"Yes, Majesty."

She heard movement and looked to see Prathad setting a tray with wine and dainties beside her. The lady poured two goblets full, handing one to Medeoan and one to Peshek.

Medeoan did not drink. She just looked at the dark depths of the wine. "Lien said Ingrid arrived safely home."

"Yes, Majesty," replied Peshek.

"She is carrying Avanasy's child, Peshek."

"Yes, Majesty."

She swirled her cup gently. "I want to send for her, when we know we have found all the real traitors and that our borders are safe. Avanasy's child should be raised in Isavalta. He should be given the honors due to him as the Avanasyn."

Peshek was silent for a moment. Then, he said, "I miss him too, Majesty."

She looked up at him then, and saw how bright his blue eyes were. Lien's healing had worked well, and his scars were almost completely gone. He was again the handsome, loyal soldier who had taken her to safety when she was so beset.

"His life is part of Isavalta now," she said. "It is because of him that we have a chance to be safe in our borders. Our task is to see that what he has begun is completed."

Peshek laid his hand over his heart, his blue eyes sparkling. "I live to serve, Majesty."

She lifted the wine cup to him and smiled, feeling a thread of warmth working its way through the chill of her soul. "As do we all, Peshek. Isavalta will in truth be the Eternal."

But even as she spoke those words, Medeoan knew the Firebird, away in its cage, locked in the cells of Vaknevos, heard, and cried out its defiance.

The empress of Isavalta shivered and turned her face away.

Main Characters

Avanasy Finorasyn Goriainavin (AHV-ahn-AH-see FIN-OR-ah-sin GOR-ee-ahn-ay-AH-veen): A sorcerer of Isavalta. Tutor to High Princess Medeoan.

Baba Yaga (BAH-bah YAH-gah): The Old Witch, the Witch with the Iron Teeth.

Bakhar (BAHK-har): Keeper of the Imperial God House.

Black Night: One of Baba Yaga's mystical servants. Only seen after sunset.

Bright Day: One of Baba Yaga's mystical servants. Only seen during daylight.

Cai Yun Shen (KAI YUN shen): Niece of Lien Jinn.

Chandra *tya* Achin Ireshpad (CHAN-drah *TEE-yah* AHCH-een AY-RESH-pahd): Oldest son of the ruling family of Hastinapura, former Emperor.

Dieu Han: (DYOO HAN) Dowager Empress of Hung Tse.

Edemsko (EH-DEM-skoh): Emperor of Isavalta, father of Medeoan.

Eliisa Hahl (EH-lee-EE-sah HAHL): Serving girl in the Isavaltan imperial household.

Everett Lederle: Friend and suitor of Ingrid Loftfield.

Grace Hulda Loftfield: Younger sister of Ingrid Loftfield.

Girilal (GEER-ee-lahl): Ambassador from Hastinapura to Isavalta.

Hajek Ragdoksyn Kraichinivin (HAH-jayk RAHG-dohk-sin KRAI-cheen-EE-veen): Keeper of the God House for Demska of the Tears.

Hamsa (HAHM-sah): Bound-sorcerer to Emperor Samudra of Hastinapura.

Harshul (HAHR-shool): Deceased bound-sorcerer to Prince Kacha of Hastinapura.

Iakush Vtoroisyn Gabravin (EE-ah-kush VEET-or-OY-sin GAHB-rah-veen): Lord Sorcerer of Isavalta.

Imperial Voice: Speaker for the Emperor of Hung Tse.

Ingrid Anna Loftfield: A young woman from Sand Island, Wisconsin.

Kacha *tya* Achin Ejulinjapad (KAH-chah *TEE-yah* AHCH-een E-jool-EEn-jah-pahd): Prince of Hastinapura, son of Chandra and husband of Medeoan.

Kseniia (KAH-sen-EE-ee-ah): Empress of Isavalta, mother of Medeoan.

Leonard Loftfield: A young man from Sand Island, Wisconsin, brother of Ingrid.

Lien Jinn (LEE-en JEEN): A sorcerer and pirate of Hung Tse.

lokai (LOW-keye): The fox spirits.

Malan'ia (MAHL-ahn-EE-ah): A fisherwoman of Isavalta.

Medeoan Edemskoidoch Nacheradovosh (MEH-deh-OH-ahn EH-DEM-skoh-EE-doch NAH-cher-AH-DOH-vawsh): High Princess of Isavalta, wife of Prince Kacha.

Minister of Air: One of the Nine Elders of Hung Tse. Personal name: Lok (LAWK).

Minister of Earth: One of the Nine Elders of Hung Tse. Personal name: En Lai (EHN LAI).

Minister of the East: One of the Nine Elders of Hung Tse. Personal name: Nha My (NAH Mai).

Minister of Fire: One of the Nine Elders of Hung Tse. Personal name: Xuan (JOO-ahn).

Minister of Metal: One of the Nine Elders of Hung Tse. Personal name: Shaiming (shy-MING).

Minister of the North: One of the Nine Elders of Hung Tse. Personal name: Ahn Thao (AHN T-h-AH-oh).

Minister of the South: One of the Nine Elders of Hung Tse. Personal name: Quan (KWAHN).

Minister of Water: One of the Nine Elders of Hung Tse. Personal name: Chi Tahn (CHEE t-AHN).

Minister of the West: One of the Nine Elders of Hung Tse. Personal name: Minh (MIN).

Nanabush (NAHN-ah-boosh): A trickster god in Wisconsin, often taking the form of a rabbit.

Ofka (OFF-kah): Lady-in-waiting to Medeoan.

Pa K'un (PAH k-UN): Emperor of Hung Tse

Peshek Pachalkasyn Ursulvin (PEH-shek PAHCH-ahl-KAH-sin UR-sul-veen): Captain of the Imperial House Guard of Isavalta.

Prathad (PRAH-thahd): Head lady-in-waiting to Medeoan.

Prithu (PREE-thoo): Head gentleman-in-waiting to Kacha.

Ragneda (RAHG-neh-DA): Lady-in-waiting to Medeoan.

Red Sun: One of Baba Yaga's mystical servants. Only seen at twilight or in the Land of Death and Spirit.

Samudra *tya* Achin Ireshpad Hariamnapad (SAHM-oo-drah *TEE-yah* ACHA-een HAHR-ee-AHM-nah-pahd): Emperor of Hastinapura, father of Kacha, younger brother of Chandra.

Valin Kalami (VAHL-in KAH-LAH-mi): A sorcerer from the island of Tuukos.

Vixen, The: Queen of the *lokai*.

Vladka (VLAHD-kah): Second lady-in-waiting to Medeoan.

Yamuna *dva* Ikshu Chitranipad (YAH-MOON-ah *DEE-vah* AIK-shoo CHEET-rahn-EE-pahd): Bound-sorcerer to Chandra.

Place Names

Apostle Islands, The: A chain of islands in Lake Superior off the coast of northern Wisconsin.

Bayfield: A town in northern Wisconsin on the east coast of Lake Superior.

Camaracost (KAHM-ah-rah-KOST): A port town on the southeastern coast of Isavalta.

Dalemar (DAY-leh-MAHR): A coastal fortress in Isavalta.

Devang (DEH-vang): A temple complex in Hastinapura dedicated to the Seven Mothers.

Durah (DUR-ah): An ancient and abandoned temple city in Hastinapura.

Eastbay: The settlement on Sand Island.

Erh Han (ER-hahn): A peninsula between Isavalta and Hung Tse. Called Miateshcha in Isavalta.

Hastinapura (HAHS-teen-ah-POOR-ah): A southern empire sharing a continent with Isavalta.

Heart of the World: Home of the Emperor of Hung Tse. A complex of palaces and official buildings.

Hung Tse (HOONG-SAY): The central empire between Isavalta and Hastinapura.

Isavalta (IS-ah-VAHL-tah): A northern empire sharing a continent with the empires of Hung Tse and Hastinapura.

Ishbushka (ISH-bush-KAH): The hut belonging to Baba Yaga.

Land of Death and Spirit, The: The space between worlds inhabited by ghosts, demons, fairies, gods and spirit powers. Also called the Silent Lands and the Shifting Lands.

Makashev: City near Vyshtavos.

Miateshcha (MEE-ah-TEHSH-chah): See Erh Han.

Padinogen Passage (PAHD-een-oh-gehn): Passage through the mountains leading to Miateshcha.

oblast (OH-blast): An Isavaltan word meaning 'province.'

Palace of Autumn, The: The women's palace in the Heart of the World.

Palace of the Pearl Throne, The: Imperial seat of Hastinapura.

Sand Island: One of the Apostle Islands in Lake Superior. Home to Ingrid Loftfield.

Shifting Lands, The: See Land of Death and Spirit.

Silent Lands, The: See Land of Death and Spirit.

Sol'uyche oblast (SOL-oo-EECH OH-blast): A southern province in Isavalta.

Sze-Leng (ZEH LENG) River: A major river in Hung Tse.

T'ien (T-YEN): The city surrounding the Heart of the World.

Tuukos (TOO-kohs): An island which is the northernmost province of Isavalta.

Vaknevos (VAHK-neh-VOS): The summer palace of the Isavaltan imperial family.

Vyshtavos (VIESH-tah-vohs): The winter palace of the Isavaltan imperial family.

Vaceta (VAH-say-TAH): A town near Vaknevos.

About the Author

Sarah Zettel, author of two fantasy and five science fiction novels, has won the Locus Award for the Best First Novel, for *Reclamation* (1996), and was runner-up for the Philip K. Dick Award for the best paperback original SF novel, for *Fool's War* (1997). *The Usurper's Crown* is the second fantasy novel in her Isavalta series. She lives outside Ann Arbor, Michigan, where she is working on *The Firebird's Vengeance*, the final novel of Isavalta.